A WOMAN
OF OUR TIMES

Also by Rosie Thomas

BAD GIRLS, GOOD WOMEN

ROSIE THOMAS

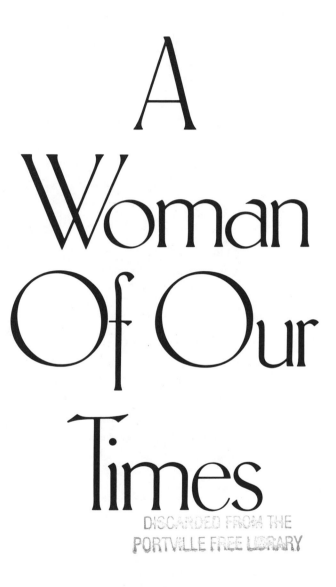

A Woman Of Our Times

Bantam Books

NEW YORK · TORONTO · LONDON · SYDNEY · AUCKLAND

A WOMAN OF OUR TIMES

A BANTAM BOOK / OCTOBER 1990

Library of Congress Cataloging-in-Publication Data

Thomas, Rosie.
    A woman of our times / Rosie Thomas.
        p.   cm.
    ISBN 0-553-05795-2
    I. Title.
    PR6070.H655W6 1990
    823'.914—dc20   90-470
                                                             CIP

Published simultaneously in the United States and Canada

PRINTED IN THE UNITED STATES OF AMERICA

BVG   0   9   8   7   6   5   4   3   2   1

The following people gave me the benefit of their specialized knowledge of the City: Paul Barry, Robin Boyd, John Nash, and in particular Philip Baldwin. Any errors of fact or interpretation in the book are mine, not theirs. I am also grateful to Peter Wilson, Julia Muddeman, Professor and Mrs. James Meade, Judy Hilsinger, Gordon Smith, Isabel McCabe, Linda Grey, Ellen Levine, my editor Susan Watt and, as always, to my husband, Caradoc King.

The game "Meizu" is based on a game devised by Professor James Meade, who retains the copyright.

For women friends,
Judith and Ellie and Susan,
and my sister Lindsay

A WOMAN
OF OUR TIMES

One

HARRIET LOOKED AT HER WATCH.

In less than an hour, the car would come to take her to Heathrow. In a little more than twelve hours, she would be in Los Angeles, with Caspar.

For a moment, she let herself think about him. She didn't expect that he would be waiting for her in the crowd at the barrier. Of course he would not. But there would be another car, and then a suite or an apartment somewhere with a view of the ocean, or the blue on blue geometry of a pool. Caspar would be there, wearing a white shirt, with the beginnings of a tan. He would say something, nothing significant, "Baby, are you dead from the flight? Come here to me," and the resonance of his voice would make it important. He would put his arms around her.

The television reporter, sitting across the desk with her list of questions ready, saw how Harriet's face softened and brightened. The electrician noticed it too, and glanced at his lights.

Then Harriet checked her watch again. She was used to apportioning her time with care, and the technicians' business with lighting and sound levels was taking too much of it.

"Are you going to need very much longer?" she asked. "The car is coming for me at three." The producer's assistant gave her an encouraging smile. "Nearly ready for you now."

While she waited, Harriet looked at the wide expanse of her office. The producer of documentaries and his P.A. murmured together on one of the pair of low sofas, while the sound man and the electrician hovered over their metal boxes. The cameraman waited too, behind the cold eye of his lens. It was a bright day outside, but the brighter television lights dimmed the glow of it. They created, within their circle, an artificial atmosphere of intimacy.

The P.A. stretched her long legs in dark stockings, stood up and came across to the desk. She produced a hand-mirror and gave it to Harriet.

"Do you want to make a quick check before we begin?" At the same moment, the reporter cleared her throat, sat upright in her chair. Harriet looked dispassionately at her own reflection. Her face, unremarkable, looked the same as always, except that it wore more make-up than usual. She handed back the mirror.

"That's fine, if it's all right for you," she said politely.

"Ready to go," the sound man announced with one finger pressed to his headphones. The producer sat forward and his P.A. held her clipboard like a breastplate.

In the moment before the producer murmured, "Two, three, and *go*," Harriet looked down at her hands, loosely clasped in her lap. The big square diamond in its Thirties platinum setting glittered on her right hand. Harriet wondered fleetingly if she ought to have taken it off for the interview. But then she thought, *Rewards. I bought it, I earned it. Why not?* She had not taken down the Emma Sergeant portrait of herself from the end wall, nor had she removed the Chinese silk rug from the floor.

Harriet lifted her hands and rested them on the desk. A few inches from her fingertips, on the pale polished wood, lay a cracked and splintered fragment of packing case. It looked like a piece of driftwood that had been battered by the sea before being cast up on a silver beach.

The reporter had been looking at it too. Now the two women lifted their heads and their eyes met. Harriet's ring shone in the full glare of the lights.

". . . three, two, one . . ." counted down the production assistant.

There would be a preamble, of course. Alison Shaw, the reporter, would write it, and record it as a voice-over. To go with her commentary there would be establishing shots of the game, in its resplendent boxes, piled to suitable heights in some suitable store. Perhaps this same crew would film a cash-till in the same store, with a close-up shot of hands passing over money in exchange for Harriet's box. Then there would be one more establishing shot, of the huge peacock's fantail that was the company logo, on the wall of the reception area outside her office, before the cut to Harriet herself. Harriet, sitting behind her big desk in her Jasper Conran suit, her anxiety about missing her flight to Los Angeles and Caspar entirely masked.

Now the viewer would know that she was a one-woman success story, a girl who had seen an idea and had run with it, taking her own company from a table-top in a borrowed flat to a stock market launch, and winning business and export awards on the way. The program was one in a series called *Success Story*.

Harriet Peacock, newly declared Entrepreneur of the Year, had been an obvious choice for it.

"Looking in from the outside, the Peacocks success story seems to have an almost fairy-tale quality," Alison Shaw began. "A game, quite a simple if ingenious game, is launched on an already overcrowded market in the face of cautionary advice and financial problems. It catches the imagination of the public overnight, and becomes a best-seller. Within a year it has sold in hundreds of thousands, within two years its parent company is beginning to diversify into other games, with apparent success, and within three it is thriving, publicly quoted, and one of the darlings of the investors and the financial press. Harriet Peacock, how has all this been achieved?"

Harriet laughed, warmly and quite naturally. She answered, "Less easily than you make it sound."

At the beginning, when she was just starting out and the sharp-nosed reporters had come with their questions, she had been a less confident interviewee. She had been hungry for any crumb of publicity—anything that would help Peacocks, her company, her baby. But she had also been defensive, and defensiveness made her awkward. Now she was on familiar ground. She had fielded all the questions before, in different interviews, and she was ready for them.

"The first, the only really important thing, was that I knew the game was good. I felt it, I felt the hairs rise at the nape of my neck whenever I looked at it. Because I believed so strongly in it I was ready to risk everything for it. Any entrepreneur will tell you that is the spark that lights the fuse. Belief, and more than belief. *Certainty*."

Out of shot, Alison Shaw was nodding, making little rolling gestures with her hand. *More, tell us some more.* Fully practiced, Harriet swept on.

"I also believe that you can regard life as a game of chance. You can play it like that, letting the currents carry you, or you can wait for the right current and then paddle furiously with it, as I did when I recognized the potential of the game. Someone said you can reach the same conclusion in life by more or less circuitous paths, by going straight for what you want or by hoping to be swept there. There's a direct route and an indirect route, and the game itself is a metaphor for that."

It was Simon who had said it, a long time ago. Harriet's direct gaze wavered.

The hand-waving had continued, now it stopped. If they were good program-makers, Harriet thought to distract herself, they would cut away from her to the game board, and the colored balls rolling.

Taking the straight path, or going the long way around.

Alison Shaw said, "Could you define 'paddling furiously'? What exactly did you do, after the prickle at the nape of the neck?"

Harriet was on firm ground again. She had described the steps she had taken in setting up her business often enough in other interviews. She went through them fluently, counting them off like beads on a string.

Alison nodded, letting her talk, occasionally prompting her, working through the questions on her list. Harriet had discussed some of them with the program's researcher, others were unexpected. Alison was a good interviewer, it went smoothly.

The producer began to make tentative wind-up signals. Harriet was pleased. A useful job had been done for Peacocks, she would easily make her flight.

The last question came.

"There's a poignant story behind this particular success story. Harriet, you didn't devise the game yourself, that's fairly widely known. As a postscript, could you tell us something of its history?"

Harriet caught her breath. She became suddenly acutely aware of the radio mike clipped to her lapel, of the faces of the technicians watching her, of spools of tape that would be imprinted with the sound of her own voice. Out of shot, Alison looked at her watch. Harriet knew they could only want another two or three minutes from her. It would not be the first time she had talked about Simon. She thought, *If only it could have been.*

"The game was devised by a British army officer who was a prisoner of the Japanese, in Hong Kong, during the Second World War. He built it from scraps of rubbish. He kept it with him for four years, and when he was liberated it was the only thing he owned."

Harriet's right hand, with the big ring, reached out to touch the broken wood that lay on her smooth desktop. The cameraman moved to bring it into shot. Harriet remembered the story, much longer and much more painful to recall, that Simon Archer had told her in his cold, comfortless house in the gloomiest quarter of a featureless Midlands town. She could clearly hear his words. She could remember the exact phrases he had used.

She listened to them now, within her head.

When she looked up again, she found it hard to believe that only a second or two had ticked by while the camera's greedy eye lingered on Simon's packing case. Evidently Alison had either no wish or no time to probe deeper. The success story had been told, and she was ready to wrap up one more program.

"A remarkable testament to one man's will to survive. As, in a different way, the success of Peacocks is a testament to Harriet Peacock's skill and determination."

"And to that of my staff and suppliers," Harriet insisted. She was briefly amused, thinking of the acceptance speech full of the same sentiments that Caspar must make if he won his Oscar. Alison smiled back at her.

"And now, in true executive style, you're going direct from here to Heathrow to take a flight to Los Angeles. Is this a business trip, or will you have time to go to the Academy Awards?"

Harriet's expression changed. Her response was chilly. "My trip to Los Angeles is a holiday. It was agreed at the outset, wasn't it, that there would be no questions about my private life?"

Alison made an acquiescent gesture that said, *Worth a try.* They would edit the exchange out, of course.

There were a few more concluding remarks, mutual thanks, and the interview was over. The technicians stuck their thumbs up. "Super," the producer said.

Harriet looked at her watch once more. The car would arrive in a little under fifteen minutes.

"If we could just keep you with us a couple of minutes longer, Harriet, while we check we've got everything? Noddys now, Alison, okay, love?"

The camera would focus on Alison now, for the footage that would be used as cutaways. Harriet waited. Across the room she saw the door silently open and her assistant's head appear. She mimed, *Telephone.* Harriet shook her head. As far as the rest of the world need know, she was already on her way to Heathrow. But Karen refused to go away. *Urgent,* she signaled.

Harriet sighed. "Excuse me. I have to take a telephone call." She circled around her own desk, and went out to Karen's office. Karen held the receiver out to her.

"Hello? Harriet Peacock speaking."

It was Charlie Thimbell. Harriet knew him well. His wife was one of her closest friends.

"Charlie, is everything okay? Is Jenny all right?"

"Yeah, nothing like that. Listen, Harriet, I heard a rumor. I thought you'd better know about it." Charlie Thimbell was a financial journalist, the city editor of one of the national dailies.

"What rumor?"

"More than a rumor, then. A tip-off. Are you watching your back, Harriet?"

"You're talking about a raid, are you? We were at two twenty-five this morning. Steady."

Charlie said nothing for a moment. Then, very quietly, "Are you overstretched?"

Harriet laughed. "If we are or if we aren't, I wouldn't tell *you*, Charlie. Which would you put first, me or a good story?"

"Difficult one, that. Well, I just thought I'd let you know. You might want to think again about making your trip."

"I'm going. Caspar's up for an Oscar, and he deserves to win it. I want to be there when he does."

"You'll be a long way from home."

Karen had taken another call. She told Harriet, "Car's waiting downstairs."

Harriet was impatient. The television crew had finished, they were carrying their gear out of her office. "Charlie, I'm not going up the Amazon, I'm going to L.A. They have telephones there. I can be back here in twelve hours, if I'm needed."

"Sure thing. Well, enjoy yourself. Tell the old tosspot I'm rooting for him."

Charlie had never met Caspar Jensen, but he made a joke of pretending familiarity with the man and his habits.

"Thanks, Charlie. Thanks for ringing. Give my love to Jen."

"Come back soon."

Charlie hung up. Karen was looking up at Harriet. "Problem?"

"I don't think so," Harriet said. She would not have admitted anxiety to Charlie. The anxiety, in any case, was well within bounds. She could live with it. She wanted to see Caspar more than she wanted anything else. Her luggage, two small neat suitcases, was waiting for her by the door. If she didn't go now, she would miss her flight.

"Shall I ask the driver to come up for your suitcases?"

Harriet picked them up. "No, I can manage. Traveling light." One Bruce Oldfield evening dress for the big night, not much else.

Alison Shaw came out of Harriet's office. She was wearing a full skirt that bunched over her hips, and a loose jacket. An unnecessary Burberry was folded over her arm.

"Thanks for the interview," she said.

"I enjoyed it," Harriet lied. They looked at each other for a moment. "I must go."

"Have a good trip," Alison and Karen said, together.

In the car, as it turned into the westbound traffic, Harriet was thinking again about Simon. Her thoughts embarked on a predictable circuit and, with a touch of weariness, she let them follow the familiar groove. She sat hunched forward in her seat, containing the discomfort that they gave her. Looking out of the car window, from the little height of the Westway, she saw the cold sparkle of the city. A moment later, her spirits lifted. The groove had led her, as it sometimes did, to her mother. Harriet imagined Kath at home, in her kitchen, at Sunderland Avenue. The big, modern house would be humming with Radio One, and with the sound of vacuum cleaning or the buzz of the electric blender. They were the sounds of Harriet's adolescence, but not her childhood. Harriet loved her mother. She thought that they were alike, for all the differences in their two lives.

Unusually, Kath had not telephoned her to wish her bon voyage, and Harriet had not found the time to call today. If there was no time to do it from the airport, she would telephone as soon as she reached Los Angeles.

On the left of the car, a 747 dipped toward its destination. Harriet watched it as it slid through the sky, and wondered if the sun was shining on the West Coast.

She wouldn't think about what Charlie had said. When she came home, she would find out where the rumor had sprung from.

Two

IT WAS HALF PAST FIVE.

The street outside Harriet's shop was crowded with office workers flooding toward the tube station.

Harriet finished checking the till, and left a float for Karen who was assigned to open the shop in the morning. She bagged the rest of the day's takings, ready to be dropped into the night safe on her way past the bank. Then she went through the shop turning off the lights, so that the dazzling mirror-walls became blank, dark curtains. She locked the inner doors and set the alarm, then stepped out into the street. The shop was secure for the night. She paused to look up at the facade. It was pristine white, with the shop's name, *Stepping*, in black, identical to the other shops in the chain.

All the Stepping shops sold dance- and exercise-wear, and ranges of associated products. Most of them, as Harriet's was, were owned as franchises. Franchise-holders ordered from a central range of products, but they chose from the range to suit their own shops. Harriet knew her customers, and had the knack of offering them what they wanted to buy. The shop was in a good location, almost prime, and it was turning over well. Harriet was proud of it, and of her foresight in predicting the dance and exercise boom. She knew that she was doing all the business she could hope to do. *If I was in Covent Garden,* Harriet thought. But she wasn't, and she wouldn't be, not with Stepping.

She had been running her business for nearly five years. She had found the shop when she was twenty-five, and her step-father had bought the lease for her. She was paying back the principal now. She was grateful to Ken for his generosity, but she was aware that it had been a sound investment for him.

She was less sure, now, whether she was satisfied with it herself. She knew that it would never make her rich, but more importantly it no longer gave her the charge of excitement that it once had.

Harriet had turned away from the shop, and dropped the

keys into her handbag. She checked to make sure that the envelope containing the cinema tickets was there, too. It was Leo who wanted to see the film, and she had booked the tickets to surprise him. Afterward she planned to treat them both to dinner at the new Thai restaurant.

Harriet forgot about the business. She began to walk briskly, looking forward to the evening with her husband. She reached the bank, with the bag of the day's takings hugged to her chest. She opened the polished slit of the night safe and slid the bag into its mouth. She heard it bumping softly as it passed into the entrails of the bank, and the home-going crowds flowed reassuringly past her. Harriet went on with them, toward the tube station.

A few moments later she reached the street where Leo had his studio. Leo was a photographer, quite a successful one. His studio was on the first floor of a small warehouse building, with a garment manufacturer below him and a design company above. Harriet looked up at his windows. It was an automatic gesture, there was nothing to see, not even a light. It was a summer's evening, there was no need for lights. She could see a drawing board angled at the window above.

Harriet would have pressed Leo's entry-phone but the front door opened just as she reached it. Two smiling machinists in saris came out, and held it for her. Harriet slipped inside the building, and ran up the stone stairs to the first floor. She was cheerful with the idea of her surprise, picturing Leo at the light table, his back to her, examining transparencies. It was dark at the top of the stairs, there were no windows here.

Click. Harriet pressed the button of the timed switch beside the door and light washed over her.

She had the impression, in that fleeting second, that the *click* had sounded a warning. There was a scuffle on the other side of the door.

Harriet was holding the key to the door in her hand. She had hardly ever used her studio key; Leo must have forgotten that she had it. She fitted it deftly into the lock, and the door swung inward.

Harriet looked straight ahead of her.

Across the studio and through another open door there was a black leather and chrome sofa. Harriet had helped Leo choose it from an Italian furniture catalog. In front of the sofa was Leo, a lock of his dark hair falling boyishly over his eyes as he tried to pull up his 501s. They were too tight and he hopped, off balance and then—ludicrously—snatched up his shirt and held it in front of his collapsing erection. Clearly the girl was more used to exposing her body. She made no coy attempt to cover herself with her hands, and her composure made Leo look even more ridiculous. She simply stood, gracefully, her body composed of dark angles and smooth, colorless planes. She was taller and thinner than Harriet. Perhaps she was one of Leo's models.

After the first current of shock, Harriet's reaction was incredulous laughter. Leo saw it, and his embarrassment lit up into fury.

He dropped the shirt, took two strides, and slammed the connecting door.

For a moment or two Harriet stood looking numbly at it. Leo would open the door again, of course, and he would be dressed and there would be no model and he would thank her for buying the cinema tickets, and they would go off for their evening together.

She waited, but there was only silence and the closed door. It was impossible to imagine what Leo and the tall, thin girl were doing on the other side of it.

Slowly, silently, Harriet closed the outer door too and stood in darkness again on the wrong side of it. She didn't bother to press the switch for its premonitory *click*. She went quietly back down the stairs, with her hand pressed flat against the cold, shiny curve of the wall to guide her.

Harriet didn't remember, afterward, how she got home. She supposed that she must have followed the route mechanically, borne along by the home-going tide.

When she reached the flat, she found herself walking through the rooms, touching things, picking up vases and books and ornaments as if she had never seen them before. She went to each window and pressed her forehead against the glass, looking out at the familiar vistas. She found it hard to believe that she had lived in this place for four years, ever since her marriage. It seemed unfamiliar now, the house of strangers. She didn't know what to do with herself in these rooms. There was no food to cook; usually one of them shopped on the way home. Tonight, there would have been the Thai dinner.

At last, she sat down in a Victorian chair that she had re-covered herself. She ran the tips of her fingers over the smooth heads of the upholstery tacks, looked out of the window at the changing light. The day was ending and the sky was thinly clouded, suffused with pink.

Harriet felt the fingers of shock beginning to loosen their hold on her. She began to think, effortfully at first, as if she had forgotten how to do it. The flat was silent, even the road outside seemed unusually still.

She thought about her marriage to Leo. She wondered how long it was exactly since they had stopped making each other happy, and then found that she couldn't recall the precise dimensions of happiness at all. She knew, in the same way that she knew the multiplication tables or the words of certain songs, that they must have been happy together once. Leo was Jewish and his prosperous parents had been opposed to their only son marrying out. Their opposition had only strengthened Harriet's and Leo's determination to marry at once. They had been happy then, in their blithe certainty. And afterward? She could remember certain times, a holiday when it had rained and it hadn't mattered at all, a long drive that they had made together, little domestic events that she could no longer recall, only the joy that went with them. That had gone. She wished she could at least remember when. They lived together now, but that was only living, the plain mechanics of it.

Harriet wondered how long her husband had had other women. How many, and how often? The memory of the tall girl with her planes of light and shadow came back to her.

Harriet thought about Leo himself. Leo was handsome, stubborn, amusing. Women were always drawn to Leo, as she had been herself. He was a man like others she had known, who found it difficult to put his feelings into words. Or perhaps not even difficult, but unnecessary.

The light was fading fast. Harriet had the sense of ordinary life fading with it, the edges of reality softly crumbling and falling away into fine dust. It made her feel sad, the more sad because it was irrevocable.

It was dark when she heard Leo's key in the lock. She had sat on in the darkness without moving and now she felt stiff and cold. He came in, clicking the light on at the door so that she blinked in the blaze of it.

They looked at each other, trying to gauge the precise gradations of mutual hostility. Harriet knew Leo well enough not to have expected contrition. Like a small boy, Leo would cover his guilt with defiance. But now she couldn't read him at all; his face was flat and cold. She heard the smallest noise, the ground around them softly crumbling into dust.

"I'm sorry you had to see that," Leo said stiffly. "You should have telephoned, or rung the bell."

There was no tentative bridge in the words, if that was what she had hoped for. She knew, in any case, that there were no foundations for a bridge. Harriet said the first thing that came into her head.

"You looked ridiculous."

He stared at her. "You're such a bitch, Harriet, do you know that? You're cold-hearted and self-righteous. You operate like a machine."

Probably he was right, Harriet thought. She didn't believe that she was any of those things, but she was willing to accept that they might know each other better than they knew themselves.

"Have there been other times, Leo? Before tonight? Could you tell me the truth, please?"

"Yes."

"Yes, you'll tell me the truth, or yes, there have been other girls?"

"There have been other girls."

"How many? How long have you been doing this?"

"Three or four. Eighteen months. Perhaps two years."

"Don't you even know for sure?"

"Does it bloody well matter?"

Harriet stood up abruptly. She went to the window and looked out. The streetlights had come on, but there was still a child skateboarding on the pavement. She watched him weaving in and out of the lamp-posts. She wanted to close the curtains, but she didn't want to shut herself in here, in this flat. Behind her she heard Leo go into the kitchen and take a beer out of the fridge. He came back into the room, dropping the ring-pull into the nearest ashtray with a tiny clink. Harriet turned to face him. Her legs and back ached with sitting motionless for so long.

"So what do you want to do?" she asked him.

She felt the ground dropping away, faster and faster, in ragged chunks now. Chasms had opened up everywhere, and there was nowhere to put her feet.

"Do? I don't know. What is there to do?"

Harriet's lips felt stiff. In their quarrels before now she had made similar suggestions but it had been to test him, even to test her own aversion to the idea. But this time, when she said, "Call it a day, Leo. Agree to separate," she spoke the words flatly because she knew what would happen was irrevocable. Tonight they had passed the last possible turning-point.

Leo's bounce, the cocksureness that had been a part of him for as long as she had known him, seemed to have drained out of his body. He sat down heavily in the Victorian chair, his hands dangling loosely between his knees.

"If you want to. I don't know. I don't know what I want."

"Are you unhappy?"

"Yes, I'm unhappy."

"So am I," Harriet whispered.

But there was no path left that they could safely tread to reach one another. In the silence that followed, Harriet went into the kitchen and began mechanically to tidy up where no tidying-up needed to be done. After a moment or two, the telephone rang. She glanced at the digital clock above the door of the oven. It was ten past eleven. Late, for a social call. She lifted the receiver from its wall socket, leaned back against the counter-top.

"Harriet, I'm sorry, were you asleep?"

"Charlie?"

It was Charlie Thimbell, husband of her old friend Jenny. Charlie was a friend too.

"I'm sorry," he repeated. "It's late, I know it's late."

Harriet gripped the receiver tighter. "Charlie, what's happened?"

"It's Jenny. She started to bleed."

Jenny was thirty-two weeks pregnant. Harriet had begun to count the days with her.

"When?"

"Tonight. Seven o'clock. The ambulance came, rushed her in." Harriet could tell that Charlie was shaking. Even his voice shook. Harriet was aware of Leo appearing in the kitchen doorway, his eyes fixing on her face. "They did an emergency cesarean. The placenta had just come away. I've never seen so much blood."

"Charlie. Oh, Christ. Is Jenny . . . ? Will Jenny be all right?"

"They didn't know. Not for quite a long time. I've just seen the doctor. He says they'll pull her around. She lost a lot of blood, you see."

"Charlie, listen to me, I'm coming. I'll be there in—in half an hour." She was looking into Leo's face. He had gone pale, his eyes were wide and dark.

"No. No, don't do that. There's nothing you can do. They've told me to go home, and they'll call me. I just wanted to talk, to tell someone."

Harriet knew that Charlie's parents were dead. Jenny's elderly mother lived in the north of England somewhere. "Have you told Jenny's mother?"

Charlie said very quietly, "I . . . I thought I'd leave it until the morning. Now that they say she'll be all right."

Full of fear, Harriet asked, "What about the baby?"

"It's still alive. It went, it went without oxygen for quite a long time, they don't know exactly how long. It's in their intensive care unit. It's a little boy. I haven't seen him. I don't know if they'll let me. They let me take a quick look at Jenny. She opened her eyes and saw me."

"Charlie, please let me come. Or let Jane come. I'll ring her now. I don't want you to be on your own."

He sounded exhausted when he answered, "I'll be all right. I'll go home and sleep, if they won't let me stay here with Jenny and the baby."

Harriet nodded. Leo came around the counter and stood in front of her, trying to decipher what had happened.

"Call me first thing in the morning. Or as soon as you hear anything, it doesn't matter what time it is. Will you, Charlie?"

"Yes. Harriet?"

"What is it?"

"Nothing. Just, thanks. Jenny'll be glad to know you're . . . there."

"Don't worry. She'll be all right." Harriet groped for words of proper reassurance, but found none. "Everything will be all right."

Charlie hung up. Leo put his hand on Harriet's shoulder, but she felt the distance between them. She told him what had happened, and saw tears come into his eyes.

"Christ," Leo whispered. "Oh God, that's terrible. Poor Jenny. The poor little baby."

Harriet was practical. Her concern had all been for what could be done, for what Charlie or Jenny might need. But Leo was different. She knew his grief was genuine, there was softness buried under his swagger, a deep streak of something vulnerable that was almost sentimentality. Tonight this underside of Leo irritated her, and she turned away in order not to witness it.

She put the kettle on and made coffee, performing each step in the sequence with careful attention. She was thinking that it seemed a long time, much more than the few hours of reality, since she had hurried toward Leo's studio with the cinema tickets folded in her bag.

Harriet poured the coffee into two cups, and gave one to Leo. They sat facing each other across the kitchen table, in the positions they always sat in.

"Will the baby survive?" Leo had sniffed and cleared his throat, then lit a cigarette. His face had regained some color.

"I don't know. I don't suppose they do, either. Oxygen deprivation is critical, isn't it? I imagine if he does live, he may be badly damaged." She tried to imagine the small addition to humanity, suspended under lights and wired to machines, but she could not. Her feelings were all for Jenny.

Leo and Harriet talked for a few minutes about the possibility of the baby's survival, the significance for Jenny and Charlie if he should be handicapped.

"Perhaps it would be best in the long run if he didn't live."

Harriet shook her head. It felt very heavy. "I think they will just want him to be alive. However bad the reality is, they'll still want him to survive."

They were doling the words out to one another, aware of the diminishment of their own unhappiness by comparison, but all the same unable to forget it, or to hope of overcoming it.

Harriet drank her coffee. When she looked back at Leo she saw that he held his head in his hands, and that he was crying again.

"Leo . . ."

His head jerked up. "If we had had a baby, Harriet."

Harriet thought, *Had had.* As far in words as it was possible to get from will have, or even might have. That distance made her understand more clearly than the longest explanatory speech could have done that their marriage was finally over.

"If we'd had a baby." Leo shouted this time. Anger licked up in him. Harriet saw how he seized on his own anger almost with gratitude, as though giving vent to it eased his pain. "I would have loved a child, but you wouldn't consider it, would you? That's what marriages are for. They're about creating families. Not about all this, shit." He arm swept sideways. Her eyes followed the movement of it. He meant the tiled floor and the ceramic hob and the dishwasher, the Spanish plates hung on the wall, the wedding presents on the shelves and the painting and decorating they had done together.

"I wanted a whole tribe of kids. I'd have been a good father, a great dad. Like my parents were to me."

Harriet thought briefly of Harold Gold, a blandly bonhomous man fond of delivering advice on how to succeed in business, and Averil, her mother-in-law, to whom Leo was a religion with its own commandments, most of them to do with food.

"But there was never any chance of that, was there? Your own concerns came first, your fucking career, your little business. You're a chilly bitch, Harriet. It's like living with a robot, living with you. You do what's expected of you because you don't like criticism, but it's all an exercise, isn't it?"

Harriet stopped listening. He went on, with his familiar mixture of selfishness and arrogance and childish disappointment. He wasn't wrong, Harriet knew that. He could make every complaint against her with justification, but she no longer wished to change herself for him.

This is what you feel when you stop loving someone, Harriet thought. You see them quite plainly, in all their dimensions, with no blurring into hopes or expectation. It was the absence of hope that made it final.

She stood up and went to the coffeepot for a refill. Too much coffee would keep her awake, but she wasn't optimistic about sleep in any case.

Leo was right to protest that she had refused him a baby, too. They had talked about it, although not often. Leo had always been interested in other people's offspring, much more than she had ever been, except for Jenny's. She had watched the progress of her friend's pregnancy with interest, but without envy. Jane, the third member of their trio of old friends, had been envious. Harriet shied away from the possibility for herself. She felt too precarious to contemplate it, believing that stability, such as Jenny Thimbell had possessed, was as much a prerequisite for motherhood as a womb.

It came to her that she had simply felt precarious with Leo. She wondered why she had never reached the obvious conclusion before.

She had felt, too, that there was still time. She was not yet thirty, and there were other things to be accomplished first. If pressed she might have admitted that she meant business achievements, although she would not have been able to say what kind of achievements. Something more than Stepping, she would have said, with uncharacteristic vagueness.

Leo's spurt of anger had died away. Her silence had denied it its necessary fuel. He sat and stared dully at the table-top.

Harriet found that she could imagine Jenny's baby now. She could see his tiny, folded limbs and his birdlike chest heaving as he took painful breaths.

Live, baby, live, she commanded silently. She wondered if he was living at this moment, or dying.

She picked up her own coffee cup and Leo's, and rinsed them in the sink. She left them on the draining board, turned off some switches.

"I'm going to bed." There was no answer, but she had not expected any.

In their bedroom she undressed, and lay down under the

double quilt. After a moment she sat up again, took the telephone extension off the table on Leo's side of the bed and brought it around to her own. She lay down once more and closed her eyes. She wondered if Leo would come to bed. They couldn't both stay here, after tonight. Then she remembered that Leo was going away for three days from tomorrow, on an assignment. Before he came back, she would have to find somewhere to go. She didn't mind very much that she would be the one who would have to leave. The idea of staying here, alone in this house of strangers, was less appealing still.

She was awake when Leo came to bed. They lay back to back, without speaking. Later Harriet fell into a heavy, unrefreshing sleep.

In the morning, very early, Charlie rang to say that Jenny had woken up properly. She was in pain, but she was only concerned for her baby. The baby's condition was stable. The next few days would be critical, and if he survived them his long-term chances would be good. They would not be able to tell for some time yet how severely his brain had been damaged, if it had been damaged at all.

"That's good," Harriet said warmly. "That's better than it seemed, isn't it?"

"I suppose so," Charlie said. He was normally an ebullient man, but there was none of it in his voice this morning.

"Can I come in and see her?"

"Tomorrow, Harriet, perhaps."

"All right. Give her all my love."

Harriet dialed Jane's number. Jane was a teacher, at a huge comprehensive school in east London. It was impossible to reach her during the day, and it was still early enough to catch her before she left.

"Jane? Have you heard what's happened?"

"Charlie just rang."

"What do you think?"

"It doesn't sound very promising."

They murmured their concern together. Jane was a forthright, single woman, a feminist and espouser of causes. Sometimes she exasperated Harriet, but she also loved her for her warmth and honesty.

"I wish I could go over there and just hold her," Jane said.

"I'm sure Charlie will do that."

"Hmm." Jane took a less positive view of the relationships

between men and women, never having achieved a satisfactory one herself.

"We'll go tomorrow."

"Yes. God, I wish this hadn't happened. If anyone deserves a normal healthy baby Jenny does. I can't think of anyone who would make a better mother. How are you this morning, Harriet?"

"I'll tell you tomorrow, when I see you," Harriet said, without emphasis. "Bye, now."

While they talked Leo had been putting shirts and socks into a canvas grip. Now he tossed a sponge bag and a camera body in on top and zipped up the bag.

"I'd better go. I've got a couple of things to organize at the studio before I leave for the airport."

"Yes. Well, you wouldn't have had time for that last night, what with everything else, would you?"

He straightened up, with his bag in his hand. "I've said I was sorry, Harriet."

"No, you haven't, actually. You said you were sorry I had to see what I did. That's something quite different, isn't it?"

Leo hesitated, somewhere between contrition and petulance. Then he sighed. "There just isn't time for another bloody great row this morning. I'm going to Amsterdam, and that's it. I'll be back on Sunday. We'll talk then."

Harriet lifted her face to him. "It's too late."

He stared at her. "I've got to go," he repeated. Harriet knew that inside himself, within all the layers of bullishness and sentimentality, Leo also knew that it was too late.

He went, closing the door between them, without saying anything more.

Harriet went to work, came home again, and spent the evening alone. The news from the hospital was that Jenny was recovering well, and the baby continued to hold his own. Charlie seemed encouraged by the doctors' predictions.

The next day Harriet left the shop early, to go and see Jenny. She stopped on the way to try to buy her something, but every magazine she picked up seemed to have a picture of a rosy baby on the cover, and every book the word *mother* or *child* in the title. In the end she settled for flowers, late-summer blooms that seemed touched with weariness.

As she walked up the street toward the dull, red-brick bulk of the hospital she saw Jane, hurrying in the same direction ahead of her. She was easily recognizable by her everyday ensemble of loose trousers with numerous pockets and flaps, a shirt with the sleeves rolled up, and her pale hair pulled into a thick plait down her back. "Combat gear," Jane called it, saying "I need it in that place." Harriet had never visited the school, but she had heard the stories about it.

She had asked Jane more than once, "If it's so bad, why don't you leave? Get a job teaching nice, bright, motivated children in a private school somewhere?"

And Jane had looked at her from under her thick, blonde eyelashes. "One, you know that I am not a supporter of private education. Two, to leave the school would be to diminish it further. Don't you think I should stay and continue to do my best for it?"

Harriet could only answer, "If you say so," knowing that it would be useless to embark on an argument about it.

She smiled, now, at the sight of her and ran to catch up. Jane turned in response to Harriet's shout. In one hand she was carrying an old-fashioned battered leather briefcase, probably stuffed with sixth-form essays on *Wuthering Heights*, and in the other a bunch of flowers more or less identical to Harriet's. The two women hugged each other, awkward with their separate armfuls.

"What else can one bring?" Jane said wryly, nodding at the flowers. "Everything I thought of seemed too celebratory or too funereal."

"I know. Jenny won't care, anyway."

They went into the hospital, following signs, and climbed some stairs. At the end of a long corridor they came to the maternity ward. There was the sound of newborn crying and a glimpse of cots at the ends of beds. Harriet and Jane looked at each other, but said nothing. They found Jenny alone in a sideward. She was propped up against pillows, with her arms outstretched, palms up, on the smoothed covers. She looked as if she might have been dozing, but she opened her eyes when they came in.

"I'm so glad to see you," she said, which was Jenny's familiar greeting. It was a facet of her appeal that she made it invariably convincing, but today Harriet thought she might have preferred to be left alone. Her smooth Madonna-face was white and drawn, and there were shadows like bruises under her eyes.

"We won't stay for long," Harriet promised. "Only a minute or two."

"I'm tired because my mother's been here most of the afternoon. She needs more looking after than I do. She's gone now to do some shopping and some tidying-up at home for Charlie. I told her he didn't need shopping for or tidying-up after, but she wouldn't have it." She put her hand out to touch the flowers. "Thank you for these. They're beautiful, aren't they?"

"This is all right," Jane said, looking around the little room.

"Tactful," Jenny said. Her mouth gave an uncharacteristic twist. She had been put in here away from all the perfect babies in their cots in the big ward, of course. They all knew it, there was a strong enough bond between them for anxiety and sympathy to be unspoken. Harriet and Jane sat down on either side of the bed, their hands touching Jenny's.

"How is he?"

Jenny didn't answer at first. Then, with a smile that contradicted the rest of her face, she said, "We've called him James Jonathan. The hospital padre baptized him, you know. Charlie and I were there, the nurses let us hold him for a minute. It was, oh, I didn't mean to cry on you, it was very moving, that's all." Her face collapsed, disfigured with pain. Jane bent forward silently until her forehead touched Jenny's bare forearm. Harriet sat motionless, aware of how much she loved them both. By contrast with the enduring, unemphatic resonance of friendship her concluded marriage seemed over-colored and dissonant. She saw that Jenny's face was shiny with tears. Gently she released her hand, took a handkerchief and dried it for her.

"The news sounded all right this morning," she ventured.

"It was, to begin with. I'd started to make plans. You know, in a month, taking him home. Not expecting too much, just finding out what he could or couldn't do. Then they came to tell me that there was a problem with his breathing. They're ventilating him because his lungs don't want to work. Then they said there was something wrong with his kidneys. There's a blockage in his intestine. They're watching him now, to see if they can operate to clear it."

"It all happened as quickly as that?"

"He's very small. They can . . . they can deteriorate very quickly. But he's much bigger than some of the babies in there. If he can survive the operation, and it's successful, he may still be all right."

They saw the equal and opposite currents of hope and fear in her, and understood some of the tension that made her arms and fingers seem stiff.

"The doctor said not, not to be too hopeful yet. One day, even one hour is critical."

Harriet and Jane said what they could, making little more than small, soothing sounds. They sat quietly for a moment or two when they had come to the end even of that, listening to the hospital noises. There was the metallic rattle of big trolleys, and a smell of boiled vegetables. Early institutional supper was on its way.

"Do you want us to go, Jenny?" Harriet asked gently.

"Stay just for five more minutes." Jenny wearily closed her eyes.

"Where's Charlie?" Jane half-mouthed, half-whispered to Harriet.

But Jenny answered, "His editor wanted him to go and do some story. I told him to go, there's nothing for him to do here. I wish I could do something, other than just lie here. If I could do anything, anything in the world to make him live, I'd do it."

They waited, holding on to one another, saying nothing.

Harriet didn't know how long it was before a doctor came in in his white coat. All three of them stared frozenly at him.

"Mrs. Thimbell, if I could just have a quick word?"

Harriet and Jane bundled themselves into the corridor. They leaned against the green-painted wall, listening to the sound of babies crying. The doctor came out again, his hands in the pockets of his coat. He nodded encouragingly at them and swept away.

Jenny's arms stuck out even more stiffly. She told them, "They're going to operate to clear the blockage this evening. They can't tell me anything else until it's been done. Will you wait until Charlie comes? He said he'd be here at seven."

They sat down again on either side of the bed. They tried to talk, but the words trailed off into silence again, and Jenny seemed to prefer that. Jane spoke once, in a low, ferocious voice. "Come on, James Jonathan. Come *on*."

Charlie came.

He was normally a noisy, red-faced man who was fond of beer and gossip. He used the saloon-bar manner as a cover for his sharp intelligence. But there was no noise tonight.

He sat down and put his arms around his wife, resting his head against her pillows. After a moment, Jane and Harriet crept away.

In the street outside, Jane said, "Let's go and have a drink. I really do need to have a drink. Poor Jenny, the poor love."

There was a wine bar on the corner, one of the green paint, wicker furniture and weeping greenery variety. They ordered wine without deliberation, and sat down at one of the wicker tables.

There seemed little to say that would not be a pointless reiteration of anxiety. Harriet watched people arriving, greeting each other. They all seemed to make tidy couples.

"What's up?" Jane demanded. "It's not just this, is it?"

Harriet shook her head. "But this makes it seem not particularly tragic. Not even particularly significant. I was thinking that, when we were sitting in there with Jenny."

"*What*, Harriet?"

"Leo."

Harriet described what had happened. Jane's thick, fair eyebrows drew together sharply. She had never been particularly fond of Leo, but she was always scrupulously fair.

Fairness made her ask, "Are you sure?"

"Sure? I suppose he might have been doing some calendar shots, and I suppose he might have taken his own clothes off to keep the model company. But then he would have needed a camera, wouldn't he, and a couple of lights? No, it's not funny, I know. He admitted it, anyway. It wasn't the first time, or even the first girl. It's been going on for quite a long time." Harriet paused for a moment and then added, "If I was being honest, I suppose I'd have to say that I half-knew. Only I didn't want to know, so I closed it off."

Jane took a mouthful of her wine. "So what happens?"

"I'm going to leave him."

"Isn't that a bit precipitate? You've been together for a long time. You're Leo-and-Harriet, aren't you? Can't you work it out, build on what you've got, or whatever it is the advice columns tell you to do?"

Harriet had been thinking about Jenny and Charlie, and wondering how their marriage would survive a handicapped baby, or the death of James Jonathan. A little absently she answered, "I don't think any of us can see into each other's marriages."

"No. Especially if you're not married at all, like me."

"I didn't mean that."

Jane's expression softened. "I know you didn't. Don't be stupid. I just wanted to say something obvious like, 'Don't be proud and hasty,' or 'Give each other another chance.' "

Deliberately Harriet told her, "No. There isn't anything to work out or build on, you see. I'm quite sure it's over, and it would only be weakness to try to hang on. Leo's kind of weakness, what's more. There would be more mess, and subterfuge, and undermining one another. I would rather be hard about it now, and then start to get over it."

"Yes. That's you."

"Don't you agree with me?"

"I don't know. I don't know what people promise when

they marry each other. I do imagine promises aren't so easily undone."

But they are, Harriet thought miserably. They are undone, and without love or affection there is no reason for them anyway. It would be different if we had children. *Had had*. She didn't say that, remembering where they had just been, and remembering that Jane wanted a baby, and could never find anyone to father it for her. She took refuge in asperity.

"I don't know why you're defending Leo's sordid behavior."

"I'm not. You know what I think about Leo. I'm just trying to see both sides."

"And that's *you*."

That made them both laugh, a little bubble of welcome laughter that grew out of tension. They leaned together so that their shoulders touched.

"What are you going to do?"

"He's away until the day after tomorrow. I think I'll go home, for a little while. I'd like to tell Kath, as gently as I can. She thinks Leo's as perfect as Averil does. Well, no, not *quite* as perfect. That would be impossible."

They laughed again. Jane knew Harriet's mother-in-law.

"Then I'll look around for somewhere to rent. I suppose, in the end, I'll get half the proceeds of our flat. I haven't thought about it very clearly yet. I'm only sure that we can't be Leo-and-Harriet anymore. It will be a relief just to be Harriet."

Jane looked soberly at her. "All right. You know you can come and stay with me, for as long as you want, don't you?"

Jane had her own tiny house in Hackney, a welcoming place that was often full of people.

"Thank you," Harriet said, meaning it.

Jane sat back in her chair. "I wonder what's happening across there."

"Helplessness makes it worse. Think how it must be for Jenny and Charlie."

They stayed at their table in the wine bar, finishing their bottle of wine without relish, and talking somberly. It was hard to think for long about anything except the baby and what his tiny body must have to undergo.

At last they paid their bill and went out into the warm night. Neither of them felt that they could eat anything; Harriet was reluctant to go back to the new strangeness of her home, but she knew that she must begin to be on her own so that it could become familiar. She had no choice.

They walked a little way together, then paused at the point where they had met earlier.

"Are you sure you won't come back with me to Hackney?" Jane asked.

"No, but thank you. I'll take you up on your offer another time."

"Good night, then." They held on to each other for a minute. Jane's cheek was very warm, and soft.

"Talk to you tomorrow."

"Tomorrow."

Harriet went back to the flat that wasn't home any longer. She walked through the rooms once again, touching possessions that had been Leo-and-Harriet's, thinking.

At five minutes to midnight the telephone rang, only once because she snatched it up.

Charlie told her that James Jonathan had survived the operation, and had been returned to the special care unit, but then his heart had stopped beating. The pediatricians and the nurses had restarted it once, but the rhythm had slowed, and grown irregular, and at last it had faded away.

"Jenny was holding him when it stopped."

Charlie was crying. Harriet's tears rolled down her face.

"I'm sorry, Charlie, I'm so sorry."

James Jonathan's life had lasted just a little more than two days.

Harriet went into her bedroom, lay down in the darkness, and cried for him.

Three

WHEN SHE SET OUT for Sunderland Avenue, for her mother's house, Harriet didn't take her car. It was parked outside the flat and the keys were in her bag, but she didn't even glance at its shiny curves as she passed. She walked to the end of the road, turned right and went on, away from the river and toward the tube station.

In the early days of her independence, before the onset of Leo and the flat and the car, Harriet had always gone home by tube to see Kath. Her mother and stepfather lived on the southern fringe of London, where the narrow streets of terraced houses gave way to the broader, suburban avenues and closes. It was an awkward, boring journey, involving two changes and then a bus ride from the tube station, but it seemed fitting to do it this way, today.

Harriet smiled faintly as she negotiated the local street market, skirting the stalls piled up with cauliflowers and Indian cotton shirts and cheap cassettes.

Going home to mother? she taunted herself, experimentally.

But it wasn't that. She was close to Kath, and she felt the need to explain to her what had happened. She was going home to do that, as if to a friend.

Harriet came out at the other side of the market and saw the tube station ahead on the corner. The pavement outside the entrance was smeared with the pulp of rotten oranges, and littered with vegetable stalks and hamburger cartons. A handful of post-punks and market traders' boys were lounging against some railings. They inspected her as she passed. Harriet had begun to think of herself as too old and too married to be a target for street-corner whistles, but now she reminded herself that she was not quite thirty, and that she was no longer quite married.

She caught the eye of one of the market boys. He stuck out his lower jaw and whistled through his teeth.

"Ullo, darlin'! Can I come wiv yer?"

It wasn't much of a tribute, but it heartened her. She smiled, more warmly than was necessary, and shook her head.

"Aw right, I'll wait for yer!" he shouted after her.

Harriet went on through the shiny mouth of the ticket hall and the dense, stuffy tube smell closed around her. She pressed her money into the ticket machine and moved through the barrier in a sea of Saturday morning shoppers. The escalator swept her downward, making her one of an unending ribbon of descending heads like intricate skittles. The train was crowded. Harriet squeezed in with a press of bodies, and reached up to a pendant knob. A newspaper was folded in her bag, but she could not twist around to reach it, let alone open it to read. Instead she studied the passengers around her.

A young black couple sat immediately beneath her elbow, with a small girl perched on her father's lap. The child's hair was twisted into springy pigtails and she wore a spotless white ruched dress. The child beamed up at Harriet and Harriet smiled back at her. The young parents nodded, conscious and proud.

The smile lingered on Harriet's face as she looked beyond. Standing next to her were three teenage girls, going up west to spend their week's wages on clothes. Beyond them was a fat man in overalls, two boys with headsets clamped over their ears were hunched next to him. There were old ladies, tourists in raincoats, foreign students, wax-faced middle-aged men, all wedged together, patiently perspiring.

Harriet didn't mind being a part of this pungent mass, even felt affection for it. She thought of it as a slice of the city itself, pushed underground, with herself as a crumb of it.

When she changed trains the crowd thinned. She was traveling against the tide of Saturday shoppers and there were plenty of empty seats. Still Harriet didn't unfold her newspaper. She stared through the window opposite at the unending runs of pipework, thinking.

At the end of the line she was almost the only passenger left on the train. She ran up the littered steps, through the various layers of station smells, and boarded a bus outside. Harriet climbed to the top deck. She had always ridden upstairs with Kath, when Liza was a baby, enjoying the vistas and the glimpses into lives behind first-floor windows.

It was a short ride to Sunderland Avenue. Harriet had long ago decided that somewhere in the course of it came the dividing line between London, proper London, and its dimmer, politer suburbs. Shopping streets gave way to long rows of houses fanning away from the main road. There were steep hills, lending the impression that woods and green fields might be glimpsed, in the distance, from the top of the bus. Harriet knew quite well that there never was anything to be seen, even on the clearest day, but the spread of more streets, winding up and down the hills.

The bus stopped at the end of Sunderland Avenue, and there was a steep climb from there to her mother's house. Harriet walked briskly under the avenue trees, past front gardens full of asters and dahlias and late roses. They were big, detached houses built in the thirties, and their owner-occupiers took pride in them. It was a neighborhood of conservatory extensions and new tile roofs and house names on slate plaques or slices of rustic log or spelled out in twisted metal.

The house belonging to Kath and her husband, facing Harriet on a bend at the hilltop, had the look of being even better-tended than the rest. The original windows had been replaced by bigger, steel-framed ones. There was a glassed-in room that Ken called a storm lobby enclosing the front door, a rockery beside the front path and new garden walls of yellowish reconstituted stone. A big pair of wrought-iron gates across the short driveway were painted baby-blue.

Ken owned a small engineering company, with a subdivision specializing in domestic central heating. "My house is as much an advert for my business as my offices, I always say," Ken was fond of remarking.

"You do always say," Harriet would agree, earning a sharp look from Kath and a titter from Liza. But Ken would only ever nod with satisfaction, as if she had simply agreed with him. He was a kind man and fond of his stepdaughter.

Before Harriet even reached the glass door of the porch, Kath appeared among her begonias that sheltered there from any storms that might sweep across south London.

"Harriet! You never said that you'd be coming."

"I took a chance that you'd be in." Equally, she had taken a chance that her half-sister would be out and that Ken would be working.

"Well, if only you'd rung. Liza's at Karen's, and Ken's on a job."

"Never mind." Harriet kissed her mother, then took her arm. "We can have an hour to ourselves." Thinking of what she would have to say in the hour, she added, too brightly, "The garden's looking lovely."

Kath peered over her shoulder. "But where's your car, love?"

"I left it at . . . home. Came on the tube."

Kath looked horrified. "It's not broken down already, is it?" Harriet knew that her mother was proud of her in her smart hatchback, proud of the shop and of Leo whose name appeared alongside photographs in glossy magazines.

"I just wanted to come the old way."

"Well, what a nuisance for you," Kath commiserated, as if conceiving such an odd notion could only be an inconvenience.

They went into the house together, passed through to the kitchen at the back. It was a big room looking through sliding doors on to a terrace and the garden beyond. There were quarry tiles and expanses of pine units with white laminate work-tops, rows of flowered cereal and biscuit jars, a radio playing morning music. Kath spooned coffee powder into floral mugs, flicked the switch of the kettle, and embarked on a piece of news about Liza's latest boyfriend. Harriet stood by the patio doors, half-turned to the garden, looking up the slope of the lawn to the spreading tree of heaven at the end. She listened carefully to the story, putting in the right responses, but Kath broke off midway.

"What's wrong?" she asked. "There's something, isn't there?"

Sometimes she surprised Harriet with her shrewdness. She supposed that she didn't give her mother's insight sufficient reckoning.

"Jenny lost her baby. He lived for two days, he died last night."

She was ashamed of her means of prevarication, putting Jenny's tragedy to Kath at one remove, instead of admitting to her own.

Kath's face reflected her feelings. She knew Jenny only slightly, but her concern was genuine.

"The poor thing. Poor little thing."

Harriet told her what had happened. They drank their coffee, leaning soberly against the pine cupboards.

"Perhaps it was for the best," Kath said at length. "Better than him being handicapped forever. They can start again, when they've put this behind them."

"Maybe," Harriet said sadly.

Kath faced her. "There's something else, isn't there?"

Harriet thought briefly that it would be much easier to talk to someone else, anyone at all, rather than her mother in her dream kitchen.

"Harriet?" Kath was anxious now.

There was no point in choosing mollifying words. Turning her back on the tree of heaven Harriet said, "Leo and I are going to separate."

As soon as it was said she wished that she had wrapped it up a little. Kath went red, banged down her coffee mug, didn't even notice the little pool of spilled liquid that collected on the white work-top.

"No, you don't, my girl. You're a married woman. You don't come back here and say you're giving up after your first quarrel. You have to work at marriages, don't you know that? You'll work it out between you, whatever it is. You'll be all the stronger together after it's all blown over."

Harriet saw that Kath was already smoothing over the damage, making it orderly again in her mind, as if her daughter's life was her own kitchen.

"Don't talk like an advice columnist," Harriet said. "We've been married for four years and had a thousand quarrels. I'm not leaving him because of the quarrels. The truth is that we don't make each other happy. It's time we admitted to the truth. It's quite clear-cut, really."

She hadn't expected Kath would be so upset. Her mother cried easily, but she looked too shocked even for tears to come.

"How can you say that? You make a perfect couple. You always did, at the wedding, ever since."

The wedding, Harriet thought. *I should never have let myself be put through all that.* It had been a big white one, of course, mostly paid for by kind-hearted Ken. Harriet herself in a tight-waisted long dress with a sweeping train and a veil; her half-sister, then fifteen, trying to hide her puppy fat inside folds of corn-gold satin, two other small bridesmaids in cream silk. A hired gray Rolls with white ribbons, and a lavish reception following the carefully ecumenical service. Leo's parents had decided to make the best of the inevitable. Harriet could have spoken their reasoning for them; Leo's girlfriend was presentable and was no fool. She had her own little business and was making a go of it. His family had turned out to the wedding in force and had sent absurdly generous presents.

Now Harriet imagined Averil Gold shaking her well-groomed silvery head and murmuring, "These mixed marriages often come to grief." Before adding, adoringly, "But Leo always was a naughty, headstrong boy."

She looked across the expanse of pine and tile at her own mother. "We're not even a couple. We never were, probably. It's a difficult notion, for people as selfish as we are."

"You're not selfish," Kath insisted. "And Leo's a good husband. He looks after you."

Harriet's forbearance deserted her. "He's a filthy bloody husband," she snapped. "Do you know what I found him doing?

Can you guess? No, don't try to guess. I found him in his studio, screwing a model."

"Are you sure?"

Jane had asked the same question. The realization made Harriet laugh, a gasp of real laughter that made her eyes water.

"Sure? What else might they have been up to?"

"How can you laugh about it?"

Yet Kath seemed more shocked by her daughter's flippancy than by the news itself. It occurred to Harriet that even her mother might have guessed at what she had taken so long to discover for herself. Anger strengthened her determination.

"I'm not going back to the flat. It can be sold, we'll each take fifty percent. I'll use my share to buy a smaller place."

"You're very cool about it."

"Am I? I want to know my own mind, that's all."

Kath was recovering herself. She mopped up the spilled coffee, took her mug over to the sink and dried the bottom of it.

"You always did. Always, from a tiny thing."

Kath remembered how Harriet had been, long ago, when there were only the two of them. Single-minded and possessed of her own unshakable certainties. She shook her head now, sighing. Kath wanted to see her daughter happy and believed she deserved it. But for all her other capabilities, Harriet was always restless rather than contented.

"I think you should give him another chance. Probably he'll never do it again."

"No," Harriet said, leaving no margin for contradiction. "He will do it again, because he's done it before."

She laughed once more. "Do you know, I think it might have been different if he hadn't tried to cover himself up with his shirt?" The absurdity of it made her want to laugh harder. "As if he had something mysterious down there, that I shouldn't see."

Then she caught sight of her mother's face, and the laughter subsided. She went to Kath and put her arms around her. "I'm sorry if you're disappointed. I'm sorry for Leo and me, too."

"Is that all?" Kath demanded.

Harriet thought. It seemed so little, after so much.

"Yes," she said quietly. "It appears to be."

She dropped her arm from her mother's shoulder, walked back to the garden doors and looked out at the big tree again. Its leaves were beginning to show autumnal colors. The tree of heaven drops its leaves every winter, Harriet told herself bracingly. It would be a sentimental mistake to regard it as an emblem.

"May I stay here for a day or two? Until I can rent a place? I can go to Jane's, if it's a nuisance."

Her childhood bedroom was across the landing from Liza's, kept neat nowadays for visitors.

"How could it be a nuisance? Of course you can stay. What shall we tell Ken and Liza?"

"The truth, of course."

As Harriet had guessed, Kath's anticipation of their shock and outrage was much greater than the reality.

"He's a stupid bugger," Ken pronounced. "You do whatever'll make you happy, love. Or I can go around there and thump him for you, if you want."

"Well no, thanks," Harriet murmured.

Liza came back only just in time to change for a date with her latest love. Harriet sat on the corner of the bed and watched her half-sister diving between the wardrobe and the dressing table.

There were too many years separating the two of them, and too many differences, for them ever to achieve friendship. As children they had fought bitterly, too different even to enjoy the satisfaction of being in the same competition. It was to Kath's, and especially to Ken's, credit that the girls had always been treated even-handedly. But still, even in adulthood, the two of them didn't fully trust one another. They existed in a state of uneasy truce, always aware that hostilities might break out again.

Kath's younger daughter had her mother's fair, curling hair and the same full, soft lower lip. Harriet's features were thinner and stronger. Liza was easy-going to the point of laziness, except when there was the faintest threat that she might not get her own way. She was like her mother, too, in that she would go to any length to avoid scenes, preferring that everything should be pleasant and comfortable. Harriet preferred clarity and justice.

"I think Kath believes I'll go back to him," Harriet said.

"And will you?" Even before she had finished speaking, Liza's attention returned to her mirror. She was busily painting her mouth with a fine brush. Harriet remembered that ten years ago she had been absorbed in similar preparations herself and Liza had been a plump, complaining nine-year-old. She had no desire to go back to those days, with or without the help of hindsight.

"Of course not."

Liza snapped the cap back on to her lipstick, rolled her lips inward over her teeth and then pressed them forward into a pout. "I can't say I blame you. But it's a big decision, isn't it? Couldn't you try to forgive and forget? Leo's not bad, even though he's usually the first to tell you so."

Harriet accepted that for Liza this was an unusually profound speech.

"I don't love him."

Liza shrugged. "Then that simplifies it. Are you afraid of being on your own?"

Harriet thought of her married home, with all its symbols and reminders, stuffed with domestic comforts, the possessions of strangers.

"It would be a relief."

Downstairs the doorbell delivered its double chime. Liza sprang to her feet, no longer listening. "Have a good time," Harriet called after her, feeling her age.

Kath and Ken were watching television downstairs. Harriet read a book, an Agatha Christie belonging to Kath, and went to bed very early. She lay in the dark in her old bedroom. She could hear the drone of the television below her. It reminded her of being a little girl, dispatched to bed so that adult life could go on in her absence. From those long wakeful evenings she knew the contours of this room and its predecessors, the patches on the ceiling and the exact, unseen position of the picture rail and wardrobe and armchair. The creak of furniture and the hissing of pipes behind the skirting boards was like a language spoken after a long silence.

The familiarity of the room, the very smell of it, should have been oppressive, but after she had been lying there for a few minutes Harriet began to experience a strange sensation. She felt light, lighter than air. She felt as if she might bob up off the mattress, if it were not for the weight of covers over her. It was as if she had had a great deal to drink, but without the dizziness or the confusion of drunkenness. Her mind felt very clear, and she knew that sleep was a long way off.

It occurred to her after a little while that what she did feel was *free*. She was on her own again.

It was exhilarating and also frightening. With her fists clenched on the bedclothes, as an anchor, Harriet reflected on what she might do. Her responsibilities to Leo, to marriage itself, seemed leaden in retrospect. The future possibilities, by contrast, shimmered around her. They were limitless, and there for the taking. She was afraid, but her fear was of failing to recognize the opportunities when they came. The thought of missing more of

her chances than had already slipped past her, while her hori-
zons were obscured by Leo, made her heart thump and panicky
gasps rise in her chest. She made herself breathe slowly, in and
out, to calm herself again.

The visions of freedom that came to Harriet, lying in the
darkness in her old bedroom in Sunderland Avenue, were all of
what she might achieve. She was briefly, thrillingly convinced
that she could direct herself whichever way she wanted to go.
She could reach out and pick off success for herself, as if it grew
on the tree of heaven outside her window. She felt the power of
it in her fingers.

The images of success and fame and happiness drifted in
front of her. None of the visions had anything to do with love.
She had had Love, and it had turned out to be Leo.

Everything that Harriet saw for herself was clear and vivid,
but it was like a hallucination. When she tried afterward to
recapture the splendor of it all, or even to remember the simple
steps that had carried her to such glory, she could come up with
nothing at all. It had gone as conclusively as a dream.

She didn't know how long the sensation lasted. After a
while she felt her limbs growing heavy once more. She closed
her eyes and was immediately too tired to open them again. A
moment before she had felt that sleep was impossible, now it
was catching up with her. She made no effort to resist it. Harriet
gave a deep sigh of contentment and fell into a dreamless sleep.

Harriet and Kath were talking. At Harriet's suggestion, because
the pine bastion of the kitchen oppressed her, they went out into
the garden and sat on folding chairs in the shade of the tree of
heaven. It was a warm day for late September and the garden
was suffused with yellow light. The buzz of Sunday afternoon
lawnmowers drifted over the fence.

Harriet saw the neat suburban tableau with extra clarity, as if
layers of dust had been washed out of the air by a thunderstorm.
The memory of her waking dream had stayed with her, through
a night's sleep, through a family Sunday morning spent with
Kath and Ken and Liza. She knew that the dream had been
profoundly significant, although she had no specific recall of the
alluring images that had danced before her in the darkness.

She moved carefully in her sharpened awareness, as if there
was a physically tender spot inside her that must be protected.
As she looked at familiar things her clear sight seemed to give
different, surprising perspectives.

Kath was wearing summer sandals on high cork heels, her toenails were painted with a dark, jammy red varnish.

Looking at her mother's feet Harriet said musingly, "You used to have a pair of sandals like that when I was small."

She remembered a blue skirt, too, and a small sandpit, perhaps in a playground. Kath in her blue skirt bent down to her with a cigarette curling blue smoke between her fingers.

"Cork wedgies, that's right. What a memory you've got," Kath said. "You can't have been more than four or five."

"I can remember all kinds of things," Harriet answered. There was something else about today that reminded her of long ago. Perhaps it was the light, oblique and golden, the standard illumination of memory.

Kath looked at her with curiosity. "Can you? What things?"

"Places where we lived, before Ken came. The one up a lot of stairs, where you could look down on the railway lines."

"That was a horrible place. I wish you'd forget it, I certainly have." Kath's voice was sharp. They rarely talked about the time before Ken, before the advent of comfort and respectability.

"It was all right, wasn't it? I remember playing on the stairs. There was a fat woman who used to take me into her room and let me touch some china animals. Where were you?"

"Working. Sybil used to mind you while I was out."

"Those days can't have been easy for you." Harriet often wondered how she had managed, Kath who liked things nice and who hated rows or scenes, or even passion, any demonstration of naked feeling. Yet she had supported herself and an illegitimate daughter, in a series of menial jobs, until Ken Trott had come along to rescue them both. Except that Harriet hadn't wanted to be rescued.

"I had you, love. I wanted to look after you. I wasn't going to let anything come between us, whatever else I had to do."

Except Ken and Liza, Harriet thought, and then almost laughed aloud at the tired old resentment that still came creeping up to assault her. Harriet was eight years old when Ken took Kath and her daughter into the first house and embarked on the processes of refurbishment, bathroom after bathroom and kitchen after kitchen, that had reached their high point here in Sunderland Avenue. Liza was born when Harriet was ten. Adult Harriet knew that she had hated them both, stepfather and half-sister, until late into her teens. Young Harriet did not know what the feeling was, only that it cut her off. She dealt with it, and with other emotions that did not seem to fit in with being a Trott, by suppressing it. She played up the aspects of herself that were approved of, or at the least tolerated, and so she became Harriet the clever one, the determined one, the self-reliant one. Harriet with the wild temper, if you provoked her. Liza was the pretty one, the one who was the image of her mother, the good little girl. The very memory made Harriet want to grind her teeth. She knew that she must have been a difficult child.

"Poor you," she commiserated with her mother.

Kath was shocked. "I don't know why you should say that. I've been very lucky. I could have ended up anywhere, considering the way I began."

Harriet knew that the euphemism meant *considering I was pregnant at eighteen, not married.* She understood her mother's fear of it, even now. It was serious, getting into trouble in the English provinces in 1952. Kath hardly ever talked about it.

Suddenly, in the sunny garden, Harriet's consciousness of her dream suffered a dizzying change of focus. From feeling light and free, she felt sickeningly cut adrift. Her marriage was over. She was grown up, twenty-nine years old, without dependents, without a center to her life. Kath had her center, here with Ken, and Harriet felt ashamed of her adolescent, submerged resentment of it. For herself she had a job, perhaps a dozen real friends. It seemed little to show for thirty years of existence. Thinking of her mother's much more frightening isolation at eighteen, Harriet was possessed by a longing to link herself with that vanished girl.

"Tell me about it. You never have, not really."

"It's all too long ago, love. Ken's your dad, isn't he?"

"Please." Harriet hadn't speculated for years about the existence, somewhere, of a real father. Even in her most intensely separate years she had barely imagined him, and she was not asking about him now. It was Kath she wanted to hear about. She was afraid for herself and drifting. Kath's story would expose the roots that went back before Ken's time. The roots were buried deep; she could hold on by them.

"Tell me," she begged. "Tell me about what you were like then."

Kath was touched by her eagerness. She sat for a few seconds looking down the garden to the open patio doors that led into the quiet house, seeing beyond them. Then, surprising Harriet, she tapped her hands on the metal arms of her chair and began to laugh.

"I was a bright spark in those days. I thought everything I wanted was just there for the taking."

"How strange," Harriet said softly. "I thought that too, last night. I had a peculiar dream about it, except that I wasn't asleep." She wondered if their visions of *everything* were the same, linking them across thirty years. Kath was busy with her own memories, not listening.

"I was very pretty, and I knew it." She turned to Harriet and pushed out her soft lower lip in a flirtatious pout that her daughter had never seen before. They both laughed.

"I had plenty of boyfriends. There'd be the cinema on Friday nights, dancing on Saturdays. One or two of them even had cars. On Sundays we'd go for a drive, right out into the country, to a pub."

"What were they like, the boyfriends?"

"I can't remember. Brylcreemed hair, they all had. Jackets and ties."

One of them, Harriet thought, had been her father. *Which* of them didn't have any significance at all. She tried to imagine him, with his Brylcreemed hair, undoing the knot of his tie before unbuttoning Kath's cotton shirtwaister. The picture would only come to her in black and white, like a still from a fifties movie. She wondered if she had been conceived after the cinema, the dance or the country pub. There seemed no point in asking, "What was *he* like?"

"I do remember someone from those days. Very vividly. I still think of him, sometimes."

Harriet lifted her head. "Who is he?"

"Oh, he was much older than me. He was a neighbor of your grandparents. We lived on one corner of the street and he lived on the opposite corner. Only his house was different, it was turned sideways so it looked in a different direction, and you couldn't see into it from where we were, across the road. He kept to himself, and we hardly ever saw him. It was funny, the way we got to be friends."

"What happened?"

But Kath was simply absorbed in the recollection. She went on, when she was ready, without needing Harriet's prompting.

"I used to ride an old bike. I was doing a typing job for a shoe company and I'd cycle to work when the weather was good to save the bus fare. The day I properly met Mr. Archer I think I must have been talking to a boy around the corner, where your gran couldn't see me. After I said good-bye to him I got on the bike and swung around the corner on it, on the pavement. I ran straight into a lamp-post. Blinded by love, I suppose."

Kath produced the pout again and Harriet laughed once more, although she was impatient for the story to continue.

"I fell off, with the bike on top of me and the bike playing a tune because the wheel was buckled and some spokes had come loose. Mr. Archer was coming up the road the other way, and he helped me up. I was half in tears, with the shock and with feeling a fool, and seeing my bike all bent."

It came back to Kath as if it had happened a week ago. More than thirty years, she told herself, unwilling to believe it. Simon Archer had lifted the bike off her and held out his hand. She had taken it, and with her other hand she had pulled her skirt down to cover her knees. She had struggled to her feet, with his arm around her waist to support her, and the tinny tune wound down as the bicycle wheel stopped spinning.

"The bike will mend," he said. "What about you?"

Kath had never said more than a good-morning to him before. She noticed that he spoke in a smart voice, like an announcer on the radio. She looked up at him and smiled, although her shin was smarting under a fierce graze and her hip and thigh throbbed from where she had hit the pavement.

"I'm all right."

"Shall I fetch your mother?"

Kath made an imploring face. "No, please, unless you want to see me get a telling-off."

"You'd better come in with me, then. That leg needs a dressing."

He wheeled her crippled bicycle into his garden and propped it behind the tall hedge. Kath had hobbled after him, up the path to the front door.

Inside, the house was bare and not very comfortable, but quite clean. Her rescuer made her sit on a wooden chair in the cream-painted kitchen, with her leg up on a low stool.

"Dear me," he murmured. "Now then, first aid kit."

Kath looked around, trying to focus on something other than the stinging cut. There was an old stone sink in the corner with a single dripping tap, a blue-and-gray enameled oven on bow-legs, an old-fashioned wooden dresser with a few plain plates and cups, and a table in the middle of the room covered with an oilcloth.

It was shabbier than the kitchen at home and different from it not so much in its furnishing as in its feeling. Her mother's kitchen was warm, busy, and scented with cooking. This room was cold, and Kath guessed there wouldn't be much food stored behind the zinc grille of the meatsafe. She wondered about Mr. Archer as she watched him filling a small metal bowl with hot water from his kettle. She knew that he was a widower, because she had heard her mother mention it, and she also knew that he did small electrical and mechanical repair jobs for people. That was all. She couldn't even remember when he had come to live in the corner house, although he hadn't been there forever, the way her own parents had.

When he carried the bowl over and knelt down in front of her, she studied him carefully. She guessed that he was almost, but not quite, as old as her father. He had fair, rather thin hair, with a high parting, and a tall forehead. He was rather handsome, she thought, in a Prince Philip way, except that his face was lined and grayish. He glanced up at her, and she saw that he had pale blue eyes.

"You'd better take your stocking off, before I bathe your leg. I'm afraid it's ruined, isn't it?"

"I can't mend a huge hole like that." As if he was a doctor, Kath drew up her skirt and unhooked her suspenders. There was a tiny bulge of white flesh above the brown mesh stocking top, and she knew that they both saw it. She rolled the stocking deftly down until she reached the graze, and then she winced. "It hurts."

"Here." He slipped his thumbs inside the nylon tube and eased the torn edges away from the oozing graze, then twitched the stocking over her toes. "Done."

Kath noticed that he had small, precise hands. He washed the wound, dabbing away the fragments of grit, and then lifted a piece of antiseptic gauze from its tin of thick, yellow grease and laid it in place. He finished off the job with a roll of bandage and then sat back on his heels to admire his handiwork.

"Thank you," Kath said. "That feels much better." She wondered if they ought to shake hands, now that the emergency was past and they were looking at each other in an ordinary, social way. But he had taken off her stocking: it had created an intimacy between them that couldn't be handshaken off.

"I don't know your name," he said, as if he had been thinking the same things.

"It's Kath. Katharine, really."

"Katharine's pretty."

"I'm always called Kath," she said firmly, shaking her head to flick the hair back from her face. It had come loose in the fall.

"Simon," he said. "Would you like a cup of tea, Kath?"

She still felt shaken, and it was comfortable, sitting with her leg up on the stool.

"Yes, please, I would."

While he boiled the kettle and set out two cups and saucers, Simon talked to her. She liked the sound of his voice.

"Are you still at school? I haven't seen you in your uniform lately, so I suppose not."

So Mr. Archer watched her coming and going. Kath was surprised to find that she was pleased with the idea. She pretended to be offended by the question, but went on smiling at him.

"I'm *seventeen*. I work in an office, typing invoices, mostly. Not very interesting."

"And what else do you do?"

"As much as I can."

That was how they talked. Kath would tell him about herself and laugh, and he would ask more questions. He was friendly, but there was a hesitancy about him, as if he didn't enjoy many conversations.

That first time, she remembered, he had told her that he would repair her bicycle. She had promised to come back a few days later.

When it was time to go she glanced down at her legs, and saw one glossy and smooth and the other bare and bandaged.

"Better take the other one off, too," she had said. She had peeled off the other stocking and then dropped the two of them, one perfect and one shredded, into her pocket. Simon made no attempt to look away, nor did she try to be coy. He didn't leer, as most men she knew would have done. He simply watched her, with an openness that she found flattering.

"I'll be back, then," she had said.

"That's good." He had held the door open for her to walk through.

They had become friends. He mended the bicycle and came out to see her ride away on it. She called on him again and sewed the hem of a pair of curtains in his living room, where before they had hung down in neglected loops. After the third time, she visited him without pretext. It was understood between them that she came when she felt like it and that it wasn't necessary for him to visit her at her own house in return.

Kath's mother referred to him as "Kath's friend," with a touch of pride. Mr. Archer was gentlemanly, he had been an officer in the war, and had lost his wife tragically young. She didn't, as she often protested, have any idea why he put up with listening to Kath's nonsense. But he seemed to enjoy it, and it would do Kath no harm to talk to someone with a bit more sense than the boys she was endlessly running off to the pictures with.

That was how it was. Kath's friendship with Simon Archer lasted for less than a year. Toward the end of that time Kath's full skirts were no longer concealing the bulge underneath them, and her pretty face had taken on a pinched, defiant look.

Kath stopped talking. Busy with the threads of recollection, she didn't see that Harriet was sitting stiffly upright in her chair. Kath was remembering one winter afternoon, early on, when she had knocked on Simon's door after walking back from shopping. She had been wearing a scarlet wool scarf, and a matching knitted hat. She had followed him into the kitchen, laughing about something, and had dropped her hat and gloves on the oilcloth. She had taken off her coat, too, because she was warm after her walk. Simon had turned from the sink where he had been filling the kettle, and seen her. She knew that her cheeks must be rosy from the wind, because she felt the heat glowing in them.

Simon put the kettle carefully down on the stove. He came to her and put one hand on her waist. It rested very lightly, curving with the hollow. He lifted his other hand and touched her cheek, brushing it with tiny movements of the fingers, as if he wanted to feel the texture of her skin.

Startled, she jerked her head back to look into his face. She was still smiling, from what she had been saying before, but the smile didn't widen or fade. It seemed to stiffen on her mouth. They had stood quite still, just like that, for one or two seconds. And then Simon had nodded, as if he was sure now of something that he had only suspected before. He had let her go, only he hadn't really been holding her. He had gone back to the stove and she had chatted on, but watching the back of his head because she wanted him to look around at her like that again.

When he did turn, after quite a long time, she wondered if whatever it was had ever really happened at all. There was nothing in his face to show it, and she didn't know how to tell him that she understood.

"Where is he now? Is he still alive?"

Harriet's voice startled Kath. She had forgotten that she was there.

"What did you say?"

"I asked, is he still alive?"

Harriet was sitting on the edge of her chair, with her knees drawn up against her chest. Her face had turned pale and her eyes shone. They were fixed on Kath.

"Simon? I don't know, love. I left home before you were born, because your grandparents wouldn't hear of me staying. I came down to London, you know all this, and lived with my cousins until after I had you."

Very quietly, Harriet asked, "Didn't Simon look after you?"

She saw the light that had softened Kath's face begin to fade. There were lines in the loose flesh around her eyes and beside her mouth; her hair was permed in graying ridges. Her mother wasn't a girl of eighteen at all, although for a moment Harriet had glimpsed that girl. She wanted to hold on to her, denying the years.

"Why should he have done?" Kath answered. "It was my own problem. *You* were. I wanted it that way, once I knew I couldn't marry the father. They'd have had me back, at home, if I'd let you go for adoption. But I wouldn't let you go, so I never went up there again."

Harriet knew about that. Kath had told her, often, it was part of her childhood creed, *I wouldn't let you go.* Kath's possessiveness had made her both father and mother. There was no need to speculate about him. He was faceless and nameless, an ejaculation. A physical spasm, like a yawn or a shiver. *The* father, Kath called him, not *yours.* Harriet couldn't remember her ever having said even that much before.

But today she had seen something different in her mother. She had seen youth, but she had also seen sex, with its face scrubbed bare, clean and wholesome. She had caught sight of Kath as a girl, and that girl had emitted a powerful signal. Now, at once, Harriet wanted to know about the man who had intercepted and returned that signal. She felt the crackle of its electricity, even over the remove of years. She was hungry because she had never experienced that charge herself, jolting through her bones, not with Leo nor with anyone else.

She would have to find the man, because he belonged to her. It was important to know him as part of her own history. Harriet felt herself both set free and dangerously adrift, and she needed a new anchorage before she could set a fresh course. Names, places, even the smallest details, if she was too late for anything more, would help her to fix herself.

She left her chair and went to kneel beside her mother, resting her head against Kath's knees.

"Harriet? Are you all right?"

"Yes. Yes, I am."

Ever since she had been old enough to understand her own story, her father had had no name and no face, because that was how Kath had wished it. Harriet had felt no need for anything more, because her mother gave her all she wanted. The fierce exclusivity of their love had only been disrupted by Ken, and later by Liza. But now, Harriet was certain that he had both a name and a face, and she understood what a chasm there was to be filled.

She was certain, without needing to ask, without changing the rule of years between Kath and herself, that Simon Archer was her father. Leo had gone, and it was both ironic and apposite that his disappearance should expose a deeper bond waiting to be uncovered.

In a light, clear voice Harriet said, "I'd like to go and see where you grew up. Perhaps he . . . your friend is still there."

"He probably wouldn't remember me, even if he was. It's a very long time ago."

Of course, all my lifetime.

"I'd still like to go."

"But there's no family left up there."

There had been a reconciliation, naturally. From the age of five or six onward, Harriet remembered visits to her grandparents. But by then they had moved away from the Midlands town, and then they moved on again. Now they lived in a retirement bungalow on the coast, with photographs of their two Trott granddaughters displayed on the mantelpiece.

"It doesn't matter," Harriet said. "Even if there's nothing there at all. It's where I began, after all. I can just walk along the streets and look at it."

She stretched up and kissed her mother, then scrambled to her feet. Looking down at her she hesitated, and then asked, "Why did you tell me all this today?"

Kath answered dreamily, "You just made me remember it."

Of course. Beginnings and endings, one separation and another coming together.

Harriet picked up the tea tray from between their chairs and walked away down the garden, in through the patio doors.

She was going to look for her father. And when she had found him, from that point she could start again.

Four

THE TOWN HAD LONG AGO been consumed by the city.

In the local train, looking out, Harriet imagined that in her mother's childhood there might have been a green ribbon of woods and fields separating the last housing estate from the first filling station. Now there was no dividing line, of trees or anything else, and the backdrop of houses and shops and small factories flowed seamlessly past her.

At the station, she bought a local street map from the bookstall and sat on a bench to study it. The other passengers from the train passed her and crowded out through the ticket barrier. When Harriet looked up, the train had pulled out and the platform was deserted. At once, she was aware of her isolation in an unfamiliar place. The place names on the train indicator above her head meant nothing to her, and she was ignorant of the streets that led away from the station entrance.

There was no sense of a homecoming. If she had arrived expecting anything of the kind, Harriet reflected, then she was being sentimental. But still she had felt herself irresistibly drawn here, and there had been complicated arrangements to make before she could allow herself the time off from her business. The urban anonymity she had glimpsed from the train was less than welcoming, and she allowed herself the irrationality of a moment's disappointment. Then she stood up, closing the street map but keeping her finger in place to mark the right page, and briskly walked the length of the platform. Her heels clicked very loudly, as if to announce her arrival.

The ticket collector had abandoned his booth, and so Harriet passed through the barrier without even cursory official acknowledgment of her arrival. There were two dark-red buses waiting beside a graffiti-sprayed shelter, but neither of the destination boards offered the area she was heading for. There was also a taxi at the rank, and the driver eyed her hopefully. Harriet hesitated, and then passed him by. She didn't want to arrive at the house on the corner by taxi, proclaiming her lack of familiarity to

whoever might now live in Simon Archer's house. If the house
was even still there, she reminded herself. Her mother's home
town had changed in thirty years.

Harriet bent her head over the map once more, then hitched
her bag over her shoulder and began to walk.

The scale of the map was deceptive. She walked a long way,
more than a mile, and her shoes began to rub. It was a long time
since she had drunk a cup of coffee on the InterCity train from
Euston, and she thought of going into a pub for a drink and a
sandwich. But she knew that sitting alone in a bar could only
heighten her sense of displacement, and she walked on instead.

The road was busy with a constant stream of heavy traffic
that left a pall of grime in the air, and over the houses and
shopfronts. The shops that she passed were small, with meager
and faded displays behind the dirty glass, and the houses looked
cheerless and hardly inhabited.

Harriet was disconcerted by the anonymity of the streets,
and by their barrenness. There was nothing to tell her, *You are
here, a thin thread links you to us, Sam's Superette and Madge's Wool
Shop and S. Walsh, Turf Accountants.* The disappointment that she
had felt on the station swelled, and to counteract it Harriet told
herself that she hadn't come looking for a place, only for the
people it had once sheltered. As she plodded on, Kath's astonishment at her pilgrimage seemed justifiable. Even Harriet found
it hard to believe that she would discover her father in this gray,
ugly, and exhausted place.

To stifle the thought, she resumed her observation. The one
place this could not be, she thought, of all defeated urban
wildernesses, was London. Even in its parts that were sadder
than this, London had an unmistakable vitality. There was no
liveliness here. Harriet felt a wave of affection for London, like
the surprising warmth that had overtaken her on the crowded
tube ride to Sunderland Avenue. There was home, after all, and
there was everywhere else. Had Kath felt that, once, about these
streets? Presumably not, Harriet decided. She had left and never
come back.

The responsibility—was it responsibility, or simply need?
—had devolved upon herself.

A dark-red bus trundled past her, the board on the back
bearing the same destination as the one she had rejected outside
the station. Harriet quickened her pace, but the stop was in the
distance and even as she half-ran it slowed, dropped a single
passenger and gathered speed again. She stopped to consult her
map for the last time, and saw that her goal was only a handful

of streets away. She turned a corner, and then another, away from the main road.

There were houses here instead of shops. This was where Kath had lived, ridden home on her bicycle to save the bus fare. Harriet's senses were all primed, ready for the impressions to crowd in on her, but now that she was here there was nothing to feel. The rows of houses were neither inviting nor as seedy as the ones that lined the main road. They were simply ordinary and insignificant.

Almost too quickly, she found herself at the right turning. She checked the street name and looked across at her grandparents' house. It was the same as all the others, the windows masked with net curtains, a patch of garden separating the front door from the pavement. Harriet turned away from it to look at the house opposite. As Kath had described, it faced in a different direction, presenting a high, blind wall of reddish brick directly to the street.

Very slowly, she crossed the road and walked around in the shelter of the wall. She came to a dusty hedge, too high to see over, enclosing the front garden of the house. When she found the gate, she had to push past scratchy branches to reach the path and the front door. As she looked for a bell to press she discovered that she was breathless, almost gasping. There was no bell-push. She pressed the flap of the letterbox and it snapped back on her fingers. The sound generated no answering sound within the house, and the windows remained sightless. Harriet knocked, hard, with bare knuckles.

Then she heard someone coming. She rehearsed her lines. A friendly smile, *I'm looking for a man who used to live in this house. A long time ago, I'm afraid. How many years have you . . .*

The door opened.

Harriet's smile never materialized. She had tried to envisage all the alternatives that might confront her, the Bengali housewife with no English, the surly night-shift worker, the transitory bed-sit dweller—absurdly, she had made no provision for facing Simon Archer himself.

The man who opened the door was in his late sixties, stooped but still tall, with strands of thin, colorless hair brushed back from a high forehead.

"I'm sorry," Harriet said. "I'm looking for Mr. Archer."

The man regarded her. Harriet felt half deafened by the blood in her ears, pounding like surf. *I'm looking for my father.* The enormity of what she was doing threatened her, made her wish herself somewhere else.

"I am Mr. Archer."

"Did you . . . were you living here thirty years ago?"

He didn't like questions, Harriet saw that at once.

"What relevance can that possibly have? Are you from the Social Services? I don't want Meals on Wheels, or large-print books."

"I'm not from the Social Services, nothing like that. I just want to ask you about something that happened a long time ago."

"Department of Oral History at the Polytechnic?"

He did have a cultured voice, clipped and precise. Harriet understood Kath's comparison with a radio announcer, but an announcer of the old, dinner-jacket days. The recognition drew her closer to the eighteen-year-old with the torn stocking, giving her the determination to press further. Harriet found her smile, although the warmth of it wasn't reciprocated.

"Nothing like that, either. I'm Kath Peacock's daughter. Kath, who used to live across there. She was a friend of yours." *And more. You must remember.*

For a moment Harriet was afraid that Kath was right, and Simon Archer had forgotten her. Then, with an imperceptible movement, he let the door open an inch wider.

"Kath's daughter?" There was a pause. "Come inside, then."

She followed him into a dim hallway. She had an impression of cracked yellow paint, a narrow stairway with bare boards, a curtain with musty folds smelling of damp. At the end of the hallway there was a kitchen, with a small window looking over a garden at the back. In this room, Harriet thought, Kath had sat the first time, with her leg propped on a stool. She wondered what else had happened here.

Simon Archer jerked his chin at the room. There were piles of newspapers on every surface, jars with brushes stuck in them, tools and crockery intermingled, dust and a smell of mildew everywhere.

"I won't ask you to forgive the state of things in here. Why should I, and why should you?"

Harriet held her hand out. "I'm Harriet Trott."

Simon took her hand, briefly and formally. His was bony and cold. "Harriet Trott," he repeated. "But you're a grown woman."

"I'm nearly thirty," Harriet said gently. "It's almost exactly thirty years since Kath left here."

He looked at her, still unconvinced by her claim. "And you're her *daughter*?"

"Yes."

Simon shook his head. "I forget. Kath can't be eighteen any longer, can she? No more than I am."

"Next year she'll be fifty."

"I suppose so." He moved away from her, edging around his kitchen, lifting one or two of the pieces of clutter and putting them down again elsewhere as if to establish his dominion over this much, at least. "Would you like a cup of tea?"

"If it's not too much trouble."

Harriet watched him lifting and filling the kettle, wiping two dusty cups with a matted cloth. She was studying the shape of his head and his hands, the set of his features, wondering if she might see herself. She could only see an elderly man in a green cardigan and oil-stained trousers, no more. Her neck and jaw muscles ached with the tension of her gaze.

"Do you know why she called you Harriet?" The abruptness of the question startled her, so that she only shook her head numbly. "Rather than Linda or Judy or something that was fashionable then? No?"

He put the cups into a clearing on the table, an old brown earthenware teapot beside them, with a clotted milk bottle. "Not very elegant. I don't get many visitors. Well, she called you Harriet after Harriet Vane."

She had been expecting a revelation, perhaps an admission that would connect the two of them. "Who is she?"

Simon laughed, a little dry noise in his chest. "You're like your mother. She wasn't a big reader either, but she did like detective stories."

"Still does. The shelves at home are full of Agatha Christie."

"Don't you?"

"Not really. I don't read anything much. I work hard, I manage quite a big shop that sells fitness equipment, dance-wear, things like that. In fact I own the franchise, so it's my own business. I'm at the shop all day, and in the evenings there's paperwork to do. There isn't much time for anything else." The words came spilling out. She wanted to impress him, Harriet realized. Why else should she need to boast about her responsibilities?

"How modern," Simon said. "To answer your question, Harriet Vane is a character in the Lord Peter Wimsey books written by Dorothy L. Sayers. I lent them to your mother, long ago, and she fell in love with Lord Peter. Her favorite was *The Nine Tailors*, although Harriet doesn't appear in that one." There was a pause. "I remember her telling me that you would be either Peter or Harriet."

Deliberately, Harriet said, "I never knew that. I think there are all kinds of things I don't know about."

Simon poured the tea. "Perhaps that's for the best?"

She was certain that he was sparring with her. He must know why she had come. She took the cup that he held out and drank some of the tea. It had an oily film on the surface, with whitish flecks caught in it. *Tell me,* she wanted to say, but Simon headed her off.

"What about Kath Peacock?" he asked. "I'd like to hear what has happened to her. Who is Mr. Trott?"

Harriet relaxed a little, some of the stiffness ebbing from her neck and head. "I can tell you all about Mum. She's well. I think she's very happy. She didn't want me to come to look for you."

"I don't know why you've come to look for me. Go on about your mother."

"She married Ken while I was still quite small. He's an engineer, a nice man. As a hobby he likes buying houses and putting in new bathroom suites and building retaining walls and then selling the house and starting all over again with a different colored bathroom."

Simon raised one eyebrow and looked around him, and then their eyes met and they began to laugh. The laughter was spontaneous and easy, as if between friends. It warmed Harriet and it convinced her that, after all, she had been right to come. Simon took out a handkerchief and blew his nose. "That gives me a very vivid picture. Carry on, please."

In the beginning, Harriet just talked about Sunderland Avenue, Ken's work, Liza and her boyfriends and Kath in her kitchen. Simon Archer listened and drank his tea. Then, with more confidence, she went further back, to Liza's birth and her own furious jealousy, and beyond that to the arrival of Ken to rescue her mother and herself.

"Not that we needed rescuing," Harriet said. "Kath and I were fine. I thought we had everything we needed, just the two of us."

"Yes."

Simon's responses were never more than a word or two. He watched Harriet closely as she talked, but his own expression didn't change.

"I didn't want to share her with anyone. When Ken came, she wasn't all mine anymore. He had a car, and a house with proper plumbing and a garden and all that, but I'd rather just have had Kath to myself, like before."

And then she told him about *before,* about the succession of furnished rooms, the times spent waiting for Kath to come home from work, and her unformulated but clear childish understanding that they must be everything to one another because there was no one else.

Simon's eyes still held hers, shrewd, without any sign of distress. "Kath needed more," he said. It was a statement rather than a question, the verdict of someone who knew her well. Harriet nodded, disappointed in him. She had expected more return for her story.

Simon smiled, sensing as much. "Thank you for telling me all this. It's comforting to rejoin broken ends, or to have them joined for me, since I'm long past involving myself in anything of the kind." A small gesture indicated the chaotic kitchen, hinted at the decaying house beyond it, and told her that Simon was indeed past involvement in the common processes of life. She felt both sorry for him and angry at his withdrawal from the world. For the first time since she had arrived she saw him as himself, not illuminated by Kath or herself. As a result her need to know, father or not, released its choking grip on her a little.

She asked, "Why are you?"

He chose to ignore the question, but disarmed her. Talking almost to himself, he said, "Kath was unusual. She was alive, vibrating with life, like nothing else around." This time the gesture took in the extinguished town, as it must have been in the post-war years. Then and now, Harriet thought. "I used to love to see her, and listen to her. She lit everything up."

"I know. For a long time I haven't bothered to see her as anyone but my mother. In the kitchen, cooking meals. Ordinary. Then all of a sudden I saw a young girl looking out of her face, when she told me about you. It's one of the reasons why I wanted to meet you. I came from London to find you."

As soon as the words were out, she knew that they would have been far better left unsaid. That she had come at all was a threat all over again, to have come a long way, with a list of reasons, was too much of an intrusion.

Simon looked at an old kitchen clock, almost obscured on the mantelpiece by sheaves of yellowing bills and papers. Harriet knew that they had been sitting at the table for almost two hours. Stiffly, but deliberately, he stood up.

"I'm glad you came. I'm pleased to hear that Kath is well, and happy. She deserved that." He had asked her in, and she had accepted his hospitality. His courtesy would continue, but it was clear that she couldn't hope for anything beyond it.

He held out his hand now, and reluctantly she shook it.

"Perhaps you'll give her my best wishes," Simon added. "I don't think any other greeting would be appropriate, after thirty years." If there was a twitch of a smile, it was gone before Harriet could be sure. "This way," Simon said. "I'm sorry the passage is so dark."

There was the crumbling hallway again, the front door and then the empty street. Simon shook her hand once again, as if she was the well-meaning but unwelcome official he had first taken her for, then closed the door.

The autumn afternoon was already almost over. There were yellow lights showing in two or three of the windows opposite, and in contrast with the coziness Simon's house seemed morbidly chilly and dark. Angry with herself, smarting with the rejection, Harriet began to walk away.

A small boy on roller skates rattled over the uneven paving stones, wobbled, and almost fell. He grabbed at her arm to save himself.

"Be careful," Harriet warned, and he gaped up at her, dirty-faced and cheerful.

"You've never been in there, have you?" He jerked his head at Simon's gate.

"Yes, I have. Why not?"

He whistled, pretending admiration. "Cos he's mad. My sister said. You want to watch he doesn't get you." Delighted with his dire warning he launched himself off again.

Harriet watched him almost collide with Kath's lamp-post. Even in her girlhood, Kath had said, the little children tended to avoid Simon's house. Now, a solitary old man existing in a nest of newspapers and rubbish, he was a bogeyman to frighten another generation. Sadness for him overcame Harriet's bitterness and hungry curiosity once more, and made her want to know about him for his own sake. She looked up at the house but it was obstinately dark.

Harriet turned away without any idea where she was heading. She walked the length of her grandparents' old street, looking through the still-open curtains at the blue eyes of television sets, tea tables, homework. She rounded a corner, went on without the intention of going anywhere.

At length she came to a park with elaborate railings, and took a tarmac path under some trees. A boy and a girl in school uniforms stood against the peeling bole of a plane tree, arms wrapped around each other, faces pressed together. Harriet passed them, came to a bench next to an overflowing litter bin. She sat down on the bench, and dead brown leaves scuttled like insects around her feet.

She sat on the bench for a long time, without moving. She didn't even think of going back to the station and the conclusion of the London train. The boy and girl drifted by, white faces turning to peer at her in the dusk, frightened of being spied on. Harriet waited until they were out of sight, then stood up and shook herself. She was cold, and swung her arms to warm her fingers as she headed for the sound of traffic on the main road.

In the center of a parade of shops she came to an Indian restaurant. It was opening as everything else closed up, and Harriet peered past the menu, mounted in an arched wooden frame and set off with plush drapes, into an interior of white cloths and twinkly lights. She was hungry as well as cold.

The restaurant was completely empty. A waiter in a white jacket came forward, beaming at her, and they went through a pantomime of deciding which table would suit her best. She chose one beside a green-lit tank of morose tropical fish, and ordered a bottle of wine to go with her food, because there were no halves.

Harriet couldn't remember ever having sat down alone to dinner in a restaurant. It seemed appropriate that she should do it here, where she had felt her isolation so strongly. Her awareness of it was just as strong, but it seemed to matter less now. She thought about Leo, and the hundreds of dinners they had shared. Her memories were affectionate, but Leo himself seemed a long way off. She didn't wish that he was here with her, or that she would be going back to him.

The smiling waiter brought her lamb pasanda, paratha and sag ghosht, and poured out the wine for her.

"You are living near here?" He had a very dark face, and a gypsyish gap between his top teeth. Harriet smiled back.

"No. I've come from London."

"Nice place," he told her. She wasn't sure whether he meant here or there, but it didn't matter. She suddenly felt comfortable, wedged between the fishtank and the tablecloth that looked purple and green under the multicolored lights.

She ate everything, and drank most of the wine because she was thirsty and because the food was so spicy it made it seem innocuous. Afterward, while she was drinking a cup of watery coffee, some other customers filtered in. A young couple stared covertly at her, and two businessmen talked in loud voices. The feeling of being at home vanished at once. She called for the bill and hurriedly paid it. Her waiter shook her hand as she left. "Come back again."

"Perhaps."

Outside she took a deep breath. She knew that she was rather drunk, but perhaps that would be a help. Without needing to consult her map, she retraced her steps to Simon's house.

It took a long time for him to answer the door. Harriet's knuckles were bruised with knocking. At last the door creaked open and he loomed in front of her. When it was too late she thought of running away, like the children.

"I've come to ask," she said, "whether I could borrow *The Nine Tailors*?"

She thought she saw relief in his face. She didn't know if it was because she had come back or for the harmless idiocy of her question.

"I told you, that one doesn't have Harriet in it. You could begin with *Busman's Honeymoon*, if you like."

"If you think that's a good idea."

He stood aside, to allow her to come in again. In the kitchen, Harriet saw that the remains of two boiled eggs had been added to the mess on the table. Simon reached into a cupboard and held up a bottle of whiskey, two-thirds empty. She nodded gratefully at it. "Yes, please."

"I haven't seen those books in years. It might take me a while to find yours, in all this." The slight, comprehensive gesture again.

"There's no hurry." Harriet laced her fingers around the sticky glass, took a gulp of the whiskey. "Simon, there's something I want to ask you."

Simon. She had avoided calling him anything, before. The whiskey hit her stomach. Now or never.

"I know you don't like questions, I'm sorry. Is there any possibility that you might be my father?"

Simon drank, looking at her over the rim of the glass. His face was creased.

"That was really what you came to find out."

"Yes."

"There isn't any possibility at all. I wish I could say something different. I wish I really were your father."

As soon as she heard it, she knew that it had been a ridiculous quest. If he had been, even if only perhaps, Kath would have found a way to tell her. Harriet had longed for the idea of him, denying every likelihood, to fill a void. The void was her own, inside her, nothing to do with Leo because the history of it went back much further than her brief marriage. Simon couldn't fill it. Nor should she ask him to. Harriet stood up. She moved with exaggerated, half-drunken care, around the table to Simon's side. She put her arm around his shoulder and rested her cheek against the top of his head. Tears ran out of her eyes and down her cheeks.

"I wish, as well. I hoped, all the time."

"Come and sit here." He took hold of her arm and guided her so that she half-leaned, half-sat on the table, where he could see her face. With his other hand he poured himself another drink.

"I've got some catching up to do."

Harriet rubbed her face with the palms of her hands, raggedly exhaling like a child recovering from a crying fit, and then smiling woefully. "I needed Dutch courage. Didn't do me much good."

"Cry if you feel like it, Harriet. I do."

"Here, by yourself?" The image pierced with sadness.

"Where else? Listen, I'll tell you about Kath and me. I loved her, you guessed that. I would watch her across the street. She used to come and visit me, tell me about her adventures, and I'd look at her sitting there, where you are. I'd have done more, of course, if I could. I only touched her once. Put my hands *here*." Stiffly, watching the hand with its brown blotches and twisted cords as if it belonged to someone else, he touched Harriet's waist. "She was so shiny, her eyes and skin. She was surprised. Not offended, or saucy, just surprised. I took my hand away. That's all. That doesn't get you a daughter thirty years later, does it?"

Harriet shook her head.

"Let's finish the whiskey," Simon concluded.

"That isn't all the story. Kath's only a tiny bit of it." With relief, Harriet forgot her own concerns. It was Simon himself who drew her now, the more sharply because he was free of the miasma of her clumsy hopes and expectations. The neon strip light suspended over his kitchen table cast harsh shadows, focusing them in their postures of almost-intimacy.

"You're not my father. It doesn't matter, I never even wanted one until Kath told me about you. But the fact that you aren't doesn't take you or me away, does it, now that we're both here? Perhaps we can be friends."

In her own ears, it sounded brash. A facile solution. But he had said, *I wish I were your father.*

"I don't have any excuse for asking. Except that I've drunk a bottle of wine and a double scotch. Why do you cry, Simon?"

"Why not?" The evasiveness, she was discovering, was characteristic. She felt suddenly tired, and Simon perceived it.

"What are the responsibilities of friendship? You'll have to remind me."

Harriet considered. "To talk. And to listen. Very important, that."

"I can listen. Most competently."

"I'd rather you talked. I have, far too much. Go on." Harriet picked up the bottle, pushed it toward him. "Talk to me."

"What a very odd girl you are. Nothing like your mother. What do you want to know?"

She smiled at him, then. "I want to know what sort of father you might have been, if you had turned out to be him."

"A disappointing one, I imagine. This is what I do, look. I repair things." He held up a small brown rectangle, nibbled with cut-outs and colored wires and brightened with drops of silver. From among the dirty plates and greasy papers he picked up an instrument that looked like a tiny poker at the end of a cord. A curl of silvery wire lay next to it. "Resin-core solder," he told her. An acrid smell momentarily overpowered the kitchen's other odors and a tiny silver tear fell onto the circuit board. "This is part of a transistor radio. Hardly worth repairing. It would be cheaper to go and buy another. The Japs overtook me long ago." He picked up another small, disassembled mechanism. "Quartz alarm clock. Same thing, but I like clocks."

"The one in the hall?" Harriet had noticed it in the dim light. It was a grandfather clock with a handsome moon-face, incongruous in the dingy surroundings.

Simon's expression changed. "Come and look at it."

She followed him into the narrow space. Simon stroked the smoothly patinated case, then opened the door so that she could look inside. She gazed at the cylindrical weights on their chains. The ticking sounded thunderous in the silent hall.

"I rebuilt the mechanism," Simon said. Harriet thought about the springs and coiled wires behind the painted face. "If you're interested," he added abruptly, "you can come in here."

He opened a door to the front room of the house. The kitchen was neatly ordered by comparison. In here was what seemed to be the forlorn detritus of many years. Harriet blinked at the skeletons of chairs, their legs and arms tangled with coiled wire, a bicycle frame, a standard lamp with the scorched shade hanging broken-necked. Cardboard boxes were piled high, sagging and spilling over between broken picture frames, rusty tins, a roll of carpet, a backless television set. Against the far wall, with a tin bath propped against it, stood a lathe with its ankles immersed in a small sea of silvery metal curls. There was a smell of oil, and damp, and persistent cold.

In the middle of the room, in a clearing, was a rough wooden workbench. It was scattered with tools, drills and files and screwdrivers curled with woodshavings, reels of solder, and used tobacco tins containing screws and drill-bits and colored capacitors. A modern desk lamp was screwed to one side, and Simon clicked it on. He began to hunt among his tools, Harriet seemingly forgotten. She watched him, aware that here, at his bench, was where he spent his time. She shivered in the cold.

"Put the heater on," he told her. She found it in the tangle, a single-bar fifties model, and dust sparked and smelled as the element began to glow.

"Here it is." Simon held up a tiny nugget of hairsprings and cogwheels. "And here's the case." He fitted the mechanism into a silver sleeve engraved with flowers and leaves, then turned it over to show her the glass face, and the web-fine numerals. "It belonged to my grandmother. An exquisite piece of fine watch-making. I used to be able to take it apart, and put it together again, just to admire it. It has a perfect economy of form and function. I couldn't do it now. Eyesight's gone."

Harriet took the watch and examined it, following the leaf-patterns in the silver.

"What else do you do?"

"Apart from repairing worthless modern clocks and radios? Yes, I make things. I enjoy that, meeting a challenge. There's no practical relevance, more an abstract pleasure, like solving a puzzle."

"What sort of things?"

Simon looked around his room, then scooped a pair of alarm clocks and a kettle on a bracket from the nearest cardboard box. "Why do you want to know about this? Here's a perfect example. I was without electricity for a while." He didn't explain why, and Harriet could guess. "I thought it would be interesting to make myself an early morning tea-machine that worked without it. Here it is. *This* alarm clock goes off, operates a flint-lighter under the kettle, lights a wick over a spirit reservoir. Heats the water, which takes a measured amount of time. When the kettle is boiling nicely, the *second* alarm goes off, operates this lever that tilts the kettle over the teapot, and wakes the sleeper at the same time. Hot cup of tea all ready and waiting. It worked perfectly the first time, then I came across an unforeseen snag."

"Which was?"

To her surprise, Simon began to laugh. The laughter began as a low rumble, then he put his head back and the sound swelled to a roar. "On the second morning, the reservoir holding the spirit cracked. The meths ran down the bedclothes and ignited. I woke up in flames. I didn't need a cup of tea to get me out of bed."

Harriet laughed then, too, in snorts that stirred the fine dust and made her splutter. It lasted a long time, this second laughter that they had shared, and it dissolved another invisible barrier between them. When it had subsided, and Simon had replenished his whiskey glass, Harriet perched on the arm of a wrecked chair and listened as he talked.

"I'm glad you came back," he told her, and she glowed at the compliment.

Much of his talk, a disjointed commentary on the fragments littering his bench and the abandoned schemes littering his workroom, was too technical for Harriet to follow. She was happy to look on and to absorb what she could. An impression formed itself of Simon's life given over to ideas that shone briefly and then lost their luminosity. The ideas became dead bodies once his enthusiasm had been withdrawn, and then dry skeletons, encroaching from the shadowy corners of the room. Soon, she guessed, the skeletons would fill the whole space and Simon would be swallowed up by them.

He finished the last of the whiskey. His voice was beginning to thicken. He held up the empty bottle and tilted it, then seemed to come to a decision. Not quite steadily, he moved to the end of the bench and opened a drawer. He took out a rough wooden board, and propped it at an angle among the shavings and discarded tools.

"This is the only thing I ever did that could have come right," he said. "If I had only known what to do with it. If I could have made myself look properly at it again, after we were liberated. Set free. That's a notion, isn't it?"

Harriet's first thought was that he had descended without warning into drunkenness. He had been good-humored and relaxed while he was pottering among his skeletons, but now his face had contracted, drawing itself into iron lines.

"Set free," he repeated with bitterness and laughed, nothing like the tea-maker laugh. "Here. You've seen everything else. Don't you want to look at this?"

"What is it?" Harriet asked in fear.

"It's a game, of course. A wonderful game if you can play it right. Like life, Kath Peacock's daughter."

Harriet was frightened by the change in him. He took hold of her wrist and she had to stiffen to stop herself drawing it away from him. Into her open palm, Simon dropped four wooden balls in worn, faded colors, and four plastic counters bright in the same colors, red, blue, yellow, and green. He raised their linked hands and let the wooden balls roll into a groove at the top of the board. Harriet saw that it might once have been the end of a packing case. There were marks on it, but she couldn't decipher them. They looked like pictographs, Chinese or Japanese. Or perhaps they were something else altogether, faded and rubbed beyond recognition.

"Now. Put the counters here," he commanded. "Any order you like, together or separate." He pointed to the foot of the board, where there were four slots. Harriet dropped the counters in, at random.

"Watch."

Simon drew back a spring-loaded tongue of wood to open a gate in the upper groove. The colored balls fell out and rolled, one after another, down seven inclined struts, glued in a zigzag down the slope of the board. In each of the struts, Harriet saw, there were three more gates, all closed with wooden pegs. As they rolled over the gates and dropped from one strut to the next, the balls made a pleasing, musical sound. They dropped one by one off the end of the lowest strut and formed a column in the last slot. Harriet's counters lay in different slots, in a different color sequence. She smiled uncertainly, pleased and oddly soothed by the sound of the rolling balls and by the neat way they had plopped into their resting place, although she had no idea what was supposed to have been achieved.

"How is your mathematics?" Simon demanded.

"Quite good." It was true. Harriet enjoyed figures.

"Then tell me how many different ways the counters could be arranged in those slots."

Harriet frowned.

"Four to the power of four," he prompted her.

"Two hundred and fifty-six."

"Exactly." Simon was delighted. Some of the iron lines faded from his face. "Do you understand?"

"I think so," Harriet said, who was only beginning to.

"Go on, then. Your counters are your markers. Make your colored balls drop into the same slots in the same order."

"I think I can do that."

"Would you like to make a little bet?"

Harriet grinned, fired by the challenge. She had forgotten to be afraid of Simon's strange expression. "A fiver," she offered.

"Thank you."

"Don't thank me. You haven't won it yet."

The key to the game, Harriet saw now, was the little gates in the sloping struts. She touched one, and then saw that it would lift out, leaving a hole in the strut, big enough for a ball to drop through. The gate was made in the shape of a Y, and when she examined it she saw that it was made from matchsticks, painstakingly glued together. She studied it for a long moment, wondering, and then slipped it back into its place. It fitted, but at a different angle. She tried it one way and then another, and discovered that there were three possible positions for it. The gate could be locked open or locked shut, that was simple enough. But in the third position, the gate stood open to let a ball through. Only then, as it passed, the weight of the ball closed and locked the gate behind it.

Harriet took a deep, determined breath, sensing Simon watching her. Her head was still fuddled with food and wine, and the day's jumbled impressions.

She saw that the green ball would roll first, but that she must coax it into the next-to-last slot. The red ball would drop last but must occupy the first slot. Without giving herself too much time to think and change her mind, she flipped the gates, trying to visualize the path the balls would take as they rolled and dropped.

After two minutes she was satisfied.

She brushed Simon's hand away, flicked the spring-loaded tongue, and the balls merrily rattled. She held her breath as they trickled and dropped, making the same musical sound. As if drawn by magnets, they completed their course and fell, color by color and slot by slot, on top of the right, bright counters.

Harriet shouted in triumph.

Simon only nodded. "Good for a first try."

"What do you mean?"

"Look."

He pointed to the little gates. A number was penciled on the strut beside each one, high numbers at the top, lower all down the length of the zigzag path. Harriet's gates stood open, breaking the smoothness of the route. Counting aloud, Simon added the numbers to make a total. "Seventy-nine," he said. "Now, watch again." With a flick, he obliterated Harriet's solution and substituted his own. She saw that fewer gates stood open, all lower down the board. Then he scooped out the balls and rolled them again. They dropped inexorably to the same resting places, but Simon's score was only twenty-seven.

"You see? The same conclusion, but achieved by a more or less circuitous route."

"I see, like life," Harriet murmured.

Simon unfolded a piece of paper. In neat, spidery writing he had plotted the lowest scores for each of the two hundred and fifty-six possible permutations. Harriet glanced at it, then rear-ranged the counters at random. She drew her lower lip between her teeth, frowning in concentration as her fingers danced over the gates. But now, when the balls were released, the yellow and the green fell into the wrong slots.

Simon moved to show her, but she stopped him. "No. Let me try again."

This time she was right, but there was no triumphant shout. She was staring at the board hypnotized by it. The power of the game, she saw, lay in its simplicity. It was made from a packing case and spent matches, but its brilliance shone out of it. It drew her fingers, tempting another try.

"It's very clever," she said. She felt the fine hairs at the nape of her neck, down the length of her spine, stir and prickle. She shivered, but not from cold now. "Very, very clever."

Harriet felt a moment of pure, clear excitement. It was like her waking dream back in her childhood bed. It possessed her completely, making everything she contemplated seem fine, and simple, and infinitely inviting. And then, just as quickly, it was gone again, leaving her wondering just what had happened to her. She touched the splintered wood and the faded markings, puzzled by them.

"So when did you make it? Where, and why?"

"So many questions," Simon said.

Ever since he had let her in, her history and her questions had probed his defenses. Kath would never have asked such questions. Kath had been absorbed in herself. Not unhealthily, but with the normal, sharp appetite of youth. Even thirty years ago she had made him feel old, because she was so fresh and full of juice. He had loved that. With Kath's different, surprising daughter—who had come too close, in so short a time—beside him, he wondered whether he had loved the real Kath, or even known her. He felt angry with this girl because she threatened to distort a happy memory, a cherished one because so many other memories were not happy.

Simon didn't want to look at the game now because it reawakened those other memories. He didn't know what impulse had made him bring it out. He studied Kath's daughter instead, as her fingertips explored the old wood from Shamshuipo camp.

She didn't look like her mother, even. Kath had been all curls and satiny curves. She had full, soft lips and a ready smile. This girl was lean and flat, and her close-cut hair made her look even more like a boy. As well as asking questions, she listened to the answers as if trying to memorize them. And her eyes moved quickly, taking in everything. Unlike her mother, she didn't smile very often. She did laugh, in startling bursts, but it was a fierce kind of laughter, more like a man's.

Simon didn't think Harriet Trott was happy, but he did not attribute much significance to that. Happiness was not an expectation of his own, either.

"Is this lettering? Chinese lettering?"

Questions.

"It's Japanese," Simon told her.

The dam burst with the words. Sights and sounds, smells that choked him, all flooded up. The stinking tide swept him away from his workbench, from his redoubt, to another place. He became another man.

Lieutenant Archer, Royal Artillery. Shamshuipo Prisoner of War Camp, Hong Kong, in the spring of 1942.

Simon stared into the gloom of his kitchen, not seeing the girl, blind to everything but the horror of the camp. He was back there in an instant, and he knew as always that nothing he had done or ever could do would obliterate what he had known in that place.

The smells were the worst.

Forty years later Simon Archer could try to close his eyes and muffle his ears, but the smells still crept inside his head to rot the bones of his skull.

There were dying men all around him. The dysentery buckets overflowed onto the concrete floors of the prison, and the sick men lay in their mess too weak to move.

The scents of putrefaction and death were part of the air itself, the principal flavors of the meager portions of gray rice.

The smell had become a fifth limb that Lieutenant Archer

dragged with him everywhere, even outside the camp to the working parties at Kai Tak airport, to the munitions dumps, wherever their Japanese captors herded them. The pains of hunger and sickness, perversely, seemed to be part of another man's body, so that he could observe them without emotion. Sometimes he could hear other men moaning or screaming, but he made no sound himself. He could turn away from the sights, pitiful or nauseating, until quite soon he had no need to do even that much because they grew familiar through repetition, and he became as indifferent to them as were the rats that ran over them all where they lay.

It was only in the later years that the sights came back to torture him. Starvation, maltreatment, and disease. In Shamshuipo Simon knew that was all that lay ahead for him and the five thousand other men in the camp. He began to regard the men who were dying, and those who were already dead, as the lucky ones.

But in answer there always came the thought of Rosemary, his wife, and the baby son he had never even seen, at home in England. Even though he knew in abstract what war meant at home, Simon always imagined his family with a soft glow around them, as if of firelight, and then he would painfully remember the sweetness of love and domesticity. The will to live returned, burning more brightly.

Lieutenant Archer, naked except for a loincloth knotted between his legs, crawling with vermin and exhausted from malnutrition and hard labor on building the Kai Tak runway, sat on a concrete floor and played with the broken end of a packing case. He turned the wooden strut in his hands and numbers raveled in his head. In the filthy labyrinth their unassailable logic helped him to stay deaf and blind to everything around him.

Slowly, tenaciously, Simon began to devise a kind of numbers game. He needed markers, and so he collected buttons from decayed battledress. Out on a working party, he watched the ground for round, smooth pebbles and when he found them he held them in his mouth until the return to Shamshuipo.

While some of the men screamed out their misery and others gnawed silently on it, Simon tilted his packing case at an angle and let the round pebbles run down the slope. He thought of choices and options, all the fruitful possibilities of freedom that had been closed off to him, and he built them into his game instead. He tried to carve wishbone shapes from twigs, although he was past wishing, but he had no knife blade or other sharp instrument. He began to collect spent matches instead. The Japanese guards all smoked, and they dropped the matches like largess. Even the men were able to smoke sometimes. They collected flies that swarmed through the camp and plagued their captors as indiscriminately as themselves. They sold them to the guards, one hundred dead flies per cigarette.

So Simon shuffled between sprawled bodies and picked up the burned matches. He made a kind of glue from hoarded grains of wet, cooked rice, kneading them into a fine, gray paste. He stuck the matches together to make wishbones. The balls rolled, and dropped through the wishbone-gates when Simon opened them. He could open or close the gates, and so he had created minuscule choices for himself. With increased concentration he added the numbers, challenging himself with new and harder combinations, scratching the columns of figures with a white stone on to the concrete floor.

He hunched over his packing-case board as if it offered him freedom.

In time, the game attracted the attention of the other men, those who were still able to take notice of anything around them. Simon showed one or two of the men how to position the button markers, and to set the pebbles rolling to meet them along matchstick paths. None of them had energy or ingenuity to spare, and interest in Simon's contraption soon flagged. He was able to keep it to himself, refining the apparatus and allowing the numbers to replicate cleanly inside his head.

The guards saw no reason to bother themselves with a contraption of sticks and stones, but still Simon generally kept it hidden under his scrap of blanket whenever one of them was near.

Then came a day when he was absorbed in watching the pebbles following the paths he had decreed for them, and so he didn't see a guard they called the Fat Man making his way between recumbent prisoners. The Fat Man was stopping every few yards to point at a man, who was then jerked to his feet and hustled away. The Fat Man was choosing those men who still had some strength left. There was clearly some task waiting to be done by the few who still might be fit enough.

It was too late when Simon looked up. His eyes met the corpulent guard's, who responded by pointing straight at him. With an automatic, belated movement Simon tried to cover up the packing case with his blanket. As the Fat Man's fellows pulled him to his feet, Simon saw the guard's eyes flicker inquisitively to his game. The pointing finger moved to it, and beckoned.

The game was pulled out for the Japanese to inspect.

Simon waited. There was nothing for him to do but watch. He saw the Fat Man's big, shiny round face bend to the game, the rolls of flesh distending his filthy tunic, and the broad, black half-moons spreading under his armpits. As he stood there Simon caught his richly oily and fishy scent in symphonic contrast to the common stench of Shamshuipo.

The guard glanced at him, curiosity making sharp points of light in his flat black eyes.

"What?" the man asked Simon.

The Fat Man was hated for his knowledge of a few words of English as much for his appearance and behavior. Simon masked fear and disgust with a polite smile. He looked like a grinning skull.

He answered, "It's a game. A game of skill and numerical calculation, involving the setting of two-way gates in various combinations to permit balls to reach pre-positioned markers via a kind of maze, or labyrinth. Each of the gates is awarded a numerical value, and the points scored are totaled when the balls reach their markers. Lowest score wins."

The guard was staring at him, his face a suspicious mask. Simon knew that he couldn't have understood more than two words of his mannerly explanation. He broadened his smile, and scooped up the tunic buttons to reposition them.

"It goes like this. The numbers form a labyrinth of their own, a wonderfully logical structure that is colorless, odorless, beautiful and safe. Unlike this terrible place." The guard blinked. Simon let the pebbles drop along the matchstick gullies. Everyone watched them as they went.

The Fat Man's face split like a pulpy fruit into a wide smile, to match Simon's.

"Crever," he said, and held out a huge hand for the buttons.

Simon let him play for himself. He could smell the man

too strongly now, and he realized that his proximity was making him shiver with fear. The Fat Man was engrossed, but his companions called roughly to him. Reluctantly he lifted his head, and then thrust the packing-case end back at Simon. He jerked a banana thumb to indicate that it should be stowed away again beneath the blanket. Simon did as he was ordered.

There was a moment then when the Fat Man considered him. Simon shrank, but there was nowhere to hide himself. And then, miraculously, the Fat Man shook his head. Simon understood that, whatever ordeal was being prepared for the few strong men, he was not going to be made part of it. The Fat Man lumbered on down the lines. Simon sat down in his place. He had no choice but to sit, because his legs gave way beneath him. His terror was the final weakness. None of the men who had been picked out ever came back. Simon never knew where or why they had been taken, but he supposed that in some way his game had saved his life. Afterward, the Fat Man ignored him.

Simon kept the game hidden from that day on. It became a kind of lucky talisman. He believed that if he could keep it, he would survive.

When at last the Shamshuipo prisoners were moved from Hong Kong to Japan, Lieutenant Archer managed to smuggle his piece of packing case with him. It stayed with him in the new camp, thrust under his tatami mat. He sat on it and slept on it for two years. The years were terrible, but they were better than the ones that had passed in Hong Kong. Simon survived because he was set to work on the docks, and he could steal enough food to stay alive.

On August 15, 1945, he heard a formal, measured voice speaking ornate phrases out of a Japanese foreman's wireless. Soldiers and civilians were running, or standing frozen into stillness, some of them weeping. At the end of the Emperor's speech, an interpreter scrambled up onto a platform of oil drums.

"You are free, gentlemen. The war is over."

A lorry-load of U.S. paratroopers came to liberate the camp. They brought bread, and fruit, and tinned ham, candy and the unthinkable luxury of American beer. Simon took his packing-case game from under his mat and walked out of captivity with it wrapped in his arms. It was his only possession. Simon Archer reached England after four years spent as a prisoner of the Japanese. It was not, however, a

return home. His wife and the baby son he had never seen
had died in the bombing of Coventry, and he was not
looking for a home without them.

This was what Simon told Harriet as she sat on his bench in the
cold, cluttered room. She listened in silence, with only her eyes
moving from the game to his face and away again, over the
room's shadows.

At the end, she touched the rough wood once more. Simon
saw that he had told her enough. Her questions, at least for the
time, had been answered. His body ached and his eyes burned.
The assault of memories had left him feeling weak and helpless.

"I'm tired," he told her. "It's too late for you to go anywhere
now. You'll have to stay the night here."

In silence, Harriet followed him upstairs. The room at the
back of the house was chilly and dusty, but otherwise clean. He
gave her yellowing sheets from a chest of drawers. They said
good night soberly, each of them stripped of the warm, temporary blanket of drink.

"You won your five pounds," Simon said.

"No, I didn't. I prefer to take the direct route."

"Of course." There was perfectionism in her, as well as
persistence. It didn't surprise him that she was unhappy. But he
didn't pursue the thought. He wished that he had left the game
in its hiding-place. He was exhausted, and if he slept he was
afraid that he would dream of Shamshuipo.

Harriet lay down wearing most of her clothes. The day
seemed to have lasted for a very long time, or to have been taken
up by a complicated journey. She was glad to have arrived at a
destination, to bed in this unfamiliar room, where she could
examine her impressions. They fitted together, after Simon's
story. The withdrawal and denial that had puzzled her became
bare and understandable fact. She felt ashamed of her probing,
now, and more ashamed because it had been motivated by her
own self-centered hunger.

Harriet knew that she couldn't offer Simon any comfort. Her
own resources were meager, and she doubted that even the most
generous warmth could touch him now. But he had said that he
was glad when she came back, with the courage of her curry and
cheap white wine. And he had told her that he wished she was
his daughter. There had been that, and the spurt of laughter,
between them.

More than that. Harriet took the last of her impressions and
fitted it into the picture. He had drawn the old packing case out

of its hiding-place and shown it to her. She lay still, hearing the musical descent of the wooden balls as they followed their separate paths. It was simpler and more elegant than life, she thought. The only common factor was the will to win that they both engendered.

She hadn't expected to sleep. But she did doze, and then fell into a series of disturbed dreams. When she woke it was in the dirty light of very early morning and the house was silent. She slid out of bed and put the top layer of her clothes on again, then crept downstairs to the kitchen. She had been intending to make herself a cup of tea because the drink of the night before had left her parched, but the chaos of the kitchen was uninviting. She used the kettle of boiling water for washing up instead, and worked her way through the piles of dirty plates and pans.

When that was done she cleared and wiped the table and the other surfaces, removing the most obvious rubbish and taking care to put the tools and clock pieces back exactly as she found them. She found herself humming as she worked, enjoying making order out of the mess. In the cupboard under the stairs, among more of Simon's abandoned skeleton projects, she found a long-handled broom and ancient mop and bucket. She swept and washed the floor, and then peered into the shadowy larder that led off the kitchen. There was nothing in it. Simon must have produced yesterday's teabag and eggs from some other hiding-place.

It was nine o'clock. Harriet picked up her bag and let herself out into the street, leaving Simon's front door unlocked. She didn't think that anyone would try to get in while she was away. She walked briskly to the Pakistani-owned corner shop that she had noticed two streets away.

"Do you know Mr. Archer?" Harriet asked the woman in a sari who helped her to pack two bulging plastic carriers. She described him and the street.

The woman shook her head regretfully. "I do not. And we know most of the people here."

Harriet was unpacking the shopping, arranging her purchases in the larder, when she heard Simon behind her. She swung around, almost guiltily. He looked at the packets and tins.

"You should have accepted your winnings. That must have cost more than five pounds."

"The money isn't important. I just wanted to get you some supplies."

Simon regarded her and she blushed. He didn't say anything, except, "I'll make some tea."

They sat in the same positions as the day before, and Harriet drank her tea gratefully and ate slices of bread and marmalade.

"When is your train?" Simon asked. He didn't try to soften the implication. He wanted her to go and leave him alone again, in peace. Yesterday's precarious intimacy had disappeared with his dreams of Japan. He didn't want this girl interfering with his possessions, clumsily imposing a sort of order that only reminded him of how a different, parallel life might have been lived. He didn't want her food, either. The bright packets belonged in the other, fertile life.

Harriet's eyes dropped to her plate. "There are plenty of trains. I'll catch one this morning. I should get back to work," she offered, making a necessity of departure.

Simon said, "Yes."

When they had finished breakfast she washed the plates, put away the remainders. When that was done she surveyed the room, glad that she had been able to do something, however small, out of her impotence.

"Thank you," Simon said kindly. He put out his hand and they shook, formally, as they had done at the beginning. He escorted her past the grandfather clock, back to the front door.

"Wait a minute," he said. She watched him return to the kitchen, and come out with one of the empty bags from the corner shop. Then he went into his front room. Harriet saw the corner of one of the dismembered armchairs, and heard a drawer pulled open. When he came out again he was carrying the plastic bag, made square and heavy by the packing-case end from Shamshuipo. He held it out to her.

Harriet looked at him in wonder.

"Take it. It's yours."

"You can't mean that."

"I do. Do whatever you want with it."

He was suddenly eager to have both of them out of the house. They had become entwined, in the dreams fueled by unaccustomed whiskey. He wanted them both gone, although he didn't expect that the memories would vanish with them.

Harriet reached out, stiff-fingered, and took the bag from him.

"Thank you," she said awkwardly. "I'll take great care of it."

"Do whatever you want with it," he repeated. His voice was harsh.

He didn't echo her final good-bye, but he stood with the door open until she had turned the corner.

Harriet walked back toward the station. This time she didn't see the shops, or the people, or the relentless traffic. The carrier bag bumped rhythmically and aggressively against her legs. With each step she took, she heard the faint click of the wooden balls rolling together. It was as if the game had a life of its own.

Five

A COLLECTION OF PACKING CASES stood in the middle of the living room; pale rectangles framed with cobwebby dust showed where pictures had hung on the cream walls. Harriet and Leo were dismantling their four years.

Leo abruptly stopped packing books into a box and sat down on the sofa. He was listening to Harriet opening and closing drawers in the kitchen. Goaded by the sound, he shouted at her, "Your mixer, my toaster, is this what everything's come to between us?"

Harriet appeared in the doorway. She looked tired.

"This is the nasty but inevitable aftermath of something that has already happened, don't you understand? Who owns what isn't significant. You can have the whole lot, if you want. But the flat has to be cleared because we're selling it, and all this stuff has to go somewhere. Why don't you help instead of sitting there?"

"I don't want to help. I don't want us to do it. Can't we stop, and forget about it?"

Wearily, because they had traveled this ground a dozen times already, Harriet said, "It isn't forgettable. You know it, and I know it!"

They had fenced with each other, like this, for weeks. They had met only a handful of times but each time they had trodden the same exhausting paths.

Leo wanted to go back to where they had been, before Harriet had seen the play of light and shadow over the girl's body in his studio. He wanted to pretend that nothing had happened, obliterating by denying, and he wanted to compound the deception by pretending that they had been happy except for his own insignificant lapse. He talked about babies, fantasizing himself into fatherhood, reproaching Harriet for her refusal.

Yet Harriet knew that his insistence on all these things grew out of his need to oppose her, on any grounds. Bitterness had driven between them. If she had wanted to stay, she thought, to cling to the debris, it would have been Leo demanding brutal severance. There is no such thing, Harriet reminded herself, as an amicable separation. She clung to her decision, with a steeliness that surprised her. She remembered, too, that her husband had accused her of coldness and rigidity. Well then, she was only behaving in character. And she was glad, with chilly relief, that there were no children to witness or to be hurt by this disengagement.

Leo looked up at her. She thought he was going to take her arm and pull her down beside him, and stepped instinctively backward.

"Don't do that," Leo whispered. "Don't act as if I'm going to hurt you."

You have, Harriet answered silently. *You won't, anymore.*

"Harriet." Leo had never had to beg for anything before. It was clear that he was making his last bid. "Stay with me."

She knew that his insistence was based on a false premise, because she didn't love him any longer. Nor did she believe, although his obstinacy prevented him from seeing it for himself, that Leo loved her either. The finality of it was sad, the insignificance of what was left was pathetic.

"I can't."

Leo scowled. He looked like a small boy who had unexpectedly been denied a treat. That was it, Harriet realized. She had spent four years of her life married to a twelve-year-old boy. A twelve-year-old, tricked out with broad shoulders, a rakishly tumbled mop of black hair, and a well-developed libido. Unbidden, but as sharp as one of his own photographs, her last sight of his most prominent feature came back to her. And the vision of her husband trying to hide it behind his shirt.

A tremor passed through Harriet. It rose from her chest and concentrated at the back of her throat, and then escaped as a snort of guilty laughter. Her hands flew up to her cheeks as she tried to suppress it.

Leo stared at her, dislike clearly visible in his face. "I think you've gone mad."

"Just the opposite, I think," Harriet said. "If you really won't help, I'll have to divide things without you."

She turned away from him and went back into the kitchen. Sabatier knives, maple chopping board, Le Creuset casserole dishes. Harriet felt faintly shocked herself as she laid them out. There was nothing to laugh at, Leo was right. In truth she found this dismemberment of their domestic life, the lifting of utensils from hooks and extraction of cutlery from snugly shaped trays, as painful and difficult as anything she had ever known.

As suddenly as the laughter had come, she felt the weight of tears in her eyes. To hold them back she stopped work and went across to stare out of the kitchen window. The view was familiar in every detail from married hours spent at the sink, filling kettles, washing dishes, preparing vegetables. The dingy curtains in the opposite windows would be taken down, and fresh ones put up by new owners. The flowering cherry on the corner would blossom and shed its leaves, but Leo and she would not be here to see it. She turned her back on the view. She hadn't cried, and she wouldn't cry now.

It would be easier to stay, of course.

She knew their life, and the patterns of it. Leo provided a husbandly shelter for her, for all his faults. She was used to being a couple, to parties and holidays and Christmases spent as one half of a whole. It would be simpler to stay in the shelter and look out on the world, believing her husband's assurances.

Only it would be wrong.

It would be a capitulation, and Harriet in her controlled and decisive way hated capitulation.

She bent to the job again. She took up a melon baller that had been a Christmas present from Averil, never used, and hovered with it between Leo's packing case and the one intended for herself. After a moment she put it in with her own things. There came another irrational urge to laugh. She was sending back the son, but she didn't want to give offense by rejecting the melon baller as well.

When she looked up again she saw that Leo was watching her from the doorway.

"You've made a terrible mess."

"Completion of the sale is in ten days' time. We have to empty the place by then. There isn't any point in maintaining the House Beautiful, Leo. It's all over."

Seeing his face, she thought for a moment that he too might be going to cry. They faced each other awkwardly, and then Harriet picked her way through the coils of newspaper packing. They put their arms around each other and then stood still, looking in different directions, saying nothing.

At length Leo let her go. He picked up a coffeepot, asking, "Where's this going?"

"With you, if you like. If you've got room."

Leo was partly living in his studio, partly still at the flat, and spending an occasional regressive night at his parents' house in

Hampstead Garden Suburb. Harriet had rented a basement flat in Belsize Park. It wasn't convenient for the shop, and north London felt like foreign territory after the west, but it belonged to a friend of hers who had gone to Paris for a year, and it was cheap because two cats came with it.

"I don't want it," Leo answered. "I've got one at the studio."

He hovered beside her, getting in the way, taking out utensils that she had already packed and staring at them as if he had never seen them before. She worked on for a few minutes, controlling her irritation, then gave up.

"I've got to go soon. There must be a carload here anyway."

"Where are you going?"

"Home." She meant Belsize Park, said it defiantly. "To drop this off and change, then I'm going to Jane's. She's having a party."

In the past, of course, Leo would have been coming as well, even though he and Jane had never felt much affection for one another.

"Yeah. Well, I might have a night out, too."

"Good idea."

They were defending themselves, and masking the defense with cheerfulness. Harriet wanted to get away.

Leo helped her to carry her plants and cardboard boxes down the stairs to the street. Harriet felt humiliated by this public admission of their mutual failure. She wished she could have removed herself in the middle of the night, and willed the door of each of the other flats to stay closed as they passed. Once safely inside they heaved the boxes into her hatchback, piling the things up almost to the roof. The last box was squeezed in and Harriet slammed the tailgate. Leo stood looking at the loaded car with an expression of baffled misery.

"I've got to go," she repeated, wishing that this was over, that it had already subsided into history.

"Shit," Leo said. He drew back his foot and gave the nearside rear tire a vicious kick. "Oh, shit."

Harriet scrambled into the driver's seat. "I'm sorry," she mumbled. "I'm sorry about it all." And then she drove away.

She reached her Belsize Park basement and staggered to and fro on her own with her arms full of possessions. She left her houseplants in a drooping thicket inside the front door and the other things stacked in the middle of the living room floor. She was already late, so she showered quickly in the bathroom that still smelled of another woman's perfume, and wrapped herself in a bath towel to survey her limited choice of unpacked clothes.

Without wasting any time on deliberations she pulled on a bright red shirt and a pair of tight black trousers with black suede ankle boots. She ran a comb through her short hair and rubbed gloss from the same tube onto her mouth and cheekbones. Then she picked up a bottle of red wine from Oddbins still wrapped in its paper, and a bunch of daisies she had bought from the florist's on the corner. With her hands full and her pouch bag swinging from her shoulder, she stepped in front of the living room mantelpiece.

Leaning against the chimney breast, from which she had removed the owner's Saul Steinberg print to make room for it, was Simon Archer's game.

Harriet had spent hours sitting on the sofa opposite, knees drawn up to her chest, studying it. She knew the gates and their numbers, the faded markings, even the cracks in the wood.

All the time she looked at it, sitting on her own in the silent room, she was thinking and wondering. And each time she looked, she felt the same shiver travel the length of her spine.

The friendlier of the pair of cats, a black one with white paws, wound between her legs and rubbed itself against her ankles. Harriet glanced down. "That's enough thinking, for now," she told it. "Time to do something. Definitely time."

She left the flat once more, locking her stronghold carefully behind her.

Harriet liked driving in London. Today's journeys, from the home she had given up with Leo to the party, would criss-cross it from west to east and back to the north again. Jane lived in Hackney, in a tiny house in a terrace pinned between tall warehouses and a rundown shopping street. But Harriet had barely noticed the first leg of her drive. Normally she enjoyed the stirring sweep of the Westway that carried her along level with the rooftops. She liked to drive a little too fast, with music playing. Today, with the unaccustomed weight dragging the tail of the car, there had been no music or display of speed. She had been oppressed by a sense of failure, by loneliness, and by a sudden desire to turn around, to capitulate after all, and go back to Leo. Yet she had driven doggedly onward, in the press of taxis and delivery vans that she felt too miserable to try to overtake.

This evening, with her thoughts focused on what lay ahead and on her germ of a plan, her spirits rose.

Instead of following the bold curves of the urban motorway, this second part of the route led her through a net of streets, now up the big road that had once been the old coaching route northwards from the City, now veering sharply to the right to

short-cut through residential streets where the pavements shone
under a film of drizzle. She passed corner pubs done up Victorian-
style, lit up for Saturday night's business, little late-opening
mini-markets, and big, darker, windy spaces that opened around
railway embankments or factory buildings. She knew the route
well, but she watched it unfold with satisfaction, whistling softly
as she drove.

When she reached Jane's neighborhood there were fewer
people out on the streets, and those that she did pass were
mostly groups of spindly black youths with huge knitted caps on
their heads. The shops were nearly all barred with metal grilles,
although their haphazard, neon-lit windows piled with dusty
toys, and bleached packets seemed to offer minimal temptation.
It wasn't a comfortable-looking landscape, but Harriet never felt
threatened by it. She often came to see Jane and had spent part
of the last three weeks staying in her house. Jane liked the area
for its busy mixture of West Indians, Greeks and Turks, and
Harriet shared her affection for it.

Harriet turned, at length, into Jane's street. It was lined with
parked cars and the first one she saw was the Thimbells' battered
Citroën. That was good. She was happy that Jenny had felt like a
party; Charlie would not have come without her. And she wanted
to talk to Charlie. She needed his advice.

The door was opened by a man Harriet didn't know. He had
thick hair pulled into a ponytail at the nape of his neck, and he
was wearing a kind of artist's smock.

"Hi," he greeted her.

"Hi," Harriet answered. She held up her Oddbins bottle and
the daisies, as if to establish her credentials.

"Come in, if you can." The hallway was so narrow that as
she squeezed in Harriet found herself momentarily wedged against
the man, hip to hip. Then they both laughed, and she broke free.
There were more people further into the hall and sitting on the
carpet that ran up the stairs.

Seeing that the press of people was thicker still in the kitchen,
Harriet left her offerings on the bevel-mirrored and be-hooked
piece of shiny brown Victoriana that Jane used as a hallstand,
and pushed her way into the living room. It had been created by
knocking two tiny rooms together to make one medium-sized
one. The floorboards had been sanded and sealed, and Jane had
prudently rolled her Flokati rugs back for the evening. The furniture consisted of a pair of Victorian plush-covered sofas, one at
each end of the room, and intermediate heaps of outsize cushions covered in Indian cotton. The alcoves beside the chimney

breasts were lined with books. The stripped pine shutters at the windows enclosed the conviviality of talk, laughter, and music.

The party was clearly well under way, but there were fewer people in here. Harriet wondered why people always did cram themselves into the kitchen at parties. She looked around, and saw that she knew most of these faces.

"Harriet! Have a drink, where have you been all evening?"

The man who greeted her was a teacher, one of Jane's colleagues from the comprehensive school. Harriet smiled at him and accepted a glass of Bulgarian cabernet.

"I've only just arrived. Late, as usual."

"Where's Leo?"

She had met this teacher at dinners and at parties, but she didn't know him well.

"Not here tonight."

"Watch out, then." He grinned at her.

She nodded back, as neutrally as she could. Over by the bookshelves she saw Jenny. Jenny's Madonna-face had developed hollows and her hair was pulled tightly back as if to punish it for unruliness. But she welcomed Harriet with her smile.

"I'm glad you're here."

"Jenny. You look fine."

Jenny nodded. "Everything back to normal. All over and forgotten about."

Harriet hesitated. "Is that what you want to feel?"

"It's what my mother wants me to feel. Even Charlie, most of the time. But I can't forget I had a baby. I shouldn't, should I?"

"No, I don't think you should," Harriet said softly.

"I want to remember him. We only had him for a few hours, but that doesn't make him any less important, does it? It seems like another . . . yet another hurt to him, to go about as if he never existed."

Harriet listened, believing that that was what was needed.

"I like to talk about him. Charlie doesn't, you know. Charlie believes in looking to the future, and being realistic. Losing James hurt him as much as it hurt me, but he can't admit it. It hasn't been very easy for us to live together, since I came home."

Harriet put her arm around her. "It will be all right," she said, believing that it would be. For Jenny as well as for herself she wished that time would speed up.

Jenny sniffed. "Yes. Sorry, Harriet. Not very festive. This is supposed to be a party." They held on to each other.

"That's what parties are for. Seeing your friends. Talk all you like, and I'll listen all evening."

"No, that's enough. I haven't asked how you are, even."

Harriet acknowledged her concern. "I'm all right," she said briefly, knowing that she would be. "Here's Jane."

Jane drank hardly anything herself, claiming that it disagreed with her, but she poured out liberally for everyone else. She was carrying a bottle of wine in each hand. Tonight she had exchanged her combat trousers for an all-in-one made of some plum-colored, silky material, with a wide belt that bunched the shimmery fabric over her hips and breasts. She was wearing a liberal amount of plum-colored lipstick, too, and eyeshadow in a slightly lighter tone, but the effect was not in the least voluptuous. She looked exactly what she was—matter-of-fact and uncompromising. Harriet was pleased to see her.

"You know, I miss you, now you've moved out," Jane said. "I was beginning to get used to having you around. Perhaps I should stop looking for a husband, and hunt about for a wife instead?"

"I don't think I'm your type," Harriet answered. "Get one who can cook."

"Of course."

The three of them laughed. Harriet felt the weight and the warmth of friendship. Its fuel was the interlinking of their ordinary lives, and their trust in one another. They never spoke of its significance, but her awareness of it buoyed her up. She felt happy, and wealthy, because she possessed it.

"What have you been doing since you left me?" Jane asked. "She looks okay on it, Jen, doesn't she?"

"She looks great."

"I've been packing, clearing the flat. Leo was there this afternoon."

"Was it grim?"

"It was, rather," Harriet admitted.

"It will be better when you've sorted out the domestic details," Jane said decisively.

"What you need now, what we all need, is a drink followed by some food followed by some dancing and more drink." She called out to the room, "Come on, everybody."

In entertaining, as in everything else, Jane believed in leading from the front. Jenny and Harriet smiled covertly at each other, but Jane intercepted the look.

"Could you two please mingle a little?"

"I'm going, I'm going," Harriet protested. "I'm going into the kitchen to find Charlie."

She eased herself across the room and into the hall, and

down the two steps to the kitchen at the back. From this room french windows opened on to Jane's sunny patio garden where she grew herbs and Alpine strawberries in pots. Tonight the dining table had been pushed right up against the doors, and it was laid with baskets of French bread, brown earthenware dishes of guacamole and aubergine dip and garlic pâté, and dimple beer glasses filled with sheaves of celery. There were quiches, already half-eaten and spreading freckles of wholemeal pastry crumbs, and a whole uncut Brie. On the back burner of the gas stove there was a big pan of hot soup, probably carrot and coriander. Harriet had helped Jane prepare for parties in the past.

The tiled work-top along one wall was a jungle of bottles, all different colors and shapes, interspersed with glasses, plates, and party tins of beer. Charlie Thimbell leaned against the work-top, with a full glass of the Bulgarian cabernet in his hand. He was talking vehemently to a nervous-looking girl in an embroidered blouse. They were pinned in place by more groups of chattering, laughing people. The girl looked to be in two minds about their tête-à-tête.

Charlie was only about the same height as Harriet, but his broad shoulders and thickset figure made him seem a much bigger man. Beneath the bluster, he was a shrewd financial journalist.

"Totalitarianism," Harriet heard him shouting. The girl shrank beside him.

Harriet reached them and touched his elbow. "Charlie?"

He stopped in mid-tirade. "Hello, darling." He kissed her noisily and then glanced over her shoulder. Harriet realized that he was looking for Leo. In the same instant Charlie remembered that Leo would not be there. His face turned a shade redder.

"It's all right," Harriet said mildly. "I forget, too, and turn round to ask him something. Force of habit is surprisingly strong." She turned to the embroidered girl, intending to introduce herself, but she was already backing away.

"What did I say?" Charlie demanded, when she had gone. "Or was it you?"

"It was you. When did she last get a chance to say anything?"

"I gave her plenty of chances. She just didn't take them."

Harriet put her arm through his. "Charlie, I want to ask you something. Can we go somewhere quieter than in here?"

He looked alarmed. "About you and Leo? Not my strong point, all that sort of thing. Ask Jenny."

His unwillingness was a pose, Harriet understood that, but she also knew that like most poses it exposed more truths than the poseur might wish. Charlie could talk all night about the money supply, or Arsenal's prospects, or the Booker prize, but he didn't like to talk about what he felt, or feared. As if to do so was to become vulnerable, in some way less than entirely masculine. Harriet remembered what Jenny had said. At least Jenny had her and Jane, the network of women, to talk to. It was probably harder for Charlie.

"Business advice," Harriet said carefully.

"In that case," he winked at her, "come upstairs."

In the end they perched at the top of the stairs, looking down on the heads below. The man in the smock was still doing door duty. Harriet took the first mouthful of her wine.

"How are you, Charlie?"

"I'm fine. What is it you want advice about?" Deflecting her from his own concerns, of course. What was it Jenny had said? *It hasn't been very easy for us to live together.* Harriet thought of Leo, and then of the unspectacular strength of women's friendships.

"Are you sure you don't really need a solicitor?" Charlie prompted her.

Harriet smiled. "I've got a solicitor."

Her plan had become important to her. More than important, almost a lifeline. Charlie would be the first person she had shared it with and she didn't want him to laugh at it or dismiss it, because she valued his judgment. She took a breath, launched herself.

"Listen.

"I've been given a game, a game of skill and calculation, by a friend of mine. He invented it, and it's very clever, very original. I want to develop the game, market it commercially. I think it will sell."

She glanced sideways and saw that Charlie was staring gloomily down the stairs.

"I've never seen anything quite like it."

To her relief, Charlie's face cleared. "That encourages me a little. Originality is the first requirement."

"What's the next?"

Behind them, on the landing, someone stumbled against the bathroom door. Downstairs the music suddenly boomed out at double volume. The party was warming up.

"If you've really no idea, then you should abandon this scheme at once. Go and ask that man in the blouse to dance with you, to take your mind off it. *I'll* dance with you, if it will help." He looked at her face then, and changed his tone. "You work in retailing. You own a shop selling fashion goods, don't you? You tell me what your first step should be."

"I do know," Harriet said. "I just wanted to . . . rehearse it with you. When you're married you get used to someone being there, don't you? To listen to you thinking aloud, setting your ideas straight? You notice the loss."

She had told Simon, she remembered, that to listen was one of the duties of friendship.

Charlie was contrite. He took hold of her hand. "I'm sorry. Go on then, rehearse."

"Research." She began ticking off points on their linked fingers. "Look at the market, establish what the competition is, study their figures. Define my own market. Get a prototype made, establish manufacturing costs. Figure out how to sell. Make a business plan, taking a best-possible and a worst-possible set of results. Go into the City and raise the capital. Or something like that." She made a sound that was half a nervous laugh, half a groan of dismay.

Charlie nursed his drink in his free hand. "Do you want to do all this?"

"Yes," Harriet said. "Oh yes, I want to. I need to do it."

Charlie looked at her again. It seemed incongruous to hear this talk of business plans and market research in Jane Hunter's impeccably homespun house. To Charlie, Harriet looked hungry and just a little driven. Need, he thought, was probably just the right word. And if she was to make her scheme work, it would take all the drive she could muster.

"There will be a heap of work to do," he told her, "even before you're ready to go out and get your requests for investment turned down."

"I'm not afraid of work." A shrug of Harriet's shoulders told him, eloquently, that she had nothing else to focus on. He felt the vibration of sympathy. Work was a useful palliative.

"Have you got any capital of your own?"

"My half of the flat, once the sale goes through. Twenty thousand. I've rented somewhere cheap for a year."

"Yes. Harriet, do you know about the risk/reward ratio?"

"Not exactly." She was reluctant to admit not knowing anything that might be relevant to her plan.

"You have to ask yourself whether all the effort and energy and time that you will have to put into developing this business will pay off for you in the end. Will you get enough out of it to make it worthwhile?"

Harriet didn't hesitate. "I want to do it. The game exists, I

want to go with it. And I *could* make a lot of money, couldn't
I?"

Charlie laughed, looking cheerful again. "There would be no
point otherwise. You'd better let me have a look at this wonderful game of yours. Are you sure there's no problem over the
rights?"

"I was told that I could do what I like with it. But I'll make
sure, don't worry." For a moment, in place of Jane's cream-
painted stairwell with its framed prints and hanging plants, and
the rising scent of carrot soup, she saw Simon's dim house and
smelled the damp and decay. She shivered a little and, mistaking
the reason for it, Charlie put his arm around her.

"Do you remember Crete, Harriet?"

"Yes, I remember Crete."

They had been traveling in Greece, half a dozen of them, in their
last student vacation. Charlie and Jane and Harriet had all been
there; Jenny had been doing something else that summer.

They had reached Vai on the eastern coast, finding a cres-
cent of white sand and a fringe of palm trees, and underneath
the palms there were the painted camper vans and orange tents
of other travelers. They pitched their tents beside this company,
hung up their travel-dirty clothes, and ran down to the sea to
swim.

The days were hot, and the hours stretched or telescoped
under the eye of the sun. They basked in the sunshine, swam in
the iridescent water and read their paperbacks in the shade of
the palms. They exchanged travel stories with bearded German
boys, although their fund was meager compared with the Ger-
mans who had quartered Europe in their Volkswagen campers.
In the red light of beach barbecues they talked to the blonde,
beautiful Scandinavians and smoked joints and listened to guitars with the friendly Dutch.

"It's perfect," Harriet said. "It's Utopia."

Jane sat cross-legged, with her hair crinkled by sun and salt
loose over her shoulders. Even the soles of her feet looked
tanned.

"No violence, no greed, no theft." The sun had hypnotized
them all, they had few possessions, and less money. "No vanity,
no competition, no racism."

"No prudery, nothing to hide."

A few yards away, on a blanket, Geza and Inge the Swedes
were making love. They took a long time over it, and appeared

to have endlessly healthy appetites for the banquet of one another. Charlie opened his eyes.

"Are they still at it? Would you really be happy to go on
living like this?"

"Forever," Jane murmured.

"And the work ethic?"

"I could sublimate it."

"Man lives to work as well as to love," Charlie reminded
them. "One could point out as much to our friend Geza."

At night, under the formidable stars, they sat around their
driftwood fires and set about changing the world. For all the differences in shades of opinion, they were all certain that when they
had drunk enough retsina and when the angle of the sun in the sky
had declined enough to suggest autumn instead of high summer,
they would return home to inherit systems that could be altered
to suit their visions. They were full of innocent optimism and zeal.

One evening, as the talk eddied in circles, someone had
asked, "What do you want, then, Harriet?"

Someone else had responded, "Harriet wants to be rich and
famous."

Defending herself with a quick retort she had answered,
"Just rich will do."

It was such an unfashionable response, such a bathetic contrast
to the hours of high-minded talk that had preceded it, that just
as she had intended everyone laughed. In the days afterward she
was teased about her bourgeois ideals and exploitative intentions.

And then not long after that, as if governed by the same im-
pulses as swallows gathering on telephone wires in English villages,
the campers began to put on their tattered clothes once more and
to talk about the long trek northwards to Munich and Amsterdam
and Manchester. Harriet's remark was forgotten as sleeping bags
were rolled up and stored in the camper vans, and the tents were
collapsed and folded away. A cold wind had started to blow from
the east, whipping the sand up the beach. They slung their guitars
from their shoulders and tied on their headbands, then set off in
twos and threes down the rutted track that led away from the beach.

Utopia seemed a long way behind them even before they
reached Heraklion.

"Yes, I remember Crete." Sun and salt water, retsina and talk,
endless talk. Harriet no longer felt young or innocent, and she
knew that it was illogical to feel a shiver of regret for ten years
ago. But she felt the shiver just the same.

"I remember that I said I wanted to be rich."

"Have you been nursing entrepreneurial ambitions all this time?"

But Charlie had misunderstood her. They were not entrepreneurial ambitions, but ambitions for Simon's game.

"I said what I said, all that time ago, as a kind of joke. A joke that was forced on me."

"There's no need to excuse it, then or now. I admire you Harriet. If you want to do it, go ahead. The financial climate is good, as you know, this government approves of enterprise, as you also know. I wish you the best of luck, if that's what you want to hear. If there's anything I can do to help you, you know I will."

Harriet stood up, as if he had given her his blessing. She kissed Charlie's cheek, finding it solid and warm. At the same moment she felt the blood in her own veins, and the bones under her skin. There was no husband downstairs. There was nothing, except her plan. She felt weightless, intoxicated with excitement all over again.

Charlie looked up. "I'm sorry about Leo," he said, surprising her.

"It's nobody's fault," Harriet answered. "We didn't make each other happy. Someone, or something, else will." She didn't think he heard the qualification. It was for herself, in any case, not for Charlie. "Thanks for your advice. I think I'll take the rest of it, and go and dance with the man in the blouse."

Harriet was leaning over him. Without thinking, Charlie reached up and slid his hand inside her red shirt. He held one warm, bare breast in the cup of his palm. The weight of it felt nice, comforting.

Harriet smiled and gently removed his hand. She had lived naked for a month on a Greek beach with Charlie Thimbell; it would be prudish to object to his touch. And it gave her a small shock of pleasure that was not particularly sexual. It was more a thrill of novelty, of freedom.

"Thanks," she said again. Charlie watched her as she retreated down the stairs. It was years since he had asked himself whether or not he found Harriet physically attractive. He supposed that at some stage he had decided not, because he preferred women who were pretty, and seemingly pliant, like Jenny. Yet tonight he had felt some charge in Harriet that was definitely stimulating. It was probably a good thing, he reflected, that she had separated from Leo Gold. He was afraid that it would be less of a good thing for her to divert her energies into marketing some game.

Charlie's thoughts completed a circle and returned to Jenny. He felt a mixture of tenderness, exasperation, and the chafing of his own grief. He wanted to find a way to assuage Jenny's sorrow, but the extent of it seemed as daunting as the sea. She had retreated into the depths of it. They had not made love since the baby had died. The brief flicker of desire that Charlie had felt for Harriet transferred itself to Jenny, and steadied.

Charlie stood up. It was time to take Jenny away from this party, away home to bed.

Downstairs again, Harriet was drawn into the party. There were other friends to see, some who were close and others she was glad to catch up with. She drank some wine, found herself laughing, and talking over the music as the circles formed and reformed. It was a good party. Harriet caught a glimpse of Jane dancing with a man in a blue shirt, and was pleased that she was enjoying herself, too.

Charlie and Jenny looked in at the door, both wearing their coats. Harriet waved, and blew a kiss.

The dancing started seriously. Jane's teacher colleague found Harriet and drew her into it. He was quite drunk, and he wound his arms around her as if without her support he might fall down. He mumbled hotly in her ear, "You're asking for trouble, coming without your husband." Harriet removed his hands, less affectionately than Charlie's.

As soon as she could she disengaged herself and wandered through to the kitchen. The smock and ponytail man was noisily drinking soup from a Royal Wedding mug. Harriet introduced herself and discovered, in quick succession, that his name was Bernard, that he was a vegan and an amateur astrologer, and that he wasn't the kind of man to whom she wanted to talk for a second longer than was necessary. To her relief, the girl in the embroidered blouse came to claim him.

Harriet turned away and with automatic energy began to clear the empty bottles from Jane's tiled work-top. When that was done she emptied the sink of dirty plates and glasses, and stacked them neatly on the draining board ready to be washed. As she worked she was reflecting that she had come to the party in search of something, and that she had failed to find it. It wasn't as a replacement for what she had lost with Leo, not love, of course, and equally certainly not sex.

She picked up a tea towel and began to dry some plates, wiping carefully and then stopping to stare into the black glass of the window that reflected the room behind her. She saw Jane's plum-colored outfit move in a blur of other people. Jane had given up hostessing in favor of having a good time. Harriet smiled. What she had found at the party was the company of friends. The warmth that had greeted her stayed with her, buoying her up.

When she looked into the window again, she saw the reflection of a man behind her. He was wearing a bright blue shirt, the sleeves rolled to the elbows. She had seen the same man earlier, dancing with Jane.

Then from behind her shoulder he asked, "Is that more interesting than mingling with your fellow guests?"

He spoke with an accent, Yorkshire or perhaps even further north. Harriet turned around. She was irritated by his suggestion, but at the same time she saw how she must have looked, back turned to the room and arms plunged in the sink.

"I have mingled," she said. The man was very good-looking. She wondered why she hadn't noticed him before, then tried briefly to work out how much wine she had drunk before abandoning the calculation. "Then I saw that this needed doing. I thought I'd help Jane out a bit." There was no need to justify herself; she hoped she wasn't doing it because he had black curly hair and a face that made her think of a prize-fighter's before the puffy disfigurement.

"Jane?"

Harriet was startled. "This is Jane's party. Jane's house. You were dancing with her an hour ago." She felt light-hearted. She didn't immediately connect the light-heartedness with relief at finding that he didn't know who Jane was.

"*That* Jane. I've just met her. I'm staying with some people and they brought me along. I didn't know anyone when I arrived, including Jane."

He shrugged, an attractive, apologetic shrug, and Harriet smiled at him.

"I'll stop washing up if you can find me a drink."

He rummaged among the half-full bottles and poured out two glasses of wine. They stood in the corner by the fridge, where Harriet had found Charlie at the beginning of the evening, and made the conversation of strangers meeting at a party. The man's name was David. The more Harriet looked at him, the more attractive he appeared.

"Are you married, Harriet?" David was looking down at her hands.

"I was," she said neutrally.

"So was I."

A moment ago they had been talking about restoring houses. The mutual admission seemed at once to put them on a different footing. Harriet breathless and then surprised. The music from the other room had stopped for a while, but now it suddenly began again. The party was in its last, noisy throes. David took her glass out of her hand.

"Come and dance with me."

The living room was darkened, almost empty now. One other couple was dancing, with the music booming around them. David took her hand and they began to dance. He held her differently from the drunk teacher. The difference was that he did it right. Harriet closed her eyes, letting the music take her over. David was humming under his breath, his face close to hers. She thought how good it was to be held. How good, and how easy. They danced for quite a long time, and then something happened. David shifted his position slightly, moving from one side to squarely in front of her. He put his hands around her waist, and she knew that he was going to draw her hips against his. Then he would kiss her.

Harriet opened her eyes. The music became just a noise, although The Police were singing the same song. She didn't want anyone to kiss her. It was a long time since anyone but Leo had done so, and she didn't want this now. But all the time she was thinking *don't*, Harriet also knew that it would be exciting to take this man home with her, and let him warm her bed and her body. It was a long time since she had done anything of the kind, but she hadn't forgotten. They would steal into a dark room, and then blink at each other in the unwelcome light. They would take hold of each other, and their clothes would drop in tangled heaps as the two of them fastened together.

She remembered how imperative it was, and all the myriad welcome demands that came afterward. Not just for a night and a day, something told her, but for a long time afterward.

Only Harriet was impatient. She didn't have any time, now, to give to the absorbing conspiracies of love.

She looked carefully at David's face. It was a good face, one that would have stared out of a crowd at her. And behind David she saw two more of her friends, preparing to leave. Harriet slipped neatly and definitively out of the grasp of his hands.

"I must go and say good night."

In the good face, the undamaged pugilist's face, she saw a shadow of irritation. It was like a man, Harriet thought. At the same rebuff a woman might have revealed hurt, or anger, or anxiety. In a man, it was simply annoyance. She crossed the room quickly and rather unsteadily. She told herself that she had had a lot to drink, that she mustn't drink any more.

After she had said good night to the couple who were leaving, Harriet went upstairs. She locked herself into the bathroom and sat on the edge of the bath. She studied Jane's asparagus and spider plants grouped in their wicker basket, the bowls of soap and jars of cosmetics and creams, and the moon-face of the bathroom scale. She breathed deeply and evenly, remembering that she had felt breathless, like a silly girl. She decided that she had had a fortunate escape, and ignored the steady impulse to run downstairs and find the man again. That would be the first of the inevitable steps that would lead them back to her borrowed flat. When they reached it she would unbutton the blue shirt and wind her fingers in the black curls. It would be good and it would hurt nobody.

"Shit," Harriet said aloud.

She stood up and looked at herself in the mirror over Jane's washbasin. Then she rummaged in Jane's quilted make-up bag and found the plum-colored lipstick. She applied it to her own mouth, and found that it didn't suit her either.

She didn't know how long she had been locked in the bathroom; it was absurd to cower in there any longer. She flushed the lavatory unnecessarily and unlocked the door.

In the kitchen Jane and the last stragglers were drinking coffee.

"I'd love some," Harriet said. She took the wedding mug that Bernard the vegan had used earlier and tried to interest herself in a conversation about gender bias in nursery education. She was looking out of the corner of her eye for the blue shirt, hoping that it wouldn't reappear. When it did, there was a thick, dark sweater over it. David had come, with the couple who had brought him, to say good night to Jane. He kissed Jane on the cheek and thanked her, but he held out his hand to Harriet. She shook it, with the certainty that he was laughing at her.

"Perhaps we'll meet again," David said. The northern accent seemed pronounced now.

"Perhaps." Perfectly straightforward, neither encouraging nor unnecessarily chilly. Harriet was proud of herself but although she couldn't see his grin, she knew it was there. She formed some words experimentally in her head, *smug* and *arrogant* among them.

As she watched him go, ducking his head in the doorway, she discovered that she was quite strongly tempted to run after him. She stood absolutely still, and heard the front door open and close.

Then she let her shoulders drop. It had indeed been a narrow escape. Was this going to happen, then, this knock-kneed surge of barely focused lust, whenever she met a new man, just because Leo was no longer glowering at her side? Harriet smiled at the thought. She didn't have time to indulge herself with anything of the kind. Tonight was an aberration, and the man's impact was fading already. She couldn't even remember the configuration of his boxer's features.

"I'll make another pot of coffee, shall I?" Harriet volunteered to Jane.

At last, the stayers drifted away. They engaged themselves, as late guests always did, in vehement conversations held half in and half out of the front door. But finally only Jane and Harriet herself were left to survey the damage in the kitchen.

Jane shoved a line of dirty glasses to one side and sank down on one of her pine chairs.

"I'm not doing anything with any of this until tomorrow," she announced. Her hair had half-freed itself from its plait, and the last vestiges of the plum-colored maquillage had disappeared. She looked as if she was relieved. She rested her chin in her hands and beamed across the table at Harriet. "Isn't this always the best bit of a party? When everyone's gone, and you can sit back and talk about them?"

"I had a good time. Did you?"

Jane gave a long sigh. "I don't, usually, not at my own parties. All that scurrying about with drinks and dips. Husbands are useful for that, at least."

Harriet grinned. "Leo was never much good at it. You'd do better to hire a butler."

Jane wasn't listening. "But I did enjoy tonight. Did you see him, in the blue shirt? Yes, of course you did. You danced with him, didn't you? What did you think?"

Harriet opened her mouth but she heard the warning bells. She had felt relief that Jane didn't know him a little prematurely, it seemed.

"About who? Oh, yes. Him. Quite nice, I suppose." Harriet stretched her feet out on the chair next to her. She saw that someone had neatly dropped ash in the suede folds of her boots.

Jane was listening carefully enough now. She looked narrowly at Harriet. "Did you fancy him?"

"What? No. Or only from afar." She had locked herself in Jane's bathroom, run through the entire future sequence of events, and decided that she couldn't spare the time. That was all. "I'm too busy for that sort of thing."

"Hmm. He's staying with the Greens. He's some sort of a builder."

"So I gather."

"You talked to him as well?"

Harriet held up her hands, laughing, defending herself. "Only for five minutes. He's yours, take him."

Jane sighed again. "I'd welcome the chance. Well, he knows where to find me." She frowned at Harriet, not quite soberly. "What do you mean, *you're too busy for that sort of thing*? Perhaps a short sharp affair is just what you need at this point?"

"I don't think so. I haven't told you what I'm going to do. Can we forget the builder for a minute?"

"If you say so."

"I'm going to start a business." Harriet jumped to her feet, unable to keep still while she talked. She began to clear up, cutting a swathe through the debris. Jane watched her, blinking, her chin still resting on her hand.

At the end, Harriet leaned back against the sink and folded her arms. "So what do you think?"

Jane pondered. "I think . . ."

Harriet waited, knowing that Jane's approval was as important, in its different way, as Charlie's had been, and also knowing that she would go ahead with her plan whatever Jane said.

"I think it sounds a fine idea."

"Thank you." Harriet bent down and hugged her, and the fraying plait tickled her cheek.

"So put that bloody tea towel down, and tell me how you're going to get started."

"Homework. Lots of homework, and then trying to raise the money. Charlie made it quite clear that it wouldn't be easy."

Jane thought for a moment. "I've got some money saved. A couple of thousand, that's all, but you could have that if it would help."

Harriet was amazed. Jane's generosity was on a far grander scale than her embryo plan called for, and she was touched by it. To hide her feelings she teased, "It might be a good investment. You'll get a healthy return on your money, I promise."

Jane was scandalized. "I offered it for you, not because I want to make money out of you."

"I know that," Harriet told her. "And I'm grateful."

"I hope so. Oh, God, look at the time. It's nearly four o'clock."

"I'm going home alone to Belsize Park."

"To slip between the balance sheets."

Their laughter acknowledged their singleness, and their affection for each other.

"Won't you stay the night?"

"I'd rather go home. I'll come back and help with this in the morning."

Harriet was thinking about the game, propped up against the wall in the empty flat. It drew her back, as if they needed one another's protection.

"You've done more than half already. Call me."

Jane stood in the circle of light from her porch to watch her go.

The streets were empty as Harriet reversed her zigzag journey. The gangs of youths had filtered away and even the few cars that swept past her seemed to travel without human intervention. It was as if she was alone in the world. It was pleasant to be warm and safe and isolated in the darkness. Harriet smiled. She wasn't thinking about Charlie Thimbell reaching up to touch her breast, or about the man in the blue shirt. She was thinking about friendship, and the evening's confirmation of it. She hummed as she drove.

Six

THE SHOP WAS EMPTY, at the end of a rainy Monday afternoon, except for two girls trying on leotards in the mirrored cubicles at the far end. Harriet knew that they might end up buying headbands, or leg-warmers at the very most, most probably nothing at all, but she left them in peace because that was the shop's policy. They would come back, perhaps, when they did have money to spend. Besides that, she liked the look of them. They were young and skinny, with their hair done up in asymmetric tufts like plumes on the tops of their heads. They admired the diminishing perspectives of their own back views in the mirrors, then collapsed into choking giggles.

One of them emerged from behind the curtains in a shimmering tube of bright pink Lycra. She made a few stiff movements at the bar that ran around the shop, the plume hair nodding in a dozen mirrored reflections.

"Makes me look like a horrible ice-cream," she sniffed.

"The leopardskin one would be better," Harriet encouraged her. "Go on, try it on." It was the first time she had spoken to them, and at once they looked startled and guilty. Harriet went to the rack where the folds of leopardskin print lay and shook one out.

"Go on," she repeated. "I'd like to see you in it."

The girl was thin. Her spine was a chain of knobs, and her hipbones jutted out. When she put the leopardskin on and sidled out between the curtains, she was transformed into a cat. A small, hungry but confident cat. The girl pirouetted and her friend whistled between her teeth. Harriet tried to remember what it felt like, to be just their age, not a woman nor quite a girl any longer. It seemed a long time ago.

"It suits you," she told her.

Without making any more suggestions, Harriet went back to her place behind the counter. She looked out of the tall shop-window at the rain. The street lights were just coming on, and the light refracted off the raindrops on the glass in tiny, optimistic sparkles.

"Perhaps tomorrow," Harriet thought. "This time."

There were dozens of boxes of soft leather dance shoes waiting to be unpacked and checked in the stockroom, as well as a delivery of new Italian body creams and oils. Harriet knew that the cosmetics would sell well, and she was looking forward to displaying them. But on Mondays she was alone in the shop, without one of her three part-time sales assistants. She couldn't leave the till, and there was nothing that needed doing within reach of it. The clothes lay in colorful folds in their pigeon-holes, or hung tidily on the chrome rails. The boxes and bottles and packets of the other stock were neatly arranged; the whole shop was a warm, shining cavern of mirrors.

At the far end, the girls were whispering together. Harriet reached under the counter, and took out the new game.

One of her tasks in the last four hard months had been to seek out a manufacturer who would do what she wanted. At length, not very many miles from where Simon lived, she had found a small plastics factory. By traveling up to work alongside the owner, Mr. Jepson, cajoling him and chivying him and making promises that she had no certainty of being able to keep, she had encouraged him enough to produce a prototype that very nearly satisfied her.

It was smaller than Simon's original, made in heavy, glossy black plastic that looked almost like lacquered wood. The gates were Y-shapes in glistening white plastic, and how bitterly Mr. Jepson had complained about the difficulties of getting those just right. The four balls and their matching disks were brilliant blobs of color against the stark black and white.

Harriet dropped the disks at random into the slots, and fed the balls into their groove, ready to roll. She made a quick calculation and flipped the gates.

Because the board was smaller, the balls didn't make quite the same musical cadence as they dropped. Harriet frowned, listening and watching. The bright spots of color zigzagged down the path she had chosen for them, and fell one by one to their predestined places. Automatically Harriet scooped them up, and scattered the counters again.

"Excuse me."

The two girls were standing at the counter. They were clutching the scraps of leopardskin fabric between them, offering it to her.

"Can we take this, please?"

"Of course you can."

Harriet took it and wrapped it in tissue, and put it in one of the silver Stepping carrier bags. The girls' heads were bent over their purses. Harriet saw that they were colored plastic ones, reminding her of the kind Liza had hoarded in Kath's old hangbags, playing shopping. They were pooling their resources. After counting and recounting the money, most of it coins, they pushed it across the counter to Harriet. She found that it was right to the penny.

"Have you left yourselves enough to get home?" Harriet asked.

"Yeah, it's expensive, isn't it? But we had to get it, once we'd seen it on, didn't we? We're going to take turns wearing it."

Harriet felt the glow of pleasure that selling always gave her. There was a positive satisfaction in fitting customer and merchandise together, as she had just done, and the recognition that the girls could hardly afford their purchase increased rather than diminished it. She knew from her own experience that she always loved most of the things that she didn't really have the money for, and she imagined the girls taking turns to appear at parties with the leotard swathed under a black shirt, their hair in ever more exotic dressings. They would get their money's worth from it.

Earlier in the day she had sold the same leotard in the biggest size to a fat woman who could clearly afford to buy it fifty times over. The only pleasure she had derived from that had been in an efficent transaction.

"Enjoy wearing it," Harriet said.

"What's this, then?"

One of the girls ran her fingers over the inclined tracks of the game. She picked out the gates, like white bones, and jiggled them. She dropped one, and it slid across the polished floor.

"Sandy!" her less confident friend remonstrated.

"It's all right," Harriet said, as the little wishbone was retrieved. "It's mine, it doesn't belong to the shop. Have a try."

Harriet showed them. Sandy rattled the counters in her fist as if they were dice, kissed her knuckles as she must have seen in the films, and cast the disks into the slots. The two of them hung over the shiny board, contradicting each other and pushing one another's hands out of the way.

"You're daft, Nicky."

"Daft yourself. If you open this one it'll only go like this, see?"

Harriet watched their faces. The spring was released and the musical rattle came again.

The girls' eyes and mouths were fascinated circles as they watched the balls follow their paths. They dropped, with finality, into the wrong slots.

"Bugger."

"Give us another go. That was your fault."

There was more jostling, more contradicting.

Good, Harriet thought. She had tried the game on everyone she knew, but she was always afraid that the responses reflected an urge to be kind and encouraging, or to play devil's advocate for her own good. She liked it best when strangers became instantly engrossed, as Sandy and Nicky had done. Their bony shoulders were hunched over it, and the plumes of hair sparred with a life of their own. There was a yodel of triumph as their second attempt was successful.

"But your score's too high," Harriet said. There was another outcry, and then they set to work again. The reaction was beginning to be familiar.

Harriet had done her research. She had spent two entire Sundays riding on the top deck of a 73 bus, north to south London and back again, through the dim streets at either end of the route and along the great channel of Oxford Street in the middle. Sunday was a good day for the buses. They weren't too crowded, the passengers were bored by the slow journey and glad to be distracted. They only bothered to climb up to the top deck, Harriet discovered, if they were traveling some distance. She attracted their attention with the rattle and plop of the balls.

It took some courage, at first, to approach people and ask if they wanted to play. But they almost always agreed. Soon she had developed a professional patter. *I'm doing some informal market research. Do you mind if . . . ?* Harriet enjoyed her encounters on the isolated, swaying top deck. She played with gangs of teenage boys, with pairs of old ladies, mothers and children and solitary middle-aged men. Once, on the last leg of her last journey on an empty bus, she played with the West Indian bus conductor. She thought that in a fairer world he would have been a professor of logic. He set the paths unhesitatingly, even for the hardest of all the permutations.

"It's good," he told her. "It's fun. My children would like this."

"Would you buy it?" Harriet asked, as she always did.

"Maybe." He patted his ticket machine on its worn leather strap. "We've all got a path to follow, haven't we?"

"I don't know," Harriet answered quickly, thinking of Simon's path. All the gates closed. Or were they?

"Would you buy it?" she asked Nicky and Sandy.

"Might do, for Christmas or something," one said, relinquishing the smooth disks.

The other added, "If it was cheap. We've got to go, Sand. You promised your Mum."

They scuttled out of the shop with their silver bag, promising Harriet that they would come back another time. When they were gone she packed the game away in its box.

She knew it was good. Sometimes her earliest conviction of how good it was came back to her, and she shivered down the length of her spine. She had only to convince the cold men who had money to lend of the same thing. She had to show them how the game had been enjoyed on the buses. And she had to convince the money men that she could sell to the bus passengers, and those people multiplied by thousands. Perhaps tomorrow, Harriet encouraged herself. She felt the bite of adrenaline in her blood.

Harriet locked the shop and began to walk toward the tube station, turning the familiar equations over in her head as she went. When she was buying into Stepping, Harriet had found the shop and Ken had bought the lease for her. She was paying him back but the property still did not belong to her, and so she couldn't offer it as collateral for a bigger loan. She would have done so if it had been possible; as she felt now she would have done anything, she wanted the money so badly. But the lease belonged to Ken, and although he had listened sympathetically to her proposal he was too careful to advance her the money for a second, much riskier enterprise. She needed too much money, in any case.

She wanted to launch her game in the way it deserved. With a splash, with sumptuous packaging, with advertising, and with piles of it in every window, in every outlet. The figures were set out, with the rest of her calculations, in the proposals she had spent the last four months poring over. The equations had become very familiar, but the size of them still daunted her.

Harriet had just under twenty thousand pounds of her own, her share of the proceeds from the sale of the flat she had owned with Leo. She had managed to add to her capital another pitifully small amount, by living on air in Belsize Park.

Almost as soon as she reached her rented flat and unpacked the prototype once more, the telephone rang. It was Charlie Thimbell.

"Harriet? Jenny's up in Newcastle for a publication party tonight, and I'm not going home to cook for myself. Let me come over and take you out to eat. We can go to the Chinese place."

Jenny was back at her job as a publisher's editor. From time to time she had to spend a night away, and Charlie was famous for his unwillingness to fend for himself. Harriet knew that there was nothing in her own fridge, and that even if there had been she probably wouldn't get around to eating anything. She thought longingly of the little Chinese restaurant that Charlie was fond of, with its tasseled lanterns and kitschy mural.

"Charlie, I can't tonight."

He made a disgusted noise. "Why not this time?"

"I'm working. I just want to go through it all one more time. I'm seeing the venture capital division at Morton's in the morning."

"Are you, now." Charlie was professionally interested. "What d'you reckon?"

"I've got a feeling this could be just the right connection, at long last. They're funding a lot of other small ventures, some of them just as much long-shots as mine."

The notion of *small* amused Harriet now as it had done before. Small in the vocabulary of a big merchant bank like Morton's meant a loan of less than a quarter of a million pounds. In her fruitless rounds of the banks and other funding institutions Harriet had been told more than once that she would find it easier to raise money if she was looking for a million or more. And yet she was shaking at the notion of a hundred thousand. She caught herself wondering if she had the right entrepreneurial qualities.

Firmly, she told Charlie, "I want to be word-perfect."

"You can over-prepare, you know. Come on, let me take your mind off it."

"Thanks. But not tonight, honestly. You can take me out to celebrate when they agree to fund me."

"Okay, okay," Charlie said, and hung up. When Harriet refused, he knew that she meant it. He left his office and went to the newspaper's pub instead, where he had several drinks with two sports writers.

Harriet made herself a cup of tea and sat down at the table she used as a desk. She set out the glossy black board beside the cracked packing case, and sat looking at the two of them for a moment. She had studied them so hard and for so long that she wasn't even sure that she saw them clearly any longer. The numbers, the patterns and permutations, made long chains in her head.

Impatiently, she drew a sheaf of papers toward her. Everything was there.

The production estimates came first. Working with Mr. Jepson, she had established the unit cost of each game, based on a first production run of thirty thousand. Thirty thousand was ambitious, but Harriet was convinced that to aim high was the only way. It would be cheaper to manufacture in the Far East, but from the other companies who she had persuaded to talk to her, through a mixture of bluff and guile, Harriet had gathered that these sources were not all reliable. She calculated that it would be better, in the beginning at least, to pay for reliability and proximity. She could always drive up the motorway to see Mr. Jepson at Midland Plastics. And she was sure that, on the spot, she could get what she wanted.

In fact the board itself had been the least of her problems. The balls and counters could be bought from another company who specialized in such things, and the spring mechanism that released the balls would come from yet another source. It was the packaging that had troubled her most. During her four-month crash course in manufacturing methods, Harriet had learned that all her game components must be assembled for sale in a molded plastic tray. An injection molding machine would have to be specially built to produce it, and that alone would cost her nearly twenty thousand pounds. And after that came the cardboard box to enclose everything else, with the color artwork to decorate it, that must be designed and proofed and then printed. The cost of quality color printing had startled her more than anything else.

At last, when the components were all ready in their plastic trays, the instructions, and the bright, beautiful boxes must all be brought together and shrink-wrapped ready to be sold.

But none of this could be done until she had orders from wholesale and retail buyers, and perhaps only firm orders would enable her to raise the money to start a production run that would allow her to meet those orders.

It was like a shivering house of cards, in which the collapse of one corner would bring down the whole shaky structure. Wearily, Harriet rubbed her eyes.

She had come this far. She was going to show Morton's that, if only they would back her, she would go much further. There would have to be no shaky corners, that was all. She returned her attention to her papers. The manufacturing details wouldn't interest the money men, only the figures at the bottom of the neatly typed pages. At the wholesale price she had established, not quite as low as she could have pitched it because she wanted her game to appear a quality product, and assuming that she could get all her thirty thousand units into the shops in time for Christmas, she could accommodate a start-up loan of one hundred thousand pounds, and clear another hundred thousand for reinvestment, expansion, overseas sales. Break-even point was fifteen thousand.

The prospect glittered at her.

But again, her card house trembled. To get the games into the shops in time for Christmas selling, the manufacturing must be completed by July, August at the latest. The buyers would place their basic orders at the Toy Fair in London at the end of February, and reorder later when selling got under way. Harriet had booked a stand at the Fair without any certainty that she would have anything to display on it except a split packing case and a lonely slab of black plastic adorned with white wishbones. And it was already mid-January.

The urgency of her need to raise capital gnawed at her all day, every day, but now it gripped her like a physical spasm. Harriet got up from the table, stretching her stiff limbs, and went over to the window. She hadn't bothered to close the curtains before sitting down, and she looked out at the dingy basement area and the railings above that separated it from the street. She rested her forehead against the cold glass and breathed slowly, reassuring herself. She would get the money. She would get the orders at the Fair. The game would be in the shops by the autumn. And her own efforts would make sure that it sold out of the shops again.

Harriet looked up and saw the two cats winding in and out of the railings, mewing at her. She had forgotten to let them in, forgotten to feed them. Stricken with guilt she went to the door and opened it. The cats bounded down the steps and streaked between her legs and into the kitchen. Harriet followed them and spooned meat out of a tin into two bowls. The yelping subsided at once into satisfied chewing, punctuated by bursts of purring. Harriet absent-mindedly cut herself a slice of bread and ate it leaning against the kitchen table, watching the cats' complete absorption in their food. If she could only bring the same attention to setting up her company, she thought, the obstacles would probably melt away.

The tea had gone cold in the pot, but she poured herself another cup anyway and settled down to her figures again. Replete, the cats followed her to her seat. One settled itself like a hot cushion against her feet, and the other launched itself into her lap. Harriet stroked the soft fur. She was glad of the company of the cats. They didn't distract her, as Charlie Thimbell would have done.

Beyond the practical details of manufacturing and sales, the bank would want to know about the structure of the company they were being asked to invest in. Weighing up her requirements very carefully, Harriet had concluded that it would be best kept very small. She calculated that at the beginning she could run it herself, as the sole proprietor. She would need a secretarial assistant, and a part-time bookkeeper. She would also need an accountant, the best possible accountant. But in her card-house world she would need to raise the capital before she could appoint one.

With clear sight, Harriet knew that she was really asking for investment in herself. It was her own energy, her own selling skills, that would make her venture work. From careful analysis of her market—not at all scientifically done, but with the intuition that she would have to let herself rely on—she believed even a bad game could be made to sell well. If it was packaged right, and cleverly marketed, and if it was enough talked and written about where people noticed such things, then it would sell. It might only be played once or twice, but the price would still have been paid for it.

Harriet was convinced that she could package and sell and promote as well as anyone else; better, even, because it was all she had to concentrate on. There were no other demands on her, she had nothing else to give herself to. She would present herself to Morton's.

And she had the added satisfaction, the added insurance, of knowing that her game—Simon's game—was good. It was better than anything else she had seen or could remember.

The rain cleared overnight. Harriet reached the bank's new black-glass building in thin sunlight, seven minutes early. She stood looking at the City edifices rearing up around her, at sooty stone and concrete and glass, feeling her irrelevance in their weighty shadows.

Of course, she told herself. *What else should you feel?*

At exactly two minutes before the appointed time, she presented herself to the reception at a desk in the marble lobby. Behind Harriet's back a fountain expensively trickled among green fronds. As the receptionist telephoned to announce her, Harriet thought about the different languages that money spoke. This soft one, of quiet voices in harmony with polite water and smooth, cold stone was becoming familiar to her. She was aware that if she penetrated further she would have to learn to interpret other, coarser tongues.

Following the receptionist's instructions she took the polished box of the lift to a lofty floor. Up here there was a long carpeted vista and a plate-glass sweep at the end that gave a further vista of towers and blind eyes of glass. It was quiet, like being in the nave of a church, looking toward some vast altarpiece. In the distance, yet all around her, Harriet could hear a low humming. She knew that it was machinery, the bank's electronic heart, but it reminded her irresistibly of the murmur of prayer.

A man came out of one of the doors that opened, like pew-ends, into the nave. In his dark clothes against the bright glass he seemed featureless, an acolyte.

"Mrs. Gold? Would you come this way, please?"

Obediently she went with him. Beyond the door there was a conference room. It was so ordinary, with its empty oval table and glass ashtrays and unmemorable pictures, that Harriet felt momentarily disoriented. The acolyte had become a middle-aged man in a conservative suit. There were two other men waiting in the room, surprisingly young, in just the same clothes. All three of them had pink, smooth, pleasant faces, as indistinguishable one from the other as the pictures on the walls.

Harriet made an effort to collect herself. Unthinkingly, she smoothed the hem of her own plain, dark jacket. The skirt of her suit was narrow, but not too narrow, to the knee. Her shoes were plain, dark, and low-heeled. She was dressed right, reflecting the bank men exactly.

"Won't you sit down?"

The youngest of the trio held out a chair. Harriet sat. She smiled at each of them but she refused the formal offer of coffee.

"Well, Mrs. Gold. Won't you tell us about your project?" The invitation came from the oldest one. He rested his wrists on the table, hands clasped, ready to give her his full attention. The other two, on either side of him, adopted almost the same position. Harriet looked at each of them in turn, remembering the names by which they had introduced themselves, and then she began.

Softly, without emphasis, she told them, "The game is called 'Conundrum.' "

It had taken her a long time to fix on a name. Simon had never called it anything. For a long time, in her own head, it had just been *Simon's game*. After meeting the logician bus conductor she had thought about his pathways, and his theory of predestination, and also of Simon's words, *It's a wonderful game if you can play it right. Like life.* But Harriet had rejected all the portentous names that went with such ideas. They would make the game seem too serious to be played with.

"Conundrum" sounded light, with the right element of mystery. People would read their own further significance into the shiny tracks if they so wished. Harriet just wanted them to give it to each other for Christmas.

In the conference room of the venture capital division of Morton's Bank, Harriet opened a small suitcase. As she had done on each of the previous similar occasions, she felt like a peddler displaying her wares.

Inside the suitcase was a box, only a dummy as yet, but still looking enough like the box that Harriet wanted for the final "Conundrum." The artwork for the design, bold Deco lettering backed by a sunray motif in brilliant colors, had been produced, after a dozen other attempts had been rejected, by a design studio recommended to Harriet by Jenny. The artwork had been proofed, using a five-color run to give depth and richness, by an East End printer recommended by the design studio. Harriet had found her own manufacturer of boxes, and had a sample made up to her own specifications. All the experiments had been expensive. Harriet had paid out of her capital, knowing that she must practice no economies yet.

When the time came the design would be printed onto the packaging, and then laminated to give it sparkle. For now, Harriet could do no better than stick a laminated proof to the sample box.

Even so, she was delighted with the fresh impact of it.

The bankers inspected the packaging carefully. Harriet opened the lid to reveal the game itself. There were printed instructions, but as yet the sheet was only pasted inside the lid. There was no molding to cradle the board or to offer little cups in which the counters and balls would neatly rest. That could come only when Harriet had raised the money for it.

Please, she wanted to implore the three pink faces. Instead she lifted out the black shiny board, fitted the white wings in their slots.

"This is how it works."

The three men gave their attention to playing "Conundrum." Two of them were good at it. The third was not, although he was clever at concealing it by deferring to the others when his turn came, and by masking his deliberations with a knowing smile. Harriet thought that probably she was the only one who noticed his shortcoming.

Rather noisily, the other two challenged each other to produce the lowest score over three games. The atmosphere in the
conference room became frivolous. Harriet kept the score, and
declared the senior man the fair and square winner at the end.
She thought that was probably important. The third man slipped
out of the room, and came back again with a sheaf of papers as
the game finished.

"Quite intriguing," was the senior man's verdict, and his
assistants nodded. "And most strikingly presented." More nods
followed.

Harriet allowed herself to begin to hope.

"Now, shall we take a look at your plans for the business?"

All frivolity ebbed away at once.

Harriet took out her projections, one copy for each of the
three pairs of fleshy pink hands, and she began to talk. She had
rehearsed her pitch so thoroughly that the points came fluently
one after another, in logical and convincing sequence. The dates
and figures and the estimates fitted together, as neatly as the
wishbone gates into their slots. Harriet convinced herself as she
talked. She could have sung, although she kept her voice dispas-
sionate and level. They couldn't refuse her now.

A hundred thousand pounds. In this financial cathedral, it
was so very little.

As soon as she finished her pitch and answered their questions, she knew that they would indeed refuse her. She barely
heard the formulas as they were reeled off, but the meaning was
quite clear.

"This is a fashion product, Mrs. Gold, of course."

"The most unpredictable market of all. If only we *could*
predict . . ."

"The high risk attached to small ventures of this kind . . ."

The third one, the one who had failed to solve the game's
riddle, read from his sheaf of papers. It contained the financial
histories of other companies, the proprietors of games and toys
and fashion products that had failed to capture the market's
imagination. As they were afraid "Conundrum" would also fail.

Harriet rallied herself. "I believe you are misjudging. 'Conundrum' has nothing to do with fashion. Its appeal is timeless. I
know the market will respond to that appeal."

They were shaking their heads, each with his own interpretation of polite regret. Harriet thought savagely that they looked
like the three wise monkeys, possessed of the wrong kind of
wisdom. The senior man stood up, and held out his hand.

"You may well prove us wrong, Mrs. Gold. I wish I could be

sure that you won't, and at the same time I wish you the best of luck.''

Harriet shook his hand, although she would rather have bitten it. She listened to his thanks for her kindness in letting them see her proposal, and his repeated regret that it appeared not to be quite the right investment for Morton's, while many of their rivals might well take quite a different view of it. The one who couldn't play the game held open the door for her, and then escorted her to the lift. She wondered if it might have been different had he been as good at it as her bus conductor.

She found herself in the street again, under the tall towers. All she knew for sure was that she had failed again. The game was good, she reasoned, so the fault must be her own. Her awareness of that, and the optimism she had felt about this meeting, made the disappointment harder to bear. She tried to think back over everything she had said, and to pin-point the moment when the tide had turned against her. But it was no use. She couldn't work out exactly where she had gone wrong. They had given her a fair hearing, a long one she saw now, when she looked at her watch. And at the end of it they had simply decided not to back her.

Harriet hurried on. She was due back at Stepping, where Karen would be needing help. Tuesday afternoons were often busy, for no particularly obvious reason.

She was already recovering her balance. There wouldn't be any failure if she refused to acknowledge it. This connection had been one possibility, and she had been wrong to place too much faith in it. There would be other connections, and one of them would hold. If she couldn't believe that, she told herself, then it would be better to give up right away.

By the evening, when she let herself into the basement flat again, she had decided what she was going to do. She would get Mr. Jepson to make up more samples of the game, a dozen at least, and she would have boxes printed and the best packaging she could manage. She would print posters and leaflets and lots of powerful, bright promotion material. She would take a bigger stand at the Toy Fair, instead of a modest one, and she would staff it with her own sales people, and she would give "Conundrum" the showiest splash she could possibly devise.

She had enough capital to do it. Just enough.

Then, when the buyers had seen and ordered, she could go out and borrow the money for the production run ten times over.

Harriet fed the cats, and they subsided into a purring dome of bicolored fur in the only comfortable chair. She opened the small suitcase that she had taken to Morton's with such misplaced optimism, and placed "Conundrum" and its bright box beside Simon's original on the mantelpiece. She was standing back to look at it when she heard people coming down the steps to her basement door.

The visitors were Charlie Thimbell and a man called Henry Orde. Henry was an old friend of Charlie's. Harriet knew him a little, and liked him. But she sighed inwardly at the sight of the two of them. She wanted to think about the day's defeat, and to marshal her reserves of confidence once more, and now she would have to descend into the realm of sociability.

"Come in," she invited, not opening the door very wide.

The men came in anyway, in their bulky overcoats, bringing cold air with them and making the room seem tiny. Harriet blinked at seeing the place so unfamiliarly crowded, and Charlie stared around him.

"We were having a drink around the corner," he announced, "so we came on to see you. Harriet, what is this place? I'm worried about you. Jenny is as well, she says she hasn't seen you for weeks."

"We've talked on the phone," Harriet automatically defended herself. "Thanks for being concerned, but there's no need, really. Hello, Henry."

She knew that she sounded stiff, and wondered if she had been so absorbed in her scheme that she had forgotten how to talk normally. She knew, too, that her visitors had come out of friendship, but she felt the intrusion even more strongly. "Conundrum" was hers, succeed or fail, and until it had succeeded her protective instinct toward it was as strong as a mother's. But still she took the men's coats, and pitched the cats off the chair, and brought a bottle of wine and glasses from the kitchen.

They settled themselves as comfortably as they could in the small space.

"It's fine for me," Harriet said quickly. "I don't need a lot of room, and it's cheap because I take care of the cats. Sort of take care of them."

"How did it go today?" Charlie asked, dismissing the flat.

"Today? Yes. Well, it didn't go, exactly."

She told them, briefly, and they listened, nodding their heads with their accumulated financial expertise. Suddenly they reminded her of the three wise monkeys at Morton's, and she felt a flash of anger.

It strengthened her determination to launch "Conundrum" in her own way, with her own money.

She took her sample down from the mantelpiece again and gave it to Henry to play with. She walked up and down the cramped room, talking about her plans for the Fair and the compelling promotion that would bring the buyers flocking. She made ideas up as she went along. She would have the box's sunray motif made up in three dimensions to back the stand. She would have her sales team in black and white shiny outfits, she would invite celebrities to play. With the force of her enthusiasm alone, if necessary, she would get the buzz going. As she talked Henry Orde flicked the release spring. The rattle and roll of "Conundrum's" balls counter-pointed her words.

"When I've got the orders I can go back and choose who's going to lend me the money," Harriet finished triumphantly. "It's the best way to do it. I know it's the best way."

There was a little silence.

"Well?" Harriet demanded.

Charlie sucked at his wine, and Henry appeared to be intent on rearranging the colored counters in the slots.

"Don't you think I can do it?"

Charlie looked up at her at last. She felt like a termagant standing over him, but she stood her ground.

"You could lose everything you've got," he said. "I've seen it happen. So has Henry." Henry was a solicitor.

"And equally, I've got everything to gain. I can only go bankrupt, can't I?"

Henry looked at her then, too.

"Perhaps you're right," he said. He had a nice, bashful smile that Harriet had always liked. "You could just be right. I think it's worth going for. They're a very conservative bunch at Morton's. And this isn't their field. They prefer telecommunications, electronics, the heavy stuff. I know someone you could try."

Henry took a business card from his wallet and scribbled on the back of it. When Harriet looked at what he had written she saw the words *Landwith Associates*, and an address in SW1.

"They're a small firm of venture capitalists. With a reputation for risking long shots." Harriet returned his smile, and put the card away. "Thanks. I think I'm going to do it my own way, just the same."

"Good luck."

Twice in one day she had been wished it. It would do her no harm, Harriet thought.

"I saw Leo the other night," Henry said, interrupting her reverie.

Harriet had not seen Leo for weeks, since the completion of

the sale of the flat. She felt a twinge of guilt when she realized that he was fading out of her life, and then reminded herself that she had no reason to feel guilty about Leo.

"How was he?"

Harriet saw the two men exchange a half-glance. She guessed what it meant. Henry and Charlie thought that if she wasn't alone, stranded here as they imagined in a poky flat, then she wouldn't need to chase after entrepreneurial rainbows and risk losing the little security she had.

They didn't believe that she could make it, and they were old friends. No wonder Morton's had turned her down.

The realization was comforting. It might just be that the fault was not hers after all, but only the shortsightedness of the huge, hermetic, male-dominated business world.

"He asked about you," Henry told her. "Not that I could tell him anything."

"I'll have to give him a call," Harriet said mildly.

They sat for a little longer, talking and drinking wine, until Charlie looked at his watch.

"Time for home."

"Is Jenny back?"

"Yes. I must go, or I'll be late for supper."

Henry stood up, too. Harriet wasn't sure what his current domestic arrangements were, but he clearly also had somewhere to go. Yet they both hesitated, and it struck Harriet that they felt badly about leaving her. They were sorry for her, abandoned in reduced circumstances with the cats and the balance sheets for company.

"I'll come out with you. I need some fresh air."

"Listen, Harriet, why don't you come, too? Jenny'd like to see you. I'll just give her a call and tell her we're on our way . . ."

Harriet shook her head. "Not tonight, thanks, Charlie. I want to do some things. Just give Jenny my love, and tell her I'll see her soon."

"You can't work all the time, Harriet."

"I don't."

It wasn't the truth, but there was no need for anyone to know that. Harriet opened the basement door and almost shepherded the two of them up the iron stairs to the street level. A taxi came by, and Charlie flagged it. It pulled in to the curb and the driver opened the window, his breath visible in cumulus clouds in the January murk. Henry paused before he climbed into the back, his hand on Harriet's arm.

"Do one thing for me. The rights in this game, whoever they belong to. Secure them, before you do anything else."

"I will," she promised. "I'm going to do that next."

Harriet didn't know why she had procrastinated. Only that the cathedral of Morton's, and everything else that she had been pursuing in the months since she had left Leo, seemed far removed from Simon among the flotsam in his cold house. She was afraid, perhaps, of being unable to find a language that would bring them together. Henry and Charlie were right, however. This was just one of the new languages that she must learn.

The taxi drove away. Harriet stood for a moment looking down the street at the lights behind drawn curtains. The thin fog blurred the yellow squares, so that the light seemed to spill beyond the window frames. Then she shivered in the cold air, and turned back down the iron steps.

This time, Harriet drove up to see Simon. She went first to visit Mr. Jepson at Midland Plastics, and ordered a dozen more "Conundrum" samples. She sat in his office with its chipped metal filing cabinets and girlie calendar, drinking thick tea and listening to the subterranean pounding of machinery down on the shop floor.

Mr. Jepson wanted to be paid in advance. Harriet leaned forward over his desk.

"Can I have everything by February the twentieth? Without fail? With a written undertaking?" Mr. Jepson appeared to be offended that she would not accept his word as his bond. Harriet opened her checkbook and wrote out a check for the full amount that he had quoted. She held it out to him.

"My written undertaking," she said, "in return for yours." He buzzed his secretary, and dictated the brief letter to Harriet's satisfaction.

"And then there's the production run. Thirty thousand units, price quoted, for delivery at the end of May. Can you guarantee that, too?"

"Those wishbones are the devil's job."

"Can you guarantee it?"

"Aye. If it gets to that."

Mr. Jepson was a Northerner. His voice reminded Harriet of the man in the blue shirt.

"It will," she said grimly. "It will, I assure you."

They shook hands. Mr. Jepson was a small man. Over his

head the January girl winked out of the calendar at Harriet. She was wearing a white fur tippet and mittens, and long white boots. Nothing else. Harriet's jaw and neck ached with the wire-tightness of her determination to pin Jepson down. She thought, suddenly, how comforting it would be to have a good cry.

"Good-bye, Mr. Jepson," she said. "I'm sure we can do business together, now we understand each other."

Harriet had written to Simon, announcing her visit. He had no telephone, of course. But she had to stand for a long time in rain driven horizontally by the wind, before she heard his steps on the other side of the door. Still the door didn't open. The movements stopped, replaced by interrogative silence.

"It's Harriet." And more emphatically, into the blanket of it, "Kath's Harriet. Do you remember?"

At last the bolts were being drawn back. A moment later, Simon confronted her. She had forgotten his height, and the milky, frosty eyes. "I did write," she reminded him lamely. "I thought you'd write back and tell me not to come, if you really didn't want to see me."

"You'd better come in," was all he said. The door opened another frugal slice. Harriet followed him down the passageway. She hadn't forgotten the smell, or the gnawing cold, much worse in January than it had been in the mild autumn. The kitchen seemed even more forlornly lumbered.

"Would you like some tea?"

Harriet didn't, but she said cheerfully, "Let me make it for you, this time."

She went to the sink and tried to clear some of the slime of crusts and potato peelings and tea leaves before rinsing and filling the kettle. Behind her she could hear Simon moving busily. She had the impression that he was putting things away, out of her sight. The notion that her visit was an unwelcome intrusion stabbed a little dart inside her. She had allowed herself to imagine that he might have been looking forward to it. Harriet brushed aside her own disappointment and began to tell him little, inconsequential snippets of news, mostly about Kath and Ken and the house, or about Liza and her boyfriend. At length it sounded as though Simon had finished his rites of concealment. She could hear him breathing now, noisily, as if with a degree of difficulty. She plugged in the kettle and washed and dried two cups before turning unhurriedly around.

"Have you got a bad chest?"

"It's winter."

The economy of the response made her smile, in spite of her

discomfort. "You think I sound like a busybody from the Council or somewhere."

"That's right." A smile, but as wintry as the weather. Gratefully Harriet accepted the moment of rapport. She put his cup of tea down at his elbow and bent down to open her case, placed on the floor for lack of a clear space anywhere else. She took out "Conundrum," Mr. Jepson's expensive "Conundrum," with the ritual incantations of the three wise monkeys somehow still clouding its polished flanks. She put it into Simon's hands like an offering and laid its box beside it, its resonant colors almost too bright for the meager room.

"You've done this?"

"I brought it to show to you. I want to tell you all about it."

In his eyes Harriet saw a dark spectrum of responses, from disgust to fear, quickly shuttered, and wished that she had not. She stooped on her haunches, to bring herself to his sitting level.

"It's all right," she said gently. She didn't know about what she was trying to reassure him.

"What do you mean?" He wouldn't admit her through the smallest chink in his armor. Harriet wished for the disarming surprise of her last visit, or for the leveling of whiskey. There was no excuse for whiskey at three o'clock in the afternoon.

"Where is my game? My packing-case game?"

"It's safe. It's at home, but I can bring it straight back for you, if you want that."

"No. It's funny, I've kept it with me all these years. But I feel better with it out of the house." He picked the gates out of the slots and shook the white bones in his cupped hands. Then he swept a clearing in the table's litter and laid out the bones in a line, a series of Y's, two narrow paths diverging from each broad central one, offering choices. "You'd better sit down properly," he told her, "and say what it is you've come for."

Harriet described everything, from the first tentative plans she had made alone in the rented basement to this morning's confrontation with Mr. Jepson. Her words came out in a rush. She didn't weigh them or try to modulate them. She simply told Simon what had happened, in a rapid, fervent, breathless outpouring. And when she had finished, there was silence. It was particularly cold and weighty silence after the heat of her delivery.

"You told me I could do what I like with it," she said, very humbly.

"I know I did. I meant it." Simon studied her face. He was realizing that, in the time that had passed since her last visit, he had been recalling Harriet as prettier than she really was. Somehow he had superimposed Kath's soft, bloomy features on the daughter's thinner, sharper ones. Kath had never looked threateningly famished, as this girl did.

"Simon?" she was prompting him, in a voice that still and yet carried the echo of her mother's, just as her face carried the print of the other one.

"What is it?"

"I . . ." Harriet's words dried. Glancing at it she saw that "Conundrum" looked meaningless, and its box garish. She had been wrong to come bearing her bits and pieces to Simon in search of approval and praise for her industry and cleverness. His game, to him, was Shamshuipo camp and so it was nothing to do with this shameless, glossy reflection of it.

There was another thing to remember, also. Simon was not her father. She had no right of filial expectation, no right to resent his lack of paternal pride. He could not be her father, however much she might wish him to be.

"I'm sorry," she said. "It's not very appropriate, this, is it?"

Simon gave a cough of laughter. "I hadn't tried to gauge the appropriateness. What exactly is it that you want, Harriet?"

She would be businesslike, then. "I want to launch your game commercially, under the name 'Conundrum.' " She went on, spelling out her plans. She couldn't tell if Simon was listening or not, but at the end he said, "I see."

"Before I can do any of this, I have to establish who owns the rights in the game. As we stand, they are yours. You could lease them to me for an agreed period. You could make them over to me. Or we could come to some other arrangement. But we must do it legally. Do you understand?"

"I'm old, but I'm not a fool. What will I have to do? Because I don't want to have to do anything, anything at all outside what I do here. Do *you* understand that?"

They regarded each other. Simon had reared up in his seat, as if to protect his narrow territory.

Harriet said, "Yes. You only have to sign something, a simple document, if you're willing to make over the rights completely. If we make a more complicated arrangement it might mean a visit to a solicitor together." She was trying to be impartial. She wanted to do what was right, but she needed the simplest solution that would leave no loopholes.

Simon sighed. "You can have it. I told you the first time. Give me what I have to sign." He read her intentions. He was shrewd enough to know that she wouldn't have made the journey unprepared. Harriet felt grubby as she took out her papers.

She had taken legal advice, not Henry's but specialist advice. She held out her simple, watertight contract. There was an interval in which Simon shuffled in search of his spectacles, another in which he read the words she had presented him with.

At length he looked up. "That seems very thorough," he said. He took up a pen, and signed.

"It should be witnessed."

"Do you think I will renege?"

She bent her head. "No."

"No other intrusion?"

"None, I promise. Only we must decide between us what your share of the profits will be." There was another dry sound, neither a cough nor quite a laugh. "What will I do with profits, Harriet?"

She held her ground. "Heat your house adequately. Repair the roof."

"And if I told you that I am happy as I am?"

"Are you?" But as she said it she felt her impudence. He would share no whiskey-confidence with her today. "Money never hurt anyone," she defended.

Simon swept the Y-shaped gates together into a heap, and funneled them from his cupped hands into the mock-up box. He put all the components neatly together, fitted the lid in place, and held it out to Harriet. "Here. Take your game."

She was being dismissed. Well, she would make the division of the money between the two of them as and when the time came. The time seemed a long way off. Harriet was afraid of everything she must do before it could come.

"Thank you for giving me the game," she said quietly. "I'm grateful."

This time the desiccated laugh did turn into a cough. "You should get some medicine for that," she told him. Simon's face altered. He fell against the back of his chair. "You sounded like your mother, saying that. Here."

She went to him. He lifted her hand and held it, very briefly, against his cheek. A moment later he had disengaged himself, impatient, unfolded his height from the chair. "You'll want to be on your way."

The touch had been a father's gesture, Harriet thought. She felt lighter, happy now. He came with her to the front door, peered briefly into the rain before retreating into the shell of his house. Harriet left him, and drove back down the motorway to London.

*   *   *

In the next month, Harriet worked harder than she had ever done in her life before. By the last week of February, using the Toy Fair directory, she had mailed five hundred publicity kits to every buyer, every store representative who might have the remotest interest in "Conundrum." She had designed the dressing for the bigger stand, in white parachute silk and black PVC, and supervised its making-up. She wanted black, shiny curves and cloudy white billows to back her sunray trade-mark. She had found a team of props designers who had made the huge, polystyrene sunray itself, and painted it in the rainbow colors of the boxes. She had dozens more boxes made, ready to be heaped in apparent profusion on the ledges of the sunray. Through an agency, she had booked two girls to man the stand with her. Remembering Sandy and her friend, Harriet had chosen young students, part-timers, whose hair could be dressed in the same nodding plumes.

She had bought three black-and-white outfits, and replaced the buttons with penny-sized ones in rainbow colors. Through Jenny, who knew his agent, she had cajoled a television personality to be on the stand for the busiest day, to challenge buyers to solve "Conundrum." His fee was enormous. Jane and Jenny and the others helped her to stuff envelopes for the mail shots, and Jenny machined yards of parachute silk. Her friends worried gently about her, and tried to persuade her to slow down, but she was driven beyond the ability to rest. Only Charlie Thimbell told her that if she was going to do it at all, she might as well give it all she had.

Harriet did everything she possibly could, and she neglected Stepping. There was very little left of her fifteen thousand pounds.

Three nights before the Fair opened, Harriet had a nightmare. When she woke up, sweaty and disoriented, she couldn't remember the details of it. But an oppressive fear made her head and limbs heavy. She felt deathly tired but she couldn't go back to sleep again; in the morning the weight of it was still with her. She felt drained of all her strength, ill without any symptoms.

The feeling was the exact opposite of the euphoria she had experienced after the strange, waking dream in her old bedroom at home. It was as if all the anxieties and weaknesses she had suppressed had surfaced at once, to cripple her. She was afraid of everything she was doing, of the ballooning enterprise she was trying to launch on such shaky foundations. Harriet lay in bed, with her knees drawn up, her arms folded around her head.

The thought came to her, effortfully, *I need help. I can't do this alone.*

After a time she got up, and groped painfully around the flat. She found the card that Henry Orde had given her.

As soon as she judged the working day to have started, she telephoned Landwith Associates.

Seven

LANDWITH ASSOCIATES OCCUPIED A stucco-fronted house in a quiet side-street. There was no marble entrance hall, and no opulent fountain. A discreet brass plate gave the company's name, and an equally discreet bell placed beside it brought an immaculate girl to open the door.

"Harriet Peacock," Harriet announced herself.

She had christened her embryo company Peacocks, and since the meeting at Morton's she had resolved that there would be no more Mrs. Gold. Nor would she go back to calling herself Harriet Trott. The direct identification of herself with her company, and also with Kath in the years when there had been just the two of them, with Simon's Kath even, gave her pleasure.

"Mr. Landwith is expecting me."

Armed with an introduction from Henry Orde, and once past the barrier of an ingeniously defensive secretary, Harriet had found it quite easy to achieve an appointment with Martin Landwith. It had been harder to find the time in her own schedule. The Toy Fair opened the next day. Harriet knew that she should have been on her stand, organizing the pinning and draping and positioning.

"This way, please, Miss Peacock."

The hall was paneled and empty, except for a Persian rug on the floor and an oval table with a big bowl of fresh flowers. Harriet followed the girl up the shallow curve of the stairs, passing three serious, gloomy still lifes in weighty frames. Harriet suspected that they were worth, individually, about as much as the total amount she was trying to borrow.

The girl opened the double doors facing the top of the stairs. Harriet saw Martin Landwith stand up at once, and come around his desk to greet her. He was a stocky man, not very tall, but dressed in a dark blue suit of such magical cut that he seemed perfectly proportioned. He was wearing a pale blue shirt and a sober tie. Narrow, shiny, hand-made shoes emphasized the smallness of his feet. His dark hair was graying at the temples; it seemed sculpted rather than mundanely cut. The silver threads glittered as he turned his head. He had dark eyes, and his naturally dark skin had the healthy polish of a real suntan. Harriet judged that he was in his early or mid-fifties. The fingernails of the hand he held out to her were professionally manicured.

"Please sit down, won't you?"

His voice was friendly, his smile followed the invitation only a second or two later. Martin Landwith made no attempt to disguise his scrutiny of her. Harriet accepted it, looking coolly back at him, and then sat down in the chair opposite his desk. She glanced around the room. To her right, there were tall windows overlooking the street. They were framed in curtains of some honey-colored material, with deep, soft scallops above and long rippling tails that were fringed in dull gold. Opposite the windows stood a Chinese Chippendale cabinet, the glass front reflecting the light in lozenges over the plain walls. Over the mantelpiece was a Victorian portrait. The whiskered subject might have been Mr. Landwith's grandfather. His grandson, if he was his grandson, sat beneath the picture at a partners desk probably inherited from the old man. Only the telephones, dictating machine, computer terminal had been added at some later date. On the floor there was a rug whose subtly glowing colors and intricate pattern spoke to Harriet of tiny silk threads, and thousands upon thousands of hand-knots. There wasn't much else in the room. It was a masterpiece of understatement that still shouted *money* as clearly as if the walls had been pasted with layers of notes. It made the glass and steel temple of Morton's seem by comparison like a hamburger bar in a new shopping precinct.

Harriet's mouth curved. She sucked the corners of it inward to contain her smile. But she saw at the same time that Martin Landwith had noted her inventory, and her amusement, and seemed to approve of it.

"This is my son, and partner. Robin Landwith."

Harriet turned. He must have come silently in behind her.

He was taller, and thinner, than his father. He had the same dark coloring, but there was no gray in his hair and it was thicker and more casually cut than his father's. Clearly they shared the same tailor, but Robin's lapels were two hairbreadths wider, and there were discreet pleats at the front of his trousers. His hand, when Harriet shook it, was larger and warmer.

He looked her over, just as Landwith senior had done. There was more open appreciation in his smile, but afterward his glance flickered back to his father, as if for approval. Only that made Harriet notice how young he was. He was younger than herself. Perhaps only twenty-five, twenty-six at the most. Not quite ready, yet, to be given free rein. It struck Harriet, seeing him take his place beside his father, that Robin looked like a particularly fine thoroughbred colt. He had been sired for this particular course, for races in which the stakes were pure risk and the prizes were all the multiplications of money. Clearly the bloodlines were faultless, whatever the running he would finally make.

For now, father and son together made a formidable combination.

Martin Landwith was sitting with his chin resting on one hand. With the other hand he made a small, polite gesture of invitation.

"Won't you tell us how we can help you?"

Harriet told.

She left nothing out, nor did she add anything, but she avoided the operatic performance that had failed her at Morton's. If the proposal was good enough, she reasoned, these two would spot it even if she made her pitch in Swahili. She spoke quietly, without emphasis, letting the information do its own selling.

When she took out "Conundrum" and set it up on the broad desk, they examined it carefully and asked half a dozen questions about the manufacture, but they didn't try to play the game. Instead, when they had finished with the board itself, they scrutinized the box and the point-of-sale roughs and all the leaflets and promotional material that the design studio had expensively prepared for the Toy Fair. But the time expended even on all of that was brief.

"The package is probably good enough," Martin Landwith judged. Then he moved on with practiced speed to her business plan.

They went through the figures line by line, and they accepted none of her forecasts without query. Harriet was glad of the thoroughness of her preparation and relieved that they couldn't fault her calculations. She wouldn't care to have stumbled in front of the two Landwiths. But she had to admit, under their questioning, that she had only investigated the performance of roughly similar products.

"There's nothing on the market quite like 'Conundrum,' " she told them. "A direct parallel between potential performance and real sales is impossible for that reason. But that is 'Conundrum' 's strength, too, isn't it?"

She saw that they didn't glance at the game but kept their attention fixed on her. She felt a small beat of triumph. She was right, it was herself and her own capabilities that she was trying to sell. If the Landwiths would buy her, she would show them that she could make the world buy "Conundrum."

"I think we should discuss your marketing strategy now," Martin Landwith said.

That was more difficult. Without having tested the water at the Fair, Harriet wasn't quite sure what direction her marketing thrust would follow. But she brought out the research notes that showed the performance of the most nearly similar products out of the big chains, and talked about targeting W.H. Smith, Menzies, Toys 'R' Us and the rest.

Father and son listened attentively, but without any encouraging sign. When she finished, she saw Martin glance at his watch. Then he put his fingertips together, looked at her over the crest of them.

Harriet's heart began to thump unpleasantly.

"I like your game," Martin said. "It may well be a seller. But I wouldn't want to try to predict how strong a seller, or how durable. I don't see any convincing way of doing so and—I'm sorry—I don't see that your due diligence succeeds either. The FMCG world is unpredictable . . ."

Fast-moving consumer goods, Harriet translated silently. *Oh, please.*

". . . and we prefer our risks to be calculated. Can you demonstrate the value of your 'Conundrum' other than theoretically?"

Harriet wondered if she should tell him about her Sundays on the top deck of the 73 bus, and the enthusiasm and friendliness she had met there. But she doubted that Martin Landwith would know where to go to catch a bus, and doubted even more strongly that he would accept the vote of its passengers. And Robin Landwith, with his long legs stretched out to one side of the desk, didn't look as though he had ever ridden a bus in his life.

"Only by having the opportunity to sell it. I shall be doing that for the next four days, at the trade fair. Why don't you come and take a look?"

There was no direct response to her invitation. The two men appeared to think symbiotically without even needing to look at each other. Their silence maneuvered Harriet into the attack.

"I know you've got to calculate your risks. But wouldn't a real venture be interesting? I'm not asking for a huge investment, I'm sure you can spread it around. And I know this will work. *I know it.*" Harriet's words seemed to echo mockingly in the plush quiet.

This time it was Robin who spoke. "Tell us what our exit strategy will be."

"USM float in three or four years."

They approved of that. It was ambitious enough.

Martin was consulting his watch again. The meeting had reached an inconclusive finish. Harriet stood up briskly, so that she could appear to control the endgame.

"Thank you for your time. I hope you'll decide in my favor, Mr. Landwith. Peacocks could work well for us both."

He looked up at her; it was an odd, sidelong glance. The atmosphere in the room changed with it. It had been cool and crystalline, now it became warmer, as if thick velvet curtains had been drawn somewhere. Harriet understood that Martin Landwith had finished his appraisal of her investment potential. Now he was examining her as a woman. His eyes traveled from her mouth to her breasts. Such practiced attention might have angered her, but she was interested to discover that it did not. She let him look, even squaring her shoulders and holding her head higher.

If he wants to play the game this way, she thought, *I can do it too. I can play any way he likes, for the right stakes.* The realization of how much she would do for the sake of "Conundrum" didn't shock her. She felt charged by it, rather, as if Martin Landwith's deft, over-dainty fingers had already worked on her. But it was the recognition of her own freedom, to do what she wanted with herself, that had excited her, not anything Martin Landwith would or could do.

Robin had seen the shade of Harriet, too, through the opaque business dress. They had stepped, an awkward threesome, onto different ground. Harriet looked from the father to the son, meeting their eyes squarely. *Funny*, she thought. *Do they compete, or run together?*

"Thank you for coming, Miss Peacock," Martin said quietly. "We'll consider your proposal." It was Robin who touched her elbow, guided her back through the double doors and down the staircase to the paneled hall. There was a scent of clove carnations from the flower display that Harriet hadn't detected on the way up. She breathed it in luxuriously. She felt lighthearted, now that she was released from the strain of the meeting, and Robin became a part of the lightness. When he smiled at her they were almost co-conspirators, released from the oppressive company of the grown-ups. They shook hands, still smiling.

"Try to come to the Fair," Harriet repeated.

"I'll do my best for you," he said. Harriet wasn't sure whether he meant the Toy Fair or persuading his father to back "Conundrum." She went down the steps into the street, knowing that he was watching her go.

The glow of powerful well-being only lasted as far as the corner. By the time she reached it she was out of the patinated smoothness of the Landwith offices and back in the real world. And in the real world there were no Chinese Chippendale cabinets, no silk rugs, and no empty taxis either. It was nearly lunchtime, and every cab that passed was occupied by men, singly or in pairs, on their way to clubs and restaurants. Everyone else in the world was on the pavement with Harriet, pushing and jostling.

She paused for long enough to look back at the stucco-fronted terrace. She wondered what the father and son were doing behind the tall, shining windows. She doubted that they were studying the copies of the plan that she had left for them. She didn't even think they were urbanely agreeing that their visitor had been unfortunately flat-chested. She imagined that they were in some mahogany and silver washroom, ivory-brushing their beautiful haircuts ready for separate lunches with identically rich men in twin trend-setting restaurants.

The fantasy didn't make her smile.

"Smug shits," Harriet murmured. "I hate you." But she said it mechanically. She didn't hate them enough not to long to join them.

There were still no taxis, and Harriet was due to meet Jane in five minutes' time at the Earls Court exhibition hall main entrance. They were going to work on the stand together. Clearly there wasn't going to be a taxi for the rest of the day. Harriet hoisted her heavy case under her arm and dived for the tube.

"Harriet? Where have you *been*? They wouldn't let me in without an exhibitor's pass."

Harriet was hot and flustered and guilty. Jane, loyal Jane, had freed herself from school for an afternoon in order to help her and she had kept her waiting for three-quarters of an hour. She gasped her apologies, waved her pass at the security man, and they were inside. She took Jane's arm and steered her forward.

"I'm sorry, I'm so sorry. Landwith Associates took longer than I thought, then there were no cabs. I thought I'd never get here."

They were half-running, half-stumbling down a long aisle.

On either side there were stands where giant teddy bears reared up, where ranks of dolls smiled sweet persuasive smiles, and the rattle and whir of mechanical toys mingled and multiplied. The dim roof-space overhead was noisy with the drilling and hammering and sawing of last preparations.

"Slow down. Calm down," Jane ordered her, but Harriet rushed them faster. At last they reached a bare rectangle of space with packing cases tipped haphazardly in the center. Harriet consulted a docket, looked at the number fixed to the stand frame, and back at the docket again.

"This is it," she said. "This is ours." She couldn't keep the flatness out of her voice. The space was so bare, and dusty, and uninviting.

"Not even a giant teddy to lend a hand," Jane said. Two young women in red and white Queen of Hearts costumes were eyeing them curiously from an apparently complete display across the aisle. "Come on, we'd better get started."

It seemed impossible that they could ever make the stand look like anything. When she unwrapped the parachute silk and draped the creased swathes over the chipboard walls, Harriet thought she saw the Queens of Hearts covertly smiling. If it had not been for Jane, she would have turned tail, even at that last moment, and run away from the exhibition hall, right away from "Conundrum" itself.

But Jane raised her eyebrows by a fraction and twitched the corners of her mouth, conveying her opinion of the Queens with such perfect economy that Harriet laughed, and instead of running she climbed a stepladder with a staple gun ready in her hand.

"How'd it go this morning?" Jane called, over a mouthful of pins. Harriet perched on her ladder, dipping her splayed hand from side to side.

"The smoothest pair of operators you ever saw. They're thinking about it."

Jane returned to her pinning. It seemed the wildest optimism to have come this far, with prototypes and printed glossy leaflets and swathes of bloody parachute silk, on the strength of two smooth operators consenting to think about further funding. Harriet had cheerfully spent all of her own capital, Jane was sure of that. If she had been in the same position she would have been too frightened to become absorbed in getting white folds of fabric to hang just so. But then, Jane reflected, she was no entrepreneur. If she were it might have been Harriet patiently waiting on the steps and herself arriving, with blazing eyes and cheeks, in a crackle of energy that made everyone turn around to look. The image didn't attract Jane in the least. Even trying to teach *The Catcher in the Rye* to recalcitrant fourth-years was more appealing. Even stapling black PVC until her thumbs bled.

By the end of the afternoon, working without stopping, they had mocked-up black shiny pillars and puffy white clouds. The air in the hall stirred just enough to make the clouds drift. It was also warm enough to have caused the creases to drop out. The Queens of Hearts had stopped smirking and yawning. Before they left they had begun to stare quite openly.

Harriet and Jane only ran into trouble when they unpacked the painted polystyrene blocks from which to construct the ambitious sunburst. There had been a measuring or a marking error, and they didn't fit together. The structure lurched at a drunken angle, offering slopes instead of smooth display shelves.

Harriet pushed her knuckles against her teeth. She closed her eyes and opened them again, but instead of disappearing the list only seemed more pronounced.

"I can't believe it," she whispered. "We'll have to get a saw and cut the blocks at one corner to even the thing up."

Jane understood that Harriet contained her own kind of fright, and that she was close to letting it spill out. She left her and went to the exhibitors bar, full now of exhibitors who had finished putting up their stands and were greeting each other with annual boisterousness. She pushed her way through them and bought two plastic tumblers of gin, carried them back to Harriet and put one into her hand.

"Drink first, problem-solving afterwards," she commanded.

"I don't know how to solve it," Harriet moaned.

Before they had finished the gin, Jenny arrived on her way home from her publishing house. She took one look at the mismatched heaps of painted polystyrene.

"Oh dear," she said.

"We're going to try to cut the blocks to make them even," Harriet told her.

Jenny had a strong practical streak. "Don't *cut*, whatever you do. You'll never get them even, and you'll end up cutting more and more off until you've got blocks the size of matchboxes. You'll have to shore up with something." She glanced around, and then cocked her head to the sound of sawing. "Hang on here."

Five minutes later, she was back with a handful of rough wooden wedges.

It was fiddly work, but an hour later the sunburst stood

level. "Conundrum" boards and the sunburst-bright boxes had to be balanced on it with infinite care, but they stood level too.

"Finishing touches now," Harriet commanded.

She had rented black folding tables and chairs for each side of the stand. When they were put in place there were boxes of leaflets and information folders and printed order books to be unpacked.

They worked silently, because it was ten o'clock at night and they were tired and hungry. But they were not too tired to notice that the other exhibitors, the last ones who were straggling out toward the exits and their hotel beds, all stopped to look at the "Conundrum" stand.

At last, the job was done.

They stood back, shoulder to shoulder, to admire it. Their backs and arms ached, and their faces were smeared with dust. Harriet completed her scrutiny.

"It's all right," she said slowly. "In fact, it's more than all right."

"It's bloody brilliant," Jenny corrected her. "So long as no one breathes on the sun thing."

Jane stuck her hands into the pockets of her overalls. "I'll get us another drink. We've earned it." She went to the bar, but came back with the news that it was closed. "This is all I could get, from a machine." She held up three cans of fizzy orange and three vending-machine packs of sandwiches.

They sat down on the edge of the stand, very carefully in case they upset any of their handiwork.

"Thank you," Harriet said. She was dirty and exhausted, but she felt full of hope. Tomorrow she would be able to show off "Conundrum." Tomorrow would tell. "Thank you for being here. You've made everything seem possible."

Jane bent her head closer, so that her thick plait of hair touched Harriet's cheek.

"You're doing something I couldn't begin to do." *Wouldn't begin to do*, Harriet silently filled in for her. "But I wish you all the luck."

That this business world was so far from what Jane believed in, or truly approved of, made the good wishes seem even more valuable. She thought momentarily of Crete, reflecting that even if their goals were changing, the ties of friendship still endured.

Jane nodded at the white clouds and the shiny boxes that represented Harriet's small capital. "Remember what I said about the money? Do you need it?"

Harriet did, but she didn't want to take it. Not until she was certain that it wouldn't be lost . . .

"I've got plenty for the launch," she said determinedly. "After that, we'll see."

Jenny leaned back and stretched out her legs in front of her. She lifted her tin of Fanta. "I've got some good news, too," she told them. "I'm pregnant again."

Their shout made the last of the toy exhibitors turn around to stare again. Jenny's face was bright. "It's a bit soon. But it happened, and it felt like the sun coming out. It was so dark, before."

They came closer to her, so they could put their arms around her shoulders. Jane raised her tin of orange drink, too, to make a toast.

"Here's to your twin projects," she said. "May they both grow and prosper. Harriet, Jenny."

If she felt the lack of a project of her own, Jane didn't let it show in her face. They drank and then ate their stale sandwiches, their optimism making the meal a celebration.

It was the last afternoon.

Briefly, surreptitiously, Harriet rested her head in her hands. Before the Fair she had had no idea how much energy it would take, just to go on smiling and shaking hands, to go on demonstrating "Conundrum" one more time, until she was sick of the merry rattle of the balls, and the colors of the counters and the slick boxes and the jaunty buttons on the girls' dresses danced in front of her eyes.

The air in the exhibition hall was hot and dry, and her feet had swollen until they felt ready to burst out of her shoes. Yet all around Harriet, on other stands, salesmen were still selling, smiling and shaking hands and cracking the same jokes that they had been cracking for the last three and a half days. Not many of them were subtle or sophisticated any more than their jokes, but admiration for her competitors was newborn in Harriet. She had seen them working, and she could appreciate their stamina if only because her own had failed to match it.

She glanced around her own stand. Her television personality had come yesterday, and he had duly challenged buyers and the press to play the game against him. A crowd had gathered around the "Conundrum" stand; Harriet had posed for photographs with the star's arm around her shoulder, and her salesgirls in their jaunty dresses had shown an adequate expanse of thigh on either side of the shaky sunburst. Kath had been there, too. She had been determined to come and see Harriet's pitch, and as her mother timidly watched the television man sucking up the well-paid publicity, Harriet had seen that she was surprised and impressed, but anxious and uncomprehending, too.

"Aren't you nervous of all this?" Kath had whispered.

"I'm not nervous, Mum. I know what I'm doing."

Only a white lie, Harriet thought.

There had been plenty of interest, the girls and the stand itself had been enough to guarantee that. "Conundrum" had been endlessly played, and admired, and much talked about. There had been orders, too. Only not quite as many as she had hoped. Not as many as she needed. Harriet was left, on this overheated and oppressive afternoon, with the realization that she had accepted orders and guaranteed delivery on not quite enough "Conundrum"s to allow her to break even.

She hadn't heard from Martin Landwith either. There had been messages every evening on her machine at Belsize Park, including one from Leo who sounded slightly drunk and promised to come and see "her show" at the Fair, but not the one message that she wanted to receive.

Harriet saw that the prettier of the girls, the one with bronze-colored hair and the least make-up, was making an energetic sales pitch to a store buyer from the north. He released the spring mechanism, the balls played their over-familiar tune, and dropped into the wrong slots. He groaned, and the girl commiserated prettily.

"Here you are, try again." She winked over his head at Harriet. There were no other customers on the stand, and the other girl would be back soon from her lunch. Harriet decided she could slip away for a moment or two.

She threaded her way through the thinning crowds, past the ranks of teddy bears, to the row of telephones in the foyer. She was panting a little as she dialed the Landwiths' number.

Mr. Martin Landwith was not available. *Still at lunch, the fat cat*, Harriet thought savagely. But Mr. Robin Landwith would speak to her, should the receptionist put her through?

"Yes please," Harriet murmured. She was holding too tightly to the receiver.

"Robin Landwith." The voice more like his father's over the telephone, silky with self-assurance.

"Harriet Peacock. Mr. Landwith, I hoped you might be able to come to the Toy Fair to see 'Conundrum' on display. The Fair closes this evening, so this is your last chance." She tried to sound warm and humorous, feeling neither of those things.

"One of our companies has gone public this week. It's been a busy few days for us."

"I'm sure," Harriet said, then reminded herself that she would gain nothing by sounding scratchy. "Look, the exhibition is hardly any way from you by cab." *If you can get one. People like you invariably can.* "The Fair's open until six. Come on your way home."

She heard him laughing, a rather surprisingly nice laugh.

"On my way home, at five-thirty? What kind of hours do you think venture capitalists work? Don't expect me, but I'll try to get there. How has 'Conundrum' been selling to the trade?"

"Very well indeed. There'll be more orders later, of course."

"Hm. Harriet, we haven't taken a decision either way, yet, you know."

Harriet? Had he called her Harriet? "That's all right. I can wait, for the right answer."

After she had hung up, leaning against the wall of the booth, Harriet was overtaken by a cold wash of terror. She couldn't afford to wait at all, not even a day. She was taking orders for thousands of games that she didn't have the funding to manufacture; and if she managed to get the money she didn't have enough orders to push herself into profit.

It took Harriet two minutes to stop herself shaking. In the end she drew a deep breath of the overused air. *Sell,* she told herself. *That's what you're here for. You're not far short of break-even. Not disastrously far short.*

Back on the stand, the salesgirl greeted her with a triumphant smile. "He took two hundred and fifty. I put the order in the book."

Harriet nodded wearily. She knew that the order should have been for five hundred, the buyer was responsible for a group of shops. "Conundrum" was selling, but it wasn't selling enough. The game was good. It deserved a better response, so what was she doing wrong? She stood back now, and looked at the stand she had been so proud of. Perhaps, a suspicion gnawed at her, perhaps it was *too* wholesome and bright? What the buyers saw was all there was. There was no story here, there was nothing to beckon or intrigue.

The challenge rekindled a little fire in her. *What can I do?* Harriet wondered. *What's the extra little thing that will make them all take notice?*

"Conundrum" was only a game, however intriguing a game

and however powerfully packaged. She needed more than that for it. She needed a human face.

A tiny worm of an idea began to wriggle, but Harriet pinched it dead.

"Harriet?" Startled out of her reverie, she swung around. It was Leo. He had arrived at the stand with metal camera cases in either hand, tripod tucked under his arm, as if for a shoot. She stared at him.

"There's no need to look so furiously bloody angry."

"I . . . I'm sorry, Leo, I'm not angry at all. Just surprised."

"I telephoned, didn't I?"

It was a long time since she had seen him. Already they were wrong-footing each other. Leo was the last person in the world she needed to see at this moment, particularly Leo in an injured mood. He needed more attention than a small boy. She had had the time, once, but she didn't any longer. She became aware that the two girls on her stand were staring curiously at them.

"You did. My fault, I wasn't expecting you right now, that's all. Why all the gear?"

"I thought you'd like some decent pictures of your stand."

It was kind of him, and Harriet felt guilty. "I'd really love some pictures," she said warmly. "What do you think of it?"

He put his head on one side, studying it. "Lighting's a bit harsh. I'll have to filter."

Harriet smiled, her guilty feeling evaporating. She shouldn't have expected a response to her own achievement. Leo only ever regarded things through his own eyes.

"I'll let you set up, then," she said neutrally.

Leo busied himself with unpacking his cameras. Harriet had rather pointedly not introduced him to her two helpers, and he spent a moment or two importantly assembling lenses and filters before glancing across at them. Immediately, and so distinctly that it made her want to laugh, he became the different Leo that she had fallen in love with. He even reproduced the crooked, faintly diffident smile that she had once found irresistible.

"I'm Leo Gold," he said. "I wish you'd tell me who you are."

The two girls loved him, of course. He became a very bright spot in a dull afternoon's work. They fluttered about, seeming to be very interested in photography, while Leo made them move things and hold lights. He winked, once, at Harriet, making her a part of a conspiracy she didn't care for. But the business of the photography created another little flurry of interest around the stand, and one or two of the late-visiting buyers drifted over to talk to Harriet.

In the hope of attracting a few more potential orders, Harriet had left the "Conundrum" stand intact. She would start to clear it after six o'clock, when the Fair officially closed. But many of the other exhibitors were already beginning to dismantle their displays. There was an air of the day after Christmas, with unraveled streamers littering the aisles, screwed-up paper beginning to form drifts, and up-ended toys waiting to be scooped up and carted away.

Leo made Harriet and the two girls pose in front of the sunburst. Harriet hated having her picture taken, particularly by Leo. The lights flashed in her eyes, and she knew that she was scowling into the lens.

"How much longer?" she was asking, when she saw Robin Landwith. He was picking his way through the debris, his expression of interest tinged with mild surprise at finding himself in an unlikely place. Among the salesmen in chainstore suits his handmade gloss seemed doubly exotic.

"I'll finish the roll," Leo said, his head bent over his lens.

Harriet was pinned against her sunburst, in her buttoned outfit with the two identically dressed girls posing on either side, while Leo's lights clicked and flared. Robin stopped to watch, off to the side in the welcome shadow. Harriet endured the humiliation for a minute longer, then said brusquely, "That should be enough, shouldn't it?"

She stepped off the stand. Leo straightened up with a shrug of irritation, but his eyes followed her. Harriet held out her hand and Robin Landwith shook it.

"Thank you for coming."

He looked at the stand. "It's impressive." His tone seemed to indicate to Harriet that it was anything but. Seeing it through his eyes she noticed that the silk was grubby and marked with hand- and footprints, and even torn in places so that it hung down in little sulky mouths.

"It's seen a lot of hard wear, the last few days," she defended it. "Crowds of buyers and sightseers. When we first put it up it stopped everyone dead." She was conscious of the girls in their dresses the same as her own, and Leo with his paraphernalia of lights and tripods. She could hardly avoid introducing them.

"This is Natalie, and Caroline, who have been helping with selling and P.R. on the stand. And Leo Gold, the photographer."

"Harriet's husband, also," Leo said coolly.

Harriet didn't know which one of their tight group stepped

awkwardly sideways in the narrow confines of the stand. It might even have been Robin Landwith. All she did know was that someone trod on the corner of the precarious sunburst. It had survived for four days but now there was a small crunching sound, and then a much louder rattle and bump as the colored platforms tilted and fell forward, dominolike, and unstoppably. The "Conundrum" boards and boxes that had been arranged on the ledges slid and bounced to fall over the four people beneath. For a few seconds it felt as if they might all be buried beneath an avalanche of shiny black frames and rainbow-colored boxes and counters.

And then there was a moment of appalled silence as they stood in the wreckage.

It was funny, but it was too catastrophic for any of them to laugh. Natalie and Caroline caught each other's eyes, and looked quickly away again. Harriet moved stiffly, over to the collapsed sunburst, and pushed it roughly upright again. Polystyrene and plastic crunched under her feet. A small crowd of people was gathering in front of the stand.

"Grand finale, eh?" one of them called. She bent down and began to collect spilled counters in the cup of her hand, her eyes and her face red.

"That's right," she answered. "Big finish."

Immediately Leo began to extricate his lights and tripod. It was Robin who waded in to help Harriet followed, after another risky exchange of glances, by the two girls.

"There's no need," Harriet said to him, gripping shiny black boards against her chest like a shield, fending off anger and humiliation. "I don't want you to do this. *Please.*"

"Why not?" Robin asked, all sweet reason.

Out of the corner of her eye Harriet saw that the tiny crowd was splitting into individuals again. The show was over.

"Because Natalie and Caroline and I can do it. It's time to dismantle in any case." And she gestured at the wasteland of the exhibition hall.

Afterward, when it was all done and the stand had been stripped to an empty slot once more, Robin took Harriet out to dinner. They were dusty beyond repair in the exhibition center cloakrooms, but the restaurant was small and satisfyingly dimly lit.

"Thank you for helping with that," Harriet said.

"Why didn't you want me to?"

"I didn't want to see someone I'm trying to borrow money from picking up embarrassing wreckage. Of course."

"If you're embarrassed by wreckage, perhaps you shouldn't be trying to borrow money in the first place? Disaster's always a possibility."

"I should. I want everything to fit, not to fail. Failure should be private, success is for celebration. I'd prefer to be successful."

Robin looked at her through the meretricious candlelight. He saw a face that was too angular for beauty, but which seemed to offer other interesting possibilities. Robin liked women as well as enjoying them, which marked a difference from his father, and he liked what he had seen of Harriet. Her declaration of preference impressed him less, because he had heard the same from every would-be entrepreneur he had ever encountered.

"I think you'll be successful," Robin said. If he could influence Martin, he added silently, and he was almost sure he could.

They didn't talk anymore about money, or about Peacocks and its prospects.

Robin ordered champagne, a marque that Harriet had never seen before in a bottle that appeared to have been hand-painted with scattered flowers. She was susceptible to champagne. The bubbles always went to her head, and tonight was no exception. She had thought, when she chose her food from the rather startlingly expensive menu, that it would be impossible to forget the anxiety of the Fair and the final catastrophe. But after two glasses of champagne, and with the arrival of *salade d'artichauts et cailles aux noix*, pretty as a picture on a plain white plate, the obsessions of the day drifted away. They were replaced by an unlocalized sense of well-being, and a sharp appetite.

What the hell, Harriet thought.

Robin watched her with approval as she attacked her food.

After the quail and artichoke came *faisan de mer au basilic*, and more champagne. Harriet sighed and leaned back in her chair, releasing her heels from her shoes. Her feet seemed to have grown after four days spent standing on them. Her shoulders and back ached, too, but champagne bubbles prickling at the back of her throat dispelled the pain.

"You were hungry," Robin commented.

"I haven't had time to eat. Sandwiches and filthy coffee, that's all."

Robin gave an automatic, gourmet's shudder. He was interested in food and wine in almost the same knowledgeable, academic way that he was interested in the movements of the money market. Both were there to be studied and their benefits, in different ways, to be enjoyed. Tonight, however, he had barely noticed his food as he concentrated on Harriet. He had seen her soften, as they talked and drank, by slow degrees. So far, but no further. He wondered what it was that she kept so tightly contained, and the speculation excited him. He shifted a little in his padded chair.

"How long have you been married?" he asked.

Leo had packed up his gear into his silver metal boxes, and then looked at his watch. It was the watch that Harriet had given him for Christmas the year before, an assemblage of buttons and bleepers waterproofed to a depth of two hundred meters, because Leo loved gadgets and mechanisms of all kinds. Robin Landwith's watch, emerging from the cuff of his pale blue shirt, was so thin and pale by comparison as to be hardly a watch at all. Leo had noted the time, muttered about his lateness for some other appointment, and kissed Harriet on the cheek. She had been relieved to see him go, but Natalie and Caroline had followed him with wistful stares.

"I was married for about four years. We separated a few months ago. The arrangement seems to suit us both better."

Robin had guessed as much, but he felt a tidy beat of satisfaction at hearing it confirmed.

"You must have some pudding," he told her. "They're very good here."

Because he was so young his assumption of authority over what she ate amused Harriet, but she submitted gracefully.

"What shall I have?"

He chose for her and ordered wine for them both. When the wine came it was dark gold and viscous-looking, but on her tongue Harriet tasted honey and flowers.

"It's good," she said.

Robin smiled. "It is, isn't it?"

Her dessert was five different tiny puddings, with petals of marbled raspberry sauce fanning between them. Food that looked as beautiful as it tasted was new to Harriet. She closed her eyes as she sampled each separate taste, and broke the pink and cream ribs of the petals with the edge of her spoon. As she ate, it struck her that her pleasure in it was sensual, as in making out-of-the-ordinary love.

She looked up and met Robin's eyes. She held out her spoon for him to taste. He acknowledged both the food, and her enjoyment of it.

"That was all wonderful," she said.

Robin inclined his head. "And now?"

"Now I have to go home. Work tomorrow." Back to ne-glected Stepping, and to a dismal reexamination of order books for "Conundrum." Back to the necessity to decide, and plan, and to find a way of selling more games. The cold touch of anxiety was the more unwelcome in the glow of the restaurant. Harriet pushed the thoughts back, examining the faces at the other tables instead, deciding that she would allow herself to escape just for tonight.

"What is this place called?"

Robin told her, and she guessed that she should have heard of it.

"I don't know it."

"You do now. I'm glad it was me who brought you."

"Thank you," Harriet said, meaning it. She had enjoyed his company. He had let her talk, without cross-examining her, and he had told her a little about himself. Not very much, his style was hardly confessional. He had steered the evening, for all its unpromising beginning, with rather likable adroitness.

"I think we probably live in quite different worlds," Harriet said, half to herself. She was still looking at the sleek customers at the other tables. *Money* was as clearly written here, in its penetrable code, as it had been in Martin Landwith's office. With Leo, she had eaten for years in noisy Italian restaurants, along the Greek strip of Charlotte Street, and in garlicky little French places. Too late, she realized that Robin might imagine she was offering him an opening to invite her a few paces further into his enviable existence. But if he did think anything of the kind, he was too subtle to show it, let alone to respond.

He only said, "I wouldn't care to try to define *worlds* in terms of restaurants. It's a tempting idea, but much too superfi-cial. I go to all kinds of places. I'm sure you do, too."

"All kinds," she agreed, liking him even better. "Robin, I must go now."

He paid the bill, which Harriet estimated must be huge, after checking the addition. Then he drew back her chair, and guided her toward the door, hand under her elbow, as he had done from his father's office. He had perfect, faintly old-fashioned manners.

It was raining outside, and it felt very exposed after the restaurant's intimacy to be standing on a wet pavement in the cold wind. Robin unfurled a big black umbrella and held it over their heads.

As Harriet might have predicted, a yellow-lit taxi rounded the corner a second later. When it stopped, Robin opened the door for her, asked for her address, and relayed it to the driver.

"Will you be all right?"

"Of course. I enjoyed this evening."

What happened next she also might have predicted, but it still surprised her when it came. Robin bent his head and kissed her on the mouth, very lightly, and then he placed two more kisses, one to each side of her mouth. The whole exchange took no more than three seconds. Harriet scrambled into the taxi and he closed the door, and the cab carried her away. She sat back in her seat, catching her breath, trying to work out what had happened to her.

"I was struck all of a heap," she told skeptical Jane the next time they met. "Like a teenager, with the class heartthrob."

The right word came to her as the taxi wandered in the approximate direction of Belsize Park. It was *tender*. Robin Landwith had treated her with tenderness, and she had responded to it.

But by the time she reached the basement flat, with its unwashed dishes waiting in the sink and hungry, complaining cats, she had control of herself again.

Don't be a fool, she had told herself. *He's years younger than you are. He's not much more than a boy. And he's a venture capitalist from whom you want to borrow a hundred thousand pounds. Don't let three kisses blur your sight of that, will you?*

Eight

NOT MANY DAYS AFTER THAT, Martin Landwith telephoned Harriet.

She was at Stepping, and she turned away from the till with her hand pressed to her ear.

"Harriet Peacock speaking."

She heard Martin say that Landwith Associates believed that they could help her. If she would be willing to meet them again, they could discuss the possibilities in greater detail.

Harriet was willing. When she hung up, Karen asked her from the other end of the counter, "Good news?"

"The best possible. Everything's going to be all right."

Anxiety fell away like a stone. With backing, she could manufacture to meet the orders she had already taken. And with capital behind her, she could promote "Conundrum" in the way she wanted to bring in the orders she needed. With the Landwiths' help, she could support her house of cards.

A spring of energy bubbled up inside her. It happened, once it had begun, with surprising speed.

There was the meeting in Martin's office. To Harriet's relief, there was no chink in Robin's businesslike manner, even when Martin told her that it was his son's enthusiasm for her project that had influenced his own judgment, and that because of that same enthusiasm Peacocks would be Robin's particular concern in the future. Harriet understood that this was probably a test for him, his first opportunity to back his own hunch. She was pleased with the idea, assuming that Robin alone would be easier to deal with than Robin in formidable conjunction with his father.

There were stringent requirements. As she had been aware, Harriet would have to appoint an accountant to work with her. Martin suggested that she should get the best possible, and arrange for him to meet Robin. It was a condition of the agreement that she should also appoint a technical director who would assume responsibility for production, and leave Harriet free to devote herself to marketing, sales, and promotion.

"I can do both," Harriet said. She didn't want any part of this, her new baby, to be embraced by an outsider.

"I don't think so," Martin disagreed. Harriet glanced at Robin, then accepted the condition. She would find someone else to deal with Mr. Jepson and Midland Plastics. Then, drawing a thin folder toward him, Martin outlined the bones of what was to become their deal.

Landwith Associates agreed to invest the sum of one hundred and twenty thousand pounds in Peacocks, for the manufacture and sale of the game "Conundrum."

And in return . . .

Harriet sat without moving, listening with every fiber of herself. In return for their investment, Landwith Associates would control thirty-five percent of the company and Robin Landwith would assume a seat on the board. Harriet would also take thirty-five percent, and the balance would be divided between key staff and other directors. The accountant and technical expert would also have seats on the board, and a fifth director might be nominated by Harriet. Martin raised his eyebrows at her.

She thought of Simon, but she knew at once that he would recoil even from the suggestion. Then she remembered Kath timidly watching the business on the "Conundrum" stand.

"My mother," Harriet said immediately.

Martin nodded. "Ten percent for staff members, the remainder for family investment."

His silky manner lulled her. Harriet moved to sit on the edge of her chair.

"At flotation, or vesting date in say three years' time, the company's performance will be analyzed in the light of your business plan. The proportion of our participating preferred stock in relation to your own holding will be adjusted accordingly."

If I do well, Harriet translated, *I get a bigger percentage of the company. If I don't, Landwiths take more.* It required no great effort to assimilate the terms offered, but Harriet drew her note pad toward her, seemed to give them due consideration. She was unafraid of the scale of it all. It even gave her added confidence. If the Landwiths believed in her to such an extent, she reasoned, she could match the faith with her own, and more. Given their investment, she would create the upside for Peacocks.

"That seems quite straightforward," she said calmly.

She looked at Robin again. His hands were folded on the partners' desk, and he smiled at her. Robin would be her co-director, not his father. Harriet was aware of invisible threads criss-crossing between herself and the two men. If her attention had not been fully engaged by the business between them, she might have wondered which way they led, and where they would tauten when the time came.

Martin turned a page of his notes. There was much more, of course, but Harriet had accepted the essentials. There had never been any question but that she would accept.

At the end of the deftly steered meeting, it was Martin who stood up to shake her hand. There had been no signatures yet, the documents and those would come later. But they shook hands; they had struck their deal. Robin gathered up his papers and retreated to his own office. It seemed to Harriet inconceivable at that moment that he had kissed her, let alone that she had been disarmed by his tenderness.

Martin watched his son leave the room. Then he walked with Harriet to the head of the stairs and stood under the gloomy, significant pictures.

"We shall work well together. I have great hopes for Peacocks," Martin Landwith said. His speech was formal, but Harriet saw his oblique, appraising glance again. He was weighing her appeal once more. She was being looked over and deliberated upon.

Then he said, "You will be working directly with Robin, of course. This is his project, and he has argued very eloquently for it. But you should also know that I am always available, if I am needed."

And she was being handed over, Harriet understood. Perhaps not her physical self, and Robin had already managed to touch that for himself, but her acumen. Her potential upside. The father was bestowing her on the son, as she had no doubt he had bestowed other benefits, and strictures, for the whole of Robin's life. Briefly, wickedly, Harriet allowed herself to imagine it. There would have been toys and bicycles and horses and finally cars; there would have been treats and travel and skiing, tennis and cricket coaching, and expensive education. In return, because there would always be such an equation for Martin, Robin would have been expected to work hard, to behave well, and to shine where his father put down his money. To bring home the school prizes. As he was still expected to do, although the prizes were different, and might even be seen to include whatever she herself could come up with.

Poor Robin, Harriet thought, and the corners of her mouth drew into a small smile. She held her head up, looking straight at Martin. She was realistic enough not to mind the idea of herself as a commodity, to be bestowed and accepted. She had not minded, either, the skillful sexual summing-up that Martin had seemed to subject her to on her first visit.

If I have to do that for "Conundrum," she had thought, *then I will.*

There would be no need for it, she saw now. The possibility had been dismissed, whether or not it was directly in favor of the son. Only there was no suggestive kindling of Martin's dark brown eyes as they shook hands for the last time. Harriet felt a cobweb brush of regret. Martin Landwith was extremely attractive. What, she wondered, of Mrs. Landwith, wife and mother?

"Thank you," Harriet said coolly, giving none of her speculations away. "I'm sure we shall have a successful partnership."

Outside once more, where the sense of stepping from expensive seclusion into the struggle of reality was as strong as it had been the first time, it struck Harriet that she ought to be celebrating.

It was five o'clock in the afternoon, the low-point of the day. The thin, greenish light in the sky showed that the coziness of early winter darkness would soon give way to the intrusive pallor of spring evenings. Harriet thought of her friends. She imagined Jane in the thick of a smoky staff-meeting and Jenny in her office shadowed by heaps of manuscripts and proofs. Charlie would be on the telephone, his shirtsleeves rolled up. Karen would be checking the till at Stepping, getting ready to turn off the lights and lock up for the night. Harriet didn't feel that she fitted into any of those bright pictures, not tonight.

She went to collect her car, and then she drove across London to Sunderland Avenue. As it always did, the drive through the intricate grid of the city soothed her. She left the Peugeot, engine running, outside the off-license on the corner nearest to Sunderland Avenue. She ran in and scooped two bottles of Moët et Chandon out of the chiller cabinet. When she reached home she carried them under her arm through the baby-blue gates to the storm porch. The light came on over her head as soon as she rang the bell.

"Harriet! Ken, love, it's Harriet. Is everything all right?"

Harriet put her arms around her mother, laughing and bumping awkwardly with her burden of champagne.

"Everything's fine. Everything's wonderful. I've come with some news that I want you to celebrate, and I want to make a proposal as well."

Harriet swept them into the kitchen where Ken had been sitting in his overalls, reading the newspaper.

"I can't drink champagne dressed like this," he protested.

"Drink it anyway," Harriet ordered, pouring out.

She felt euphoric, temporarily released from the weight of worry. "A toast, Mum, Ken. To Peacocks." She jerked her arm up, and silvery froth from the glass ran down over her fingers.

"To Peacocks," they echoed her.

"You've done it, then?" Ken asked. "You've got the money?"

"I have." Harriet could have embraced the kitchen—pine and laminate and flowered mugs—the tree of heaven beyond the window, the whole world in her happiness.

Ken drank, unconcernedly smacking his lips, but Kath only fingered her glass. Her eyes were fixed on Harriet.

"It's a big commitment for you. Just for a game, like that."

"Not just one game. There'll be others, once I've launched this one successfully. I'll be expanding, making a whole empire. The sky's the limit, as they say."

"Tell us the whole story," Ken said, adopting his shrewd expression that indicated he was the head of a business himself, and understood such matters.

Harriet explained the Landwiths' proposal. "They put up a hundred and twenty thousand pounds, and take an initial thirty-five percent of the company. I have an equal holding, for a token investment of twenty thousand pounds."

That had been one of Martin Landwith's final stipulations. It was a sort of gesture of faith, a mere token, Martin had suggested.

Harriet had spent almost every penny she had in getting "Conundrum" to the Toy Fair. She had still looked Martin Landwith straight in the eye.

"Fine," she said. "I can do that."

"I'm going to sell Stepping," she told Kath and Ken now. "It's the best way to raise the money. And I can pay back your loan, Ken."

They were both horrified. Kath gasped, "You can't. Not after all your work. You'll have nothing."

Harriet was prepared for their response. She smiled reassuringly. "I can. I must repay Ken before I take on new commitments. I can put the rest of the money into Peacocks, and have a little left over to live on until the new business starts to pay. It's a good thing; Stepping is worth something now, and I couldn't have run it properly at the same time as trying to launch this. Everything will be all right, I promise it will."

She was repeating herself, trying to convince Kath, who only shook her head. Harriet understood that fancy titles and big talk of shareholdings were one thing, and real customers and proper takings were another, altogether better thing in Kath's view.

"You've got no proper home, and now no proper job either." *No husband to look after you,* Harriet filled in for her. Kath had the security of Ken and his ideal home; she had suffered for long enough without either, it was natural she should want the same safety for her daughter.

Gently, Harriet stroked her mother's shoulder, looking down at the pewter threads in her hair. She remembered the young girl's face that she had seen peeping out at her through Kath's older features.

She felt none of Kath's fears, not at this moment. She knew that she was poised up on high, with vertiginously steep cliffs falling away on either side of her, but she felt the firm rock of a ridge under her feet, and she was sure that she could tread safely along it. The certainty was exhilarating. She did have a real job ahead of her, whatever Kath thought; she didn't need a home, or a husband.

"Listen," she said. "I haven't finished telling you yet. I want to repay Ken for a good reason. Eighty percent of the new company will be owned by me, the staff and the venture capitalists. That leaves twenty percent for other investors. If you and Mum want to invest in me all over again, Ken, I'd be very pleased. And if you agree, Mum, I want you to be on the board. You'll be one of five directors."

Kath went pink. "Me, a company director?"

But Ken only leaned forward, resting his hands palms down on the table-top with the glass of champagne disregarded between them.

"I don't know, love," he said bluntly. "Bricks and mortar make good sense, always have done. Some game and a lot of percentages up in the air is different."

Kath looked quickly up at him. "Ken," she implored.

"It's all right," Harriet put in.

"Now just wait, both of you. Harriet's done well in her little shop, and I'm glad of the return on that investment, don't get me wrong. But I know business, and I'm not keen on this new idea. Just how much cash are you talking about, Harriet?"

"Ten thousand pounds." Martin Landwith had suggested that it would be an appropriate investment from family shareholders.

Ken pulled down the corners of his mouth and shook his head. "Too much to put into a mad idea."

"Landwith Associates are prepared to put up twelve times

that much," Harriet pointed out stiffly. Ken's outright refusal annoyed her, even though she had decided beforehand to accept cheerfully whatever decision he made.

"They're welcome. But I'm not a sheep to follow their lead, am I?"

"Ken, let me speak." The pink flush in Kath's cheeks had concentrated in two spots, high up on her cheekbones. "I'll help her myself. If Harriet believes in this new business, and she wants me to be part of it, then I want it as well." She turned to Harriet. "I've got some money put by. There's what your Aunt Dorothy left me that I've never used, and some I've added over the years. I'll give you your ten thousand."

She glanced sideways at Ken. It was rare for Kath to oppose him, and she was as apprehensive as she was determined on Harriet's behalf.

Harriet was reminded of Jane's offer. She thought with a touch of wryness that she was willing to risk her mother's money where she had refused her friend's. But Kath had her husband to look after her and Jane was alone.

To Kath's evident relief, Ken only slapped his hands down on the table-top. "It's your money. I'm not going to argue with you. If you want to pour it down the drain, Kath, it's your own affair." And then he winked at Harriet. He had taken his stand, she thought, and now he was prepared to be magnanimous. She also knew that ten thousand pounds was not such a very big sum to her prosperous stepfather.

"You won't be pouring it down the drain," she said clearly. "I promise you. It's a good investment. But thank you, Mum. Thank you for your faith in me."

A little faintly, as if shocked by what she had promised, Kath said, "I'd like to do it for Simon, too, in a way. What about Simon, Harriet?"

"He won't take anything now. There isn't anything to take, yet. I'll see that he gets a fair share when the time comes."

"I know you'll do what's right," Kath pronounced.

"So. I propose ten percent for you, Mum, and five each for Ken and Liza. If you want to count them in, of course."

Kath looked pleased. "Of course I do. I'd like that."

Harriet held out her hand. "Deal."

They shook hands, the three of them. "Drink your champagne," Harriet ordered. "This is supposed to be a celebration."

*   *   *

They saved the second bottle of champagne for Liza's arrival. She came in a little later, irritable with her day's work and the rush hour, sulkily pretty in a bright pink padded jacket. Her eyes went straight to the bottle and glasses.

"What's going on, Mum? Have you won the pools?"

"Harriet's landed her big loan for starting the new business." Kath's expression was a cocktail of sensibilities. She was proud of Harriet as well as anxious for her, but she was ever-conscious of the long-standing rivalry between her daughters and would never over-praise one to the other. She was also eager for everything to be nice, as she always vaguely put it to herself. There must be no quarrels, tonight or ever, if only that could be possible. As she watched her mother's small internal battle Harriet was exasperated by her, and loved her very much for it.

"That does call for a drink." Liza held her glass out to be filled.

"We're all going to be shareholders. Isn't that smart?"

Liza raised her eyebrows at her sister and Harriet explained the arrangements.

"For me?" Liza crowed. "I'm going to be a rotten capitalist at last?"

"Thanks to Mum. But you won't be able to get your clothes at cost from Stepping anymore."

Liza looked at her. "Good luck. Good luck to all of us. Tell you what, shall I make a special dinner? Are you staying?"

Harriet had inherited her lack of enthusiasm for the kitchen from Kath. Ken and Liza were the cooks.

"Just for this evening." No encroachment beyond that on Liza's territory. "I'd love some dinner."

Liza cheerfully rattled and sang over the stove, and Harriet set the circular pine table in the dining room. Kath found new pink candles in a drawer and stuck them into glass candlesticks, and Ken came downstairs in a clean shirt and a green cardigan with leather-covered buttons.

The candlelight was warm and flattering, and they were a family around the table when they sat down to eat.

After the meal Kath held up her hand, preparing to say something important. The other three, after some good-humored protests, fell obediently into quietness.

"I just want to say, Harriet, that whatever happens—don't interrupt me—whatever happens, and I'm not as clever as you so I can't predict what that will be, whatever it is I want you to know that we're all on your side. We're all behind you, Ken,

Liza, aren't we? If there's anything we can do to help you, love, you only have to ask us."

And Ken lifted his glass, charged now with celebratory Niersteiner Gutes Domtal from his own cellar, and bellowed, "Here's to it, love. I'm all for what Kath says."

"And me." Liza's eyes were bright, and her pink lipstick exactly matched the swaying pink plastic bobbles of her earrings. They drank, Trotts and Peacock, undifferentiated.

"Thank you," Harriet said simply.

She was lucky, she reflected. She had friends and family, and no need of anything else.

Spring came. It was a wet, cold spring, but it might have been sub-tropical for all Harriet noticed.

She sold her interest in Stepping, repaid Ken's loan and deposited twenty thousand pounds in the Peacocks account. The money from Landwith Associates was credited to the same account, and Kath's with it. Harriet and Robin officially became business associates. She appointed a partner in a firm of high-powered accountants to the board, on Martin's personal recommendation, and employed a technical expert from the toy industry to work for her on a part-time basis. The expert, whose name was Graham Chandler, took on Mr. Jepson and won hands down. Tooling up was completed, and "Conundrum" went into production. Landwith capital flowed out of the Peacocks account as fast as blood from a severed artery.

"Conundrum" was selling, and yet it didn't sell.

Retailers ordered it in tens and twenties, instead of in hundreds. Harriet became an automaton, a machine that telephoned people she had never met, numbers and names one after another, disembodied voices, and talked sweetly to them, injecting a smile into her voice. She talked to everyone, anyone who might mention "Conundrum," journalists in their columns, disc jockeys on their programs, editors and assistants, assistants to assistants, all the way down the line to the recent hires who made the tea. She talked to anyone at all, so long as there was the faintest chance that they might help her to produce some publicity. She could buy advertising space, and she spent on that as liberally as she dared, but it was much harder to get the gossipy little mentions, half news-items that were completely free except for her own efforts in securing them. Harriet began to understand, as she reviewed the orders, what she had only guessed at before. Only by generating the right kind of publicity could she create a buzz about "Conundrum." It was harder still that she couldn't even define her buzz except as a ripple in the ether that would wash people into the shops to buy the game.

It was April, and "Conundrum" was to be launched in August. She needed the pre-publicity now, the whisper in the air that would stimulate the buyers just enough to draw their attention. Without it, "Conundrum" would sink in a mass of other Christmas games. Harriet frowned and drew the telephone toward her again. Her ear ached from the pressure of the receiver against it. She dialed a number from one of her lists, asked for a name.

"Cindy speaking."

Harriet had spoken to Cindy before. She was a researcher at a commercial radio station in the north of England.

"Hi, Cindy, how are you?" The smile in the voice, imperative. "This is Harriet Peacock. You remember, I talked to you about 'Conundrum'?"

"Oh, right, *hello*." The sound of illusory friendship. "I talked to John, and he was really interested." John was the presenter of a self-consciously wacky music and chat program. Harriet was trying to persuade Cindy to persuade John to play "Conundrum" on the program, perhaps inviting some local celebrities in to play with him, or some nurses from the hospital, or the winners of the week's phone-in quiz. Anyone, to do anything, so long as it was with "Conundrum."

"That's great. When can he do it?"

"Well actually, the thing is, John feels it's a bit early for it yet."

Harriet was also beginning to realize that it was invariably too early, or too late, or else the wrong season altogether. She doodled a face on her scrap pad as she listened, then scribbled an arrow piercing the skull.

"He wondered if it would be better to do it around the launch date, you know, when the game is actually in the shops? When is the date, by the way?"

"August. I'll send you another press-kit. There'll be a lot of interest in it then, Cindy. Press as well as radio. Feature it now, and people will have heard it from you first. I know John likes to be first." There was the delicate suggestion that, if somehow he failed to be, it would all be Cindy's fault.

"Oh, sure, I see that. Look, we've got the game here, all right? We'll hold on to it, and put an item together nearer the time."

"That'll be marvelous. I'll come back to you." Admitting defeat, for now.

"By the way, Harriet, there's one thing I want to ask about it, and I'm sure John'll say the same."

"What's that, Cindy?"

"Well, it's just, where's the *story* behind this? It's a great game, right, but I'd like to know something else about it as well. Where do you come in? How did you invent it? Did the idea come to you in the bath, like *eureka*?"

Like hell, Harriet thought. But Cindy was right, curse her. Harriet had been aware that something was missing right back at the Toy Fair. The pristine backdrop and the rainbow boxes were bright, and they were also bland. The dark idea that nested in the back of Harriet's mind raised its head again, and she pushed it forcefully away from her. Cindy was rattling on. She must be lonely, up there in her windowless little office in the boxy modern building on some windswept industrial estate. "Can't you sell yourself a bit more? Are you a parachutist or an ex-nun, or anything? That would make a good one for us."

Harriet laughed. "I must get a press release together. I'll call it All About Me." She was even beginning to talk like these people, she thought bitterly, and it didn't make her any more successful at selling to them. But this wasn't selling. It was beginning to feel more like begging.

"Thanks for the idea, Cindy. It's been lovely to talk. Bye now."

Harriet made two more calls, and finished with two more open-ended assurances that there would be the right item, not to worry, when the time was right.

At last, she pushed her chair back in despair and stood up to stretch her stiff legs. The two-and-a-half offices that she had taken for Peacocks in a grubby Bayswater mews were silent. It wasn't one of Graham Chandler's days, and the typist-receptionist must be daydreaming behind her switchboard in the little front cubicle.

Harriet felt lonely and depressed. Her head was full of telephone voices, and yet there was no one to talk to . . .

Stop it, Harriet commanded herself. There wasn't any reason to be depressed. These were only obstacles besetting her now, not failures. And loneliness only attacked her when she wasn't working, which was hardly ever.

She went to the dust-streaked window and looked down into the mews. She saw two or three parked cars, people passing by, and pigeons in a comical line on a window ledge. Harriet turned back to the lists on her desk, then dropped them impatiently and went through to the front office. As she had guessed, the typist was sitting staring blankly in front of her, her hands slack on the keys. She started into awareness several seconds too late. Harriet asked, not very mildly, if she didn't have any work to do, and went on into the cramped washroom without waiting for an answer.

The office kitchen was a corner of the washroom, equipped with an electric kettle and a cold tap. Harriet poured water onto a teabag in a mug, too impatient to let the kettle boil. She took the resultant tepid brew back to her office and drank it, wincing at the assault by tannin.

When she went to the window again, she saw Robin Landwith getting out of his car. He had arranged their meeting for four forty-five, and when she looked at her watch she saw that he was punctual to the second. She also saw that he was driving a white Porsche.

Well, she told herself, *he would be, wouldn't he?*

Robin paused briefly by the nameplate to one side of the street door. *Peacocks*, it announced in an austere typeface. Beside the name there was an engraved fan-shape, feathers of the bird's tail, that Harriet had adopted as her company's logo. Robin nodded, signifying approval. Harriet had style and good taste, whatever her other talents might prove to be.

He went briskly up the steep brown stairs and found Harriet's typist pounding away as if trying to beat a speed record. The girl smiled at him from beneath her eyelashes, stopped typing, and buzzed through to Harriet.

"Mr. Landwith is here."

The announcement was a formality that amused them both, as Harriet was separated from them only by a door so thin and warped that there were inch-wide gaps at top and bottom. Robin was smiling as he went in to her.

She looked up, and something sharpened in her face. She didn't smile back at him.

"Sit down, won't you? It's not very comfortable, I'm afraid."

Robin took the second chair, too big for the small space. He glanced around at the wall-charts, the piles of paperwork on Harriet's desk, the print-outs of sales data placed ready to hand. "Conundrum" boxes and boards made the only bright spots in the room. Robin also noticed that there were dark, puffy bags of skin under Harriet's eyes. The two of them had met only twice, briefly and formally, since Landwith's had set her up in business. They had talked perhaps a dozen times on the telephone.

"You seem well established," he remarked.

Harriet didn't even try to respond to his polite formula. The offices were horrible, she was well aware of that, because she had deliberately taken the cheapest possible. They would do, it would all do, for now.

"Thank you for coming," she said.

"You don't have to thank me, Harriet. I work for the company, too. Shall we look at the figures?"

Harriet handed over the print-outs and a short covering report. She looked expressionlessly out of the window while Robin went through them. When he had finished his reading he asked the necessary questions and she answered succinctly.

There was a short silence and then Robin said, "Not good."

"No, not good," she echoed him.

Robin didn't waste any time on laments. "What are you going to do?"

"I've got two options. I can either keep plugging on as I am doing, and hope that things will pick up just before and following the game actually appearing on the market. Or I can stop everything now and make radical changes."

He regarded her steadily. "So, which?"

Harriet felt slightly sick. The black idea had grown inside her, fed by Cindy. She didn't want to admit to it, but at the same time it was powerfully attractive.

"I need a little more time to think it out."

Procrastination might bring a different, easier idea. Or "Conundrum" might start selling just as it was.

"Okay, good." To Harriet's surprise Robin didn't press her any further. With apparent relief he gathered up the print-outs and replaced them on the desk, put his gold-nibbed pen away in his inside pocket. Business was over. He leaned back, crossing ankle over knee to show an expanse of silk sock, and clasped his hands behind his head. He made a picture of relaxed good humor. Harriet felt a twitch of tiredness pulling at the corner of her eye.

"And so, what now?" Robin asked. She could see his father's features very clearly, softer in the son.

"Now, this minute do you mean?" Harriet indicated the loaded desk, gave a faint shrug.

"You look miserable."

"Thank you very much."

"Let me try that again. I . . ."

"Robin, don't you want to discuss Peacocks any further?"

"No, not now. It's in your hands and I'm confident you'll do whatever must be done."

"Thank you for your confidence." *If only it were justified,* Harriet thought. "And if I need additional funding?" She would certainly need it, if she had to do what she feared.

"Ask."

He spread his hands, as if it were the simplest thing in the world. Harriet nodded, slowly. Lack of funds would be no excuse. She felt an invisible net closing around her, twisted automatically and uncomfortably on her hard chair.

Robin had put his fingers together. He tapped the end of his nose with the joined forefingers, studying her over the tips of them. *He's damned pompous,* Harriet thought irritably, *for not much more than a boy.*

"Stop work for this evening," Robin ordered. "Let me take you out to dinner."

"Thanks, but no."

From the outer office came the sound of the receptionist putting on her coat and gathering up her plastic shopping bags. Harriet didn't need to look at her watch. She knew it must be exactly half-past five. *I must replace her as soon as I can,* she resolved.

"Please come. I'd like it very much if you would."

Harriet had forgotten, for a split second, what he had been asking her. She was very tired. The momentary blankness must have shown in her face, because Robin stopped tapping his nose and stared harder at her.

"Robin, I'm sorry. I'm not deliberately trying to be rude."

"I know you're not. I'd like it very much if you'd let me take you out to dinner." He put no sarcasatic emphasis on the repeated invitation, and spoke more softly than before. Harriet saw at once that he did want her company, and that he was concerned for her.

She felt a rush of exhausted self-pity. She could have dealt easily with accusations or aggression, or anything on a business footing. But direct sympathy was too much for her. Her eyes filled up with tears.

"Harriet."

Robin stood up and took a folded handkerchief out of his pocket. He put it on the corner of the desk and then went over to look out of the window with his back to her. Harriet blew her nose furiously. The boy was pompous, but he was also tactful.

Still turned away, Robin said, "If I don't move my car soon, the owner of that garage over there is going to come home and find me blocking the doors."

ʹ Harriet thought of sinking into the black leather seats of the white Porsche. She imagined the comfort of letting someone else make decisions for a whole evening. Somewhere in the inviting picture, too, was the prospect of a meal that would not involve a visit to the Belsize Park late-opening supermarket to see what the freezer cabinet would yield. She sniffed, and refolded the sullied handkerchief.

"Thank you. I would like to come."

"Good." As soon as he had got what he wanted, Robin became brisk again. "Let's go, then, shall we?" He swept Harriet out of the dingy office and down into the mews.

The car wrapped her in its leathery embrace, exactly as she had imagined. It was pleasant to bowl down Park Lane, past the cold clumps of daffodils showing in Hyde Park. They shot between the buses and taxis. Robin was a slightly flashy driver, like Harriet herself. Harriet's spirits lifted. London looked bright and busy, full of people going somewhere.

She wanted to brush aside her moment of weakness. "There's been a lot of hard work, just lately." A half-explanation. She didn't want him to know that she was vulnerable to his kindness.

"It doesn't do to overwork," Robin answered. *Lucky for you, if you don't have to,* Harriet thought. "Would you like to come home for a drink first, then we can go out to eat later?"

"That sounds nice." Decisions, administrative ones at least, could be his for the evening. Harriet sat back and admired the performance of the Porsche.

If she had imagined where he lived she would have pictured a stiflingly carpeted flat, perhaps in a mansion block in one of the gloomy streets behind Sloane Square. But Robin drove on over the river, where the strings of lights were coming on against the dark trees of Battersea Park. He stopped the car in a pretty street lined with flowering cherry trees.

"Is this your house?"

"What did you expect?"

Harriet laughed. "I don't know. Something different, not this."

The two downstairs rooms had been knocked together, just like Jane's. But the similarity went no further. There was only the best, here, in the most carefully understated way. There were big pale gray sofas and marble mantels to the pretty polished grates, polished parquet and, beside the french windows at the back of the room, a single serious piece of furniture. It was a Biedermeier secretaire with two dozen tiny, ivory-knobbed drawers. Harriet was involuntarily drawn to it, and she stroked the flat of her hand over the warm, smooth birchwood. She noticed that there was not even the finest film of dust. Everything in the room was very tidy and clean, no doubt kept in order by some faithful cleaning lady. Harriet imagined her partiality, "My young Mr. Landwith, he's a lovely boy," and almost laughed.

"Pretty," she said, of the desk, to cover her amusement.

Robin was pleased. "I saw it in a catalog and went to bid for it myself, so there was no chance of losing it. The interior decorators did most of the rest." He waved dismissively and Harriet saw that home for Robin was merely a place to live, necessarily as superior in appearance as the cut of his suits, and requiring about the same amount of emotional involvement. Robin had plainly chosen the right decorator. To put further energy into homemaking would leave less to spare for making money, she supposed.

She felt the superiority of her own experience. She had made a home of her own already, and deconstructed it into packing cases layered with knives, casserole dishes, coffeepots, and wedding china. Was it better to have done that much, she wondered, than to have done nothing at all?

And now at Belsize Park there was no time for homemaking. The cases remained packed, containing the trappings of her marriage. But it wasn't money for the sake of money that she was in pursuit of, Harriet distinguished for herself. It was success for "Conundrum," and through it success for herself, and Simon.

The day's concerns came back to her, but she dismissed them. She sank down into one of the gray sofas. There were even fresh flowers, she saw, arranged in a bowl beside the fireless hearth. Fires were messy, of course, and needed tending.

"I don't spend a lot of time here," Robin said, apparently following her thoughts.

"I don't see a lot of my home, just now, either," Harriet smiled at him.

"It is possible to work too hard."

"Not in the position I'm in now. Next year, it'll be different."

He put a drink into her hand and they raised their glasses to each other in a silent propitiation of whatever demons might stalk the interval.

They had their drinks, and then another one apiece. When those were finished Robin said that he intended to take a shower before going out to dinner, and inquired politely whether Harriet might like one, too.

She considered. She felt tired and grubby, and the idea of a hot shower was inviting. But to take off her clothes in Robin Landwith's house, who although not an adversary was not yet quite a friend, wouldn't that make her vulnerable again?

Harriet decided that she was being foolish. If she wanted a shower, she should take one. "Thank you," she said briskly.

He showed her upstairs. The pictures hanging up the staircase wall reminded her of the Landwith Associates offices. Perhaps they had bought a job lot somewhere? Robin's bedroom, with a big bathroom opening through double doors beyond it, was decorator-masculine. There was plenty of solid mahogany, and some serious drapes, and framed photographs that seemed mainly to feature sports teams with crossed cricket bats or rugby balls on knees at centerfront. Everything was in impeccable taste, but Harriet felt irritated by the display of premature prosperity. Robin Landwith ought to be sharing a chaotic flat somewhere, with rock or political posters on the walls and a smell of unemptied trash can pervading the dense kitchen air. Leo had been living in just such a flat when she had first met him. She had begun by imposing a measure of hygiene on the kitchen, then they had moved on to live on their own together.

And why, Harriet wondered, *am I thinking so much about Leo this evening?*

Robin followed her through into the bathroom and gave her thick, clean white towels. Then he went away, closing the double doors behind him.

Harriet wandered around, looking at things. There was more mahogany here, and gray-white marble, and heavy, old-fashioned white ceramic fittings. There were hairbrushes with initials, and various jars of unemphatic toiletries. She drifted to the window and looked down, her irritation evaporating in the soothing quiet. At the back of the house, there was still just enough light for her to see, was a little square of garden, paved in brick and made summer-private by tall trelliswork. She imagined it in daylight, with the new green leaves showing on the twiggy sticks of the climbers.

"Pretty," she said again.

Harriet returned to her investigations, after pulling down the white blind. It took her a moment or two to find the shower, but then she located it behind a door with opaque glass panels. She undressed, dropping her clothes haphazardly onto a chair. When she was naked, she examined herself critically in a convenient mirror. Probably she was too thin. Certainly her ribs were clearly visible under pale skin, and her hipbones stuck out sharply on either side of a concave expanse of flesh. But her waist was satisfactorily slim, she had decent legs, and her breasts were neat and firm, even if there wasn't enough of them.

Leo used to say that she looked much better with her clothes off than on, unlike the majority of women. Well, she supposed that Leo should know. Harriet turned the shower on full blast, and stepped under the luxurious flood of water. One of the drawbacks of the Belsize Park flat was a viciously unpredictable heating system. She hadn't yet cracked the code that would enable her to predict when there would be enough hot water in the half-sized tank to allow her to enjoy a half-sized bath. Water this hot, and in this apparent abundance, should be enjoyed to the full.

The steam and the rush of water and the opaque glass were an effective insulation from the outside. As she lathered herself with Robin's Czech & Speake soap Harriet hummed a little, and indulged herself with a fantasy about what she should do if she stepped naked out of the shower and found Robin sitting in his bathroom chair, waiting for her.

She would be graceful and dignified, she decided. Unhurriedly, she would reach for one of the big white towels and swathe herself in it. With one corner she would pat the silvery drops of water from her throat and arms, and he would watch her guiltily. She would say nothing, but still Robin would recognize at once that he had made a serious mistake. He would stand up and then slip away, murmuring a stricken apology. Later, when she came downstairs, neither of them would refer to the incident.

Very satisfactory, Harriet thought, as the last of the soap rinsed away. She turned the control to cold, and spluttered for a few seconds under the icy jets. Then she opened the door again, feeling her skin glowing.

The bathroom was empty except for her own clothes, lying exactly where she had discarded them and looking unfortunately crumpled. Harriet caught sight of herself in the mirror again, only now she was beetroot-faced with heat and her hair was plastered flat to her skull, so that she looked as if she had just come last in some swimming race. She made an inventive face at herself. So much for vanity and fantasy. No one was going to lurk in any bathroom for a glimpse of this brick-red captain of sports. Harriet snatched up a towel and scrubbed unforgivingly.

She was not pleased either to recognize that the fantasy role she had cast herself in was much too close to the real reaction of Leo's model girlfriend when she herself had burst in on them in the studio. Leo and Harriet had split the Robin role between them.

"Damn it," Harriet said aloud. "And *bugger* Leo."

She found a clothes hanger and hung her clothes up in the shower cubicle so that the steam could work on the creases. She splashed her face with cold water until it returned to approximately the right shade, and then towel-dried her hair because she judged that Robin was too butch to make it worthwhile searching for a dryer. Finally she remade-up her face and put on her clothes again. The end result was just about acceptable. *Vanity, vanity*, she reminded herself.

Harriet flung open the double doors. The bedroom was empty, too. She strolled across it, stopping deliberately to examine the photographs. The various teams featured a younger, more eager-looking version of Robin. Of course, he would have to be a games-player, too. Martin would have expected nothing else than the First Eleven. She warmed to the son in sympathy all over again, even though he had dealt her a fantasy-rejection.

On the bureau, in an oval silver frame, was a photograph of a woman. Harriet picked it up and turned it toward the light in order to get a better look. She saw a heart-shaped face set on a long, fragile neck, cloudy dark hair, and a sweet, thoughtful expression. Robin's mother, Martin's wife. Probably at least fifty, but still lovely.

For some reason, Harriet found herself blushing. She put the silver frame down and tiptoed out of the bedroom.

She found Robin sitting on one of the gray sofas reading *The Spectator*. He was wearing a different suit, and a different tie, and a fresh shirt. He must have taken his shower in some guest bathroom or downstairs cloakroom-cubbyhole, leaving his own bathroom free for her to use.

His formal, respectable, *Spectator*-absorbed appearance was so different from the hopeful satyr she had imagined upstairs that she bit the corners of her mouth to contain her amusement.

Robin put aside his magazine and stood up. "You quite often look," he remarked without rancor, "as though you are enjoying some succulent private joke. Is it a reaction to the world in general, or just to me?"

Harriet was shamed into honesty. "I can't take you quite seriously," she admitted. "It's because you're so young. And yet there's the business, and the car, and all this." She nodded at the room.

"I am twenty-six." A little older than he looked, then. "All of four years younger than you." Harriet was thirty. She had passed the milestone without celebration, or analysis of what had gone by. Her attention was fixed on the future.

Robin had crossed the room to stand in front of her. He looked down, with the advantage of his height. Harriet was conscious of having to stand her ground, and also of something more. A scrutiny, or appraisal, not unlike Martin's. She looked back, making her own judgment.

"You should take me seriously," Robin said softly. And he leaned forward to kiss her cheek. Harriet stood still, waiting for what would come next, remembering her bathroom fantasy. But that was all. She felt faintly foolish, as though she had closed her eyes and pursed her lips, although she had done nothing of the kind. Into the small silence that followed she said, "I will from now on, okay? I promise." She spoke very lightly, and then she turned away and picked a book up off a table, examining the author's photograph on the back cover with interest.

"Would you like another drink? Or shall we go straight out to dinner?"

"Dinner, I think, please."

It was dark now. They drove back, over the river where the lights shimmered. Harriet realized, a little to her surprise, that she was enjoying the evening in prospect. The restaurant was Japanese. Evidently Robin was a favored regular, because the waiters greeted him as a friend. Harriet had never eaten Japanese food before, and she exclaimed with delight over the tiny, perfect dishes and parcels as they arrived in front of her. She ate with enthusiasm, enjoying the clean flavors. Robin was pleased. He liked showing her how to unwrap and slice and sample, and ordered more than they needed to eat for the satisfaction of demonstrating.

They drank sake. Robin poured it out, and Harriet laughed and spluttered when she tasted it.

"Good?"

"Well, interesting. It probably improves on acquaintance, like many things."

"I hope so."

They talked, not very significantly, about books and films, and then about friendship. Harriet couldn't remember, later, at what stage of the meal she became aware that she was positively attracted to Robin Landwith. Her interest seemed to have transferred itself from father to son with extraordinary smoothness. The symptoms were pleasant. They heightened the significance of their easy conversation, gave the bleached decor of the restaurant a rosier glow, and made Harriet think, momentarily, of the man in the blue shirt at Jane's party.

It was a welcome change from work, and anxiety, and the depressing surroundings of Peacocks' offices. Harriet sighed comfortably and drank some more sake. This attraction would come to nothing, of course, because she would not allow it to. But it was diverting to sit in a restaurant again, regarding the object of her interest across a starched white tablecloth, and imagining what would happen when he kissed her.

Robin was handsome and self-possessed, and she was sure that she was in no danger from him.

"Is that your mother, in the picture with the silver frame, in your bedroom?" She was interested, now, in weaving a history for him.

"Yes. We're supposed to be very alike."

"She's beautiful. What does she do?"

Robin looked surprised. "Do?"

"Do. Is she a venture capitalist, too? Or a doctor, or a singer or a naturalist?"

Robin laughed. "None of those. She doesn't do anything. She looks after my father, used to look after me. Still would, if I'd let her."

Harriet nodded. Robin thought that it was enough for Mrs. Landwith to be a wife and mother to Landwith men. *A different woman from me*, Harriet thought. More like Kath, only Kath had fought her battles at the beginning. She deserved her security now. Harriet wondered about Mrs. Landwith of the cloudy dark hair and innocent, sweet expression. There would be a big house, somewhere in the country, to be looked after. Husband and son to be looked for.

Harriet glanced around her. Sake and satisfaction seemed to have given the restaurant light a warmer tinge. There seemed to be a golden nimbus of it around Robin's head. She watched it with affection, a little in awe of the glamour of privilege. She felt no resentment. She only saw, quite clearly, how he had come to be all the attractive things that he was. It was, as she had perceptively imagined weeks ago in the Landwith offices, like rearing a thoroughbred. He would run well now, and repay the investment. She would have liked to lean across the table and put her mouth against his. She wanted him, she would have forgiven him anything in the afterglow of warm rice wine.

Robin was turning his thimble glass on the tablecloth, making interlocking circles with the heavy base.

"I thought we should talk some more about 'Conundrum,' " he said quietly.

Harriet opened her eyes wider, shook her head a little, to clear it of golden light and images of a big house in green gardens.

"Why not?" And seeing at once that the response was too frivolous, added, "in what respect, exactly?"

"In the important respect, selling it." Harriet watched his mouth as he talked. "I've got a board in the car. Will you excuse me a minute if I go and get it?"

"Of course I will."

She watched him walk across the restaurant, still with the light around him. *Nice shoulders,* she thought. *Nice long back, and narrow hips. Oh dear, Harriet.*

There was nothing to be done about it, of course. It was unprofessional to sleep with a business partner. It was probably unprofessional even to imagine it.

Robin came back with the familiar box tucked under his arm. He cleared the sake to one side and put the box on the table, then looked around the restaurant. They had taken a long time over their meal, and there were only a handful of diners remaining. The waiters had begun to congregate in a corner, but two of them hurried to Robin's summons. Robin was on friendly terms with both of them. He said something and all three of them laughed, then one of the waiters answered a question and the other chipped in, correcting him. Harriet wasn't listening. She studied Robin's profile, then glanced down at the "Conundrum" box on the table between them. Robin's fingers were resting on the box, but not idly.

Harriet stiffened.

She looked at his face again. He was still chatting genially to the waiters, but his eyes were sharp. He was watching, waiting for something, and his fingers made little impatient movements on the rainbow-colored packaging.

What are you up to? Harriet thought, but she knew as soon as the question had formulated itself.

"What do you think of this, by the way?" Robin asked lightly. His fingers now described an elegant little flutter over Harriet's box.

The waiters looked, then shrugged. Neither of them had focused on the box before, and now they examined it politely.

Harriet saw what Robin was intending.

He opened the box, stripped off the shrink-wrapping, and lifted the shiny black frame out of the injection molding. He set it up, and shook up the colored balls and counters in his fist. The waiters leaned closer, their interest kindling. The younger one stopped glancing over his shoulder to see who might be coming to direct him back to work. Robin threw the counters, frowned over setting the gates. Harriet waited, and then came the over-familiar rattle and roll. The waiters' faces split into identical beaming smiles.

"Clever," the older said. Only he said, *Crever*. He reached out and took the counters, as people always did, to play for himself.

Harriet felt cold. The waiters were friendly, and attentive. The restaurant was elegant, cool and quiet with paper screens and tranquil flower paintings. She had sat here all evening, eating sushi and drinking sake, and admiring the golden boy who was paying for it all. Now she saw the Japanese lettering on the menus, and she remembered the split packing-case end resting on the mantelpiece at home in Belsize Park. The waiters were laughing and Robin was watching, narrow-eyed, as if he saw everything.

Simon had been in Shamshuipo, had almost died there. He had created "Conundrum"—*the name was wrong, hopelessly wrong*—to save himself.

I can't do it, Harriet thought. And even as she decided that she couldn't make use of what Simon had suffered she saw Robin Landwith's expression, and knew that she would do it. She would do it because it made hard sense, and Shamshuipo was forty years ago.

"Good game. Very good game," the waiters chorused. "Is yours, Mr. Landwith?"

"Something we're working on together," he murmured deprecatingly, and then added, "I hope I haven't kept you from whatever you should be doing . . ."

The waiters collected themselves, as they were intended to do, and went on their way bowing and smiling.

Robin turned back to Harriet, and raised his eyebrows. Harriet was ready to defend herself. Being defensive made her angry, and the fact that she was drawn to Robin only increased her anger. She sat silently, unwilling to give any ground.

"And so?" he pressed her. He sounded almost like a clumsy parody of one of his waiters.

"I'm sorry? And so what?"

With a show of patience, Robin answered, "I was watching what happened then. Weren't you? Neither of those chaps displayed any curiosity about the package when it was sitting on the table. It was only when the game itself was put in front of them that they came alive. They didn't want to open the box themselves. They didn't even crane their necks to read what it *said* on it."

"No, they didn't." Harriet's lips barely moved. Robin rapped his knuckles on the cloth.

"So your packaging is no bloody good." In spite of what his own father had said.

"Months of work have gone into that. Months of research. Colors, logo, everything. It's as good as it damn well can be." Harriet's voice was raised. The lingering diners peered covertly at them. Harriet defended her work furiously and pointlessly. She knew it was wrong, and had known it since the Toy Fair. It was maddening to have Robin demonstrate its deficiencies so elegantly.

"Two Japanese waiters is hardly a representative sample."

"Take any sample you like."

They found that they were glaring at each other, like children quarreling. Harriet was fighting him off, because she was afraid of what she must do when she acknowledged he was right.

"In the office this evening you said, 'It's in your hands and I'm confident you'll do whatever must be done.' " Harriet smiled, trying to regain her equilibrium.

"I did, and I am. But I'd like to know what, and when."

"I'll need some more money." She disliked the petulant sound of it.

But Robin only said calmly, "I know you will." He lifted one hand to call for the bill.

Help me, Harriet wailed silently. They walked out, past the screens and the pictures, the Japanese lettering and the bowing, smiling waiters.

When they reached Robin's sleek, white car he opened the passenger door for her.

"I'll drive you home."

"Thanks, but there's no need. I'll get a cab."

He only held the door wider. Harriet climbed in, with all the confusion of her feelings, and let him drive her back to Belsize Park. The trip passed mostly in silence; Harriet was thinking.

"This is it," she said, breaking the silence when they reached her street. It would have been ill-mannered not to have asked him in for a drink. Robin accepted, and they descended clanking iron steps to the basement front door. The cats appeared at once, and twisted between their ankles and the uncollected empty milk bottles.

"Come in," Harriet invited, making an ironic sweep of her arm.

Even to her own accustomed eyes, the flat made an unhappy contrast with Robin's house. The chairs were heaped with books and unread newspapers, and on the table in the window was a thicket of cups and plates and papers and letters. It occurred to Harriet that Robin was standing looking about him in rather the same way as she had done in Simon Archer's kitchen. She noticed that the air in her room was cold and yet stuffy, and there was a distinct smell of cat.

"They belong to the girl who owns the place," Harriet explained, surprised to find that she was embarrassed by the squalor. "They came as part of the rental package. Would you like some whiskey?" Like Simon, she thought she must have part of a bottle somewhere. Involuntarily, her eyes went to the original game, propped up against the mantelpiece.

"Just some coffee," Robin said. He had been looking at it, too.

Harriet went through to the kitchen. Robin followed her and leaned against the door-frame to survey the further chaos. Harriet had had little time lately for cooking; there had been no time at all for clearing up afterward. There was a smell of sour milk, probably the cats', that reminded Harriet of the kitchen in Leo's old flat. *God damn Leo.* She snatched up the cats' bowls and washed them, then doled out food from the half-tin in the fridge. The cats yelped and subsided into noisy chewing. Harriet put the kettle on.

"Do you *choose* to live like this?" Robin asked from the doorway.

"I don't choose anything just now, beyond what I do for Peacocks," Harriet said angrily.

"What happened to the rest of your life?"

Harriet knew what he meant, but she misunderstood deliberately.

"I have a perfectly satisfactory life." Her stiffness fended off any more of his questions.

They took their coffee into the living room. Harriet cleared a chair for Robin, but he went over to the boarded-up fireplace and stood looking at the piece of packing case. He touched the faded lettering, and then stood back again.

After a long moment he said, very quietly, "That makes me shiver."

"Yes."

That was it, of course. They both knew it, neither of them spoke of it.

Robin sat down on the chair that Harriet cleared for him. He drank his coffee and one of the cats jumped on his lap and kneaded with its paws. It was a cheap picture of domesticity. They talked a little about the game, and Simon. Robin knew the story, of course. Landwith's had been careful to establish it at the beginning. Unwillingly, Harriet spoke of Shamshuipo and Simon's survival.

Robin nodded, as if his opinion had been confirmed. Then, when he had drunk his coffee, he stood up. He let the cat go without regret, came to Harriet and put his hands on her shoulders.

"And so what are you going to do?"

Harriet didn't know if he was threatening or cajoling. She closed her eyes before she answered. "I'm going to change it. Give the game a new title. Repackage and relaunch." The scale of the job threatened to crush her. She opened her eyes again and looked toward the mantelpiece.

"Good girl," Robin whispered.

"What about the money?"

"Readily forthcoming, as I told you. We'd have to take a further piece of the equity, say fourteen percent. And, just as a formality, a floating charge on the assets of the company."

He glanced up, once more, at the piece of packing case.

"Including the game itself."

Harriet nodded slowly. She hadn't expected that they would give her more funding for nothing. If that was what it would cost, then that was what she must pay. Robin leaned toward her and kissed her hard. His mouth jarred against hers. It was a bite almost as much as it was a kiss. When his hands dropped from her shoulders Harriet put her fingers to her mouth as if to rub his imprint away. She was attracted to him, disturbingly so, but she was also faintly repelled. There was another side, then, to the golden boy.

"Good night," Robin said, as if nothing had happened. "I'll see myself out."

She listened to his footsteps as they clanged up the iron steps.

When she was sure that he had gone, she crossed the room and lifted Simon's game down from its resting place. She studied the familiar lettering, trying to see it again for the first time.

It makes me shiver, Robin had said.

It was Simon's story itself that would sell the game for
Peacocks. Cindy and all the others like her would fasten onto the
British officer who had fought to survive, through his game, in
the particular hell of Shamshuipo. Harriet could already imagine
what the Cindys would say and write.

The bright, bland "Conundrum" packaging would have to
go. Instead, the box would be a somber replica of what Harriet
held in her hands. Even the clever, tricksy name would have to
be changed. The game must have a Japanese name. Perhaps the
unintelligible symbols she had so often stared at would themselves yield the name.

A thread of excitement twisted in Harriet. Now that the
decision was made, now that she had committed it to Robin, she
felt the power of what she could do with it. She wished now that
he hadn't gone, so that she could share the thrill of the planning
with him. Before she put it back in its place, she studied the
wooden rectangle for another moment.

Then, to the inanimate wood, she whispered, "I'm sorry."

Nine

SIMON HAD BEEN ILL. It had been his chest, as it usually was, and for several days he had felt unable to leave his bed except for brief expeditions to the kitchen, where he made messy meals that he didn't want and often couldn't eat. But when he woke up this morning he felt better and stronger, and so he got up and dressed in a collarless shirt and his warm trousers, and put his dressing gown on over the top of them. It was the end of June; although from the bedroom window Simon could see sunshine and flowers in his neighbors' gardens, his own house still seemed to contain the chill of winter.

Or more probably, he thought, the cold was just in his bones. It was not particularly significant.

He went downstairs and made himself a cup of tea, and then he sat in the kitchen chair and listened absently to the grandfather clock ticking in the hallway. He lived so much with the silence of the house that it had become a companion, with different moods. Today's was benign, and so the knocking at the front door, when it started, was doubly unwelcome.

Simon sat still and waited for it to stop. Sometimes people did come to the door, people he thought of as busybodies or do-gooders, and usually they gave up quite quickly and went away again. But this knocking was more than usually persistent, as well as loud and heavy. At last, with the half-hope that it might be the girl Harriet, Simon hauled himself out of his chair and shuffled down the passageway to the front door.

Standing on the step was a young man he had never seen before. He had a flat, bristly haircut that made him look aggressive, and he was wearing jeans and an anorak with some kind of logo or slogan on the sleeves and breast. Incongruously, it seemed to Simon, he was carrying a briefcase in his left hand. His right hand shot out to Simon and, when Simon didn't take it, vibrated accusingly between them.

"Hello there." The young man had a big, friendly smile.

Perhaps he was an estate agent or a property developer, Simon guessed. He must get rid of him as quickly as possible.

"Barry Buchan." Only when the young man saw that his name meant nothing to Simon did he elaborate, "From the *Mail*."

The *Midlands Mail* was the popular local paper that served the whole urban area. Simon had at least heard of it, although he never read it.

"I'm afraid you're at the wrong house." He began to close the door, but Barry Buchan's hip and shoulder were in the way.

"I don't think so." The intruder was still smiling. "You are Mr. Simon Archer, aren't you? Lieutenant Archer, as was, Royal Artillery?"

Surprise undermined Simon's defenses. He stood back from the door and a second later Barry was inside the house with him. He rubbed the flat of his hand over the flat top of his head and then brushed invisible dust off the sleeves of his anorak to give the unshaken hand something useful to do before he put it back, where it clearly belonged, in the pocket of the jeans.

"Great. Thanks very much. Sorry to turn up on spec like this, but you're not in the phone book, are you?"

"What do you want?" Simon managed to say.

"Just a chat, a bit of background, that kind of thing. It's a great story, you know. It'll make a wonderful feature, with the local angle. Shall we go through there, Simon?" Barry nodded down the passage to the slightly brighter light in the kitchen.

Simon pulled his dressing gown closer around him, over his thundering chest, afraid of this ferret in his burrow. He knew that there were men like this outside, of course there were, but not here behind his defenses.

"A chat about what? There must be a mistake, there isn't a story here." He felt, and sounded, weak and stupid.

Barry looked amazed. "Of course there is. This 'Meizu.' It's not the usual publicity guff. This is a real human story, isn't it?"

"I don't know anything about 'Meizu.' I've never heard of it. It's a mistake." But even as he said the word, faint memory and sharp apprehension stirred together. This ferret-boy was right and he was wrong. There might be a story. And he was afraid that part of it was some unseen connection between this visitor and Kath Peacock's hungry daughter.

The newspaperman hustled Simon into his own kitchen, settled him into his chair, and took a notebook and papers out of his briefcase. From the sheaf of papers he selected some thick, creamy pages and passed them over to Simon. "There you go.

'Meizu.' Craze of the year, if the P.R.'s to be believed. Now, correct me if I'm wrong, but you are that POW, are you not?"

Simon read. His premonition was fully founded.

The press release told him about Shamshuipo and the Japanese torturers, and the British officer who had clung to sanity by way of a numbers game. It also described the game's forty-year hibernation, and rediscovery by "Peacocks." This last was mentioned only lightly. Now, the piece concluded, the game had been rescued and launched so that everyone could enjoy its intricacy and simplicity. The board was a close replica of the prison-camp original, as a tribute to the bravery and ingenuity of that British officer. There were photographs of the game. The resemblance to the packing-case end that Simon had given away was close enough.

Harriet Peacock had done a good job. Only not quite good enough. She had changed the officer's name, but either through innocent oversight or a more likely wish to keep as enticingly close as possible to the real truth, she had given his actual rank and regiment. Only a handful of Simon's fellow officers had survived Shamshuipo and the years that came after it. Harriet could hardly have known how very few they were.

It would have been worth the gamble of a few hours spent with regimental records to follow those men up. For an eager journalist, just such a keen young man, it would not have been a difficult task to find the right one. It didn't matter whether it was Barry Buchan himself who had done it, or one of his contacts who had then traded the information to the local man.

It didn't matter. He was here now, inside Simon's redoubt. Simon studied the last words on the thick cream paper.

"This is a true story. *Meizu* is the Japanese word for maze or labyrinth."

Simon folded the paper neatly into its creases and tossed it back across the table to Barry Buchan.

"True?"

What did ferrets do to their prey, Simon wondered, once it was caught?

There was no need, in any case, for him to answer. Barry was nodding in satisfaction. "Pulled a fast one on you, have they?" He spoke with evident knowledge of a world of fast ones. He had opened his notebook.

Simon's lips and tongue were dry, but he made himself say stiffly, "It's quite legal. There's nothing to tell beyond what you've already got there."

Barry Buchan wouldn't care. It was all story to him, the

dirtier the better. It occurred to Simon that perhaps Harriet had done only too good a job. Perhaps she had made the veil deliberately thin so that young men like this could find him, search him out, just to sell more "Meizu" . . .

Simon stood up. "I'd like you to go now. I didn't invite you here, nor did I give you permission to come into my house. If you won't go, I shall have to call the police."

"Steady on." Barry was still grinning. "I can see it's been a shock, and I'm sorry about that. Shall I put the kettle on for you, or something?"

Simon gripped the back of his chair. "Just go." Barry began to gather up his papers.

Simon pointed at Harriet's press release. "Take that with you."

To his great relief, the reporter really was going. His bulk went away down the hall, and then his voice called with cheery imperviousness from the front door, "Anything I can do, Simon. You know where I am."

There was a rattle, and a decisive bang.

Barry walked down the path in the June sunshine, relieved to be out in the light and fresh air again. Some place, he thought. He felt sorry for the poor old bugger in there, in his dirty dressing gown. It didn't matter that he hadn't said much. He was the right man and Barry was the one who had found him, that was enough. He could write a good story about him sitting alone in that kitchen while "Meizu" rolled into the shops and out again, and made some fat cat fatter still. A touch of pathos, a touch of concern for our old folk, and a good war story. It would make a good Friday center spread. Barry didn't care either way about "Meizu"—or whatever the bloody game was called. He just liked the story. He was sure the *Express* would like it, too, he'd give them a call. He whistled as he climbed into his Golf, forgetting about his moment of sympathy for the poor old bugger. It had been worth the effort of tracking him down.

Simon was still at the kitchen table. His hands were shaking and his legs, and his neck felt too brittle to bear the weight of his head. He kept looking at the place where the cream pages had been lying. There was a piece of buttery paper there, there would be a semi-transparent grease stain on the last sheet folded in Barry Buchan's briefcase. Those were not the only pages, of course. Simon could imagine just how publicity worked. The words would have been duplicated, Harriet's cleverly unhyperbolic filleting of his life, and sent out to all kinds of people. Thousands of them. Simon could imagine the crisp piles of creamy pages, and the trim envelopes to be torn open . . .

He stood up, bumping against the chair. He swept the butter paper off the table and screwed it into a ball, then pushed out of sight anything else that Harriet's pages might have touched. But then the space in the middle of the cluttered table stared up at him like a knowing eye. Panicked by the stare, Simon ran out into the passage. The face of the grandfather clock was another eye watching him. Now, when he turned, there seemed to be knowing eyes everywhere, in the dim corners, behind the door, even in the walls themselves.

Simon slid the bolts at the top and bottom of the front door, even though he knew it was too late. He went upstairs, the focus of all the eyes. In his bedroom he closed the curtains against the sunlight. He lay down on his bed and drew the blankets over himself, gritting his teeth as he did so.

"Graham," Harriet said. "I think we're going to do it."

Graham Chandler was at his desk in his cubbyhole office. He had just finished talking to Jepson at Midland Plastics. Jepson could deliver a "Meizu" shipment in time to follow the first wave out of the shops. He was standing ready to put another into production as soon as it was needed. It had been hard work, remaking the whole package in a matter of weeks to meet Harriet's deadlines, but it had been done. There was new artwork, new film, new boxes, and a game board that looked as much like splintered packing-case wood as modern technology could make it. "Conundrum" had become "Meizu," and the market loved it.

Graham looked up at Harriet. Her eyes were shiny. Graham felt himself blushing a little, as he always did when Harriet confronted him too directly.

"I hope so. After all the work," he added, in his diffident manner.

Harriet came and perched on the edge of his desk. She was wearing leather trousers, and some kind of top that seemed to be all zips. Graham sat very still, and stared at the sheaf of papers that spilled out of Harriet's hands. There were order print-outs, sales sheets, and photocopies of newspaper and magazine articles.

"Look," she said. "Look at all the editorial we're getting. *Daily Mail, Cosmo, Woman's Own, Weekend, Good Housekeeping,* just in this week. Listen to this one." She read to him. " ' "Enter the Labyrinth." That's what *Meizu* means, and once you've played this fascinating game you'll know what it means, too. But "Meizu" isn't just another game for the Christmas market. There's a touching story behind it. It was dreamed up by a British officer in a Japanese prisoner of war camp . . . mmm, mmm, . . . playing his game literally kept him alive through his terrible ordeal. Forty years later the game was spotted by businesswomen Harriet Peacock, who snapped up the rights. Now "Meizu" is hotter than hot cakes, but the real identity of the officer is still a close-kept secret. I wonder what my old Grandad invented when he was with the ARP?' "

Harriet laughed. "Awful, isn't it? But it's just what we want. The game goes into the shops in August. And if you can't wait until then, enter our fun family competition and you could win your own "Meizu." We've got twenty games to give away.' "

"Graham, I tried so hard to get this kind of buzz going before, and no one was interested. Now we can't keep up with it all."

Karen put her head around the door. "Telephone. Radio Brighton." Karen had been unhappy at Stepping after Harriet had sold up. She had come to Peacocks to beg for a job, and Harriet had gladly taken her on in place of the clock-watching receptionist. Karen had taught herself word processing in two and a half days.

"Coming." Harriet stood up. She touched Graham's shoulder. "Thanks for all you've done," she said seriously.

"It's what I'm here for," he mumbled. But he was pleased, just the same. He felt that he would willingly go through the pandemonium of the last weeks all over again.

Harriet was good at commanding loyalty.

Karen gave up her evenings for Peacocks' sake, even Jeremy Crichton the marmoreal accountant worked his hardest for Harriet.

"Jeremy will be pleased with us," Graham said. "Have you talked to him?"

"Yep. B double plus." Jeremy's pessimism was a company joke. For Jeremy, the rating was a rave.

"And Robin?"

Harriet paused in the doorway. "Not yet. I'm saving that one up." She winked at Graham, and went away to her telephone call. He returned, with some reluctance, to his work.

Radio Brighton wanted Harriet on the morning show. She was going to play "Meizu" with nurses and doctors from the children's hospital, as part of a fund-raising week. It had been her own idea, enthusiastically received. Now the program researcher wanted to know if she would be willing to be interviewed herself, to talk about discovering and marketing "Meizu."

"Of course," Harriet said. "I'd be glad to. Anything you like."

She would talk about anything under the sun, to anyone who wanted it, she thought, so long as it generated publicity for her game.

"And what about the man himself? Would he come with you? I do understand he doesn't normally do publicity, but . . ."

There had been many other offers, of course, from television companies and national newspapers. Harriet thought, for the thousandth time, *If only Simon would.*

"I'm afraid not."

"*Is* he in fact your father?" the girl persisted, as if that was what everyone assumed.

Harriet turned very firm. "No, he isn't my father. There's no more I can tell you, either. What time would you like me to arrive?" She made the necessary arrangements, and then hung up.

Harriet sat back in her chair for a moment, biting her lip. Then she reached out for the sheaf of press cuttings that she had taken through to show Graham, and looked up from those to the sales chart on the opposite wall. There was no need for it to be there, all the sales information was carried on disk, but tending it was the single time-wasting activity that Harriet allowed herself. Optimism seemed to radiate from her chart. The dingy office, that had so oppressed her in the "Conundrum" days, now seemed only temporarily inconvenient.

Harriet sprang up from her desk and walked the three or four steps to the window. When she swung back again she passed the new "Meizu" boards and boxes displayed on top of a battered filing cabinet. They seemed to fill their space much more effectively than the old rainbow ones had done.

Musingly, Harriet picked up a board. She turned it, admiring the verisimilitude that Graham and Mr. Jepson had achieved.

"Meizu."

She was thinking of Simon. It had been a bad thing to do, to take his privacy, she was all too aware of that. But she could also defend it as a good thing. As she had told Graham, Peacocks was going to make it. There were enough orders already to put the company healthily into profit. There would be reorders before the game was officially on the market, yet more in the long run-up to Christmas. The first hurdle had been triumphantly cleared. If she could get the balance right now. Not to manufacture too many units that couldn't be sold, not to under-order so that stock couldn't be supplied to the shops rapidly enough to meet demand.

Harriet paced up and down, her fists clenched in her pockets.

She had stolen Simon's story, turning his tragedy into a marketing tool. But she had protected Simon himself. She wasn't proud of what she had done, but she had been practical. "Meizu" was selling, better and faster than she could ever have hoped. Harriet was frowning, but her steps were springy. She felt charged with energy, it radiated out of her and fired everything she touched. The sensation suited her. She was strong. She felt happier and more alive than she had ever felt in her life before.

And so, Harriet thought, perhaps it was time to stop being cautious, and practical, and businesslike. She returned to her desk, forgetting about Simon and about balancing supply and demand. Just for an evening or so, she told herself.

She hadn't seen Robin Landwith for some time. Landwith Associates had advanced the necessary capital for the repackaging and relaunch of "Conundrum," and then had left her to get on with the job. Presumably Jeremy Crichton reported back to them.

Harriet crossed her legs in supple black leather and dialed the Landwith number. She stopped frowning, and smiled wickedly instead.

"Robin? It's Harriet. I think it's my turn to buy you dinner, isn't it?"

"What a good idea." She liked his voice, even on the telephone, she realized. "I'll look in the diary."

Harriet's smile broadened. "I was thinking about this evening, actually, Robin."

He sounded startled. "*This* evening? Well, I don't think . . ." She waited. She could almost hear him thinking. Then, a second later, "But why not? Where would you like to go?"

"I'm taking you, remember?" Harriet answered. She named a place, a French bistro much frequented by journalists and publishers, an old favorite of hers. She was sure that Robin would never have heard of it.

"I'll look forward to it," Robin said.

Harriet replaced the receiver, quite satisfied. To *feel* powerful, she reflected, was to *be* powerful.

Harriet had arranged to meet Liza, first, for a drink. They had made the date a week before, and the wine bar they had settled on was near enough to the French bistro. Harriet called good night to Karen and Graham and was, for once, the first rather than the last to leave Peacocks' offices.

When she stepped out into the mews she looked up at the domes of tall trees just visible over the line of rooftops, and decided that she would walk instead of waiting for a bus. It was a clear, warm evening of the kind she loved, when the summer was still new enough to be fresh and green, and the city was full just of Londoners, good-humoredly *en fête* to celebrate the fine weather.

Harriet passed the tall, crumbling terraces of the immediate neighborhood, where sunshine had drawn shady inhabitants out of curtained rooms to perform more publicly on front steps between peeling stucco pillars, and where pairs of policemen strolled up and down in their shirtsleeves. She plunged across the main road, between shimmering red buses, catching a whiff of warm tar that reminded her sharply of some childhood game in a street not much different from those she had just left. Ahead of her, beyond some railings, was the park. The trees' shade, when she reached it, was welcomingly cool. Harriet took off her zippered jacket and walked on in her white T-shirt, one finger hooking the jacket over her shoulder.

The grass was lush after a wet spring, but there were bare dusty patches under the great trees. Predatory urban squirrels chased through the dust, then shot up tree trunks as smoothly vertical as stucco pillars. They were undisturbed by the joggers who thumped past, stirring hot air in their wake. Harriet smiled and went on at her own pace, her head empty. It was pleasant to be walking without the weight of a briefcase at her side, without the immediate pressure of work to be done. She felt as though she was taking a tiny holiday. The evening in prospect lent a stimulating edge, even meeting Liza. They didn't often see one another alone, away from the upholstery of Sunderland Avenue.

When she reached the opposite side of the park, Harriet saw a group of people gathered near the tall gates at a point where a much narrower path diverged through dense shrubs. When she came closer she saw that they were passers-by, mostly home-going office workers taking a shortcut like herself, standing in a circle around an elderly woman. The woman was crying. She let the tears roll down her face, making no effort to stop them. A policewoman was holding her arm, a policeman was listening to a man in a suit who was describing what he had seen. As Harriet drew level with them, a police car turned in through the park gates, blue light languidly flashing.

A woman had been attacked, mugged perhaps, in the shelter of the thick bushes. Harriet passed by, looking exaggeratedly in a different direction to spare the woman the sense of being stared at. There was nothing else to be done.

The sight of the incident changed her perceptions of the evening; she knew that the woman's wet face would stay in her mind. The green colonnades of the park were as dangerous as the sleepy, tarry streets on the other side. And yet, thought Harriet, it was the very rawness that sharpened her appreciation of the mundane, lovely familiarity of the city.

Out from under the trees, the roar of the traffic clamped around her again. She went on more soberly, her senses sharper, feeling the warmth of the pavements striking up through her thin shoes. She was passing big shops now; from the opulent windows mannequins in summer tableaux stared out over her head.

When Harriet reached the wine bar she saw that tables had spread out onto the pavement. Every chair at the tables was taken, and there was a buzz of talk and laughter from customers pretending that London was a Mediterranean city. Harriet squeezed between the tables, but Liza was nowhere to be seen. She passed through the open doors, and peered into the gloom within. She did see Liza then, sitting on a high stool drawn up to the bar. She was talking to a man and it was a full two seconds before Harriet realized, with a guilty beat, that the man was Leo.

Liza saw her, waved, and when Harriet reached them offered her cheek for Harriet to kiss.

"I bumped into Leo outside the tube."

"Really?"

Liza enjoyed making mild mischief, but Harriet was inclined to believe that it had just been a chance meeting. There was no point in bringing Leo along for a surprise confrontation because no sparks would be struck from it. Their marriage had simply ended, so conclusively that Harriet found it difficult to imagine how it had ever existed. She looked at Leo as he stood up, leaned across to kiss her. Their cheeks brushed, dry and cool. She didn't feel that she knew this particular man any better than the one next to him who was drinking kir royale with a silent blonde, or the Australian barman, or any of the others in the crowded room.

It was chilling to think of the years that they had spent together, years that seemed now to have evaporated without a trace, putting Leo on the same footing as the men in suits and herself with the silent blonde. Strangers, having a drink together. As she studied her husband's face Harriet guessed that it was the same cold sense of waste that gave Leo his baffled, irritable air whenever they met. Her own response was to cling more tenaciously to the idea of her work, and her determination to make a success of Peacocks. That, at least, would not evaporate.

She wanted to put her hand up to touch Leo's face, to say *I know*, but she didn't. She smiled at him and said, "I'm glad you're here."

They found a barstool for her and she perched on it, accepting a glass of wine.

Leo asked, "So how's the entrepreneur?"

The question was mildly sarcastic, in Leo's irritable mode, but Harriet took it straight.

"Busy, but reasonably optimistic."

"When will you make your million?" Liza inquired.

"Probably not until Peacocks goes public." Harriet noticed that Liza was looking a shade older, although no less pretty. The touch of maturity suited her. Liza felt her scrutiny and reached out to touch the soft leather creases of Harriet's trousers, choosing to ignore her half-sister's threat to become rich.

"Aren't you hot in those?"

Harriet laughed. "Just a bit. I didn't look at the sky very carefully this morning."

There was always this same friction between them, inflamed by tiny things too small to be called jealousies or resentments. Sometimes the two of them achieved a truce and Harriet thought, *Now, we're adults, at last.* But then the abrasion came back again. Tonight it seemed stirred up by Leo's presence. Harriet wished he was somewhere else.

"How's Mum?" she asked neutrally.

Liza told her, retelling some tiny snippets of Sunderland Avenue gossip. Then, relieved of the possibility of having to give Harriet's affairs first mention, she added, "Mum thinks it's terrible, what you've done."

"What?"

"Taken Mr. Archer's story like that and made a sales gimmick out of it."

"It's not a gimmick," Harriet said harshly. "It's a story that deserved to be told."

Liza shrugged her shoulders. "That's not what Mum says. She was wondering how he must feel, having his life served up in front of everyone."

"No one knows it's his life. His identity is a secret."

"*He* knows, doesn't he? Mum was so upset about it, she said

she'd have to give you her shares back and resign her directorship. Actually, I said I'd take them off her hands."

Harriet stared at Liza. She hadn't seen Kath for a little while,
the relaunch of "Meizu" had taken all her attention.

"Mum's never mentioned anything to me."

"Well, you know what she's like. Anything rather than have
a fuss, or a scene."

Liza was right in her judgment of that, of course. Harriet
twirled her glass. She must go and see Kath, and explain that she
had only done what had to be done. And she must also make the
journey to see Simon, to put it to him as gently as she could.
She had put the duty off, out of a sense of distaste that she had
later suppressed, and then she had been too busy, and then it
had seemed too late. She consoled herself with the certainty that
Simon would not have heard anything about "Meizu" in any
case, living in isolation as he did.

To Harriet's surprise, Leo defended her. "As a commercial
decision, it makes perfectly good sense."

Liza glanced sharply at him, betraying a kind of complicity.
Harriet wondered what they had talked about on their way from
the station, and sitting over their wine while they waited for her
to arrive.

"I'll go and see Kath," Harriet murmured. "She'll understand, when I've had a chance to talk to her."

Her mother's approval was important, and so was her support. Harriet was dismayed to hear that "Meizu" had upset her.

Liza appeared to have lost interest. "By the way," she said
breezily, "I'm moving out, leaving home at long last. I'm getting
a flat in Blackheath, Ken's given me the deposit."

"That's good," Harriet said, glad of a change of subject. "A
very good thing. It's time you had your independence." It would
do Liza good to have to fend for herself, Harriet thought. "No
more coffee and walnut cake for everyone who calls." Leo laughed,
like the old Leo, with his own recollections of Kath's hospitality.
"How *is* the big love?" Harriet continued.

Liza pushed back her curtain of hair. The man with the
blonde glanced at her, then looked with appreciative interest.
"I'm not seeing him anymore," she said flatly.

Harriet's eyes met Leo's. Just like that, just like us. She felt
pity again for the waste of it, but she knew it was incontrovertible.
There was nothing more, but neither of them had mentioned
divorce. She supposed that would come, in time. She had heard
somewhere, perhaps from Henry Orde, that Leo was now seeing

someone else. She hadn't inquired who it was. For her own part, there had been no time for anything of the kind.

Harriet looked away first. She felt the complicated knots of family business enmeshing the three of them, and then she remembered the taut and enticingly separate thread of her evening with Robin Landwith. The thread drew her with surprising force.

Leo and Liza and Harriet finished their bottle of wine. They talked about the layout of Liza's new flat and her plans for decorating it, and Leo and Harriet agreed that some of their equipment from the old flat could be unpacked and given to Liza, who needed it. Then they talked about some work Leo was doing, and his prospects for the rest of the year.

The wine bar was beginning to empty, and there was space at the tables outside. Harriet glanced at her watch. It was nearly eight o'clock, and time to go to meet Robin.

"Let's have dinner," Leo said. "Where would you like to go?"

Out of the corner of her eye, Harriet saw Liza frown.

Harriet said, "I can't, tonight. I'm meeting someone else for dinner. In fact I should go now, or I'll be late."

They didn't say anything, but both pairs of eyes demanded *who?*

"The man from the venture capitalists. The one who put up the money." That was too explanatory, of course. "Robin," she finished. "I've really got to go." She put down her glass and gathered up her jacket and handbag.

Harriet saw that she had separated herself from them. They were resentful of her business elsewhere, and of her talk of capital. Their small circle had been uncomfortable but she was wrong to remove herself from it.

"Good night." Harriet kissed them both, and extricated herself. Her last glimpse of them, through the windows of the wine bar, revealed them watching the doorway that had swallowed her up.

It was cooler now. Harriet put on her jacket and fastened the zips. She was glad to have escaped the knots of the evening, and she deliberately put the ravel of them behind her. Just for tonight, it was her holiday.

She was walking quickly, almost running. She breathed in the city smells of street dust and engine fumes, mingled with the mold and leafy scent of the park. It was good to be free, she chanted silently, in time with her own footsteps. It was good to be in charge of her own destiny. She had come to it late, but she would make the most of it now.

Thinking of the months since she had separated from Leo, she realized that she had been cold and preoccupied. What she needed now, what she wanted, was some fun, some love, and a rest. Or if not a rest, than a change from the relentlessness of work.

Robin was already at the restaurant when she arrived. He stood up when she reached the table, and she saw pleasure and admiration in his eyes.

She was breathless. "I'm sorry I'm late. I've been having a drink with my sister."

"It was worth waiting for," Robin said simply.

They sat down facing each other, wedged into a cramped space under a Lautrec poster and a framed collage of claret labels. Robin was less formally dressed than usual, not even wearing a tie. He might have been one of Charlie's friends. He looked as at home among the checked tablecloths as in the grand restaurant where they had first eaten dinner together.

Harriet thought she probably underestimated Robin Landwith.

He poured wine, and they touched glasses. Their fingers touched at the same time.

"How is Peacocks?"

Harriet told him. Robin's smile showed his beautiful teeth.

"I thought you'd do it."

"I hoped we would do it."

He put his other hand out to cover hers, on the checked bistro cloth. Harriet's fingers were naked. She had taken off her wedding ring, a long time ago.

Afterward, Harriet didn't remember much about that dinner. They talked a great deal, about themselves and not at all about business, and they laughed almost as much. They were the last diners to leave, when the Gallic waiters grew openly impatient.

The street outside the restaurant was deserted. Harriet looked up to see the stars, just visible through the orangy film of street lighting. She felt a little drunk, but also clearheaded and excited.

Robin put his arm around her waist. "Would you like me to come to your flat," he asked, "or would you rather come home with me?"

Chaotic and cat-redolent Belsize Park or tidily opulent Battersea, Harriet mused.

"Neither," she answered. "I think I'd like to go to a hotel."

"Small and intimate or large and anonymous?"

"The bigger and more impersonal the better."

Harriet loved hotels, all the bathroom paraphernalia of shower gels and shoeshine kits, the impromptu picnics out of mini-fridges, and the sense of a tiny, complete world temporarily created behind a numbered door.

"We'll go to the Hilton, then," Robin said, as if nothing could be more obvious.

Harriet grew suddenly giggly. "We can't go without luggage, can we?"

"I got back from Milan this morning. I have perfectly respectable luggage in the boot of my car."

"You'll have to lend me a shirt and a toothbrush."

"That will be my pleasure."

"Robin, it's way past midnight."

"I don't care what time it is. If you want a hotel, a hotel it shall be."

Harriet let him take charge. She discovered that receptionists and hall porters hurried to do what he asked. She no longer felt that Robin was pompous. It was comfortable to have arrangements made for her, it was charming and flattering to be the subject of this handsome boy's attentions.

Within minutes, it seemed, they were in possession of a room with two huge king-sized beds, a tiled bathroom, a mini-bar stocked with half-bottles of champagne, and a window that promised a view of Hyde Park, a long way below them. The porter who had brought Robin's suitcase bowed his way out. Robin was a confident tipper.

Harriet went to the window and lifted the heavy net drapes. Far beneath she saw the dazzle of red and gold lights of cars negotiating Hyde Park Corner, and facing her across Park Lane the black curtain of the park itself. She looked at the familiar landmarks from this unfamiliar perspective, across to the lights of Knightsbridge Barracks and northwards to Marble Arch.

Robin came up behind her, put his mouth against her bare neck. "Now," he said. "Please." Harriet let the curtain drop.

He unzipped her complicated jacket and the tight leather trousers. Harriet wriggled out of them, and folded them carefully on a chair. She glanced at each label, not knowing whether she was putting off the moment or prolonging the anticipation. Robin watched her while she took off the rest of her clothes. She was surprised to discover that she was shaking. She stood up straight in front of him, spreading her hands in a small gesture.

"I'm not pretty. I wish I was."

He caught her wrist. "Pretty is superficial. You have much more than that."

His face had changed. His eyes were very wide, with anxiety and something like awe in them. He was suddenly young, much younger. Harriet was touched, and also more profoundly excited. She wanted him very much now.

Together, awkward in their haste, they pulled off his clothes. There was no tidy folding now. They clung together for a second, and then Robin pushed her back onto the wide, smooth bed. He kissed her mouth and then her skin, trying to cover every inch of it, as if he wanted to devour her.

"Robin . . ." Harriet tried to whisper. She had thought to establish her liberated, experienced credentials, to take some of the control and to tell him that she preferred to be on top. But, instead, Harriet closed her eyes on the pastel decor and the blank square of the television, and gave herself up.

It had been a long time, months, and she had been dry and diligent. Now, with Robin, she remembered all the intricate pleasures, and beguiling diversions that still led to the same engrossing destination. She let herself be carried deliciously toward it, without trying to touch the polite markers of *now you*, and *do you like this?*

It was a wonderful feeling.

She came quickly, much too quickly. Harriet, who never cried out in lovemaking, put her head back and blindly screamed, without a thought for the sleeping occupants of the other numbered rooms to either side of their private dominion.

Robin was quieter when his turn came. But the spasm went on for a long time, like a boy's. Harriet held him in her arms, and they lay silent. Robin's eyelashes were wet and black.

At last he said softly, "That was wonderful."

She smiled, near to tears. "It was." There was no need to cry, after all.

Harriet listened to the sound of the traffic. It was so muted that it might just have been the sea, or the wind in the trees. After a while, beginning to feel cramped, she moved an inch or two. Although he tried to hold her closer she propped herself on one elbow to look down at him. She saw well-developed shoulders and a flat stomach, a sparse triangle of dark hair spreading over his chest to his belly.

"You look as if you're enjoying one of your private jokes again. Bad timing, I call it."

"I'm not," Harriet defended herself, laughing. It was nice to laugh in bed. "I was just thinking, you're such a perfect specimen." She was teasing him, made confident by the homage he had paid her. She was, she realized, peculiarly happy. "Is there anything you don't excel at?"

Robin pretended to consider. "Let's see. Hmm. Well, I can't sing."

"Oh, in that case . . ." Harriet made as if to scramble out of bed, but he pulled her back and kissed her.

"If you're going anywhere, you might just bring some champagne from the fridge on your way back."

They sat up in bed, drinking the champagne and eating fruit from the bowl provided by the management as if they were ravenous.

"What's the time?"

"Late, late."

"Don't you have work to do tomorrow?"

"Of course I do. So do you, I hope. But it's too early to go to sleep yet, don't you think?"

"Possibly. Or no, not possibly. Definitely. Robin . . ."

This time, Harriet had plenty of opportunity to express and to exercise her preferences. She straddled him and he looked up at her, spreading his arms, young-faced again, so that she rolled over with him and took his face between her hands.

It was very satisfactory.

They fell asleep, at last, knitted together.

In the middle of the night, or perhaps toward the early morning because there was dim gray light showing at the window, Harriet woke up again with Robin's hands on her. She turned to him, reaching out, and he came inside her at once, without words, without preliminaries.

At that hour, even the distant tide of traffic was stilled. Harriet cried out again into the sleeping silence.

"I love you," Robin said. She put her fingers to his mouth.

"No, you don't. We shared something, a little holiday, that was it." She remembered her cool decision to let herself off the leash for one evening. "Anything more wouldn't be businesslike. Would it?"

"Fuck business," Robin said. "This is what matters. I love you."

They slept again.

When it was fully light, Robin drew back the curtains so that they could look at the trees. He ordered breakfast from room service, and went into the bathroom to shower. When he came out, in a white toweling robe with his damp hair standing on end, he looked about fifteen. Then he dressed in a clean shirt and a tie from his suitcase, and turned into the businessman again. Harriet watched him happily from the bed.

When it came, Robin brought the tray of breakfast to her. She sat up, naked in the coil of sheets, drinking coffee and licking drips of honey off her fingers.

"Good?" he asked her.

She told him, "Very good."

He whistled as he poured more coffee. Harriet remembered the words of the middle of the night, and her denial of them. Now, in this morning's intimacy, she thought how conclusively she had forgotten the luxury of being loved. And what would happen if she accepted the luxury all over again, she wondered. Which one of them was vulnerable?

"What are you doing today?" he asked.

"Going to see my mother, first." That was important, after what Liza had told her. "Then back to Peacocks."

"What time shall I pick you up this evening?"

Harriet was startled. "This evening?"

"Of course. I don't want to let you out of my sight for a minute longer than necessary."

The luxury and the liability.

Her choice was either to go home alone, to Belsize Park and the cats and a folder of work, or to be with Robin. In truth there was no choice, she knew which she wanted. To hell with it, Harriet thought. We're both grown up. We can deal with whatever happens when it happens. Luxury lapped around her; she gave herself up to it.

"Seven o'clock."

"Good. And do you crave hotel anonymity?"

Harriet looked around at one smooth bed and one rumpled, crumbs and honey on the tray beside her, Robin's discarded white robe.

"One night is enough to remember."

"The *first* night," he corrected her. He was very confident, as he appeared to be in everything. Except in the secret moments, Harriet remembered. Perhaps she loved him for those. A little bit, just a little bit.

"Perfect specimen," she teased him. He kissed her, and went on his way.

Meditatively, Harriet put her clothes on and traveled against the morning tide from Park Lane to Sunderland Avenue.

*   *   *

"You look well enough," Kath said. She had come to meet Harriet practically at the baby-blue front gates.

"I am well," Harriet said tranquilly. Kath was looking intently at her. "Let's go inside and have some coffee, Mum. I need to talk to you."

Kath bustled about her spotless domain. Harriet waited, looking out of the patio doors at the roses in the summer garden, knowing that her mother wouldn't listen until a tray was properly laid and the right sorts of cake and biscuits laid out for Harriet to refuse with her coffee.

They went out into the garden, Harriet carrying the tray. They sat in deckchairs, in the same places as when Kath had first told Harriet about Simon Archer. *If he had really been my father,* Harriet wondered, *would I have done any of this any differently?* "Meizu" was so close to her heart, and her hopes for it so fierce, that she didn't think it would. Does that make me a good businesswoman, a bad daughter? she wondered. Robin was a good businessman and a good son. To Martin, in any case, the two were synonymous.

"Liza said you were upset about my telling Simon's story."

Kath was flustered, as always, by the threat of a scene. Her fair face turned a dull red, and she looked wildly around for an excuse to head off what might be coming. But both coffee cups were full, the milk jug was covered against the possibility of flies, and the chocolate biscuits were safely in the shade.

"I don't want you to be upset," Harriet prompted.

"I know what he's suffered," Kath said breathlessly. "You shouldn't use that, for making money. You made me feel involved in it too, owning those shares, being on your board of directors. If I am a director, shouldn't I have a say? I'd have said no, Harriet. I don't want to be part of a thing like that."

Harriet felt scolded, a child again. She hated to make Kath angry, hated it more if her mother was unhappy. She left her chair and knelt on the grass in front of Kath.

"I run a company. The decision was mine, and I had to take it. I'll tell you why." Kath listened while Harriet explained. The flush ebbed from her cheeks and throat but her expression was still anxious, the soft lower lip stuck out. Kath wanted to believe what she was told. She was proud of her daughter.

"It can't hurt Simon. I didn't use his name, there's no question of any of the publicity touching him. You could think of it as a generalized tribute even, to all those POWs, to their will to survive."

"As well as your determination to make money out of it, do you mean?"

Harriet flinched. "There isn't any money yet. Only a negative amount, the huge sum I've borrowed from Landwith Associates." The name, absurdly, made Harriet redden in her turn. She went on quickly, "Without the change of direction I didn't even have a hope of paying that back. I didn't have any choice. I had to go ahead and do what I did, or go under. Simon will understand that, when I go to tell him about it."

"When are you going?"

"Um. Not before the weekend." There were press and radio interviews, a chance of TV-AM. "On Monday," she added, deciding. "And when I have made the money, I can do something valuable with some of it, can't I? Which is better than 'Meizu' not having existed at all."

Kath sighed, but her face had brightened. The scene had been negotiated, with no serious damage resulting. She leaned forward to Harriet, putting one hand on her shoulder.

"You're a good girl, Harriet. You always have been, you know."

Harriet was pleased, and touched. "Have I? Keep your shares, and your directorship, won't you? It's important to me." She put her hands over her mother's, feeling Ken's wedding and engagement rings sharp under her palm.

"If that's what you want. If it makes you happy. Are you happy, Harriet?"

"Of course I am." More so than yesterday. Surprisingly so, when she thought of the neutral hotel bedroom and the unneutral scenes the pastel walls had witnessed. Harriet suddenly felt so hungry that she let Kath cut her a piece of chocolate cake, so ensuring further satisfaction for her mother before she had to return to the demands of Peacocks. "Good girl," Kath said. "You look as thin as a stick."

"Is Harriet in yet?"

Monday was one of Graham Chandler's days in the Peacocks office, and he had arrived early. But Karen was there first, opening the morning's mail at the front desk.

"No. She rang yesterday to say that she was driving up to see Simon Archer first thing. She's doing Midlands Radio, and a couple of other things as well."

Graham had a newspaper under his arm, one of the national dailies. He unfolded it now, and put it in front of Karen.

"Will she have seen this, do you think?"

Karen read the paragraphs, where his finger pointed. Then she looked up at Graham. Her eyes were round and horrified. "How can they have done that? They can't, can they?"

"They have," he said. "And I don't suppose this will be all. How can we reach Harriet? Or Mr. Archer himself?"

Karen shook her head. "We can't. Harriet's driving, she'll have left long ago. And there isn't a phone at Mr. Archer's."

Harriet had left home very early. The drive seemed familiar now. As she drove, smiling a little, Harriet thought about the weekend she had just spent with Robin. She also carefully rehearsed how she would explain to Simon the change from "Conundrum" to "Meizu." A replica-board, in its packaging that showed the faded Japanese characters of the original, lay on the back seat of the car.

When she reached Simon's house Harriet saw that the curtains, grown colorless with age, were drawn at all the windows. At once, anxiety tightened in her throat. The house looked worse than blind; it looked dead.

She stumbled out of her car, her legs stiff after the long drive, and ran past the barrier of the overgrown hedge to Simon's front door. Fear made her bang rather than knock, her clenched fist thumping on the blistered paint. There was no response, nothing but silence into which street noise from beyond the hedge seeped as if leaking from a different world.

"Simon!"

Harriet tilted her head back, peering upward, trying to see if there was any movement behind the upstairs curtains. There was nothing there, and even though she pressed her face to the grime-encrusted downstairs glass she couldn't find even a chink in the closed curtains.

"Simon!"

Her knocks brought tiny flakes of paint, like scabs, off the old door, but not a sound from within. She knelt down to the trap-mouth of the iron letterbox, pushed it open and peered through the slit. She had braced herself for the sight of him collapsed in the dingy passage, but she discovered that she could see nothing at all. Some thick, dark material that smelled of dust had been hung over the wire letter-basket inside. He must be afraid, she realized, that eyes would look in at him, just as her own were doing. She let the flap of the letterbox snap shut and, still kneeling on the step, she thumped at the door and shouted, "Simon! It's Harriet. What's happened? Please, open the door. Just let me see that you're all right. *Please, Simon.*"

Nothing. Harriet became aware that she was being watched. She looked back over her shoulder and saw two women staring over the gate.

"He won't open it," one of them pronounced. "All kinds of people have been here knocking, but he won't open up to any of them."

"All kinds of people? What sort of people?"

The woman was offended. "*I* don't know. It's not my business. I keep myself to myself as well."

"Council, are you?" the other one inquired.

"No," Harriet said hastily, "nothing like that. I'm an old friend. I'm worried about him."

"I try to keep a look-out for him," the first one said, lugubriously. "Going down the street for his few bits. But you can't push yourself on people, can you, not if they don't want it?"

"He's in there," her friend announced. "And he was all right first thing."

"How do you know?"

"He's lit his fire, hasn't he?"

Harriet walked back to the gate, and all three of them craned upward. A fine wisp of smoke, so pale as to be little more than a hazy distortion of the blue sky beyond, rose from the chimney.

"A fire, this time of year?" the other woman demanded.

"Old bones, isn't it? Just like ours, Doll."

"Thank you." Harriet cut short their laughter. "Thank you, I'll just stay here and keep on knocking until he does answer."

As soon as the two women had gone she knelt on the step once more and put her mouth to the letterbox. "Simon, it's Harriet. I know you can hear me. I'm sorry. I'm very, very sorry." Because Harriet knew whatever it was, whatever had happened to Simon behind his closed curtains, must in some terrible way be her fault. She had done it to him, and she must find out exactly what it was. "*Please.*" She pressed her palms flat against the solid wood. "Please, won't you let me in?"

At last came the sound she had been waiting for. There was a faint, slow shuffling and the rattle of the doorchain following less identifiable bumping and scraping sounds. Harriet waited, levering herself up from her knees.

At last, the door opened by a grudging crack.

Harriet's instinct was to dash forward and wedge her shoulder into the crack in case it should close up again, but she stopped herself in time. Instead she even stepped back a little.

In a low voice she said, "May I come in? I won't stay for very long."

After another interval she heard the chain being taken off. The door opened wide enough for her to see Simon standing in the passage. Harriet almost cried out.

He looked like an animal, trapped in its lair. He also looked very sick. His face, under a coarse mask of gray stubble, was collapsing inward. His cheeks and eyesockets were pronounced hollows, his filmy eyes stared at her out of pouches of tobacco-colored skin. Harriet was appalled, and she was also frightened. She thought at first that he was beyond recognizing her, but then she saw in his eyes that he did know her and, more than that, that he had been waiting for her.

She made herself say, in her calm voice, "Can I come in, Simon? It's hard for me to talk, out here, with your neighbors going by . . ."

That was enough. He shot a vicious glare at the gate, then beckoned Harriet to follow him inside. Once past the door she saw what had created the bumping and scraping sounds. An old sewing machine on a stand, a broken-down armchair and a long wooden joist had been dragged up against it. Simon had tried to barricade himself, against the invaders.

In the kitchen, the smell was like a wall. Newspaper had been pasted over the windows. Harriet edged around the table, mounded with debris, to Simon's side. "What's wrong?" she asked pointlessly, seeing that everything was wrong. "What's happened? Tell me, and then I can help."

The animal eyes regarded her. There was fear in them, making her ashamed of her own, but also the threat that like an animal's his fear might lead to a wild leap forward.

"What can I do?"

Simon made a lunge with his shoulder. Harriet nearly flinched, but she stood her ground.

"You could put something on the fire." It was the first time he had spoken.

She understood that he was gesturing at the old range at the other end of the kitchen. She had never seen it lit before, but now there was a low, sullen fire burning in it. She went and rummaged in the clutter beside the range, found a yellow plastic sack empty except for some black grit. There was nothing else that looked obviously like fuel. The rationality of the request encouraged her, however.

"The coal's all gone. Is there any more?" There was no answer. "If you're cold, Simon, shall I make you a hot drink?" He looked as if he had a fever. Harriet went to the sink, and tasted sour juice in her own mouth at the sight of what lay in it.

"Don't you have any fresh food? Any milk? Have you been out to buy anything for yourself?"

At once, at the word *out*, Simon lunged forward and slammed the door that connected to the passage. "I won't go out. They're all out there, watching for what they can see, all of them. The job is to keep them out of here. They think they can look in, free and gratis, see what they want, any time they like. Spy on *me*. But I lock them out, don't I, and stop their staring." He went to the small window and ran his hands over the newspaper lining, almost crooning at it, "I did a good job. Kept those staring eyes out." Then he faltered, his head sagging into his shoulders. "Most of them. Some get in. I don't know how. Even upstairs." He frowned, and turned away from the window. In a different voice, as if an uncovered window had opened briefly on to normality, he added, "I only let you in because . . . because, you're Kath Peacock's daughter, aren't you?"

"Yes," Harriet said softly. "That's right. I'm Kath Peacock's daughter. Harriet. After Harriet Vane, do you remember?"

"If you were a boy, you were going to be Peter."

Gently, so as not to startle him, she took Simon's arm and led him to a chair beside the last glow of the fire. She brought up another chair for herself and sank into it, letting silence settle around them while she tried to think what she could do.

Simon had been eccentric before, a recluse with odd ideas even in Kath's day, but he had been sane. Now something had happened to upset what must have been a precarious balance. Harriet thought of the watching eyes that he seemed so afraid of. He had overbalanced into paranoia, into a persecution complex. Harriet grimly rehearsed the superficial, color-magazine labels for depths she knew she didn't understand.

"It's because of you, isn't it?" His eyes were fixed on her.

Harriet took a breath. "I'm afraid it might be, yes. Can you tell me what has happened? So that I can do something about it?"

Simon laughed, and the laughter was more disturbing even than the look in his eyes.

"I've done everything." He pointed at the newspaper over the windows. "Fixed 'em, haven't I?"

"Tell me, Simon."

"The first one came banging at the door, got in here before I could stop him, with his questions. *I was that POW, wasn't I?* What does he know? What do any of you know?" He was shouting, not at Harriet but at observers she couldn't see.

"You don't like questions. He should have known that,"

Harriet soothed him. But Simon turned to look full at her, with sudden plain rationality. "He had a piece of paper of yours, about me and my game. *Lieutenant Archer, isn't it?* That's what he said. Like a spy." Harriet understood what had happened. Some clever journalist had uncovered the tracks.

"What did he write?"

Simon stood up, shuffled unsteadily across the room. He came back with a crumpled, torn newspaper. Harriet took it, noticing that it was a popular local tabloid, wondering which neighbor had brought it for Simon to see.

She found the piece, and read it.

It was titled, *Heroism's Reward?*

From the horror of Shamshuipo emerged spectacular courage, and a game that was literally a game of life. Now, the same game is all set to break every sales record. While the tills ring, the same brave officer sits alone in a comfortless room.

The journalist named the town and the street, where Simon lived, and gave his real name. Harriet put the paper aside. She knew, now, just what she had done. The knowledge felt like an ugly weight lying beneath her heart.

"It's just a newspaper story. A horrible, intrusive story, but they print stories like this every day. It's gone now. It's wrapped the chips, and been forgotten. I'm sorry, Simon. I thought I'd done enough to protect you."

"They follow each other. One comes, and the others follow, like rats, looking for more. They knock on my door and look in through my windows."

So there had been other journalists, after the story. Harriet saw that it was a reflection in dirty water, of her own energetic pursuit of publicity.

"I'll stop them coming."

Simon began to cry. The tears dropped down his face and he made no attempt to rub them away. Harriet remembered the weeping face of the woman who had been attacked in the green avenue of the park. She went to Simon, leaned over his chair, put her arm around his shoulder. Even through the thick clothes he wore, she could feel that his skin was dry and very hot.

"Simon, listen to me. I think you might be ill, perhaps some kind of fever. If I call your doctor will you see him, let him give you some medicine?"

The reaction was as violent as she had feared.

"Is there a neighbor then, someone you trust? To do some shopping for you?"

"I don't want them looking at me, seeing in." He repeated the words mechanically, as if they made a constant chorus within him.

Harriet knelt down so that she could see his face. It was impossible to tell where the dividing line came, between clarity and confusion, and how finely it was drawn. Now that she was close to him, she was as afraid for his physical condition. His arms were bone-thin, and she could hear the rasp of his breathing. And at her back, there was the squalor of the rotting kitchen.

To bring help was essential, but she shrank from the responsibility of bringing more intruders into this precarious sanctuary. It was easy to imagine white coats, brisk professionals, Simon's helplessness at their hands.

I've done enough to him already, Harriet thought.

But she must do something.

Still kneeling, with her back to the room, Harriet saw a sudden clear picture of her mother's kitchen. It was sharp-edged, scoured, scented with pine cleaner and aerosol polish. With the image, the idea came to her of her mother as her own sanctuary, as invincible as she had seemed in early childhood. Harriet longed for Kath, here and now.

With Kath, she could confront the decay within the walls of Simon's house. Between them, they could go out and find the right kind of help for him. With her mother's help, only with Kath, she could try to undo what she had done.

Harriet seized on the idea, like a spar floating in a shipwreck.

Gently, she asked, "Would you like to see Kath? Would you let her come?"

In the following silence Harriet was afraid that he had forgotten Kath, beset as he was by hostile eyes, real or imagined.

But at last Simon murmured, "She's a pretty girl, Kath Peacock. A good girl, too, whatever she thinks herself. I always like to see Kath."

Harriet wondered if he had lost the intervening years, if he was still imagining a soft-faced girl. But she touched his hand and said, "I'll go and telephone Kath. She would like to see you, too. While I'm out I'll buy some more coal, and some groceries. Will you let me in, when I come back? I'll just knock once, very softly."

Simon looked straight at her. His tears had dried. "Just once," he repeated. "Very softly."

From the telephone kiosk at the end of the parade of shops

two streets from Simon's house, Harriet dialed the Peacocks number first. She wasn't sure when she would be back at the office again, Karen would have to hold the fort.

"Peacocks," Karen's warm voice answered after two rings. The thought of the office, piled high with "Meizu" boards and orders and P.R. leaflets, made a vicious contrast with what Harriet had just left. Karen's voice turned anxious at the other end.

"Have you seen today's *Express*?" she asked.

"Read it," Harriet ordered.

It was the same story. Lieutenant Archer, the real-life hero. Life and death, "Meizu" and money. There was a little more, even; a picture of Harriet, a particularly glamorous headshot, and of the new "Meizu" packaging. And another, of Simon's house with the curtains all drawn, just as she had left it five minutes ago.

There had been a photographer, then, pointing his lens eye into Simon's windows.

"The implication is that we're ripping him off, Harriet," Karen said. "We're not, are we?"

"The only people we've ripped off so far are Landwith Associates," Harriet answered grimly. "And they're well able to stand it. If anyone calls about this, Karen, I'm away on business and you've no comment."

"Right. Robin Landwith called, asking for a contact number for you."

"Yes. I'll get back when I can, Karen." Harriet replaced the receiver.

There was nothing else to be done, she told herself. *If "Meizu" was to survive.*

She had got what she wanted. Publicity bred publicity, and she didn't bother to hope that the other papers wouldn't carry their own stories, in their turn. She reflected heavily that it would do "Meizu" itself no harm. She could even hear her own voice, jauntily repeating the truism about all publicity being good publicity over some celebratory drink.

All she could do now was try to shield Simon from good publicity. There was no undoing what had already been done.

Harriet picked up the telephone once again and dialed her mother's number.

Ten

IN THE WARM AIR, the Christmas tree gave out its scent of anticipation and celebration. Harriet stopped to breathe it in, admiring the frosty sparkle of the decorations.

"A designer tree, no less."

The lights were tiny white points, the balls were of translucent glass, and the silvered branches were tipped with white ribbon bows. There was no red and green tinsel, no plastic lantern lights, and no cotton wool blobs of the kind that Kath brought out every year for the tree that stood in the awkward angle of the stairs at Sunderland Avenue. Harriet had ordered the Peacocks Christmas tree by telephone and it had materialized this morning in a van marked "Decorations for All Occasions." Harriet enjoyed finding the right people to do the right job. If she gave a big party, she mused, a really big company celebration, she would have Decorations for All Occasions design a theme for it.

"It's so pretty," Karen said.

Her desk was at the opposite side of the reception area. She sat at a right-angle of pale blonde wood, with a huge Peacocks logo, a stylized fan of feathers, on the wall behind her. At one end of her desk, supplied by the people who had brought the tree, there was a Christmas arrangement of ivy, holly, and Christmas roses. Harriet went to examine it, touching the waxy curls of the holly leaves, and the boss of stamens at the center of the ivory petals that left a sooty print on her fingertips.

"And this, too," Harriet agreed.

"I love Christmas," Karen said. "I tell myself that I'm too grown-up to get excited about it, but every year it still happens."

She had glanced at Harriet before initiating the conversation. Sometimes Harriet was too busy to chat, and when she was she didn't care for the implication that any of the others had time to spare. Karen didn't blame her for that, she knew Harriet drove herself hard, but it made her treat her with more circumspection.

"Anyway, she is the boss," Karen had said to Sara, Harriet's secretary, when they discussed it.

Harriet smiled at Karen now. "I know. Me too." She looked around her, from the strong lines of the feather fan against the pale wall, to Karen's neat workstation beside the switchboard console, and back to the shimmering tree. She sighed. "This place is my Christmas present. I still can't believe we're here."

They had been in the new offices for a month. Harriet was prudent; they were not over-luxurious, but they were newly decorated, and they were in Soho. There was carpet, matching and unstained, throughout, solid doors that fitted tightly so that conversations held behind them were inaudible, and enough space for a full-time staff of eight. Peacocks was still expanding.

"It's been quite a year," Karen breathed. She felt, sometimes, as if she was being washed along on a flood tide. In the sixteen months since its launch, "Meizu" had outsold every game on the market. It had been written about, talked about, been bought and gift-wrapped and accepted until it seemed that every household in the country must possess one. "Meizu" had been launched in America, and this Christmas it was being sold under license in thirteen other countries.

To do it, Karen reflected, Harriet had turned herself into a selling machine. There had been a time, the summer before, when it seemed there was nothing she would refuse to do for publicity's sake, so long as the attention focused on her and on no one else. *Meizu Girl*, the tabloids had called her.

Karen looked quickly at the switchboard. Two lines were busy, Graham Chandler was still talking to a printing company in Italy. No one was waiting, that was all right. It wouldn't do to let a caller hold on for more than two rings with Harriet standing right beside her. Even if it did look as though the festive spirit had mellowed her.

"Quite a year," Harriet echoed. "But just you wait for the next one. Karen, we've only just begun."

I could do with my Christmas holiday first, Karen thought. *I need a rest.* "What are you doing for Christmas?" she asked Harriet.

"A bit of time with my parents; seeing some friends, if they still remember who I am. What about you?"

"The same." They smiled at each other, acknowledging the irrationality of feeling excited at such a prospect. But the scent of the Christmas tree, the garland of ivy and holly, had worked on both of them. Harriet took a last look at the white and silver sparkle of the tree, picked up the afternoon's mail that Karen had put out for her, and carried it, with less enthusiasm than usual, into her own office.

The room was still bare; there had been no time yet to collect pictures or personal ornaments. The only decorations against the pale walls were "Meizu" boxes. This Christmas, to sell alongside the original version that had been last year's runaway success, Harriet had introduced a new design. The board was black, with white wishbones, the balls and counters and packaging were in bright primary colors.

Harriet smiled at the sight of the rainbow boxes. They were almost identical to the original "Conundrum" ones. It was a satisfying vindication of her original concept that this year the rainbow version was outselling the Shamshuipo board.

Shamshuipo.

Harriet's expression changed. She sat down at her desk and began to work her way through the mail. It was mostly Christmas cards from suppliers and wholesalers. She arranged the bright rectangles on top of a cabinet, then looked to see what she must do next. Work was the easiest thing to do. She opened a folder and immersed herself in the proposal of a game inventor who wanted Peacocks to develop and launch his idea.

The afternoon passed like most afternoons, between telephone calls and talk with Graham, now full-time production director, and Fiona who was now in charge of promotion. Harriet was used to being too busy to think beyond the world of Peacocks.

She was surprised, as she always was, when Sara put her head around the door to say good night.

"Is that the time?"

"It is. And I must go, Harriet, I've got a date."

"Enjoy yourself," Harriet said. She made her own more leisurely preparations to leave for the night, taking an armful of work off her desk and packing it into her briefcase, reading a final set of figures, then checking the open diary on her desk for tomorrow's appointments. *Lunch, Jane, 1:15*, she read, frowning a little. It would have to be a quick one. She had a meeting with the game inventor at three.

In the reception area she admired the tree once more, then turned off the last of the lights. She felt a little reluctant to leave, and smiled at herself. There was nothing wrong with that. It was good, to feel this symbiotic closeness with her business. Both of them would continue to thrive on it. Harriet swung her heavy bag, and locked the doors behind her.

She drove northwards, up Wardour Street and across under the suspended stars of the Oxford Street decorations. In the no-man's-land to the north the darker streets were inscrutable after light-washed Soho in its Christmas mode, but Harriet negotiated the route with confidence, letting her mind run comfortably over the day. It had been a good one. She was pleased with the new game idea, and was certain that she could sell it. *That's what I'm after*, the owner had told her, *your marketing skills. I hear you can do it better than anybody.* Harriet braced her arms, swung the wheel and took a right turn into the mainstream of homebound traffic. That was how Peacocks must develop, she was thinking. To work with game designers, developing ideas, manufacturing and selling.

There would never be another "Meizu," it would never work quite like that again. In her new car, a faster model than she really needed but an indulgence that she justified because she loved driving, Harriet swept on up the hill toward home. She passed the turning that would have taken her to the old Belsize Park flat because she had graduated, now, to the top of the hill and Hampstead. The cats had been restored to the care of their proper owner, without regret on either side, and Harriet had bought a flat of her own.

It was hewn, or carved, as her estate agent insisted on expressing it, from what had once been a huge family house in a quiet side street. Harriet owned the ground and garden floors. There were only three proper rooms, but they were vast and high-ceilinged, with intricate cornices and marble fireplaces and tall, solid, paneled doors. After the boxy conversion that had been her married home with Leo, and the cramped confines of her rented flat, her new home felt like a palace. Harriet loved it, for its space that was all hers, with secret, almost guilty triumph. The asking price had seemed enormous. But Jeremy Crichton had advised her that it was a sensible investment, and Robin had agreed with him.

"Live somewhere decent," he had urged her from the comfort of his own well-organized house. "If you won't come and live with me, that is. Won't you?"

It was an invitation that he repeated, nowadays, almost as often as he saw her.

Harriet shook her head. "I'll buy the Hampstead place," she said gently.

She had felt reluctant to leave her elegant offices, but now when she reached home she felt an equal pleasure in arrival. She ran up the wide steps, unlocked the front door and scooped up the mail that was waiting for her. It was mostly Christmas cards, a thinner sheaf than the one at Peacocks.

Harriet unlocked the second door, that led her into her own flat. She switched on the lights and felt a beat of simple, straightforward pleasure. Here was warmth, light and space, all her own. She moved slowly through the small, enjoyable rituals of being at home. She kicked off her shoes and left them by the door. Feeling polished parquet warm and slippery under her feet she padded through into her kitchen, admiring pools of light and the watery shine of marble surfaces. She opened the fridge (packed with all the latest German appliances, the estate agent had crooned about the kitchen), took out a bottle of white wine, poured herself a drink. Nursing the glass she stood for a moment at the huge window, looking down into the black expanse of her own garden, before lowering the white blinds. Downstairs, her bedroom opened on to the same view from a more immediate angle. There was a bathroom, with black and white tiles and a huge old-fashioned tub, not unlike Robin's.

Harriet sighed with satisfaction. Sometimes she could map the sequence of achievements that had earned her all this with unsurprised logic but at other times, like now, it seemed too good to be true, as if she had won a lottery, or would wake up in a moment to find herself sitting stiffly at the rented table down the hill, her business plan in front of her and the cats hungrily crying around her ankles.

Harriet hesitated, enjoying the moment. She was aware, through her preoccupations, that she didn't always allow herself time to savor having come this far.

I'm here, she told herself, *this is what I believed in, wasn't it?* And as always, she heard the antiphonal response, *At whose expense . . . ?*

Perhaps, she thought, not to permit the reflection at all was best, and just to go on, making more progress, as she seemed designed to do.

She went through double doors into her sitting room, carrying her weighty bag like a shield, sat down and spread some work on the cushions beside her. She would work now, and if she felt hungrier later she would cook herself some food. She could recapture the pleasure she had felt in reaching her beautiful flat, of course she could.

Harriet worked for two hours, forgetting everything else. It was nine-thirty when she closed what she thought was the last folder, planning to go into the kitchen to make herself a sandwich, and then watch the ten o'clock news.

But at the bottom of the pile there was another folder, blue, without a label on the front. Harriet flipped open the cover and looked down at a neat catalog of press cuttings. She remembered now, Sara had been looking for something in the cuttings file.

She had put the folder back on Harriet's desk instead of replacing it in the file cabinet, and Harriet had swept it up with the rest of her work.

There was the story, and although she knew each one she still turned the plastic-cased pages, her eyes running over the columns of newsprint with their accompanying semi-opaque windows of photographs. Her own blurred face looked up at her, smiling too much, and the cracked packing case, and the blank eyes of Simon's house. There was a little series of the last, all from eighteen months ago, the time when "Meizu" had been appearing in every shop in startling pyramids, the time when Simon had been taken away to hospital.

Harriet had telephoned Kath from the public phone box two streets away from Simon's house. Her voice had been sharp with anxiety.

"Please come. He's ill, and confused, and he won't have the doctor or anyone to help him, except you. He thinks people are spying on him."

"Are they?"

"Some reporters came, about the game."

"Oh, Harriet," Kath had whispered. "What have you done?"

Kath came, driving Ken's car that looked too big for her. Harriet was looking out for her, watching through a narrow slit in the front curtains. She saw her mother climb out of the big car, stiff with driving, and look up and down the old street. There was no visible connection with the fair-haired girl whose bicycle had collided with the lamp-post. Harriet ran to open the door to her. She had to resist the urge to throw herself into her mother's arms in relief.

"Thank you for coming," she mumbled, childishly. "I couldn't think what to do, here on my own."

Kath's face was clouded. "Where is he?"

Harriet led the way back into the kitchen.

Simon was still sitting in his chair. Gray light came through the newspaper-pasted windows, the fire in the old range had a low red heart in a hummock of gray ashes. Kath didn't glance at the shambles of the room. She crossed straight to Simon's side and put her hand lightly on his arm.

"Simon. It's Kath." When there was no answer she repeated, "It's Kath. Look at me, Simon."

Obediently he looked up into Kath's face. Watching, Harriet saw blankness dissipate. She saw recognition in his eyes, startled recognition, and following it an expression of exhaustion, and infinite sadness. In the confusion of his dislocated world Simon must have been looking for the sweet, fresh, unbruised eighteen-year-old that Harriet had glimpsed just once. Kath had faded hair and a lined face, and a body rounded into a cylinder.

"Getting old, aren't we?" Kath said simply.

"I'm always glad to see you, Kath," Simon said. "Nobody else."

Harriet bent her head, accepting the rebuke in silence.

"You haven't been looking after yourself, Simon. And you've got a fever. Will you let me call the doctor, just to take a look at you and give you some medicine?"

Simon caught at Kath's wrist. Harriet could feel the tightness of the grasp at her own flesh.

"Only you, Kath. None of them out there. They stare in at me, as if they want to eat me."

Harriet could still remember the look that Kath had given her then. Accustomed to her mother's love and support and admiration, it made her want to run away and hide herself.

"You'll have to listen to me then, and do what I tell you," Kath said briskly.

Simon nodded his head, submissive.

Between them, they maneuvered him upstairs to his bedroom. They found clean linen for him, and made him comfortable in his bed with pillows and hot-water bottles. Simon's eyes stayed fixed on Kath as she moved around him. She went to the window and looped back the curtains, saying, "The sun's shining out there. It would be nice to let it in, wouldn't it?"

He shrank into the bedclothes, and Harriet saw the fear and bewilderment in him. She would have done anything to lessen it; the knowledge that there was nothing she could do flicked her like a whip.

"All right, then," Kath said quietly. "We'll leave the curtains as they are." She sat down on the edge of the bed. Very tentatively, as if trying to work out if she was really there, Simon touched her hand.

Harriet left them. She almost fell down the stairs in her hurry. In the kitchen she rolled up her sleeves, put water on to boil, and took the bucket and mop that she had used on her first visit from the tangle of rubbish in the cupboard under the stairs. She began to clear up, working quickly, breathing through her mouth to keep the cocktail of sour smells at bay. She was thinking about the first visit; she had washed up and cleared the table then. That Simon had still possessed the strength to be frightening. Now her fear was for him.

If she had it in her power to go back to that first time,

Harriet challenged herself, would she hand "Meizu" back to him, to be obscured once more among the heaps of junk deposited in the room next door?

She knew, even before she had finished asking herself the question, that she would not. If she could do anything differently, it would be to change the story enough to protect Simon's identity, so that no zealous journalist could ever find him. And in reality, she couldn't even do that much for him.

Harriet hated the feeling of powerlessness that the awareness gave her. She worked with grim energy, washing and scouring.

At length, Kath came downstairs. "He's asleep," she said. The two women faced each other. Harriet knew that her mother was hoping for her explanation, justification. She sensed again Kath's pride in her, her own need for her mother's approval.

"I should have been much more careful," she said at last. " 'Meizu' need never have touched Simon, nothing should have connected it to him. It's my fault that people came here, prying into his life."

"You need never have used his story at all. You could have sold your game some other way."

Harriet said quietly, "I didn't think I could. Even now, I still don't."

There was a silence. When Kath spoke again, it was with the implication that there was no more to be said. "He'll need a doctor, whatever we do for him. Probably a hospital. They won't want to leave him here, and we can't stay indefinitely, can we?"

Harriet imagined the intrusion of *them*, what it would mean for Simon. "Let me finish what I can here. If I make it look cleaner, get in food and coal and whatever else he needs, perhaps the doctor will let him stay at home. A nurse and a home help could come in, would Simon accept that? There's plenty of money, we could get a private nurse for him. Peacocks owes him money, from the sales of 'Meizu,' we sent him checks but he never banked them. I opened an account in his name, the money's all there, whatever he needs it for . . ."

Harriet heard herself talking very quickly. Listening to it, she knew that money made no amends.

"I'm sure that'll be a help, love," Kath said without conviction. "Let's do what we can for him first, then, shall we?"

Kath and Harriet stayed for twenty-four hours. Kath slept the night in the dusty back bedroom that Harriet had once used, and Harriet took a room in a nearby bed and breakfast. The proprietor, in a scarf over blonde ringlets puffed up in readiness for some celebration, recognized Harriet from a magazine article about "Meizu." Back issues of the magazine were stacked up on a stool in her sanctum at the back of the house. She invited Harriet in and made her wait while she shuffled through the copies, found the article, and presented it to Harriet for her autograph. She was curious about what Harriet was doing, and Harriet answered evasively that she was visiting friends nearby. Harriet was afraid that the woman might have seen the piece about Simon in the local paper, but she appeared not to have done. She paid her bill for the night before going up to her room, and left very early in the morning to start work again at Simon's house.

Between them, Kath and Harriet made the house as clean and cared-for looking as they could manage. While they worked Simon slept behind his closed curtains. He accepted some of the hot drinks they carried up to him, but he ate almost nothing.

A doctor was found who would agree to visit. He came on the second evening. Kath led him upstairs, and Harriet waited in the kitchen. Kath's prediction was correct. The doctor, a young man with a prematurely furrowed face, insisted that Simon must be admitted to the hospital. He was suffering from bronchial pneumonia, dehydration, and probably malnutrition.

"There is also some mental confusion," the doctor added. He was obviously overworked, but sympathetic enough. Kath and Harriet waited. "That can be assessed while they are treating him. You're doing the right thing for him," he added, in encouragement.

Kath went upstairs again, to pack a bag for Simon. Harriet walked to the nearest chemist's shop and bought a new tooth-brush, soap and face flannel and disposable razors, packing her purchases into a zippered sponge bag patterned with bright bands of color. The toilet items looked too new, and too cheap at the same time, as if Simon was a long-standing inmate or pris-oner, who was now being hastily discharged for reasons of convenience.

Harriet put the package under her arm and walked slowly back through the hazy streets, overtaken by children on BMXs, passing pairs of teenage girls who wandered with their heads close together.

Kath was sitting on Simon's bed; his fingers rested against her arm. Harriet waited with them until they heard the sound of the ambulance stopping in the street below. Simon's eyes flickered.

"I don't want to go with them," he said.

Kath leaned forward. "You must go, to get better. Then you

can come home again. It won't be long, Simon. I promise it won't."

Suddenly, to Harriet's surprise, he smiled. "You're a good girl, Kath. I remember."

Kath recalled his hand, on the curve of her waist, when her waist had been narrow and supple. "I remember," she told him.

The ambulance men came up the stairs in their blue shirtsleeves. They helped Simon down the stairs again, into a waiting wheel-chair, wrapped a red blanket around his knees. One of them pushed him out of his front door and past the overgrown hedge-barrier. A small group of neighbors stood watching on the oppo-site pavement, and three small boys—one of them might have been the roller-skater who had warned Harriet of Simon's ferocity—peered curiously into the ambulance's interior. Simon saw them all. There were no curtains or newspapers to screen the eyes. He bent his head, and put up one arm to shield his face.

The ambulance man wheeled the chair briskly up the wait-ing ramp, locked the chair in position inside, and came forward to close the doors. His colleague went around to the driver's door. Harriet and Kath stood side by side, looking up. They had encouraging smiles, and Kath lifted her hand in a wave.

"He'll be having a good time," the ambulance man said, coming forward. "Isn't that right?" Simon made no movement. The doors closed, shutting him inside with the sympathetic, staring eyes, and the big white ambulance rolled away.

Harriet and Kath went slowly back to the house and locked it up. They came out once more without looking back, and stood between their two parked cars.

"I'll ring the hospital every day," Harriet said. "And I'll get up to visit him as soon as I can." He would rather see Kath, she was sure of that, but Kath had Ken and Sunderland Avenue, and Ken didn't like his wife to be away from where she belonged. There didn't seem to be anything else to say. The two women kissed each other, and climbed into their separate cars.

Harriet tried to keep her mother in sight as she drove, but she lost her almost immediately in the tangle of traffic that blocked the heart of her old home town.

In her own home, Harriet turned the stiff plastic sheets of the cuttings file. She knew the next batch as if she had written them herself—it had been harder work, earning these ephemeral para-graphs, than almost anything else she had ever done. She read the headlines. *Life and Death Game. Into the Labyrinth. It's a Gamble. "Conundrum" by Any Other Name.* These were the write-ups she had wanted, focusing on the game itself, her own gamble in deciding to publish it, the decision to change its name. She had done everything she could think of to generate publicity, re-creating her Oxford Street bus rides with a photographer, turning a city chess garden into "Meizu Maze" for a day, challenging mathematicians and sports personalities and soap actors to find a "Meizu Master."

She would do anything to get "Meizu" talked about, or herself talked about, so long as it meant at the same time that Simon was forgotten. In the end, her determination to make a story in itself became a story, and "Meizu Girl" was born. And to become "Meizu Girl," Harriet developed a secondary self, an extrovert, bright-smiling and quick-talking pseudo-Harriet who wasn't quite real, was too thick-skinned and determined to be real, but who at the same time provided an outlet for many of the energies that had warred uncomfortably in the primary Harriet.

The second Harriet became the best friend of gossip reporters and feature writers. The coverage developed from little snippets puffing "Meizu" to longer profiles of Harriet as a new-wave businesswoman, as a hard-edged success story, as a career girl who put her work before her private life.

For the sake of Peacocks, Harriet talked about the failure of her marriage to a sympathetic girl from one of the women's magazines. The story had appeared under the heading, "Why My Business Meant More Than My Marriage." Leo had complained, coldly, that she made him sound like a bad bottom line, to be obliterated at all costs.

"You know I didn't mean that," the real Harriet had answered.

There had been other pieces, on the theme that there was no one special in Harriet's life now because Peacocks came first. "I like to be taken out to dinner, yes, I love to go to the opera with someone special," she was quoted as saying, "but being in love takes time, and I don't have much of that to spare."

"Is that true?" Robin asked her one night, when they lay in the dark. "I was being discreet," Harriet answered, which they both knew was no answer to the question.

Harriet's theory had been that all publicity was good publicity, all publicity that did not touch upon Simon. And she believed, as she turned the plastic-covered sheets, that she had been right. "Meizu" and Peacocks and Harriet herself had become the focus of press attention, and interest in Simon had correspondingly dwindled away. There was no mileage in pictures of an empty house, and the Real Officer story in any case led nowhere once it had been told, whereas Harriet was available, visible and endlessly inventive.

Simon had spent a few weeks in hospital and had returned home to find his privacy restored. Harriet and Kath had visited him, separately, more than once. He was quiet, newly passive, but seemingly well again. He appeared able to look after himself as he always had done. He showed no interest in the Peacocks money that was accumulating for him when Harriet tried to persuade him to make use of it.

And in the past twelve months Peacocks had experienced a growth rate of almost four hundred percent. The company had acquired new offices, a distribution manager, a customer services manager, and would soon be needing a sales manager to take on some of Harriet's workload.

Martin and Robin Landwith were pleased with the progress of their investment.

Meditatively Harriet closed the blue folder, and slipped it with the others into her briefcase.

When the telephone rang on the table beside Harriet she answered and found that it was Robin, as if he had known that she was thinking of him.

"What are you doing?" he asked.

Harriet smiled. "Looking at the feasibility of 'Travel Meizu' in a blister pack, thinking about point-of-sale for an extra fast sell-through. I've been doing more or less that since I came in, and now I'm going to stop." That was close enough to the truth. She wouldn't tell him that she had submitted herself to trial by press-cutting, and found herself guilty.

"And what now?"

"Bed, I think."

There was a small silence, then Robin said, "Shall I drive over and join you?"

It was an unusual request. By an unspoken agreement that had seemed to suit them both, Robin and Harriet spent one or two weekday evenings together, at the theater or the opera or simply over dinner. Sometimes they went to parties or night-clubs, usually at the invitation of one of Robin's friends or business associates, but Harriet preferred the earlier nights because she needed to be able to think clearly in the mornings. At the weekends they spent all or a part of their time together, depending on their separate commitments. Robin was often abroad, and lately Harriet had been traveling, too.

After their evenings out they returned either to Robin's

house or to Harriet's new flat. It still surprised Harriet how much she enjoyed going to bed with Robin Landwith. Sometimes when she thought unguardedly about it, of how he had last touched her and what he had said, it made her inner muscles contract and a small hiccup of breath catch in her throat.

It happened now, as she thought, twenty minutes from Battersea to here . . .

But yet, to succumb to that need would be to put herself at risk of other needs, her own and Robin's. They had made clear definitions, she thought, and they worked well. It was responsibility and dependency that she had been afraid of in the beginning, and if the definitions between them were changed, what might happen then?

So it was against her immediate inclination that she answered, "Well, no. Perhaps not tonight, Robin. I've got a serious day tomorrow." And at once she thought, what *are* you afraid of? Robin isn't dependent, nor do I need to feel responsible for him. It's my own weakness, the fear that I might give way and admit to needing him . . .

"That's a pity," Robin said. His voice sounded husky, almost blurred. Harriet wondered for a moment if he might be drunk, before realizing that what she could hear was tenderness. It reminded her of the beginning.

"Shall we have lunch tomorrow?" he asked now.

Harriet bit the corner of her mouth. "I'd like to, but I can't. I'm having lunch with Jane and I've put her off once already."

At the end of the line she heard Robin laugh. It was a low, warm laugh that made her remember again what it was like to have him lie beside her, to feel his hand move over the slope of her thigh to the folds between her legs. Harriet stood up abruptly, carrying the telephone with her. She walked over to the gilt-framed mirror above the mantelpiece and stared with hostility at her own reflection.

"In that case," Robin said, "I shall have to do this by telephone. It isn't how I imagined it, but I shall have to make do. You must take the appropriate posture as adopted, even though I might be standing on me head for all you know."

"Robin, what are you talking about? *Are* you a bit drunk?"

"No, darling. Never more sober. Harriet, will you marry me?"

She saw the shock leap in the eyes of her reflection. She saw something else, too, a light and warmth in her face that made her look pretty, rubbing away the preoccupied lines at the corners of her mouth. Her fingers felt damp. Harriet found that she was exactly half-way between laughing and crying.

"I'm married already," she whispered.

"That is not a serious obstacle, as you must know."

Harriet wished that she had said yes, drive over here tonight, come now. It would have been easier to say this to him directly, rather than to this touching disembodied voice.

"No, I won't. Robin, are you there?" She had said it too abruptly, she couldn't call back the words. "I can't, rather. I feel as if Peacocks has taken everything, for now. I haven't got enough, what is it, *essence* left over to marry with. I'm very happy being with you, Robin. I love what we do, everything we do together. I can't get married again. Are you still there?"

"I'm still here. I think I'll get up off my knees."

"Were you really kneeling down?"

"You'll never know, now, will you?"

"Damn." Harriet was crying, now. She saw a pair of oily tears swell at the corners of her eyes and roll, gathering momentum down the sides of her nose.

"I love you, Harriet."

She listened to the silence, hearing him breathe, twenty minutes away from her by white Porsche. She wiped the tears away with her free hand, wanting to sniff, wanting to cry some more.

"*Say it*," he commanded.

"I love you too." It was half of a truth, enough of a truth to suffice, like many of the truths she dealt in nowadays.

Softly Robin said, "That's good. Enjoy your lunch. See you on Friday," and he hung up.

Harriet dropped the telephone back into place, walked slowly down the stairs to her big, luxurious bathroom, stripped off her clothes and stood in the hot shower where it didn't matter that the tears were running down her face. She cried without fully understanding why she needed to cry, and when it was over she dried herself and put cream on her swollen cheeks. She went to bed, telling herself to be happy, and eventually fell asleep.

Jane had arrived first. She was sitting at a corner table in the restaurant with the *Guardian*'s education section folded in front of her. She looked up as Harriet came between the tables toward her.

"I'm always late," Harriet said. "I'm sorry."

"It doesn't matter. You look good, Harriet." She did, too, Jane thought. It was nothing definable, except that Harriet seemed to have acquired presence. Two or three people at the nearest tables turned to glance at her as if they half-recognized her. *Meizu Girl,* Jane remembered. The nonsense of the title made her smile with her lips together. Harriet saw her expression and tugged apologetically at the peplum of her scarlet jacket, thinking Jane must be meaning her clothes. Jane was wearing one of her standard outfits, a shade less war-zone than usual because it was the school holidays. The two of them made an odd contrast.

Harriet explained, "I've got a day of meetings. This is my bid to look significant."

"It's very successful."

Harriet sat down quickly. "What shall we eat?"

The restaurant was busy, noisy with office Christmas lunch-parties that were already growing boisterous. Harriet started to worry about her three o'clock meeting.

"I'm just going to have mozzarella salad," she said, not looking at the menu.

"I'm hungry. I'm going to have linguine."

When they had ordered they leaned back, looking at each other. It was more than two weeks since they had last met; Harriet found herself trying to remember what news they had exchanged then. Jane had been producing the school's Christmas show, Harriet had listened to her descriptions of backstage dramas, and had talked in her turn about Christmas sales peaks and the relaunch of the rainbow version. "Remember the night before the Toy Fair?" Jane said, and they both laughed at the memory.

Even so, when they kissed good-bye at the end of the evening Harriet came away with the feeling that they hadn't talked about anything much. Covertly, now, she looked at her watch. There was no time for anything in what was left of this lunch hour.

"It's been a long time." Jane spoke Harriet's thoughts. "What's been happening?"

Last night the venture capitalist you all disapprove of asked me to marry him. Harriet knew she wouldn't mention it, and the realization made her aware that a space had opened between Jane and herself. Nor had Jane talked much, lately, about her own love affairs, or lack of them. Harriet told herself that next time they met, the very next time, whenever it was, she would make sure they had a proper talk.

"Just work. We're looking at a travel 'Meizu,' for next year. And looking at the possibility of publishing some new games. Two ideas look quite promising, I'm meeting the designer this afternoon."

Jane nodded.

"What about you?"

Jane considered for a moment, as if about to say something, but their plates of food arrived between them, and once the waiter had left them alone again she only said, "Just work, like you. Are we getting old and dull? I had dinner at Jenny and Charlie's." She told Harriet who the other guests had been; they were old friends from the Crete days. Harriet wondered why she had not been invited, too, and then remembered that in any case she had been in Germany that night.

"How are they?"

"Good. Harry's walking."

"Already? How long is it since that day we went to see him?"

Jenny's second son was more than a year old. Harriet and Jane had gone to the hospital together, to a different ward that was still almost identical to the one they had looked fearfully into before finding Jenny shut away on her own. This time Jenny had been ensconced in the center of the row of beds, with the hospital crib beside her and Harry asleep in it. Exhaustion and relief had stripped her face bare, so that every flicker of feeling showed in it.

"I can't believe it," she had whispered to them. "I still think, I'm still afraid that he'll die. But he's perfect, isn't he? Look at him, he's perfect. He weighs eight and a half pounds."

Jane had leaned over the crib to touch the warm, peach-skinned, naked head.

Harriet smiled at the memory. Jane's head was bent over her plate, although she wasn't eating.

"How is Jenny?" Harriet asked. Jenny was pregnant for the third time. Charlie could even joke about her fecundity now.

"She's okay. Like a ripe fruit."

Harriet's anxiety about the time and the afternoon ahead of her conflicted with concern for Jane. Guiltily aware of her hope that whatever it was wouldn't take too long.

Harriet asked as gently as she could, "What's the matter?"

"Oh. Not much, really. School gets me down. It's seemed more of a pointless struggle against apathy and underfunding than ever, just lately."

Harriet sighed. "Get a job in a better school."

Jane tapped the newspaper beside her. "I'm looking. But it's all complicated by wanting a baby, isn't it?"

Harriet studied Jane's face. It had darkened, and there were sucked-in hollows at the corners of her mouth.

"Is it? Do you want a baby now?"

"The clock's ticking."

"You're only thirty-two."

Jane leaned forward. "Harriet, I'm desperate for a baby. All the powers of reasoning ask *why*, and I can't answer. I just am. I pick Jenny's baby up, I look in every pram, and I feel it like a pain. Don't you?"

Wonderingly, Harriet shook her head. "No. Never like that. Not with Leo, and not since. But if you do, why don't you just go ahead and have one?"

"On my own? Just get inseminated by whoever's to hand, you mean? I'd rather have a baby with a father to its name." She paused, twisting the strands of pasta on her plate, and then put her fork down. "There was somebody."

"You never told me."

"No. Well, it never came to anything, much."

In the past, Harriet would have extracted the story and then commiserated or consoled. Now she just stared miserably, aware of constraints that had never existed before.

Jane ignored the silence. "If I did decide to do it by myself, there are the practical considerations, aren't there? I'd have to go on working, so I'd have to find someone to look after it. I'd have to move house, I wouldn't want to bring up a child in my neighborhood."

Harriet thought of the streets, either threateningly teeming with life, or ominously deserted. She felt a twinge of irritation, like the beginning of toothache, and resisted the need to look at her watch. "So look for another house. There are plenty of houses."

Jane's head jerked up. Her throat and cheeks began to flush dark red. "Have you seen what's happened to property prices?"

"Yes, I've just bought somewhere, remember? It isn't like you to be so defeated."

"Perhaps I'm just tired of the struggle. Whereas you're such a go-getter, aren't you?" Jane was angry. "It's all right for you, Harriet."

Harriet was silenced by her bitterness. She could have demanded, *Why is it all right for me? What's the difference between you and me?* She supposed that Jane meant money. Yet the truth was that she had very little money because she took almost nothing out of the business. Her car and today's clothes were necessary expenses, and her beautiful flat had only been bought on Jeremy Crichton's recommendation. Yet because Peacocks was successful, she could imagine how Jane thought she was rich and therefore different.

"I'm sorry," she said at length, because she felt she had to. The color in Jane's face began to fade. They looked at each other, and found the grace to laugh. Jane reached out and put her hand over Harriet's.

"I think I'm going a little bit mad. It must be the thwarted maternal hormones."

"What will you really do?"

Jane shrugged, flicking her plait of hair back over her shoulder. "Probably go on just as I am. Let's have some coffee, shall we?"

They tried to talk about other things while they drank it.

"Are you coming to my party?"

By tradition, Jane gave a lunch party on the day after Boxing Day.

"Of course I am."

Harriet had not decided yet whether or not she would ask Robin to come with her.

It was half past two. The office parties were settling in for the afternoon; Harriet couldn't pretend any longer that she was not in a hurry. She called for the bill and paid it, insisting rather too forcefully, and they hustled out onto the cold pavement. They exchanged kisses again and Jane went on her way.

"Happy Christmas," Harriet called after her.

She turned and walked in the opposite direction, back toward Peacocks, hoping that the wintry air would clear the fumes out of her head. It had not been a particularly reassuring lunch. After Christmas, she decided, she would ask everyone to come to Hampstead for supper, Jane and Jenny and Charlie and the others, and they would have one of the old evenings, and then she would be sure that everything was as it always had been. Then she reached the office, and having made the plan she forgot about it.

Robin opened the bedroom curtains and looked out onto Harriet's garden. The flowerbeds were covered by a thick layer of dead leaves, and the margins of each leaf carried a thin beard of frost. The sky was clear, colorless. It was Saturday and Christmas Eve. Turning back into the room he saw that Harriet was still asleep, her long, thin shape curled into a round hump under the covers. They had been out late last night.

The party had been given by an old friend of Robin's, a girl

he had known since they were both small children. He had gone
to his first birthday parties with Rosalie Fellowes, and he had still
been her partner for her "coming out" dance held at her grandfather's house in Gloucestershire. Even though they had known
each other for such a long time, Robin had never actually made
love to Rosalie. At one weekend party, when he was seventeen,
he had progressed as far as removing her white lace pants in an
orchard as the sun came up. It had seemed incestuous to attempt
to advance beyond that, and they had eventually made their way
companionably back to the end of the party, his arm around
Rosalie's waist and her head resting on his shoulder.

   Now, Rosalie had been married for over a year to the elder
son of a banking dynasty. They lived in an impressive house on
the river at Chiswick and last night's party had been their Christmas celebration. There had been perhaps two hundred people at
the party, at least half of them known to Robin from school, or
from Oxford, or from the City. There had been a disco in the
strobe-lit conservatory, little round supper tables in a long dining
room, and a starry Christmas tree in the paneled hallway that
soared above the gallery of the landing overhead.

   Robin had enjoyed being at the party with Harriet. They had
moved through the connecting circles, part of the talk and laughter, and he had been drawn to look at her over and over again,
admiring her. Among strangers she was attractive and animated,
but she also maintained a kind of separate coolness. It was a
combination that he found particularly alluring. He also liked the
way that she observed everything, with amusement, as if storing
up information and impressions. They were separated at dinner,
and from across the room he watched her talking and carefully
listening. He knew that she would remember what had been
said.

   Robin had no doubt that Harriet would be a considerable
success as an entrepreneur. He hadn't persuaded his father to
put up Landwith capital just because he found her personally
attractive. But now Robin wanted more than Harriet's success,
he wanted Harriet herself, and the force of his wanting was
highly stimulating. Robin was used to getting what he wanted,
but he also understood and enjoyed the groundwork that was
necessary to achieve his ends.

   Harriet had turned down his proposal once, but he fully
intended that she would accept it in good time, to their mutual
pleasure and satisfaction.

   After the little tables had been cleared away, Harriet's dinner
partner threatened to monopolize her. They went off to dance

together, and so Robin danced with Rosalie, and then with a girl he had been briefly in love with at Oxford, now married to a broker. Everyone was marrying, he thought. They had reached that age. He was suddenly impatient with observing Harriet from a distance. He went to claim her, and they moved under the ribbons of light, their hands touching.

Harriet was wearing her expression of secret amusement.

"What is it this time?" he demanded.

She had been observing Rosalie's English prettiness, envying it but also thinking that it would look better in a stately ballgown than in Lagerfield black with a river of sequins down the back. Harriet raised her eyebrows at Robin.

"All this. English society, *grande luxe.*" She had been intrigued by the sprinkling of famous faces among unfamiliar ones that were still somehow printed with the heredity of money and power, and all of it commanded here by a pink-and-white girl younger than herself.

"Rosalie has some useful connections, and so does her husband," Robin shrugged.

"Why didn't you marry Rosalie?" Harriet's eyes were wickedly bright.

He jerked her against him, bending her backward, his mouth against her ear. "Because she'd bore the balls off me within two years, that's why."

Harriet stepped away from him again, composedly reentering the dance. "I see. That would be a problem." Her coolness made him feel hot. The party was becoming an irrelevance. He thought briefly of upstairs bedrooms with rose chintz valances and long-skirted tables, and then dismissed the idea. He didn't want a hasty party screw. He wanted to spend a long time making love to Harriet, doing it very slowly and very thoroughly.

"Have you enjoyed your evening?" he inquired formally.

"Is it over?" She smiled openly at him now. "Yes, I have, thank you. Quite an eye-opener for me, coming from Sunderland Avenue."

He took hold of her wrists, drawing her against him more gently. He could feel her nipples through the thin fabric of her dress. Harriet moved her hips, teasing him with the evidence of his erection. He kissed her mouth, drawing her tongue with his own. He heard the little hiss of her indrawn breath.

"I don't care where you've come from, so long as you're here. I do know where we're both going."

"Now?"

"Jesus, Harriet. This very second."

They said their good-byes, and went out under the black sky. They found the Porsche, valet-parked in a semi-circle of BMWs and Mercedes. Harriet's evening slippers made a ripple in the gravel, Robin sounded heavy-footed beside her. In the car he asked her, "Where?" "Hampstead," she answered, and he thought, *Too far*. As they drove she put her loosely curled hand to rest on his thigh, her knuckles brushing against him. He jerked his head sideways for a glimpse of her quarter-profile, serenely turned away from him. He knew that he had never wanted a girl as much as he wanted Harriet tonight.

It was late, and he blessed the empty roads. There was no traffic at Hammersmith, and the Westway beyond was an empty, orange-lit ribbon. Robin slammed up through the gears and the Porsche howled through the tunnel of light. He drove faster, until Harriet's head was pressed back against her seat and her lips just parted.

When they reached home, and stood facing each other, the silence seemed thick enough to touch.

Robin's desire was intense, but the urgency had gone with the whirlwind drive. He was clear-headed now, and meticulous in his intentions. He stroked her cheeks with the tips of his fingers, and she looked straight back into his eyes as if she could see deep into his head. He traced the line of her neck to her shoulders, thinking that he would like to put diamonds around her bare neck. When the time came he would buy her jewels, when they were married. Now he turned her around and unzipped her dress and let it fall at her feet. He put his mouth to each breast, in turn.

Robin took off his own clothes, butterfly bow tie and pleated shirt and silk cummerbund, and folded them carefully aside. When they were both naked he put his hands to Harriet's hips and lifted her against him. Her legs twined around his waist and her head fell forward, the wings of her hair feathery against his skin.

It was Robin who was cool now. He was aching for her but he enjoyed the fine degrees of his own self-control. He made her smooth back arch up to him and her head fall back to offer up her throat to his mouth. He peeled away the layers of her party self-possession until he possessed her himself and she whispered, *"Please, please,"* in her submission. It was a powerful stimulus. And when he came, Robin gave himself up in his turn. "I love you," he cried out. "I love you. I love you." Harriet put her hands over his ears, cradling his head, so he heard the words trapped inside the bones of his skull.

Afterward they lay quietly with their faces touching.

"Good?" Robin whispered. She smiled, all her muscles loosened, amused by the small-boyishness following the grown man's performance. She felt wonderfully warm, and drowsy, and comfortable.

"Are you looking for compliments?"

For a second, he was disconcerted. "Of course not."

"Well then, not good. Wonderful."

He looked like a small boy who had won a prize. With their arms around each other, they fell asleep at the same moment.

When he woke up, to see the light strengthening in the corners of the room, Robin lay still with his mouth touching Harriet's bare shoulder, contemplating his happiness. He was used to succeeding, but he felt that this was the best moment of success. It was uncharacteristic for him to feel the following opposite beat of fear, and when it came now it was as strong as nausea. If he *couldn't* have her . . . Robin sat up, and swung his legs out of bed. He went to the window and looped back the curtains to look at the frost in the garden.

When he turned into the room again, to see Harriet still asleep under her covers, he had taken hold of his certainty once more.

Robin went upstairs and whistled softly in the kitchen, boiled the kettle and laid a tea tray. Across the gardens, between the black twigs of shrubs, he could see the lights of a Christmas tree winking in someone's window. He made the tea, enjoying the quiet of the kitchen, and then carried the tray down to Harriet.

"Wake up. It's Christmas Eve."

She was sleepy, stretching and clenching her fists. "What time is it?"

"Late." He gave her her cup. "Drink your tea, and then we'll go shopping."

"What shall we buy?"

"I'd like to buy you everything. Furs, and jewels, and silks. Pictures, and porcelain, and gold."

Harriet laughed. "You'd make me a kept woman. A concubine."

"*My* concubine." He put the tip of his finger to the warm hollow at the base of her throat. "I'm going to begin by buying you something to go here."

Harriet looked at the little clock beside her bed, then lifted her arm and put it around his neck. "There's plenty of time," she murmured. "There are at least six more shopping hours until Christmas."

*   *   *

In the fading light of the short afternoon, when the last shoppers were already hurrying away with their last-minute purchases, Robin drove Harriet in the white Porsche down the glitter of Bond Street. He left his car to the Christmas goodwill of the traffic wardens and led Harriet into Aspreys. And there, from among the fire and ice that was brought out for their admiration on black velvet trays, he chose a diamond shaped like a teardrop. He fastened the necklace around her throat and the stone lay in the hollow. Harriet looked amazed.

"Do you like it?"

"It's beautiful."

He kissed her. "It's only the first one. Happy Christmas."

"Robin, I—" She wasn't sure what kind of protest she intended to make, but he stopped her anyway.

"Don't. I just wanted to buy you a present. Why not?"

It seemed mean-spirited to mumble, *I can't accept this, I shouldn't*. The diamond was growing warm against her skin.

"Thank you," she whispered.

Robin made payment of the seemingly enormous sum apparently effortless. An assistant bore one of his rectangles of plastic away, came smiling back with it, and the diamond was Harriet's.

They came out of the shop, with Harriet's hand protectively at her throat, into the blue-gray light. The opulent shop windows still beamed their seductive messages, but the day was nearly over. Soon the streets would be deserted and all the people would retreat behind doors for the rituals of Christmas. The dormancy would end in three days, with the abrupt springtime of the sales. Harriet felt a glow of happiness, and a corresponding reluctance to let Robin go home to the senior Landwiths. She was expected herself at Sunderland Avenue. At this moment, Kath would be flushed with the business of preparation. Harriet put her arm through Robin's. "Let's walk, just for half an hour."

They went on down Bond Street and crossed Piccadilly into Green Park. It was cold, with damp in the air that made the street lights shine through greenish halos. The blackness of the trees made them seem two-dimensional, less substantial than the clouds of breath that preceded Robin and Harriet as they walked. Harriet could feel the warmth of Robin's body through the weight of his overcoat. He held her hand inside his pocket, matching the length of his steps to hers.

"Harriet, will you come and live with me?"

"Oh, Robin. Is that what the diamond was for?"

"No. The diamond is just a compliment."

"I can't. I lived with Leo for so long. I don't want to live with anyone else." After a second she added, "Even you."

His fingers tightened on hers. "Thank you for that. Don't expect me to stop asking."

It was a luxury to be loved, Harriet thought. To be loved like this, and wooed with diamonds. She wouldn't make the mistake of confusing it with necessity.

"My parents are having lunch for some neighbors in the country on the thirty-first. Will you come down for it?"

Harriet had a momentary picture of one of her mother's occasional family lunches, with the best vegetable dishes set out on a heated trolley. She was curious to meet Robin's mother, and to see the house where he had grown up. She had only a hazy idea of what it would be like, except that it would bear no resemblance to Sunderland Avenue.

"In what capacity will I be attending?" she asked, only half-joking.

"As a friend of mine," Robin answered patiently.

"Thank you. I'd love to come."

They turned, and began walking back the way they had come. There was no one else in sight, the park was deserted and almost completely dark. Piccadilly made an ocher glow ahead of them.

"And in return, will you come with me to Jane's?"

Robin sighed. "I don't think Jane likes me very much."

"Jane doesn't approve of some of the things you represent. That isn't the same as not liking you. I wish you would come."

There had been many similar parties. Harriet was too loyal to admit it even to herself, but she was afraid that without Robin's company the day might not be very interesting. She excused herself with the reasoning that her free days were few and precious now, and she was less willing to let them drift by in the old way.

"Of course I'll come," Robin said. He stopped walking, took their linked hands out of his pocket and kissed Harriet's knuckles. "I love you."

Then he took her arm in his again and they walked on toward the emptying streets.

Eleven

CHRISTMAS AT SUNDERLAND AVENUE followed the usual pattern in every detail, even down to the presence of Leo at dinner.

"You've invited *Leo*?" Harriet stared at Kath in amazement when her mother made the casual announcement on Christmas Eve.

"Why not? Averil and Harold have gone to Eilat. Leo always enjoyed his Christmases here with us, he said so when he rang up, and so I asked him for this year, too."

"He enjoyed himself? You could have fooled me," Harriet muttered. As far as she could remember Leo had complained routinely about Kath's cooking, Ken's heavy-handed humor, their insistence on watching the Queen's speech, and his own tendency to fall asleep on the sofa in overfed boredom.

"Leo and I separated two and a half years ago. Why should he want a family Christmas now?"

"I don't know, love. He rang up to wish us Merry Christmas, I invited him, and he accepted. Liza thought it was a good idea."

"What's it got to do with Liza?"

Kath sighed. "Don't make one of your awkwardnesses about this, Harriet. It's Christmas. Here, chop this up for me, will you?"

Obediently Harriet sliced vegetables and wondered if her mother was making a misguided attempt to bring herself and Leo together again. Kath worried about her being alone, she knew that. *You know what they say, Harriet. All work . . .* Harriet smiled a little, and tried to imagine what Robin was doing at his parents' house. She must find the right moment to tell Kath, very lightly, that she wasn't alone, but that she had no plans to marry again either. The only reason she had never mentioned her affair with Robin, she reflected, was because she didn't want her mother making elaborate schemes for their future together. But it would be worth running the risk of that if it would stop Kath trying to engineer reconciliations with Leo.

"I've been so busy," she said, "I haven't seen Leo for months."

Kath pressed her lips together. "I know you're busy. Don't busy yourself out of your life, will you?"

Harriet laughed, and hugged her. "No, I won't do that."

Leo came, on Christmas morning, in a good humor and bearing appropriate presents for all of them. He listened to Ken's jokes and contributed his own, flattered Kath and carried plates and dishes for her, was brotherly to Liza and friendly to Harriet, and behaved throughout like a model son-in-law. His presence made the day more enjoyable; even Harriet was glad that he had come.

After the lengthy ritual of the meal, Leo and Harriet insisted that they would wash up. Liza, who had lost weight and looked almost ethereal in a white knitted dress, yawned delicately and said, "Good, so I can watch the film."

In the kitchen Harriet dried the dishes after Leo had washed them. She said, "Leo, don't you think we should make this arrangement between us formal now?"

"Get divorced? Yeah, we've been separated more than two years. It is only a formality. Why not?"

That was all. Harriet was surprised, although she had no particular reason to be.

As he swished Kath's dishmop through the greasy water, Leo was thinking how much Harriet had changed. She had always been firm; now she seemed positively metallic. She had always been brisk; now she seemed in perpetual driving motion. He had loved her competence once, and had imagined himself bereft when she left him. But from what he had seen of Harriet lately, he was relieved to have nothing to do with Peacocks, or with bloody "Meizu." Any man coming within twenty yards of his ex-wife these days, Leo thought, was running the severest risk of having his balls crushed. He preferred women, or one woman in particular, to be pliant and yielding.

The dishmop made a satisfied twirl in the water. The situation was a little tricky for Leo, but he was confident that it would sort itself out in good time.

Harriet went home to Hampstead on the morning of Boxing Day. Ken carried her overnight bag out to her car for her, opening his blue gates as if they enclosed acres of park land. Harriet felt a surge of uncomplicated affection for him.

"Ken," she asked on impulse, "are you happy, you and Kath?"

"Of course we are," he answered sturdily. "We've got every-thing we want, haven't we?"

Harriet wasn't sure that that was quite the same thing as being happy, but she didn't press him.

"Are you?" he demanded, startling her.

"I'm interested. I'm excited." Those were not the same things either. Hastily she said, "Yes, I am. Everything's going very well for me, isn't it?"

"You be careful," Ken said enigmatically.

"I will. Thank you for a lovely Christmas."

Kath waved from the storm porch, Ken waved from beside his gates. Liza was still in bed.

The next day Harriet and Robin went to Jane's.

The little house was crowded on two levels. At the higher level people were talking and laughing and drinking, their mouths opening and closing on glasses of wine or ragged cuts of French bread or baked potato. And at the lower, children lurched and tottered between the adult legs, or sat placidly on the floor where they had been parked, poking fragments of food between the cracks in the pine boards with fat, sticky fingers. This company of teachers and social workers, journalists and academics had spawned a secondary race of toddlers, seemingly overnight.

Harriet saw Jenny's fourteen-month-old among them. He was absorbed in running a toy truck along the line of a floor-board, but he turned every few seconds to make sure that his mother's ankles were still in sight. Jenny was nearby, half-leaning against Jane's upright piano. She was enormously pregnant, the bulge looking not quite part of the rest of her body. She was wearing a dress of thin Indian cotton, and her everted navel made a tiny, secondary bump on the summit of the first.

Harriet kissed her, patted the trophy. "How much longer is it?"

Jenny's hair was parted in the middle, falling in straight curtains beside each cheek. She pushed one curtain back behind each ear, made a weary face. "Another month, would you be-lieve? I don't think I'll be able to walk if it gets any bigger."

Harriet looked down at a pair of matted-curled heads, push-ing at knee-height. "There are such a lot of them, all of a sudden."

Jenny smiled her new, tranquil, maternal smile. "It's the age we're at."

Making connections, Harriet asked, "Where's Jane?"

"In the kitchen, I think."

"You remember Robin, don't you?" They had met, at some similar gathering.

"Of course I do." Her smile was just as warm. Robin maneuvered politely beside her; his lean height and dove-gray cashmere sweater looked incongruous beside such uncontrived fecundity.

Jane bore down on them, brandishing a bottle. "You haven't got any *drinks*. Harriet, you look amazing." Harriet was wearing her diamond, because she knew that Robin would have wanted her to. Jane saw it, and her eyes widened a little, but she only said, "Is that thing you're wearing silk? We'd better try and keep the babies at bay."

Harriet had dressed to please Robin. He had come up behind her and fastened her bra, then looked over her shoulder into the mirror. Harriet let her head drop back against his shoulder, his hands fitted over her breasts. She had wanted to get undressed again, but they had smiled conspiratorially at each other and he had taken her shirt off the hanger. He had done up the buttons, with regret. Now Harriet felt she was faced with a choice of saying, "No, I'd love to cuddle all of them," or "Yes, do, I don't want fingermarks on my St. Laurent." She did say, crisply, "They're only clothes."

"Hello, Robin." Robin and Jane exchanged the coolest of kisses, and Harriet was struck again by an awareness of incongruity. But it was hardly Robin's fault, she thought, if he stood out among the beards and corduroys and Marks & Spencer jumpers.

It was her own fault for trying to mix the immiscible. She wouldn't attempt it again.

"There's Charlie," Robin said, with relief.

Robin and Charlie Thimbell liked one another. "He's a bit of a prat," Charlie had said. "But quite a clever one. Are you two giving each other a little whirl, Harriet?"

Harriet had laughed in spite of herself. "Not very elegantly expressed, Charlie. But I suppose that's what it amounts to. I like him, I enjoy his company."

"And why not?" Charlie had agreed cheerfully.

The two men converged now and immediately began a conversation about some uproarious Liffe pre-Christmas party they had both been to. Harriet left them to it, and followed Jane through toward the kitchen. At the end of the hallway, in a niche beneath the stairs, they found a corner empty of both levels of guests. Jane drew Harriet into it.

"Hattie, I'm sorry." She only called Harriet "Hattie" in moments of vulnerable friendliness. Harriet was startled. "What for?"

"I'm not very nice to your lover-boy. I can't bring myself to be. He looks so bloody superior all the time, and so stiff and proper."

"He isn't any of those. He's a nice man. He's just not much like . . ." Harriet gestured.

"Us?"

"Us, then, if you like." Which was she, herself, more like now? Harriet wondered. "But he is amusing and lively, and rather clever."

"Generous, as well." Jane touched the diamond, and Harriet felt herself blush.

"Yes."

Jane looked doubtfully at her. "Is that what it's about?"

"Of course not. I don't want to have to defend him, or it, to you."

It was Jane's turn to be startled. "I wasn't expecting you to."

Harriet knew there was no point in being angry with her. Unlike Harriet herself, Jane said what she thought as a matter of honor. She was also her oldest friend. Harriet exhaled a long breath. "We have dinner, go to the opera, go to bed together. He's not at all pompous, and if he acts superior I don't notice it." She laughed then, almost a giggle. "Not in bed, anyway. If you want to know, the sex is amazing."

"A-ha." Jane laughed, too, her face collapsing into creases, reminding Harriet of all the conspiracies they had shared. "I can relate to that better than to Porsches or diamonds or Thatcherism."

"We don't discuss politics much. Deliberately."

"Too busy, eh? What exactly does he do that's so amazing?"

"Mmm. It's not so much what he does, as how he does it. With great conviction, and an exemplary attention to detail."

Jane sighed. "I can see it, now I look closely at you. You look as though you've had a few collagen treatments, an unmistakable sign. I envy you, God, I envy you. I think for conviction and attention to detail where it counts, I could even overlook possession of a gold American Express card."

"Wouldn't that be a bit too much of a compromise?"

They emerged from their niche, relieved to have found grounds for laughter, and went on into the kitchen.

A dozen people were sitting at the kitchen table. Harriet and Jane edged behind them until they found empty chairs, then squeezed into the group. When she looked around the circle of faces Harriet stopped at a woman she didn't know, sitting beyond Jane. The woman was breastfeeding her baby. The baby sucked, and the curve of its cheek mirrored the white, blue-veined curve of the breast. The woman unconcernedly forked up her own food, and talked across the table. At the rim of the baby's mouth there was a whitish, glistening bubble of milk.

Harriet felt a sharp contraction within herself. It was as if a thread knotted between her two ovaries and running through her womb was drawn tight, and then sharply tugged.

Beside her, Jane seemed to be frozen into stillness. Harriet was going to murmur something to her, but Jane stopped her. "Don't say anything," she whispered. "Please, don't say anything."

At a loss, Harriet turned to her other side and looked straight into a face she knew and had forgotten.

It was a prize-fighter's face, marked but handsome, of the kind that stood out from a crowd. Harriet remembered the man in the blue shirt, who had tried to kiss her at another of Jane's parties, and from whom she had hidden in Jane's bathroom. David, that was his name.

"I keep reading about you in the papers," he said in his northern accent, as if their last conversation had been half an hour before.

"Not much of what you read is true. It's just publicity."

"What do you want publicity for?" His tone was abrasive.

"Because I can spend money on advertising my product range in the press and on television, or on posters stuck all over the country, but I'll get twice the response from editorial promotion which is also free. I just have to think of the right angle, and push it for all I'm worth."

He shook his head in mock amazement. "And do you think it's all worthwhile?"

"Yes," Harriet said shortly. "Tell me, how's the building business?"

He grinned at her. "Booming. In the south-east, that is. I'm working on an interesting project now. Would you like to come and see it? It's not far from here."

Harriet glanced away. The woman had finished feeding her baby. She held it loosely in the crook of her arm and did up the front of her bra. Her breasts looked huge, the nipples dark brown and distended. Harriet's pain had disappeared. She wondered if Jane felt that temporary ache permanently, if that was what shadowed her face when she looked into other women's prams.

"I . . . I'm very busy," she said to David. She turned away again and found that Jane was still sitting motionless beside her.

Jane didn't look up to meet her eyes but she said in a low voice, "I'm going to try to have a baby. I'm going to throw my bloody cap away and grow a baby, and the two of us will manage because we'll have to."

"Yes," Harriet said. "Yes. If you want it so much, you must do it. I told you I'd never felt it, didn't I? But I did, then. Like a string pulling."

"It never goes away," Jane said.

Harriet was going to ask, *Why didn't I know, we never talked about this, did we?* Then she saw Robin in the doorway, seeming too tall for the low-ceilinged kitchen.

"Why are you so busy?" David persisted, as if he wanted to draw her attention away from Robin.

"Because I run a business."

David was calmly studying her face. She remembered how she had hidden from him, and then when he had gone she had been tempted to run after him. She had even imagined how it would be if they had gone home together, and then dismissed her attraction to him as a dangerous weakness.

The recollections irritated her now.

She had decided at the time that she couldn't allow herself the intricate distractions of a love affair, and she was sure that she had been right. At the same moment she knew that whatever she was doing with Robin now it wasn't falling in love with him.

"I thought you didn't know Jane. But you're here at another of her parties."

Jane stood up abruptly. She gathered up some dirty plates and glasses, making a small, unnecessary clatter. David watched her, and then asked, "Can I help you with that?"

"No, thanks," Jane said. "You talk to Harriet."

She left her place and went away with her hands full of washing-up.

"I didn't know Jane then, but I do now," David said. "I moved to London, not very far from here. It's a good house, Georgian. You should come and see it." Harriet opened her mouth. ". . . But you're very busy," he supplied for her.

Robin came and put his hand lightly on Harriet's shoulder. It seemed a mark of possession.

"Shall I bring you a plate of something to eat?"

"No, thank you," she said with a touch of sharpness. "I'll go and get my own."

When Robin had moved away again David raised his eyebrows. "Who was that?"

"My lover," Harriet said. She noticed amused lines deepening beside the man's mouth, and she suspected that he had taken sharp-eyed note of Robin's handmade shoes and forty-pound haircut. He had already scrutinized her diamond teardrop. But he ignored her bald statement and looked at his watch.

"I've got a business to run, too. And how is it that you can manage long lunches like this?" Before Harriet could answer *It's the Christmas holidays*, he added pleasantly, "I must go. I'll give you a call. Perhaps the pressure of business will ease off, one of these days."

Harriet stood up. "Excuse me," she murmured.

Robin was at the counter where the food was laid out, prodding at a bowl of lettuce. They both watched David on his way out, moving with outdoor clumsiness in the confined space.

"Who was that?"

"A friend of Jane's. I met him here once before. He's a builder of some sort."

"A builder? I wonder if he's any good? Perhaps he'd like to come and take a look at the damp in my chimney breast."

Harriet laughed. "I don't think he would, somehow."

In the car on the way home, Robin asked her, "What was the matter today?"

She sighed and closed her eyes. "I felt scratchy, that's all. I'm sorry if you didn't enjoy yourself."

"I did enjoy myself," he said smoothly.

The trouble was, Harriet thought, that Robin Landwith didn't mix with Jane, and Jenny and Charlie, and all the rest of her old friends. He didn't now, nor would he ever, the sight of him in Jane's house today had convinced her of that. She would have to keep the two halves of her life apart, although the notion displeased her. She had, once, enjoyed the idea of friends as separate individuals securely joined by the webs of common experience and understanding. But her life had changed. From now on there would be Robin and Peacocks in one compartment, her old friends and her family in another. She would also trap the moment of sharp maternal desire that she had shared with Jane in the second compartment. It wouldn't, and couldn't, so much as touch the first. They drew up outside the tall Hampstead house, fresh with white paintwork and newly restored brick and stone.

"Home," Robin said with satisfaction.

The next day, they both went back to work. Because of their separate commitments they didn't meet again until New Year's Eve, the day of their visit to the senior Landwiths.

Robin's father and mother lived in a village on the London side of Oxford, less than an hour's drive from Hampstead. It was a cold, clear morning and Harriet stared out at the scraped brown fields and black patches of somber woodland as Robin drove. She was a city girl, and thought of the countryside as a faintly mysterious environment that existed for other people, with no relevance to her own life.

"Have you always lived in the same place?" she asked now. "Little Shelley?"

"If that's where we're going." To Harriet, civilization in a westerly direction didn't extend much beyond Hammersmith.

Robin smiled. "No. They've had the present house for ten years. It's the furthest they've ever been from town. Before that it was near Henley, and Maidenhead before that. When I was born they lived in Surrey."

"Why did they keep moving?"

"Why do you think? Martin is interested in property, my mother liked doing up houses."

"I've tried to imagine what it's going to be like, and I can't. I can think of lots of details but no overall picture."

"You'll see soon enough," Robin said tranquilly.

The road swept through the great V of a hill cutting, and dropped away to a wide, cold, bleached landscape. The light was sharp and bright, and Harriet shaded her eyes. In spite of the traffic all around them, the world seemed empty out here.

Robin pointed down into the middle distance, into space. "Little Shelley is there, not far away now."

A little distance further on they left the motorway for a smaller road, then turned into an even narrower one. Flocks of birds rose from the bare trees and wheeled in arcs over the plowed fields. Robin slowed the car to overtake an olive-coated rider on a big white horse; as they slid past his boot in the shiny stirrup was at Harriet's eye level. She saw the milky cloud of the horse's breath, then they passed a road sign announcing Little Shelley.

There was a church with a square gray tower and a pretty lych-gate, and a row of cars parked beyond a pair of imposing stone gateposts.

"They can't be at church today, can they?"

"That was the old vicarage. It's a restaurant now, rather a grand one. People are lunching, not praying."

That gave Harriet the key to Little Shelley. As they drove into the village she realized that there was going to be no village green with a cluster of shops and a picturesque pub. Little Shelley seemed to be mostly very high, very well-kept walls, over the tops of which she could just glimpse majestic trees and clusters of tall chimneys. Every few hundred yards the walls gave way to high gates, with speaking grilles and remote control buttons set into the gateposts beside them. By craning her neck as they swept by she could sometimes see up a short drive-way to a handsome house. Each house, as they passed it, seemed to be larger than the last.

They had arrived in rich country, Harriet realized.

"Where are the shops?" she asked.

"Oxford."

"Where does your mother's cleaning lady live, then?" she persisted.

"On one of the new estates in Great Shelley, I think. Why?"

"I just wondered."

They reached what seemed to be the last majestic gateway. The road wound out of the village, into the tidy countryside again.

The gates were wrought iron, with intricate curlicues, but they stood open. The Porsche rolled between them, gravel crunch-ing under its fat tires. The driveway was lined with green-black sentinels of conifers, rigorously clipped. Beyond them there were lawns dotted with bigger trees, bare branches dipping toward the wet grass.

The driveway widened to a semicircular sweep; there was a handful of big, shiny-looking cars parked here, and enough space for a dozen or so more. Harriet looked up to the house itself.

It was built of stone, gray today but probably golden in sunlight. There were three rows of small-paned windows, an-other row of mansard windows above those in the steep-pitched roof. There were the clusters of tall chimneys that had been visible over other walls, but more of these. The house had a main front, but there were also shorter, projecting wings that made it look as if the building had grown comfortably, but haphazardly, on a human scale.

There must be at least fifteen bedrooms, Harriet thought. The house was huge, but it managed to look intimate. It was grand, but at the same time it fitted comfortably into the setting of this opulent village.

She couldn't fault Martin Landwith's taste. Parts of his house must date from the sixteenth century, it was clearly the jewel in a remarkable collection of gems that made up the necklace of Little Shelley. Martin must have had to trade up with particular dili-gence to achieve it.

Robin's car slid into place beside a bronze-colored Rolls Royce.

"It used to be the manor house," he remarked. "Lord Nuffield owned it at one time, the estate of the Earls of Oxford before that. The rest of the village grew up around it."

He came around to Harriet's side of the car and opened the door for her. Politely, he helped her to her feet. For a moment, she needed his arm to lean on. She had had a sudden glimpse of the meaning of real wealth, and it had made her dizzy.

"It's very impressive," she said because, in a way, it was.

The lawns and the gravel sweep were divided from the house by a paved terrace. On the terrace, guarding the front door, sat a pair of seemingly life-sized lions, the carved stone pocked with age and softened with lichens. Harriet and Robin passed the lions' scrutiny and entered the house.

Harriet had a brief impression of a high hallway with a flagged floor and a pair of carved chests in dark oak, before Robin steered her through double doors into a long drawing room.

At first glance, the effect was of discreet but extreme opulence, created equally by the room and the people gathered in it. A woman detached herself from the group and came across the Aubusson to greet them.

"Robin, darling."

Harriet recognized her instantly from the silver-framed picture in Robin's bedroom. The cloud of dark hair was casual by way of expensive artifice, the heart-shaped face was strikingly lovely, but the expression was less innocently sweet than in her photograph. There was level appraisal in her eyes, and a readiness to disapprove and then to dismiss. Robin kissed her and she cupped his face, briefly, in her long, manicured hands.

"Harriet, this is my mother. Mummy, this is Harriet Peacock."

Robin's mother held out her hand and Harriet took it. "Mrs. Landwith, how do you do."

"Hello, Harriet. Won't you call me Annunziata?"

I'll try, Harriet thought, with a touch of hysteria. *What does Martin call you in bed, surely not that? Nancy?*

Annunziata Landwith scrutinized her. Uncharacteristically Harriet had not been quite sure how to dress for the occasion. In the end she had opted for a chrome-yellow Kamali tunic and black leggings, hoping that if it was too informal it would at least look youthful and wacky. But it clearly didn't pass muster with Nancy. Any more, she guessed, than she did herself. Probably Robin's mother didn't approve of any of his girlfriends whose families and financial pedigrees were unknown to her.

For her own part, Harriet noted that Robin's mother was

wearing couture Chanel, a long-jacketed suit in ecru wool with gilt buttons, and heavy ropes of pearls. There was, in any case, no competing with that.

Harriet followed her hostess across the room to be introduced to her fellow guests. Second impressions of the drawing room confirmed the first. The effect of luxury had been achieved by padding every surface, not once but twice.

There were deep buttoned sofas piled with antique embroidered cushions. The thick curtains were secondarily curtained with deep swags, draped tails and tassels, and the side tables were skirted with silk cloths and then draped again with silvery blue and green Fortuny overskirts. Over the thick carpet an enormous antique rug had been laid, on which soft pink embroidered roses coiled against a background of misty blues and greens. There were lamps with shades of pleated silk and even the frames of photographs, dotted all over the room, were padded with velvet and petit point.

As all the softness and richness rose up to swallow her, Harriet felt a moment of longing, and of deep, pure affection, for Jane Hunter's house in Hackney.

What do I like? she thought wildly. *And where do I belong?*

Not here. Anywhere but here.

There were perhaps a dozen other people, standing in a loose semicircle with glasses in their hands, in front of a log fire. They were all older than Robin and Harriet, silvery-haired men still exercise-fit, and slim-waisted women with swollen coiffures whose clothes carried the sheen of money. There was no cause for Harriet to feel conscious of her diamond here. As she shook hands she saw creamy-varnished fingernails offset by rows of diamonds, cabochon earrings the size of golfballs, and an emerald pin at the neck of one woman's blouse that made her remember the jewel-house at Topkapi Palace through which she and Charlie and the others had passed with their backpacks more than a decade ago.

"Robin's friend, Harriet. All of you know Robin, of course, don't you?"

Robin passed among them, urbane, secure behind the screen of his expensive manners. Harriet thought, *What can I say to these people?* There was no sign of Martin, even, who might perhaps have been counted as an ally.

Then she saw that one of the guests had been overlooked in the round of introductions. She was sitting to one side of the room, in an armchair half-turned to the windows that looked over the garden. Her skinny legs, in tartan trousers, were drawn up beneath her and her shoes might just, unthinkably, have been in contact with the honey-colored upholstery. She was perhaps ten years old, and she was wearing an expression of mutinous boredom.

A man in a dark jacket and striped trousers, carrying a silver tray, passed between Harriet and the child. Harriet took the champagne flute that he offered her, and watched him bend slightly to offer a tumbler of plain orange juice to the child. She took it, not looking at him, her expression unaltered. A child of these people, without question, Harriet diagnosed. She wondered which of the silky, silvery couples could be her parents.

Harriet sipped her champagne, and then slipped sideways around the chattering group. There was a buttoned ottoman with gilded claw feet close to the child's chair and Harriet sat down on it, bringing their eyes level.

"I'm sorry, we weren't introduced," she said. "My name's Harriet."

The child looked at her, but said nothing.

"What's your name?" Harriet prompted.

The girl frowned. "I'm only a child, you know," she pointed out in a clear voice with a distinct American accent. It was a surprise in this room full of drawling and baying English. "Children should be seen and not heard."

Harriet grinned. "Do you believe that?"

"As a child, I can't really believe or disbelieve, can I? It's a grown-up thing. Do *you* believe it?"

Harriet thought of Jane's two-level party, giving the girl's question proper consideration. "Children are people, too. They deserve the same hearing as everyone else. Not more, as some of them seem to expect, but certainly not less either."

Now it was the girl's turn to consider. "Where I come from, children are to be brought out and shown off once in a while. In the right clothes, for parties or horse riding or all that stuff. Then they're to be put away again until the next time."

"I see. Where do you come from?"

The child shrugged. "Sometimes I live in Little Shelley, sometimes in L.A. In Bel Air," she added, unnecessarily.

Harriet wondered which of these men was in film finance, dealing in picture-budget millions. Any one, or quite possibly all of them.

"I see, again. Aren't you going to tell me your name?"

"It's Linda."

Harriet put her hand out. "How do you do, Linda."

The child shook hands, and then she sighed. "Okay, you've done your stuff."

"What do you mean?"

"You've been nice to me. You can go back to the party now."

Harriet was amused by her rudeness, rather than rebuffed as Linda had probably intended.

"Suppose I don't want to?"

The child eyed her. She had a pale, peaky face and colorless hair cut straight with a square fringe, but her eyes were wide, dark brown and lively. "You could come for a walk in the garden with me. There's a swing. Not much else, but it's better than in here."

Harriet glanced around the room. Annunziata's straight back was turned to her, and Robin was sitting on a distant sofa between two coiffures.

"Aren't you allowed to?" Linda challenged her.

"I'm *allowed* to do anything that doesn't embarrass or inconvenience other people," Harriet said pompously. "That's grown-up manners, and worth remembering. I can't see any reason why I shouldn't take a stroll in the garden with you."

They stood up together, Linda wriggling in her tartan trews and shetland jersey. As they passed Robin's sofa Harriet leaned between the rival auras of Joy and Arpège and murmured, "I'm going out into the garden for ten minutes, for a walk with Linda. She's a very nice child." Either of those women, of course, could be her mother. "Will Annunziata mind?"

"Of course not," Robin was obliged to answer. But Harriet was left in no doubt that her behavior was eccentric. Smiling a little, she shepherded Linda through double doors, out into the hallway where the man in the black jacket sprang to open the front door for them, and on out into the colorless sunshine.

Linda ran in a wide circle, her arms windmilling, like a big dog let off the leash. She leapt onto the sloping back of one of the lions, clinging on like a monkey and scraping long weals of the mellow lichen with her old-fashioned barred shoes.

"You'd better not do that," Harriet observed. "At least, not in full view of the house." Linda smiled for the first time, her face suddenly sunny. She scrambled down and ran to Harriet's side. "Okay. Let's go and do things out of sight."

Linda ran and Harriet followed, slowly at first and then sprinting to catch up. Their feet left skidding tracks in the wet grass. It was cold, but a burst of speed made Harriet's blood sing. It was exhilarating to be in the clear air after the muffled drawing room, and she sympathized with Linda's mutinous indoor appearance.

They headed for the most distant corner of the garden, and there they found the promised swing. The metal frame was rusted, but the structure looked safe enough.

"Push me," Linda commanded.

"Can't you swing yourself?"

"I like it better if I'm pushed."

"I'll give you five big ones to get you started."

Linda swung, stretching the sodden toes of her shoes higher and higher, and Harriet surveyed the garden. There were big flowerbeds with geometrically neat edgings, the bare earth well turned and the twiggy shrubs regimentally pruned. There must be a gardener somewhere, to whom these beds were a pride and joy.

Linda swept in more exultant arcs. "Look at me! Am I higher than the bar?"

"Be careful." Harriet tried to imagine Robin swinging as a little boy, muddy and defiant, and failed.

"Have you been here to play before, Linda?"

"A couple of times. Their pool's bigger than ours."

Harriet walked to an opening in a box hedge and found the swimming pool enclosed by its formally clipped walls. There was a pool house like a tiny classical temple. The springboard had been removed and its brackets poked up forlornly. Harriet peered down into the empty blue rhomboid, suddenly depressed by the garden's barrenness. She went back to Linda and when the child saw her she dragged her feet to slow the swing's momentum and then leapt to the ground.

"What shall we do now?"

"I think we'd better go back to your mother."

Linda stared scornfully at her. "My mother? My *mother's* in Phuket. She doesn't like Christmas. Or England."

"Your father then," Harriet wasn't sure where Phuket was.

The sullen expression was back. "All right, then. But he won't be bothered, you know."

They walked, Linda stabbing her toes into the lawn as if she wanted to dig it up. Harriet longed to ask her inquisitive questions about the Landwith set-up and her father's relationship to it, but it seemed faintly dishonorable to milk a child for information.

She contented herself with, "Do you live near here?"

Linda tilted her head without enthusiasm. "Over there."

One of the big houses, hidden behind walls, rich sanctuaries. Harriet couldn't think of anything else to say. They were almost back at the house before Linda broke the silence.

"I really like your clothes," she said.

"Do you? Thank you very much."

"Yeah. They're neat. I hate mine."

"You look fine." She did, in fact, look slightly old-fashioned, like a child in a fifties picture-book illustration. She also had the air of being deliberately under-dressed for the Landwiths' elegant party.

"My dad likes me to wear this sort of stuff. He thinks it's appropriate, like from his childhood. My mom likes fancy things, I told you. I've got two wardrobes, kind of, and I hate them both."

"What would you like to wear?"

"You know, Levis, sweats, all that. Neat leggings, like yours."

They passed the lions again and came into the hall. "You'll be old enough soon to pick your own clothes."

"Oh, yeah," Linda said, as if Harriet had told her she would soon be old enough to make an excursion to the moon. From her own childhood Harriet remembered the enticing, unattainable prospect of adult freedom.

"You don't believe it now, but you will."

They were in the drawing room again. After the chill outside it felt like a hothouse, and it was as overpoweringly scented. More guests had arrived and the big group had fractured into smaller ones; the noise level had risen perceptibly.

Linda frowned. "Thanks," she mumbled, without looking at Harriet. "See you." Staring straight ahead of her she marched across the room and reinstalled herself in her armchair. She drew her legs up once more, and this time her muddy shoes were defiantly in contact with Annunziata's chair-cover. Harriet looked away, suppressing a smile. She was very conscious that her own feet were wet, and that her cheeks were red and glowing from the fresh air.

Robin materialized at her elbow.

"There you are. Come and meet Tom Sachs. He runs TKS, and he might be useful to you."

Harriet let him lead her over to one of the silver-haired men. Tom Sachs shook her hand and wished her Happy New Year, and they began to talk about Peacocks and media buying, with particular reference to Tom Sachs's company.

Harriet accepted another glass of champagne from the butler, and a canapé from a salver offered by an impassive-faced woman who was probably the housekeeper. She ate the tiny morsel whole, listening to Tom Sachs with as much attention as she could muster.

"Your TV commitment, of course, must be related directly to existing market awareness . . ."

Harriet realized that someone new had entered the room behind her.

Tom's eyes flicked to the door and then dragged themselves back to Harriet. There was the smallest lull in the general conversation but it rose again immediately, louder than before, as if to confirm that there had been no break.

Harriet resisted the urge to turn and look.

A moment later Martin Landwith crossed into her line of sight. He was as handsome and suave as always, but next to his companion he seemed smaller, and lusterless.

Harriet's first thought was that she had known the man with him for years. She even made the beginning of a move to greet him. Then she realized with a sense of foolishness that of course she had never met him. Nor had she ever met anyone who held himself and moved in such a way, as if he were inevitably the center of attention, the focus of all other eyes.

It was a famous face, familiar from cinema and television screens.

Annunziata swept toward him, the chilliness that Harriet had sensed entirely obliterated. "Caspar, you haven't got a drink. Martin, you've neglected him." She almost clicked her fingers at the butler. Champagne materialized at once at the man's elbow. As, Harriet reflected, most things he wanted probably did, and many more that he didn't. He was Caspar Jensen. Harriet recalled the last of his films that she had seen. It was *Thundercloud*, not a very good movie and Caspar Jensen had played only a cameo role, but his face had appeared on all the posters. He had given a spate of interviews, there had been Jensen features in most of the glossies and color supplements.

Harriet felt, probably in common with most of the other people in the room, that she knew his life history from humble origins in Durham through Oxford and the stage, two failed marriages, to stardom in a series of highly successful films and then, latterly, less successful films. Harriet couldn't recall when she had last heard of him making a stage appearance, although it was as a classical actor that he had first made his name. There had been rumors of other problems, implicitly denied in the upbeat publicity interviews.

"Not at all, Annunziata, I've done very well," she heard him say, enunciating as if he were delivering the opening lines of

Twelfth Night. His voice was as familiar as his face, coming from his chest and sounding as if it emerged through honey and smoke.

Caspar Jensen carried his champagne glass over to the chair where Linda sat. He stroked her hair, then stepped back again as if following a director's blocking.

"How are you, baby? Being good?"

Harriet understood, then. She had been walking in the garden with Linda Jensen. Linda was Caspar's youngest child and only daughter. She had been conceived by Clare Mellen, an actress of luminous beauty and reputedly limited intelligence, with whom Caspar had been co-starring just as his twenty-year-old first marriage had been breaking up. Caspar and Clare had later married, and the marriage had survived a surprising nine years. It had come to an end in the last twelve months.

There were two sons by the first marriage, the older of whom was beginning to make a name for himself as a film actor.

Understanding who the pale, sulky child was, Harriet was no longer surprised that she had got away with putting her feet on Annunziata's cushions.

Tom Sachs was still talking, and Harriet had been making the appropriate responses. Now they exchanged the briefest of glances, a glance that said, *We've seen who's here, and we're impressed, but we're going to act as if we run into such people every day.* The civilized conversation resettled into an even hum around them once again.

Harriet recovered from an urge to laugh, and focused on the technicalities of successful media buying. Caspar Jensen had been swallowed up into a group in the middle of the room, and Linda sat on in her chair, her gaze directed out of the window.

Annunziata, with Martin to help her now, orchestrated her party with high skill. The groups of guests were combined and rearranged, Harriet among them. She came close to Caspar, but never reached the point of being introduced to him. Observing him, she noticed that he was smaller and stockier than he appeared on screen, that he held himself straight and moved with grace, and that he possessed physical magnetism that seemed natural rather than bred from his celebrity. She found that she wanted to look at him, even to move closer, to be within touching distance.

Harriet had been talking to, or rather listening to, one of the slender women who had a more golden tan than the others. She had been extolling the joys of a Sydney summer against an

English winter. "A terrible journey, but once you've recovered from that it's paradise. Truly it is."

"I'm sure it must be," Harriet agreed politely.

The woman suddenly broke off and moved closer. "He *is* rather special, isn't he? I've met quite a lot of stars, of course, through Dick's business, but there's no one quite like Caspar."

"Do you *know* him well?"

"I don't *know* him, actually, even though he has this house in the village. Not that he spends a lot of time here. He's quite a recluse, I believe."

So tactfully that the mechanics were unnoticeable, Annunziata had been dispersing some of her guests and marshaling others. Harriet realized that several couples were leaving, and that those who remained were being corralled ready for a move elsewhere. Lunch must be ready for the chosen in another room. She found Robin at her side.

"Glamorous company," she murmured, watching Annunziata escorting Caspar with her fingertips lightly at his elbow.

Robin's eyebrows made amused peaks. "Are you going to fall for him, like everyone else?"

Harriet laughed. "Everyone? I shouldn't think so. Did you know he was coming?"

"Certainly not. If I'd had a choice, I wouldn't have risked you within fifty miles of him. Shall we have some lunch?"

Harriet followed Robin obediently.

The dining room was a long room on the opposite side of the hallway. French windows framed with more heavy curtains looked out on the barren gardens, on which darkness already seemed to be falling. There was a big oval table laid for twelve, with miniature battalions of knives and forks and thickets of crystal glasses. Harriet saw that there were place cards at each setting, and sighed inwardly.

"That's her," Linda Jensen said, pointing. "That lady."

Linda was holding her father's hand. They had come into the dining room a little after everyone else, with Martin. Linda was pointing at Harriet.

Caspar came straight across the room, with his daughter beside him. He held out his hand, smiling, and Harriet saw the color of his eyes. Blue, but not the intense on-screen blue that she expected. The whites were bloodshot.

"I'm Caspar Jensen."

Harriet shook his hand. "I know. I'm Harriet Peacock."

"Linda says you're great." There was an American intonation in *great*, incongruous with the magnificent Shakespearean voice.

"We went for a walk in the garden. I enjoyed it, too."

Caspar put his arm around her shoulders, hugging her like a bear. "Well, you're a good girl. Booze and talk are fun for us, but they're no entertainment for kids. Hey, look, we're holding everyone up. Here, come and sit down by me. I want to find out what my daughter's fallen for."

He pulled out a dining chair for her, and sat down alongside. Quick as an eel, Linda wriggled into the place at Harriet's other side. Out of the corner of her eye, Harriet saw Annunziata's expression. A second later Annunziata had made a complete circuit of the table and scooped up all the place cards.

"Let's be quite informal," she called. "Sit anywhere you like, *just* so long as husbands and wives are apart."

After another second she was directing the seating from behind the chair next to Caspar. When everyone else had found a place she managed to look gracefully surprised by the position that had fallen to her. Martin and Robin faced one another from opposite ends of the table.

The butler and the housekeeper moved behind the chairs, placing a plate in front of each guest. Harriet glanced down at her portion. There was an artfully curled prawn, a fan of coriander leaves, and some small hummocks and pools of mousse and sauce. The first of her glasses was simultaneously filled with pale gold wine.

Beside her Linda hissed, "I can't eat stuff like this. I like french fries."

In as stern a whisper as she could muster Harriet hissed back, "How old are you, Linda?"

"Nearly eleven."

"You're old enough to know that you can eat almost anything, if you really must. Anyway, this is probably delicious. I should think you can have french fries when you get home."

Linda sighed and prodded the hummocks with a spoon. "He doesn't like this kind of food either. He likes steak and kidney pie."

"But he'll eat this."

"I wouldn't be so sure," Linda said darkly.

Caspar had been talking to his hostess. Now, with an exaggerated movement that rocked his chair, he swung around to Harriet. He hooked one arm over the back of his chair, his free hand lifted the glass of gold wine to his mouth and then replaced it, empty.

"Now. Tell me everything."

Harriet noticed something that she had overlooked before, probably because he contained it so skillfully. Caspar Jensen was three-quarters drunk.

"Everything? I think that might be a rather boring catalog."

His laughter warmed Harriet. It was big, rich and noisy, bigger than the artfully decorated room with its silver and porcelain, and much noisier than the surrounding conversations. Harriet felt rather than heard the talk petering out, and the pairs of eyes turning to Caspar.

"Let us not bore one another, at any price." His hand descended on hers, perfectly familiar. Harriet sat still, not wanting him to feel that he must move it. Caspar examined her face. The effort of focusing made lines deepen between his eyebrows. "Is it the new big sin, do you think? Deadlier than the seven? Wha'd'y'all think?" He lifted his hand from Harriet's and made a beckoning gesture to draw the rest of the table into the talk. He nearly swept his empty glass over, but he caught it in time and held it up for the butler to refill. Harriet picked up her knife and fork and bent her head over her plate.

"Well? Sin or not?"

"Of course it isn't sinful to be a bore," ventured a woman from beside Martin. "How could it be?"

Caspar leaned toward her, prodding his fork in her direction. "How could it *not* be? I have known some Olympic-class bores. Men who could divert a lava stream with a single speech. Women, dear God, women who could extinguish the sun in the sky. The obsessive interest in the self, that is the sin. It stifles all else, all joy, dams all the streams. Bores are the true villains in our world. Give me some decent sloth, or gluttony. Lust, best of all."

Harriet wished that she could see Annunziata, but her profile was hidden behind Caspar's bulk. The room seemed unnaturally silent when his booming voice stopped.

"I think I would also include it in the list of sins," Martin said mildly. "But it would be rather low in the ranking."

"What about stupidity?" Tom Sachs drawled.

"Stupidity is an affliction, not a sin." It was the woman who had defended bores.

"Bores are not always stupid. Nor are stupid people invariably boring. But it is my experience that the two conditions are closely associated. Triumphantly. Magnificently."

Harriet judged that Caspar had now tipped over the edge into being completely drunk. She knew that she should say something quiet to him, aiming to confine his attention to herself and so to limit the potential damage to Annunziata's party. For her own part, she knew that whatever Caspar said or did while he was drunk wouldn't affect the liking that she already felt for him. She sensed that here was someone large, to whom ordinary rules could not apply because they would always be broken, and who possessed as much capacity to charm as to disrupt. She felt awkward, and angry with herself, because she didn't know what to do or say to divert his course.

Harriet glanced around the table once more. Martin was smiling, apparently unruffled. Robin was smiling, too, but there was annoyance in his dark eyes. Robin didn't like the unexpected or the uncontrolled, Harriet knew that. Linda had made a praiseworthy attempt to eat her food. Now she was crumbling bread and marshaling the fragments into little heaps beside her plate.

However, Harriet had underestimated Caspar's self-control, and his ability to dominate a room. When he spoke again, he seemed to have shrugged off the effects of the drink.

"Talking of bores, as it seems we must—" he broke off, and the uncertain eyes studied Harriet again. "You will tell me, darling, if I'm committing the sin myself, won't you?" And then, to the company in general once more, "I'll tell you about the time I was in Tokyo, with John, filming *Gemini Too*."

The anecdote, about a famous film director, was a funny one, made funnier by Caspar's timing. There was a burst of relieved laughter. He told two more stories while everyone else around the table ate lemony soup with tiny vegetable florets drifting in it.

The guests relaxed, and separate conversations began again.

Harriet saw Robin looking at her. His expression didn't change, but she felt that she could see through his eyes into his head. She clearly saw that he loved her, and that he was proud, and possessive of her. Instead of happiness the realization gave her a moment of panic, which was followed by guilt. She smiled across the table at him, a smile with her mouth which she knew was perfidious.

The servants had taken away the soup bowls. Caspar had tasted only a mouthful of his. The main course was being served from a pair of huge silver-domed dishes that had been placed on the sideboard. Listening to Caspar talking, Harriet didn't immediately look at what had been placed in front of her.

It was Linda's gasp of shock and disgust that alerted her.

On each plate, resting on perfect ovals of gravy-richened toast, lay a pair of whole, tiny birds. Their eyes were closed by tiny, opaque lids and their long, straight beaks were tucked against their breasts in a parody of sleep.

"What are they?" Linda asked in horror.

"I'm not sure. Snipe, or woodcock. Something like that."

"Poor little things," Linda whispered. "They should be flying over the woods. They look so dead." Her face was white, and her eyes were red. Harriet knew that she was on the point of tears. Harriet felt coldly angry with Annunziata for serving such a dish to a child. The tiny, filmed, unaccusing eyes of the birds made her feel sick, and so how much worse must it be for Linda? She felt profound dislike for the soft, tasteful, ostentatious display of this house, and for Robin's mother who was responsible for it. She knew that she would not come here again.

"Don't worry," Harriet told Linda.

She lifted her hand to summon the butler. She murmured to him, "Would you take Linda's plate away, please? She will just have some vegetables."

The exchange was swiftly and discreetly made. If anyone noticed what had happened, no one made any comment. Linda's color slowly came back, and she picked at her tiny sprouts and carrots and thumbnail-sized parsnips.

Harriet tasted the flesh of one of her birds. It was delicious, of course.

The course lasted interminably. A fine burgundy was served, provoking much discussion among the men. Caspar contributed little to it, but he drank his share.

At last the plates with their minute, dismembered carcasses were removed.

"Thank you," Linda whispered miserably to Harriet.

"You'll enjoy the puddings," Harriet tried to comfort her. "And then it will be all over."

She had thought that Caspar was engrossed in his own performance, and in any case too far gone to have been aware of what was happening on Harriet's other side. She was startled when he turned his attention full to her. "You did right," he said, in a low voice. "You did just right. I'm grateful."

But when she tried to suggest that Linda had had almost enough, and might be glad to be taken home soon, the blue stare turned glassy. She had the impression that Caspar had forgotten who she was, if indeed he had ever known it. He had thanked her, in obedience to some dim formula that persisted from sober hours, and immediately blotted it out. She recognized just how drunk he was, and had to admire his ability to stay at the table, still talking.

Linda had brightened up a little. The puddings were as elaborate as the rest of the meal, but one of them was chocolaty enough to interest her. She dug enthusiastically into her portion, only pausing to ask Harriet if she thought there might be second helpings. It was totally dark outside. The braided tie-backs that kept the curtains looped up had been unfastened, and the heavy folds had dropped across the windows. Candles had been lit in silver holders, creating instant night out of the winter afternoon. The meal seemed to have been going on for hours. More wine was being served, viscous and deep straw-golden this time, in tiny thimble glasses. Probably Château d'Yquem, Harriet thought sourly.

The crisis came, as in retrospect she knew it had to come, very quickly. The company had been talking about money. The topic had swelled from a specific debate about some aspect of venture capitalism to a more general discussion of monetarism and from there, lubricated by the straw-gold wine, to the morality of wealth. Harriet listened, fascinated. To sit among these people and hear them talk about money was like sitting amid ermine and strawberry leaves for a celebration of the rights of aristocracy.

"It's money that makes the world go round," one woman said. She had been resting her chin on one hand, but it slipped and she jerked herself upright. Harriet would have excused her fatuity on the grounds of too much wine, but she heard Caspar gasp beside her. It was as if patience, or diplomacy, or self-control had finally, and sharply, deserted him. He levered himself to his feet, resting with his thumbs on the tablecloth.

"To answer your cliché with another, money is the root of every evil in this world. I've made more bloody money than any of you, pissed most of it away instead of *investing* and *buying and selling* and fucking *counting* it, which was at least amusing while it lasted, but I can tell you now, with no charge, that I have seen what it does. I've seen the rot and the rubbish. I haven't got any money now, thank Christ. Piss it away, that's my advice to you for yours." He made a grand gesture, half a flourishing bow. "Money stinks. Can't you *smell* it?"

There was an appalled, ominous silence. Linda sat motionless, holding her chocolate spoon. She gave no sign of having heard anything, except that her ears burned dull crimson. Martin was already on his feet, and Robin stood up, too. Apparently intending to leave the table before they reached him, Caspar pushed his chair back. It would have fallen if Annunziata had not caught it. He lurched, caught at the table to steady himself, and found the rim of Harriet's pudding plate instead. The plate and its contents tipped into her lap.

Caspar looked down. With the unpredictable, exaggerated politeness of the very drunk he said, "I beg your pardon. I do most sincerely beg your pardon."

Martin took him by the arm. Quite kindly, he said, "Come on, old boy. I think that's enough." Robin stationed himself on the opposite side. Caspar let them steer him away. When they reached the door he turned to look over his shoulder at the silent room.

"The condemned man was led from the courtroom," he intoned.

Harriet put the plate back on the table. The mess in her lap looked disgusting, as if she had vomited over herself. Beside her, Linda stared down at her hands, folded in her own lap.

"It's all right," Harriet mumbled.

The women crowded around her. There were low murmurs of dismay and sympathy. The spilled food was mopped up, Harriet was spirited briskly upstairs to Annunziata's bedroom. There was a four-poster bed and carpets the color of full-cream milk, and silver-framed photographs of Robin at various ages that Harriet would have liked to peer more closely at. Annunziata laid out some of her own clothes for Harriet to change into, the housekeeper bore away her soiled ones.

"I'm so sorry," Annunziata said. "Who could have known that he would behave like that?"

"It's all right. I liked him."

Harriet had certainly liked him, especially for his gloomy humor as Martin had hustled him away. She would have defended him against any of these people, except for Robin, but it was hard to forgive his implication of Linda.

When she came back downstairs she found that several guests had left, and the remainder were in the drawing room, sitting or standing in a circle around the child. She looked up as Harriet came in, with clear relief in her face.

"I'd really love to go home." Her knees were drawn up and her locked arms thrust down between them. She looked small and thin, and shivery with cold. Martin Landwith was patting her shoulder, as if he couldn't think what else to do.

Harriet glanced at him. "Where's . . ."

"Taking a little nap," Martin said dryly.

Harriet went and knelt in front of Linda so that their faces were level. "Is there anyone at home?"

"Ronny's there."

"Shall we telephone him?"

"Her. She looks after me." Linda's voice had shrunk, almost to inaudibility. Harriet thought, at least she's got somebody.

Robin appeared beside Harriet. "I'll drive her. It's only a few hundred yards."

"Will you come, too?" Linda begged.

"Of course I will," Harriet said.

There was an air of relief in the room at the prospect of getting rid of at least half of the problem. Very quickly, they found themselves outside. The air was cold and sweet.

"The car's over there," Robin said.

"Could we . . . could we walk?" Linda asked.

"Yes, if that's what you'd like." Harriet understood her need to be in the forgiving dark. Robin looked as if he would like nothing less. "I'll take her. I'm sure Linda can show me the way," she added.

"I'm not going to let you wander around the lanes on your own in the dark."

Harriet smiled inwardly at the thought of legions of high-waymen lurking in the manicured byways of Little Shelley at seven o'clock on a winter's evening. She said nothing, and they set out together. They walked the short distance in silence, beneath high walls and thick hedges, their footsteps clopping unevenly. About halfway there, Linda slipped her hand into Harriet's.

They reached the right gates. Robin pressed the bell and announced their intentions into a speaker. The gates swung silently open. Ahead of them lay the bulk of another big house. There were lights showing in only two small upstairs windows, but as they passed through some security beam across the drive-way, floodlights snapped on to illuminate the entire housefront. Harriet blinked, wanting to put her arm up to shield her face. The front door opened as they reached it.

A middle-aged woman in a tweed skirt stood in the harsh light. She looked more like a secretary or assistant than the homely nanny-figure Harriet had been imagining. Behind her, what was visible of the house looked as if the occupants were in the process of moving in or moving out. Packing cases piled haphazardly with books stood everywhere.

"Thank you for bringing her," the woman said pleasantly. "I'm Veronica Page, by the way."

"Daddy's asleep," Linda told her. Miss Page nodded, her mouth in a straight line. It was clearly a familiar occurrence.

"Come on inside, then."

Linda released Harriet's hand and went to stand by her Ronny, without much show of enthusiasm. "Thank you," she said mechanically to Robin. But when she looked at Harriet her face changed, filling with imploring anxiety. "You will come and see me, won't you? Will you come and see me at my school?"

Harriet went and hugged her, drawing her head against her. Her colorless hair felt fine and silky under her fingers. "I'm sure we'll see each other again."

They left her with Miss Page, and retraced their steps to the gates. Behind them, the probing lights snapped off again.

In the darkness of the lane, Harriet asked Robin, "What was it like when you were small, when you were Linda's age?"

After a moment he answered, "Secure. Comfortable."

"Did you rough around with other little boys?"

"Not much. There was only me. I spent a lot of time with adults."

"Yes," Harriet said. Robin seemed old for his years now; the same control must have been required from him as a child. Harriet felt sorry for him, but she felt sorrier still for Linda Jensen.

Robin and Harriet refused Annunziata's invitation to stay for dinner and to see in the New Year. "What a wretched day it's been for you," she said to Robin rather than Harriet. "But there's always next time to look forward to." She did turn to Harriet now. "We've hardly had time to talk. You will come again, won't you?"

"Of course I will," Harriet lied.

Martin walked out with them to the Porsche. He told Harriet, "I'm glad you and Robin are seeing something of each other."

Harriet remembered the sensation of being looked over, and then of being dismissed in favor of the son. She still didn't know if Martin merely summed up women in his sleek head, or whether he took their analysis any further. But having met his wife, she couldn't blame him if he did all the investigation that was possible.

The Porsche wound down the narrow road, turned into a wider road, and then reached the motorway. Harriet's spirits lifted like a balloon.

"I'm sorry if you didn't enjoy yourself," Robin said.

Harriet wondered if he was deliberately echoing her own words to him as they drove away from Jane's house.

"I did enjoy myself," she said. In a way it was the truth. She wouldn't have missed the day, she was sure of that.

After a moment she added, "We don't have much success, do we, in conjoining our separate worlds?"

Robin's response was fierce. "I don't care about worlds. I'm only interested in you and me." He lifted his hand from the wheel and let it rest against her thigh. "Happy New Year," he said, in a softer voice.

Harriet repeated the words after him. His touch didn't affect her quite as strongly as it usually did.

That was all, except that two days later a big oblong package was delivered to Harriet at Peacocks.

Inside the wrapping paper she found a big cellophane box, and inside the cellophane lay a sheaf of orchids. The petals of the swollen blooms were bruise-purple, lime-green and velvet-brown, spotted and furred and blotched like small, exotic animals. Harriet lifted the flowers. They were still moist, as if they had just been flown in from the East, or wherever it was that orchids bloomed in January.

The card enclosed with them read, *Sincere and sober apologies. Perhaps I may make amends in person when I am back in England? Thank you for taking care of my daughter. Caspar Jensen.*

Harriet wondered how he had found her office address. Perhaps he had, after all, been perfectly well aware of who she was.

She didn't take the flowers back to Hampstead, where Robin would see them, but kept them on her desk. When at last they faded, turning over-ripe and then dropping their petals to lie on her papers like sloughed skins, she lifted them out of their vase and tipped them into the dustbin.

She thought no more about them and very little more about their sender.

Twelve

HARRIET TOOK HER PLACE at the big oval table. Beside the draft copy of the Peacocks prospectus that had been set at each place she laid her blank notepad, and the gold-nibbed pen that Kath had given her for Christmas.

Harriet was the only woman in the room. Six men were taking their seats to the right and left of her, laying out their papers and their notes in busy silence. Harriet folded her hands in her lap and waited. Under the table, out of the sight of the six men, she pressed the balls of her feet against the boardroom carpet. She pressed harder, until she felt the bite of cramp in her instep, but she couldn't control the shaking of her legs.

After almost six months of preparation, of minute scrutiny of her company and its performance by accountants, bankers, brokers and lawyers, this was the pricing meeting. Harriet's lawyers, Piers Mayhew, sat on her left, and Jeremy Crichton the accountant on her right. They had come to the offices of A.R. Allardyce & Co. Ltd., their sponsoring merchant bankers, to hear the valuation that they would put on her company, and the figure at which they believed Peacocks' shares should go to the market in six days' time. Harriet had come to hear what price they would put on her baby. After the months of work, Peacocks was ready to be floated. Harriet was about to become the head of a publicly-quoted company.

The date of this meeting had been fixed weeks before. All the necessary procedures had been completed according to City formulas, but now the hour had come Harriet could not stop herself shaking. She was afraid, but she was also enthralled, and she felt as high as if her veins had been pumped full of heroin.

She glanced covertly to her right. Piers Mayhew's plump moon-face was impassive behind his heavy-rimmed glasses. His white hands were quite steady as he unpacked documents from his briefcase. On her other side Harriet saw that Jeremy's marble features were disturbed only by the involuntary twitch of a muscle at the corner of his mouth. Harriet looked up at one of the clocks on the wall facing her, the one labeled *London. Come on, please come on*, she begged silently, as the thin black second hand swept around the face to three p.m., exactly.

"Gentlemen?" James Hamilton, the senior member of the bank's team, spoke with authority.

The meeting came instantly to attention.

Hamilton began his prepared speech. Harriet and her advisers leaned forward in their chairs to listen. Harriet was too intent to notice, but her legs stopped shaking. She had chosen these people, A.R. Allardyce and McGovern Cowper, the brokers who were acting in association with them. Months ago, Harriet and Piers had made the rounds of merchant banks who were eager to act as the issuing house for the stockmarket launch of her company. She had taken particular pleasure in their visit to Morton's, although she had not seen the three wise monkeys at the meeting. The process of vetting the interested banks was known as a beauty parade; from the parade Harriet and Piers had chosen Allardyce's for their enthusiasm for and high estimation of Peacocks.

The time had now come for it to be made clear whether their enthusiasm and Harriet's choice were mutually justified. Deep inside herself, Harriet knew that there was no real cause to feel afraid. She had done everything that could be done, and she believed in Peacocks with every fiber of herself. After six months' investigation, Allardyce's could only do the same.

James Hamilton was coming smoothly to the point. The room was quiet enough for the sound of traffic in Cornhill, far below, to be audible through the barrier of the double glazing.

"In giving our most careful consideration to the potential placing of Peacocks within its sector of the market, we have made a careful study of the performances of competitors, and of your accountants' long-form report . . ." James Hamilton tapped the copy of the prospectus in front of him. Harriet did not even glance down. After so many weeks spent helping to prepare the forecasts it contained, she knew the figures by heart. ". . . as a culmination of many hours of discussion, and a final analysis by the head of corporate finance, we are of the confident opinion that Peacocks, as a dynamic growth company with prospects of leading its sector in due course, has a market value of . . ."

Harriet saw that the faces were impassive. Allardyce's probably sponsored twenty issues a year. This was a day's work to Hamilton and the others. She wondered how much her face betrayed her own feelings, at this climax of more than three years of solid work.

". . . sixteen million pounds, give or take a narrow margin
of perhaps half a million pounds."

The room was still quiet. Harriet was surprised that it was
not filled with the thumping of her heart. It felt as if it might
burst out of her chest.

"Your current after-tax trading profit of one point three
million pounds," Hamilton intoned, "historical profits and profit
forecasts . . . indicating a price to earnings ratio of sixteen. We
suggest therefore that an appropriate share price for a company
of this weight, to place it in the highly marketable range . . ."

He exchanged nods with the two brokers and then looked
directly at Harriet over the rim of his spectacles. She waited. The
bankers and brokers would pitch the shares at a price a little
below their estimate of their real worth, to ensure a rise once
trading began. But if the price was too low, she could justifiably
accuse them of not getting the best price for her.

". . . is one pound twenty-five pence. We therefore propose
flotation on impact day next Tuesday at this price."

Harriet took a breath. It was what she had been hoping for.
A shade better even. Figures began to unwind in her head,
reeling faster and faster like a line once a big fish had taken the
hook.

"Miss Peacock?"

Harriet took up her notepad and wrote briskly. Piers and
Jeremy edged their chairs closer to hers. With the benefit of their
advice, Harriet had to decide whether to accept the sponsors'
proposal.

They murmured briefly together. The bankers and brokers
talked politely among themselves while they waited.

Harriet lifted her head. "Two or three questions," she said.
"With which other companies have you compared Peacocks?
And why do you suggest a P.E. ratio lower than that of Dy-
namic, which stands at seventeen?"

She listened carefully to Hamilton's fluent answers. At length
she nodded. "Mr. Mayhew has some points to raise also."

And then, when Piers was satisfied, Harriet looked to Jeremy for his approval. Only now did she allow herself to smile.

"Thank you, Mr. Hamilton," she said softly. "Your proposal
is acceptable. We shall be happy to float on Tuesday at one
twenty-five."

They stood up, all six of them, and shook hands.

"Very good," Hamilton answered. "All being well, we shall
have impact at ten a.m. next Tuesday morning."

Impact day, Harriet had learned to call it. Tuesday, June the twelfth. The date had been allotted by the Bank of England all of three months ago, but the lengthy lead-up had only increased Harriet's excitement. The figures continued to dance in her head. The sale of five percent of her own equity would net her several hundred thousand pounds, but the remainder of her holding now had a paper value of rather more than four million pounds. The dividend on her holding alone would amount to more than eighty thousand pounds a year, to add to her salary as managing director.

Harriet was still smiling as dizziness took hold of her. She had estimated all this, of course, a thousand times over, but now that the bankers had confirmed it it was as if she held the money in her hands.

I'm rich, Harriet told herself, chanting the words as if they were part of a rhyme, *I'm suddenly, suddenly rich.*

She remembered Crete, and the half-joke that had just become wholly truth.

She remembered also, with pleasure, that Kath's investment had brought wealth to the Trotts, too. Paper wealth, as yet, because Robin had convinced the family that they should hold on to their shares and wait for the post-launch rise.

Then, with sudden clarity, imprinted on the jumbled images of her friends and her family, she saw Simon's face. He was in a dim place that might have been his kitchen or the half-imagined horror of the camp, but his features were sharp. He was looking past her, over her shoulder, as if in expectation of someone else. There would be money for Simon, too, she thought. And the blankness of the following question, *What can it do for him?* brought her up short, in bewilderment.

Deliberately, carefully, Harriet steadied herself again. There was still work to be done. That was what was important now, at this minute.

James Hamilton's number two was holding up the draft prospectus. Harriet nodded her approval to him. The figures that the seven of them present at the meeting had just agreed upon would now be inserted, and the whole document would be whisked away to the security printers. The final prospectus would be printed overnight, and on the morning of impact day McGovern Cowper would issue it to their clients and potential subscribers.

The months of work, the planning and calculating, would find their measure in the interest of the market at impact on Tuesday morning.

There was another job, too, that must be immediately at-

tended to. A report of the meeting must be sent to Peacocks'
public relations company, who would arrange for the story to be
fed to the press—the business and financial press. There would
be stories in the City pages about the forthcoming issue, the
P.R. people would make sure of that. James Hamilton had described Peacocks as a dynamic growth company with real prospects of leading its sector in due course. The press release would
repeat the phrases, Harriet would see to it, and the journalists
would paraphrase them and add their own interpretations of
Peacocks' performance. The stories would catch the eye of the
investors, most of whom would have seen "Meizu" somewhere,
probably played it, perhaps read about "Meizu Girl."

The other stories, in the blue cuttings file, were all justified
now, Harriet believed. Today's pricing meeting justified them,
the "Meizu" stunts and "Meizu Girl" and even the British POW
stories. All the work, all the marketing and the pushing and
pleasing, had led to this; James Hamilton of A.R. Allardyce,
looking at her over the rim of his spectacles, had announced that
her company was worth sixteen million pounds.

Harriet felt a shock of triumph running through her like an
electric current. She could take the figures to Martin and Robin,
to Kath and Ken, and say, *You see?* I did do it. She could even
go to Simon and lay in front of him whatever he wanted, whatever he needed, in return for "Meizu."

And she would do that, Harriet determined.

As soon after impact day as she could she would take the
figures, and the benign, impersonal business cuttings, and show
them to Simon. It was a long time since she had seen him,
although she ensured that money continued to accumulate in the
bank account she had opened for him. But now she could go to
see him and tell him that although she had taken his story, taken
his suffering, she had translated it into success.

What else was there?

The meeting was over. Harriet gathered up her papers and
replaced them in her briefcase. James Hamilton and his number
two shook her hand, followed by the two men from McGovern
Cowper.

"Until Tuesday morning," Hamilton murmured. "At eight
a.m., for breakfast?"

"Of course," Harriet smiled at him. "I'm looking forward to
it."

Harriet rode down in the lift, through the intestinal tracts of
the bank, with Piers and Jeremy. In the daylight outside she saw

that Piers's round face was flushed with excitement, and that even the accountant's marble complexion was tinged with color.

"Good?" Harriet demanded, ready to dance on the city pavement.

"So far," and "Tuesday will tell us for sure," they answered, with professional circumspection. Jeremy flagged down a taxi.

"Are you coming back to the office?"

Harriet shook her head. "I'm going to Landwith's first. Then I'll go on to do the press release. I'll be in the office after six-thirty, if you want me."

Harriet hadn't been home very much, lately. She had found the capacity to work harder, and longer, than she had ever done before. But she did it with pleasure, finding that work increased her appetite for work, until even busy Robin complained.

She took a taxi to Landwith Associates. Robin had been working at his desk in his blue and white shirtsleeves, but he was putting his jacket on when his secretary showed Harriet in. He came around the desk to greet her. It was part of their agreement, their unwritten contract, that formality was preserved between them in everything to do with business.

Harriet sat down and after one look at her face Robin ordered, "Wait. Martin will want to hear, too." Harriet folded her hands in her lap. While they waited, Robin asked for tea to be brought in.

Martin came, his habitual suavity masking his eagerness for the news. Harriet looked at them, father and son with their lean, dark, clever faces, waiting to hear what she had brought home for them. The word *home* triggered another thought. She realized that for what must be the first time she did feel at home in here. She had crossed some divide, and landed on the same side as Robin and his father.

The secretary brought in the tea, and laid it out on a low table. Harriet crossed her legs while she waited, and then saw that both the men were looking at them. She smiled, inwardly. She was stimulated by the feel of her own muscles, knitting smoothly under her skin, the strong sheet across her stomach and the tiny wings at the corners of her eyelids. Her shakes in the Allardyce boardroom were forgotten. Now her body was powerful enough to contain her bursting excitement, holding her in repose as calm as Martin's while the teacups made their tiny, civilized clinking.

The secretary went away again and Robin poured from the silver teapot into white-and-gold cups. Harriet was too taut to think of eating any of the decorative morsels of bread or sponge, but she drank China tea, thirstily.

"And are our friends at Allardyce prepared to do Peacocks justice?" Martin drawled.

Harriet put her cup down slowly, loving the moment.

"I think so," she said. "I hope you'll agree."

She took her notes out of her briefcase and set them in order. And then without referring to them she told her backers what she had done for them.

Landwith's was offering for sale fourteen percent of their equity, taking their holding back to the original thirty-five percent.

Harriet didn't need to spell out what Tuesday's flotation would net for them, or what their remaining equity would be worth in a healthy aftermarket. Their investment in Peacocks had been a flyer; now it was coming triumphantly home to roost, on golden wings.

She saw, as she talked, an identical light kindle in their eyes. They didn't smile, either of them, nor did they rub their hands, but she knew that she had set their juices flowing just the same. This, then, was their private and mutual buzz. It wasn't the money that excited them, because they didn't need more money. It was simply hearing the numbers, and calculating the power, yes, and the glory, that the additions made.

Watching them, Harriet wondered whether she really liked these men at all. But she also knew that, like them or not, she belonged with them. She had crossed over to their side. And she felt the charge, too. She felt it in her toes, and fingers, and in the center of herself.

"There it is," Harriet concluded softly. "Robin, may I have another cup of tea?" Martin took her cup, and refilled it. When he stood in front of her again he held out his hand, and Harriet took it.

"Congratulations," Martin said. "I'm sure you know that I was less convinced by your proposal than Robin was. I'm sure that Tuesday will prove me wrong, and I'm pleased. Well done, Harriet."

"Tuesday will tell whether congratulations are in order," Harriet answered.

She knew there were other things that would not be said. From the way he looked at her, and from the touch of his hand, Harriet knew that Martin wanted her. She had speculated in the past: now she knew for sure. She also knew that his desire for her was as clear-cut and as measurable as a closing price, and equally that tomorrow would bring another hot issue to displace her.

She accepted the tribute and looked past him to Robin.

Martin said cheerfully, "Annunziata's expecting me to take her to hear Pavarotti this evening. I'd better think about going to change. Good night, both of you."

The door closed behind him.

Robin stood up at once, and came to Harriet. She read the satisfaction in his face; it was for the fact that she was here with him and Martin had gone as much as for Peacocks, as much as for Harriet herself. She accepted that also.

"How do you feel?" Robin asked.

Harriet smiled, meeting his eyes, then let her head drop forward so that her forehead rested against him.

"Hot," she whispered.

Robin drew her closer. "Hot, like this?" With one hand he undid the buttons of her linen suit, and dropped the jacket on the floor at their feet. He undid the smaller pearl buttons at the front of her blouse, and opened it. His hand touched her breast.

"Cooler?"

Harriet shook her head. "No. Just the opposite. But this is the office, Robin. This is business."

"You think too much about the bloody business." His face had darkened. She saw that he wasn't playing anymore. "Now, take it off." He twisted her silk blouse and she heard the sound of a tiny tear.

Harriet looked around her, at the desk and the screens with their closing prices, and the row of telephones, waiting to ring. "Here?" she murmured.

"Here. And *now*," Robin commanded. He pressed a button. "No more calls. No interruptions."

Then he went swiftly to the door and locked it.

Harriet might have laughed but she was aroused. She took off her blouse and let her skirt fall in another heap. Then, with Robin watching her, she peeled off her underclothes. When she was naked she turned slowly on the balls of her feet, stretching, feeling the cool air on her skin. It was erotic to find herself standing here, under the good pictures, with the nice rugs under her bare feet, while the London closing prices danced on Robin's screens in front of her eyes.

"Come here," Robin said softly.

He stroked her arms, and her thighs, and closed his hands around her waist. When he touched her, Harriet felt herself catch fire. She loosened the knot of his tie and undid the buttons of his shirt, feeling the crisp cotton under her fingers. Her hand moved down, found the zipper of his trousers, and deftly released him.

Driven by a sudden imperative, Harriet knelt down and took his cock into her mouth. Her tongue moved along the shaft and her lips closed over the smooth head.

As she moved, lifting and lowering her bent head, Harriet became quite sure of what she wanted.

She wanted to fuck Robin and Martin and Landwith Associates all together, taking them into herself, taking them up and using them for her own pleasure, as a tribute to her power and her success. She felt the power; it stirred her own response more deeply than Robin alone had ever done. Robin filled her mouth and her throat, she wanted to swallow him, consume him. Above her he murmured, "Harriet, I shall come."

She raised her head and then stood up. Robin leaned back against the corner of his desk. His eyes were fixed on her, greedy, his appetite matching her own. With one movement Harriet lifted herself, and then with delicate concentration fitted herself over him. She wrapped her legs around his waist and he drove up into her, filling her with a wash of warmth and light that spread upward, into her heart and head.

Fiercely, Harriet took what she wanted—not just Robin, but everything he stood for. It was intensely, profoundly exciting.

She wanted to bury her teeth in Robin's throat, to dig her fingers deep into the muscles of his back. They were solid, both of them, but they were also abstract and floating, practice and theory coming together. Harriet closed her eyes on the walls and the picture and saw equations instead, the intricate formulae that linked sex, and power, and money. She thought in that instant that she saw the world clearly, and read its secrets. She was also blind, and helpless, a bewildered witness to her own longing. Harriet's head fell back.

She didn't see the almost identical scene from a different perspective, the door of Leo's studio. Nor was there a wife to appear, silent and accusing in the doorway. The door was locked, and Robin's secretary stood unconscious guard beyond it. Harriet was oblivious. She had never given herself up so completely, nor had she ever taken what she needed so ruthlessly. It was like being shaken awake, and set free. She whispered, "Robin," but it was much more than Robin that she was really calling on. Her mouth opened in a long, silent cry.

Afterward they clung together, breathing in the same short gasps. Harriet's head lay on Robin's shoulder. She saw, close up to her eyes, the red marks that her fingers had made.

Robin lifted her up and then lowered her into a chair. She felt as limp as a rag doll, and as inarticulate. Robin opened a drawer and took out a shirt in rustling laundry wrapping. He tore the bag open, discarded the paper stiffening and undid the buttons. Then he handed the shirt to her.

Harriet wrapped herself in it, looking around the room again. She felt surprised, now that she was in possession of herself again, and faintly embarrassed.

Robin went into the bathroom that led out of his office, and came out again dressed, with his hair smoothly brushed. Harriet drew the cool cotton shirt more closely to her and tucked up her legs beneath her. Robin came closer, then knelt down in front of her, looking into her face. Harriet met his eyes. She knew that her hair stood up in a ruffled crest, and that her mouth was bruised.

"Harriet?" Robin said. "Look, here, it's me. It was me just then, too. Are you there, Harriet?"

She shook herself out of her silence. "I know it was you. I'm here."

"Will you marry me?"

She studied his face, familiar and separate from her. She didn't know if it was Robin who had lit the flame, or if she had done it herself. But the feeling of having crossed some divide, of belonging here, remained with her. She reached out to touch the corner of his mouth with her fingertips.

"Ask me after Tuesday," she answered.

Robin smiled. "How does it feel to be a millionairess?"

"A paper one, only."

He bent his head to her curled-up thigh and kissed it. "Flesh and blood," he contradicted her.

"It feels fine." Harriet knotted her fingers in his dark hair, disheveling it again.

"Robin, I have to go and see the P.R. people now."

He lifted his head. "Go on then, witch."

In his bathroom, Harriet studied herself in the mirror. There was no difference to see, for having become rich. She put on her clothes again, linen suit and silk blouse, and repaired her face. She emerged once more, the corporate executive. Robin was installed behind his desk. But there was a feeling of complicity that made her want to stay a little longer, to play truant.

"Good-bye, Mr. Landwith," she said firmly.

"Good-bye, Miss Peacock."

Harriet closed his door behind her, nodded to the secretary in the adjoining office, and went blithely on to the meeting with her publicity agents. There was plenty to do, before Tuesday.

*   *   *

Five days to impact, then four, then three.

Harriet woke up, already looking at the digital clockface beside her bed. She had been getting up at six, to be in the office by seven-thirty. Preparing for the stockmarket float had taken up so much of her time the routine work had been shelved. Now she was trying to catch up on it.

The red digits told her that it was eight o'clock. Confusedly she reached out for her watch and then remembered that it was Saturday. She had deliberately not set her alarm the night before, to allow herself some extra sleep. Now she lay quietly, still curled up, enjoying the sense of waking to a special day, like a child in the week before Christmas, that had been with her since the pricing meeting. The brokers at McGovern Cowper were canvasing prospective investors by telephone, and reporting considerable enthusiasm. Press reports were encouraging. Harriet could look forward to impact with confidence, still pleasantly flavored with uncertainty.

But as soon as she was fully awake, she couldn't lie still any longer. She had never been able to enjoy languishing in bed. Now she got up, put on her bathrobe and went upstairs.

She did like being able to wander around her kitchen, without the pressure of having to get to work. It seemed a very long time since she had had a Saturday morning like this.

She took a handful of coffee beans from a tin and ground them, enjoying the rich smell. While the coffee brewed she made brown toast and spread it with honey, then stood at the window eating it and looking down at the rosebushes in the garden that had survived her regime of neglect to produce blooms. The sun was shining. Harriet wondered whether later on she might walk up to Chic, in Hampstead village, to find something suitably powerful to wear to the sponsors' breakfast on Tuesday, or whether she might just spend the morning sitting in the garden with the newspapers. She realized with a little shock that the second option, nowadays, would be the more luxurious.

It was not that she didn't take pleasure in having money to spend, of course. It was still a luxury to walk into expensive shops and to look critically along the rails at the whispery silks and crisp linens and melting tweeds, choosing or rejecting among the designer labels. She had not forgotten how it had been when she had only been able to admire, before going elsewhere to search out cheaper lookalikes. It was just that now, so quickly, the prospect of a few hours doing nothing was even more beguiling than the hunt for the most covetable outfit in the world.

Harriet heard the rattle of the front door letterbox. She let herself out of her own flat door to collect the morning's mail.

Most of her mail came to the Peacocks office. This morning there was only a bill, a credit card statement, a circular and a bright yellow envelope addressed in a child's handwriting. Harriet took the little sheaf back into the kitchen and poured a cup of coffee. Then she sat down at the table and opened the yellow envelope, neatly, with a table knife.

The top lefthand corner of the single sheet of yellow paper was decorated with a dancing Snoopy. On the right hand there was the address of a school near Ascot that Harriet had never heard of. Frowning, she turned the sheet over to see the signature. It read, *Love, Linda.*

Harriet took a mouthful of coffee, then started at the beginning again.

Dear Harriet,

Linda Jensen had written, more or less; her spelling and handwriting were like a seven-year-old's:

You never came to see me did you? And you said you would so you havent been very nice. I am as good as a prisonner heer in this school, I reelly hate it, reelly, reelly hate it, the girls and the teachers are so stupid and boring. Daddy and my Mom said I would love it, but they were wrong werent they!

I found your adress which was quite clever and I even called you but all I got was your machine and I hate those, so I hung up.

Will you come and see me now? Pleese? I think you should stick close with your friends. Harriet, I would come and see you if you were in jail.

Ronny says I must join in and make friends but who wants to be friends with these assholls. Mom is busy in LA and Daddy is filming abroad as usuall so I am COUNTING ON YOU, Harriet, to have a plan.

Love, Linda

Harriet read the letter through, twice, with some difficulty. Its imperious, unhappy demands touched her. She also felt faintly guilty. She should have made some effort to stay in contact with the child.

"Poor Linda," she said aloud.

She vaguely remembered having read somewhere that Clare Mellen was stormily involved with a new actor, younger than herself. She didn't know what Caspar Jensen was doing, but she could guess. And so Linda had been put into—Harriet glanced at the address next to Snoopy again—a good, safe, conventional English boarding preparatory school. Harriet supposed that it had become Ronny's responsibility to drive over from Little Shelley at weekends to take her out to tea, or whatever it was that the school permitted.

"Poor Linda," Harriet said again.

She went through to her desk in the next room and, after a few moments' thought, wrote an answer to Linda's plea.

> Dear Linda,
>
> You are quite right, I should have come to see you, and I promise that I will. I won't make excuses for not having been before, because I'm about to make another excuse, and one at a time is quite enough.
>
> I can't come to St. Brigid's this week, because it is going to be the busiest and most important week of my life. I'll explain why, and tell you all about it, when I see you. If all goes well, and if school and Ronny will allow me, I will come two weeks today and take you out to tea.

Harriet couldn't check her diary because it was at the office. If there was something else, she decided, she would have to cancel it for Linda's sake.

> In the meantime, I know you won't like to hear this, but I'm sure Ronny is right. If you do join in and make friends, you will find that school is more fun than if you are angry with everyone. It's easy for me to say so, because I haven't got to be at school anymore, but I can remember what it was like. You also have to trust what your friends—if you count me as a friend, and I wish you would—tell you. We can talk some more about this when we meet.
>
> I'm sorry you are unhappy. I'll do whatever I can to help.
>   With love, Harriet
>
> PS. Can you tell me EXACTLY what makes them assholes? If you're going to use words like that, you should know how to spell them. Do I sound like a teacher? H.

She sealed the letter and addressed it.

Harriet decided that she would ask Robin to ask his mother for the telephone number of the uncozy house that Caspar Jensen owned in Little Shelley, so that she could ring Linda's Ronny and discuss the problem with her. Harriet sighed. She didn't suppose that the woman would welcome her interference, but that couldn't be helped.

And then, having done what she could for the moment, Harriet put Linda's letter aside. She didn't go shopping in the end, nor did she do more than glance at the business pages of the newspapers. She opened her briefcase and took out some paperwork, becoming absorbed in it. She worked until the telephone rang beside her.

The caller was Jenny Thimbell, reminding Harriet that she had promised to come for a family tea, before going out to the theater with Robin.

"I'll be there at four o'clock," Harriet promised briskly. "I hadn't forgotten."

In the afternoon Harriet drove over to the Thimbells' house in Islington. Jenny and Charlie lived in a tall, thin, Georgian house that seemed to have more stairs than horizontal floor-space. The house seemed also to be in a perpetual state of structural mobility as walls were re-sited, plasterwork exposed and shutters divested of decades-worth of pastel gloss paint. As she rang the bell Harriet tried to estimate how long the restoration work had been in progress, and then gave up the attempt.

Charlie opened the door. He was wearing overalls and brandishing a paintbrush.

"Prominent Financial Editor in Cupboard Crisis," he announced. "The painter didn't show up all week, so how is the kitchen to get to the next stage? You guessed. Charlie does it." He leaned forward, holding the paintbrush approximately away from her, and gave Harriet a kiss. "God, how svelte you look. How can you bear to come in here? But come in anyway. Jenny and the kids are in the garden. I'll do one more cupboard while Harry's out of the way, then I'll be out."

Smiling, Harriet picked her way along the hallway to the back of the house. The floorboards were all exposed, and on the equally bare stairs there were heaps of baby clothes in laundry baskets, toys and books and shoes, piled up waiting to be carried up to the floors above by whoever next undertook the steep climb.

A door at the end opened on to a tiny semicircular wrought-iron balcony, and a narrow wrought-iron spiral stair led down to the garden.

Jenny was sitting on a rug spread on the grass below. The

baby was kicking her bare feet beside her, and Harry was pottering in his sandpit with a wooden spade.

The sun shone on Jenny's smooth blonde head.

"What an idyllic scene," Harriet called. Jenny looked up in surprise.

"Harriet! I didn't hear the door. Come down here."

Harriet hitched up her narrow skirt and climbed over the safety gate at the bottom of the stairs. Harry rushed at her, waving his spade and scattering sand in a wide arc. Harriet swung him off his feet.

"How's my best godson?" He beamed at her, showing small teeth in a mouth circled with sand and earth. He smelled of sugar, hot skin and diapers.

"Watch out, Harriet, he's filthy."

"Doesn't matter," Harriet said. "He's grown so *big*. Do they all grow like this?"

"I think so," Jenny said happily.

"And Alice?" Harriet leaned over the bundle on the rug. The baby stared up at her, serious-faced. Harriet imagined how she must seem, a huge dark moon blotting out the light, and quickly sat back again.

"Alice is fine. She's a better sleeper than Harry was. We're down to only one feed a night, already."

"Is that good?"

"It is. Life begins to seem distinctly possible again." Jenny's eyebrows drew together.

"I don't want to sound as though I'm complaining. I don't, do I? You and Jane, of all people, know how much I wanted them." She reached out then, for Harry, as if an unseen hand might snatch him away, and held him until he gave a wail of complaint. Jenny laughed at herself. "Sleep just becomes a precious commodity."

"I sympathize with that," Harriet told her. "Tell me what you've been doing."

Jenny gestured at the little walled garden, shady, planted with ivy and lady's mantle and London pride, with the sunny patch in the center, and the tall house at her back. Harriet looked up at its windows, and the windows stretching away on either side of it, the other houses of the terrace in which probably lived families like Jenny's, husbands and wives and children growing up.

She suddenly felt conspicuous, sitting on the corner of the tartan rug in her theater-going clothes.

"Just this," Jenny said. "One o'clock club, tea with other

mothers, the park and the shops and the baby clinic. It doesn't sound much, does it, compared with what you do?" Harriet didn't look at her. She was picking blades of grass from the lawn and laying them out in neat lines on the rug.

"You could argue that you're doing much more important work than I am."

It wasn't an argument that Harriet wanted to pursue. She knew that they could laud one another's roles, and that the praise wouldn't change their estimation of their own in any way. She was glad when Alice began to fuss and then to cry properly. Jenny hoisted her up, undid the front of her dress and put the baby to her breast. Harry came within whacking distance with his spade, and Jenny gently fended him off.

"What does it feel like?" Harriet asked, watching the greedy sucking.

"Comfortable," Jenny answered. "Reassuring, to be able to give her everything she needs." She added, "For now."

Harriet sighed. "I think I'm too selfish to be a mother," she said half to herself.

"No, you're not. You learn that you can't be selfish, except for them. Have you seen Jane?" she asked abruptly.

Harriet shook her head. "No. I haven't seen anybody. I've been so busy, you know, with preparing for the launch." It sounded so drab, and so preoccupied, that she added, "I've seen Robin. He wants me to marry him."

Jenny studied her, her head on one side. "Will you?"

Harriet grinned suddenly. "Perhaps, I'm not sure. I've told him to ask me again after Tuesday."

"At least he could buy you a house that doesn't breed concrete mixers and dust and builder's rubble like this one does."

"I'd rather buy my own house," Harriet said, and then regretted the stiff sound of it. The french doors leading from the basement kitchen swung open and Charlie, divested of his overalls, backed out with a loaded tea tray in his hands.

Harry saw him and made a tottering lunge across the grass with his fists waving.

"Bicks," he shouted. *"Bicks!"*

"It's a fine thing when your son's only attempt at the glory of language is *biscuits*," Charlie complained.

"He says other words, too," Jenny said mildly.

"Not half as often as he says biscuits. Pour the tea, Jen, will you?"

They sat in a circle on the grass, drinking tea and eating strawberry cake.

"It's nice here," Harriet said, recognizing envy in the complicated net of her impression of the calm afternoon. "It's really nice." She laughed at the inadequacy of the words but Charlie and Jenny didn't hear. They had embarked on a disparaging duet about the dilatory builders and their prompt bills, but they looked affectionately at each other. Harriet felt her conspicuous singleness again.

If she married Robin Landwith, she wondered, would they have children together, and a garden with a mown lawn, and a humorous duet of their own?

She tried hard, but she couldn't imagine how it would be.

Charlie leaned over and patted her thigh.

"So, Tuesday's the big day? The issue's heavily underwritten, I hear."

"It looks promising," Harriet answered with circumspection.

"Oh, come on. Do you know what Harriet stands to be worth after Tuesday, Jennifer? Guess? No. Something like four million. Isn't that right?"

Amazement turned Jenny's face into a set of circles, absurdly like Harry's. "Four *million*? Oh, I see. I see what you mean about buying your own house. You could buy anything, couldn't you? You're rich." She made it sound like, *infectious*.

"Harriet will be head of a publicly quoted company, Jen. It's big league. Real, proper, serious business."

"I know what it means," Jenny snapped. "I'm not an idiot."

There was an awkward silence. To break it, Harriet tried a self-deprecating laugh. "It doesn't mean anything, really. It's only on paper. I'd only get the money if I sold my interest in the company, and I won't do that."

But Jenny didn't answer. Harriet saw that she was staring at her, and that Charlie was looking at her, too.

"It doesn't make any difference . . ." Harriet began. But evidently it did make a difference. She saw the distance that the news had created between them. In a matter of minutes she had become an object of curiosity, a specimen of self-made womanhood instead of a trusted old friend. She wondered how she could apologize for her money, somehow rub the effect of it away, and then she thought, *No. I did it, I worked for it, and I'm proud of it*. Apology would be hypocrisy.

"What will you do, Harriet?" Jenny asked.

She said quickly, "Nothing. Go on working for Peacocks, selling 'Meizu' and the new lines. If I sold up I'd have the money and the time to spend it as well, I suppose. But now, all it means is that there will be an injection of funds for the company.

I can expand, perhaps look at my own factory." She went on a little, talking about the intricacies of recapitalization, until polite boredom replaced astonishment in Jenny's face.

It was Jenny who apologized. She leaned across Alice, asleep on the rug, and put her hand over Harriet's. "I'm sorry. I hadn't realized how big it all was. I'm proud of you, I really am."

There was another small silence, and then Charlie began lazily to recount some City gossip. The moment passed, but Harriet knew that it would not be forgotten.

The sun had moved off the patch of lawn. It shone on the windows overhead, turning them into polished metallic plates. Harriet scrambled to her feet, and ran to Harry in the sandpit.

"Come on, Harry. Let's make a huge castle for you to knock down and jump on."

A little later they went into the kitchen. Harriet sat at the table with Harry in his high chair beside her. He scooped egg and slices of toast up from his dish and squeezed them between his fingers, then pressed the remains into his mouth. Alice sat in her bouncer in the middle of the floor, watching Jenny's cat weaving between the adult legs. There were toys underfoot, more baskets of ironing, and photographs of the babies pinned to the unpainted walls. Charlie was cleaning his paintbrushes, whistling, and Jenny was slicing vegetables. Harriet thought of her own clean, elegant, silent flat. It was warmer and brighter here, in the family muddle.

She drank some of the gin and tonic that Charlie had brought her, and then caught Jenny's eye over the rim of the glass. They both started to laugh.

"I don't know what's the matter with us all," Harriet gasped. "Why aren't we satisfied with what we've got?"

Charlie looked up from his brushes. "I am," he said.

"Yes, you are," Jenny answered him. "That's why I love you."

Harriet finished her drink.

"I'd better go," she said at last. Charlie and Jenny followed her down the dusty hall.

"Come and see us soon. Harry'll forget what you look like. Good luck for Tuesday." Charlie stopped her on the front step. "I'm proud of you as well, Harriet."

She smiled at him. "Thanks, Charlie."

She left Islington behind, driving west toward Shaftesbury Avenue where Robin would be waiting for her in the theater stalls bar. As she drove, Harriet looked around her, at cars and houses and shop windows.

You could buy anything, couldn't you? Jenny had blurted out, in her amazement. Harriet had recognized the complicated equations of money and power and money and sex long ago in the Landwith offices, although she was no nearer to solving them for herself. But she had never, as far as she could remember, analyzed her possible wealth simply in terms of the *things* it might buy her.

Is that naive, she wondered, *or preoccupied, or rather morally admirable?*

She wished that Jane or Jenny were with her to share the joke.

I could buy that. Or that, or half a dozen of those. By the time she reached the West End she had sized up and rejected a large swathe of central London. The ideas were so ridiculous that she was light-headed and giggly by the time she found Robin in the bar. He looked hard at her, and then asked exactly how many drinks she had had with the Thimbells in Islington.

Two days, and then only one.

On the night before impact day Harriet went to bed early, but she found that she could not sleep. She got up again, pulled on a tracksuit, and let herself out of the front door. The big houses in the street were dark and silent behind their screens of limes or chestnuts. The sound of late-night traffic was only just audible in the distance. Harriet breathed in deeply. She felt better outside in the cool air. The tension that had knotted inside her, making her twist to and fro under the bedclothes, began to slacken its hold. She padded the length of the street, a dark shadow under the trees, looking up at the blind windows. The corner of her eye caught sight of a movement and she jumped around, and then saw a cat sliding beneath a privet hedge. They had the night to themselves.

Harriet came to the end of her street and hesitated. The silent network of residential roads fanned away from her, possessed by other people's sleep. She knew that she should go back, but the sweet-smelling air and the silence drew her on.

She crossed the road and began walking faster, but with no sense of purpose. She straightened her back and stretched her legs, and as she swung her arms the back of her hand brushed against the garden hedges. She broke off twigs and smelled them, distinguishing the rank flatness of common privet and aromatic choisya. A long way off, she heard the rising wail of a police siren. Awareness of violence or danger somewhere at hand made her draw closer into the deep shadows, but her pace did not slacken. A long road sloped away to her right. She followed it, and a single car passed her. She turned her face away from the yellow wedge of the headlamps. At the bottom of the hill she came to the fringe of Hampstead Heath. The darkness was wide and completely impenetrable. She stopped for a moment and stood looking across the road. The airy, invisible space drew her, but she knew that it would be madness to walk across there. Instead she turned and walked up the hill parallel to it, in and out of the cones of light thrown by old-fashioned street lamps.

The hill grew steep here and the climb made her pant for breath. She began to veer left again, away from the open space of heath and through more deserted streets.

Harriet felt exhilarated. The city's quietness made it seem an unfamiliar place, but at the same time she felt that she possessed it by the simple act of being awake, and walking through it. She thought of nothing as she walked. The rhythm of her footsteps was soothing, her mind emptied.

Once she thought she heard footsteps behind her. She shrank into a gateway and looked back the way she had come, but there was nothing there. When she started walking again she could only hear the soft lick of her own feet.

At last, without being aware of the direction she had been heading, she reached the street that ran at right angles to her own. She came to the corner and looked down toward her own house. The light she had left on in her hallway seemed so bright she thought it must be the only one she had seen in all her hour's walk. Harriet knew she would sleep now.

She let herself back into the flat, dropped her clothes in a heap, and climbed into bed.

At eight o'clock the next morning, Tuesday, June 15, Harriet arrived by taxi at the offices of A.R. Allardyce & Co. Ltd. For her sponsors' breakfast Harriet had not, in the end, bought a new power outfit. Instead, she had taken out of her wardrobe a navy-blue suit by Karl Lagerfeld for Chanel. The buttons of the slim jacket were embossed with the linked C's, the lapels bound with braid. The shoulders were almost unpadded, the narrow skirt reached to the middle of the knee. It was the least aggressive of her business suits, but it was also the one that remarked *money* in the most muted but patrician tones.

Harriet had smiled when she put it on. It reminded her both

of Annunziata's Chanel that had so impressed her at the New Year's Eve lunch, and of Robin's old friend Rosalie Fellowes in her Lagerfeld sequins at her Christmas party.

I'm here, now, Harriet told herself. She smoothed the waist of the jacket that fitted her own as if molded to it, and picked up her bag. It was not her customary briefcase, because the paperwork was all in the hands of others now. Today she was the star. A small quilted bag in the exact navy of her suit swung on its chain from her shoulder.

At the bank Harriet stepped out of her taxi, crossed the strip of sunlight that lay across the pavement, and walked without hesitation through the great doors.

James Hamilton and his minions were waiting for her. They formed a phalanx around her and swept her up to the directors' dining room on the top floor of the bank. As doors opened ahead of her and closed soundlessly in her wake, Harriet felt exactly as if she were the Queen.

A final pair of double doors, leading to the sanctum itself, was opened by a real-life, country-house butler in a black coat and striped trousers. Harriet blinked at a room full of people all gathered around a white-clothed table. They made way for her, smiling and greeting her, and she found herself seated at the center of the table on James Hamilton's right hand.

Harriet glanced around the circle of faces. The gathering was an amplification of the pricing meeting, and of all the other meetings that had taken place over the six months of preparation: She saw the members of the Allardyce team and the Mc-Govern Cowper people; there were the bank's lawyers and representatives from their accountants; there were public relations executives acting on Peacocks' behalf; Jeremy Crichton and two of his assistants; Piers Mayhew and Graham Chandler; and directly opposite her, Robin and Martin Landwith. Martin nodded a suave good morning, Harriet thought she saw Robin give the shadow of a wink.

This was the ceremony of the meeting brought to its apotheosis, as a celebration of itself, over a formal British breakfast.

The room was oak-paneled as if in a country house; the walls were hung with English landscapes, less impressive than Martin Landwith's but lending the right atmosphere of stateliness. The carpet was very thick and new, with the bank's logo discreetly woven into the wide border. It provided a tell-tale link between all this baronial splendor and the humming technology beyond the double doors.

Harriet smiled and unfolded her huge starched napkin.

"How do you feel this morning?" James Hamilton inquired.

"Nervous. Regal," Harriet said.

"It's a big day," he murmured. "Now, what about some breakfast?"

On the sideboard running the length of one paneled wall there were a dozen big, silver-domed chafing dishes presided over by the bank's butlers. Under the silver lids lay Finnan haddock and Caister kippers, kidneys and kedgeree and eggs, bacon and grilled tomatoes and mushrooms.

Harriet discovered that she was hungry.

She ate eggs and bacon and drank excellent hot coffee. She listened to the city conversations and reflected that these people were here because of her, because of what she had achieved. She felt a moment of pure self-centered triumph.

There was champagne in silver ice-buckets, but Harriet had refused it when it was offered. She drank a silent toast in coffee, instead, to "Meizu" and Simon Archer. Then she looked up and saw that Robin was watching her. Their eyes met, then Harriet looked away, inclining her head to listen to something James Hamilton was saying.

At exactly eight forty-five a McGovern Cowper man slipped in through the double doors. The twenty heads around the table all turned to him. He had come to report on the state of the financial markets overnight. Harriet heard him announce that it had been a quiet night with no major moves. Tokyo had closed a few points up on the preceding day.

The brokers nodded calmly. Harriet understood that there had been no shock to the market that would affect Peacocks' issue. Her company would go to the market as planned. She spread thick orange marmalade on her toast and went on eating. The food seemed to calm her last-minute nerves.

At nine-fifteen a telephone rang. James Hamilton stood up, excusing himself to her, slid his chair into place and went to take the call.

He returned a moment later. He bowed to her, a little, formal bow and then he announced, "Ladies and gentlemen, we have impact."

Harriet hadn't expected what happened next.

There was a burst of spontaneous applause. More chairs were pushed back and the men in their dark suits crowded around to shake her hand and kiss her cheek. Piers and Jeremy hugged her, and Martin Landwith's kiss came closer to her mouth. Now, laughing and with her face flushed with excitement, Harriet felt more film star than monarch.

Robin wrapped his arms around her. "That's my girl," he whispered.

My girl? Harriet thought giddily.

When the hubbub of congratulation had died down a little, the lawyers and accountants gathered in a separate group and then slipped out of the room together. They were on their way to the less glamorous but more vital sealing and exchanging of completion documents. Harriet knew that once that business was done, a copy of her prospectus would be dispatched by moto-cycle messenger to Companies House.

She looked at her watch. It was nine-forty. From ten o'clock onward the McGovern Cowper equity brokers would be placing her shares with their institutional clients.

In a moment of panic she thought, *What if they're all wrong? What if no one buys?* It made no difference to know that the issue was underwritten. Peacocks felt more like her baby than it had done since the very early days, when she huddled over Simon's broken packing case in the Belsize Park flat.

The minutes ticked by. Most of the breakfasters were slipping away to their day's work, but a handful remained gathered at the end of the table with Harriet. Martin Landwith was deep in conversation with one of the brokers. Robin sat calmly beside Harriet, sipping champagne.

At ten thirty-five the head of the McGovern team came in. He stood at Harriet's shoulder and said, "We have a full subscription."

The issue had been taken up. Harriet's face split into a wide smile. "Well done," she said. "Well done, all of you."

The broker made a small gesture. "We could have sub-scribed it six or seven times over," he told her.

That, Harriet thought, was her proudest, dizziest moment. It was a day of moments, but *six or seven times over* was the one she remembered best.

Harriet's next engagement of the day was a lunch for a group of prominent journalists. She found herself in the strange position of making a speech extolling Peacocks' past and future performance to, among others, Charlie Thimbell. Harriet remem-bered the Cretan beach; Charlie's face was impassive as he took brisk shorthand notes.

"Give me a nice write-up, Charlie," she demanded as the lunch party broke up.

"I don't know," he grinned at her. "I have to maintain professional detachment."

Harriet went back to the Peacocks offices to give some more

interviews. Some were serious, others were the "Meizu Girl
Makes Good" variety. She submitted herself to them cheerfully.
Her secretary came in and out with sheaves of congratulatory
messages, and enough flowers were delivered to turn the reception area into a scented hothouse.

Harriet was too busy to take calls, but she did speak to Kath.

"Thank you for your faith in me, Mum. Do you know what
your holding in Peacocks is worth now?"

"Yes, love. Harriet, are you doing the right thing?"

"Going public?"

"I meant more, sacrificing all your young life to it. Harriet,
are you there?"

Harriet sighed. Kath's anxiety seemed to have become per-
manent. "It's not a sacrifice. Today's the most exciting day of my
working life. Won't you let me enjoy it, and take pleasure in it
with me?"

Quickly, guiltily, Kath answered, "Of course I will. I'm your
mother, Harriet. I only want you to be happy."

"I am happy."

Sarah came in with more flowers. Harriet read the card, and
saw that they were from Mr. Jepson and everyone at Midland
Plastics.

At six o'clock Harriet gave her own party for Peacocks' staff.
They crowded into her office and toasted each other and the
company's success in more champagne. Harriet began to feel
that she was floating on a tide of it. She scrambled up on to a low
table to make her speech of thanks. She told them that Peacocks
would not have come this far nor would it go any further without their help, and she reminded them of the long hours they
had all put in and the value of the team effort. Harriet was being
quite sincere, but even as she talked she was thinking that
Peacocks was still her baby. She looked at the faces turned up to
hers, Karen and Sarah and Fiona, Graham and Jeremy and the
others. She felt buoyed up by their liking and loyalty, but her
pride and her possessiveness for Peacocks was undiluted.

Later, when the party was ending, Graham Chandler edged
her into a quiet corner.

"I wondered," he said with his usual diffidence, "whether
you'd let me take you out to dinner tonight? When you've done
everything you need to do here, of course."

"I'm really sorry, Graham. I'm meeting Robin. In fact," she
looked at her watch, "He should be here now. Can we do it some
other time?"

"Of course we can." His face had turned slightly red.

Robin came a few moments later, and the Peacocks people dispersed. He drove Harriet to the restaurant where they had had their first dinner together, and at the end of the meal he produced a small package in Aspreys' wrapping.

"This is to celebrate a successful flotation, and a successful professional partnership. It is also to celebrate the fact that I love you."

Harriet opened the little velvet box. Inside was a pair of diamond earrings, cold fiery teardrops that exactly matched her Christmas necklace.

She lifted her eyes to Robin's face. "They're beautiful. They're extravagantly beautiful." Robin reached across the table and removed her Butler & Wilson clips. Then he fixed the diamond drops in place.

"Like you," he told her.

Harriet knew that she wasn't beautiful, but for this evening she was willing to believe that she might be.

It was midnight when Robin's latest Porsche drew up outside Harriet's house. She looked at her watch and laughed softly. "Will it all disappear when the clocks strike twelve?"

He leaned across to kiss her. "How could it? You're the fairy godmother, not Cinderella."

As they reached the steps leading up to the front door Harriet saw a darker shadow moving in the front garden's shadows. She was fleetingly reminded of her walk the night before that seemed separated from this moment by much more than a day. Then the shadow came forward and grew solid.

It became a small figure in a shapeless checked cotton dress, a V-necked jersey and white socks. Harriet recognized the school uniform before she recognized the child herself.

Then she said slowly, wonderingly, "Linda? Linda, what are you doing here?"

"I ran away," Linda Jensen answered. "I got your letter, and I wanted to see you. I've been waiting here for hours and hours."

"Oh, *God*," Harriet said. She put her hand out to Robin for support. "For God's sake, Linda." She suddenly felt how tired she was. And at the same time she noticed that Linda was shivering. Wearily she added, "Come on. We'd better all go inside."

In the warm light of the kitchen Linda stared coldly at Robin.

"What's *he* doing here?"

"I invited him," Harriet said pointedly. "Sit down on that stool, Linda. I'm going to make you some hot chocolate. Don't say anything, I don't want to hear anything about this until you've drunk it. Then we'll try to sort it out."

"Can I have some toast as well?" Linda asked. "I'm really hungry."

With food inside her she stopped shivering. But her eyes were over-large in her thin face, and the shoulders in the maroon jersey looked very small. Harriet knew how young she was, however old she might try to act. She could also guess at what Linda had gone through to reach Hampstead at all, and she began to regret the brusque reception she had given her. She pulled another stool close to Linda's.

"Now. Do you want to tell me about it?"

Linda gave a small shrug. "I already told you. I wanted to see you."

"I was coming to take you out to tea." Harriet had meant to telephone Ronny. Only she hadn't, yet.

"In how many weeks? I can't *stand* that place. It's horrible, gross, the things they make you do all the time."

Over Linda's head Harriet caught Robin's eye, and had to suppress a smile. "All schools are pretty much the same, you know."

"Are they? Well, I'm finished with this one. I'll tell you what I did. I just climbed out through the hedge and walked down the town to the station. There are day girls, you know, so no one paid any attention to me walking around. This was before tea, when all the lucky ones are going home, to people who care about them."

Harriet's eyes met Robin's again. She put her hand out, to Linda's maroon shoulder. "People care about you, you know. Go on."

"I bought a ticket to Paddington and got on the train. Some creepy woman in the carriage asked me what I was doing on my own and I told her I was going to an appointment with my orthodontist in Harley Street and my father's chauffeur was meeting me off the train." Linda smiled at the recollection. "That shut her up. At Paddington I made sure she was out of sight and then I got in a taxi and it brought me here. A long way, it took all the rest of my money. As a matter of fact it wasn't *my* money. Arabella Makepeace keeps a whole pile of it in her creepy hand-bag, so I borrowed some, temporarily. Ronny never lets me have enough. Will you pay Arabella back for me?" Linda's face looked stiff. "I don't want to owe her anything. I wonder if she's found out it's gone?"

"Linda, what time did you leave the school?"

"I told you. Before tea."

"And it's now half-past twelve at night. Have you thought, at all, about how worried the school must be? And Ronny? I'll have to ring them now and tell them you're safe."

The shrug came again. "Ring whoever you like. But I can stay here with you, Harriet, can't I? Please let me stay?"

Linda's voice quivered. The chink in the child's precarious armor touched Harriet. She put her arms around her. "Where's your mother?"

"At home in L.A. I wish I was. Let me stay, Harriet."

Harriet held her. "You can stay tonight, at least," she soothed. "Robin, do you think you could telephone the school? St. Brigid's, Ascot. They must have half the police in the country out looking by this time."

"It would be better if you did it," Robin muttered. "They'll think I've abducted her, or something. Whereas, in fact, nothing could be further from my mind." But he went through to the next room, and they heard him obtaining the number and then talking in his calm voice.

"Linda, where's your father? Don't you think we should talk to him about all this?" Harriet asked.

"No."

The child drew a long, ragged, frightening breath. Then, at once, the remnants of her bravado deserted her. Her face contracted like a baby's and she began to sob.

"Don't tell Caspar. I'll do anything if you don't tell Caspar. You don't know what he's like when he's angry. You don't know anything." Linda pitched forward and wept in Harriet's arms.

Harriet stroked her hair. There were small twigs caught in it, left from her long hours, hiding in the garden hedge. Harriet found that she was suddenly near to tears herself.

She could imagine Caspar Jensen's fury as clearly as she remembered his charm.

"It's all right," she whispered to Linda. "It's all right. We'll think of something, between us."

Thirteen

ALL THE WAY BACK TO ASCOT in Harriet's car, Linda sat in silence, staring without interest out of the window. Harriet glanced at her from time to time, but said nothing.

When Harriet had telephoned Linda's headmistress the night before, Mrs. Harper's relief that Linda was safe had swung quite quickly into suppressed anger. Nor could Harriet entirely blame her. She suspected that if she herself were responsible for Linda Jensen she might react in the same way. She listened patiently to what the headmistress had to say.

The police had been called, did Miss Peacock realize? Linda's nanny had driven straight to the school and was even now trying to contact Mr. Jensen, *overseas*, you understand? Harriet pressed her lips together, knowing that she mustn't show a flicker of amusement. Linda was watching her closely.

Had Miss Peacock by any chance *encouraged* Linda to run away?

"Of course not," Harriet protested. "But she had told me that she is unhappy at St. Brigid's."

Linda's brown eyes fixed on Harriet's face.

After a pause Mrs. Harper said, "Yes. It's not a very easy situation. We're trying to do all we can to help her, you know."

Harriet imagined her, a competent and probably kindly woman shaken out of her calm routine, and sympathized with her.

"I understand that."

There had been some more talk. Veronica Page had wanted to drive straight to Hampstead to collect Linda. Harriet had spoken to her, and under Linda's unblinking stare had suggested that that was unnecessary. She could be regarded as a family friend, Harriet had continued, and so would be glad to look after Linda overnight and drive her back to St. Brigid's the next day. Miss Page could meet them at the school, perhaps. There had been an agreement. Linda had come forward to mumble a few words to Ronny to convince her that she was perfectly safe.

Harriet accepted Mrs. Harper's and Miss Page's thanks and hung up.

As soon as the receiver was replaced Linda had rounded on her.

"I won't go. You can't make me. It all stinks, you don't *know.*"

The words had come out in a jumble, fury competing with tears. Linda had swung out with a fist, intending to hit Harriet, but Harriet had caught her arm and the tears won out. Linda stood and cried noisily, her narrow shoulders vibrating. Harriet held her and looked over her head to Robin.

Robin was embarrassed, and impatient, and irritated. With the sobbing child between them, Harriet sighed.

"What are you going to do?" he asked. He made Linda sound like a business decision, to be dealt with briskly before moving on to the next item on the agenda. Harriet found herself looking at him with an edge of dislike. She put her hand up to touch Linda's fine straight hair and picked out a tiny twig that had been caught in it. "I'm going to put her to bed, and in the morning see if she wants to talk. Then I'll drive her back to school."

Linda broke away from her. She hesitated, trying to make up her mind which way to run, and then dashed past Robin in the direction of the door. Robin caught her this time, not very gently, and Linda drew back her foot in the round-toed school shoe and kicked his shin. Robin swore.

"You can't run away from here as well, Linda. Where will you stop, if you do?" Harriet asked.

"You can't kick people who are trying to help you, either," Robin said between his teeth.

"*Are* you?" Linda demanded. "I hadn't noticed."

"Robin," Harriet said quickly, "Why don't you go on home? I'll call you tomorrow."

Robin hesitated, unwilling to yield. He had made other plans for what was left of the night. But he saw that there was no alternative, and gave way with apparent grace. He crossed to where Harriet was standing and kissed her. Harriet made no movement.

"I'll see myself out," Robin said.

When they were alone, Linda hung her head in order not to meet Harriet's eyes. "Sorry," she mumbled. "Did you want to go to bed with him, and you couldn't because I was here?"

Harriet couldn't tell if it was a provocation or a straight question. She ignored it, and put her arm around the child's shoulders again.

"Linda, what do you really want?"

There was a silence. Then, in a voice that through its layers of truculence and bravado touched Harriet directly, Linda confessed, "Just my mom. And to go back to L.A."

"When can you?"

"In the summer vacation."

"That's not very far off."

"It's *weeks*." It was a cry of desolation. "And I'll only have to come back here after it's over. To horrible St. Brigid's, and Ronny, and Little Shelley. My dad wants me to grow up to be English. To have an *English education*."

"Your father's British. And he loves you, you know."

"Yeah. If he didn't, he wouldn't be so heavy about where I am and what I'm like, would he? Plus it suits my mom for me to be over here. She's busy, and all that."

Harriet didn't much like the sound of mom. She also thought that Linda Jensen might send letters that gave the impression she could barely read or write, but she was very far from stupid. She tilted the child's head up now so that she could look at her. Linda's face was white under the hedge dust and dirty tear marks.

"Don't you like Ronny? And Little Shelley?"

"Ronny's okay. You saw Little Shelley, didn't you?"

"Yes, I saw it." They both laughed, then.

"It's time you went to bed, now, Linda."

Harriet left her and went to fetch sheets and bedcovers. She let down the sofa bed in the sitting room and began briskly to make it up. Linda followed her and stood watching.

"Where's your bedroom?"

"Beneath this room."

"Can't I sleep down there with you?" Linda was suddenly much younger than her years. Harriet smiled at her. "There's only one bed. And I kick."

"I don't suppose you kick *him*."

"That's none of your business." Harriet wondered if all children could change like kaleidoscopes.

"I know what happens, you know."

"I'm sure you do, Linda. But there's a difference between knowing and understanding."

"And that's the kind of crappy thing my dad says."

"I like your father." I *do*. Harriet remembered the orchids that had shed their petals like sloughed skins on her desk. And she reflected that liking Caspar Jensen was something close to liking the QE2. It would sail on, whatever her feeling for it.

"Come on, Linda. I'll find you a toothbrush, and a T-shirt to sleep in."

In bed, between the fat cushions, Linda looked very small. "I won't be able to sleep," she announced.

"If you need me in the night, you can call and I'll come up," said Harriet, who hated to have her sleep disturbed. She thought with new respect of Jenny and her babies.

But when Harriet looked back into the room after having made herself ready for bed, Linda was fast asleep, lying in the same position as when Harriet had left her. Harriet stood and studied the visible half of the smooth face. She might have bent down and kissed the cheek that offered itself, but she reflected that it was the waking Linda who needed affection, and to make the gesture to Linda sleeping, someone else's child, would have been sentimental.

Harriet closed the door firmly and went to her own bed. There was no cry in the night.

In the morning, while Linda ate her breakfast and Harriet made the necessary telephone calls to rearrange her morning, they said almost nothing. Linda looked mulish, and Harriet ignored her. It was only when Harriet gathered up her jacket and handbag, and handed Linda her maroon jersey to put on, that Linda understood there was really to be no reprieve.

"Please, Harriet," she begged. "Can't I stay here with you? I'll be good. I can be, you know."

Harriet gestured around her. "Look. Don't you see? I haven't even got a proper spare room. There's nothing here that doesn't belong to a grown-up life. I don't know anything about children." *If I was Jenny*, she thought, *or even Jane. Then it might be different. Except that it wouldn't, because you're Caspar Jensen's and Clare Mellen's daughter, and not ours.* "I've also got work to do, Linda. Work that's important to me, and takes up a lot of my time."

"Now you sound like Clare. Only she pretends that not having time is to do with education and being for my own good. At least you're honest."

Harriet was rebuked. "I didn't mean that I don't have any time for you."

"Oh, that's okay."

There was silence in the car, lasting until they were almost in sight of the school.

Harriet made one or two attempts at small talk, and then gave up.

They reached the school gates, set open on a driveway lined with horse chestnut trees. Harriet read the discreet sign as they passed it: BOARDING PREPARATORY SCHOOL FOR GIRLS AGED 7–11. Seven sounded very young for both boarding and preparation for anything.

Linda hunched her shoulders. The car turned a corner and a large, gray stone house was revealed. Bicycle sheds, modern classroom buildings and tennis courts were discernible beyond it.

"You're just like all the others," Linda said hopelessly. "I thought you were different." Harriet accepted the dismissal. "I know you did."

The front doors, between stone pillars, looked imposing, but inside there was the invariable smell of polish and lunch. Sniffing it, Harriet felt her own heart sinking. She tried to take Linda's hand, but Linda held her arm stiffly away.

The school secretary led them up some stairs and along squeaky corridors. They passed two or three groups of quiet little girls in their unflattering uniforms. They all gawked at Linda and then nudged each other.

The headmistress was at her desk behind a door labeled "Headmistress." She stood up to greet them. She was wearing a pleated skirt and a bow-necked blouse, exactly as Harriet had imagined she would. There was a row of small silver cups in a glass cabinet behind her chair.

Harriet shook hands, accepting the headmistress's thanks for taking care of Linda and her offer of a cup of coffee. Linda listened to Mrs. Harper's grave recital of the trouble and anxiety she had caused by running away. Harriet and Linda learned that Miss Page was on her way back to the school and would be here at any moment, that Mr. Jensen had been spoken to, and that Mrs. . . . er, Jensen would be calling from California that evening. Between them, they would all decide what was best for Linda.

"Because we're all on your side, dear. We only want you to be happy and comfortable, Linda. But you have to help us, don't you?"

Linda nodded. There seemed nothing else to say.

The coffee and Veronica Page arrived together. There was more handshaking and thanking, and more description for Linda of how all would be made well.

The three women drank their coffee, and Linda studied the top of the bookcase.

At length, replacing her empty cup on the tray and leaning forward to examine Linda's filthy white socks, Mrs. Harper said, "I think you might go back to your dormitory now to change, Linda, and then I think you should rejoin morning school."

"Please can Harriet come with me? Just so I can show her my dorm?"

"I'd like to see," Harriet said quickly.

"By all means."

Closing the door behind them, Harriet felt exactly as she had done on leaving Annunziata Landwith's drawing room on New Year's Day. She wanted to run down the corridor and slide down the banisters.

"See?" Linda demanded.

"I thought Mrs. Harper seemed kind and sensible." But this time Linda didn't reject her hand.

They climbed more stairs, narrower and steeper, to the top of the house. Through open doors Harriet caught sight of neat beds and rows of washbasins. Linda pushed open another door and they came into an attic room, cream-painted, with six iron bedsteads painted the same color, and six bedside lockers. There were teddy bears on the beds, and pink and cream curtains at the windows.

"This is it. Isn't it disgusting?" Linda yanked open a drawer and took out clean, folded clothes.

"It's perfectly cozy." Harriet looked at the other five beds, wondering about their occupants. "How much money did you say you borrowed from Arabella Makepeace's creepy purse?"

Linda laughed. "You've got a brilliant memory. Ten pounds."

"I'm good at some things, actually. Here." Harriet gave her the money. Linda banged open another locker, took out a little leather bag and stuffed the notes into it.

"Probably she'll never notice. Thanks, Harriet."

While Linda wriggled out of her dress Harriet wandered around the room. On Linda's locker, as on the others, there were family photographs. Harriet picked one of them up and studied it. She saw Caspar's big, handsome head and Clare's milky blondeness. They looked as if they were on the way to some Hollywood party. Clare was wearing a dress of pale, shiny material with a wide, low neckline. There was a limousine in the background, and the suggestion of popping flashbulbs.

Harriet put the photograph back in its place. She didn't look at those displayed by the other girls but she could imagine the Pony Club portraits, the sensible mothers and dogs and Army or City fathers, and the brothers at Fourth of June picnics. She had such a strong sense of Linda's oddness among these people that sympathy overcame her determination to be rational. She turned around abruptly and said, "You think I've let you down, don't you?"

Linda only shrugged.

Harriet went on, "I don't want to let you down. I can't take you away from here, or do anything like that, because your mother and father and Ronny make those decisions. But I can do some things. I can take you out for the day, can't I? You can come and stay with me in London at the weekends, whenever you like, whenever they let you. We can call each other and talk, you can tell me about Arabella Makepeace and Mrs. Harper and I'll tell you what I'm doing. It's easier, in a way. It's easier to be friends if you don't have duties to each other. Like providing an *English education*, and *making the best of it*."

Linda's smile was the answer to Harriet's fear that she might have over-committed herself and her reward. It spread over the child's face, changing its shape, making her pretty.

"Really?" Linda asked. "Will you really?"

"Yes, I will. For as long as you want."

The smile was followed by a bear hug. Harriet staggered under the fervor of it.

"Really? Weekends?"

"Whenever you want." Harriet thought of Robin, and the just faintly staid routine that they had established. For some reason the idea of its disruption by Linda Jensen made her smile. "You'll have to ask your father and Ronny, and get permission here first."

"They'll let me. Harriet, I didn't mean what I said before. You are different. You're better than different, even. You're . . . *like me*."

"Well thanks," Harriet said, smiling at her.

It was time for Harriet to go. Satisfied with her promise, Linda let her leave without protest. She waved good-bye, and then went back to her class with apparent resignation. Ronny Page walked with Harriet to her car. She cleared her throat before she spoke, making Harriet think that she was uncomfortable about what she wanted to say.

"I'm sorry you've been troubled with all this."

Harriet glanced at her. Ronny was neat and correct, but somehow bloodless. She would be efficient at her job, but not very imaginative. Not much of a companion for Linda, in her parents' absences. Harriet felt the wash of sympathy again.

"I think perhaps I should apologize, too. I've made a promise to Linda," she explained. Ronny nodded as she listened, with only a touch of color showing in her cheeks.

"I don't have any objections personally, of course. But Mr. Jensen would have to be consulted."

"Yes. How can I get in touch with him?"

Ronny's manner changed. "That may be a little difficult, just at the moment, because of his commitments." She was the efficient P.A., protecting her famous employer from the intrusive hordes. Harriet smiled faintly and remembered how the great man had deposited his pudding plate in her lap. "I'll tell him everything that has happened, of course. I know he'll be very grateful for everything you are doing for Linda."

"Thank you," Harriet said. She drove her car back down to the gates, relieved that she was not obliged to stay behind at St. Brigid's herself. The realization made her more determined to do, or to be, whatever Linda Jensen needed.

Harriet went back to the Peacocks offices. It seemed much longer ago than last night that they had been celebrating the successful launch, although there were still champagne bottles and overlooked glasses in corners to remind her.

Harriet closed the door of her office on Karen and the banks of flowers in reception. Sarah had put a list of calls and messages on her desk, and Harriet saw Robin's name among them. Sarah had also been through the mountain of mail and arranged it neatly, and had marked the first reports of the Peacocks flotation in the business press for Harriet's attention. Harriet sat and looked at all the work spread in front of her, and at the names of people who were waiting for her decision, or her comments, or her acknowledgment.

Surveying it all, Harriet felt disturbingly flat. It was a feeling that stayed with her all through the days that followed.

Six months had been spent preparing for the stockmarket flotation. Harriet had been busy for every hour of every day, and whenever she had had time to think beyond the immediate demands on her, there had always been her goal to look forward to—Peacocks' launch as a publicly quoted company. The work had been a pleasure and it had been powerfully stimulating.

The demands of it had also meant that Harriet had been forced to neglect other things, some of them the day-to-day decisions that had accumulated to await her now. She had to turn her attention to new game proposals, to the decision whether or not to invest in her own manufacturing concern, to the expansion of her team, and dozens of smaller, related questions.

Harriet tackled the work diligently. But she felt the lack of the excitement that had given her her edge in the past. She watched Peacocks' share price creep satisfyingly upward, and read the favorable press comments. Yet she and her company were no longer, as they had been for six months, the focus of minute and flattering attention from lawyers and bankers and brokers. Once again they had become just another young outfit with a position to hold in a difficult sector of the market, and others took their place as the hot issue of the day.

Harriet continued to grit her teeth and wade through what needed to be done. Karen and Graham Chandler and the others trod carefully around her.

She canceled an evening at the theater with Robin, even though it was a play she had been looking forward to, claiming that she had far too much work to do. She did spend the evening in her office, but her old ability to concentrate evaded her. She wasted more than an hour in sitting with one of the old Shamshuipo "Meizu" boards on her desk, watching the colored balls rolling inexorably to their rendezvous with the counters in the slots. Harriet could play the game now. She knew all the routes, circuitous and direct. The only thought that came to her was that it had been a long time since she had seen Simon Archer.

During this time she spoke twice to Linda on the telephone. Linda didn't complain when they talked. Surprisingly, it was as if simply knowing that Harriet was there had given her the security or the reassurance that she needed. In one of their conversations Linda told her that she was in her house rounders team ("It's a dumb sort of game, not like American baseball, but I'm pretty good at it"), and in another she described an essential skirt that all the big girls were wearing, and which Ronny claimed was no different from the summer skirt Linda already possessed. Harriet listened carefully to Linda's description, then went to Top Shop at lunchtime and bought the closest thing in the smallest size. She packed it up and sent it off, and earned a rapturous thank-you note from Linda (*"Harriet you are BRILLUNT"*).

The last days of June went by. Harriet told herself that she must see some more of Jane and Jenny, now that the drama of the launch was passing into history, but that she must solve her manufacturing problems before giving her attention to her social life. For the same reason she refused Robin's invitation to Glyndebourne, and as far as she was aware he took Annunziata in her place.

At the beginning of July, when the trees in Hyde Park had already lost the sappy freshness of early summer and Oxford

Street and Piccadilly were noticeably more crowded with bri-
gades of tourists, Harriet's sense of anticlimax grew deeper instead of diminishing. The days were sunny but cool. It was
energizing weather that worried her because she couldn't respond to it.

One morning she found herself listening to Karen's plans for
a holiday on Kos with her boyfriend. Harriet reflected that she
probably needed a holiday herself. Should she go on her own,
she wondered, to stroll around the Uffizi or to lie on the sand
beside the Adriatic? (*You could go anywhere*, she heard Jenny say.
You're rich. As if it was, *infectious*.) She could go to Crete, and
stay in one of the luxurious resort hotels that had been new, and
way beyond their means, that first visit. She wondered if she
could, perhaps, persuade Jane to accompany her. She knew that
she didn't want to go on holiday with Robin. Their time together, she realized, had been so industrious. It was hard to
imagine how they would handle the diffuse constraints of a
holiday.

Harriet shook her head impatiently. She pulled a folder
toward her. It contained details of several small industrial premises that might be suitable for her manufacturing operation. She
was reading the specifications of the first when Karen buzzed
through to her.

"Harriet, there's someone here to see you." Her voice sounded
odd, as if she had swallowed something too hot. Harriet frowned
a little, glancing across at her diary.

"Who is it? I'm not expecting anyone."

"It's Mr. Jensen," Karen said.

Harriet half-stood, the door whirled open and Caspar appeared. It was as if a strong wind had begun blowing.

"Will you look at all this? Why didn't you tell me you were
'Meizu Girl'?"

"As far as I remember the opportunity didn't quite present
itself."

He gave a healthy trumpet of laughter. "You remember
more than I do. It wasn't one of my better days, but then it
wasn't a very memorable occasion, was it? But I do remember
you."

He had come across to her desk. Harriet stood up straight.
She saw the blue eyes again, and a light suntan that didn't quite
hide a network of fine veins spreading over his cheekbones. He
carried with him the scent of cologne, expensive clothes and
dark, smoky bars.

Caspar held out his hand and Harriet took it. The first time, his voice had made her think of honey and smoke. Now that he was sober she perceived it as much more complex, a matter of levels as discrete but inseparable as the rings of a tree trunk. He had the gift of making the banal sound significant; he made her want to go on listening to him, whatever he said.

"I have never thanked you properly."

"You sent the most beautiful flowers. I like orchids."

Caspar let go of her hand, still looking at her. Harriet withdrew her own, slowly. She was nonplussed by the materialization of this famous face, this more-than-real presence in her office. But she was glad that he was there. She did know that.

"Now I owe you more thanks."

"I'm pleased Linda came to me. She stayed the night and I drove her back the next morning. That's all. We've talked a couple of times on the telephone. I told her she could come at weekends, sometimes, if you would let her."

Caspar put the edge of his thumb to the corner of his mouth, rubbed it contemplatively, without taking his eyes off Harriet.

"Let's go and have some lunch."

Harriet had the feeling that whole chunks of dialogue that should have taken place between them were being cut; complete scenes, even, being elided. It wasn't a disagreeable feeling, but she did protest, "It's ten past eleven."

"The morning is progressing nicely toward lunchtime. And I think we should talk about my daughter."

"I'd like to," Harriet agreed. Then she indicated her laden desk, and the open desk diary. "But I just can't, not today."

"Oh, Jesus, why ever not? Talk to your boss."

Harriet straightened her shoulders. "I'm the boss."

"Exactly. And what's the point of it unless you get to call the damned shots? Let's go to lunch."

Caspar Jensen was inviting her. You didn't say no twice, Harriet thought. "Okay," she said meekly. "Lunch it is."

Caspar swept her along. Harriet remembered Karen's startled expression, Sara cut short with an armful of printouts, two or three other faces staring in doorways as her staff witnessed their departure.

"I'm going with Mr. Jensen," Harriet said, like a prophecy. "I'll call in this afternoon, to see if anything has come up."

From beyond the door she knew that Caspar's trumpet laugh would be clearly audible behind them. She followed him out into the street. Outside, she saw it was a beautiful day. Caspar's car, a black Jaguar, was parked at the curb. Harriet knew that more heads turned as Caspar opened the passenger door for her. He was whistling as he climbed in beside her. They pulled away, leaving Peacocks behind them.

Caspar turned to look at her. "You see? It's easy."

"You're right," Harriet answered. She stretched her legs and leaned back, looking out at the shoppers as if they belonged to another world. She was doing her own kind of running away. She felt gleeful, irresponsible.

"The Waterside, today, don't you think?" Caspar asked.

Harriet knew that the Waterside was out of town, beside the Thames. "Definitely." They drove westwards.

"Why didn't you tell me who you are?" Caspar asked her. He took out a cigarette and lit it one-handed, then drew on it and squinted at her through the smoke. Then he took it from between his lips and offered it to her. Harriet rarely smoked but she took it and turned it in her fingers, looking at where his mouth had been.

After a moment she asked, "Would it have made any difference? Does it make any now?"

"I think so." He was quite candid. She saw that he was looking at her thighs, exposed by the hem of her skirt rising when she leaned back in her seat. She didn't try to tug it down again.

"I like it. I like success," Caspar told her, and then returned his attention to the road. Harriet watched the sun sparkling on the traffic, enjoying the drive and their enclosure together behind the Jaguar's tinted windows. Caspar was also enjoying himself. He began to hum, and then in his resonant voice to sing.

> Gentlemen songsters out on a spree,
> damned from here to eternity.

The song was an old favorite of Ken's. Harriet remembered it from her childhood, how she had watched him shaving, striking swathes of white lather from his cheeks and singing. She joined in now as she had not done then, her voice sounding thin and dry in union with Caspar's.

> Oh, Lord, have mercy on such as we,
> Baa, baa, baa.

Caspar was delighted. He drummed his fingers on the steering wheel. "Encore!"

They sang most of the way to the river at Bray.

Their singing made Harriet feel as if she was on a delicious outing, a rather old-fashioned outing like a Sunday school trip. The sight of the river, when they reached it, heightened the effect. The water shivered with points of light and the weeping willows' fronds lifted in the stiff breeze. Pleasure boats passed with their flags fluttering, and bright pennants strained on the bank. Snatches of music drifted from the boats, and then were swallowed up by the ripple of their wash.

Caspar had been warmly greeted.

"For two? But of course, Mr. Jensen. A great pleasure to see you."

Caspar had made no reservation. Harriet supposed that for Caspar tables always materialized, always the best tables. The impromptu quality of this day appealed to her. It was very different from the way she and Robin did things together. They consulted their diaries and compared their schedules, and booked opera seats and theater tickets well in advance. Robin's secretary booked tables, and telephoned Harriet's secretary to confirm times. Robin and Harriet planned their time carefully, because they allowed themselves so little of it. At that point, Harriet caught herself. Robin would like more time with her, only she denied it. She wasn't sure that there was much they could do with more time.

Caspar had decided, with satisfaction, that it was still too early to eat lunch. They had come to sit in the garden and watch the river traffic. He had ordered Bellinis and the drinks came in frosted glasses, looking to Harriet too pretty to taste. Caspar had no such reservation. His was gone very quickly, and a fresh one ordered. He leaned back in his white-painted chair and lit a cigarette.

"Linda," he said.

Harriet listened while he talked, absorbing the details of a story she had largely guessed for herself.

Linda had reacted badly to the breakdown of her parents' marriage, choosing at first to deny that it was happening at all. Then, faced with what could no longer be denied, she had swung violently between the two of them, first refusing to visit Caspar in his rented house at the beach, then insisting that she could no longer live with Clare on their Bel Air estate.

"The usual kids' stuff," Caspar said.

Harriet wondered about the kids for whom this was usual. The only children she knew herself were Harry and Alice, safe in Islington with Jenny and Charlie to look after them. The sympathy for Linda renewed itself.

Then Caspar had been offered a short theater season in London. He had bought the Little Shelley house in a great hurry, moved in, and left Linda with her mother in Los Angeles. Linda had been particularly difficult and then Clare had been offered, in quick succession, two unmissable scripts. Both had involved long periods of location work. The first had also involved Marco Rey, the young actor, Clare Mellen's new love.

The obvious solution to the problem of Linda had been boarding school in England, under the direct care of Ronny Page and the more distant supervision of her father.

"Poor Linda," Harriet observed.

"She wasn't learning a damn thing in grade school. I wanted her to have an English education."

"So she told me."

"She likes you very much. She did from the first day, when you got rid of those bloody little birds off her plate. Which her father was too high to do."

"I like her, too." Harriet spoke coolly.

Caspar appraised her. There was something of Martin Landwith in the way he did it, but Caspar was bigger in every dimension, and more lustrous, than Martin Landwith. Harriet's memory of the Landwiths seemed to break up, like mist, in the sun of Caspar's proximity.

"Are you willing to be a friend to her, in her mother's absence, in a way I can't be?"

"I have already told Linda that I will. I need your permission. Probably St. Brigid's requires it in writing. In triplicate."

Caspar ignored that. He leaned forward suddenly, touched Harriet's hand. "Thank you," he said.

"I'll do whatever I can. Linda needs something. I doubt if anyone can give it to her except you and her mother."

Caspar sat back in his chair again. He reached the bottom of his second Bellini as Harriet finished her first.

"Tell me," he said. "Did I disgust you, that day we met?"

Harriet thought. Then she answered, truthfully, "Not at all. In fact, I thought you were the only person in that room who was properly alive."

The truth pleased Caspar. And Harriet wanted to please him. She wanted to sit in the sun, in the regatta festivity of the garden, and listen to his voice.

As she listened, feeling that she was colored and animated by Caspar, as if she had been pale and lifeless before he came, realization delivered itself to her. The understanding came fully formed, needing no exploration or qualification, that she could fall in love with Caspar Jensen. That indeed she had already fallen in love with him, while they had been sitting here in earshot of the music from the pleasure boats, and the ripple of their wash.

If he wanted her, she decided simply, she would go to him.

The simplicity itself was alluring. Harriet had spent so long thinking, and planning, and calculating. Even Robin had seemed to be another issue that required appraisal, and informed judgments. Caspar called for none of those things. He drew her in, sweeping her into the current around him, and that was enough.

While she was thinking these things Harriet went on talking and laughing, because it seemed quite natural to do so. Whatever happened, today or after it, there had already been this. The flags in the trees and along the waterside had been put out for her.

A waiter came to murmur that their table was waiting.

"Are you ready?" Caspar asked.

"Yes," Harriet said. The admission made her smile, and Caspar put his arm around her shoulder as if to confirm a pact as they walked to the restaurant.

Harriet remembered how the Landwiths' guests had covertly stared when Caspar made his entrance among them. The same glances followed him and Harriet now as they were shown to their table. Caspar seemed unaware of them, as he had been then. He brushed the maître d'hôtel aside and drew out Harriet's chair himself. White wine was waiting in an ice bucket beside the table, and as soon as they were sitting opposite each other he lifted the bottle and poured it. He raised his glass, one arm hooked over the back of his chair, and inspected her over the top of it.

"What shall we drink to?"

She studied him in return, noting the screen looks that were a little blunter and coarser in the flesh, but were more attractive for that, and the blue eyes that lacked the celluloid dazzle, but seemed more humorous. She liked what she saw.

"Let's drink to truancy," Harriet said.

"Very good. I am a perpetual truant. And what about you, Meizu Girl? Are you playing truant from that sleek boyfriend who looks as if he has been raised on a diet of cream and capital gains?"

"I think I've been playing truant from Robin for quite a long time before today."

"Good."

Harriet ate a mouthful of food from the plate that had been placed in front of her, without tasting it.

"Now. I think you should tell me about yourself. Childhood, marriages, all those things." He emptied and refilled his glass.

"Couldn't we talk about being a film star instead?"

"Of course, when my turn comes. We have a certain amount of ground to cover." As in a script, Harriet thought, before the action can get fully under way. She unbent under his questions, still, and talked more about herself than she had done for a long time. More food came, was no doubt perfect, and the plates were removed again. Caspar drank steadily, calling for a second bottle when the first was empty.

Caspar talked, too. He told her well-honed stories that made her laugh, Hollywood stories, but he also told her about his Tyneside upbringing and the days when he worked in provincial rep. It was enough to make her feel that he was offering her something of himself, beyond the public face. She forgot the covert glances of the other diners.

If it was all a performance for the benefit of the surrounding tables, of distinguished actor amusingly lunching with young businesswoman, then it was a performance that Harriet couldn't fault him on.

With his coffee, Caspar drank Calvados. Harriet had drunk less than half as much as he had done and her last glass of wine was untouched, but she could feel the walls of the dining room seem to ripple and dissolve, and the carpet to undulate beneath her feet. She was not quite certain that she would be able to stand up steadily when the time came, but she had also reached the point of happiness and relaxation that made her not care, particularly, what the walls and the floor were doing.

The same carelessness made her ask Caspar, "Why do you drink so much?"

As at Little Shelley he had been showing almost no signs of it, but now his expression changed and she was reminded of how he had looked when he had lost his temper at the inanities of the table. She had a moment to be afraid, and then the anger was gone again. He leaned closer to her.

"Are you afraid that I'll empty your plate into your lap again? Or that I'll assault the waiter? Or you?"

"No, none of those things. I think I *am* afraid of anger."

"Harriet, I'm not angry."

It was the first time, she thought, that he had used her name.

"I drink because I like it. When you reach my age"—fifteen or even twenty years older than herself, Harriet had already estimated—"you learn that you may as well focus on your pleasures. The spread of them is not as wide as it once was. Also, Harriet, if you knew any drunks you would be aware that they have good days and bad days. You have already witnessed a bad day. Today, up to this point, has been a good one."

Harriet lifted her head. "For me, too," she told him.

Caspar seemed to be thinking. Then he said quietly, "We're not here because of Linda anymore, are we?"

"No."

Harriet's chin had been resting on her hands. Caspar circled her wrists with his fingers.

"Now I should tell you that I propose to take you back to Little Shelley. There I will ply you with more drink, a little Mozart, and attempt to seduce you."

Harriet let him see that she was considering.

"Is that the usual pattern? With starlets, and so forth?"

"In my experience, more or less."

"I should tell you that in *my* experience everything works much better if there is a mutual agreement. I'd like to come back to Little Shelley with you. I'm fond of Mozart, too. But I don't have to be seduced, Caspar, because I can think for myself."

The blue eyes gave her a longer look. And then he nodded. "I recognized that two hours ago." Caspar stood up, and held out his hand to her. "Come on, Meizu Girl. Let's go home."

Harriet was also on her feet. The ground remained firm. "Only people who don't know me call me that."

Caspar said, "I don't know you yet. But I intend to."

Outside they blinked in the bright sunshine after the cool dining room. The Jaguar had been valet parked. Caspar turned back from giving instructions for it to be brought around, and as he put his hand on Harriet's arm a man jumped into their path. Harriet wheeled instinctively against Caspar, looking for his protection from the attacker. Too late, her brain registered the black weapon that the man had raised to his face, and she heard the click, click, click, and the hum of the motor-drive. The man was a photographer.

Caspar briefly patted her shoulder as Harriet lowered her arm from her face, still blinking in the harsh light. She saw him walk over to the photographer and turn him out of their path.

"Fuck off, friend, will you?"

The man had his pictures. He stepped back out of Caspar's reach, nodding. The black nose of the Jaguar came around the corner and drew up smartly in front of Harriet. The attendant opened the door for her and she slid gratefully inside, slipping right down in her seat. Caspar sank down beside her and the car leapt forward. Harriet remembered the ice bucket. "Can you drive?"

"Do *you* want to drive?"

She was conscious of the photographer and the parking attendant and a waiter or two watching their tail end. "I couldn't."

"Then you will have to let me."

They whirled up the lane, away from the Sunday-outing riverside. When she felt that they were safe Harriet asked, "Who was that?"

Caspar shrugged. "One of Dempster's people. Or someone like him."

"How did he know?"

"One of the waiters tipped him off. Or one of the customers. You never know."

It must happen to Caspar Jensen all the time, Harriet realized.

"You'd better be prepared to read all about it. *Caspar's New Love. High-Life for Business Girl Harriet.* They'll drag in whatever they already know about you."

Harriet watched the road. It seemed to unwind steadily, reassuringly slowly. She let her head fall back against the seat, aware that her heart was thumping.

"There isn't very much to drag. My P.R. people will probably be thrilled. Any publicity, as they say."

So long as it isn't Simon, she thought. Just so long as it isn't Simon.

Caspar began to whistle softly. *Gentlemen songsters out on a spree . . .*

It was not far to Little Shelley. When they were almost there, Harriet asked, "*Are* you drunk, Caspar?"

There was his loud laugh. "I'd have difficulty producing much evidence to the contrary."

They drove along the leafy road, past the big houses invisible behind their screens of trees, and came to Caspar's house. Harriet hadn't tried to imagine what would happen once they were here. It had been enough to obey the simple urge to follow Caspar. Now she looked up at the expressionless windows. The house didn't look much more inviting by day than it had done at night.

Inside, the big square hallway was faintly chilly. The same boxes and cases that Harriet had seen at New Year still stood against the walls. Caspar led the way to a large kitchen with a refectory table and too many empty chairs, and a heater that, when Harriet put her hand to it, she found was cold. It was a family house without a family.

"Where's Miss Page?" she asked, wondering a little what the pale creature would think when she saw her here with Caspar. Caspar made the same connection, jumping some links in the sequence.

"In her own flat, I dare say. It's my house, you know." And what I do here is my business, Harriet supplied for him. She wondered what exactly he did do. "Would you like a drink?"

She shook her head. She went to the long windows at the end of the room and looked out at a colorless garden, hearing the rattle of ice cubes. It made her sad to think of Linda wandering through these deserted rooms. Caspar's touch startled her.

"Come with me."

She followed him past so many doors that she couldn't imagine enough uses for the rooms within and up a wide staircase to more rooms. He opened a door at the far end of the house and led her inside. Caspar's bedroom was spartan, almost monastic, except for the books and manuscripts that were heaped on every surface. He made a gesture that signified apology, and dismissal, and put his drink down on the floor beside the bed.

"You did say that I didn't have to try to seduce you."

"Yes."

"Well then, will you come to bed with me?"

"Yes."

Harriet felt neither urgency nor diffidence. She simply knew that to do this was right. Caspar began to undo her buttons. His fingers were clumsy and he fumbled. Harriet half-closed her eyes. She didn't want to think of all the other bodies that Caspar must have explored, bodies much more beautiful than her own, and all the pretty, eager faces that he had kissed as he was kissing her now. Nor did she even want to remind herself that she was in Caspar Jensen's bedroom, that this was Caspar Jensen removing her clothes. That way, she could only have been frozen with self-consciousness.

Instead she focused on a separate, warm, and ordinary Caspar that she was sure she knew, and wanted to love.

They lay down together on the bed. Caspar's lovemaking was direct, without any of Robin's imaginative finesse. He entered her quickly and Harriet let him lead, although with Robin she had learned to direct as well as to accept. His breath made a small snicking sound in his throat as he reared up and down.

He came quite quickly. Harriet watched his face contract, the spasm seeming almost to cause him pain. When it was over he lay with his face against her neck, his mouth warm and loose against her cool skin. Harriet lay still, too, feeling the muzzy pressure of happiness at the periphery of her consciousness.

After a little while Caspar moved. He raised himself on one elbow and rubbed a hand over his face. Then he touched Harriet's cheek.

"Thank you," he said gravely. He reached down, beside the bed, for his whiskey glass. He drank from it, saw Harriet watching, and kissed her again. His tongue was cold, from the dissolving ice.

"You asked me why I drink. Tell me something, Harriet. Did you feel it, down at the Waterside, while we were sitting in that restaurant with the flowers and the drapes and the silverware? Did you begin to suspect that it was all a set, and that we were playing a scene that involved you and me having lunch together, and that somewhere the cameras were merrily rolling? That none of it was real at all, not the food nor the silver and least of all us?"

"I did, a little."

Caspar laughed, a drier laugh than usual. "I feel it all the time. Sometimes I have to stop and think, really quite hard, where the hell am I today? In character or out? That's why I drink. There comes a point toward the bottom of the bottle when you're too drunk to bother anymore, too drunk to care either way. That feels good. *That's* what I drink for, Harriet. Don't look down your nose because of it, because it won't do any good."

"I won't," Harriet said softly.

Caspar sighed. His glass empty, he lay back against the pillows. "Your breasts are pretty," he told her. "Round and pretty."

"They're too small."

"I like small ones. Clare's were too big, they rolled like the sea."

Harriet had seen them in enough films. She suddenly felt the absurdity of the moment, of finding herself in bed with Caspar discussing Clare Mellen's breasts. She laughed, and then saw that Caspar was falling asleep. He had thick, grizzled hair on his chest and she let the palm of her hand rest on it. She could feel his heart beating beneath.

While Caspar slept, Harriet lay in her contentment and watched the sun fading outside. It occurred to her that she had forgotten to telephone her office, and the omission seemed not very important. The house was utterly silent. She was thinking, as she lay there, that this conjunction between Caspar and herself was real enough. It should not need fixing with whiskey.

*   *   *

Harriet drew up in her car at Jane's front door. She climbed out, rested one hand on the shiny top and reached into the back for a bunch of flowers in florist's wrapping. With the flowers in the crook of her arm she walked up the path through the tiny front garden. Jane had watched her arrival through the window and she bit the pad of her thumb reflectively, waiting for the bell to ring, instead of going straight to the door.

There was a brisk ring. Jane went, then. Harriet was smiling on the step, holding out the flowers. She looked elegant, and incongruous against the backdrop of drab houses.

Unusually, they didn't kiss each other. Jane stepped backward, hands in the pockets of her khaki trousers, murmuring her welcome. Harriet's scent and the proferred flowers combined powerfully in the confined space of the hallway.

"Come into the kitchen," Jane invited. "Lovely flowers. How are you?"

In the slightly bigger area of the kitchen Jane saw that there was no need to ask. Harriet seemed burnished, not by the sun although her skin glowed, but by some less definable and equally powerful influence. To her irritation, looking away from the gloss of Harriet, Jane noticed that the surfaces of her kitchen were covered with a film of greasy dust, and that the marigolds in a stone jar on the table must have been dead for at least a week. She scooped them up, dripping greenish slime, and dumped them in the already full trash can.

"Shall I put these in water?" Harriet offered. "Where's a vase?"

Having lived here, in her pre-millionaire days, Jane thought impatiently, Harriet bloody well ought to know where to look for a vase instead of drifting about expecting one to materialize.

"I'll do it," she said. "Sit down and have a drink."

She took an already-opened two-liter bottle of Soave out of the fridge and poured two glasses full. It would probably make her sick, she thought, but she needed a drink quite badly enough to risk it.

"Cheers," she said, watching Harriet briefly inspecting the seat of the wooden chair before committing the folds of her maize-colored linen skirt to it. She took an unattractive green glass vase out of a cupboard and thrust Harriet's irises into it.

"What's wrong?" asked Harriet.

Nothing, Jane wanted to say, that a haircut like yours and a dab of Chloë and a Ralph Lauren jacket not to mention a few hundred thousand pounds in the bank wouldn't solve. But instead of saying it she flopped into the chair opposite Harriet, easing the belt of her trousers that bit into her middle, and took a defiant gulp of wine. Harriet was her friend, however little they appeared to have in common at this moment. She let her face crease into a smile.

"Where shall I start? With feeling jealous because you look so good?"

Jane disapproved of jealousy as a principle. It was not constructive. But she felt it now, and the feeling wasn't eased by admitting it. *It's easy for Harriet,* she caught herself thinking, and then wondered if she was going slightly mad. She had always prided herself on her rationality.

"You don't want to hear all that," she said quickly, "Cheer me up. Tell me something interesting." She refilled their glasses, although Harriet had only sipped at hers.

"Shall I?" Harriet was saying, "Shall I tell you what's happened?" She looked almost dazed with well-being.

"Go on."

Harriet needed no further invitation. She had kept the secret of Caspar for three days. After the first he had telephoned her and then telephoned her again to ask her to come to Brighton with him for the weekend. He had assumed that she would be free, and Harriet had made herself free although she had arranged to see Robin.

"Brighton is essential," Caspar had told her, "for the proper conduct of a love affair. Sea air and seedy grandeur, a stimulating combination."

Harriet hugged to herself the words *love affair*. She felt her happiness and excitement fomenting inside her, ready to spurt out under the slightest pressure. She needed to talk, to spill some of it, and so had come to Jane.

"You'll never guess. It's very extraordinary," she laughed.

"Don't make me guess. Just tell me."

Harriet told her that she had fallen in love, and then told her whom she had fallen in love with, and how.

Jane listened, in spite of herself, intrigued. The images of fast cars and restaurants by the riverside, orchids and runaway children and big, empty houses were powerful enough, and then there was Caspar Jensen's famous face to animate them. Was it *this* Harriet, she wondered, who had cooked lasagne in this kitchen and occupied the upstairs spare bedroom because she had nowhere else to go?

"I don't care what happens, you see," Harriet finished simply. "I just want to be with him. I can't not be with him. I never felt it before."

Jane nodded, although she had never felt it. *If I had*, she wondered, *would I have looked like Harriet does now?* In the situation in which she now found herself, the speculation struck her as ironic.

"That's quite a story," she said aloud. "No wonder you looked fit to burst with a secret."

"It's not much of a secret," Harriet answered, less thoughtfully than she might have done, "as from this evening." She took a folded tabloid newspaper from her handbag and passed it across the table, confident that Jane would only have seen the *Guardian*.

"I'm happy for you, if you're happy," Jane said primly and unfolded the evening paper.

It was a gossip column snippet, and a photograph. Harriet had turned to Caspar for protection, startled by the man who had reared up in front of them, but in the blurred picture she appeared to be nestling against his shoulder as coyly as any starlet. Jane read the brief paragraph. It was mostly about Caspar and Clare, but Harriet featured as "go-getting businesswoman Harriet Peacock, better known as 'Meizu Girl.' " "Meizu" itself was described as the "tragic POW game that became a world-wide craze," and the piece concluded with the inevitable speculation, "What game can Caspar be playing now?"

"Jesus," Jane said, curling down the corners of her mouth. "Can you bear to have this sort of stuff written about you?"

"There's been worse," Harriet said. "As you know." She looked harder at Jane and then asked, "What *is* the matter? You've gone very white."

"I'm going to be sick," Jane announced, "That's what the matter is."

She was gone for ten minutes. Harriet had got up to try to follow her, but Jane had pushed her back into her chair as she rushed past. Harriet sat still, trying to think, but she had been unable to think properly for three days. She sat down in the office to study the relative advantages of different factory sites and her thoughts looped back to Caspar. She sat still now, staring unfocusedly into Jane's back garden, busy with her dreams.

When Jane came back she leaned weakly against the doorframe, but spots of color were beginning to show in her cheeks again.

"Evening sickness," she said drily. "Wouldn't you know nothing goes according to plan?"

Harriet stared stupidly at her. "You're pregnant?" she said at last.

"I'm pregnant," Jane confirmed, with no inflection in her voice.

"Is that good? Or bad?" Harriet asked gently.

"Oh, shit," Jane answered. "I really don't know." She was aware that she was going to cry and that she didn't want this new Harriet to see her crying, not after her stories of Caspar Jensen and Brighton and sudden, startling love.

"How pregnant?"

Jane sniffed and rubbed her nose with the back of her hand. "One hundred percent. There are no half measures, you know."

"I meant how long."

"Ten, eleven weeks. They tell me the throwing up will stop in another two or three."

Harriet was absorbing the new information, setting in its context. Bringing logic to bear on problems had become a habit. After a moment she said, "You told me at Christmas how much you wanted a baby. Do you remember? You said you felt the need, like a pain."

"I know I did." Jane felt that her own powers of reasoning were deserting her. Familiar standpoints seemed to have shifted, leaving everything else awry. She had wanted a baby, Harriet was right. Specifically, she had wanted David's baby, in a partnership with David, although Harriet knew nothing about that. She had tried hard enough for both, in the short time that they had been together, but the elements had obstinately refused to unite and so, in the end, had their begetters. David had moved on as, she suspected, he was bound to do. Jane was far too matter-of-fact to think in terms of broken hearts. And that, she remembered, had been the stage she was at when she met Harriet for their uncomfortable lunch before Christmas. That was the time that Harriet had failed to disguise the fact that she was in too much of a hurry to talk about anything much.

"I did want a baby."

It was merely ironic that, after all her wishing and wanting with David, this baby should be the result of a two-night stand with a teacher from Chatham, met at a conference on computerized teaching aids, and not contacted thereafter by mutual consent. The pain that she had described to Harriet had turned into an altogether different pain, of anxiety and uncertainty, heightened by loneliness.

"Then what's wrong?" Harriet asked in the same patient, analytical voice.

"I suppose I wanted it in different circumstances. With a man."

"There must have been a man."

"Not really so you'd notice. Not a venture capitalist or a film star, for example."

Harriet heard the bitterness and tried to reach out. "What do you want, Janey? It's not too late to decide not to have it."

Jane lifted her head and looked full at her. "Yes, it is. I do want the baby. I want . . ." She made a little circle in the air with her cupped hands. "*It*. I'm afraid of the practical things. Where to live, how to look after it on my own, how to go on doing my job. Just earning a living, for the two of us."

"Be practical, then. Will the father help you?"

When Jane only looked, but didn't answer, Harriet went on. "All right. Move to a better area. Think about changing your job. Think about child-minders, crèches. This is *your* area, Jane, not mine." And, with a touch of exasperation, "What does Jenny say?"

"That you start feeling better after three months."

Jane felt as if her familiar self was beginning to crumble, slipping and trickling away like fine sand, while Harriet faced her cast in stainless steel, bright and definite and invincible.

Jane was jealous of more than Harriet's appearance. She was jealous of her success, of her independence of the men that she could, seemingly, take or leave or choose to fall in love with, and of the strength that her money brought her. If Harriet had a baby, she could employ a nanny or two to take care of it. Contemplating the distance between them, Jane knew that it was money that separated them. Money cushioned and comforted, and Jane needed comfort now. The change of perspective that Harriet's wealth forced upon her heightened her sense that all the old values were changing, leaving her adrift. She had been certain, once, that it was the common good that mattered and that individual ambition was in some way suspect. Equally she had believed that wealth was for distribution not personal accumulation.

But I worked for my success, she could hear Harriet say. *I earned it.*

I worked, too, Jane answered silently. *I did more valuable work than you. And what have I earned?*

"This isn't like you," Harriet said.

"I'm not like me." Jealousy made her feel even sicker than pregnancy. She didn't want to feel it but it was there, rising like bile in her mouth. And Harriet sat opposite, calm and business-like and judgmental. Separated from her, when they had once been close. I need a friend, Jane thought. If Harriet was still poor, she would share my problems. Suddenly her resentment was directed not against Harriet, but against money, the subtle rival, that had come between them.

"Sorry," Jane said, without a clear idea of what she was apologizing for.

Harriet was wishing that she had not rattled on quite so euphorically about love and Brighton. She took the evening newspaper off the table and stuffed it back into her bag. She was wishing that Jane had told her her news as soon as she had arrived, and that they could begin the evening again, following different paths. She wished that they could go further back, to some point—when?—when they shared the same perspectives. With the new distance between them what she felt now, mostly, was a kind of baffled impatience.

Jane would have her baby; surely the only problems were practical ones?

"Look," she said cheerfully, "If you are fit, and the baby is healthy, there's nothing that can't be fixed. If you need money, you know, you've only got to ask."

Jane appeared to rouse herself from more engrossing thoughts. "Ask for what? How long are you offering to provide for us? Six months? Six years? Until it's grown up?" The vista of her child's long life opened terrifyingly in front of her as she spoke. She would be responsible for another human existence, responsible alone, when she felt that she could hardly control her own destiny.

Misunderstanding, Harriet said, "Don't ask. I'll just send the checks."

"I don't want your money." Jane was cold.

"I'll *be* here, too."

"Of course you will! You have been lately, haven't you?"

Harriet stood up, horrified to find that they were quarreling. She went to Jane, intending to hug her, but Jane shrank away from her, her arms wrapped protectively around herself.

"My tits feel like septic footballs."

They might have laughed, so recently, but now they did not. Harriet found herself thinking back, trying to work out when, and how, this gulf had opened.

"Isn't there anything I can do?" she whispered.

"You could put the dinner in the oven. It's in the fridge, the dish with foil over it."

That was all; Harriet did as she was told.

They talked in circles, after that, with a pretense that everything was normal. They discussed what Jane's doctor had said, and the maternity leave she expected to take, and Peacocks and Harriet's plans, and other, ordinary things that had made up the currency of their friendship. They didn't laugh very much and they were wary of each other, too careful to shy away from threatening topics.

The talk was bland and the kitchen seemed chilly.

It was still early when Harriet said she must go. Jane came with her to the front door, as she had done so many times.

"Keep in touch," she said dryly. The porch lamp, shining down on Harriet, picked her out like a spotlight against the dark street. The incongruity of Harriet, here, struck her afresh, reinforcing all the evening's impressions.

"I'll call you after the weekend," Harriet promised. "Have a rest. You'll feel better."

It would be nice, thought Jane, as she closed her door, if everything were as simple as it seemed to Harriet. If rest really would solve anything; if real life was simply a matter of hiring and firing, or making the right telephone call at the right moment. Instead of being messy, and murky, and complicated by our ignominious selves.

Harriet drove back to Hampstead. She was disturbed by the faltering of their friendship, but she believed that it was only temporarily interrupted. And she was confident that Jane herself would triumphantly survive. She was confused now but she had always been strong. She would make the necessary decisions and she would act on them. She would have her baby and her life. She deserved to win both races.

There were two messages from Robin waiting for Harriet on her machine. It was ten to eleven, and she decided that she wouldn't call back tonight. It was late, and she didn't know what she would say to him.

She left the machine on and went to bed, thinking about Caspar and Brighton.   .

On Sunday evening Kath and Ken were at home in Sunderland Avenue. Since Liza had left home their routines had set firmly into rituals. On Sunday evenings they had a cold supper, the remains of the lunchtime roast that Ken enjoyed. Ken liked to spend the rest of the evening finishing the newspapers, scrutinizing the sports pages and shaking his head over the scores. On weekday evenings he often retired to his little study off the hallway to catch up on business paperwork, but Sunday, he usually remarked, was his day of rest.

Kath would sit in the armchair opposite him, reading her book. Tonight she had a P.D. James that she was particularly enjoying. It had been a still, humid day and they had eaten their meal sitting at the white wrought-iron table out on the patio. Kath had cleared the dishes afterward and turned on the dishwasher. It had been pleasant to come into the cool sitting room, turning on the lamps and picking up her book from the nest of tables beside her chair.

The only sounds in the room had been the crackle of Ken's newspaper and the just audible hum of the dishwasher changing gear in the kitchen.

Kath had just been going to say, "Would you like a cup of tea, love?" knowing that Ken would answer, "You sit there. I'll put the kettle on," when she heard someone at the front door. She heard the sound of footsteps on the path before the knock came. The footsteps were slow and they dragged. Her nervous senses primed by the book she was reading, Kath's flesh pricked. She raised her head but the person outside was already at the door, out of the range of the wide bay window that looked toward the road.

Ken only heard the knock. He put his paper down impatiently. "Who's this? Bothering people at this time of night?"

It was only a little after eight o'clock. But visitors on a Sunday evening, unannounced, were unheard of in Sunderland Avenue. "I'm coming," Ken muttered, hoisting himself to his feet, although there had been only one knock, neither loud nor imperative.

Kath heard him open the front door. There was a mumble of voices, Ken's clear and abrupt and another, much softer, that she could only just distinguish. But still the sound of it was familiar, and it set up reverberations of a different anxiety.

She was already standing up when Ken called sharply, "Kath!"

She ran out into the hallway. In the glass shelter of the porch, amid her begonias and pelargoniums, Kath saw Simon Archer. He was sagging forward, half-supported by Ken. His clothes were filthy, and he had a patchy growth of white and gray stubble. His hair was matted, uncut.

Ken looked at her in bewilderment. "I thought he was an old derelict, on the cadge. But he *asked* for you."

Simon pulled himself upright, holding on to Ken. He looked through the frame of flowers at Kath. He said in his precise, announcer's voice, "You'd better get inside and shut the doors and windows, Kath. They're right behind me."

"Simon, Simon."

She went to him, drew his dangling arm around her shoulder. Between them Kath and Ken helped him forward, avoiding their lamplit sitting room, into the clear white light of the kitchen at the back of the house. They lowered him into a chair. Kath's hand went involuntarily to her face as she looked down at him. She dropped it again when she caught the smell that clung to it, where she had touched him.

"Who *is* he?"

"Simon Archer. I knew him when I was a girl. I told you."

"Simon Archer. Harriet's friend?"

Simon twisted in his chair, peering up at them. "Harriet Peacock," he said. "After Harriet Vane." Then he sat back, his eyes closing. The flesh had shrunk over his face, leaving his eyes bulging. There were shreds of food, or vegetation, caught in the stubble around his mouth.

"It's all right," Kath said. "You're all right, now. Ken, will you get him a drink? And bring me a cloth, a towel, something to wipe his face."

Ken brought a very small whiskey. Simon sniffed at it, then drank. He began to shiver.

Kath said very gently, "Simon, can you hear me? How did you get here?"

He opened his eyes then. There was a look of pure, intense cunning in them. Kath knew at once that Simon had been driven somewhere beyond their reach.

"Ha. It wasn't easy. I had to take a long route, lie low, you know. But I did it. I had to, didn't I? They came back, when I thought they'd gone. They were at my door, eyes looking through my windows. All over again, watching me."

"Who was watching you?" Ken asked.

"Who's *he*?" Simon said to Kath.

"He's my husband, Ken. He's here to help, too."

Simon ignored him. "So what did I do?" He laughed, cracked laughter. "I left them to it. Left them an empty house, for their voices and their staring eyes and their questions. I came to you, Kath. I know you'll keep your doors and windows locked. But they might be here already." His protruding eyes went to the patio doors. "Close those curtains, Kath. They'll see in, otherwise."

"There's no one out there," Ken protested. "Just our garden."

"Close them, Ken," Kath said quietly.

When it was done Simon seemed to relax. His head dropped back again. Kath saw that he was on the point of exhaustion.

"Sit still," she ordered him. "You need some food, and a

bath, and some rest. I'm going to get you a rug, because you're cold."

He nodded, like a child.

Ken followed Kath out into the hall. "What are we going to do with him? Poor old bugger, he's not playing with a full deck, is he?"

Kath took his arm. "We're going to give him some hot food, a bath and some clean clothes, and put him to bed. In the morning we'll have to get the doctor." Her soft lower lip stuck out more prominently, as it did when she was badly disturbed.

"It's our fault that he's like this. It's because of us, you see. Harriet, and me." Her words came out almost as a wail. "It shouldn't have happened."

In Brighton Caspar and Harriet had had a long, late lunch and had gone to bed after it. After they had made love, Caspar had fallen asleep. Harriet lay watching him, and listening to the sea.

It was early evening when he woke up again and lifted his head. Sleep had folded red creases in his cheek and he rubbed the flat of his hand over it, pushing his jaw to one side, like a man waking up on camera.

He saw Harriet beside him, awake, with the sharp lines of her characteristic alertness rubbed out of her face. She looked soft and pretty, and he reached out for her.

"Was that okay?" Caspar mumbled.

She laughed at him, stretching so that her legs brushed against his under the coil of sheets. "Do you have to make a performance of sex, as well as everything else?"

He was surprised. "It wasn't a performance. I enjoyed it." He leaned forward and pursed his mouth against her bare breast. "Harriet, darling, is there any more Scotch over there?"

She poured it, but she held her hand over the glass.

"Do you have to drink any more?"

He leaned back, contemplating her breasts as if he had painted them, was putting the finishing brushstrokes to them.

"Yes, I do, rather," Caspar said, reaching out for the glass. But when he had taken a mouthful of the whiskey he pointed to the window, with the air of making a diversion, "Look at the light out there. Let's go for a walk on the beach."

Harriet got up and walked unself-consciously to the window. The beach was visible as an iridescent ribbon, dotted with stick people and bounding specks of dogs. The sea looked flat, with only monotonous wavelets folding at the high-tide line.

"Yes, let's do that," Harriet said absently, surveying the scene.

But Caspar's energy surprised her. He sprang out of bed and within minutes he was showered and dressed, waiting for her to put on her own clothes. He propelled her downstairs and out through the revolving doors of the hotel into the evening light.

"Slow down," Harriet protested.

"Seize the moment," he answered. "Always. Grab hold of it."

Yes, Harriet thought. *You're right to do that.* She liked his immediate appetite, feeling the contrast with her own circumspection.

They dodged through the traffic that clogged the seafront and ran between the kiosks and municipal flowerbeds to the promenade railings. Caspar stood on the lowest rail, spreading his hands along the top one to keep his balance as he leaned over to look at the shingle below.

"Smell that," he roared, inhaling so fiercely that his nostrils pinched together. "That unique mix of seaweed and piss and frying chips. Doesn't it take you back to seaside visits when you were a kid?"

The seaside had not played a big part in Harriet's south London upbringing. She wondered how largely it could have figured in Caspar's prewar Tyneside childhood, and if the stories he wove out of his own history were true, or all part of the perpetual performance.

"Not really," she answered.

"Shame," he scolded her.

Two old ladies in raincoats stopped to stare at him and then, recognizing him, nudged each other delightedly. Caspar half-bowed to them, then took Harriet's arm and marched her down the steps to the littered shingle.

"Let's move on," he said, "before they ask for my autograph, and then reveal their disappointment at having mistaken me for Peter O'Toole."

The suck of the sea became suddenly audible, and the pebbles grated under their feet as they turned westwards and began to walk, still arm in arm. Caspar was humming his favorite song, *Gentlemen songsters out on a spree, damned from here to eternity . . .* Harriet sighed with pleasure, breathing in the salty air that reminded her of nothing in particular. It was good not to be working. It was particularly good to feel that she didn't have to demonstrate her control, over herself or Peacocks or anything else. With Caspar, control was not an issue. He seemed to do

exactly what he felt like doing, with the egocentricity of the star.
Full of affection, Harriet drew his arm closer and put her hand in
his as they walked. His perspectives tilted the narrower sight-
lines of her world. He was wonderful company.

"Do you know what?" he said, pointing with his free hand
at the shabby-ground facades and curlicued balconies lining the
seafront. "Do you know, I wish I'd been born an Edwardian? An
actor-manager, like Irving. Bestowing my Lear on my adoring
public. Eating and drinking before it became a sin to do either.
Fucking in the robust, discreetly handled country house manner.
A king to my own company. Elegant and raffish, just like this
place."

"It's Regency, not Edwardian," Harriet said pedantically,
and they both laughed.

"What about you, my Harriet? What would you have been
born?"

She considered, for so long that she sensed his impatience.
So she admitted, "I'm happy with now. But then, I'm a woman.
What other time would have given me the opportunities that I've
already had?"

Caspar groaned. "Oh, Christ. A woman of our times."

"Why not?" Harriet asked. "Why not? I'm proud of what
I've done." *Most of it,* she added silently. Then she thought of
the times when she had slipped into shops, just to look at the
displays of "Meizu," to measure them with her eye and to watch
people picking up her game. She liked to watch them examining
it and then to witness the moment of decision when they turned
toward the till, satisfied with what they saw, prepared to buy.
The moment never failed to give her a kick of excitement. And
sometimes at a party, she had seen a group of heads bent in
concentration and then realized that the people were playing
"Meizu." Then someone, her hostess perhaps, would say, "This
is Harriet. She's the 'Meizu Girl,' didn't you know?"

It was different when the shield of anonymity was removed,
but it always gave her pleasure to see her game being played, as
she had planned it. She knew from the sales figures that her
instinct had been right, but all the profits didn't give her quite
the same intense satisfaction as seeing a single sale, or one
absorbed player.

Yes, Harriet thought, *I'm proud of that.* And again, *Why not?*

Caspar was nodding at her side. His attention had already
moved on. Caspar was Caspar, and he was not particularly
interested, beyond the requirements of good manners, in her
world or her business life. It was partly that, she reflected, that

made his company relaxing. He didn't ask questions, and he didn't make her feel that she should attempt vague apologies for her success. His own was on a so much grander scale.

"I like it here," Harriet said. Caspar heard the happiness in her voice.

"I told you Brighton was essential for the proper conduct of a love affair, didn't I?"

"Brighton's an extra. I like being with you," Harriet told him.

He stopped and turned to face her. Then he leaned forward, very slowly, and kissed her on the mouth.

"Thank you," Caspar said.

They walked on for a long way. The sun set and the beach emptied of people before they turned back. Harriet's calves began to ache from walking on the shingle. Lights came on in the hotels and apartments along the front, and the sky over the sea faded to vanishing green.

"Are you tired?" Caspar asked, and Harriet nodded. "Then let's go briskly back and have a bottle of champagne while we're thinking about dinner."

He walked as springily as if they had just set out, drawing Harriet down to a stretch of more level beach exposed by the ebbing tide. He murmured, "One, two. One, two," coaxing her along. Harriet found that she could imagine how he had been with his children when they were small, in the happy times.

The more gentle slope of the beach drew them closer to the water's edge. They were at the point where the foam drained into the pebbles when a seventh wave raced out of the dusk and broke, and Harriet and Caspar were sent scrambling and stumbling away from it, much too slowly. The sea swirled merrily around their calves as they staggered. They clung together as the undertow sucked at their feet, and then were left dripping on the innocent shiny stones.

Caspar cursed inventively. He was wet to the knees and Harriet's shoes were full of sea. "Bloody hell, Christ," Caspar bawled until Harriet reminded him, "Brighton is essential." A wave of laughter as irresistible as the sea took hold of them.

They slopped back to the hotel together and dripped across the elegant foyer, still smiling, oblivious to the stares that tracked them.

In the lift, as they swept upward, Caspar took Harriet in his arms again. She leaned contentedly against him, thinking of her champagne, of dinner and bed, thinking of nothing.

Fourteen

ON TUESDAY MORNING, Harriet was up early. She had come back to London with Caspar the previous afternoon and had spent an edgy, distracted evening alone at home with her paperwork. She had left her answering machine on and had taken no calls. She wanted to work but there were too many things that needed her attention, and she was unable to focus on any one of them.

Caspar had flown to Los Angeles. He had telephoned her from the airport, before he left. He had called her *"baby"* and Harriet wondered if it was her imagination or if he really did sound different, belonging already to unknown Hollywood and not to her in any way. He had told her that he would be back soon, and asked her if she would be Linda's supporter until then.

"You know I will," Harriet had promised.

Now that he was gone, she resolved, she would pick up the threads and pull them tight again. She would be at her desk early, before any of her staff arrived, and she would reconfirm her empire. The intention gave her satisfaction.

In the early morning she drew the protection of fine, dark stockings over her pale legs and buttoned herself into her clothes, as if they were plates of armor. She looked once out of her front window and saw the empty street, and then her eye caught the slow movement of a milk truck rolling under the lime trees.

When she looked again, Robin's car stood outside.

She took one quick sideways step that brought her within the shelter of the curtains. She thought, *Don't hide*. But her heart was beating with unpleasant insistence. She took two or three breaths, trying to make herself calm, then left her shelter to answer Robin's knock at her front door.

As soon as she saw him, Harriet knew that for all the seeming irrationality of it, she had been right to be afraid of Robin today. His features seemed to have hardened and sharpened, all the angles of his face slicing at her. She was aware of his height, and of the dark, stiff correctness of his clothes, different from

Caspar's rumpled jackets. Her fingers curled around the door-knob, as if she could still hurl the door shut.

But she only said, "Robin? You're very early."

He followed her inside. Harriet glanced at her briefcase, already packed, waiting to be taken out to her car. The cushions on her sofas were plumped up, there were flowers in a vase on a low table, the Sunday business pages, her life neatly arranged. There was nothing here to give her away, and as soon as the thought came to her there was the corollary, I don't need to worry about giving myself away. I don't belong to Robin or to anyone.

She turned to face him.

"Have you come for breakfast? Coffee?" She looked at her watch. "I wanted to get in quite early . . ."

Very softly Robin asked her, "Where have you been, Harriet?"

A cold finger touched her spine. He was standing too close to her.

"Working. Why? Yesterday I took a look at the prototype for 'Alarm.' You know, I think the unit cost is going to be twelve or fifteen percent too high . . ." She was angry at her own coward-ice, and the anger fought with her physical fear of him.

"Not yesterday, I know where you were yesterday. At the weekend. Last week."

"I went to Brighton." Harriet made herself face him. The dislike that she had begun to feel, before last week, and her anger, and her fear all solidified within her.

Robin was reaching into his inside pocket. Her eyes followed the movement. He took out a piece of paper and unfolded it, and Harriet saw the photograph from the evening newspaper. Of course. She was struck by her own stupidity in imagining that it would somehow escape Robin's attention. Probably Robin saw everything, knew everything. It was not a comforting thought.

"With Caspar Jensen?"

"Yes."

"I called you, you know. I left messages. Only you were in Brighton." He gave the cutting a little shake, like a cat with a bird.

"I should have told you," Harriet began. She swallowed against a hard knot in her throat. "I don't know why I didn't. We seem only to have lived together in one dimension and to break out of that, to say, 'Robin, I've fallen in love with somebody,' seemed too hard. I suppose I thought we could go on in our single dimension. Going to the opera, having dinner together twice a week. I know that wasn't very clever, I hadn't even thought it out. But it is the truth."

She lifted her head, relieved to have worked out as much for herself.

Robin grabbed her wrists. She might have screamed, but she did not. He was big and cold. Thoughts of assault, or rape, flitted out of sequence through her head. She looked longingly at the telephone on the low table across the room. A red digit showed in the front of the answering machine beside it the number of recorded messages waiting for her. She couldn't see at this distance if the number was a six or a nine. She realized that she had let the calls mount up, not even playing the tape back, because she had been avoiding even the sound of Robin's voice. *For God's sake*, Harriet thought. *I'm like some stupid girl.* She owed it to Robin to be honest with him now.

"Please let go," she asked, reasonably. "You're hurting me. Let go, then we can talk."

He drew her closer to him, instead. They stood touching, parodying an embrace.

"Have you?" Robin asked.

Somehow she knew he meant, had she fallen in love with somebody?

She told him, "Yes, I have. I didn't mean to."

"But I love you," Robin said.

Then she saw hurt in him. The coldness, the violence in him was because of the hurt. Harriet shook her head, unused to the spectacle of his vulnerability.

"I'm sorry. I haven't done any of this intelligently. I met Caspar, and that was all, somehow." She tried to twist her wrists in Robin's hold, but he would not let go.

"You started seeing him because of the child?"

"Linda." She remembered Robin's indifference, his reaction to her simply as a nuisance. *Not very nice, either of us,* she thought. "Yes. He came to thank me. He took me out to lunch, the same day, when that picture was taken." We deserve not each other, but better. Then we would be better ourselves, perhaps. Was that how it worked?

"And then?"

"It doesn't matter, except that it happened."

"I want to *marry* you."

"I couldn't have married you, Robin. I tried to be honest about it. I couldn't have married you even before this."

She looked at his face. In the silence that followed, Harriet imagined the toys and the pets and the treats that had been lavished on the small Robin, and the promises that must always have been kept for him, and the cars and the deals and the profits that the grown man had wanted, and won. It was bizarre that she had become one of Robin Landwith's targets, unfortunate that it was apparently the first denial he had ever suffered. She could not work out, from his face, whether he was about to cry or to break her in half.

Harriet's anger began to gain the upper hand. She knew this body, the shape and the weight of it, like her own. It was sufficient violence that she should have felt threatened by it. Her submission was over.

"Let me go, Robin."

His answer was to jerk her head back and begin to kiss her, kisses that were more like bites, with teeth that scraped her skin. Harriet breathed in sharply, twisting her face away, struggling as if she were drowning. The disconnected images of assault came back to her, but she was not frightened any longer.

She lifted her foot, in a gray suede shoe with the sides sculpted into a suggestion of tiny wings that made her think of Mercury's sandal. The shoe had a high, slim heel. She brought the heel down with all her strength onto Robin's black brogue. Linda had kicked him, she remembered, with a stout school sandal.

He gasped, and lurched backward, but Harriet was not nearly quick enough. Robin came back at her at once, with a wide swing, palm open, that smacked her jaw, knocking her head backward and rattling her teeth. She half-fell against the open door, more stunned by the ringing noise of the blow than by the slap itself. The door supported her and rage inflated her again. She would give no more ground. She stood up, square to him.

"Is that it? Is that one of the family secrets? Does Martin knock Annunziata around, down there among the cushions in Little Shelley?" She wiped her mouth with the back of her hand, panting for breath. "Like father, like son, is that it? You want to be like him, don't you? Are you afraid you won't measure up?"

"Harriet." His expression had changed. His face looked puffy now, his eyes fixed on her. "Harriet . . ."

"Don't hit me again. Don't touch me again. You are . . ." she searched for the word but she could only come up with—like Linda's schoolmates—*pathetic*, and he was pathetic, watching her, ". . . like a little boy. A spoiled little boy, turned class bully."

Only then she saw something else. Robin was coming at her again, but this time it was because he was excited, the violence had excited him. His mouth hung a little open and she could hear his breathing.

"I didn't mean to hurt you." His hands groped for her. She

was caught against the door, with nowhere to escape to. He held her with one hand and the other pulled at her blouse, tearing the buttonholes. He gave a sharp jerk and her breasts were exposed. He put his face down, biting and sucking.

Harriet looked down at the crown of his head. It was very familiar, the way the hair grew in dark whorls. She had looked down like this at other times, willingly, when he had given her pleasure. Anger gave way to deep, smothering weariness.

She said very quietly, "I don't want you to do this. You make yourself seem disgusting. Please, Robin."

He stopped moving, seemingly frozen. At last, very slowly, he lifted his head, but his eyes never met hers. His fingers groped, clumsily, drawing her clothes back over her reddened skin.

"I want you," he mumbled.

"I'm not a Porsche, or a property deal, or a hot share, Robin."

She thought that he might hit her again and waited for the blow, but it didn't come. Harriet lowered her arm that she had involuntarily lifted to protect herself.

"No, you're not," he agreed, the mildness of his tone surprising her. She caught a glimpse of the old, assured Robin. The mention of familiar totems must have revived him. "My father never hit my mother, you know. Or me."

"I wonder where you acquired your taste for it?" The reemergence of the other Robin did nothing to lessen her distaste for the darker man.

He looked levelly at her now, seeming to appraise her as his father had done at the very beginning, weighing each of her attributes in fine balance.

"Don't make an enemy of me, Harriet." His voice was smooth. It was difficult to tell whether he was threatening or offering advice.

Harriet smiled. "*I* can't make an enemy of you. Only you, and your responses, can do that. I would like us to be friends."

The level stare again. "We can be lovers, but I don't think we can be friends."

"In that case, I'm very sorry." Harriet spoke coldly.

Robin was in control of himself again. He walked away from her, and as if he was in his designer-masculine bedroom at home he checked his tie and smoothed the cuffs of his shirt. Harriet thought of all the things she knew about him: that the shirt was Turnbull & Asser, made to measure, and that under the dark suit he wore boxer shorts from another shop in Jermyn

Street. That he liked Verdi, chocolate, and conversation in the bath. That he could assimilate a page of figures more quickly than anyone she had ever met, and, the latest tiny piece of the mosaic, that he was sexually stimulated by a touch of violence. It seemed such a small, insignificant catalog of data to have accumulated from all the time they had known each other. Harriet felt profoundly depressed as she thought of it. By contrast, Caspar seemed both infinitely mysterious, and warmly expansive.

She wondered what he was doing now, at this moment, while Robin Landwith smoothed his hair in the gilt mirror that hung over her marble fireplace.

It was clear that there was no more to say. Robin looked out of the front window, to check on his car. Harriet turned sharply away from him and went into her kitchen. She heard him going out, closing the front door behind him, and after a moment came the rumble of the car as it pulled away.

She found that she was shaking. Her hands trembled uncontrollably. She made an effort, setting a coffee cup down on the work-top and pouring coffee from the jug.

She drank it standing at the window, looking down into the garden and trying to think of nothing. After a moment or two the shaking stopped. Harriet left her empty cup in the sink, changed her shirt and gathered up her briefcase and went out to her car. She didn't look at the space in front of it, that Robin's had occupied. She drove off, heading for the Peacocks office, using the white noise of early morning radio to suppress unwelcome silence.

On the same Tuesday morning, while the streets were still empty of traffic and before the weekday surge began to the station, Simon slipped out of the house in Sunderland Avenue.

He walked down the slope of the drive to Ken Trott's blue-painted gates, passed through and closed them carefully behind him, then went down the hill past the slate or wooden tiles that announced the names of the detached houses behind their flowering hedges. He didn't glance back at the Trotts' house, nor did he seem to look ahead of him to see where he was going. He walked slowly but steadily, with his eyes fixed on the ground.

Simon walked a long way without varying his pace or looking up to determine the direction of his march. He moved purposefully, but at random. Once, by taking a series of right turns, he covered an approximate square and returned to the point he had already passed twenty minutes earlier. He gave no sign of recognizing the street corner but simply walked on, looking fixedly at the ground in front of his feet.

The roads became busy with traffic and the pavements filled up with hurrying people. Simon seemed unaware of the streams of cars and buses passing within inches of him, but when a large man in builder's overalls jostled him as he passed, calling jocularly, "Sorry, mate," as he hurried on, Simon looked around in bewilderment, then shrank against the wall on his right hand that offered no protective niche in which to shelter.

He stood quite still for a moment and then began to move on, much more slowly. He was visibly tired from the long walk. Once or twice he put his hand out to the wall, supporting and steadying himself, before trudging on again. A girl passed him and then turned back to watch him, frowning, as if deciding whether or not he needed her help. Simon sensed her eyes on him. His hand, dragging along the wall, suddenly groped in emptiness. He had come to a corner, an alleyway that led down a slope. He turned the corner and half-stumbled downward, between high brick walls. The girl watched the mouth of the alley to see if he would reappear. When he did not she hesitated, then shrugged a little and walked on.

The alley ran between the high sides of two dingy factories. It was mounded with rubbish, peeling cardboard boxes and polystyrene blocks that shed white pellets like hailstones.

Simon made his erratic way between the heaps of refuse. He raised his head just once, and saw what lay at the end of the alley. Beyond the walls of the factories there was a small patch of waste ground, where panels of rusted, misshapen metal stuck up between swaths of rank, green weeds. The far side of the wasteland seemed to dip sharply downward, before rising again to the walls of more factories on the other margin of the deep gully.

The patch of ground was fenced off with sagging loops of barbed wire. Simon seemed to have found a reserve of strength as he pushed through the wire. A strand of it caught on the arm of Ken's jacket, much too big, that Kath had given him the day before. The sleeve tore almost right off as he freed himself. He brushed forward through the weeds, holding the severed material tidily in place with his other hand.

There was a metal footbridge ahead of him, spanning the divide. The bridge was fenced off with rolls of wire, too, the old right of way from the alley and across to the other side clearly disused. Simon hauled the wire to one side, scratching his hands but not noticing the blood that sprang from dotted perforations.

The jacket sleeve flapped down again and he held it up, glancing down briefly and frowning at the sight of the unfamiliar cloth.

He walked onto the bridge. There were blue-gray iron parapets on either side of him, their broad, flat tops at chest height studded with big rounded bolts. Simon ran his hand over the bolt heads as if admiring the solid Victorian construction.

Then he heard a sound behind him. He cocked his head to it for a second, then leaned forward, hooking his arms over the parapet. His feet scraped against the metal as he clawed upward, the final effort bringing his legs after his torso, up onto the flat ledge. He lay still, gasping for breath, and then hauled himself precariously to his feet.

He stood upright at last, his hand groping at the drooping sleeve, pulling it back into place. He looked down, then, at the rails running through the cutting.

He waited until the sound at his back had swollen to a pounding roar, and then he jumped.

The driver of the London Bridge train didn't even have time to touch his brakes.

Graham Chandler came into Harriet's office. She was on the telephone but she looked up and smiled at him, and indicated the chair facing her desk.

"Okay, Mr. Field, we can do that for you. But we'll be looking for some special support when we launch 'Alarm,' the new game, in the autumn. Yes, yes, I know. You're telling me." Harriet was laughing, but she stopped as soon as she replaced the receiver, and raised her eyebrows at Graham. "Promises, promises."

"Harriet, we need to make a decision about the premises. We have enough capacity for 'Meizu' and about fifty percent of the projection for 'Alarm.' If it takes off we'll need to look abroad, or alternatively if we're manufacturing ourselves . . ."

Harriet held up her hand, forestalling him. "I know. I know what we need." She leaned forward to her terminal and tapped the keys, glancing at the screen as she spoke. "Let's make the decision. I think we should go for the Winwood site. It's close at hand, offers the best access and by far the best facilities."

Winwood was a small industrial building on the motorway corridor to the west of London, one of three possible factory sites the company was considering.

"And it's the most expensive."

"Not unreasonably so. The benefits in terms of transportation costs alone will outweigh that in the long run. Winwood's my choice, Graham. Will you back it?''

Harriet was glad to be making a decision on a major issue. It made her feel properly focused again.

Graham studied her. He was less sure than Harriet appeared to be, but from experience he knew that her decisions were trustworthy, and also that she got what she wanted, out of determination. He nodded. ''I think Jeremy should go along with it, too. Can you get Robin's support?''

''Oh yes,'' Harriet said. ''That's it, then. Winwood it is. Our own manufacturing set-up.''

Graham went away appeased. Harriet considered, and then decided that she would wait a day or so before discussing Winwood with Robin. There would have to be an interval to allow them both to retreat, and put on the impersonal armor of a business relationship. After that, she had no doubt, they would work together perfectly smoothly. It had been one of the bonds between them that they put business first.

With the major manufacturing decision made, the other problems facing Harriet seemed to fall into place. ''Alarm'' could be made more cheaply by eliminating the manufacturing contractor's mark-up, and the retail price resistance that had worried her was no longer an issue because she could pitch the price lower and still maintain her level of profit. The gains would have to be offset against a big expansion loan that would need to be serviced, but Harriet knew that the loan would be readily forthcoming from the company's bank, and an afternoon's work on the figures convinced her that the benefits would comfortably outweigh the increased level of borrowing.

It was a satisfactory day.

At the end of the afternoon Karen said on the intercom, ''Harriet? Your mother's on the line for you.''

Harriet looked at her watch. ''Um. Can you just say I'm busy at this minute and I'll call her back at seven?'' She was immersed in her work, and didn't like to have her train of thought interrupted. A chat with Kath could wait until the end of the day.

''She sounds upset.''

''Mum? Are you okay?''

As soon as Kath spoke Harriet knew that everything was wrong.

''Harriet, thank God you're there.''

''I'm here, it's all right. Tell me what's happened.''

''Simon. Simon's *dead*.''

''Meizu,'' the old Shamshuipo *meizu* that was the basis of all this structure of Peacocks, sat on the table across Harriet's office. Her eyes rested on the silvery, flaking wood.

"I'm sorry, I'm so sorry. Mum, you know he . . ." she was going to say, he was ill, and lonely, but Kath cut her short. Kath was crying, choking between the words.

"It's worse than that. He was killed by a train."

"Where? How?"

"I should have stopped him," Kath sobbed. "He was here in London. At the house on Sunday night, like an old tramp, he was filthy and all his clothes—I had to give him Ken's. He said that people were watching him again, following him, and he'd got away from them by coming to us. He made us close the curtains and lock up, at eight o'clock on Sunday night."

"Why didn't you tell me he was here? I'd have come straight away."

"I tried to. I left the messages. Yesterday morning your secretary said you were away." Harriet thought of the red digit on her answering machine, winking at her. The telephone receiver slipped in her grasp now. Her palm was clammy.

"He seemed better yesterday. We got the doctor and he gave him some pills. He said he'd find a psychiatric bed for him, and I said I could look after him at home until he was admitted. Only I didn't, this morning when we got up he was gone. I waited all day and then I rang the police. They asked me what he was wearing when he went, I knew straight away. They told me an unidentified man had gone under a train, only it was Ken's old coat he was wearing. He'd jumped off a bridge, Harriet. Miles away, he didn't have a farthing on him, he must have walked."

Harriet listened to her mother's crying. She imagined Simon walking through the south London streets, toward the railway line.

"The police asked Ken to identify the body. He's gone there now. But it's Simon, we know that."

"I'm coming home, Mum. Stay there, I'll be there soon."

"Where would I go? I feel it's my fault, Harriet. I let him go off, I didn't know how bad he was . . ."

"It's no one's fault. You couldn't have known."

Harriet drove home to Sunderland Avenue. As she drove, she thought how Simon had answered her question about whether he might be her father, when they first met, by saying, "I'm not your father. I wish I were." She had wanted to hear it again, Simon wishing that he really were her father, but he had never said it. Perhaps part of her ambition for Peacocks, for its success, had been to do with making Simon proud of her. But he had not even wanted to take the money that she had accumulated for him, guilty money as she now saw it. As far as she knew he had not touched a penny of it. All Simon had wanted was to be left alone, in peace.

She would never hear him say, "I wish you were my daughter."

Harriet saw Ken's car in the driveway when she reached Sunderland Avenue. He came out to meet her and Harriet asked, "Well?" but without any hope. Ken shook his head. His broad face looked gray and flaccid with the shock of what he had seen.

"It was him. I knew it more from my old coat than what was left of anything else."

Harriet closed her eyes briefly, then opened them again on Kath's begonias and hybrid teas, only what she saw was Simon, and the bridge, and the train.

"Your mother's inside."

Kath and Liza were sitting together on the sofa. Kath was still crying quietly, and Liza's arm was round her shoulders.

"Liza?" Harriet said stupidly. "What are you doing here?"

Her sister said, "Taking care of Mum, of course." There was a subtle mixture of censure and self-righteousness and piety in the words and in her face that took Harriet back to their childhood dissonance. She wanted to snap, *I'll do that*, but Liza squeezed her mother's hand and murmured, "You sit there, love. I'll make you another cup of tea."

Kath raised her swollen face. "We're to blame, Harriet. We are."

"Don't cry so much," Harriet answered. "It doesn't help anything, you'll make yourself ill." The words came out sounding sharper than she intended, and Ken frowned at her from behind Kath's shoulder. "I'll see to the tea," she said, and followed Liza into the kitchen. Liza was opening cupboards and moving flowery jars.

"Where're the tea bags? She's moved everything around."

Harriet stood looking into the garden, making no move to find the tray or the teacups. The tea bags were uncovered and Liza clattered with the kettle.

"Leo says he would have died instantly. He wouldn't have known anything, after he jumped."

Harriet's eyes moved. "*Leo* says?"

Liza faltered, with the milk jug in her hand. Her cheeks reddened but she said distinctly, "Yes. Do you think he's right?"

"We can hope." The glazed, shocking afternoon seemed to have developed a slow-motion clarity. Harriet understood clearly and in total what she had not previously spared the time to examine. Her sister and her ex-husband were involved, an *item* as Liza would describe it, imagining that it sounded slick.

"How cozy," Harriet said. She was thinking back, beyond Christmas. Liza and Leo had been in the wine bar together, how long ago? On the night she had gone to the Hilton with Robin. Then she thought, *It doesn't matter. Simon matters, I knew it but it wasn't convenient, and now he's gone.*

"It's more than that," Liza protested, but Harriet turned away.

"I'll take the tea through."

They sat in the drawing room, the four of them, drinking it. No one said very much. Harriet felt the pointlessness of the family gathering. All they needed to complete the picture, she reflected, was Leo as the dutiful double son-in-law. Kath's tears, heartfelt and abundant, began to irritate her. Liza sat looking pensive, patting her mother's hand.

Ken stood up. He made a small gesture to Harriet to follow him and she went gratefully, leaving Kath to Liza's ministrations. Ken and Harriet walked slowly down the garden together, to the shade of the tree of heaven. Ken put his hand on Harriet's shoulder.

"I think he was bound to do it, sooner or later. He was disturbed, no doubt about it." His blunt, kindly meant words pierced Harriet's defenses. She pressed her lips together but tears still came and after a moment she let them, her shoulders shaking.

"You're not quite as strong as you'd like the world to think, my love, are you?"

"No. Oh, Ken, poor Simon. What a terrible way to have to die."

Ken was silent for a minute, then he said, "I didn't want your mother to see this. But the police gave me the contents of his pockets. Done up in a sealed plastic bag, like an exhibit. There wasn't much. A couple of things of mine, that I'd forgotten were in there. There was this though."

He held it out to her.

It was the cutting, the same as Robin's, from the gossip column of the evening newspaper. It seemed to keep on appearing, like evidence of a crime that she was trying to cover up. Harriet looked down into her own face, with its dazzled, startled, tipsy expression, nestling against Caspar's shoulder.

Distaste filled her mouth, rising so that she had to swallow it down, like nausea. She knew exactly what had happened, what had driven Simon at last to the railway bridge and the oncoming train.

Some eager journalist had seen the story, too, and in the glamorous light cast by Caspar Jensen had gone back to "Tragic POW" to ask what he thought of "Meizu Girl" now. He would have gone to Simon's sealed-up house and knocked too hard at the bolted door. Then he would have peered irritably into the windows, trying to see through the chinks in the pasted newspapers. He would have counted himself lucky when Simon crept to the door at last. He would have thrust Harriet's picture at him, Harriet was sure that was how it had been, and Simon had blinked down at the coy, smiling, horrible photograph.

I wish you were my daughter. He would not have wished it then.

After that, whether they were real or not, Simon would have sensed the presence of the intruder closing in on the house, pressing against the bricks and the fragile glass. In the end they had driven him out, to Sunderland Avenue, somehow, like an old tramp as Kath had said. Then, from Sunderland Avenue, finally to the railway bridge.

Harriet folded the piece of paper, smaller and smaller, and then held it in the ball of her clenched fist.

"Thank you for not showing it in front of Mum."

If it could only have been kept from Simon, she thought, perhaps he would still be alive. She felt as surely as if she had pushed him that she was responsible. She stood with the ball of paper in her fist, feeling how all her pride and satisfaction withered in the face of that.

Ken touched her arm. "Your mother and I don't see that paper." He seemed to be explaining the omission, as if they had failed to keep up with the proper developments in Harriet's life. "He must have been proud of you, to have it in his pocket at the end like that."

Harriet answered, "No. I don't think Simon was proud of me."

She had a sense of oppressive finality, that a huge mistake had been made and could never be undone.

"Do you know him, then?" Ken asked, with some curiosity.

"Caspar Jensen? Yes. I met him because his daughter is a friend of mine. He took me out to lunch. There was a photographer there."

Ken shook his head. "Must be difficult, for people like him. You can understand why they get nasty, some of them, can't you? People always staring, and taking pictures."

Only for Caspar there were compensations, of course.

Simon had suffered the invasion and had received nothing, except the inappropriate money that she had tried to give to him.

Harriet was silent.

"Are you all right?" Ken asked her. "It's been a shock for you."

Her tears had dried up. Her eyes burned instead, but Ken wouldn't see that.

It was a gray afternoon that smelled of grass and rancid city earth. The air was humid. Harriet looked up at the back of the house, rising complacently over the lawn. She wanted to get away and to be on her own.

"I'm perfectly all right. Shall we go back inside?"

By early evening Kath was composed again. She was clearly glad to have her daughters with her. Harriet stayed because she knew Kath wanted her to, although the house and Ken's solid goodness and Liza's tiptoeing depressed and irritated her in equal proportions. Kath recovered enough to go into the kitchen and prepare a ham salad, with hardboiled eggs sliced lengthways and Hellmann's mayonnaise.

"Let me do that," Ken and Liza said together.

"Kath and I will," Harriet retorted, with greater firmness. "I want to talk to her."

In the kitchen she peeled the shells from the eggs and washed and dried the lettuce, while Kath laid cold meat on plates.

"You mustn't talk about fault, or blame," Harriet told her. "You were a good friend to him. You did everything you could."

Kath raised her spectacularly swollen eyes. Harriet felt that they had just made the exchange that came at some point for every mother and daughter. She had become the protector, the one who told lies that she hoped were harmless and would fend off the guilt and the horrors for the protected one. Kath had become the child who needed to be comforted, while she was the mother who compromised. Harriet wondered why she had never realized that the exchange was inevitable; why, indeed, she never even so much as speculated about it. If Jane's baby was a girl, she thought, the reversal would come for them, too.

"Do you think that? I joined Peacocks quite happily, didn't I? I was glad to think of making some money for Ken and me out of Simon's game. Out of him being in that terrible camp. Yet I saw what he was like, after those reporters, that day you had me up there. I should have thought harder, Harriet, before I let you talk me into all of this."

A child, needing to be coaxed into or soothed out of its attitudes.

"You did the right thing. If there is any blame due anywhere, and I don't believe there is, I should accept it. I saw an opportunity with 'Meizu' and I took it. None of us could have guessed that doing that might affect Simon. If it did, directly."

There was the protectiveness, and the untruths could hurt no one now that Simon was dead. Kath appeared to be comforted. She began slicing into a loaf of bread.

"The doctor said he was seriously ill."

"We both knew that."

"If you'd seen him, Harriet. When he turned up here. So dirty and frightened, like a . . . fugitive." She brought out the word, an unlikely one for her to use, with a sad flourish.

Harriet put down the plate she was holding and went to her. In her arms her mother felt small and light, childlike. "I wish I had seen him," she said, more to herself than to Kath. "Just the last time."

Now there was only what Ken had seen.

Kath straightened up and patted Harriet's arm, as if it were she who had been doing the comforting and now judged it time to turn their attention back to the needs of the living.

"Let's lay these trays up. Your Dad'll be wanting something to eat by now."

There was something else Harriet wanted to say. As they counted knives and side plates she asked, "How long have Liza and Leo been seeing each other?"

"Did Liza tell you?"

"She let something slip, rather than telling me."

Kath's more habitual, troubled and flustered expression came back. Harriet was glad to see it, as a sign of her mother's recovery from the shock. "I don't know how long. It was Liza who asked him here for Christmas. He seems to make her happy, Harriet. Do you mind about it?"

"You always liked him, didn't you? Leo and I are divorced. We've no claims on each other. I'd rather have known than been kept in the dark for so long, that's all." She was thinking that if Liza was really what Leo wanted, then it was no wonder that her marriage had failed.

"I don't know why they didn't tell you. They had their reasons, I expect. You can frighten people, Harriet, you know."

"Not my own sister and husband, surely?"

Kath regarded her. "Me, sometimes."

"Well, then," Harriet sighed, "I'm sorry. I don't mean to."

She felt her isolation, and was momentarily sorry for herself because of it. She took ironed, folded napkins out of a drawer and laid them on top of the pile of plates. Caspar was a long way away and even if he were close, she was shrewd enough to realize, he wasn't and never would be a rock for her. She wanted to be a rock for him, rather. Harriet also realized that she would like Robin to be there, or at least to have the chance to talk to him. Robin had never been afraid of her.

Robin was gone, however, the old Robin. Those images of him coalesced with this morning's—was it only this morning? In future she would only talk to him about Winwood and things like Winwood, and soon enough she would hear that he had found someone else he wanted to marry and who would not elude him.

She hoisted the heavy tray and smiled at her mother. "It's getting late. Let's all have something to eat."

Lying in her old bed that night, listening to the over-familiar sounds of the house, Harriet found that she could not sleep. She tried to discipline herself into drowsiness, but only grew more alert. At last she got up again, dressed herself, and crept down through the house. Silently she let herself out into the soothing darkness.

At once she began to breathe more easily. She felt that in the dark she could see further and more clearly. It was becoming a habit of hers to walk at night. When the activities of the day were over she found that she was often anxious, possessed by a formless kind of anxiety that she could do nothing to solve, and walking helped her to contain it. Sometimes she would walk a long way, crossing and recrossing her own path; at other times not more than ten minutes in the anonymous dark was enough to calm her. Then she would go back to bed, finding either that she could sleep at once, or identify specific worries, and so begin to unpick the knots of them. She never felt afraid of the dark.

Tonight she walked for a long time, thinking of how Simon had taken the same route in the early morning. She imagined him passing through these suburban streets, brushing past the laurels and the viburnums, heading for the railway line in its deep cutting. She tried to will herself closer to him so that she might understand what had driven him up onto the bridge. Over and over again she came back to the same answer. Simon had felt hunted, and in the distorted landscape of his mind the hunters had cornered him. At last he had turned his back on them, and jumped.

Harriet stopped, putting out her hand to steady herself and

feeling brick gritty under the palm of her hand. The image of the train and the shining rails and Simon falling before being thrown up again, parts of himself instead of the whole, was as vivid as if it was happening in front of her, filling the empty and silent street with noise, and rushing wind, and terror. Harriet felt her own body lurch forward into emptiness and then cartwheel downward.

She closed her eyes and then forced them open again. There was only the street, alternate pools of light and shadow under the streetlamps. She pushed herself away from the wall, staggered, and then steadied herself against the dizziness that had taken hold of her. She made herself walk on, in and out of the lamplight.

She was close to Simon now.

And even as she realized it she faltered, slowing her pace and then quickening it, because she heard footsteps behind her. They were soft at first, almost echoing her own, but seeming to come closer. Harriet reached a corner and turned, darting a sideways glance, but she could see no one. The new road stretched in front of her, with the wider main road at the end of it leading back toward Sunderland Avenue. She walked faster but the footsteps quickened their pace, too, and with the greater speed they grew louder. She thought now that the noise was of more than one pair of feet—perhaps even as many as four or five. The individual footfalls merged together into a kind of patter, gentle at first but growing louder, and closer, threatening her.

There were the lights of passing traffic at the end of the road. Harriet didn't want to run because she didn't want the pursuers to run, but she could not stop herself. As she ran the sound of others running was almost at her back.

She was panting for breath when she reached the main road. A night bus swished past her as she hesitated on the corner and Harriet caught a glimpse of blue-lit faces inside it, dead faces drained of color, incuriously staring out at her. A scream rose inside her but she pressed her hand to her mouth and watched the bus shrink in the distance, a tail of cars drawn after it. She wondered if the blue-white faces had turned and were now staring back at her, and she understood Simon's fear with immediate and sickening clarity.

Harriet didn't hesitate any longer. She caught her breath and ran, as fast as she could, toward her mother's house.

It was as if she had become Simon. She was watched and hunted as he had been. Each breath she drew sobbed in her throat, and although she ran in silence she kept going in case she should hear the whisper of following feet again. Just once a figure stepped out of a gateway, into her path. She whimpered with terror as she almost collided with it, and then saw that he was a startled pensioner with a big dog on a lead. The dog snarled its threat but the old man called after her, "Here, are you all right?"

She flung an incoherent word back at him and ran on, until she came to the slope of Sunderland Avenue itself. The familiar, suburban stretch of it calmed her. She slowed to a walk and toiled up the hill with her hand pressed into her side. She looked back, and there was nothing there. She had fled, like Simon, although there was nothing to run away from.

Harriet came home, opening and closing the blue gates and entering through the glass porch with its moist leaf-scent. Her fear had evaporated as completely as it had earlier possessed her.

Upstairs she sat down on her bed, still in the darkness, her hands hanging down loosely between her knees while her breathing slowly returned to normal.

She discovered in a moment that the night had, in a way, worked its accustomed trick on her. She understood quite clearly now that neither she nor Kath could have stopped Simon once he was running, and that at the end of Simon's run there could only have been the jump, while for herself there was the return, and the even breathing, and the quiet again. Because she was strong and sane, and Simon was not. She was also certain that if she had left him alone, if there had been no journalists or anyone else coming to his door, he might not have begun running at all. If she had left "Meizu" as the piece of cracked board from Shamshuipo, or even if she had tried harder, thought carefully enough to disguise his identity properly, then he might still be safe within the shell of his house. But she had done none of these things, and she had tried to compensate him for her failings with her clumsy money.

That was her guilt, and that was what she would have to live with now that Simon was dead.

"I can catch you!" Linda screamed.

She ran down the long slope in pursuit of Harriet, her arms circling and her feet in red sneakers skipping over the clumps of rough grass. Harriet ran, too, down the hill toward the children's playground and the running track and the railway line beyond which small trains fussed in a loop around north London.

"You can't."

Harriet ran as fast as she could, but Linda was faster. Before she reached the bottom of the hill Linda flung herself forward, wrapped her arms around Harriet's waist and hung there, almost dragging both of them to the ground.

"Okay, okay," Harriet gasped. "You win. Let me go. You're the fastest child on Hampstead Heath."

"Hey, look up there."

They turned back to see the slope that they had descended. At the summit of Parliament Hill the kites they had climbed to watch were bright, dipping squares and lozenges of color against the sky. Linda and Harriet had walked up the other side of the hill together, from Harriet's flat, in the gentle current of Saturday afternoon strollers on the Heath.

"I don't like walks," Linda had protested when Harriet suggested it. "We have to do walks at school, endlessly, and it's vacation now."

"You'll like this one."

She had been predictably sulky at first, but as soon as she saw the kites above them she forgot her displeasure. "Look at the bird one," she shouted, and then they reached the top of the hill and she caught sight of the city spread out below.

"You never said there was a view. It's so big. I should think it's as big as L.A., only there's no ocean," she added, amusing Harriet with her loyalty to home. "What's that round thing?" she asked, pointing.

"Linda, that's the dome of St. Paul's Cathedral. Don't you recognize it?"

Linda shrugged. "I guess not. Should I?"

"Come over here."

They hung over the metal plaque that indicated the principal landmarks. Harriet was startled by how little Linda seemed to know, but she was touched by her interest in the green and brown spread of the city. Her questions about it showed her intelligence. Harriet answered with enthusiasm, their heads close together as they pointed and squinted ahead into the gray air.

Linda turned and grinned at her. "It's pretty neat. I like it because there's so much green stuff."

The heavy, domed heads of trees descended to the fringe of the railway line, became a green swell that spread across to Regent's Park further away, and then fractured into the mosaic of city squares beyond that.

"The trees are beautiful," Harriet agreed.

Linda glanced at her again. "You really love this place, don't you?"

"London? Yes, I do. It's home, I'm safe and comfortable here. It's important to feel that you belong somewhere, don't you think, like you in Los Angeles?"

"I wish I lived there all the time instead of at lousy St. Brigid's," sighed Linda.

"You're going home tomorrow, so be glad of that," Harriet said bracingly. She had discovered that briskness worked better with Linda than sympathy did.

Caspar was back in London. While Harriet and Linda were walking on the Heath he was having lunch with a director and some money men, and they planned to meet later and take Linda for supper at the Hard Rock Café. It was a last-evening treat; tomorrow Linda would be put on a flight to the West Coast, to spend the second half of summer holidays with her mother in Hollywood.

"Yeah, I can't wait," Linda said uncompromisingly. But she did add, "I'll miss you."

"I'll still be here when you get back."

"Hey, I bet I can beat you down to the bottom there."

Harriet didn't wait. She began to run, sailing over the hummocks, but Linda was too swift for her. They clung together on the level ground at the bottom, panting and laughing.

"Can we go in the playground?"

"You're too big."

"Who says?"

Linda slid, and swung, and swarmed up the climbing frame among the Saturday afternoon park-goers in their dungarees and slogan T-shirts and colored hair-ribbons. Harriet sat and watched from the sand-pit wall, with the fathers in sweaters and mothers who smoked and gossiped and pushed buggies backward and forward to keep the smallest babies quiet. Harriet was surprised by the liveliness of it all. She couldn't remember ever having taken a child to a playground before. When she thought about it, she supposed that Charlie and Jenny must spend Saturday afternoons in enclosures like this, with the other families, and the shouts from the swings, and the splashing from the paddling pool in its separate compound.

Soon it would be Jane's turn.

Watching the children, the smallest ones who walked in a series of collapsing lurches, their faces puckered with concentration, Harriet wondered how it would be to possess one of her own. To be possessed by it.

"Harriet? I want to go in the water."

Harriet followed Linda into the paddling pool area. Here

was a grayish expanse of shallow water in a concrete saucer, the blue paint long ago flaked from its sides. It was a melee of fat, pale little bodies and drooping wet pants and flying plumes of spray. Linda stuck up like a stork, paddling up to her thin ankles in the soupy trough.

A little train clicked past beyond the fence. Linda watched it pass, and then sloshed her way out of the pool.

"It's funny here, it's all so small, like a toy town or something?" Harriet knew what she meant. Looking at the scene she thought it was more like a nursery or classroom poster with the bright, primary colors and the train and the triangles of the kites, and a jet homing in the sky.

The city was homely and safe, as she had told Linda on the hilltop, but it also made her think of Simon, for whom it had been neither. Harriet heard the toy-town train braking as it came into the miniature station around the curve of the track.

"What's the matter? Are you thinking about your friend?"

After the inquest and Simon's funeral, Harriet had told Linda that a friend of hers was dead, and also a little about his life. She had listened intently to the story of "Meizu."

"It's good you made it into a real game," she judged, "So more people can play it, kind of remembering him without knowing him."

Harriet looked at her now, startled by her perception. She mumbled, "Yes. I was thinking about him."

Simon was with her all her waking hours. She did not so much think of him as work and live in continual awareness of what had happened, and of what she had unthinkingly done. She knew the necessity of living with her guilt day by day, and the guilt itself was sharpened because there was no possibility of assuaging it. The real Simon was gone, out of her reach, replaced by this memory. The pitiful fortress of his house. The railway bridge. Ken's old coat, and what Ken had seen at last.

Nothing Harriet could do, none of her cleverest efforts, could change any of this. She couldn't bring Simon back.

Linda was asking, "What shall we do next?"

With an effort, Harriet diverted her thoughts.

"We could walk down to Marine Ices, if you like."

"Okay."

They went on down the hill together and the circle of Harriet's thinking resumed. She could do nothing about what was past, only about what was to come. As she always did at the same point, she told herself, *You can make sure in the future. Whatever you do, whoever you deal with, you must never risk doing damage.*

Whoever it is, Kath or Liza, Jeremy Crichton, Graham, Robin—even Robin. You must take care. The resolution, reiterated every day, focused on Linda now. She could take care of Linda, because Linda needed her.

They came to the ice cream shop. Harriet shook off the effect of her meditations till they came around again, and followed Linda inside. Five minutes later they stood side by side at the curb, licking their double cones and surveying the dense traffic. Trucks and taxis seemed to cleave through a pall of atmospheric grime.

"It's pretty ugly and dirty here," Linda said unnecessarily.

"Dirt's part of it. Do you want to walk on down to the market?"

"Market?" The suggestion was greeted as suspiciously as the original walk had been.

"There's a big weekend market. Open-air stalls selling records and sweatshirts and bags, *neat stuff*, Linda. I'll buy you a going-home present."

"Yes, pul-lease. But we've walked a pretty long way already. How'll we get back in time for Daddy?"

Harriet had been going to say, *Oh, by taxi*. But something made her suggest, instead, "We'll catch the 24 bus."

Linda goggled at her. "A proper red London bus, one of the ones with an upstairs?"

"A double-decker. Yes, one of those exactly." Linda's arms shot around her, ice cream hanging at a reckless angle. "Harriet, going out with you is so unbelievably, perfect fun."

For a Bel Air baby, Harriet supposed, a bus ride home from the market would indeed be a kind of fun.

"And for me with you," she responded gravely, as they headed arm in arm toward the fried-onion air of the canal-side.

"How was your afternoon, ladies?" Caspar asked when they were sitting in the hamburger restaurant.

Linda beamed. "The best. You know what we did?" She had enjoyed everything, but she loved the bus ride best of all. She described everything, in detail, and Caspar sat drinking Budweiser and smiling at her. "Harriet's so great," she concluded.

"I know that."

Harriet blushed, a weakness she thought she had grown out of.

"We had a good time. How was your meeting?" It was odd to find herself sitting there, eating french fries and raising her voice to make herself heard over the music, exactly as if she was part of a family. Linda was chattering and sucking up her milk-shake and Caspar acted the benevolent father. He was in a good humor. He was a little drunk, after his long lunch, but particularly benignly so.

"Ah, a classic of its kind. Bull-talk of turning a development project into a go project as of right now. 'Caspar, we're going all the way with this one and we want you in there with us, because without your name up there, Caspar, this isn't a movie at all.' " Caspar's Shakespearean tones flattened and broadened, his eyes narrowed to match and he turned into a movie man. " 'Believe me, baby.' "

Harriet laughed. "Who were these people?"

"Producer." Caspar puffed out his cheeks and leaned forward to drop a heavy hand over hers. "Director." His face hollowed and he rubbed a hand through his hair, boyishly charming. "A couple of lawyers," with sharp eyes and wide smiles. By the time he came to the accountant, pursing up his lips and adding columns of figures on a folded paper napkin, Linda was giggling and Harriet was laughing helplessly.

"These are the people I have to deal with, while you two are riding the buses."

Caspar was a brilliant mimic. Harriet felt suddenly shy of him, and the scale of his talent. She also felt impatience, because he drank and dissipated it. She had seen his last two films.

"But it will be a good movie, won't it?"

"It will be a *lousy* movie," Caspar drawled, "but the bucks will be fine. Darling?" The young waitress jumped to his summons. "Bring me another nice cold beer, will you?"

"Is that a good enough reason for doing it?" Harriet asked, prim even in her own ears.

Caspar stopped with his glass on the way to his lips. "If you were going to mention integrity, or the Jensen *Lear*, then I advise you not to. Hollywood is where it happens. It's shit, as you'll readily point out, but it smells sweet enough to me."

Linda looked warily from one to the other.

"However," Caspar continued, "there is a small ray of light, *Open Secret*. I told you about it, Linda, do you remember? Harriet will approve of that one."

He was challenging her, with the fuel of drink, to murmur about her own approval being irrelevant. But Harriet only asked, "*Open Secret*? What's that?"

"A good movie. Only a supporting role, but a fine one.

Shooting finished at the end of last year, but because of post-production problems it won't be released until this Christmas."

"I'll look forward to it," Harriet said. Surprisingly, Caspar leaned forward and noisily kissed her cheek. For the rest of the meal he was the cheerful paterfamilias again, and they looked like any family out for a birthday or holiday treat. Harriet enjoyed herself and she thought Caspar did, too.

At the end of the evening they came out into Old Park Lane. Caspar looked up and down.

"No paparazzi here, then."

"None," Harriet agreed somberly. And even if there were, it was too late for it to matter.

Caspar held old-fashioned views as far as Linda was concerned. He would take her back to Little Shelley for the night, even though it would have been more convenient for them both to stay in Hampstead with Harriet.

"Come to the airport to see me off," Linda begged.

"No, your father and Ronny will do that. Send me a postcard of some palm trees."

Linda hugged her. Balancing her, smelling her soap and childish skin, Harriet felt jealous of Clare. She would miss Linda during this summer holiday.

"I'll call you tomorrow evening," Caspar said. Harriet watched them drive away before climbing into her own car. Linda waved until she was out of sight.

Caspar did better than calling. He arrived in person, direct from Heathrow.

While Harriet hastily changed her clothes he stalked through the flat, picking up and riffling through her sheaves of paperwork, peering at "Meizu" boxes and the prototypes of new games. He followed her downstairs and sat on her bed, looking at the neat regiment of jackets and blouses in their plastic bags hanging in her wardrobe. It seemed to amuse him to claim ignorance of her world.

"You're a business executive."

Harriet applied lipstick without looking around at him. "Yes. 'Meizu Girl' sounds as if it might be something livelier, don't you think? Disappointing for everyone."

"Do you enjoy living here?" He gestured at the room and pointed upstairs. She knew what Caspar meant; she had been seeing it partially through his eyes. It was so neatly white-painted, furnished with such silky and marbleized neutrality and hung with such tasteful pictures. For the first time since she had moved in, she felt less than wholly pleased with it. "Do you enjoy your life, Miss Peacock? Your executive apartment, your office suite?"

"It's the only life I know," Harriet answered.

Caspar beamed. He was bulky, tanned from his visit to the Coast, larger than life in her tidy rooms. "Follow me," he commanded.

He took her to what she supposed was a drinking club. It was in Chelsea, in the same street as Manolo Blahnik where she had bought her gray suede Mercury sandals. She remembered as they passed the shop that she had wrenched the high heel when she drove it down on Robin's foot, and reminded herself that she must bring the shoe in to have the heel reset. It was not proving so easy to reset her relationship with Robin into a mere matter of business, but she dismissed the anxiety for that evening.

Harriet had never noticed the discreet door, or even the building itself, which looked like a private house. She followed Caspar obediently into a wide hallway, with a glimpse of green garden beyond. There was a billiard table on one side, with a number of red-faced men gathered around it. On the other side was a crowded bar, backed up by tables crowded with glasses. A blue wreath of smoke drifted over the drinkers' heads. It looked and sounded like the height of an unusually successful party, a party that must have been under way for several hours. Looking at her watch, Harriet saw that it was still only seven-thirty.

Caspar was greeted as they pushed their way to the bar, as an old friend and not a face. He boomed in pleased response. Two or three people glanced after Harriet as if wondering what she, rather than he, might be doing here. They passed a television newsreader, holding a billiard cue javelin-fashion. His face was just as familiar as Caspar's, and no one peered covertly at him either.

"What'll you have, Harriet?"

She glanced around her. There was not a white wine spritzer in sight. Nor was there a suit, or a tie, or a calculator. It was a world of corduroy and crumpled cotton and unfamiliar periodicals. Probably also of Russian novels, Harriet thought, and the latest literary fiction. "Gin," she answered.

She was also noticing that this diverse crowd of people was comfortably and equally enjoying itself, although violent disagreement might well break out later. Caspar was perfectly relaxed here. He handed her half a tumbler full of gin, minimally diluted with tonic, no ice.

"What *is* this place?"

He looked surprised. "My club. Every gentleman needs a club. It isn't quite the Atheneum, thank God, but it is home." He lifted his glass of Scotch. "Welcome home." Caspar might like to pretend ignorance of her world, Harriet reflected, but she was genuinely unknowing of his. Thoughtfully, she drank her gin.

It was a long evening.

At some stage they did eat a meal in the club dining room, at a long communal table, but Harriet only remembered that everything had the color and texture of steak and kidney pie, and that the member sitting next to her ate everything one-handed because his spare hand was on her leg. Before the meal there was drink, and talk, and a surprising amount of laughing, and after it there was even more drink, and talk growing heated. The violence that she had anticipated broke out at last, with Caspar at the center of it. At one moment he was unsteadily on his feet, propped up by his supporters, trying to swing a punch at a little, gnomish man in a green corduroy jacket, also hemmed in by supporters. There was a great deal of shouting. Harriet was surprised to discover that she was shouting herself. But then, a moment later, Caspar and his opponent were sitting with their heads close together and the little green man was crying into his drink.

It was very, very late when Harriet and Caspar at last found themselves back on the pavement in Old Church Street.

"I'm afraid I can't drive," Caspar confessed, with an owlish expression that Harriet found very endearing. She hung on to his arm out of affection as much as necessity.

"Neither can I."

They found a taxi to take them back to Hampstead.

Caspar may not have been fit to drive, but he was perfectly well able to make love. He did it in his usual direct way, but Harriet felt confused, and tearful, and dissatisfied. She locked her arms around his neck and whispered, "I love you," but he didn't answer that.

She told herself afterward that it was the gin talking, and hoped he had forgotten it.

In the morning she left him still asleep on her bed, and went to work with a searing hangover. She confessed it to Graham Chandler who clicked his tongue at her, his disapproval only half humorous.

That was Harriet's introduction to the world Caspar liked best.

Fifteen

THE FACTORY MANAGER WAS A BIG, paunchy man whose white nylon shirt parted down the front to reveal ellipses of white vest. The shirt sleeves were rolled to the elbow exposing meaty forearms, held akimbo as he led the way across the factory floor. The machine operators stared at Graham Chandler and Harriet following behind the manager. They stared hardest at Harriet's navy blue suit with the wide shoulders and narrow skirt, at her hair and her diamond ring and her flat black attaché case she carried under her arm.

Harriet wouldn't sail by them to her meeting in the factory office. She stopped by the nearest machine, the expensive and elaborate new German installation that produced the plastic components for "Alarm," to greet its attendants. She knew two of them already and remembered their names, and she introduced herself to the third, shaking his hand.

"Is it behaving itself?" she asked, nodding at the machine. The foreman gave a gloomy nod, standing back to wipe his forehead with the back of his wrist.

"Because the production figures are twenty percent lower than they should be," she added calmly, and waited for his response.

"Teething troubles. Dies not aligning properly, see. Been sorted out now."

"So I'm told," Harriet smiled. Graham and Ray Dunnett, the works manager, were six steps away, waiting for her.

Harriet said, "I know you've been having some other problems. We'll solve those today."

She moved on across the Winwood floor, exchanging brief words with some of the men. When she moved on they turned to look at her legs, and then grinned at each other. Harriet felt their scrutiny and judged that it was curious, not hostile. There were problems at Winwood, mostly technical problems, and nothing that could not be dealt with. Production figures were an issue; her legs were not. Harriet regarded her manufacturing set-up with determined equanimity.

They reached the far end of the factory floor and a row of partitioned offices that housed desk staff. Ray Dunnett's cubicle was at one end. He held the door open for her. At the end of the line two women in overalls were checking the sets of finished plastic bits and temporarily bagging them in plastic, to await final packaging. Big cardboard boxes of filled bags stood on pallets beside them. They watched Harriet and Graham until the door closed behind them. Then one woman turned down the corners of her mouth at the other.

"She don't look very fat or happy on all of it."

"On what, Bet? Him or the money?"

"Oh, I wouldn't mind the chance of getting fat on him. Take it as it comes, I would."

"As he comes?"

Both women shrieked with laughter. Harriet and Caspar Jensen were the familiar property of the factory floor after the newspaper stories about them. There was plenty of dirty talk at Winwood. Bet lit a cigarette and leaned against a stack of filled cartons.

"Ray's busy, isn't he?" she said cheerfully. One of the men wandered over and stood beside her.

"So what are my chances, then, darling? I'm not famous, but I've got other advantages, if you know what I mean."

"Get away," Bet said, to encourage him.

Harriet sat down opposite Ray Dunnett's gray metal desk, alongside a pair of gray metal filing cabinets. Her works manager's office reminded her strongly of Mr. Jepson's at Midland Plastics. There were the same pictures of airbrushed flesh, the same well-used ashtray, probably even the identical paper cup half full of cold coffee. Ray would have to start delivering better than Mr. Jepson had done, that was the difference. Harriet snapped open her case.

"Let's deal with the technical side first, shall we? Graham?"

Graham and Ray discussed the afflictions of the new machine. The manufacturer's technical representative had made a site visit, and the faulty part had been replaced. Ray and his foreman were watching it and monitoring its performance. Harriet listened to Graham's questions. There was no doubt about his expertise, he knew what he was talking about, but he never said it forcefully enough for Harriet. She found herself sharpening his points for Ray Dunnett's benefit, stressing the importance of the machine's proper functioning. It irritated her to realize that she could not quite grasp exactly why it had been misbehaving, but at the same time was clearly aware that Graham was not handling the investigation with enough force.

Harriet also knew that it was her weakness to believe that she could do everyone else's job more efficiently herself. It was irrational, she understood, to feel impatient with her colleagues because of that conviction. She forced herself to listen politely, and to thank Graham and Ray at the end for their explanation of the technical details. But still, she saw, Graham looked annoyed.

"Let's move on, shall we?" she said.

"I'll have to call in Mick, off the shop floor," Ray announced.

The next problem, Harriet rightly suspected, would not be so easily dealt with. Mick came in and sat down. He rolled a thin cigarette with elaborate care and then began a long explanation of how his lads were not happy with the canteen arrangements. Harriet listened, frowning. The union representative was trying to tell her that he wanted a hot-meal service provided for his members.

"There are only forty-two people employed here, including clerical staff," Harriet answered at length. "It would hardly be economically sensible to equip and staff a kitchen for that many, would it? The canteen room is provided so that people have somewhere to eat their packed lunches, and vending-machine hot drinks are available, as you know. That's all we can do, while Winwood remains at its present size."

Mick appeared not to have heard what she said. "Either a full canteen," he went on, "or a longer break-time so that they can drive back and get a hot dinner."

The Winwood site was isolated in an industrial development. It would take an appreciable amount of time to drive into the nearest town and back.

"Break-times have already been negotiated, as you also know," Harriet told him. "I can't consider extending them." She thought back, with nostalgia, to the Stepping days when she and Karen and the others had arranged their hours without dispute, to suit themselves and each other. And at the Peacocks offices everyone worked, as Harriet did herself, until whatever needed to be done was finished. In contrast, Mick's bland deafness was intensely irritating. He swept on, involving all of them in a discussion of down times and working practices and demarcations that threatened to last for the entire day. Harriet fought unsuccessfully with boredom and anger.

At last she snapped, "We don't have any more time to devote to this. Down-times were agreed with your management at the outset, and the canteen arrangements remain as they stand."

Mick sucked in his cheeks but, at last, he stood up. Graham looked pointedly at Harriet, and she ignored him.

"I'll report back to my members, then."

"Do that," Harriet said crisply. Mick left the room, exuding grievance. "What's next, Ray?"

"Health and safety."

The health and safety officer had visited the Winwood factory, and sent in his report. There was a list of details that did not please him, from inadequate machine guards to the towels in the female lavatories. Harriet sighed and massaged her forehead.

"Right. Let's begin at the beginning. Where must the safety guards be fitted?"

"Well, I'll show you, but if they *are* fitted the operator'll need to remove them every time he wants to reach over the belt."

"And how often does he want to do that?"

"Two, three times a day."

"What's the answer, then?"

Ray shrugged. "Lose time or ignore the safety requirement."

"Does everyone face the same choice?"

He laughed. "Course they do."

There was no satisfaction, Harriet thought, in dealing with issues like these. She began to feel numbed by the tedium of the day. Slowly, painfully slowly, they went through the inspector's list. It took all the afternoon, and at the end of it Harriet did not even feel rewarded by a sense of something achieved.

They shook hands with Ray Dunnett before leaving for the drive back to London. They had reached solutions on two or three of the minor health and safety issues, but could only agree to try out means of solving others. The business of Mick and his canteen requirement was no further forward. Ray wagged his head morosely. Harriet knew that he wanted to be told how to deal with the issue. She should, she thought, have appointed someone more dynamic to manage her factory.

"Do what you think is necessary," she said briskly, letting go of his hand. "That's what I want."

"What you want," he echoed, as if cogitating the idea, but also with a touch of sarcasm. Again Harriet wished she had a better understanding of the technical mysteries that were plain to Graham and Ray. She would have to learn, that was all. A course, perhaps, or better still a week or a month spent here at Winwood, watching and overseeing. If she could spare the time out of the office. But then time could always be made, somehow, she had already learned that.

When they came out of the office, Harriet saw that the floor was deserted. It was a few minutes past five. The big German plastic-molder stood silent, an old man in an overall was halfheartedly sweeping in a distant corner. Out of action, the machinery seemed much bigger, veiled in its own expensive mystery. There was no overtime, Harriet was aware of that. They were well up to date with orders for "Meizu" and "Alarm" as well as for other, smaller products.

They left Ray in the empty car-park and headed along the motorway toward London.

"We have to make that place work," Harriet said. Graham only nodded. "It's costing hundreds of thousands."

"I'm not a money man, Harriet. But I do know that there's nothing to be gained by antagonizing the men. Or by letting your irritation show to people like Ray Dunnett."

"I'm not irritated," Harriet snapped. She pushed her foot down harder, and sent the car swirling in the stream of fast traffic.

The next day was a busy one. Harriet had a long meeting with her marketing manager and the packaging designers who were working on a new range of point-of-sale material for "Alarm." They spent the morning surrounded by dummy boxes and art-work, examining the effect of poster roughs and mocked-up counterpacks. It was the kind of work Harriet liked best, with the feel of the product in her hands, and she knew that she was good at it. She made instinctive decisions, but she could always justify them.

She said, "I like the cherry-red background for the lettering. It's much warmer than the blue, and the type reads off better."

"Red it is, then," the art man said.

The packaging people liked working with Harriet, too, and the atmosphere in her office was cheerful. They sent out for sandwiches and had a working lunch, still surrounded by color samples and boxes of "Alarm."

Harriet was in a cheerful mood at the end of the meeting. As soon as her office was empty, Jeremy Crichton put his head around the door. Harriet smiled at him.

"Come in, Jeremy. I'm sorry, I've been tied up all morning."

The figures that Jeremy wanted to discuss occupied them for half an hour. When Jeremy stood up to go he hesitated with his hand on the back of his chair, and said almost as an after-thought, "Robin asked me to have dinner with him."

Harriet looked up, clear-eyed. "How nice. You'll go, I assume?"

"Yes, I suppose so."

Jeremy was not gregarious, preferring to get home in the evenings to his wife and the garden, and did not particularly look forward to a social encounter with Robin Landwith.

"Good," Harriet said, raising her eyebrows by a millimeter to indicate, *Is there anything else?*

"Right, then," Jeremy murmured. He left her to get on with her work.

Harriet didn't think any further. It was useful that Robin should want to maintain social links with the other Peacocks directors, even if their own were severed. She had no doubt that Jeremy would pass on to her anything that she needed to know. She bent her head over her desk again, telling herself in passing that she should speak to Robin, too.

Several days passed before she did so, although she wouldn't have admitted that she put off making the call. She was going to tell him that she would be away from the office for a few days that was all. It was no concern of Robin Landwith's, beyond the requirements of business.

At length she did put through the call, dialing direct instead of asking her secretary to get the number for her. She swiveled in her chair while she waited, looking around her office, imagining Robin in his. When he answered, they exchanged neutral phrases for a moment. Their dealings were strictly limited to business now. They talked infrequently on the telephone and they met at board meetings. Robin was businesslike, as always. She had no criticism of him in that direction. He had even been surprisingly accommodating over the question of Winwood, and had been as helpful as he could be over the problems that had followed. But his manner was distant, opaque rather than hostile, so that she could not begin to gauge what he was thinking.

Harriet came to the point, the scheduling of the next board meeting.

"Can we change the date of this month's meeting, Robin, please? I'm going to be away on the twenty-eighth."

"Of course. Are you going somewhere nice?"

Harriet waited for one second. She wouldn't lie, there was no need to descend to that. Her private life was nothing to do with Robin now, she had nothing to hide or disclose. Briefly, she told him about the plan she had made. She had laid her plans with Caspar, full of happy anticipation, but she didn't mention Caspar's name or the excitement she felt.

"You're going to Los Angeles?" Robin's voice was silky in a way that Harriet did not much like, but there were a number of things that Harriet did not much like about him, these days. Harriet wished that she could see his face. She sat forward in her chair, looking across at the portrait of herself on the opposite wall.

"That's right. Just for a few days."

"Business, or holiday?"

A reward, Harriet thought. *There should be rewards, shouldn't there?* She didn't allow herself all that many. Probably not nearly enough, that was something she was learning from Caspar. He drank too much, and he wasted his time and his startling talent, but he enjoyed himself where he could. Caspar liked excess, whereas she herself was frightened of it.

"I'll be having some meetings." "Meizu" in its various forms sold well in the States. Its successors, "Alarm" among them, needed a boost. But she would be better to aim for that in New York, as Robin was perfectly aware.

"Well-timed to coincide with the Academy Awards, then," Robin drawled.

"I want to be there, of course," Harriet said. She was unable to keep the pride out of her voice. Caspar had been nominated for his performance in *Open Secret*, as Best Supporting Actor. She wanted to see him going up to collect his Oscar.

"Congratulate him for me, won't you? You haven't been out to the Coast before?"

"No."

"When are you going, and when will you be back?"

Harriet told him.

"Enjoy—" Robin murmured, and hung up.

"It's just family," Harriet told Jenny and Charlie when she opened the door to them in Hampstead that evening. "Just us, and Jane."

It had been a long time since she had made the space to cook dinner for her friends. She had been determined to do it before she left for the States.

"Oh, *good*," Jenny said. "We can relax. I thought it might be all brokers and bankers, and me disgracing myself by falling asleep. It's not my fault, I can't stay awake in the first three months however hard I try."

Jenny was pregnant again. Charlie followed her in, depositing two bottles of wine in Harriet's arms. He kissed Harriet on both cheeks, as Harriet thought a shade guiltily how unlikely it was that Jenny might encounter anyone from the other compartments of her life over the dinner table in Hampstead. She had learned the lesson that they were best kept apart quite a long time ago.

"Is Jane here yet?"

"No. It seems to take her a bit of time to get to and fro."

"I know how it is," Jenny sighed. "It must be even harder doing it alone."

Jane's baby daughter was three weeks old. Harriet had only seen her twice, briefly. She had a thatch of dark hair and a round, red face, and Harriet had been struck by her physical unlikeness to her mother. Jane appeared to have adapted to motherhood exactly as Harriet had imagined she would do, with her usual competence and assurance. But it was noticeable that the baby took all her attention. She was not overanxious or even particularly joyful; she was simply intent on the baby Imogen.

Jenny and Charlie and Harriet went into the kitchen, and Harriet offered drinks. Jenny shook her head, asking for orange juice, and eyed the champagne that Harriet poured for herself and Charlie.

"What are we celebrating?"

Harriet had laid the table carefully, with flowers and candles and polished glasses. She enjoyed the business of preparation, once she had decided to make time for it. Tonight she had laid out her best blue and white plates on the linen cloth, and crammed bright spring flowers into glass bowls, searching for color to offset the tasteful neutrality of the flat, as she had glimpsed it through Caspar's eyes. Her cooking was no better than it had ever been, but she was good at buying the best ingredients and serving them simply, and at chopping and slicing and garnishing to make decorations of the plates.

The plain food and the exotic presentation had amused Caspar on the few occasions when she had cooked for him. Once, at Little Shelley, he had made a meal for her and had surprised her by his familiarity with onions and thick stock and braising beef. It reminded her that he had been married for fifteen years before the advent of Clare, and made her think of a family life about which she knew nothing. Odd jealousies pricked her, as they often did about Caspar, and she told herself that there was no point in giving attention to them.

With Robin, she had almost never cooked. They had eaten in the newest restaurants, carefully evaluating the food. That period seemed a long time ago, now.

"Celebrating?" Harriet answered. "Imogen, and Jane. And us all, being here."

They sipped their drinks and Jenny looked around the pale, light, tidy kitchen as if it was her first visit. "It's nice to be here," she murmured, leaving Harriet to wonder if there was a criticism in that because it had happened so rarely.

"Here's to your trip," Charlie added, emptying his glass and holding it out for a refill.

"Is your boyfriend going to win the Oscar?"

"I don't know," Harriet smiled at him. "I want to see him there, if he does."

After a few minutes, Jane arrived. It took several trips to and from her Citroën before the baby and its necessities were installed as the focal point in the middle of Harriet's drawing room floor. Harriet surveyed the wicker cot basket, the bottle for boiled water and its carrier, the pink bag bulging with diapers and creams and spare blankets and shawls, and the string of bright plastic shapes that Jane would suspend over the cot to provide visual stimulation when the baby woke up. Imogen looked very small in the midst of it all.

"Made it at last," Jane sighed, and sank down onto the sofa.

Jenny knelt and peered into the basket. "She's so pretty. How's the feeding now? Did the spray help?"

Imogen was a demanding feeder and Jane had begun to suffer from cracked nipples. From experience, Jenny had been able to recommend the best remedy.

"Still every two to three hours but yeah, it helps. But how are *you*? Still got the pukes?"

Harriet picked up one of her pretty French plates with its extravagant tidbits of *bresaola* and *mascarpone* and offered it to her guests. Jenny shook her head and sighed again, but Jane scooped up a generous helping.

"I'm so hungry all the time. I'm never going to lose this twenty pounds I seem to have acquired." She was wearing a voluminous flowered overall which was, as she described it herself while waving one hand over breasts that were twice their old size, "front loading."

"I'm always ravenous, too, when I'm breast-feeding," Jenny said.

Charlie held out his glass for more champagne.

Steamed tiny vegetables to go with the moist cold duck were the only proper cooking that needed to be done, but at the al dente instant they were ready Imogen woke up and needed to be

fed at once. Jane brought her to the table, thoughtfully recognizing that Harriet did not want to keep her embryonic carrots and
baby beans waiting. She unloaded the front of her overall, baring
a blue-white breast seemingly bigger than the baby's head. In
response to Imogen's full-throated crying a tiny jet of translucent
milk sprang from the nipple.

"Ow, ouch," Jane said. "Here, baby."

The baby latched on, with a series of little snorts and gulps.
Jenny smiled fondly, the first time since the evening had started.

Harriet was remembering the almost identical scene, across
Jane's own table, the Christmas before last. Only then it had
been Jane gazing longingly at another woman's baby, and Harriet had felt a contractionlike cramp in her bowels. She felt it
now, watching Jane's baby feeding, and she ignored it.

"How's the business, Harriet?" Charlie asked.

"Fine. Pretty good, in fact," she lied. "Some teething troubles at Winwood, but nothing serious."

They had finished the champagne. Harriet had two bottles
of white Rioja waiting, but Charlie expressed a preference for
red. She opened a Bourgeuil instead and poured into three
glasses. Jane lifted hers at once.

"If I drink, she sleeps," she explained.

That was how the evening was. Whatever topic Harriet or
Charlie introduced, the conversation seemed to turn irrevocably
back to babies. Charlie's thick eyebrows drew together in a straight
line, and Harriet grew irritable. It wasn't particularly that she
wanted to talk about her own life, which mostly meant her work,
or even to hear it acknowledged as important, as important as
these sacred and exclusive rites of motherhood. In fact she had
been looking forward to forgetting Peacocks for an evening and
enjoying some of the old talk. In the past, Jane had been the one
who was always ready for discussion, an argument on any topic,
leaning across the table at midnight with her eyes gleaming with
conviction.

But Jane had turned into this floral mountain, who seemed
capable of talking about nothing but birth and breasts. All her
first ambivalence about having a baby seemed to have disappeared with Imogen's triumphant emergence. She was riveted,
hypnotized. She had become, Harriet thought, *bovine*. And she
suddenly missed the old Jane, as she had not done in all the time
before while she had been immersed in Peacocks.

After the three exotic fruit sorbets with *tuiles amandes*, Harriet
settled Jane and Jenny side by side on her sofa with a pot of
peppermint tea in front of them. She closed the kitchen door and

left them to their arcane talk. She wanted strong coffee, and so did Charlie. Charlie was leaning against the kitchen sink, rolling a glass of Armagnac between the palms of his hands.

"I'm sorry," he said.

"Sorry for what?" Harriet pretended.

"The mumsy phase does pass, you know. It tends to be most emphatic just after they've conceived and just after they've dropped it. You'll find out."

"I don't think so," Harriet answered, recognizing a truth. Her body, all those pouches and coiled tubes down there, might tell her one thing, but her mind's inclination was quite opposite. Charlie only laughed.

"So what's new and interesting?"

Harriet hesitated. She was torn between an urge to talk, after an evening of bored listening, and the awareness that Charlie was an astute City commentator who would not be doing his job if he didn't fasten on to the smallest hint of problems at Peacocks. It was a contradiction that was always with her when she saw Charlie nowadays, but she usually ignored it because she liked him, and she trusted him. Tonight she settled for a light-hearted shrug. "Nothing much. We've got this new German miracle machine but so far it does less rather than more . . ."

"For God's *sake*," Charlie interrupted her. "Don't you think about anything else, ever? After a good dinner? In bed? When you're asleep?"

Involuntarily, Harriet glanced at the door that separated them from Jenny and Jane. The comparison was obvious. Her own baby, Peacocks . . .

Charlie was, she saw, by now rather drunk. He was scowling at her from under his eyebrows, and she grinned at him, full of affection.

"Sorry," she apologized in her turn. Charlie left the support of the sink and came closer to her. She was leaning against the white counter, half-turned to watch the coffee drip into its glass jug. Charlie came closer still. His hips touched hers. He put his hands on her waist, swiveling her to face him.

"Mmm," Charlie said. "That's better."

Experimentally, he moved against her. His hands moved upward, spanning her ribcage and then settling over her breasts. Charlie had big hands, they swallowed everything. Harriet could not help but feel thin, and taut and springy, after so much spreading and dripping maternity.

He murmured, *"Nice."* And then prompted, *"Nice?"*

His fingers moved, rubbing a little. Harriet thought, a little dreamily, that it was nice. There had been another time, also at Jane's, when he had reached up and rather pensively put his hand inside her shirt. She supposed they were both remembering it now, although she was certain that neither of them had given it a thought in the meantime. It had also been, she recalled, the evening of the man in the blue shirt. For some reason she had thought of him, once or twice, since she had last seen him.

Charlie's caress became more insistent. It wasn't as if they had been nurturing a long-standing passion for one another, Harriet was sure of that. She had never been particularly attracted, in the physical sense, to Charlie Thimbell. And now she only wanted Caspar, to get to Caspar in Los Angeles. She could feel Charlie's erection, prodding against her thigh. His mouth slid from her ear to her neck, nuzzling under the angle of her jaw.

Harriet took a deep breath. It was nice, defiantly and mischievously nice after a dull evening, but that was its only significance. She lifted her hand to Charlie's and removed it, letting it drop by his side.

"What have you got in mind, anyway, Charlie? A quick one on the kitchen floor while Jenny and Jane rehearse episiotomies they have known?"

Charlie stood upright. "I have nothing in mind. Nothing whatsoever." He winced as he spoke, then reached inside the waistband of his trousers and adjusted himself. Harriet laughed, still in affection.

"You're pissed, Charlie."

"You are exactly right."

Oddly, he reminded her of Caspar now. At a certain stage of drunkenness they both displayed a sort of amiable male lechery, a quality that she could describe to herself as *chappiness*. She knew from her experience with Caspar that the stage didn't last long, and as she thought it she saw Charlie's face change.

"It isn't easy, the hands-off time, you know," he announced. "The beginning, and the end, and just afterward. And it's always then that Jenny seems her very softest and juiciest."

So much, Harriet thought with amusement, for her own skinny tautness.

"I haven't forgotten what it was like when we lost James, you know. I'll, never forget that. But I feel just a little bit now, just a tiny bit, Harriet darling, as though I'm being bombed with milky babies. With milk, and pee, and baby shit. While you, lovely, delicious Harriet, with your head full of the money market and your P.E. ratio, are sheathed in silk and scented with Chloë. You've got the little hard breasts and a lovely flat belly and long legs, so can you blame me, could you blame any man, for wanting to lie down with you and wrap the whole lot around him?"

Dryly Harriet said, "Put like that, not really. Not that I was about to do any blaming, in any case. Here you are, Charlie. Drink your coffee. Strong and black."

Was that what Caspar thought, she wondered, in the same condition? That she was a collection of bodily bits and pieces, in which to wrap himself? Robin had never thought as little, she was sure of that. Nor Leo, even at the end.

Charlie drank his coffee. It sobered him noticeably.

"Sorry," he grimaced again.

"Let's stop apologizing." She held out one arm, mocking him a little. "Shall we rejoin the ladies?"

Charlie laughed. "You're all right, Harriet, you know. No wonder you're a success in business. You think like a man."

Harriet didn't bother to take him up on that.

"Still at it?" Charlie inquired, when they returned to Harriet's drawing room. Jenny and Jane looked up, guiltily. Imogen was at her mother's breast again. But Harriet found that her own mood had altered. She understood that of course Jane needed to talk to Jenny at length about feeds and schedules and weight-gain. She was alone, a new mother, she had no one else except the professionals to turn to. Contrite, she went across the room to her and hugged her, including the baby in the embrace. Jane smelled of milk and baby sick. She found that she understood a little of Charlie, too.

"Don't listen to him. Talk all night, if you want."

Jenny was biting on a yawn. Her eyes were watery, and there were yellowish patches under her eyes. "I couldn't possibly. Charlie, I don't want to drag you away too soon, but could we think about going before long?"

"Now, my darling, if that's what you would like." He held out his hand to her, and wobbled as he helped her to her feet.

"I'll drive," Jenny said patiently.

Jane packed up the baby and her belongings. They divided the load between the four of them and carried it out to her car.

Jenny's face was wan as she said good night. "I'm sorry to be such a rag for your lovely dinner, Harriet. I just feel so ill, that's all. Much worse this time than with any of the others. Time to call a halt, I think. Charlie'll be glad."

Harriet consoled her, "Don't worry, after thirteen weeks you'll be fine and full of energy."

Jenny even laughed at that. "Poor Harriet. You've had to listen to all of it. Still, you'll know everything when your turn comes."

Charlie gave Harriet a chaste kiss, and Jenny drove them away.

"When are you off?" Jane asked through the wound-down window of the Citroën. Harriet told her. "Lucky you. I'd give anything to be going off for some high-life in Los Angeles." But there was not a trace of envy in her voice. Jane had her five months' maternity leave, her problems with finding a new house and a minder for her baby, her difficult job waiting unimproved for her, and she had Imogen herself. She wasn't jealous of what Harriet had, and Harriet was relieved to recognize it.

"Have a good trip," Jane called.

"I will," Harriet answered softly.

She watched Jane drive away, and then went inside to load the dinner plates neatly into the dishwasher.

Robin had been busy. Robin was always busy, but lately there had been a methodical, implacable force about his busyness. All of it was in connection with Peacocks. He was gathering a crop from seeds that he had planted long ago, as long ago as last summer. Harriet would have been surprised to discover how thorough he had been, but Harriet knew nothing about Robin's crop. Her attention had been on other things, and her preoccupation had led her to forget—or to overlook—what she already knew perfectly well about Robin Landwith.

Robin had begun, last summer when Harriet was dizzy with the exotic process of falling in love with Caspar, by making a series of telephone calls to a chosen few of Peacocks' employees. Harriet was the chief executive, of course, but Robin was the company chairman and so it was not so very unusual that he should want to speak to various key members of the staff. It was a little more unusual that they were not the most senior people, but belonged to the secondary management level, and it was noticeable that the calls were made privately, out of working hours, to the individuals' homes.

The telephone call seeds had not always germinated, but when they did they were followed up with discreet meetings, nowhere near Peacocks offices. Robin kept the details that emerged at these meetings in a dossier that was always locked in a drawer of his big desk.

More recently, he had taken to visiting Winwood. None of the machine-minders bothered to look at Robin's legs as he strolled around the factory floor with Ray Dunnett, although they did mimic his Duke of Edinburgh stance with his hands clasped behind his back. After these tours of inspection, Robin and Ray would retire to Ray's office and Robin would make casual notes as the two men talked under the eyes of the girlie calendars.

Then Robin had started meeting Jeremy Crichton, the accountant. Robin had chosen his time and prepared himself carefully, but the first of these encounters, over a good dinner at one of Robin's clubs, had not been particularly satisfying. Jeremy did not at first understand why Robin Landwith was suddenly inviting him to gossip over the beef and burgundy. But Jeremy was far from stupid, and the light dawned quickly enough. He didn't trust Robin but then he didn't trust anyone, and he was swift to work out which way the wind was blowing. When they met a second time, Robin's casually framed questions were more pointedly answered. The third time, Robin brought his dossier with him and the two of them went through it together. Jeremy looked anxious, but by the time Robin was leaning back in his chair to enjoy his port and cigar the anxiety had all but disappeared.

"You seem to have a case," Jeremy said cautiously. "Or you make it appear that you could have. I did give my agreement to the financial arrangements you indicate, however. That is incontrovertible."

Robin smiled his reassurance and recharged the port glasses from the decanter left for them by the club servant. "I don't think it will be difficult to argue, given the style of management, that there was no other course open to you. The nub of the business, of course, is that you need not worry about your previous role if the shareholders can be persuaded that a strong management is doing all that is necessary to set the company on a secure footing for the future."

Jeremy did not like cigars. He lit up one of his own Silk Cut and examined Robin through the smoke.

"And you can get sufficient showing of support from the institutions?"

"I think you had better leave that to me," Robin answered.

Robin made the last preparations for his harvest through another series of meetings. These last meetings were an odd mixture of the formal and the informal, being mostly held in the proper offices of the big financial institutions, but at which there was a good deal of Christian-naming between the dark-suited men, and even the occasional half-jocular *old boy.*

At these meetings Robin made a lot of play with his dossier, and with the information that he had gleaned from the financial controller, the production manager, the junior marketing executive, and the rest of his collection of germinated and now flourishing seeds. And after these smaller plants had been counted, he moved on to Ray Dunnett and Jeremy Crichton, his prize exhibits.

Not one of these meetings, however, for all their superficial friendliness, was easy for Robin. After more than one he had to return to his office and exchange a sweat-dampened shirt for a clean one, off the top of the cellophane stack in his desk drawer. But he never lost sight of exactly what he wanted, and it was in any case in Robin's nature to enjoy taking on these men, the fund managers of the big insurance companies with all their power and the might of the Investment Protection Committees behind them, men who had admired Harriet's entrepreneurial skill and had invested accordingly, and winning them over to his own side.

He was not successful every time. Sometimes James, or Christopher, or whichever fund manager it was at whichever institution, would glance up from the dossier that Robin had prepared and ask, with narrow eyes, "Aren't you exaggerating all this a touch, Robin? There doesn't seem to me to be all that much in it." It was then that Robin would nod, regretfully, and embellish his case with a few smooth exaggerations. Some of these exaggerations were developed enough to qualify as lies, as it happened, but Robin was a very, very skillful liar.

At the end he would fold up his papers and say, "That's it, Chris. We are all admirers of Harriet Peacock, and her abilities are unquestionable. But as chairman I have a responsibility to the shareholders and to the future of the company itself . . ."

Christopher and James and the rest would not see the dark patches under the arms of Robin's shirt, because his well-cut suit jacket masked them. And they didn't guess, either, at the delicious adrenaline that coursed through his veins as he fenced with them. The thrill was better than sex, Robin thought. Better than the time, even, when he had made love to Harriet in his office, on the day of the Peacocks flotation.

Of course, in the end, Robin would get what he wanted, because he always did and always had done.

Most of the individual holdings of Peacocks shares amounted to three or four percent. He had calculated that he needed to persuade only four of these major shareholders into his camp, four fund managers represented by the Jameses or Christophers, to give him the magic fifty-one percent that he needed.

After the last meeting, Robin went back to his office and locked the dossier away in his desk once more. He sat for a moment, thinking. The most delicate negotiations were still to be made, and he would be dealing with less familiar and predictable creatures than the fund managers of the major insurance companies. But he knew from experience that families offered much more fertile ground than financial institutions for his seeds of suspicion and dissent. The prospect and the potential prize, if he did his job right, interested him even more than all the prizes he had already gained. It was a challenge for him: he knew that simple people did not always make simple targets.

Robin left his desk and went over to some low shelves where, among mementos and plaques and other little personal possessions, the earliest production example of "Meizu" sat propped against the wall. It was the first, shiny black plastic model, that Harriet had christened "Conundrum" and which had failed to sell. He liked to see it now, because it reminded him that Harriet was fallible, whatever her loyal supporters chose to believe.

It was the failure of "Conundrum" and its rebirth as "Meizu," too, that had delivered into his hands the best card of all in the game that he was playing with Harriet. Robin smiled as he thought about it. Above everything else, he liked to win.

He picked up "Conundrum" and set the gates before releasing the balls to roll, and rattle in succession, and drop toward their destination. As they fell he saw that he had miscalculated, and the yellow ball insinuated itself before the blue one, into the wrong slot. Robin was still smiling when he put the board down and turned back to his desk, leaving the colored balls and bright disks in the wrong correspondence. It was typical of Harriet, he was thinking, and presumably also of the old man about whom she had worried so ineffectually, to imagine that the game provided some kind of metaphor for life. Robin did not see his own life as any kind of labyrinth. Rather it was a straight and well-defined path along which he progressed confidently toward the goals of his own gratification. If any obstacles appeared in his path they could be shouldered aside, and if the path deviated it could, with the application of the right amount of effort, be wrenched into the appearance of straightness again.

Setting his own path straight was, after all, what he was

doing to Harriet. Harriet had disturbed his equilibrium, she had refused him, and he could not tolerate that.

It had been Harriet's mistake not to understand as much.

Harriet was all ready. Graham and Jeremy and the others were prepared for her week's absence, Winwood appeared to be functioning acceptably, her bag was packed with her Academy Awards dress. She had even seen Linda off from Heathrow a few days earlier, at the beginning of the Easter holidays, en route for Clare's Bel Air estate.

Linda demonstrated a well-traveled familiarity with the airport's long-haul terminal and with the business of flying. She detached the badge announcing her as an unaccompanied minor almost as soon as it was pinned to her lapel, and stuffed it into her pocket. She craned her head to look up at the departures screen.

"Look, it's not even boarding yet. Can I get something to read on the flight, Harriet? The shop's at the end of the concourse, there."

"I'll buy you an improving novel," Harriet promised sweetly.

Linda scowled. "A couple of mags will do fine, thanks."

They threaded through the crowds together. The shop offered a wall of gold-inscribed paperbacks and a mounted display of Union Jack tea towels and plastic Beefeaters. Linda caught at Harriet's arm. "Look!" she crowed.

Harriet's experienced eye had already seen it, and registered the stock position as well. There was a spinner standing at one end of the display unit, one of her own spinners topped with the Peacocks feathers, and the pockets in it were neatly filled with her games. There was "Meizu" in the blister pack that had caused manufacturing problems, and in the black and silver executive version, and "Alarm" in the old packaging that didn't satisfy her.

Harriet said, "Yes, airports are good outlets."

Linda had already hurried over to the spinner. She was tidying the units in their pockets, moving them to fill slots that had been emptied. A Japanese couple were standing nearby, examining "Travel Meizu."

"It's really good," Linda said, planting herself in front of them. "You should get it." They backed away from her, balancing "Meizu" defensively on top of an armful of tartan-packaged shortbread.

"*Linda!*" Harriet protested.

"Well? It's a sale, isn't it? Don't you feel proud when you see people getting your things? *I* feel proud of you. It's like seeing Dad in a movie. You can't believe someone belongs to you."

"Yes, I feel proud. Of course I do. I keep quieter about it, that's all."

As quiet as she kept her pleasure in hearing Linda linking her with Caspar in the same admiring breath, Harriet thought. But that wasn't to deny the reality of it. She smiled at Linda. "I should have you on my sales force."

It was time for Linda to board her flight. Harriet busied herself with checking that she had her passport and her ticket and her boarding card.

"It's not a proper good-bye," Linda said. "Not as you're coming to L.A. so soon. It'll be so great to have you there."

"It's only for a week," Harriet warned. "And I don't know how much we'll be able to see of each other. You're staying with your mother . . ." *And I'm your father's girlfriend*, she had delicately not added.

Linda responded smartly. "Clare likes what keeps me happy. Seeing you makes me happy. Don't worry, we'll fix it."

Her high spirits and her confidence and her affection pleased Harriet. Linda seemed a different girl from the mutinous child she had met at the Landwiths'.

"See you in L.A." They hugged each other, not like mother and daughter and not like sisters. *Nothing like Liza and myself, anyhow*, Harriet thought. She watched and waved until Linda passed out of sight behind the airside screens.

The last day before her own departure came. There was only the television interview to be taped, and then she would be on the way back to the airport.

Alison Shaw arrived, with her television crew, to make the program called *Success Story*. Sitting in her office under her portrait, with the startling title of "Entrepreneur of the Year" just awarded to her, Harriet was evidently a success. She could remember Simon, reaching out to give her the cracked wood of the first "Meizu," but she need not dwell on what had happened. She could be confident that when she came back after her week's holiday, her deserved reward, she could make Winwood work. She had always made everything work; she was a success story.

The reporter wound up her interview. While the crew filmed the reaction shots Harriet went out to take a call from Charlie Thimbell. Charlie was relieved to have caught her. As he talked he doodled fiercely on his notepad, drawing looped circles and then slashing oblique lines through them.

Harriet, I heard a rumor.

He had had lunch that day with a P.R. agent, a lively girl who enjoyed her wine and with whom he regularly shared convivial, indiscreet lunches. But Charlie had a story to write that afternoon. He drank only one glass and the girl finished the rest of the bottle.

You're a friend of Harriet Peacock's, aren't you, Charlie? The question was accompanied by the knowing squint that suggested a tidbit of information to follow. Charlie's contact didn't work for the company employed by Peacocks, but she had her contacts, too. And although what she leaned forward to breathe across the table to him did not amount to so very much, in hard fact, it still worried Charlie very much. It also suggested the kind of City story he excelled at winkling out for his readers. He hurried back to his office, and put through the call.

Are you watching your back, Harriet? Are you overstretched?

Her laughter was confident, but it didn't reassure him.

I wouldn't tell you, Charlie. Which would you put first, me or a good story?

You'll be a long way from home.

Airily Harriet had told him that she was not going up the Amazon. She could be back in London in twelve hours if she was needed. Which she would not be.

And so there was no more Charlie could say, except, *"Enjoy yourself."*

Harriet hung up. Karen was signaling at her to say that the car to take her to the airport was waiting for her downstairs. Alison Shaw came out of Harriet's office, the thick folds of her clothes and the raincoat over her arm making her look dumpy in comparison with Harriet's elegance. The two women shook hands and Alison thanked Harriet for the interview. Harriet answered that she had enjoyed it, lying because she didn't like being interviewed, not anymore. It connected too readily back to the old search for publicity, any publicity, and Simon.

But she noticed that now the reporter's work was finished, there was warmth and friendliness in Alison's face, as well as sharp intelligence. It made Harriet think that if there were only time to share, it would be nice to make a new friend. She responded with warmth of her own.

"Have a good trip," Alison and Karen said together.

By five o'clock, Harriet was airborne.

Sitting in her first-class seat, holding a glass of British Airways champagne, Harriet allowed herself a small sigh of satisfaction that was touched with the smallest, most pleasurable tinge of disbelief. She was a successful businesswoman, by an eminent committee's reckoning the "Entrepreneur of the Year," no less. She had money, real money, and the evidence of it in a silk and wool suit with a covetable label, handmade shoes, and a diamond ring she had happily bought for herself. And now, better than any of those things, best of all, she was flying out to Los Angeles, to Caspar Jensen.

Harriet took a sip of her champagne, smiling to herself, forgetting Charlie's warning. She had come a long way.

Los Angeles exploded around Harriet like a fireworks display.

From her first glimpse of the city over the wingtip of the 747, an ivory and silver inlay within the curve of the Pacific, she was enchanted.

She forgot her flight-weariness as she came in a boiling crowd out of the terminal at LAX and took her first taste of the overheated, tainted air. She saw the car that Caspar had sent for her, a long black limousine with opaque black windows, in a press of similar cars that waited for the success stories to descend from the air and take possession of them, and she felt a bite of adrenaline in her blood that she had never known before.

The car swallowed her up with her two suitcases, and the driver touched his gray peaked cap.

"Are you ready, ma'am?"

"I'm ready."

The car swept through the gritty low-built jungle of fast food outlets and hoardings that surrounded the airport and as they drove Harriet saw that the drivers of the Fords and Buicks and beat-up Volkswagons that streamed alongside turned to peer vainly in at the opaque glass, as if they might rub so close to some celebrity.

She read a sign, San Diego Freeway, and looked ahead to see a solid ribbon of metal and glass and rubber that stretched away, shimmering in the heat. The city traffic. She could sense, rather than hear, that the surrounding air vibrated with the sound waves of a thousand radio stations. Fingers drummed on the steering wheels and the glinting metal all around her, as far as she could see, in response to some insistent and inaudible beat.

Up ahead an electronic sign flashed. 18:27. 87°. 18:27. 87°. 18:28, over and over. It was hot out there, but Harriet was cool in her air-conditioned cocoon. Instead of leaning back against the cushions and closing her eyes she pressed forward in her seat, willing the limousine to carry her faster.

Santa Monica Boulevard. The traffic here moved more freely, but four lanes abreast, past a green and black glass ziggurat of skyscrapers, past a great cream-colored edifice like a modern cathedral, and more hoardings and flashing signs and words and colors that demanded her attention more stridently than any landscape she had ever passed through. She gazed out at it all, her eyes ready to jump further and faster than the car could travel. Under her breath she repeated, "Santa Monica Boulevard." A car with the license plate ACTREZZ sprang forward, sunglasses and vermilion lips at the wheel, and whirled away in the opposite direction.

Harriet laughed out loud, hungry for and at the same time awed by the appearance of the fabled city in front of her.

Now the limousine turned out of the traffic. Harriet saw a wide, quiet street more like other streets that she had known, except this street was lined with a double guard of four lines of sixty-foot palm trees. The leaf-fronds that sprouted gracefully out of the smooth, ringed boles were so still in the heavy air that they might have been cast in metal. There were no hoardings here, no Big Boy Burger signs, no gas stations. There were only cars that swept silently under the palm sentinels, past mown grass plateaus. Beyond the grass like velvet Harriet could see houses, white and pink and cream houses behind banks of flowers. The windows stared impassively over the flowers, meeting her gaze.

Harriet leaned forward and tapped on the glass panel that separated her from the driver. The obedient panel slid away with a humming sound.

"What's this area called?" Harriet asked.

"This here? This is Beverly Hills, ma'am."

Beverly Hills, of course it was.

"This is your first visit to L.A.?"

"Yes."

The man shook his head. "Ain't no place like it. Crazy city, this is. You staying here long?"

"No."

He nodded now. "That's the best way. You come and see it, then away you go home again."

Harriet laughed. "That sounds like a warning."

As they drove on, deeper into Beverly Hills, even the houses disappeared. Now all that was visible was greenery, starred with bougainvillea and hibiscus and orange blossom, and the exclusion zones of manicured grass. There were high gates here and there, and the occasional rooftop was visible over the ramparts of foliage. It came to Harriet that this was a huge, subtropical version of Little Shelley.

The car began to climb a winding road. Turning to look back where they had come from, Harriet saw the dense carpet of city below, stretching westwards to the ocean. The sun was setting, casting an orange-golden sheet over the silver water. The view was magnificent, but there was nobody out to enjoy it. Harriet realized that they had not passed a living soul while they had been climbing the canyon road. A moment later the long black car was negotiating a tight corner between banks of lush greenery. Harriet glimpsed a sign that read, "AREA PATROLLED BY PRIVATE ARMED GUARDS 24 HOURS A DAY."

The car stopped.

She opened the door and stepped out. The heat descended immediately on her head. Harriet saw that she was in the garden of a long, low, white-walled house. The house was cut off from the outside world but there the similarity to Little Shelley ended. In this garden, instead of the familiar dripping English shrubs, there were cacti and mysterious succulents, tall white arum lilies and tangled ivies, carpets of pink and purple blossoms offset by the narrow black points of cypress trees, and abundantly scented flowering orange trees in earthenware pots. The drowsy silence was only broken, from somewhere close at hand, by the barking and rattling of chained-up guard dogs. Harriet hesitated. The low white ranch house seemed to have no front door, and the windows she could see were all shuttered. Then there was a movement in the thick of the glossy green leaves. A second later a man in an olive-green overall backed toward her, a watering-hose spraying a rainbowed arc from one hand.

"Excuse me, which way is the front door, please?"

The gardener turned and stared blankly at her. Harriet repeated her question and he beamed, showing pink and gray gums, but still offered no response. She concluded that he was either stone deaf, or spoke not a word of English. A burst of loud music and some shouts and laughter came from somewhere very near. Out of the corner of her eye Harriet saw that the limousine was sliding away, leaving her two suitcases standing on the gravel.

The beaming gardener pointed away around the side of the house, toward the music and laughter. "Sí, sí," he encouraged her.

Harriet walked slowly. She was hot in her London clothes. The leaves had swallowed up all sound again; she could barely hear the sound of her own footsteps. Hanging tendrils and stridently scented blooms brushed her face. She walked all the way around one long wing of the big house.

She turned two corners and emerged suddenly on the pool terrace.

The terrace faced southwest, over the vista, and it held the evening light. In the diamond-shaped pool the choppy water reflected strings of lights that laced the trees. There were swimmers in the water and a very fat man who floated like a pink inflatable. Around the pool were women sitting and standing and lying, all wearing tiny bathing suits, and high-heeled sandals. The girl nearest to Harriet wore a black costume with huge bites taken out of it, the remaining shreds of black latex spangled with rhinestones.

A butler moved between the nearly naked bodies, offering vermilion drinks crammed with bits of fruit. Fully dressed, in his white jacket and bow tie, he appeared to be wearing fancy-dress.

Caspar was standing on the edge of the pool. He was holding a full glass. With his head on one side, he seemed to be listening either to the voices of the girls, or to the music that had started up again. For a confused instant Harriet couldn't determine if it was incongruous or quite predictable that the tune should be the *Tea for Two* tango. Caspar straightened his head and saw her.

He didn't walk very steadily, but a moment later he reached her side. He put his arms around her, as she had known he would. It seemed to Harriet that no one else paid even the slightest attention.

"Baby. I'm so glad you're here. I wasn't expecting you yet."

He was pleased to see her. He was Caspar as he always was, magnified beyond common proportions, and she instantly became just Harriet, not "Meizu Girl" or even "Success Story." She was tired but he woke her up, making her warily alert, ready to be taken by surprise. She had missed him and she was happy to see him. She kissed him on the mouth, tasting whiskey.

"I'm glad to be here." The music trilled on her ears. *Tea for two, and two for tea. Me for you, and you for me.*

"Caspar," she whispered. "What's going on? Who are all these people?"

He answered, out of the side of his mouth in his own mogul-speak, "Ya gotta do it, babe. This is Hollywood."

The complicity drew her to him. Harriet let her head drop

on his shoulder, the moment of bewilderment forgotten. She found to her surprise that she was laughing.

"Welcome to L.A. Would you care to tango?"

Me for you, and you for me . . .

He was a good dancer. His hand splayed at the small of her back, holding her against him. His other hand linked with hers and their cheeks touched. Harriet was stiff at first, but gradually she relaxed into the rhythm of the absurd dance. She found herself smiling, her eyes closed as she listened to Caspar humming. He felt solid and warm, and she liked the way that he held her.

The music changed to a waltz. *The Blue Danube*, even. Harriet drifted, dreamily submissive. Caspar murmured affectionately, his breath warming her ear. It was a good welcome, she thought. A good prelude.

They danced until Harriet remembered that she had been on an airplane for twelve hours, that her body was telling her it was seven in the morning after a sleepless night and a busy day. She stood still and let her hands drop to her sides. Caspar studied her with concern.

"You're tired. You want to shower, and sleep. Am I right?"

Harriet nodded her gratitude.

"Of course you do. But, Harriet, this is Hollywood. This is Academy Awards week. Before you sleep, you party. Come and meet the boys and girls."

And so Harriet followed him obediently, shaking hands as she was introduced, trying to memorize the differences between the identical wide, perfect smiles that greeted her. The fat man was an agent, and the good-looking girls with their dauntingly worked-out bodies were actresses and editors and assistants. There were dark-haired men, too, who Harriet had not noticed at first. The men were writers and lawyers and accountants.

"I'm a businesswoman," Harriet answered the questions. "An entrepreneur. No, nothing to do with movies." The people were friendly, but she knew that they recognized at once that she was an outsider. It was odd to feel dismissed, however cordially, when she had grown used to recognition.

Vernon the butler was British.

"Good evening, madam," he said, as if they were all in Belgravia. "Would you care for a tequila sunrise?" The difference was that he winked at her when she took her glass off his tray.

Harriet drank her drink. She sat down and talked to a girl in a pink bathing suit who admired her Jasper Conran jacket. "But aren't you kinda hot?" the girl asked kindly.

"Stifled," Harriet said. "My luggage is still sitting outside the front door, I should think."

The friendly girl pointed to the pool house. "There are all kinds of things hanging up in there. Goes with the house, I guess."

Caspar was moving around between his guests. His voice was clearly audible, sonorously counterpointing the rest. Harriet watched him for a moment and then took the girl's advice. She took off her clothes in the pool house and emerged, self-consciously white-limbed among the tanned bodies, in a scrap of iridescent latex.

Harriet sat down at the edge of the pool, dangling her legs in the velvety water. It was almost dark, and tiny lights in the trees shone like glowworms. Los Angeles spread in front of her, a grid of lights that stretched all the way to the ocean. London seemed much further than half a world away.

Caspar was dancing with someone else. He smiled at Harriet over her shoulder. Harriet understood that this was another of Caspar's worlds. When the party was over, whenever that might be, it would be their own time. She felt perfectly at home now. The tequila, two or three tequilas even, had gone to her head.

She stood up and stretched out her arms.

"I'm going to swim," she announced, to no one in particular.

She arched her back and dived. She sliced through the water until her fingers met the bottom of the pool. Then she turned, slid upward, and bubbles like champagne fizzed around her head. When she broke out into the scented darkness again she rolled onto her back and floated. Her hair fanned out like weeds. She was unassailable within the skin of water. Her impressions of the day and night unrolled behind her closed eyelids like hallucinations.

Sixteen

AFTERWARD, WHEN EVERYTHING THAT WAS going to happen was over and she had time to recollect—there would be no shortage of time—Harriet still liked to remember the first days of her visit to Hollywood.

The place always came back to her as an assault on all her senses. If she had thought about it en route, in her armchair five miles above Greenland, she might have predicted the scents of lilies and orange blossom, and the ripple of water on her sun-burned skin. Her imagination might even have begun to grope toward the food, elaborate achievements of perfect simplicity set in front of her at Spago, or the Ivy or the Bistro Gardens, or in the pale, muted, absolute luxury of the dining room at the Bel Air Hotel. But she would never have dreamed of the silence, broken only by birdsong, that enveloped Caspar's borrowed ranch house off Loma Vista Drive and which struck her, in the middle of this vast city, as far more luxurious than any of the effects achieved by the interior decorators of Hollywood. And then, when the silence was broken, she remembered the talk. Holly-wood talk seemed to be conducted at a faster pace and with a different level of artistry from what she was used to in London. It was not that the subjects of conversation were profound or widely varied; rather that talk was conducted according to differ-ent rules. There was no reminiscence here, nor even any refer-ence to defining principles like art, or history, or human experience. All was concerned with the future, and even the present was of interest only in as far as it affected what was about to happen.

The collective enthusiasm, flowing as dangerously as lava, released Harriet's juices in response. She felt excited, charged by the proximity of so much wealth and power and energy. She loved the way that the answer to every question, any question, seemed to be *yes*. She had never been anywhere else where so much seemed possible, and then she smiled at her own misuse of the idea. Not possible. Not even probable, but sure-fire. After business in London, after cautious appraisal and sage headshaking, to discover Hollywood was to seem to discover liberation.

Harriet gave up trying to promote "Meizu" and Peacocks. They were not movies. At one party, seduced by food and music and novelty, Harriet told Simon's story to a young man as they sat together beside the sapphire oval of an illuminated pool.

"It's a great story," the young man said. "Are you working something up? Who have you been talking to?"

Harriet let her head fall back against the cushions of her seat. Above her the fronds of bamboos made a net against the navy-blue sky.

"It's not a story," she answered. "It's the truth."

"That doesn't matter," he told her, intending encouragement.

Harriet learned quickly, as she always did. By watching and listening, she began to understand some of the nuances that governed this startling society. The creative talk, for all its artistry, cost nothing.

As Caspar's companion, Harriet was both highly visible and effectively transparent. She was looked at a great deal but hardly noticed, and she accepted her temporary role in this perpetual pageant with good humor. She only wished, in the few reflective moments there was time for, that Caspar himself might see her more clearly. He escorted her to the parties and took her to bed afterward, but she was never quite certain what position she occupied in his field of vision. He was drinking heavily, but he was doing everything else with comparable enthusiasm. He talked unstoppably, told stories and generated festivity wherever he went. He was wonderful company in that week, for Harriet and for everyone else who came into his orbit. Watching him at the parties, resisting her need to jump up and stand close to him to block out his sight of everything else, Harriet told herself that she must allow him this time.

Afterward, after the Awards ceremony, she might claim him for herself.

For now, she would have to be happy with seeing him at the expansive peak of his enjoyment. It made her proud, as she grew more familiar with the inverted laws, to recognize the height of his wave.

They did not spend much time alone together. On the few occasions when they were at the ranch house without any of Caspar's retinue, he seemed to prefer to spend his time reading or sleeping by the diamond pool. He read a great deal, consuming novels and history with the same appetite he applied to everything else. Harriet did not stand in front of him and demand, "Look at *me*," although sometimes she wanted to. Nor did she ask him why he had wanted her to be with him at the Awards, although it came into her mind more than once. Instead she left him to relax with his books, took the spongy white sedan that belonged to the house, and went to explore Los Angeles.

She had been least prepared for the beauty of it. The loveliness was obvious in Bel Air and Beverly Hills, and in the smaller avenues of West Hollywood where the miniature castles and mansions were matched in exoticism by the strange vegetation that sprang and twisted everywhere. But Harriet also found that she was drawn to the urban wastelands where acres of low shacks stretched behind gas stations and fast food hoardings, and where the sun leached colors from the lurid advertisements and left a smoky, monotone landscape. Harriet cruised through it, in the air-conditioned cell of the white car, watching the city as it unfolded. Currents of excitement coursed in her blood.

She drove to Anaheim, then out through the minuscule kingdoms of the San Fernando Valley, and westwards to the ocean at Santa Monica. She was amazed to discover that a little further on, behind the beach house at Malibu, a road wound upward into the canyons and within half an hour it led her to a deserted hilltop in a landscape of scrub-covered semi-desert. The isolation was more marked because she could turn to one side and see the immense encrustation of the city around the curve of the ocean, and every thirty seconds the glint of light that was a jet turning upward from Los Angeles International in the center.

The freeways yielded everything to her. An hour after leaving her hilltop she was idling along Rodeo Drive, peering at the jewels and the little beige silk suits in the windows of the designer stores. The contrasts were so sharp that sometimes they left her winded, but still, however oddly, she felt at home in this place. Its energy seemed to match her own. Humming with it, she went back to Caspar who laughed and stroked her hair, and took her inside to make love behind the shutters before it was time to set out for the next party.

On her third day in town, Harriet took Linda to the beach. She had wanted to see her on the second day, as soon as she had slept off some of the jet lag and her tequila hangover, but any arrangement seemed to require a surprising amount of negotiation with Clare Mellen's secretary. In the end, it was settled that Harriet should collect Linda from her mother's house at two-thirty in the afternoon and deliver her back again at six prompt.

When the time came, Harriet drove up to the inevitable high, blank gates in the green depths of Bel Air, and announced herself into the grille of an intercom speaker. It made her think of Little Shelley again. After a long time, the gates swung open. Harriet parked the dull sedan beside a Mercedes limousine and a smaller, matching convertible. The secretary came out of the house, more to check her out than to greet her, Harriet thought. She looked less approachable even than Ronny Page.

Harriet waited obediently in the hallway. The house seemed to be furnished mostly in white and beige marble, set off by the most extravagantly frilled and ruched soft furnishing Harriet had ever seen. In comparison Annunziata Landwith's house was as stark as a bus station waiting-room.

A moment later, Clare Mellen and Linda appeared at the top of a shell-shaped curve of beige marble stairs. She was older than Harriet by two or three years, but Clare's face and figure were still perfect. She was wearing a dark pink dress that was tight over her hips and stopped above her knees, to show dancer's legs. Her fingernails and toenails were varnished to exactly the same shade of pink. One step behind her, Linda had reverted to the scowling child that Harriet had first seen in Annunziata's drawing room. She was wearing a dress in the same pink fabric as her mother's, but it was full-skirted, and ribboned. Her nails were unpainted, of course, but Clare had managed to find flat leather pumps in exactly the right pink, too. Or more likely had had them specially made, Harriet reflected. Poor Linda looked as if she were on her way to the stiffest kind of children's party, or perhaps to act as bridesmaid at a not-too-elaborate wedding.

Harriet felt disheveled and oversized under the full beam of Clare's examination. For her own part, she could well understand Caspar's long infatuation with Clare. She was very beautiful and she lacked only a hint of animation.

Harriet held out her hand, and Clare touched it with the tips of her fingers.

"This is very kind of you," Clare murmured, according to formula. The secretary had already made it clear that in fact Clare was doing the kindness in bestowing Linda for the afternoon. "Say a proper hello, Linda, won't you?"

Linda murmured something. She looked miserable, but stood close to Clare. For the first time Harriet noticed that her face was a smaller, plainer version of her mother's, made heavier by Caspar's more emphatic features. She felt sorry for her obvious confusion and began to wish that she hadn't come. Clare was her mother, even if they didn't immediately present the happiest mother-and-daughter picture.

If she were mine, Harriet wondered, *would we be like Jane and Imogen?*

"Linda so much wanted to see you," Clare added.

"We're good friends, I think, aren't we?" Harriet spoke directly to Linda. She disliked the way the talk was conducted over the child's head. But Linda only nodded, and the three of them began to walk across the acre of marble toward the door. It seemed inconceivable that anyone should mention Caspar, but Clare said brightly, "Linda is such a creature of enthusiasms. She's like her father, in that."

Harriet admired the neatness of the put-down, reducing her own significance in both their lives to a passing fad.

"It's a very lovable quality." She smiled back.

At the door Clare asked, "Where are you girls off to?"

Wisely, Harriet didn't mention the beach. There was no membership requirement for access to the sand and sea. Clare would no doubt consider it dirty and dangerous, as well as vulgar.

"Oh, just to drive around. Maybe do some shopping and have tea somewhere quiet."

The mild program was judged a suitable afternoon's entertainment for Linda. Clare nodded and held open the front door. She leaned forward to kiss Linda's cheek as she passed.

"Good-bye, darling. Have a lovely afternoon. *Six o'clock, then.*" The last words, delivered in a different tone, were Harriet's dismissal.

In the car, even after the gates closed behind them, Linda sat with her face turned away. She looked out of the window at the ramparts of greenery as if she had never seen them before. Harriet waited. At last Linda turned to her and said, "I really love her, you know."

Harriet was dismayed. She didn't want Linda to have to defend her mother to her. She was ashamed to have let her own estimation of Clare show so clearly.

She only answered, as if surprised, "Of course you do. You should."

After a moment Linda tugged at the skirt of her pink dress. "Dumb, isn't it? I told you what to expect. You get dressed up, rather than just *wearing* something."

The atmosphere lightened at once. Harriet laughed and headed the car toward Santa Monica.

Linda was delighted with the beach.

It was a warm, clear afternoon, but the immense sweep of pale sand was almost deserted. The lifeguard sat in his house on stilts, watching over the dozen black and Mexican families who had spread their clothes and towels around pyramids of drink cans. The breeze off the ocean and rhythm of the surf drowned all but the bass beat that pumped out of their big black transistors.

Linda ran down to the hard, shiny sand at the lip of the waves. Harriet walked a little further up the slope, holding her pink pumps and watching her skittering dashes in and out of the dying surf.

"Don't get salt on your skirt."

Linda's face was shining. "It's so neat down here."

"Don't tell me you've never been before?"

"I've been enough to Malibu, I guess, where people have their beach houses. And I used to go with Caspar to Venice beach, on Sundays, because he liked to look at the freaks and the jugglers and stuff. I don't think I've ever been here, by the pier."

"And I've only been in L.A. three days, and I've done it already."

"D'you like it here?" Linda seemed almost shy in her eagerness.

"In L.A.? I *love* it."

Linda beamed. "I told you, didn't I? But do you know something weird? When I'm here, in a funny way I quite miss England. England's greeny-gray, and sort of soft, you know? Everything's hard and really bright, here. Do you know what I mean? Or am I crazy?"

"I know just exactly what you mean."

Harriet turned her back to the sea and looked along the beach. The pier poked absurdly out into the sea, like any pier anywhere. If she half-closed her eyes she could imagine herself in Hastings. Or in Brighton. Brighton made her think of Caspar, who was sleeping off his lunch under the shade of a parasol, with *Memoirs of an Infantry Officer* face-down on the warm stone beside him. Harriet opened her eyes wide. The palm trees along the Palisades were nothing to do with Brighton or Hastings, and neither were the supine black families. Like Linda, she felt a whisper of homesickness for the little, crowded, sand-and-shingle beaches and the green mounded landscapes of home. The thought made her smile.

"Shall we go for a swim?"

"In the *sea*?"

"Of course."

"I haven't got my things."

"I've brought towels. You could swim in your pants, couldn't you?"

Linda needed no more encouragement. She stripped off her dress in a makeshift tent of towels that made Harriet think of English seasides again, and Kath providing the same protection for Liza and herself.

With her arms wrapped around her thin chest in unnecessary modesty, Linda sprinted down the slope of sand. Harriet wriggled out of her own clothes and ran, too. The water was icy cold, and they gasped and splashed and shouted encouragement at each other. After five minutes they ran back up the beach and rubbed the circulation back into one another's limbs with the warm towels.

"I'm so c-cold," Linda spluttered.

"Don't complain. In England, this would be an official heatwave."

The idea made them both laugh. "I'm hungry. Can we go on the pier and buy something to eat?"

"Why not? That would be fun."

Linda stared over her blanket of towels. "Can we really?"

"I said, why not?"

"You're really amazing, you know, Harriet," Linda told her. "I can't think of anyone who'd enjoy going on the pier. Who wouldn't do it, sort of, out of suffering, to keep me happy."

"Not Caspar?"

"I don't really belong to Caspar out here. I belong to him when I'm in England. It's what the lawyers worked out."

Harriet took her hand. She wanted to put her arms around Linda and hold her, as if she could compensate for anything, but she would only let herself link their fingers and swing them, with the highest spirits she could muster.

"Well, I want to go on the pier, and I want you to come and keep me company."

The pier, as Harriet had already observed, was exactly like piers anywhere. They ate a hamburger apiece and watched the sea fishermen hunched over their lines at the far end, and then they were drawn by the tinny music into an amusement arcade packed with sweaty, barrel-chested men and furtive adolescents. Linda ran between the slot machines, almost capering with delight.

"Quick, Harriet," she commanded. "Give me some quarters."

Harriet's role was as the provider of dollars while Linda played the machines, until they discovered the worm game. In the worm game, flat reptilian heads popped in and out of holes in unpredictable sequence. Armed with a heavy wooden mallet, the player's job was to smash each head back into its hole before the next appeared.

Linda swung wildly, but Harriet never missed a head. She flattened each contender as soon as it winked over the rim of its hole, and when her score reached one thousand a bell rang. Players at adjacent machines turned to stare. Flashing lights announced Harriet as the top scorer of the day.

"Zowee! Look, you get a free game!" Linda chanted.

Harriet dropped her mallet. She was laughing and gasping for breath.

"That's not much different from being an entrepreneur. Just keeping one deadly step ahead of the opposition. Come on, let's get out of here. I enjoyed that so much I'm worried about myself."

"Terror of the worms," Linda grinned.

Outside the light was white and hard. They idled arm in arm over the tarry decking.

"I wish the Ferris wheel was going." Linda sighed. In an enclosure to one side of the pier was a little funfair, but the rides were still shrouded in the winter's faded blue tarpaulin. Even so, from somewhere close at hand, they heard carousel music. Linda ran ahead.

"Look, Harriet!"

At the shore end of the pier, sheltered in its own glass-walled and mirrored wooden house, was a fairground carousel spinning with carved and gilded prancing horses. As they watched, it slowed and stopped. A handful of children slid reluctantly from painted saddles. The ride must have opened for the first afternoon of the summer season. Harriet stood to admire the horses' flaring nostrils and streaming golden tails, and the fine curved lines of the chariots they drew.

"I remember it," Linda said in delight. "At the beginning of that movie. Do you remember, *The Sting*? It was this very carousel, wasn't it?"

Harriet was still admiring the exuberant carving, and the colors of the mirrored reflections. "I don't think I saw that one."

Linda looked at her sidelong. "Do you go to the movies, Harriet?"

"Not all that often."

Now Linda shook her head. "You must think this place is really weird."

"I do, a bit." Linda was a native, and she was not. A faint, cold finger of premonition touched Harriet.

"Can we ride?"

"Try and stop us."

They chose their painted horses, and they turned in the stately circle. Reflected colors danced out of the mirrors, shadows in the wooden house and white light from beyond the glass doors making soothing patterns behind Harriet's half-closed eyes.

When it was their turn to slip out of the smooth saddles she had forgotten what she had been thinking.

"It's time I took you home. Your mother will be waiting."

"Mom doesn't wait. People wait for her."

Harriet delivered Linda back to the secretary at six o'clock exactly. There was no sign of Clare.

"How was she?" Caspar asked, when Harriet found him in his chair by the pool. There was a highball glass on the table beside him, and he peered up at her with one eye half-closed.

"Your daughter?"

"Of course."

"She was okay. She enjoyed Santa Monica pier."

Caspar chuckled. "That was a good idea."

Harriet knelt down to bring herself to his level. There were small beads of sweat in the mat of gray hair on his chest, and the creases at the corners of his eyes had deepened in the faintly waxy skin. His blue stare was alert, however. She felt a mixture of tenderness and exasperation. She stretched one finger to touch the sticky rim of the glass.

"Why do you drink so much?"

"I told you long ago."

Harriet thought for a moment. The Hollywood silence enveloped them. In the fading light, blue and white flowers grew iridescent. "What would you say if I told you I wanted you to stop?"

Caspar laughed, but he took her hand at the same time. Harriet's feeling of tenderness deepened. She wanted to lay her head on his chest, claiming him, but she held herself still.

"I would say that it's too late for that, Harriet. Even for your sake."

The fatalism disturbed her. With her own unfailing energy to fuel her, Harriet believed that it was never too late. But she fixed on the words, *even for your sake*, as if they held out a promise.

"*Even?* What does that mean? Why did you ask me to come out here?" She hadn't meant to pose the question, but it came anyway.

Caspar appraised her. She occupied the center of his field of vision now, as she had wished, but she was suddenly alarmed.

"Why?" He gave the word the full, declamatory weight. And then his voice softened. "I asked you because you are your own woman. You live a life, a life I don't understand, but I admire you for it. You don't want to feed on mine, you don't need to live through me."

As she listened, with her head bent, Harriet felt the distance between them, and not only between herself and Caspar but between herself and everyone she knew. She had grown up and away from Kath. Her marriage had ended in divorce. Her friends had shifted in their old, well-worn dispositions. Simon was dead. More sharply than she had ever done, she longed for the filial bond that had never existed, never been reacknowledged between them.

Harriet put the flat of her hand down to touch the paving stone at her side. She could feel how it held the day's heat. If she moved her fingers a few inches they would trail in the pool water. She could see, and smell, and hear, all the richness of the garden. She was a part of this landscape, for all her isolation.

Caspar said, "I asked you out here because you are the kind of woman who doesn't proselytize about my habits."

"So you were wrong." Harriet faced him. "But I don't ask you out of some stiff-necked sense of morality. I ask because I think you're a great actor, and because I see you pissing your talents away."

Caspar's voice was quiet now. "I think I am the best judge of that."

The hairs prickled at the nape of Harriet's neck.

But a moment later he said, "Come here." He drew her closer so that she sat against him, and her head did rest on his shoulder. "Listen. I'll strike a bargain with you. If I walk up there tomorrow for that little statue, I'll try to knock off the sauce. Will that do?"

The Oscar. In all his long career, Caspar had been nominated only once before.

"Does it matter so much?" Harriet whispered.

"Oh, yes. Yes, honey, it matters."

"You'll win it," Harriet told him. "No contest."

He lifted her chin and kissed her. As she held him, feeling the knots of his muscles that were beginning to turn flaccid, Harriet thought that the smitten intensity of new love was metamorphosing into familiarity. Infatuation would become a different, better love.

"It's a bargain," she said.

Inside the ranch house Vernon was moving to and fro, turning on lamps.

"Let's go and eat, before we go to Marv's," Caspar said. "Let's see and be seen. Let's demand the best table in the room. Tonight, I am as good as king."

"Tomorrow, emperor."

They left the soft twilight and went into the house, their arms around each other.

Robin drove home across Blackheath. It was not a part of London he was familiar with, and he was obliged to concentrate on finding the best route home.

But he was pleased enough with himself to whistle softly as he drove, repeating the same phrase over and over, a little triumphant fanfare.

Kath and Ken Trott had reacted exactly as he had expected they would. Sitting in their front room among the nested tables and well-dusted porcelain knickknacks, he had begun with such circumspection that they had not, at first, understood what he was saying.

"Peacocks in trouble?" Kath had put her hand to her throat, twisting her strings of beads into a knot.

Robin was quick to reassure. "Of course not. It's a matter of steering, that's all. So many companies, you know, under a dynamic entrepreneur like Harriet, can suffer a small setback at just this stage. As we're a small company still, almost like a family, I thought it best to come and talk to you informally, like this." And Robin gestured at the suburban lounge and the coffee tray on the low table at their knees.

"You are important shareholders, you know. And, of course, you are Harriet's family. You have a double concern."

"Just what are you getting at, lad?" Ken's arms were folded, indicating hostility.

Because Kath was a director of Peacocks, Robin had encountered her at board meetings. He had summed her up long ago as decent, but stupid. He was less sure about Ken, but he was sure that if he could win Kath, Ken would come with her.

Robin sighed, with a well-gauged combination of regret and anxiety. He opened his briefcase and took out the dossier. He began to talk in a low, sympathetic murmur, addressing most of his explanation to Ken, businessman to businessman, but directing long looks from under his eyelids at Kath, looks that were almost loverlike. Kath's lips parted a little as she listened to him.

Robin's performance with the dossier was well enough rehearsed by this time, but he spoke haltingly now, as if made
inarticulate by his own concern.

"How we can best deal with this unhappy situation . . .
spending out of control . . . not the wisest investment . . .
Jeremy Crichton and I . . . Harriet's best interest at heart . . . a
safeguard before anything further . . . and, of course, to protect
your own investment . . ."

The room had been quiet, as if the listeners were mesmer-
ized by the low voice, but now Kath's head jerked up. A blush
spread up over her throat and up into her cheeks.

"I don't care about the money, if that's what you're getting
at. I haven't wanted anything of it, after Simon died. It's tainted
money, isn't it?"

Ken's arm descended on her shoulders. He leaned forward,
restraining her.

Robin almost smiled. Families were the most difficult to deal
with, but they were also the most satisfying because of the little
doors that sprang open only after the lightest pressure on exactly
the right spot. The door yielded to him now.

"I understand that you should feel that way. It was a great
tragedy. A needless tragedy, even." He was as gentle as if he
was reassuring a baby. There was no hint of a pounce, but still
he pounced.

"Don't make yourself upset, Kath," Ken said.

Robin nodded his sympathy, watching another door silently
open. Ken would follow, because to do otherwise would upset
his wife.

Robin knew then that he would get what he wanted. He
stayed for a long time in Sunderland Avenue, accepting another
cup of coffee that he did not want and later a glass of sherry
that he never drank, but he knew from the moment that the two
little doors swung silently open that he would win, and win
triumphantly.

By the time he left the three of them were friends, united in
their friendship by their concern for Harriet. That was Robin's
trump card.That their conspiracy would, in the end, be best for
Harriet.

Out of the cold March wind in the shelter of her storm
porch, Kath watched Robin drive away.

"I don't want her to go and end up with nothing," she
justified herself. "And I'll be glad to be free of it myself, Ken."

"It's like he said, isn't it? There are the entrepreneurs, ideas
people, and there are those who know how to keep an estab-

lished business on the rails. Two different skills, isn't it? I know, I've seen it. It doesn't surprise me, what he says." Ken was knowledgeable, as he always was. "He'll do all right by her, Kath. He was in love with her himself, wasn't he, only she wouldn't have him?" He chuckled in amused appreciation of Harriet's choosiness.

Kath was back where they had begun, with her hands anxiously twisting the beads at her throat. "I wish she'd settle down. Perhaps this will give her a chance. What do you think?"

"It might," Ken answered, without much conviction. He suspected that he understood Harriet better than her mother did.

After Kath and Ken, Liza in Blackheath was easy for Robin.

"Harriet's made a few boo-boos, has she?" Liza sniffed. "Well, you can't always be perfection itself."

The door opened to Robin at once, at the very first tentative pressure. Jealousy, he reflected, was so often the key. He saw that Liza was a watered-down version of her sister, a sharp little person without the clarity of Harriet's intelligence or the unfailing sense of style that had first drawn him to her. He thought of her as he had first seen her, in his father's office, and the recognition that he would have to live without her strengthened his purpose. He bestowed on Liza a smile of particular charm.

"There are some anxieties. I wanted to come and talk to you informally, like this . . ."

Liza needed no particular persuasion. She shrugged off Robin's assurances.

"It was my mum's money. Harriet just put five percent in my name, but mum made the investment. I do what she does, of course."

Only the little triumphant smile told Robin that she was quite glad to do it, too. The thickset photographer, who was—unthinkably—Harriet's ex-husband, was less acquiescent. Robin remembered Harriet telling him that Leo had taken up with her younger sister. Confronting him, Robin saw that he was opting for the less challenging version, a kind of diluted Harriet without the bite, or the sparkle. The man himself was second-rate. Robin could hardly suppress a sneer.

"Why is this all being done behind Harriet's back?" Leo asked.

Robin spread his hands. "By its very nature, an operation like this must be swift, and decisive. And Harriet's absence, you know, at a time like this, is an indication itself." His finger rested on the dossier, the print of it as light as air, but the weight of implication behind it heavier than Leo had the ammunition to deal with.

"It's nothing to do with you, Leo," Liza said, in her half-Harriet voice.

This visit was not a long one. Robin did not enjoy the confines of the flat with the echo of Harriet and the man who had married her to remind him of what he no longer possessed.

He kissed Liza lightly on the cheek as he left. She yielded to it readily enough. Leo's expression of poisonous dislike followed him, cheering him when he remembered it. Robin whistled as he drove homeward across Blackheath, his triumphant fanfare, repeated over and over. There was no need to make anxious reckoning. He had his fifty-one percent, and some to spare.

The seeds he had sown had ripened into a field of waving golden corn. The time had come to cut it, and take it to market.

Robin did count then, but it was not shares but hours, the number of hours that separated London from Los Angeles.

Harriet was adrift on the diamond pool.

It was mid-afternoon, when the day's potent heat was concentrated between the white wings of the ranch house. The pool water was slick with heat, and the haze-softened disk of the sun reflected off the ripples as dashes of light that chased over the white walls.

The inflatable armchair drifted in a slow arc to the side of the pool and Harriet touched one toe to the steps. She sent herself at a tangent, keeping her foot raised as she sailed on so that she could admire her own suntanned instep, and the scarlet moons of pedicured toenails. The ice in her glass clinked as she drank and then she let her head sink back, closing her eyes, so that the sun imprinted copper disks within her eyelids.

She was ready for the Awards ceremony. Her Bruce Oldfield dress, pressed to perfection by the Spanish maid, hung in the wardrobe. The manicurist and the hairdresser had done their work, and Harriet held her head so that not a drop of pool water would disturb a single hair. She had even, smiling a little at the performance of wifely duties, overseen the pressing of Caspar's evening clothes. She approved of the stately, British cut, and the unfrilled reticence of his dress shirt.

Caspar sat in his usual place in the shade. She had counted his drinks. She would get him to his seat primed as far as necessary, but fully capable of the speech, the necessary ponderous banter. He would do himself justice.

It was almost time. The dictates of television, the broadcast of a live show across the nation's time zones, meant that they must take their places almost before the end of the afternoon. Harriet roused herself. She would ask Vernon to bring her one more glass of iced tea, and then she would steer Caspar inside to dress.

Harriet sighed with satisfaction. It was as if Vernon had read her thoughts. He was already on his way around the side of the pool, toward her. She saw that he was holding an envelope.

"This just came for you."

Harriet stretched out a lazy hand, the nails also perfect scarlet.

When she took it from Vernon she saw that it was not an envelope but a fax, neatly folded in two. She shook out the thin sheet of paper and read.

The words made no sense, and she read again.

It was a letter, headed with Peacocks' feather logo and signed by Jeremy Crichton as company secretary.

The language was formal, with a deadpan nastiness that made Harriet blink in bewilderment as she floated in the scent of orange blossom. It was so unexpected, so mystifying, that it seemed to be a foreign tongue.

Harriet read for the third time, trying to decipher this message that had sucked the air out of her lungs.

> In accordance with Article 14b of the Company's Articles of Association you are hereby given three days notice to run from the date of this letter of a meeting of the Board of Directors to be held at 11 a.m. on March 31 at the Company's registered office.
>
> In the event of your failure to attend, the meeting will proceed to business in your absence.
> An agenda is set out below.
> 1. Minutes of previous meeting
> 2. Matters arising
> 3. Board appointments
> 4. Any other business
> Confirmation of this letter follows by hard-copy telex, as required by the Company's Articles.

The ugly phrases jumped in Harriet's sun-dazed head. Proceed to business. Board appointments. Article 14b. What was Article 14b? There was no business without her. There could be no *appointments to the board*, how could there be, without her own nomination?

For a second she was convinced that this was a joke. It was part of some elaborate leg-pull that she didn't understand because she was so far from London and absorbed in the sunny vigor of California. She closed her eyes and let her hand fall, holding the sheet of paper. One corner of it trailed in the blue water. Only it was the water, the white light and the heat that seemed foreign now.

Harriet jerked the letter up again. This wasn't a joke. No joke would knot a band of anger and fear around her chest such as she felt now.

The armchair was becalmed in the dead center of the pool. Harriet struck out, wallowing where earlier she had elegantly drifted. She could think of nothing but reaching a telephone. Caspar rejected the Hollywood cliché of calling from his poolside. She would have to go into the house. The water seemed to have turned to molasses.

She reached the steps and floundered out of her armchair. Caspar opened his eyes as she ran by. He caught a glimpse of her face and called after her,

"What's happened?"

"I need to call London."

She was standing gripping the receiver before she asked herself, *Call who?* Where?

Vernon was crossing the room behind her, stately in his butler's white coat.

"Vernon, what time is it in London?"

"Approximately three o'clock in the morning."

Who was it, faxing her letters in the low hour of the night, and from where? Harriet dialed the Peacocks number. It rang twice, and then she heard Karen's bright message on the answering machine. ". . . Peacocks' office is closed until 9 a.m. Please leave your name and number . . ."

She tried Robin, imagining the white telephone ringing on the bedside table, the bed where she had slept, mahogany-masculine . . . The interval was a little longer, but his invitation to leave her name and number, when it came, was no more informative than Peacocks'. So where was he? Was it Robin, staging this offensive against her? Even though her thoughts skidded in bewilderment, she was beginning to be sure that it was. Robin, with Jeremy whose signature was on the letter she still clutched, and who else?

Who to call? Graham Chandler? She would have to look up

his number, in her book, on the table beside Caspar's bed. Or Charlie? In the middle of the night, while the children slept?

What was she doing here, so far away? Charlie had called her, even as she was leaving for the airport. I'm not going up the Amazon, she had told him. What was it that Charlie knew, and she didn't. I'm not going up the Amazon, I can be back in twelve hours, that's what she had said. Why had she not had the patience to listen to him?

She wouldn't call anyone. She would be on the next flight and then she would sweep in against them, her own counter-shock. The next flight, taking her home.

Harriet began to dial the airport before she remembered why she was in Hollywood. In two hours, she would be leaving for the Awards on Caspar's arm. She replaced the receiver stiff-armed and smoothed the crumpled fax so that she could examine it more carefully. Of course. It had been timed to reach her now. That explained the hour in London. It had always been intended to reach her as she prepared to set out, in her Bruce Oldfield dress on the arm of her film-star, to see her lover receive his Oscar. This piece of paper was the flimsy envoy of a calculating saboteur. He was aiming at Caspar as well as herself, at their moment of public pride, and he could be no one but Robin Landwith.

Cold fury took hold of Harriet. It set in her stomach and her heart, and made iron hooks of her fingers. She screwed the letter into a ball and flung it away from her.

"Vernon?"

"Yes, madam."

Her brain would not function. She couldn't count or remember because the anger was so corrosive. "Was it three a.m. last night, or tonight?"

"London time is ahead of Los Angeles. So tonight, if you choose to see it in that way. I personally find it less confusing just to subtract . . ."

"Yes, thank you. Vernon, will you do something for me, please? Will you book me a seat on the first available flight to London in the morning? Any seat, the first possible flight."

"Yes, madam."

Three days' notice, the letter had said. Harriet thought she remembered now what was set out in Article 14b. It was something to the effect that meetings of directors could be summoned by letter or telex, and in the case of directors' absence abroad telex or facsimile would be deemed sufficient, giving a minimum of three days' notice.

So they were giving her three days because they were obliged to, but because of the time difference twelve hours of that were already spirited away from her. Perversely, it was the realization of that that decided Harriet. Whatever was against her, even time itself, she would still stay for the Awards and defy Robin's sadistic calculation. She would stay for the ceremony and the party afterward, and reach London twenty-four hours after that. By doing so she would deny Robin one small satisfaction.

She couldn't even begin to assess how else she might thwart him, not until she knew what he was planning. It must be something to do with the balance of power within Peacocks, altering it by making new appointments to the board, and not in her favor, she was certain. But beyond that, she could only guess until she was back in London.

Harriet looked at her watch. It was time to dress.

Caspar opened his eyes once more as her shadow fell across him. "Make your call?"

When he saw her face he sat up, fully awake. "Jesus, Harriet. You look like you've eaten a handful of nails. What's up?"

She clenched her fists.

"There'll be worse than nails to eat in the next day or so. Either for me, or for Robin Landwith. He's trying to fuck my company up, Caspar, while I'm away. He's pulling some shitty trick that I don't understand yet. But I will understand it. I'll turn it inside out, and Robin with it."

Harriet tasted fury and fear and determination on her tongue, a bitterly potent cocktail. Her legs and arms twitched with some atavistic impulse to fly or to give chase. A heavy medicine ball that Caspar was supposed to use for some complex and ignored fitness regime sat on the edge of the pool. Harriet vented a ridiculous fragment of her anger by kicking it away. The ball swung in a curve and dropped into the water, sending up a glittering plume of spray. Her foot hurt after the impact.

She knelt down by Caspar's seat, gripping the arm of it.

"It's *my* company, Caspar. I labored for it and suffered all the pains of it. If he interferes with it, I will kill him."

And then she thought of Robin in his glovelike suits, living his ordered, discriminating, privileged life out of her own efforts, and those like her, because he had money to bestow. His power seemed in that moment feudal, corrupt like the touch of some medieval king conferring sickness on the faithful, instead of health. *The king's touch*, Harriet thought. Taking instead of giving. She knew that she was being irrational. But she knew that she had generated the success, not Robin. She had done it, and Simon, who was dead.

She lifted her head and her eyes met Caspar's. Hatred for Robin overtook her anger, frightening her with its intensity.

"No, I won't," she said softly. "I won't kill him. I'll castrate him and stuff the pieces in his soapy mouth."

"Harriet," Caspar said wonderingly.

She smiled then, but without softness. "I've got to go back to London. First thing tomorrow morning."

"But you'll stay for tonight?"

Caspar's first thought was for his own concerns. She had known it would be, she had always accepted that. He had never claimed any interest in Peacocks.

"Of course I will. But I must go," she repeated, "first thing tomorrow."

Caspar levered himself out of his chair. "Come on then, baby. Let's show them what we've got."

When they stepped out of their limousine, in the line of limousines that choked Hollywood on the evening of the Awards, and Harriet lifted her eyes from the tongue of carpet that ran all the way to the theater entrance, all she could see was faces and camera lenses. The faces belonged to spectators, seemingly in their thousands, ranged on bleachers that rose in tiers on either side of the carpet walk. The noise they made was a muted roar, like the sea. The television crews and reporters and press photographers made a tighter, harder phalanx, much closer, pressing around the nominees as each one arrived. The lights dazzled Harriet, and the giant microphones seemed to crane forward into her face. Seeing it all, her first impulse was to duck back into the shelter of the car. Even in the days of "Meizu Girl," she had never dreamed of exposure to such scrutiny.

But she didn't duck. She stood up straight and shook out the tiers of ruffles at the back of her long red dress. She felt Caspar's arm at her elbow and she turned to him. The expressionless camera eyes held them and relayed them to more invisible spectators, millions of them, across the world. Harriet was thinking of Robin, switching on some news bulletin that would cover the Awards, waiting to see Caspar without her . . .

She gave Caspar a smile of perfect serenity, brighter than the lights that exploded around them.

"Good luck," she whispered.

They walked arm in arm to the theater entrance. A ragged, British-voiced cheer of support followed Caspar as he went.

Inside, for all the assembly of the hot and the bankable and the powerful, Harriet's attention wandered. The preliminaries were long and tedious. Her thoughts focused on London. As she smiled, with her head inclined just a fraction toward Caspar's in case some audience reaction-shot should catch them, and transmit them across the hours to wherever Robin might be watching, Harriet was planning. Her first step must be to find out exactly what he intended to do. Her second, to put a stop to it. Before the meeting, it must be done before they came to the boardroom table.

Harriet applauded an award to a Polish animator. Even though she was here tonight, she reckoned, she would be in London with some forty hours to spare before eleven a.m. on March 31. That should be long enough. It would have to be long enough.

At last, *Best Actor in a Supporting Role.* She heard the words as from a great distance, but then the tiers of seats and the stars and directors and technicians came sharply into focus again. She leaned forward one inch in her seat, at the same time felt the infinitesimal stiffening beside her that was the only sign Caspar gave. They turned their faces to watch the brief clip of Caspar as the old spymaster in *Open Secret.* Harriet saw every frame, suffused with a particular clarity, knowing it as well as if she had directed the picture herself, admiring every nuance of Caspar within it.

The Award for Best Actor in a Supporting Role. The heavy pause and the corny business with the envelope. The recitation of a name, and the burst of delighted applause. A name, not Caspar's.

Harriet looked at Caspar, stricken. At first sight, she thought he had suffered a stroke. One side of his face, from the eyelid to the corner of his mouth, drooped as if made of wax, melting. He stared straight ahead of him as Harriet touched his arm. She saw the falling corner of his mouth turn upward as he made himself smile. He was applauding.

"Clap," he commanded her.

Harriet beat her hands together until the palms stung.

It seemed incredible now, but she had never imagined what it would be like if he did not win. There was no escape. They were pinioned with their disappointment, among other disappointments.

It was a long time, but the end did come at last. Through a mist, Harriet watched Lord Olivier presenting the Best Picture award for *Out of Africa*. Then they were retracing their steps, among the condolences, out into the blue evening.

Caspar said, "I need a fucking drink."

"Caspar . . ." Harriet was going to say, *I'm sorry, you deserved to win it*, all the other pointless clichés of consolation, but he cut her short.

"A bargain's a bargain."

It was only then that she remembered their pact about his drinking.

"I know you need a drink," she answered, "I'll have one with you." Her London flight was scheduled to depart at 9:40 a.m. Check-in 8:15. Time to drink with Caspar, to pack her suitcases, perhaps even to sleep a little. Their car materialized out of the polished grid of cars.

"Right," Caspar said grimly. "Let's party."

They were going to the night's best party. Not the official bash, but the annual celebration hosted by a super-agent, one of the legendary powerful.

As soon as they arrived, into the throng of women who cooed and men with warm handshakes, Harriet knew that Caspar was heading for a bad drunk. Everything about him, even the way he held his body, as if it hurt him a little, reminded her of the New Year's party at the Landwiths'.

The party swallowed him up. The momentum of it never allowed his glass to empty.

Harriet prowled the outskirts. She was remembering Linda's words beside the carousel on Santa Monica pier and the finger of premonition. It was true that she did not belong here. She would have to hurry on home.

Once, from across the room, she smiled her assurance at Caspar. He was talking and laughing giving the impression that he was enjoying himself. She did not want him to feel the necessity of concern for her, not tonight. But she felt the way that the people, and the occasion, and the tide of drink held them apart. The irony of it, that she had planned for their intimacy after the Awards and—laughably as she saw it now—for Caspar's salvation from the bottle, touched her and made her heavy and sad. Something was ending, not with a bang but with the hollow echo of defeat.

At midnight, Harriet detached herself from her seventh conversation with the seventh stranger and went in search of Caspar. She found him at a table in an inner room. He was sweating and his face was marked with lines. Harriet didn't recognize any of his companions.

She said gently, "Caspar, can we go home soon?"

He looked up at her. His blue eyes were dimmer offscreen and they were glazed as they had been that first day. She was not sure if he knew who she was.

"Go?" Caspar said. "Like hell. It's still early."

"May I go, then?"

He spread his hands in puzzlement. "Why not?" Then he collected himself. As she had discovered at Little Shelley, he could exert charm even in advanced drunkenness. "Harriet. Dear anxious Harriet. Take the car. Tell the driver, just take the car."

"How will you get home?"

He grinned at her, his eyes sliding again. "Somehow. It's my town. Or I'll just stay here."

She was going to say, *But in the morning I have to go . . .*

She stopped herself. She bent quickly instead, put her hands to turn up his face and kissed him on each cheek. There were whitish deposits at the corners of his mouth and his breath was loaded with whiskey.

"Good night," she smiled at him.

The limousine swept Harriet back to the ranch house, along the twinkling avenues lined with palm trees under the warm velvet sky, on her last night in Hollywood. Vernon opened the door to her. The house was dark and very quiet. Harriet packed her belongings and laid the red dress on top. The silence was oppressive, no longer remotely luxurious.

She hesitated by the telephone, then picked it up and dialed the number of Charlie Thimbell's newspaper office. To her surprise he answered. She had half-imagined that he would be out, or at lunch.

"Harriet? You're back?"

"Not quite. Charlie, what did you mean when you called me before I left? A tip-off, you said. A tip-off from who, meaning what?"

"You asked which I'd put first, you or a good story."

"Put me first. Tell me what you heard."

"I had lunch with a P.R."

Harriet listened intently. One publicist had told Charlie Thimbell over a bibulous lunch that a fund manager at Associated Assurance had been invited to use his organization's shareholding in Peacocks in support of a management restructuring. The fund manager had refused, claiming that Harriet Peacock was heading up the company through a satisfactory growth curve.

"Who was doing the inviting, Charlie?"

"I didn't hear tell. Doesn't take much guesswork, though, does it?"

"Not much," Harriet considered. It was City gossip; a thousand similar tidbits circulated every day, and some of them were given enough credence to affect share prices. Peacocks' price was steady, she had not been over-confident to dismiss Charlie's warning before she left. Only today's summons made sense of speculation. Robin must indeed have been summoning support.

For what battle?

"Charlie, will you do me a favor? Ask around some more? Without frightening the horses?"

"Yeah. I'll make some calls. What's happened?"

"Nothing's happened. I'm just suspicious."

"When are you back?"

"Tomorrow morning."

"Did he win?"

"No."

"Damn. He deserved to."

"I'll call you tomorrow, Charlie. Thanks."

Charlie sat back in his chair. Something had happened, however Harriet chose to deny it. He took out the anonymous notebook in which he kept the telephone numbers that were not stored in his secretary's Rolodex. Before he dialed the first, he checked Peacocks' price. They were down a shade, at two-twenty. Charlie's nose continued to scent a good story, but he knew that whatever was afoot was far from good for Harriet. She was doing right to get herself back to London at top speed.

Harriet walked through the silent house, picking up a magazine and putting it down again, wandering out to breathe the night scents beside the pool and then turning her back on the seductive dark. Vernon had retired to his own cottage beyond the garden.

The time passed very slowly as Harriet waited and listened. But she never even heard the sound of a single car to lift her hopes. The silence seemed absolute.

At a few minutes after two a.m. she knew that she would have to go to bed and try to sleep a little before her flight. It appeared that Caspar was not going to come home, at least not to spend this last night with her. It was the last night, Harriet knew that.

She undressed, her head and hands heavy, and went to bed.

It seemed that she had been asleep only for a matter of minutes before the telephone woke her. She groped for it, the shreds of a dream still caught together by its ringing. Her first thought was that it must be London; Charlie, perhaps, or even Robin, to explain away a mistake.

And so it took even longer for Harriet to distinguish what the thick Angeleno voice at the other end of the line was trying to tell her. She blinked at the clock-face and saw that it was 5:15 a.m.

"I think you must have the wrong number." But even as she spoke Harriet realized that it was not the wrong number, it was the right number, and the emergency room of whatever hospital it was in Sherman Oaks was trying to tell her that Mr. Jensen had been brought in following an automobile accident on Mulholland Drive.

Drowsiness fell away, to be replaced by fear.

"I'm sorry, I didn't understand. Where is he? Is he hurt?"

Mulholland Drive, under the Santa Monica Mountains with wide views across the San Fernando Valley, Harriet had driven it in her city explorations; what was Caspar doing there?

The voice repeated the address of the hospital, Harriet managed to scribble it down.

"The police do this, miss. Only seeing it was Mr. Jensen . . ."

"Thank you, thank you. Please tell me, how bad is it?"

"He's hurt, but conscious."

"I'll come at once."

For a moment, Harriet had no idea what to do. She was alone in a dark house, clutching the address of a hospital she had no idea how to reach. On Caspar's side of the bed the covers still lay undisturbed. She hesitated for only a second. Then she pulled on the clothes she had laid out for flying home and ran out of the house. The space in the driveway where the white sedan was usually parked was empty. She remembered that Vernon garaged it when it was not in use, she had not the first idea where. Harriet ducked her head and ran, across the garden and through a wall of thick, snaky greenery to the butler's cottage. Her hammerings on the door produced no response, so she ran around the little house and rapped on the windows. At last a light flicked on behind the closed shutters. Harriet ran back to the front door and as soon as it opened she stumbled into the little hallway, almost too breathless to gasp out her message. The cottage was tiny. Over Vernon's shoulder she saw a few feet into his bedroom. A Chinese boy was sitting up in the bed, unwinkingly staring at her.

Harriet turned, putting her hand imploringly on Vernon's arm. "I'm sorry, I'm sorry. Caspar's had a car accident. He's in a hospital. I need the car, *hurry*, Vernon."

The butler reacted with impressive speed. A moment later Harriet found herself bundled into a dim garage behind the cottage. The car engine fired, and they swung out of the garage and down the driveway.

"Where is it?" Vernon asked as they shot through the gates. Harriet looked at the scrap of paper in her hand.

"Moor Park Hospital, Sherman Oaks."

"Not so very far."

"Do you know the way?"

"I'll find it."

Harriet almost wept with gratitude, imagining how it would have been if she had had to drive herself.

The night's silence was gone. There were cars and trucks on the road with the approach of daylight.

"What can he have been doing over on Mulholland Drive?" Harriet was talking more to herself than to Vernon, but he answered without looking at her, "Party night."

The hospital was a slab of concrete and glass set in a small, green park. They left the car and found their way through automatic doors to the accident and emergency room. "Mr. Jensen?" Harriet asked at a desk.

An orderly indicated that they were to wait. There was a row of green chairs set against a wall behind them. They sat down obediently and waited. The hands of the clock above the orderly's head reached 6:25 a.m. Harriet knew that she would not, could not reach the airport in time for her flight. Knots of anxiety for herself as well as for Caspar began to harden in her stomach. Anxiety made her voice brusque when she strode back to the desk and demanded to see Caspar, or a doctor, or someone who could give her some proper information.

"The police are with him right now," Harriet was told.

"The police?"

"Sure. There's been an accident."

New knots tightened within her. She felt foreign, incapacitated. At last a doctor came to find them. He wore a short blue coat, he looked young and tired, like any hospital intern. He looked doubtfully at her.

"Are you Mrs. Jensen?"

"No. I'm a friend. And this is a member of Mr. Jensen's staff. How is he?"

"He'll be okay. He was quite lucky." The doctor's expression did not seem to match the news he gave them.

"So can we see . . . ?"

"I'm afraid, I'm sorry to have to say, his passenger is dead. She was dead on arrival."

Harriet stared at him. "His *passenger*? That can't be right. He wasn't driving, he didn't even have a car. I drove here in his car less than an hour ago."

"The car was registered in Miss Getz's name, but Mr. Jensen was driving it. Did you know her?"

Harriet shook her head. "No, it can't be right. He couldn't have been driving."

But she was remembering the day they went to the Waterside, when they drove away and left the sneak photographer and the regatta gaiety of the Thames behind them. Can *you* drive? Caspar had asked, and she had answered, I couldn't. *Then you will have to let me*, Caspar had said. Had he said the same to Miss Getz, whoever she was, who had died in her car on Mulholland Drive?

"The police will give you the details," the doctor said. He was awkward; Harriet could see that he wanted to get away from her denials and go back to his work. She nodded, feeling a weight of weariness descend on her.

Caspar was in a room only a few yards from where they had been waiting. The police were still with him, preparing to leave having presumably taken whatever statement they required. They were a man and a woman, flat faced, who stared incuriously at Harriet and Vernon.

Harriet did not want to ask them anything. She stood back against the wall until they maneuvered past her to the door. When they had gone, and the door was closed, she went to the bed and looked down at Caspar. A black-edged gash and a fresh bruise distorted one side of his face. He must have vomited, for a crust of it stiffened the hair at his temple. Harriet closed her eyes and opened them again. She was thinking of Linda.

Behind her shoulder, Vernon said, "I'll be outside, Mr. Jensen."

Harriet could see that Caspar was still drunk. She sat down and touched his wrist with her fingers. He looked at her and moved his head on the pillow. The movement hurt him.

"How does it feel?" Harriet asked gently.

He attempted a shrug. "I bounced, more or less. Drunks do. The doctor said so. If I'd been sober, I'd probably be dead." His eyelids dropped, but then he forced them open again. Harriet could only guess at the sight behind them, that he would not contemplate. "The girl is dead. Did they tell you that?"

She nodded. "Yes."

"I was driving the car. So the police tell me. I don't remember that part. Only afterwards."

Harriet said nothing, because she couldn't think of anything. She was seeing Linda, riding the carousel on the pier, and somehow the image became fused with Miss Getz, once a little girl with ribbons in her hair, waving from her carved and gilded horse.

Caspar said, "I wish . . ." but he didn't finish. Harriet knew that wishing belonged with the infinite optimism of the bright world outside, not here with Caspar in the hospital. She sat with her head bent, uselessly holding on to his hand.

Caspar broke the silence, saying, "I didn't mean you to have to come over here in the middle of the night. I gave them my own number. It was the only one I could think of."

"Vernon brought me. I'd have come anyway, whether you wanted it or not."

"Will you go and see Linda?"

"Yes."

"You've got to go back to London, but if you could just see Linda first."

Harriet understood that she was being discharged. She was to feel no responsibility to Caspar, for all the months they had shared. He would not let her stand close enough to suffer with him, and in that moment she realized that he never had. Their relationship had been more truly Hollywood than she had properly seen. The peak of the wave was to be ridden in glory, and the trough was to be turned away from, in the pretense that it did not exist.

Caspar's lawyers and his agents and the rest would close their professional ranks around him. There was nothing for Harriet to do here, now. There was no window in the hospital room but Harriet knew that it was full daylight outside. The last night was long over.

Caspar's face was the color of stone, except for the livid bruise marks.

"Go and see Linda before you go home," he repeated. "Don't let her know I killed someone, will you?"

She would have to know, soon enough, Harriet thought.

"I'll tell her you're hurt, but not badly. She'll want to come and see you. What shall I say?"

Caspar lifted their joined hands, but the weight defeated him and they dropped again. It was to say, *When she looks at me, what will she see?*

"Is there anything else I can do, Caspar?"

"Just ask Vernon to come in."

Harriet stood up, then leaned over him to kiss the undamaged side of his face. She hesitated, needing to give more, but Caspar was looking away, trying to excuse her even this negligible duty. Harriet could only let her cheek rest against his forehead.

"If you need me," she whispered.

Caspar didn't answer.

Harriet straightened up again and went to the door. Caspar lay against the pillows. He was diminished, smaller than life. She remembered how, when she first saw him back in Little Shelley, he had seemed to dwarf Martin Landwith.

"If you need me," Harriet repeated, but now it was a formula.

She went out and nodded to Vernon, who was leaning against the opposite wall of the corridor. As she waited, she heard Caspar issuing instructions for the marshaling of lawyers and agents.

Harriet and Vernon retraced their steps down the corridor and across the waiting area. As they approached the glass doors that opened onto the early light, Harriet became aware of a couple walking to one side of them. They moved very slowly, and Harriet saw it was because the woman was crying, her mouth open in a square, and the man was supporting her. He was overweight, in a sports shirt that was too tight for him. The woman's tears fell unnoticed onto her pink blouse. There was no reason for her to assume it, but Harriet was sure that they were Mr. and Mrs. Getz.

Ahead of them the automatic doors hissed open, and Harriet and Vernon walked out into another bright day.

"Linda will be down in a moment," Clare's secretary told Harriet. Harriet sat among pleated cushions in the marble chill, and waited. Linda came slowly down the stairs. Her eyes were dark in her white face. Harriet went to hug her, but she submitted to the embrace without returning it.

"Let's go outside," Linda said.

It was late morning, because Harriet had had to undertake more negotiation with the secretary for permission to see Linda. The sun was hot on their heads and they walked across immaculate lawns, past the glassy pool and banks of flowers punctuated with dark columns of cypresses.

Someone, either her mother or the secretary, had already given Linda the news.

"Tell me how he looked," she ordered, in a small unin-flected voice.

Harriet told her, with as much optimism as she could command. Linda considered, looking away, with seeming concentration, toward the tennis court.

"He won't die, then?"

Harriet stopped walking, moved around to stand in front of her and took her hands. "No, I promise he won't die."

Linda looked at her at last, without blinking. "Was he drunk, in the car?"

Lies and half-truths counterasserted themselves in Harriet's mouth before she answered, "Yes, he was."

"Why weren't you with him?"

"I was going back to London this morning. I went home early. Perhaps I should have stayed with him."

"The other girl did," Linda said, in the same small voice.

Clare must have told her. It was better that she should know, Harriet thought, rather than pick up distortions of the truth.

"It was a car crash, Linda. A terrible accident. Probably we won't ever know exactly what happened."

"Probably," Linda agreed politely. They walked on, in the sunlight, through the lush garden.

"Are you going today after all?"

"I have to." Harriet was booked on the evening flight. She would reach London late, with only hours in hand before the meeting. She pushed the thought away from her for now. They were at the furthest point of the gardens when the Spanish housekeeper came out to tell Linda that her lunch was ready. She was a big woman who smiled at Linda, and called her honey in her Latin accent. Linda and Harriet walked back toward the house, and Harriet was reminded again of how they had played truant together from Annunziata's New Year's party.

Beside the open door Linda hesitated, pointing the toe of her sneaker at a pebble on the path.

"I thought at first it was you," she said. "In the car with Caspar."

Harriet put her arms around her, careless of whether Clare might be watching.

"It wasn't me. I'm here with you. I'm always here if you need me." The words she had offered to Caspar, but no formula now. They were the simple truth.

Linda nodded. Almost inaudibly she said, "I love you."

Harriet smiled, looking down at the top of Linda's head.

Incongruous but perfectly sharp happiness descended on her. "I love you, too."

"Harriet? Is it wrong to be glad that someone else died, because it meant you didn't?"

Harriet told her, "You have nothing to be afraid or ashamed of, Linda. Remember that, if you can. Don't take a load of guilt that doesn't belong to you. You'll get your share in the end." Harriet tried to make her voice light, but Linda would not be deflected.

"Does it belong to Caspar?"

Harriet held her for a moment longer, before she tried to answer, and then she let her go. She wanted to go on, hugging the breath out of her, but she stepped back and stood with her arms at her sides.

"I think the only person who can talk to you about that is Caspar himself."

She could see that there were tears in Linda's eyes, but she was staring hard to keep them back. From inside the house the housekeeper was calling.

"Go on," Harriet whispered. "Remember what I said, I'll see you in London."

"Remember what I said, too," Linda said fiercely. She turned and ran into the house.

At seven o'clock, Harriet's plane climbed up, heading directly into the fire of the Los Angeles sunset. Then, as if the spectacle was overdone, it banked in a slow turn and circled back over the curve of the bay. It straightened again and headed eastwards, into the thickening darkness, for London.

Seventeen

HARRIET REACHED HOME AT ten o'clock on the last evening. She left her two suitcases in the middle of the floor and went to the telephone.

"Charlie? What did you get?"

From his armchair Charlie pointed the remote controller at the television screen, suppressing the news. Jenny raised her eyebrows, letting her mending drop in her lap.

"Nothing."

"What? There must be something."

"Exactly. The silence itself is ominous. But I couldn't get a whisper. He's covered his tracks, wherever they lead. I spoke to the P.R. again, too. All she'd heard was the one story she told me. Listen, Harriet, perhaps it's all quite innocent."

Harriet leaned wearily against her marble mantelpiece. Her eyes and mouth were gritty with dehydration after the long flight and her head felt heavy and thick. She frowned, massaging the bridge of her nose as she spoke.

"I don't think so."

"What's your guess, then?"

She hesitated and then shrugged. "I don't know. He'll be wanting to change the board structure somehow, gaining control of it for himself, putting in some sort of figurehead M.D. in my place to stop me calling the shots, perhaps. Whether he can do it depends on how much shareholder support he can call on, of course."

He would need a big slice, to set against her own and the family's. She clung to that comfort.

"Has there been trouble, Harriet? What ammunition has he got?"

Harriet reviewed the dissonance at Winwood and the expensive malfunctioning of its machinery, the sales performance of "Alarm," the new lines in the production pipeline. The problems were out of focus, seen through the distorting lens of Los Angeles and diminished by her anxiety for Linda and her sadness for

Caspar. She wished her head would clear, but she was still sure that there was nothing wrong at Peacocks that she could not solve. She described some of it to Charlie, briefly, needing a friend and forgetting that he was a journalist.

"He can't shoot me down with that much. But he can try, if he wants to."

"That's the girl." Charlie felt a surge of admiration, but he possessed none of Harriet's apparent confidence.

"I'm going to bed now, Charlie. I didn't sleep on the plane, and I only got about two hours the night before."

She heard Charlie's loud, short laugh. "Go on then, party girl."

Harriet thought of Caspar's darkened face, and Mr. and Mrs. Getz. She was too weary to dispel Charlie's illusions.

"Good night," she said tonelessly and hung up.

Jenny had readdressed herself to the buttons on Harry's dungarees, but she glanced sideways at Charlie as she bit off her thread. "Did she have a good time?"

"Sounds like it." Charlie was gloomy as he settled back in his chair, pressed the button and resuscitated the news once more.

Harriet looked at the clock. It was late to be ringing Kath, who kept regular hours, but not impossibly so. Harriet herself had lost track of time. She knew that she was exhausted, but her body gave her no indication that it was day or night. She seemed to have entered a gray zone of perpetual anxious wakefulness.

Ken answered the call. It seemed to take a very long time for Kath to come to the telephone.

At length Harriet heard, "Is that you, Harriet?"

She smiled. "Who else?"

"You're back safely, then."

"Yes. Mum, we need to talk about tomorrow."

And then, at once, Harriet heard the silence. She talked into it, telling Kath that she would be needing her support, counting her holding in with Ken's and Liza's. Kath said nothing, and Harriet's voice sharpened.

"You'll be there?"

Kath answered, "Yes, I have to be there, don't I?"

Harriet listened, trying to marshal her thoughts, wondering if tiredness was playing tricks on her. It was impossible that any of this was to do with Kath. She realized that her heart was thumping unpleasantly, but she made her voice as calm and easy as she could. "Have you seen Robin?"

"He paid us a visit, just for a chat, he said."

"What did he *say*?"

"Oh, Harriet. You know I don't understand any of it, really."

Her vagueness kindled irritation like a flame in Harriet. She snapped, "*Why* don't you? Don't you have any idea how important it is?" She knew as soon as she had said it that it was the wrong time, she was too fatigued after all that had happened, to be having this conversation.

"Don't talk like that," Kath's voice came back thinly. "You do it too much. You have, ever since you started this business. No wonder you're there on your own, you'll end up alone, is that what you want?"

"I want," Harriet answered, carefully spacing the words, "to know what has been happening while I have been away, in connection with my company. Is that too much to ask?"

"I don't know what you mean," Kath murmured. There was a familiar plaintive note now, that Harriet knew of old. Kath could draw a willful opacity around her when she wanted to, shielding herself from one of the scenes she dreaded by deflecting every challenge with resigned bewilderment. Harriet knew quite well that she would learn nothing now.

"You do know," she said softly, but she only found herself listening to the bruised silence. Fear and anger beat together in her chest. "It's me, *Harriet*," she tried.

"I know it is," Kath answered, all sadness, but Harriet was too far off balance to take her chance. She saw that it was almost eleven p.m., and that there was only twelve hours until the board meeting.

"I've got to go to bed," she said abruptly.

It was Kath who was left listening to the silence behind the dial tone.

Harriet went to bed, but she could not sleep. Jet engines still vibrated beside her and her limbs curled stiffly in the contours of the plane seat. She turned and lay flat, trying to suppress the chains of thoughts that looped together fears and speculations and fraying hopes. Figures and prices made processions in her head, and she tried to harness them to form speeches to the Board, to her shareholders, but they wheeled and turned in the wrong direction and outflanked her.

Her body began to vibrate with her anxiety for sleep, and sleep receded further. She could only think about the meeting, and whatever it was that Robin had plotted against her. In the darkness she grew more fearful, and Peacocks began to seem a real baby, bonded to her and about to be torn away. The images became confused with Linda, riding the carousel, and Miss Getz in her ribbons, and then blood and dismemberment.

Harriet sat upright to chase away the horrors. She pushed the bedclothes aside, and got out of bed. She couldn't sleep, so she would walk instead.

It was cold outside. London's spring was still weeks away. The pavements that led from Harriet's front gate were black and slick with frost. She put her hands into her coat pockets and bent her head, walking quickly, directionlessly. After the mild, scented air of the West Coast the chilled London smoke bit into her lungs, making her cough and gasp.

The night walk did not help her to unravel any of the coils in her head, but the icy air did damp the heat of her anxiety, and the rhythm of her footsteps overcame the vibrating tension that had stopped her from falling asleep. She walked until she was warm and no longer needed to huddle in her heavy coat. She put her head back, and turned at the far corner where the Heath stretched away in blackness beyond the nimbus of a street lamp. She retraced her steps to her own gate.

She did sleep, then.

Her alarm woke her again at six, precipitating her from a dream into a disorientated groping, through the fog of which she quickly distinguished the threatening contours of the day. She got up at once, turning her face to meet what was coming.

She dressed in the navy-blue Chanel suit that she had worn for her impact breakfast. It had brought her good luck then. She fastened the monogrammed buttons with deliberate care and smoothed the braided lapels. When she stopped to examine her reflection in the full-length mirror she saw that she hadn't changed. She still looked what she was, a successful woman, "Meizu Girl."

Harriet was the first to reach Peacocks' offices. The week's paperwork was neatly laid on her desk, sorted into the categories she preferred. There was a list of less urgent callers; Harriet saw Alison Shaw's name among them. She looked up at her own portrait, noting its serene expression. Everything was so much as it always was that it was hard to believe Robin could assail any of it. Harriet got up from her desk and went into the kitchen to make a cup of instant coffee. She came back and began to go through the correspondence, concentrating on details to keep the larger anxiety at bay.

At nine, the staff began to arrive. Harriet had not announced her early return and their surprise seemed genuine. But even as Harriet asked herself, *Who knows?* the atmosphere seemed to grow cooler. She rang through to Graham Chandler's office, but his secretary told her that Graham would not be in until eleven, for the board meeting. Everyone knew about the meeting, then. Harriet opened her own diary and saw that the day was blank.

She could keep up the pretense of routine working no longer. She stood up and walked slowly to and fro. She began to understand that in her brief absence Robin had made her a suspect in her own stronghold. On an ordinary day there would already have been a stream of people in her office, wanting to talk and plan, eager to tell her what had been achieved in her absence. The door that remained closed and the silent telephone gave her a clearer warning than any coldly worded official letter.

At half past nine exactly she rang Allardyce's, the company's bankers. There was some prevarication, but Harriet was insistent and at last she was put through to James Hamilton. He listened to what she had to say, Harriet all the time aware that she was not expressing her anxiety very cogently. Jet lag confused her thinking.

Hamilton's response to Harriet's incoherence was impeccable, but stony, politeness. "Allardyce's have not been approached to deal with any business in connection with this," he said.

"I'm afraid that at this time we are no wiser than you as to any possible restructuring within Peacocks. We are here to help in so far as we can, of course, at any time . . ."

Harriet struggled to decipher a subtext from the suave sentences. He knew, of course he knew, but he wasn't telling her. He left his last sentence delicately in the air, but gave her no doubt that their conversation was at an end. The contrast with the warmth and flattery he had beguiled her with on impact day—seemingly a forgotten eon ago—was painfully sharp. She might have laughed, if she had not been afraid.

"Thank you, James," Harriet whispered.

She left her office and walked the short distance to Jeremy Crichton's, bypassing his secretary and interrupting him in the middle of a call.

"What are you doing, Jeremy? What is this?"

He stared at her, pale eyes behind rimless glasses. "I think that's more properly a matter for discussion at the meeting." He looked at his watch. "In fifty-five minutes' time."

Harriet went back to her office. She knew that she was on her own. The scale of what was happening was only beginning fully to dawn on her, and as she saw it she cursed herself for her blindness and her willful overconfidence. It was going to be worse than she had feared. It seemed, now she analyzed it, as bad as it could be.

It was Robin's doing. It was only now, after so long, that she perceived it as his revenge on her. She realized that her worst mistake, perhaps her only real mistake, had been to underestimate the clever boy who always got what he wanted. Futile anger and hatred fermented inside her. She tried to suppress her feelings, knowing that they would distort her vision. She was going to need all the clear-sighted logic she could bring to bear.

Harriet waited, in the quiet luxury of her office, through the interminable minutes.

At eleven o'clock exactly she walked through to the boardroom. She went empty-handed, not knowing what to take with her. She would have to mount her defense and her counterattack off the cuff.

She took her usual place at the end of the table. Karen had been laying out memo pads and water glasses, but at the sight of Harriet she looked frightened and slipped away. Jeremy came in and began to lay out pens and papers in his meticulous way, and Graham Chandler edged in in his wake. Harriet saw his discomfort and spared him more than a surprised glance.

Robin was next. His beautiful dark suit contrasted with the chainstore clothes worn by Jeremy and Graham. His hair and his skin possessed a gloss that made the other two look scurfy and stained. He took his place opposite to Harriet and nodded gravely at her. She thought how handsome he looked. In the time they had known each other Robin had lost the last of his boyish softness. He had acquired the polish of maturity.

As she sat, still waiting, Harriet found herself remembering the time they had spent together. She recalled separate nights, isolated hours when they had been close, times when he had told her that he loved her. If she had been different, she reflected, if they had even come together at a different time in their lives, they might have made a team. The irony of the thought, here and now, touched the corners of her mouth with a smile.

She saw that Robin looked at her, with a flicker of doubt in his eyes. If he still loved her, she thought, it was much too late. And he might be handsome but he was also—although she had realized it also too late—quite deadly. She met his eyes with a blank gaze and looked quickly away. But the fuel of her anger had died away inside her. She simply felt tired, and anxious for this to be over.

Kath arrived, shown in by Karen. She took her place quickly, looking at Robin for confirmation that she was in the right place at the right time. In the past, at other meetings, it had always been to Harriet that she had directed the silent query. Harriet saw that her mother kept moistening her lips with the tip of her tongue. It showed her anxiety and uncertainty. Harriet braced herself.

Robin began very quietly, looking across the table directly at her.

"Thank you for coming back from your holiday in Los Angeles to be at this meeting, Harriet. I think you must know that the directors would not have asked it, if it had not been vitally important."

Harriet inclined her head. Her hands were folded in front of her. She was watching Jeremy Crichton taking the minutes. Usually one of the secretaries sat in on the meeting; this one was too momentous. She realized that she was shaking, and folded her hands more tightly to hide the tremors.

Robin said, "Shall we proceed to business?"

The minutes of the last meeting were nodded through; there were no matters arising.

"Item three," Robin continued. "Board appointments." There was an instant's stillness before he went on. "I think there is no point in disguising the issue. There has been grave concern among directors, managers and a proportion of the company's shareholders about the running of the company and its financial affairs, reaching a peak during the last few days during the present chief executive's absence on holiday. It is with the long-term health of the company in mind that the directors have reached a majority decision to appoint a new managing director, under whose guidance Peacocks will continue to achieve a pattern of growth that has been temporarily disrupted."

"You can't do that," Harriet said flatly.

He only held up his hand to quiet her. "You will want to know on what grounds, of course. But I want to stress that the decision has already been taken."

There was a folder on the table beside him. He opened it now and cleared his throat before he began to read. Harriet despised him for the theatricality of the gesture, but she sat as still as she could, and listened.

It was what she had expected: he was using Winwood as the spearhead of his attack. Her investment in cheaper production for the long term was interpreted as overextension, and the shortcomings of the unfortunate molding machine in particular were Harriet's fault, because she had bought it after inadequate research.

There was truth in that, Harriet knew. She had been overeager to get Winwood running and earning its expensive keep.

Different accusations centered on overspending in several areas, in particular within Harriet's favored marketing department. Robin lightly indicated the new range of packaging that had been intended to lift the sales of "Alarm," the cheerful red point-of-sale material that she had chosen at the enjoyable meeting before she left for Los Angeles . . .

Overspending, Robin said with carefully judged regret, was endemic throughout the company, and Harriet had failed to control it. She was further at fault in introducing and trying to promote too many new products that had failed as yet to meet sales expectations.

Yet how can Peacocks follow an upward growth curve, Harriet wondered, *if I don't introduce new lines?*

As she listened Harriet saw the full extent of her own overconfidence, not in her own business acumen because she was quite sure of that, but in her belief that other people would recognize it, too. And in her failure to see Robin quite clearly enough.

When Robin had finished, she lifted her head.

"I can defend my decisions on every single one of those points," she said softly.

She had no need of notes. Her head was quite clear now, except for a faint ringing in her ears, the sound of her own alarm. She answered Robin, point for point. Winwood would pay its way, although the turnaround might take a year. The German molding machine was exactly right for the job it was intended to do, and the purchase had been made in consultation and with the full approval of the technical director.

She looked across the table at Graham Chandler. He was miserable, his eyes showed her the extent of it.

"That is correct. The malfunctions were unfortunate, and no one could have predicted them. The machine is working perfectly now."

Harriet understood that Graham was on her side and that he was too weak to count. She looked past him to Jeremy, only half-visible behind the disks of his spectacles. Jeremy was not on her side. And facing the two of them, Kath. Kath, in her blue two-piece, looking at no one. Harriet found it hard to believe that this was her mother. It was just as hard to believe that all of this was happening.

Robin said, "Maybe so. But in the interim the breakdowns have lost twenty-two percent of forecast production, resulting in a revenue shortfall of one hundred and sixty-eight thousand pounds, translating into a loss of profit . . ."

It was only figures. Harriet knew that if she had prepared her own version, she could have made it look as bright as Robin made it dark. But she was not prepared, and Robin had been working, adjusting the light on his half-truths and the shade that softened his careful lies.

Harriet went on, mouthing her defense, but she felt the moment's clarity slipping away from her. Robin had been too clever. She was only shouting as she went down.

She saw a series of images, vivid in her mind's eye, superimposed on Robin's watchful face. She saw herself in Simon's kitchen, taking the packing-case end that he held out to her. And then she saw herself sitting on the stairs at Jane's house with Charlie Thimbell; and the basement flat in Belsize Park where she had propped the game on the mantelpiece, so that it overlooked the little room while she worked on her business plan in the empty evenings.

Opposite her, across the table, Robin sat while they went on through the dismal catalog of her supposed failings. At the end they came to Harriet's laxity in stealing away to Los Angeles.

Robin closed his folder with a well-judged sigh. "And in the managing director's absence on holiday, industrial action at Winwood results in a further loss of production which in turn will lead to . . ."

"What industrial action? This is the very first I have heard of it."

Robin spread his hands, as if to say, *Out of your own mouth.*

Graham said hastily, "They downed tools for two hours yesterday, in protest about the canteen facilities, and there's a further stoppage planned for this afternoon."

Robin was behind it, Harriet was as sure as she was certain of everything else. Somehow, he had fixed it with Mick whatever-his-name. Probably with Ray Dunnett as well. He would have wanted to get her at Winwood, in her Achilles heel, and his sense of symmetry led him to wind up his case with Los Angeles, and Caspar, who had supplanted him. There was an inevitable, ironical neatness in it all. Harriet realized the full extent of his determination to finish her.

She faced him, down the table, her hands folded again. "And so?"

The images still flickered in front of her. There were the two girls who had come into Stepping, with their bobbing ponytails, playing "Conundrum." There was the conductor on the 73 bus, and the precarious glitz of her black-and-white stand at the Earl's Court Toy Fair, and the moment when her sunburst display collapsed and showered Leo and the two demonstrators and Robin and herself with boxes and shards of polystyrene. An involuntary smile pulled at Harriet's mouth and she caught her lip between her teeth, because she knew she was on the point of weeping.

Robin gave a tiny gesture, that she could interpret as victorious. "And so the directors have asked me to indicate their willingness to accept your resignation from the board of Peacocks."

"I see. And if I refuse to resign?"

Kath shifted in her seat but she said nothing.

Robin smiled. It was his moment of triumph, and Harriet could see that it was sweet to him. He smiled sometimes in bed, in just the same way. When he answered his voice was almost caressing. "Harriet, I want everything to be quite clear between us. With my supporters I control fifty-two percent of the company. If you don't cooperate I will simply call a shareholders' meeting and oust you, which will be ugly for you and no more than an inconvenience for me. Why don't we behave like the friends we have been, and make a civilized agreement behind these closed doors?"

The euphemistic *we* and *the directors* had gone, Harriet noticed. It was *me* now, and *you*, the sordid personal truth of the battle.

"It would be advisable," Jeremy Crichton said.

"I don't need your advice, Jeremy, thank you. Tell me, Robin, how you control more than fifty percent? My holding is twenty-eight percent and my family has a further fifteen as you know, to Landwith's twenty. Graham has five." Harriet smiled at him as she said his name, and saw his relief. Graham couldn't save her, but he didn't want her to drown. Harriet knew what Robin was going to say but she wanted to make him say it just the same. She wanted to lay their perfidy in front of them, because it was all she had. Her eyes stung and she found it hard to breathe. She didn't try any longer to hide the shaking of her hands.

The images she saw now were all triumphant, mocking her in the face of her defeat. She remembered the giddily ascending sales figures after "Conundrum" became "Meizu," the breakfast on impact day when she had swept into the merchant bank as if she were the Queen. She had been wearing the same blue Chanel suit. Harriet looked down into her own lap. She dropped her hands and let them rest there, out of sight. The glint of her big square diamond caught her eye, the diamond that she had bought for herself as one of the rewards of success. It reminded her of

Robin's diamonds, the teardrop necklace and earrings that he had given her, and the words that he had said.

She had underestimated Robin. Her worst, most terrible mistake.

"Landwith's twenty, as you say," Robin was smiling, "Jeremy's five and the various holdings of a number of institutions, as set out here."

He held out a slip of paper to her. Like an obedient messenger Jeremy passed it on down the length of the boardroom table.

Harriet read the list; it was surprisingly short. From their non-appearance on it she deduced that those fund managers had remained loyal to her. For an instant she was almost heartened, even though she guessed what must be coming next.

"Another twelve, then. You're still a long way short of control, Robin."

His smile showed his teeth, at last. "Not if you count in the Trotts' holding. Their votes take me well past the fifty mark. I've got control, Harriet. Face it."

Slowly, stiffly, Harriet turned her head to Kath. "You'll vote with *him*?" she whispered. "With him, against *me*? You would do that, Mum?"

Harriet had never called Kath anything at any of their meetings. She had scrupulously avoided any mention of their relationship. But now she gave the word its full weight. In an echo of Robin's cheap effects she even repeated it. *"Mum?"*

Kath's head wobbled a little, so that the loosening flesh on her full cheeks shivered like milk coming to the boil. A dark flush colored her skin, but she held her chin up.

"I never liked it, Harriet. I never liked what you did to make this business. You did it at Simon's expense. You drove him off that bridge, you and your business together. You've as good as got his blood on your hands."

Harriet fended the words off, pushing them aside with an uncontrolled sweep of her arm that sent the blank notepad at her elbow flopping to the floor.

"I live with that. It isn't necessary to offer me a reminder. But you're confused, Mum. You don't think logically, because you've never needed to. You've lived your life behind Ken, and before that behind your own determination to keep up appearances. You have to have things nice, don't you? Well, listen to me. Things aren't nice. And when you tell me you want to vote me off my own board because you think I've got Simon's blood on me, then I tell you that you're confusing business with sentiment."

Harriet took a breath. She looked away from her mother's

dark red face to Robin's smooth one. "You would never have been guilty of mixing business and sentiment, Robin, would you?"

"I might have been, once," he answered her softly.

She saw the last picture then. It was the day of her pricing meeting. She had gone back to Robin's office after that meeting, bearing her news. She had felt powerful enough to take over the world, and they had made love, heated by their mutual success. Harriet suppressed the vision, pinching it into blackness behind her eyes, and it was replaced by anger that swept up hotter than any erotic impulse she had ever known.

She swung back on Kath, who seemed to shrink away from her in fear.

Harriet hissed at her. *"Don't support him.* Don't you understand? Can't you see why he wants to do this? What the little-boy reason is behind it all?"

Kath had been turning a pencil in her fingers. It was a Peacocks pencil, one of the kind that the company gave away at toy fairs and trade promotions, decorated with a little peacock's tail. It snapped in her hands now. She laid the two splintered pieces carefully on the table, beside her notepad. She jerked her chin at Robin, and the loose skin shivered.

"If you think *he's* been working on me, turned my silly head or whatever it is, then you're wrong. I've lived long enough, Harriet, with your explanations and translations and allowances as though I'm a child, or a fool. You mean well, usually. But I can make my own mind up. I have made it up. I'll vote with him. Not with him, really, but against you. I'm doing it because of Simon."

Harriet stared mutely at her. She wanted to scream, *Stupid. Do you think that will help Simon? Do you?* But she suppressed the impulse. She knew that Kath's decision was irrevocable, and no amount of screaming would change it. It was a revelation to find such determination within her soft, tremulous, conciliating mother. And even as she recognized it she felt the buried links of inheritance, surprisingly taut. In the midst of her anger at Kath's ignorant betrayal, she knew that she was like her.

There was no need to ask about Ken. Ken would support his wife, of course, because Kath must not be upset. Harriet gave a grim smile at the thought.

"And Liza? What about little Liza?"

Liza would vote against Harriet, of course. She would be glad to. It would be her revenge for all the years that Harriet had been older, and cleverer, and quicker, and closer to Kath.

"Liza, too," Robin murmured.

Harriet ignored him. She was still looking at Kath, but she was shaking so much in her anger that the graying fair hair and the blue two-piece seemed to blur into anonymity before her eyes.

"So it wasn't enough for Liza to have my husband. She wants to do it all. Take my company as well." Harriet's voice had started low but now it rose until she was shouting. The room went very still. "Not that she'd have had the wit to do it, if I hadn't been fool enough to hand it to her with a few shares. *My company.*"

Kath leaned forward. "It's only a business, Harriet. It isn't the world. It isn't life itself."

Harriet screamed at her. "How do you know? What do you know?" She had to lift one shaking hand to wipe her mouth.

Out of the blur she saw Jeremy's face, faintly colored, and Graham's pity, and embarrassment. It was an added humiliation to find that she had lost control of herself. She leaned awkwardly back in her chair, trying to steady her breathing.

At last she looked at Robin. His face was clear in the fog, and she saw that there was no embarrassment there. He was watching her with a degree of interest that had something carnal in it. It was a look that made her pull her jacket more tightly around her, with an attempt at defiance.

"What will you do if I refuse to resign?" she whispered.

He smiled again, showing his perfect teeth at her. "I could call a shareholders' meeting, as I have already said. Or there's another alternative. Do you remember when the launch of 'Conundrum' failed, and you came to me for further financing so you could relaunch the game as 'Meizu'?" His tone was light, conversational, as if he was telling an amusing story across the dinner table. Harriet nodded.

"Of course you do. And you'll also remember that one of the small conditions was that I took a floating charge on the company's assets, including Mr. Archer's game itself? Now, I'll remind you of the *security in jeopardy* clause relating to that charge. The clause states that the holder of the debenture—Landwith Associates, Harriet—has the right to foreclose if the assets on which the holder is secured appear to be threatened."

Robin laid one caressing finger on his folder. "*This* information leads me to believe that through your mismanagement and neglect, my asset is very much in jeopardy. And so, according to our very proper agreement, I can foreclose on the game itself. I can take 'Meizu,' and leave Peacocks. You don't need me to explain what that means."

He would strip the company.

Harriet raised her eyes. From the other three faces she could see that they had heard nothing of this. Robin had kept it to the end, his last trick. Perhaps he had used just a hint of it to bring one or two of his friends, the fund managers, into the fold. She didn't doubt that he would do it. He would take "Meizu" and leave Peacocks with nothing.

As she had done, to Simon.

She was defeated. She had been defeated all along, and the memory of Simon took the last of her resistance. She couldn't try to fight, and watch Robin destroy the company she had created, even though she was no longer part of it. Robin would have calculated that, too, as he had calculated everything else.

"And so what do you propose?" Harriet asked him.

He took out yet another piece of paper. She sat motionless while he read out the arrangements for the disposal of her shares through the institutions, her compensation, the formalities of the notice to the Stock Exchange, and the euphemistic wording of the announcement to the press.

"I think you resign to 'devote more time to your personal life,' don't you?" Robin murmured.

"If you say so," she answered him.

"I think that concludes the meeting," he said.

Harriet stood up. She picked up the two halves of the broken pencil, and closed them in her fist. As she passed behind Kath's chair she touched her mother's shoulder.

"I'm sorry I screamed at you. I wish I hadn't."

After the door had closed behind her, it was a long moment before Kath ventured, "I think I should go to her."

Robin was sharp. "Don't do that. She'll prefer the dignity of some privacy."

With dislike, Kath said, "You think you know her, don't you?"

Robin was packing the papers and his dossier into his briefcase.

"I do know her," he said, without emphasis.

Harriet sat at her desk. She looked unseeingly around her. After a little while, because she couldn't think what else to do, she picked up the telephone to talk to Charlie Thimbell. At the sound of her voice, Charlie waved one of his writers out of his office, with a gesture that told him to close the door behind him.

"What happened?"

Harriet told him all of it. The words spilled out.

"The devious, dirty little motherfucker," Charlie pronounced.

It was a wonderful story. A classic of its kind. He made some notes, on the lined pad he kept ready.

"I should have seen it coming. I should have acted tighter. I should never have gone to L.A."

"Well, Harriet, I'm sorry. You didn't deserve it." He was sorry, genuinely sorry, because he liked Harriet and he admired her. "You didn't deserve what your family did, either."

"Oh. I probably did."

"What's the deal, then?" Not that he couldn't have worked it out for himself.

"A placing of my shares. Twenty-nine percent's a big slice, but Robin's P.R. will convince the world that this is an amicable split, and it will be taken up. I daresay Peacocks will go down to one-ninety or so, which isn't to say they won't be back at two twenty-five the day after. With compensation I suppose it will mean about nine million. Say five to six, after tax."

Charlie's whistle was soundless.

"So what are you going to do now?" he asked.

Harriet sounded weary. "Have some time off. Take stock. Isn't that what I'm supposed to say?"

"Yep." Charlie would not have minded taking some time off, with six million to cushion him.

"Charlie? Do you know what? I feel as if I'm right back at the beginning again. All the way back to that beach in Crete."

"You're a long way from Crete, my love. A *long*, long way. You're rich."

Harriet heard the words, without comprehension. The fear and its attendant adrenaline, that kept her going through the meeting, that had brought her all the way from Los Angeles, were ebbing away. It was dawning on her what the loss of Peacocks truly meant. She couldn't think what to do now, or tomorrow, or in the weeks that were going to follow each other. "Do you want me to take you out for a drink tonight? Or, come home and have dinner with Jenny, why don't you?"

"No," Harriet said. "No, thanks, Charlie. I think I'll just go home tonight."

After they had said good-bye, Charlie drew his notepad in front of him. He began to tap at his terminal, squinting at the words as they appeared on the screen. Whatever rubbish Robin's P.R.'s put out, he could counter it with the real story. Straight from the horse's mouth. Charlie justified himself with the thought that, if their roles were reversed, Harriet would do exactly the same thing.

When Harriet had finished talking to Charlie, Karen came

into her office. She was carrying a cup of tea, in the thin, fine
china. She put it down on the corner of Harriet's desk.

"I'm really sorry," she said. "Everyone is."

Harriet looked at her. Everything was all over. "Karen?"

"Yes?"

"Leave me alone for an hour, will you? Please?"

When she had gone, Harriet opened her fist and looked
down at the two pieces of pencil. She had been holding on to
them so tightly and for so long that they had left blue-white
marks in the palm. Now she laid them out and tried to fit the
fractured ends together. She stared at them for a moment.

Then she put her head down on her desk and wept.

Later, Harriet went home. She stayed at home while her lawyers
and the company's lawyers agreed on her compensation, and
while the placement of her shares was organized. It was announced that her decision to leave Peacocks had been voluntary,
that there had been no dissension, and that the company could
only go on to further strengths under the direction of the
new chief executive, Robin's appointment. But it was Charlie's
different version of the story that was enthusiastically taken
up by the press. With the boardroom battle public knowledge,
the price of Peacocks shares fell. Harriet had no alternative but to
accept a lower price for her holding, but in the end, in exchange
for the years she had put into Peacocks, she received rather more
than five million pounds, net. She didn't blame Charlie for telling the story. As he had rightly guessed, she knew that she
would have done the same herself.

The popular press enjoyed the news as much as its City
counterpart. There was a spate of "Meizu Girl's Millions" stories,
and a siege of telephone calls and reporters' visits cut Harriet off
in Hampstead. She thought of escaping by returning to California, but Caspar didn't respond to the suggestion when she made
it. He was out of the hospital, and back in his chair beside the
pool at the ranch house.

"I think you'd best stay there, baby," he told her. It was
clear to Harriet that whatever there had been between them was
now over, as definitively as her life within Peacocks was over.

Caspar said there was some possibility that he might have to
stand trial for involuntary manslaughter, but his people were
working on it. They were evidently also working on suppressing
the news. There were few mentions of the accident in the British
press, and the brief accounts only said that Oscar-nominee Caspar

Jensen had been involved in a car accident, in which one person had been killed. More was made of Caspar's relationship with "Ousted Meizu Girl"; Harriet wished that she had advisers with the protective expertise that Caspar's possessed.

For two or three days, it seemed that she could not walk out of her door without being surrounded by intrusive questions. She grew tired of fending them off with "No comment" and "I am quite satisfied with the agreements made with the company," and she stayed at home to evade the questioners.

The tasteful, neutral confines of her flat began to seem part fortress, part prison. She began to feel that she was safe in her privacy so long as she stayed within her own walls, but to venture out was to risk something indefinable, that was still much more threatening than a few questions about her future plans. Her tall windows seemed suddenly to admit a little too much light; the possibility of spying eyes. She resisted the urge to keep her curtains closed, but it still overtook her each late morning when she finally got out of her bed. One part of Harriet was too rational not to recognize that sooner or later, the next day or the next week, another story would break and hers would be forgotten. But there was another part of her, the part that kept her doors double-locked and longed to leave the curtains drawn, that understood what Simon must have suffered. She thought about him a great deal, and talked aloud to him, the way solitary people do.

She did not cry again, after the long weeping fit in her office, but she was possessed with a weight of sadness that was more for Simon than for herself.

She could not think about the future, or her wealth, or what she might do. When she tried to, a prospect of such blankness confronted her that she was frightened, so she made herself sleep again, or sit in front of a television soap that bewildered her because she knew none of the characters or the reasons for their dilemmas.

Her existence narrowed to fit the frame of her four rooms. She slept, heated up tins of soup, watched more television. The telephone was her link with the world. It rang constantly, and mostly she left the answering machine to field the prurient inquiries. One caller who did get through to her was Alison Shaw, the television reporter. Alison wanted, if Harriet would be willing, to film a coda to the *Success Story* program. She thought it would make a pertinent comment on City practices.

"I don't want to add anything at all," Harriet said.

"It's going to be difficult for us to schedule the program without some kind of footnote after what happened."

"I can't help you with that. I'm sure you can devise your own footnote, if pressed."

"I can't persuade you?"

"No."

"That's a pity. I'm sorry about what happened, Harriet." Alison's voice held natural friendliness, once business was out of the way, as Harriet had noticed before. "Keep in touch, won't you?"

"Thanks." Harriet found that she was sorry when Alison hung up. She would have liked to talk some more. The silence in the flat was heavy. Harriet walked through the rooms. She couldn't think what to do. The reasons that had existed for everything, when Peacocks was everything, had all been removed.

Jane telephoned. They talked a little about the mechanics of Robin's coup. Jane offered her sympathies that were tinged with the faintest satisfaction, perhaps only audible to Harriet's silence-attuned ears. Jane had never much liked or trusted Robin. She asked the inevitable question, *What now?*

"I don't know," Harriet answered.

"You could do anything. Anything at all, couldn't you? Patronize the arts. Travel. Invest the great fortune and sit back and count the interest."

Harriet read the envy. In the middle of her loss, she didn't know how to contend with it.

"Money isn't everything," she said.

"Isn't it?"

Jane was sitting on the rug in her front room. She looked up as a thin shaft of sunlight came between the houses opposite and lay in a bar across the whitish fur. It made her notice that the window needed cleaning. Imogen's basket beside her was empty because the baby was asleep in her cot upstairs. Soon she would wake up, and Jane would put her in her pram and wheel her around the circuit of Clissold Park. As she talked to Harriet, Jane was thinking that she would like to look forward to an evening with some friends, going to the cinema or perhaps to a restaurant, but she couldn't because there was no one, at the moment, to babysit Imogen. But Harriet, Harriet could walk out of her expensive pale flat and buy herself a ticket to anywhere.

Harriet heard. Distance yawned between them. It was impossible to tell Jane, across the space, that she could think of nowhere she wanted to go except back to her desk, or to Winwood to vanquish Ray Dunnett and the plastic molder. She looked at her walls, beginning to hate them as her dependence on their protection increased.

Jane and Harriet talked a little more, promised to see one another very soon. When the conversation finished, both of them wondered if they would.

Jenny, Charlie, Leo, other friends, all put their calls through to Harriet. The messages came like darts, piercing her solitude. Harriet didn't want to talk, but she felt the loneliness in the intervals between the stilted conversations.

She spoke to Kath, too.

"Are you angry with me?" Kath asked. Her voice was soft, almost bland. It was a "little me" question, making Kath seem vulnerable and humbly acknowledging Harriet's right to anger. And yet, on another level, it was a challenge. *Be angry: it won't make any difference to what I did.*

Yes, I'm angry.

The words exploded inside Harriet's head, hot little pellets of rage. The thought of Kath at the other end of the line, in the secure nest that Ken had created for her lined with china ornaments and velvet cushions, sent a hot current of fury washing all through Harriet. Kath was a coward, a noncompetitor, a prettifier, an evader of reality, her own mother.

Harriet fought to control her voice, and her feelings.

"Yes. Yes, I'm angry. What did you think? You lost me my company. It isn't that you don't understand how, or why. Because you do, don't you? You're not as stupid as you pretend to be. Listen, I built that company up. Day by day, hour by hour, watching it and planning for it. I loved it. It was *mine*, can you understand that? And still, Robin Landwith comes and lies to you and you listen to him, and you throw my company away on some sentimental whim that won't bring Simon back. Nothing will bring Simon back. He's damn well *dead*."

"There's no need to talk like that, Harriet," Kath said.

Harriet thought, *It's exactly as if I was a little girl who had said* shan't *or* so there. *Why won't she admit what she's done?*

Kath was saying, in her soft voice, "What did you want? You've made a lot of money out of it, haven't you?"

"I don't want the money," Harriet screamed. The telephone receiver felt like putty in her fingers. She could have crushed it or twisted it and torn down all her tasteful, pointless surrounding possessions and destroyed them with it. "I don't give a fuck for the money. *I want my company back.*"

But she wouldn't get it back. It was gone, into the hands of Robin and Jeremy and the people she couldn't touch, and it would never be hers again.

Harriet was panting, gasping for breath, and her face was burning with tears.

Kath's voice went on, pricking at her, "I can't listen to you when you talk like this. I'll have to call you back, Harriet. You'll make us both upset."

There was a click, and then the dial tone in Harriet's ear.

She shouted at the walls, "Upset! God forbid that anyone should ever be upset!"

The walls and the curtains and the carpet absorbed the sound of her voice, and gave her back silence. Harriet dropped the receiver, letting it hang. She slid slowly down the wall, collapsing in a shapeless bundle, so that her head rested on her knees and her arms stuck out sideways, empty, palms upward.

She sat for a long time, crying. And then the tears dried up. Harriet opened her sticky eyes and surveyed the room. Nothing had moved, nothing had altered, and nothing would change however long she went on crying. She sat still, in her huddle, thinking.

She knew that she would ring Kath and apologize, and Kath would say, "That's my girl. We'll forget all about it. It was in the heat of the moment, wasn't it?" That was how it was between them. They had subsided and set fast into those roles long ago, and there was no changing them now.

We're not alike, Harriet thought. *We're quite different. That's something to be thankful for, isn't it?*

The flat was very silent. She longed for the sound of voices or a television or music from next door, or overhead, but there was nothing. She felt weary, and vacant, and peculiarly disorientated.

She stood up, awkward and stiff, and wandered into the kitchen. There were no tins left in the store-cupboard, she had never been a stockpiler. She would have to go shopping. The thought brought anxiety flicking in its wake, anxiety that intensified to the point where it caught at her breath. She was frightened to go out: recognition of it made nothing easier, only bringing further awareness of what she had done to Simon.

"Is this what it was like?" she asked aloud. "Was it?"

Only Harriet knew that she wasn't afraid of the reporters, if any of them had bothered to linger, or any of the physical manifestations of the world outside the front door. She was afraid of nothing more than the emptiness, the inaction after so many years of occupation. She could keep it at bay by denying the outside, but it also lurked inside with her, expressionless in the neutral walls, implicit in the bare cupboards, eloquent in the absence of a life in the elegant decor.

She had never felt more impotent or more hopeless.

"I wish I could talk to you," she told Simon.

Even the one-way conversation began to seem impertinent and irrelevant. Simon was gone. He had never told her again that he wished she really were his daughter.

With relief Harriet saw that it was getting dark outside. There seemed no sign of spring. The day's brief sunshine had been wintry, and now it had been extinguished by the evening's cold. Harriet shivered. Her blood was still thin after the prodigal warmth of the Coast. She told herself that it was perfectly in order now to draw the curtains on the greenish twilight, to turn up the heating and watch television.

She took a jar of Marmite out of the cupboard and spread it on the last crackers. She made tea, pouring the water onto a teabag in the bottom of a mug that had earlier held coffee. She discarded the teabag in the sink, but then she had a sudden clear vision of the throat-blocking flotsam in the bottom of Simon's sink. She snatched up a teaspoon and prodded the brown lump down the plughole. Then she turned the stopper of the waste-unit and listened to the mechanism grinding the scrap of mess away.

Harriet decided. Later, when it was completely dark, after *News at Ten*, perhaps, that would be the best time, she would go out and do some shopping. She would walk down the hill, to the late-night supermarket in Belsize Park. It stayed open until midnight, and there was rarely anyone in the narrow aisles in the last hour. Harriet remembered it very well; the shop was just around the corner from the dingy flat she had borrowed when she was struggling with the beginnings of Peacocks. She used to rush in and buy ready-made meals out of the freezer, scooping up whatever there was without wasting time on deliberation. She had been too busy to shop, too busy to cook. A long time ago, although she had been too busy ever since. Until now.

Well, then. She would walk down the hill and stock up. She would lay in plenty of supplies, it was a good opportunity. Tins, and packets of dry goods that would keep, that was what she needed. There was no point in dashing out every five minutes, after all. It was much better to have whatever was necessary right to hand, in the kitchen cupboards.

Harriet nodded in her relief. She would watch the early-evening soaps, because she was already beginning to feel that she knew who was who, and after all why not? Then there was a play she wanted to see, and the news afterward. After that she would have a walk, one of the calming, invisible night-walks that had soothed her in the past, and she would take a route that curved backward, toward home once more, past the late-night shop.

It would be good to get out for some fresh air. It was how many days since she had come home from Peacocks?

Harriet carried her Marmite crackers and tea through to the sitting room. She sat down in one corner of the sofa, shoring up the space around her with cushions. She ate her way through the small meal without tasting it, her eyes remaining fixed on the television screen. She watched the soaps and a game show, the play and then the news bulletin in which the stories from Lebanon and China and the Princess Diana end-piece seemed to come from worlds equally remote.

At half past ten she stood up, stiffly, with pins and needles prickling her feet. She spent a long time searching for a scarf to go under her coat, and a red beret that she had not worn for years but was suddenly convinced was the only thing that would keep her ears warm. Then she found her purse and put it in her coat pocket, and made a meticulous round of the doors and windows, checking the locks and bolts.

It was almost eleven o'clock when she let herself out of the front door.

She hesitated on the top step, peering into the night murk, but there was only the sound of distant traffic on the hill and music from a neighboring window. There was no one watching or waiting any longer, of course, as her rational self had always known. She would have a walk, do her shopping, and come back home again. When she reached the gate Harriet was thinking, *Tomorrow I'll go into Peacocks. I'll pack up my office, talk to Graham, have a cup of coffee with Karen. Tomorrow afternoon. Or perhaps in the morning the day after tomorrow.*

She began to walk. Recollections of other nighttime expeditions came back to her. It had been a habit of hers for a long time now, to walk off her anxieties in the darkness. She had walked the dormant streets around Sunderland Avenue when Simon died, and she had felt his fear pursuing her, just as she felt it gathering tonight in the corners and pressing itself against the windowpanes of her rooms. Her steps quickened. The steep incline of the hill drew her on, faster, toward the traffic and away from the hedged residential streets. She couldn't submit to the fear. She would go to Peacocks tomorrow, she would open her curtains wide.

Harriet's arms swung with the rhythm of her steps.

She crossed the main road and her unplanned route led her through a housing estate where blue television lights showed in uncurtained windows, and music crackled in defiant bursts over brick balconies. Big, uncollared dogs sniffed in torn black plastic sacks that spilled their greasy contents between the dustbins. Harriet hurried past the daubs of slogans on the corners of the blocks and emerged again under the orange pall of streetlights. A little further on she came to a place where she had run with Linda on the happy afternoon before they met Caspar for their hamburger dinner. It was almost a year since she had come home with Robin and found Linda hiding in the hedge.

Harriet walked further, down gritty roads, thinking about Linda. In a few days' time she would be back in England for the summer term.

Linda would not sympathize with closed curtains and locked doors, unanswered telephone messages.

Come on, Harriet. Shape up. Harriet even smiled at the heartiness of her self-admonition. There was no point in hiding with her defeat. She shouldn't allow Robin that satisfaction. It was time to turn back, if she was to reach the shop before midnight.

It was a quarter to twelve when she pushed the door open. The tired shopkeeper in a blue coat nodded at her from behind his till, recognizing her from her Belsize Park days. Harriet moved up and down the cramped aisles, dropping packets and jars into her basket. She was aware of the shopkeeper drawing down steel shutters while he waited for her, preparing to close up for the night.

She took her loaded basket to the till. She stared at the tins of Campbell's soup and jars of pâté as they were checked through, wondering a little at why she was buying all this stuff. The total, when the shopkeeper rang it up, seemed huge. *Pâté de campagne* in little glass jars bought in shops that stayed open until midnight was always expensive, Harriet reminded herself. She opened her purse. There was plenty of money. More money than she could imagine what to do with. Harriet was grinning a little too widely. She saw the shop man looking sideways at her as he piled her purchases into two brown bags. Harriet dropped some notes onto the counter and he pushed two of them back at her.

"Plenty, plenty," he muttered.

"Thank you very much. Good night," Harriet said in a friendly voice. The man followed her to the door of the shop and closed it behind her with evident relief. He pulled a blind down to cover the glass and Harriet heard the locks clicking. She hoisted her brown bags in her arms and walked again.

The underpass led beneath the main road. In daylight Harriet always took it because the main road overhead was busy.

Late at night there were fewer cars, but a fast-moving line of them must have swept by when she reached the curbside, with the mouth of the tunnel at her left hand. She was thinking with relief that her shopping was done and looking forward to being back in the sanctuary of her home. Her mind was occupied, fixed on getting back as quickly as she could, away from people and cars and streetlights. Harriet didn't think any further. She began to descend the familiar steps, her bags held tight against her chest.

She didn't glance at the slashes of graffiti or the drifts of rubbish against the grimed walls. She saw the legs of the two men as soon as they appeared, coming down the steps to meet her at the opposite end of the tunnel. She walked on, not altering her pace, all her longing focused on *home*.

Under the abrasive light she saw that they were young, white, thin-legged with shoulders broadened out of proportion by leather jackets. Their faces bore the same expression. Knowing she shouldn't meet their eyes she turned her head sideways to the threat-daubed walls. When they were two yards in front of her they stopped, blocking her path, as she had known from the first glimpse they would do. She tried to walk on, intending to push past them. One of them grabbed her arm.

"Give us your bag."

It hung over her shoulder from a broad leather strap. Encumbered by her bags of shopping Harriet tried to pin it against her side with one elbow.

"Mind out of my way, please." Her voice sounded thin, ridiculously over-modulated.

The grip on her arm tightened. "Give us—your—fucking *bag*!"

Very clearly, Harriet saw the studs in the leather, a rag knotted around one neck, chains round the other. She said, "No." She tried to hold her handbag more tightly to her side.

"What's in it?" one of them jeered.

The other tore the strap off her shoulder. "Give it here. Bitch."

A picture came back to Harriet. She had been walking across the park on a hot evening on her way to meet Robin, her head full of her own business. She had seen a little crowd gathered around an old woman who had been attacked or mugged. She could see the woman's face, as vividly as if she stood in front of her now. Fear and bewilderment. It had been a sharp little contradiction of her satisfaction in the lovely evening, London in its summer dress. She had stood watching for a moment and then, unable to contribute anything, she had walked on. She had found Liza and Leo together, in a wine bar.

They were pulling her handbag away from her. One of them lifted his arm and hit her, with casual violence, across the jaw.

Harriet had been frightened. But the shock of the blow seemed to deaden her fear. In its place, with the stinging pain, came a flood of anger. It turned the harsh subway light crimson, and reddened the dirty white walls. It braced her arms and back and drew her lips back from her teeth in a snarl. It encompassed much more than two youths in a deserted subway. It was for what she had lost, and how, and why. It was for her days as a recluse in her own home, and for the woman in the park, for Simon, Miss Getz, and Linda, as well as for herself.

Harriet let out a torrent of filthy words of her own.

Ridiculously, she clung on to her brown paper bags of shopping. She drew back one foot and kicked upward, between a pair of thin legs. There was a yell, and she heard her own shouts like a chorus, *Leave me alone! Fuck you! Don't touch me!*

"Fucking cow!"

The one she had kicked staggered back against the curved wall, then lurched upright. Once more, coming for her again. Harriet felt her head dragged back, viciously enough to snap her neck. She was propelled against the filthy tiles and pinned there. Two faces swam against hers. She sagged and one of the bags of shopping slipped out of her arms. But the anger still coursed through her. She sucked in her cheeks and then spat. One pair of hands twisted at her breasts and jabbed upward into her crotch. Close to her, one mouth breathed out a long whistling sigh.

"Like it rough, do you, darling? I can give you some."

There was one more strike in her. She swept with her free arm, and felt it connect with a force that jarred her bones. There was a grunt, almost into her ear.

The hands released her, but only for long enough to hoist her again. Anger collapsed in a wash of terror. A blow caught the side of her head, smashing it against the tunnel wall. Harriet slid downward, blind now, her mouth opened and leaving a thin shiny trail down the tiles. Blood welled between her teeth. She descended into a huddle, her head pillowed on her hunched shoulders. There was a rain of kicks, but she didn't feel them. Silence came.

The two men stood looking down on her.

One of them whispered, "Jesus."

The other bent down and disentangled her handbag. He wrapped it against his chest inside the flaps of his leather jacket. Then he straightened up again. "Come on."

They ran, their heels drumming, down the underground passage and up the steps at the far end.

Harriet opened her eyes. She could see a dirty white tube in front of her, with bright, hard points that shone out of it, and black steps that she longed to reach. Very slowly, with the back of her hand against her split mouth, she climbed to her feet. Looking down she saw that one of the bags of shopping was still intact. She hoisted it into her arms. Weaving like a drunk, with her breaths forcing little groans of pain and terror out of her lungs, she made her way down the long tube. At the steps she dropped to her knees and crawled up, dragging the bag.

When she reached the top and the night air caught her in the face she fell forward. Her chin smashed against the top step. The bag of shopping broke open and the tins and jars and bottles rolled and bounced all the way down again, to settle in the drifts of debris trapped at the bottom.

"So what did you expect?" Charlie Thimbell demanded.

Harriet's hospital bed was submerged in flowers. On the table at the foot of it stood a basket of lilies from Caspar, with a pyramid of roses next to it signed simply "from Robin." Vases and pots of every kind of blossom in every color mounted on either side of her. They seemed to have come from everyone she knew in the world, even from "All of us at Midland Plastics."

"Just like a film star," Ivy in the next bed had said.

"I don't know what I expected," Harriet answered him, looking at the glory of the flowers. There were tears in her eyes again. She cried a lot. One of the doctors told her that it was reaction. "I didn't expect to be beaten up on the way back from the late-night shop. I didn't expect . . ." She gestured at the flowers and the tears ran down her face.

Charlie shifted in the visitor's chair, took a handkerchief out of his pocket and handed it to her.

"Kindness? Sympathy? Come on."

Harriet blew her nose. The vibration hurt her cracked jaw and she winced. She knew that it was easy for Robin to take out his credit card and call a florist; she knew that it was no more difficult to do the same all the way away in Los Angeles. It was the other flowers that touched her, the flowers and the messages of loving concern from Karen and Graham and the *Success Story* team and Kath's neighbors and all the others, some of whom she hardly knew. The nurses seemed to bring fresh cellophane-crisp sheaves every hour. Harriet tried to stop herself crying. Her tears made her more aware of her own vulnerability. She felt soft and damp and helpless, a crustacean scooped out of its shell.

A passerby had found her, lying at the top of the steps. He had stooped down to her, and she had seen the cuffs of his trousers, very close to her eyes. She had tried to say something to him, but the words wouldn't come out of her broken mouth. An ambulance had come to take her away.

The hospital's casualty department had peeling paint and there were empty paper cups on the floor under the rows of chairs. It was nothing like the Moor Park Hospital, Sherman Oaks, but as she lay on her stretcher in a curtained cubicle, waiting for the doctor, it made Harriet think of Caspar. She wished pointlessly that he could be there with her, to hold her hand. Her face and chest hurt.

The doctor came, looking as young and tired as the other one. Like Caspar, Harriet was lucky. Her jawbone would knit, the stitches at the corner of her mouth would dissolve and leave barely a scar. The body bruising, internal and external, would heal itself.

"You'll be as good as new," the doctor said. "Can we telephone someone for you now? Relatives? A friend?"

"In the morning," Harriet answered. She wanted to lie behind closed curtains, in peace. She wanted to cry without anyone to see her.

Almost as soon as she woke up in the morning, it seemed, Kath and Ken came. Their concern and their outrage washed over her. Everything that had happened seemed to have taken place inside her. The fact of the attack itself was almost peripheral. Harriet recounted the bare details to a woman police officer, and was glad when she went away.

Immediately after that, Jane came. She had managed to leave Imogen somewhere—Harriet had not seen her without her since the baby had been born. She inspected Harriet's face, leaning so close that Harriet could see the down on her top lip. Jane was very angry. She kept repeating, "Why? What did they want to do?" over and over.

"They just wanted my handbag. I lost my temper. It was just a mistake, trying to resist them. I could have given them the bag, and they would have gone away."

"But you didn't, and they did *that*?" Jane was almost in tears, too. "Harriet, what were you doing? Why were you wandering around on your own, in the middle of the night?"

Everyone asked her, of course, Kath, and Ken, and the young policewoman. Harriet couldn't have explained her fear of the daylight and the busy outside any more coherently than Simon could have done. Nor could she have described the counterpoint of her enjoyment of the darkness, the way that the solitary walks soothed her, her need for the night's anonymity.

"I needed some things. The shop was open late."

She closed her eyes, then opened them again, too aware of Jane's concerned scrutiny. Worse than the bruising, worse than the splintered bone in her jaw, was the shock the assault had dealt her. She thought it was like a friend's betrayal. She had lived in London all her life, and she had taken its crowds and its diversity as allies. She had never felt lost or afraid in the City— threats had come from much closer to home, from people who knew her, not from the mass of the City itself. Yet now, at random, it had thrown up her attackers, out of the darkness that she had mistaken as protecting her. The youths, faceless because she couldn't even attempt a description for the policewoman, had taken more than her handbag. They had dispossessed her. They had made her afraid of her own place. Harriet shuddered at the thought of street corners, of empty tube platforms and windy open spaces.

Jane patted her hand. "It's shock," she said. "Shock does weird things. You'll get over it. Look, the tea trolley's coming. I'll get us both a cup."

She had become the old Jane again, capable and brisk. Harriet knew that she could depend on her to do anything she could to help, anything that was practicable. She knew that Jane would visit her every day, however inconvenient it might be for Jane herself, that Jane would make sure all was well at the Hampstead flat, would organize her homecoming. Obediently, Harriet drank her tea.

"When they say you can come out, you'll come home to me, to Hackney, won't you?" And then, *"Please* don't cry. You'll make me cry, too. You'll be all right. You'll be better in a couple of days."

"I know. I know I will," Harriet said grimly.

Charlie ate the chocolates that Harriet's jaw was too painful to allow her. "You know why, don't you? Why everyone wants to rush in, and take care of you, and heap flowers on your head?"

Like Jane, and Jenny, and Kath, and Leo, and Liza who had brought the chocolates that Charlie was busily dispatching, and even Caspar and Robin from their safe distance. Harriet nodded slowly.

"Exactly. You'd be naive if you didn't. It makes *them* feel good. You've been hurt, you need them, they can look after you.

It's not so easy to think of anything that needs doing for a self-made multimillionairess."

"I'm still a multimillionairess."

"Yeah. Just a rather battered one."

Charlie put another chocolate in his mouth and gave a little wave to Ivy who was pretending not to listen to their conversation.

"Harriet, are you okay in this ward? It's full of old ladies."

"Yes, thank you. I like the company."

When Charlie had gone, Ivy got out of bed and shuffled across to Harriet.

"He looked like a nice young man."

"Yes. He's the husband of an old friend of mine. They're both old friends. We used to go on holidays together when we were all young and broke. We went to Crete, once."

"Oh. Not yours, then." Ivy was disappointed.

"No. Not mine."

Ivy peered up and down the ward, then wrapped her dressing gown more tightly around her chest, a sure sign of a confidence about to be delivered. She jerked her chin at the tiers of flowers. "I know who you are. A lady down the other side told me. You're that 'Meizu Girl.' "

"I was," Harriet said. "I used to be."

Her most surprising visitor was Alison Shaw. She came down the ward with a bunch of tulips in her hand, her raincoat folded over her arm. Harriet was very pleased to see her, surprised by how pleased.

"I wanted to come."

"I'm very glad you did. I'm sorry about the program."

"There'll be other programs."

They smiled at each other.

Alison sat down, and they began to talk. It was not a profound conversation, but Harriet found that it was comfortable to begin the definitions of a friendship that was entirely new, and so did not have to adjust itself either to her bruising or her money. They talked about television, a magazine article they had both read about women executives, a new novel they had both admired. Alison had strong opinions; she was formally educated and widely informed. Harriet found herself drawn to her out of her own more random and piecemeal culture.

Her visitor stayed for almost an hour. At the end of the time a smell of brown stew announced the arrival of the ward supper. The two women exchanged expressions of amused revulsion. Alison prepared to leave; Harriet would have liked her to stay longer so that she could enjoy more of the conversation that did not make her cry, or feel guilty, or long to be left in peace.

"What happens now?" Alison asked. "Are you going to open a florist's?"

They laughed at the flowers. "I'll be out of here in a day or two. I don't know what I'm going to do. Or where. I'm not very keen on London at the moment." The understatement masked all Harriet's fear of the dense streets and the cold spaces.

Alison glanced at her.

"Retire to the country, then. I've got a place in Kent, my weekend bolt hole. Come and stay there, recover yourself. It's very quiet."

"That's very nice of you. I might just take you up on the offer." It was a conventional response, Harriet didn't know how seriously the invitation had been made. Alison held out her hand. Harriet remembered the unpainted nails, ringless fingers. The big, square diamond still adorned her own right hand. The muggers had missed that, somehow.

"Do you live on your own?" Harriet asked.

"Yes, I do."

They clasped hands, warmly.

After Alison had gone Ivy darted across. "I've seen *her* on the telly."

Two days later, Harriet went home. Jane was there, ready to look after her, as Harriet had known she would be. She carried Imogen in a kind of canvas pouch strapped to her chest.

"You don't look too good," Jane said, with her characteristic bluntness. The bruises on Harriet's face were turning yellow and purple, her neck and jaw were still distended.

"I'll mend."

But in truth Harriet felt weak and shaky. It had been an effort to make the mugs of coffee that they were drinking at the kitchen table. Held close against her mother, Imogen was making contented little noises. Jane's face was smooth and determined, a modern Madonna, Harriet thought.

"Come home to Hackney with me."

"I'm fine here, you know." That was another untruth. The sight of the pale walls and the neutral pictures disturbed her. The emptiness was too apparent. But Harriet didn't want to go outside either. She kept remembering the boots that had kicked her, the distorted faces, the stink of the white-tiled tunnel.

"Let me go out and do some shopping for you, at least. There's nothing in the cupboards." The last shopping had ended up as a slimy quagmire of broken jars and spilled packets at the bottom of the steps, of course. Harriet tried to conceal her shuddering.

"Is it cold in here? If you could, just get some milk and bread and stuff. I'll go out tomorrow and do a proper shop. Leave Imogen here with me, if you like."

Jane's hand cupped the small dark head. "I'll take her with me."

She brought back a mound of provisions and arranged them in Harriet's cupboards. They drank a cup of tea together, and there seemed no reason for Jane to stay any longer. After she had gone Harriet went to the window. The street was quiet, the houses opposite as mute and prosperous as always. She wondered what the facades were concealing.

She turned sharply away from the window. She went across the room and clicked on the television. Tomorrow, she resolved, she would go to Peacocks and pack up her personal belongings.

But as it happened, there was no need. Graham and Karen came with Harriet's possessions in the back of Graham's estate car. Graham brought in the Emma Sergeant portrait of Harriet and leaned it against a wall. Harriet eyed it with dislike. She thought now that it made her look smug.

Karen carried in the old packing-case game and laid it gently on the table. Harriet rested the palm of her hand on the splintery wood. She was glad to have the game back but the rest of the things—an early "Conundrum," framed photographs from launches and presentations, souvenirs of success—looked like meaningless junk. Harriet thanked Graham and Karen warmly, sat them down, gave them drinks. They stared uneasily around the room. Harriet knew that they were examining her curtains and cushions out of politeness, rather than be seen to stare too openly at her. She looked from the satisfied portrait-face to the reality in her gilt-framed mantel mirror.

The sight made her want to put up her hands to cover the damage. The swelling and the stitches, the half-closed eye and the livid marks mottling the skin appeared to Harriet as the external manifestations of her defeat. The loss of Peacocks and the beating she had suffered became connected, shaming.

She turned her back on the mirror and the portrait. She plied Graham and Karen with more drinks.

"It looks much worse than it is, you know," she said cheerfully. "Tell me what's been going on, will you? I'm starved of news."

They jumped at the opportunity. They told her about the

new managing director brought in by Robin, about his methods and innovations and the reorganization at Winwood. Harriet listened avidly, hardly able to believe that all this was happening without her, that she no longer held Peacocks in her hands.

"But what's he *like*, this new man?" she begged.

"Probably quite capable," Graham admitted. He would be, of course. Robin was no fool.

"But he's not *you*, Harriet," Karen wailed. "We all miss you so much."

"I miss you, too. But you never know. We may all get the chance to work together again some day."

Their faces were transformed at once. "Are you planning something?"

"It's too early to talk about anything yet." Harriet felt her nullity. It seemed more pronounced then than at any moment since the last meeting. *Come on,* she admonished herself. *For God's sake, Harriet.*

When they were leaving, Karen hugged her very carefully. Graham kissed her cheek. She didn't think he had ever done that before. "We'll keep in touch," they promised each other. When she was alone again Harriet carried the portrait out into the hallway and stowed it out of sight, in the back of a cupboard. Then she went back into her drawing room and picked up the old Shamshuipo board. With the tip of one finger she traced the path down the slope, examining each of the fragile gates and the penciled numerals beside them. Very gently she placed the counters in the bottom slots and set the balls behind the barrier at the top. She opened or closed the gates in their sequence, all the way down the slope. Then she released the balls. They set up their rolling and clicking. As she held the board, watching their pursuit through the maze, Harriet felt how fragile the old packing case had become. There was a long crack through the middle of the panel and the barely joined halves shifted in her grasp. The movement pushed Simon's ingenious grids a little out of alignment; wood of a slightly different color showed beneath them. Harriet gazed at the Japanese characters that even in the time she had possessed the board seemed to have faded almost to the color of the silvery wood. Soon they would no longer be distinguishable. Simon's game was slowly disintegrating.

She put the board down, but she still followed with her eyes the paths through the gates and the thickets of numerals.

She was thinking about the mugging. She was lucky, as the doctors had told her. The faceless attackers might have killed her. It was not inconceivable that she might have died, where she fell, at the top of the tunnel steps.

She thought again of Simon, joined to her by his game and by her mother, and of Miss Getz, who she would never know.

"Meizu" was a metaphor, as Simon had always been aware. Harriet touched the slots at the bottom, where the counters and the balls from her last shot lay snugly in their proper sequence. The conclusion was the same and inevitable, however directly or circuitously that conclusion was reached, and however high or low the score achieved en route. The recognition comforted her.

Harriet lifted her head. She did not want to spend any more time immured in her silent rooms, mourning the loss of her company and the failure of her love affair with Caspar, wearing her injuries like the marks of loss and failure.

She picked up the telephone and dialed the BBC. At length, she located Alison Shaw.

"Did you mean what you said about your place in Kent?"

"Of course."

"I can come and stay with you?"

"Of course. I'm going down there this evening. Can you be ready? Shall I come and pick you up?"

It was a Friday. "I'll be ready," Harriet said.

"Fine. I'll have to come back on Sunday evening, but you can stay down there for as long as you like."

Harriet packed a bag. It was a relief to put into it nothing but jeans and jumpers. No city suits, no silk shirts, no high-heeled shoes.

She hesitated over "Meizu," but in the end she put it away on a shelf in the same cupboard as her portrait. If the conclusion was indeed the same, she reckoned, then the route was everything. She was not covering any new ground by hiding within her own four walls. And if London made her feel sick and afraid, well then, she would try out some country roads.

Alison was cooking. The ground floor of her cottage was almost all kitchen. The tiny rooms of the original layout had been opened out to make one big one, a place of mountainous sofas, old pine cupboards, rag rugs and stone jars. The only other downstairs room was a small study that housed the television set and the video recorder. Alison kept the door to it firmly closed.

"I don't want the thing staring at me all weekend," she told Harriet.

Once or twice she retreated into the study to watch a program. Some of the rest of her time she spent working at a corner of the refectory table in the middle of the kitchen, books and notes and a dictaphone spread out around her. Observing her from one of the sofas, over the top of a newspaper, Harriet was reminded of her own days at Belsize Park, when she had worked hungrily and obsessively to start up Peacocks.

It was bewildering to find herself without work, without responsibilities. From time to time she would give a start, as if to shake herself out of a lazy reverie and back into full concentration. Then she would remember. There was nothing that required her concentration. She had read somewhere that amputees experienced a similar conviction, that the missing limb was still a living part of them.

Now, watching Alison assembling a complicated terrine of fish and tiny vegetables, she was aware that Alison possessed the enviable ability to do her work and then put it aside, in order to give her full attention to something else. She was absorbed, as she prepared their meal, in the rhythms of slicing and chopping and the manipulation of copper pans. She had spent the afternoon outside in the cottage's garden, clearing the winter's dead growth and freeing the new, green shoots of spring. Harriet had walked up and down the mossy paths, admiring the saffron and gold of daffodils and forsythia.

On her way to the compost heap with a barrowload of debris Alison had asked, "Are you bored? We could go to the pub, if you like. Or over to Canterbury, or something."

Guilty in the face of Alison's industry and evident contentment, Harriet had answered, "No, I'm not bored. I don't want to do anything, except exactly what we are doing." Nor did she, except that it was difficult to forget the insistent twitching of her amputated limb.

If she had Alison's reserves of interest and self-reliance, she thought, she might deal better with the alarming spaces around her.

"You're very good at everything," Harriet told her in genuine admiration. "Is there anything you can't do?"

Alison looked up from her leaf gelatin and green peppercorns. She waved one hand at the kitchen with its accretions of junk-shop finds, yellowing herbs and wildflower posters, dresser crowded with unmatched china and propped-up postcards.

"I'm not noticeably talented at making money, for example. I only have this place because it belonged to my parents."

Harriet frowned. "Perhaps you're lucky," she said contentiously.

Alison raised her eyebrow. "What are you saying? That you wish you didn't have yours?"

After a pause Harriet said, "I'd rather have my company. You have your job, and your garden, and this. A variety of other things, too, I imagine. The pursuit of wealth, although I didn't recognize it as such, precludes most other activities. Friendship. Love. As well as cookery and gardening and crossword puzzles."

"You don't seem to have done noticeably badly for love or friendship." Alison's tone was severe. "And perhaps you're just not interested in asters or anagrams? I think you'd fight like hell if anyone tried to take your fortune away from you."

"Do you think wealth corrupts?"

The atmosphere changed at once. Alison laughed, leaning against the table and wiping the corner of her eye with a tea towel. "You think you're corrupt? Listen, you're an intelligent woman assailed by guilt. You worked hard, you made a fortune on paper, then it turned into a real fortune because someone worked a slick deal. Then you went out late at night to buy some tea bags and rye crackers, and you got mugged and beaten up. Those are the facts. You can assemble them into any scenario of exploitation and retribution that suits your need to castigate yourself. You're rich. Your friends and relatives are smitten with jealousy, naturally enough. You'll have to learn to deal with that, just as they will.

"Do you think that if every possible cause of jealousy were removed, any of us would be any happier? Do you think that if all the wealth were removed from the world, all the corruption would disappear as well? Or would it simply be corruption of a more squalid and desperate variety? Come on, Harriet."

"As I keep exhorting myself," Harriet remarked.

"Good. You have to work out how to use your money and yourself. Decide how to use what you've got. If you're worried about unfashionable absolutes like goodness, or morality, you could tell yourself that it is probably easier to be a good rich person than a good destitute one. And work out the practicalities thereafter."

"That sounds extremely straightforward."

They were both laughing now.

"You can do it, you know."

"It?"

"Whatever you want. You are single-minded. You don't dissipate your energies, like most of us. When I came to interview you, you were about to leave for Los Angeles. But still you gave your entire attention to answering the questions. You were *savage* in your determination to say what you wanted, in the way you thought was best. It made a very good interview for me. If only you'd let us do a coda . . ."

"*No coda.*"

"Okay." Alison held up her hands in defense. "But me, I make a program, probably quite a decent program, then I come down here and move the shrubs I put in last springtime, and I cook lunch for people and get involved in an argument about public spending, one of those fruitless arguments that only start when everyone's drunk too much Rioja. It's not a path that leads straight to the Director General's office, is it? But you, Harriet, you are formidable."

"Thank you," Harriet said dryly. "And are you happy with the path, even if it doesn't lead to the right office?"

Alison thought for a moment. Then she said, "Yes."

"I can see you are. Whereas I haven't given any consideration to happiness since, I can't remember when."

"Perhaps you should."

"I'm sure I should. I've got plenty of time, now." Harriet got up from where she had been sitting and went over to where Alison stood surrounded by the detritus of cookery. She rested her elbows on the back of a Windsor chair and examined Alison's face. "Given our different characteristics, it's simple to work out which of us is the nicer person."

Alison shrugged volcanically. "Oh, *nicer*. If you're going to use bland notions like niceness then I don't think either of us qualifies. We aren't *nice* because we're busy, greedy, preoccupied, inquisitive and exacting. And why do you have to quantify which of us is more something than the other, in any case? Shows your competitiveness, doesn't it? You must have been one bloody awful sister."

"Poor Liza," Harriet said penitently. "I think I was. No wonder she decided to vote against me."

The realization, belated as it was, salved the affront. Harriet smiled. She found herself hoping that Leo was, at least, making her sister happy.

Alison held up the white china terrine that she had been decorating with bay leaves. "Finished. It needs to set now." She opened the door of the fridge that was adorned with half a dozen jokey magnets, and put the dish inside. "There's a chunk of beef that just wants to go in the oven. We can go to the pub while it's cooking."

"I haven't been into a pub for ages."

"You haven't missed much," Alison grinned at her.

They put on their jackets and walked down the dark lane together.

The air smelled of cold earth and animals, and their exhaled breath hung in faint, gloomy clouds in front of them. Harriet kept her eyes fixed on the single street lamp that had come on at the end of Alison's lane. The halo of chilly mist enveloping it reminded her of the light at the margin of Hampstead Heath, beyond which she had never passed in the darkness. The attack had come in the full glare of light, under the traffic of the main road, instead. As she walked, feeling the satisfactory slither of mud beneath her boots, Harriet discovered that the shivers had left her. She was out in the night, remembering what had happened to her, and she wasn't afraid.

She held her head up, walking faster so that Alison had to quicken her pace to keep up with her. She felt better, as if some sickness was at last responding to treatment.

They walked under the light at the corner, past a telephone kiosk with two teenage girls giggling outside it, and on down the village's single street to the pub. Alison pushed open the door of the saloon bar. The lights were yellow-bright, reflected from bottles and horse-brasses, making them both blink. There was a coal fire in a tiled grate, a dartboard in one corner, two or three huddles of incurious people and a fat man polishing glasses behind the bar.

It was very cozy and ordinary-seeming. The smell of beer and chalk and carbolic was familiar and reassuring. The publican greeted Alison cheerfully.

They sat down near the fire with their drinks. "It's nice here," Harriet said, looking around her. Darts plopped into the cork board behind them.

"*Nice*, again?" Alison demanded.

Harriet drank some of her Scotch. "Exactly. Safe and comfortable. I like it." From being a foreign land, the country seemed suddenly homely. They seemed to be much further from London than the two hours it had taken them to drive through the Friday evening traffic. They were sitting with their second drinks when one of the darts players came across and leaned over Alison's shoulder.

"You playing tonight, Alison?"

"Yes, I'll give you a game."

Harriet looked at her in disbelief.

"Harriet? Do you want to play?"

"I haven't played darts in a pub since I was a student."

"Dear me. Come on, we'll play doubles."

They followed the young man across the bar. He had straw-colored hair and meaty hands. "You haven't got a whole crowd down this weekend, then, Al?" somebody said.

"Not this weekend. This is Harriet," Alison said. Harriet shook hands with Geoff, and Ron, and Kenny and Liz. None of them stared at her. Ron, or perhaps it was Geoff, put his own darts into her hands.

Harriet put her toes to the line on the rubber mat, took careful aim. "I do warn you . . ." she murmured.

The dart missed the board altogether and hung at an angle from the cork shell.

"You're short of practice," Alison told her.

They lost the game, although Harriet was fired by the challenge and managed to hit the board thereafter.

"We've got to go," Alison said. "Dinner's in the oven."

"I was just getting into my stride."

"She was, too," Geoff or Ron encouraged her. "You should have your tea before you get down here, Al."

"You could be right."

A chorus of good nights followed them to the door. Harriet was smiling so widely her jaw began to hurt again. They set off back up the street, past the single shop and the bus shelter. The teenage girls had migrated there out of the drizzle.

"Last week it was L.A. and the Academy Awards," Harriet said. "Lord Olivier, Jack Nicholson, Cher." She was thinking of Caspar's diamond pool, the palm trees and the carpet of lights under the Hollywood Hills.

"Doesn't really compare with the Wheatsheaf on darts night, does it?" Alison answered.

They began to laugh, and found themselves laughing so much that they bumped together and stumbled in the darkness. The laughter made Harriet more light-headed than whiskey had ever done. "I like the Wheatsheaf a lot."

"It's very important to have contrasts," Alison told her portentously. "You might not like it so much if the Wheatsheaf was all you'd ever known."

"I think I may have erred in the other direction." Harriet contemplated the years of meetings, hotels and airplanes, and the infrequent holidays that involved more airplanes, different hotels.

"Lucky you've got me to put you straight with a game of darts."

"It is lucky." Harriet was serious, even though Alison was not. "I'm grateful. I'm not sure what would have happened if I hadn't come here with you this weekend. I think I might have gone slightly off the rails."

"Yes."

"So, thank you."

"Thank you for coming." They glanced at each other. Alison opened the front door of the cottage and the smell of roast beef came to meet them.

When they sat down at the refectory table Harriet looked at the length of it and the assortment of different chairs drawn up against it. She remembered what the man in the pub had said.

"Do you usually have a lot of people down here to stay the weekend?" She felt a touch of unwarranted jealousy.

"It varies. Sometimes I do, if I feel gregarious. Other times I'd rather be by myself. Or with just one person."

Harriet suppressed her curiosity. "And the people in the pub all know you? Call you *Al*?"

"Don't you? What if Head of Documentaries heard? I told you, I grew up here. I went to school in Tenterden. It's my home. I've known most of those people since I was small. Where do you come from? It's probably in the research notes, but I forget."

Harriet told her about Sunderland Avenue and the perspective lines of the houses preceding it, dwindling to the vanishing point before Ken, and the memories of it that Kath tried to discourage.

"I don't come from anywhere, really. I always thought of home simply as London. Only now I've been dispossessed." Unthinkingly, she put her hands up to her face. The unshelled crustacean image came back to her, and she realized that she had felt safely housed since she had come to Alison's cottage. "What's it like, still belonging to the place you grew up in?"

Alison wrapped her hands around her wineglass. Her face was rosy. "Irritating sometimes. But secure."

"I envy you," Harriet said truthfully.

They ate their meal, and Harriet did the washing up. Alison retreated into the television-study to watch another program, and when she emerged again they sat on opposite sofas to finish their bottle of wine. Alison read a book, and Harriet listened to some music with her hands clasped behind her head.

"The picture of harmony," Alison remarked at last, closing her book. She yawned. "Time for bed, I think."

Harriet's curiosity got the better of her. The question popped out. "When you come down here with just one person, is it a man?"

"When *I* tried to ask *you* about Caspar Jensen, you froze me solid with a glance."

"That was on camera. This is between these four walls. I'll tell you about Caspar, if you like."

"Fair exchange. Or not very fair, because my history isn't nearly as interesting." She drew her feet up beneath her, settling down. "Isn't this girly? Yes, sometimes there's a man. Not invariably the same one. There isn't one at all at present. I used to worry when there wasn't; lately I've started to accept that I feel just as comfortable on my own. I like my own company, and when I don't there's always the company of friends. I like my work, and it takes a lot of time. I don't need a man to complete me." She lifted her eyes to meet Harriet's. And Harriet, who on first meeting had decided that she was dumpy and plain, now realized that she was original, and, more than enviable, she was admirable. She began to wonder about all the principles that governed her own judgment.

"Don't you want to marry and have children?"

"I don't think so," Alison said calmly. She didn't turn the question back to Harriet. "Tell me about Caspar."

Harriet thought for a moment. "I thought I could reform him. I thought I could help him off the booze. The love of a good woman." After the Awards, she had thought, she would claim him. The willful optimism of it almost made her laugh now. "Every woman he's ever been involved with must have believed the same. Caspar doesn't want to be helped off the booze. Caspar likes himself the way he is. To imagine anything else is a conceit." She remembered Mulholland Drive, and the girl dead in the car. Anger and sadness fell around her like a curtain. She stared hard at the nap on a velvet cushion to hold back repetitive tears. "I loved him and then I stopped loving him." And then she added, "He's got a ten-year-old daughter, did you know? Her name's Linda."

Alison listened, and Harriet told her about Linda Jensen.

When she had finished Alison said, "You would like to have children." It was a statement, not a question.

"Not on my own, I wouldn't." Harriet was thinking of Jane and Imogen. And then of Jenny and Charlie. "I'm not even sure about with a husband, a partner. If I could find one. If I wanted one."

Alison slowly lifted her almost-empty glass. They drank a toast to each other. The salute was ironic, but they recognized the links of commonality, the beginnings of real friendship.

"Bedtime, I think," Alison repeated.

As she went up the narrow stairs Harriet knew that she had much to think about. She propped herself up on pillows in the plain white-walled bedroom, in which someone at some stage, probably long ago, had painted all the wooden furniture in shiny, harebell-blue paint. Harriet imagined Alison as a teenager, painting intently with her tongue between her teeth.

She had been intending to think, but for the second night in succession she fell asleep as soon as she closed her eyes.

In the morning Alison read all the Sunday papers with unswerving concentration. Harriet made a series of cups of coffee and wandered in the garden. There was, at last, a breath of mildness in the air. The low gray sky had softened, and there was a noise of birds in the elms that marked the garden's edge. A thin coat of fragile green seemed to have descended overnight, masking the black outlines of Alison's border shrubs. Harriet walked slowly, examining the moss that blurred the paving stones of the path, the sticky knobs of buds and the unraveling new shoots. The threat of rain in the still air made the morning seem all the more beneficent.

Harriet listened to the noises from the next garden beyond the beech hedge. A small child was riding what sounded like a tricycle on a concrete path. From time to time he called out, "Look!" and a woman's voice from further away praised and reassured him. Cooking smells mingled with the scents of earth and smoke and agriculture.

"Your garden's very pretty," Harriet said when she went inside again. "Cultivated but natural. I wish I knew what half the plants are."

"It's a mess at the moment," Alison sighed, without looking up from her paper. "Don't get interested in gardening, that's my advice. It's a tyranny as much as a pleasure. Look, there's a bit about Peacocks here." Harriet leaned over her shoulder to read it.

She learned that her company was making a smooth recovery under the new leadership of David Daventry, following the departure of charismatic entrepreneur Harriet Peacock, and that the confidence of the City in the high-performing "Meizu" outfit appeared to be unshaken.

"Who is this Daventry?" Alison asked.

"Robin's man. A capable administrator, I think. Rather gray, from what I remember." Harriet answered automatically. Realization left her winded, as if someone had hit her. Peacocks wasn't her company. It was Robin's and David Daventry's. The limb no longer twitched, her blood no longer flowed through it. It had been cut off.

After a moment she turned away from Alison's scrutiny. She

supposed that she would sometimes forget what had happened, and that remembrance would come with the same shock. All that would happen was that she would forget for longer intervals, and the shocks would lessen. She felt her body jumping with adrenaline. She wanted to run, to telephone, to launch herself into attack or defense, and it was much too late. Her hip caught the corner of the table, rattling the crockery that stood on it.

Alison said, "We need some mustard, if we're having cold beef for lunch. We finished the jar last night. The village shop will have some, it opens on Sunday mornings."

"Am I in the way?"

Alison refolded her Business Section. "Nope. We just need some mustard."

Harriet put on her coat. She walked down the lane very fast, so that her body might take up the adrenaline once more, and let her heart stop knocking. Curls of woodsmoke hung over the roofs of the neat double row of houses. Women in green padded jerkins walked dogs past gardens lined with scarlet tulips and sheets of grape hyacinths. One of the dogs carried a rolled newspaper in its jaws.

In the shop Harriet found the mustard and waited in a line of other shoppers who greeted one another and gossiped with the woman behind the till. The pace of the various transactions was noticeably slow, and Harriet shifted from one foot to the other. When her turn came at last, she was not excluded from the routine exchange of pleasantries. The shopkeeper swathed the mustard in a paper bag with minutely serrated edges and examined Harriet's face with concern as she handed over the package.

"Oh, dear. What was it, a car accident?"

"An accident, yes," Harriet agreed. Behind the woman's nylon-overalled shoulder she saw a small poster, copied on pulpy pink paper, taped to the wall between district council notices of proposed building works. The paper showed a hand, held palm upright, and the hand-lettered message, STOP BOTTRILL. For some reason, the name struck a faint association in Harriet's head.

She nodded pleasantly at the pink poster, mostly to divert the attention from her face.

"What's STOP BOTTRILL?"

The woman clicked her tongue. "Not local, are you?"

"No. Just staying a few days."

"Well, he's one of these big London men, isn't he? Bought a whole lot of land over to one side of the village there. There's a plan to build a dormitory town, or a new town, or whatever they call it. A lot of little boxes, anyhow. It's not right, is it? Not stuck on the side of a little place like this."

Harriet tracked down the association then. BOTTRILL must be Keith Bottrill, building magnate and property mogul. From what she had read about him, she gathered that his methods were not always admirable but he invariably achieved results.

"Who is organizing the opposition?"

"The Everden Association. Locals, again."

"I see."

Behind Harriet the remainder of the queue was growing restive in its turn. She tucked the mustard into her pocket and went back into the quiet street. On her way past the Wheatsheaf, she noticed that the car park was full to capacity.

At the cottage she found Alison laying the table. If Harriet had been eating a quick cold lunch she would have assembled the elements at random and consumed them standing up or walking around, if she had bothered to eat anything at all. But for Alison every meal was an occasion, even if she was sitting down to it alone. She had taken pretty plates down from the dresser and arranged the food on them, and placed a glass tumbler of dwarf narcissi in the center of the table. She took the mustard from Harriet, thanking her, and dropped a dollop of it into a tiny blue glass salt liner.

"So you don't go to the Wheatsheaf at lunchtimes?" Harriet asked as they sat down.

"Not on Sundays. It gets full of people in complicated jerseys who talk about the property market. We're only an hour's commute from Victoria, you know."

"It feels much further," Harriet mused. "How much do you know about Keith Bottrill? *Stop Bottrill*, rather."

"There's not much to know. No one is even certain whether he actually owns the piece of land this new town's supposed to be going up on. There's a halfhearted move to stop him, I think. Real David and Goliath stuff."

"The Everden Association."

"That sounds like it."

"I saw the poster in the shop. It looked like a notice for the playgroup bring-and-buy."

"That's certainly it. Would you like some wine? Beer?"

Harriet held out her glass. She was thinking. "Are you involved in it?"

Alison gave a hollow laugh. She waved a hand at her notes and files and the dictaphone perched on top. "I've got time to enter a battle in which nobody quite knows who the two sides are or on what bit of land the fight's going to be held? Besides, this is a small country. People need somewhere to live. Why not alongside the village of Everden, Kent?"

"Courtesy of Keith Bottrill? You know who he is?"

Alison laughed again, genuinely now. "It'll be courtesy of someone or other. Bottrill or clones of him put together by your friends the Landwiths or people like them."

"They're not my friends."

"I'm sorry, that was stupid." Alison put her hand out, contrite. "If you're interested, we could walk over this afternoon and have a look at the site he's supposed to have bought. It's pretty over there."

Harriet said, "Yes, I'd like that. A walk would be a good idea."

She knew that she needed the exercise. She still felt, uncomfortably, as if she wanted to run or to fight.

By the time they had finished their simple meal and cleared it away, it had begun to rain. Dark spots marked the stone path to the front gate.

"Waterproofs time," Alison said, unconcernedly. But Harriet only had her pale wool Nicole Farhi coat. Alison lent her a pair of Wellington boots and a deeply creased and scuffed Barbour jacket.

"I feel as if I'm going to a point-to-point."

Alison stared critically at her. "You don't much look it. You'll have to work on getting a few more broken veins and an authentic perm."

They took a small road that led away from the village between tall hedges. The rain and the dim light intensified the new green of the hawthorn leaves. They walked mostly in companionable silence, listening to the clop of their footfalls on the road. For about a mile they climbed a shallow incline, their view of the fields and little copses obstructed by the enclosing hedge. The road grew dark and shiny with rain, and moisture dripped from the twigs and overhanging branches. Only one car passed them, a Golf driven much too fast. They pressed themselves against the wet bank to let it pass in a jet of fine spray.

"Wheatsheaf Sunday lunchtime people," Alison said sourly.

Harriet shrugged as they walked on. She was thinking about the image of England that Linda had missed in Santa Monica. It was a soft, greeny-gray place, just like this. Linda would like Everden. It was a real place, with edges and a middle, not just a collection of fine houses like Little Shelley.

They came to the top of the hill. On the other side the ground stretched away in smooth folds, big fields bordered by oak trees, the ribbed surface of plow alternating with pasture. The land rose again in the near distance up to the crown of a thickly wooded hill, enclosing a sheltered hollow too gently contoured to be called a valley.

It began to rain more heavily. Fine gray shawls of it swept in from the north. The view was masked, and then revealed again.

Alison beckoned Harriet to a field gate. They leaned over the bars of it, watching the rain and the changing patterns of light.

"Can you see down there?" Alison stood on the bottom bar of the gate and pointed. "The chimneys of a house, just in that belt of trees?"

Harriet followed the direction of her finger. Gray chimneys were just visible over the tops of huge, old trees. The new growth of leaves did not yet mask the untidy clumps of rooks' nests in the top branches.

"The land goes with the house. The house has been empty for five years, perhaps a bit more. When I was a kid the same family had owned the place forever. Then it was sold, and sold again. I don't think either of the last owners ever really lived in it. They were probably trying to work their own deals for developing the land. I think the house is in a poor structural state now. That would be in the owners' interest, wouldn't it, claiming that it's uninhabitable?"

"What's it called?"

"Birdwood."

"And where will the new town be?"

Alison made a sweep with her hand. It covered the plowed and bitten-green fields, the stand of trees, and all the land in a circle around the house.

Harriet saw it. There would be a crop of red and yellow brick houses with dormer windows like eyebrows in the new tiled roofs and tiny porches jostling one another. There would be patches of garden turning their backs behind raw fencing, and rotary washing lines, and television aerials. There would be none of the proper, old glue of Everden to hold the new building blocks together, no shop, no proper pub, no center. The new-town people would have to get in their cars and drive somewhere else to find a center. They would simply occupy their red and yellow houses in the middle of the quiet gray landscape.

"They can't," Harriet said. "There's no reason to create a town there."

"Bottrill has a reason."

"Can we go down and have a closer look?"

It was raining hard. Harriet's hair was plastered to her head.

Alison seemed unaffected by the weather but she asked, "Are you sure you want to?"

"Yes, I want to."

They began to walk on, down the gentle hill. As they went on Harriet saw that the apparent remoteness of the house in its hollow was an illusion. They turned a corner and another village was revealed as an outcrop of houses around a church tower. From the opposite side of the road Everden was also visible. To Harriet the old villages looked like comfortable, settled accretions around their two churches. The thought of the rash of hard new houses at the third point of the triangle seemed the more incongruous. It was further than it had looked from the top of the slope to Birdwood. They were very wet when they reached the stone gateposts of the house. A heavy iron gate stood half open. The sagging corner of it had dragged a furrow in the driveway. The only sound was water dripping from the branches.

Harriet turned in a circle. The Birdwood hollow had become secluded again. Only trees and fields were visible.

"Show me the house," she murmured to Alison.

They walked up the driveway shoulder to shoulder, trying to step quietly, like intruders. The house emerged from behind its trees. Harriet saw a big, square, stone-faced facade, windows asymmetrically placed, a pillared portico, the far corner of the building rounding out into a little turret. She crossed a stretch of gravel that had erupted into thickets of weeds and looked down the southern face of the building. A veranda in a complicated design of wrought iron was half-shrouded in creepers. Turning back to where Alison stood Harriet noticed that the boarded-up windows of the ground-floor rooms had been sprayed with black aerosol paint, CAZ & FRAN, and indecipherable symbols, over and over again. She shivered involuntarily and then remembered the association of graffiti with tunnels, deserted urban corners, and felt sad for being dispossessed of the City that had always been home.

"What do you think?" Alison was standing with her head back, her hands in the pockets of her mackintosh.

Birdwood House was part minuscule château, part Victorian-Gothic folly, wholly neglected. Broken slates scattered among the weeds indicated holes in the roof. The interior must be in worse condition than the shell, Harriet thought.

"Sad," she answered. "Sad to see a house rotting away. Sadder still to think of hideous little houses covering it, and all its land."

The garden was a dripping mass of heavy foliage. There

must once have been a properly gloomy Victorian shrubbery, but now it was a tangle of leathery evergreens and bare, twiggy branches. Around a rough oval of shaggy grass were raised hydrangea bushes, last year's dead heads standing out as fists of sullen khaki.

"They need not be hideous," Alison said mildly. "They might be perfectly nice."

"Nice?"

"Okay, decent. Serviceable houses in a pretty piece of countryside for people who need somewhere to live. Why not?"

"No reason. I just know not. I can feel it."

"All I can feel is rain running down the back of my neck. Can we go home now?"

Harriet hesitated. She took another long look at the closed facade, averting her gaze from the black scribbles that disfigured its blind eyes.

Finally she said, "Let's go, then. There's nothing to be done here." They walked through the downpour back to Everden.

In the early evening Alison began to gather up her work and pack it into her briefcase. Harriet sat at the long table watching her.

"I want to be back in town by about eight," Alison told her. "What are you going to do? You can stay here as long as you like, you know that."

"Thank you," Harriet said. "I'd like to stay for a bit, if you'll let me."

She couldn't go back to Hampstead, to the rooms that seemed a shell in comparison with the homeliness of Alison's cottage, and she had no idea where else to turn. She looked at Alison's preparations for her working week with sudden suffocating envy. Alison had preoccupations, challenges to meet, reasons for leaving and hurrying and using her resources. It seemed inconceivable to Harriet that she herself had none of these things, and at the same time she knew that she must make herself conceive it, because it was the truth.

She listened numbly to Alison's instructions about the boiler and the hot water supply and the security bolts.

"Will you be all right here by yourself?" Alison asked, already half out of the front door with her briefcase. Harriet glared at it, as if it was a badge of office of which she had been stripped.

"Of course I will. Go on. Thanks for everything."

"I'll have to take the car, you know."

Harriet had accepted Alison's offer of a lift from Hampstead.

"So if I need to go anywhere I can walk or call a taxi or get a train. Go *on*."

"Will you be here when I get back on Friday?"

"If you don't mind me being . . ."

"I'd like it. See you then." Alison smiled at her, and closed the door.

Harriet listened to the car receding up the lane. When she could hear it no longer the silence seemed so absolute that she was momentarily afraid, and then overtaken by an awareness of loss and disappointment more powerful than anything she had felt since Robin's moment of victory. She put her hand out to the back of a chair to steady herself, then half-sat and half-fell into it. She folded her arms on the table and let her head drop forward to rest on them.

Harriet cried, giving herself up to a fit of weeping like a perverse luxury. She cried for a long time, but at length she lifted her head and looked around the kitchen through the slits of swollen eyelids. She had the sudden sense of apartness from herself, as if she was perched somewhere on the shelves of the old dresser, surveying herself from among the plates and flowered china cups. She saw her own hunched shoulders and distorted face, and the irregular wet patch that she had made on the table-top, and she disliked what she saw.

Harriet took a long, ragged breath. Then she went slowly upstairs to the bathroom. She washed her face in icy water, combed her hair and put on a lick of make-up. Then she changed her sweater in the blue-painted bedroom. Without another glance at her reflection she took Alison's old Barbour off the peg behind the kitchen door, made sure the windows were locked in the way Alison wanted, locked the front door securely behind her, and set off down the lane toward the Wheatsheaf.

The fire was lit again and the landlord seemed to be polishing the same glass, but the bar was almost empty. Sunday evenings were clearly not as popular as lunchtimes. Harriet bought herself a drink and sat down in a corner. Slowly, in ones and twos, the locals began to drift in. Tentatively, unsure of the protocol of the country pub, Harriet nodded and smiled at the darts players of the night before.

She was rewarded with the question, "Al gone back to London and left you, then?"

"Yes. I'm going to stay on for a few more days."

"To improve your darts?"

Harriet smiled again, accepting the joke.

As she had hoped it would, conversation became general, and she was drawn into it. Within a few minutes she was able to ask her intended questions.

"What do people think about the development on the Birdwood site? Are many of them involved in the Stop Bottrill campaign?" After that she had only to listen, and nod her head.

She learned that no one was in favor of the plan, but no one knew exactly what was proposed, or who really owned the site, or what planning permission had been granted or applied for. The opposition campaign was being run by a village committee that included the vicar and the chairman of the parish council. Whatever truth was discernible was distorted by rumor and exaggeration and hearsay.

"Why are you so interested?" someone asked, with evident suspicion. Harriet became the focus of the room's attention.

"It's only interest," she said lightly. "Alison and I had a walk over there this afternoon. It's a beautiful piece of country."

A girl in a denim jacket who hadn't spoken before suddenly lifted her head. She had a thin face half hidden by waves of colorless hair. "Yeah. And they'll put beautiful houses on it with fancy names like the Tudor or the Devenish or something, three or four bedrooms and two bathrooms and a joined-on garage, and the young executives will come and live in them and catch the train up to town every morning and their wives will shop in London or Canterbury and park their Volvos out in the street there. There's nothing over on Birdwood for the local people, is there? No houses for people from around here who haven't got a hundred thousand for the Tudor, nor a hundred and twenty for the cottages down the end there that some incomer'll buy and knock together to make one big house out of two decent little ones that would have done for Mick and me."

Her boyfriend put his big hand on her knee. She took a defiant gulp from her half-pint beer mug after her long speech and retreated behind her waterfall of hair.

"That doesn't mean Alison, you know," someone said kindly to Harriet. "The place is hers by right because it was her dad's. But what Susan says is true enough. There's no houses around here that the young people can afford. It's all executives, isn't it?"

Harriet was quiet. She was assimilating the fact that houses that looked to her like ugly little boxes disfiguring a pretty piece of countryside might equally appear to Mick and his girl as pinnacles of unattainable executive luxury.

I've forgotten, she thought. *I've forgotten what it was like not to be rich.*

"If you're interested in all this village politics, you could always go and talk to the vicar," Ron or Geoff the darts player told her.

I don't want to forget. Harriet was remembering the beach in Crete, where all things had promised to be equal.

"Or old Miss Bowlly," Geoff or Ron's counterpart added.

"Who is Miss Bowlly?"

Miss Bowlly, Harriet learned, was an elderly lady who lived in a small house on a little patch of land at the edge of the Birdwood site. Opinion had it that Miss Bowlly's two acres of ground straddled the only feasible route for the new access road, that without Miss Bowlly's corner of ground as part of the package the entire Birdwood development was impracticable, that Miss Bowlly had been offered millions, that she had refused even to contemplate selling and had chased the negotiators away with a shovel. Harriet also deduced that all of this could be mere rumor, just like everything else connected with Keith Bottrill's development scheme. Probably Bottrill intended it to be so. And then one day the bulldozers would move in.

Harriet finished up her second drink. She edged out of her chair in the corner, nodded a series of good nights to her new acquaintances, and left the discussion to meander on without her.

In the morning, Harriet was up early. She judged that there was no point yet in paying a call on the vicar. Instead she walked out of the village and up the gentle hill to the point where Birdwood House was just visible in its fringe of trees. The rain had stopped overnight and the sky was lighter, pearl-gray over the opposite lip of hillside. The view was clearer, and Harriet could distinguish a gray cottage over to the right of the big house. She followed the road onward, down the hill and past the rutted driveway. She walked on until she came to the cottage. There was a low wall separating it from the road, a square of scrubby garden overlooked by windows heavily shrouded in grayish net. Harriet put her fingers to the catch of the gate. At once, with alarming rapidity, the front door opened. A small, square woman confronted her.

"Miss Bowlly?" Harriet asked pleasantly.

The response was neither friendly nor encouraging. "What do you want?"

"I'm a friend of Alison Shaw's." Harriet had decided that the local approach was the best one.

"Never heard of her," Miss Bowlly snapped. The door almost closed, then reopened a crack.

"Netty Shaw?"

"Alison's her daughter," Harriet guessed.

The crack yielded no further, but Miss Bowlly demanded, "Well?"

"I wondered if I could come in and talk to you for five minutes."

The response was immediate, and vehement. "I'm not selling, or signing anything."

"I'm glad," Harriet said. "You certainly shouldn't sell, and I've nothing for you to sign."

The crack did widen then.

"You can come in for five minutes, that's all."

Quickly, before she could change her mind, Harriet slipped in through the front door.

"This way," Miss Bowlly sniffed. Harriet followed her down a short, gloomy hallway, into the kitchen at the back.

Fingers of indefinable familiarity had tugged at Harriet from the moment she had reached the front gate, but in the kitchen the association suddenly became clear. She looked slowly around her at the stacks of yellowing newspapers, the cardboard boxes filled with egg cartons and empty cereal packets and old telephone directories, the hoarded magazines and broken kitchen implements and domestic junk piled under a thick coating of dust on every flat surface in the room. Miss Bowlly's house reminded her of Simon's.

For a moment Harriet might have been back with him, behind the papered-over windows. There was the same beleaguered atmosphere, the same dusty scent of long entrenchment. She found herself wishing that she was indeed back in the old house, so that she might do things differently.

Miss Bowlly stared at her. Harriet knew the difference was that Simon could not defend himself against intruders, whereas she suspected that Miss Bowlly was capable of seeing off all comers. At close quarters she saw that Miss Bowlly was older than she had seemed at first glance, perhaps in her mid-seventies. She was wearing Wellingtons, a tubular tweed skirt, and a brown hand-knitted cardigan.

"It's not supposed to be the House Beautiful," the old woman announced. "And I don't know any Nettie Shaw. Said the first name that came into my head, to test your reaction. All liars, you people with your plans and schemes." She chuckled broadly, delighted with her little trick.

"I do know Alison Shaw," Harriet said humbly. "She lives across in Everden, I've borrowed her cottage for a few days. Her mother's dead, I couldn't have known her name. But she might have been a friend of yours, mightn't she?"

"Well, she wasn't. What do you want?" And after a second's gap while Harriet marshaled her questions, "Tea, I suppose?"

"Thank you. Only if you were going to make some."

The tea when it came was thick and brown, but more palatable than Simon's. Harriet drank it and found herself answering questions rather than asking them as she had planned.

"There's no such thing as *just* being interested," Miss Bowlly told her at the end. "No such thing at all. What do you want?"

Harriet shrugged gently, evading the question. "Tell me why you won't sell to Mr. Bottrill?"

"No one's ever mentioned Mr. Bottrill to me. It's all done in the name of some company. But I've seen him snooping around here, following his young men in their nice coats. And no one's mentioned selling either. Nothing as firm and solid as that. A site option's what they call it. Tuppence ha'penny now, and twenty-five percent of some pie in the sky if he gets his planning permission. I told them I wasn't signing any agreement, and I didn't want their nice slice of profit when the time came either."

"Why not?" Harriet moved a little further forward on her rickety chair. Miss Bowlly gave her alarming chuckle.

"Because I didn't like them, simple as that. Nice as could be to start with, and then when I wouldn't agree to what they wanted they started coming around here to threaten me, saying that lorries would be coming by here day and night, they'd be digging up all around to make roads, it would be noisy and dirty and dangerous and the place would be worth nothing anyway because they were going to build here whatever I did, so why didn't I be a good girl and take something for nothing now, and move to a nice modern bungalow when the time came?"

Miss Bowlly clapped her hands on her knees, rocking with pleasure at the thought of her own stubbornness.

"I decided they wouldn't get any option on my property, and I wouldn't sell either, not even if they offered me two million pounds. Which they won't, see, because they don't like tying up their capital in options." She screwed up her eyes and squinted through the slits at Harriet. Harriet recognized that Miss Bowlly knew exactly what she was talking about.

"So I'm going to stay right here, and Castoria Developments can put their access road somewhere else, can't they?"

The chuckle developed into a roar of laughter.

"They don't like it. They try all sorts of tricks, but I'm up to them all. You're probably one, whatever you say."

"I'm not," Harriet said quietly. She drained the last of her brown tea and cleared a space to put the cup down. "But would you sell, to another group with a better scheme? One that took account of local needs, for example?"

"No," Miss Bowlly said.

Their eyes met. It was Harriet who looked away first. She stood up, and stepped carefully around the boxes piled up on the floor.

"Thank you for the tea."

"Remember what I said."

She followed Harriet to the door, watched her while she latched the gate behind her, and continued to watch until Harriet had climbed the hill toward Everden. Harriet walked quickly, with her head up. She was whistling a little tune, and her arms swung in time with it.

At the cottage, in Alison's television study, Harriet picked up the old-fashioned black telephone and dialed Charlie Thimbell's number.

"Charlie," she said, after they had exchanged greetings, "you owe me a favor." And Charlie, who had written up the irresistible Peacocks story and had accordingly reduced the value of Harriet's shares for sale, could only agree that he did owe her a favor.

"I'm calling it in," Harriet said.

"What do you want me to do?"

"I want some information. As much information as possible, about a company called Castoria Developments and about Keith Bottrill, and a project development at Birdwood, near Everden, in Kent."

"Is that all?" Charlie said dryly.

"For now."

Charlie sighed and drew his book of addresses toward him. "I'll see what I can do."

"Call me tomorrow, at this number."

"Where are you?"

"At Everden, of course. Talk to you tomorrow."

When Harriet hung up again, she was smiling. She opened the local directory. She would need a taxi to take her to the station. She would go to London for the day, pick up her own car, and do some investigation of her own.

She didn't think about it as she waited for the taxi to arrive, but she no longer felt jealous of Alison's occupation.

Eighteen

"THERE'S A HOUSE," Harriet told Jane, "a Victorian-Gothic folly with a turret, and a wrought-iron veranda, half-falling down. It was built in the eighteen-seventies by a man called Farrow, who made his money as a soap manufacturer. The land is what's left of his parkland."

Jane was looking out of her front window. The Greek family directly opposite had painted the sooty old bricks of their house a brilliant canary-yellow color. Its virulence seemed to beam straight into Jane's living room, reflecting off her walls and seeping into dim corners.

"You look better," Jane said. "And I thought it was just the country air."

Harriet had driven up to the Hackney house at the end of the afternoon, color in her cheeks and a folder of papers under her arm. Jane transferred her gaze from the yellow facade to Harriet's face.

"Go on. Tell me. You've seen a soap manufacturer's falling-down Victorian folly somewhere in the depths of commuter Kent, and you want it?"

"Yes, I want the house. But I want the land as well."

"To garden in? You've never even grown a pot of marigolds."

"*All* the land," Harriet said. "The development site."

"But . . ." Jane began to say something, and then she stopped. They were both aware of the soft and mysterious weight of Harriet's money between them. Jane couldn't guess what it might be capable of purchasing. "You're not a property developer."

"Not the Bottrill kind, fortunately. But I have had an idea."

Harriet opened her folder and spread the contents on Jane's flokati rug beside Imogen in her basket. There were copies of planning regulations, developers' prospectuses, and a mass of other material. Harriet had had a busy afternoon.

Jane picked up the nearest prospectus and glanced at a pastel-tinted drawing of gabled white houses set in wide, lush gardens. She put it down again, quickly, and looked instead at the back of sleeping Imogen's head, where the dark fringe of baby hair curled in the tiny furrow of her neck. Then she looked up from Imogen, to Harriet.

Harriet's face seemed to have changed completely. The bones that after the mugging had seemed ready to dissolve under the bruised flesh were firm again. The discoloration was fading, the swellings an irrelevance. It was the old Harriet.

Jane smiled, then. "What idea?"

"If I can acquire the land somehow, as a capital investment— whatever parts of it that Bottrill doesn't own options on, yet, because he won't tie up his own capital until he's sure of planning permission—and there's at least one crucial parcel he can't option, perhaps more, then I can put forward my own scheme, win over the local support, make Bottrill see that he can't realize his own plans. He'll have to back out and leave the field to me. Putting it at its simplest, that is."

"But you're doing just the same as he is."

"No," Harriet said. "There's a difference. I'm not planning to put up three- or four-bed executive houses, dumped into the landscape for a quick sale to outsiders who won't put anything back into the local community at all. I'd like to see some starter homes, first offered to local couples, and a proportion of them available for rent. They'd be built in the local style, with none of those stained-wood windows. There'd be a mix of other buildings, too, like in any real village—some bigger houses, a corner shop, perhaps a pub or a village hall, even some workshops."

The words came faster. Her hands drew hipped roofs and streets and intersections in the air. Jane watched her, fascinated.

"There could be a proportion of sheltered housing, a village green, a pond with ducks, if you like. I can raise the money for the development three times over, once I've acquired the land and been granted planning permission. There'll be a return on investment, of course, substantial enough even though not as big as it would be on an executive dormitory."

Jane held up her hand, stopping the flow. "Why do you want to do all this?" She meant, *You needn't work at all. You could play with the money you've already got, enjoy yourself. You don't have to teach* The Catcher in the Rye *to threatening schoolchildren.*

Harriet answered simply. "Because it's there. Because I saw it."

"Just as 'Meizu' was there, and you saw that?"

Harriet remembered the shiver that had traveled down her spine when she first saw Simon's game. She had felt it again as she walked with Alison around the dripping bulk of Birdwood House, past the boarded-up windows with their black graffiti hieroglyphs. Only she had weakly dismissed it as fear. As soon as she knew that what she had felt was not fear but intuition, confidence flowed back into Harriet like fresh blood in her veins. "Yes. Exactly like 'Meizu.' "

The simplicity of her words didn't mask the moment of exultation. Sitting as close to her as she was, Jane caught a strong whiff of Harriet's fuel, compressed within her and ready to burn. The sense of it made her feel faintly awed. For the first time, she understood that it was not money that motivated Harriet at all, but a much older and rawer necessity. *Winning.*

It was not the attack in the subway that had collapsed Harriet's bones and drained the vivacity out of her. It had been loss, and defeat.

Harriet was talking again. "I'd like to restore the house. Perhaps live in it myself, while the development's under way. Couldn't you and Imogen come too? Take your own half?" She nodded through the window at the glaring yellow house. "You could leave the school, and this place. There's a school in Everden, I saw it. It would be the perfect solution."

There was generosity of a sweeping kind in the suggestion, Jane knew that. She knew also that there was no point in expressing hurt or irritation because Harriet did not understand that she might not want to subordinate herself to someone else's grand scheme, to become a Birdwood appendage. It was simply Harriet's way to see the bold outlines, and in the magnificence of the vision to overlook the small details.

"Thank you for thinking of it," she said calmly. "But Imogen and I must make our own plans." And then, with reciprocal but much deeper and more painful generosity, she made her suggestion. Even though she suspected that Harriet would never even guess at how generous she was being.

"If you're really serious about all this, you should talk to David Howkins."

"Who?" Harriet asked, as Jane had known she would.

"David Howkins. He's a builder, specializing in community projects. You met him here, once."

"Oh, yes," Harriet said. "It was twice. He was wearing a blue shirt, the first time." She had imagined, very briefly, what it would be like to go home with him. It had been her first party after her separation from Leo. It seemed a very long time ago, now. "Perhaps I will."

"How *are* you going to do it all?" Jane asked, interested.

Harriet was candid. "I don't know, yet. I'll find a way. I'm hoping Charlie can help. I said he could call me here this evening, is that okay?"

"Of course it is."

It was only a few minutes later, when Jane was giving Imogen her bedtime feed and Harriet was standing in the window bay looking blankly out into the street, that she saw Charlie drawing up in his Citroën. Jenny was in the passenger seat.

"Here *is* Charlie, and Jenny as well."

Jane looked up, smooth-faced, ever hospitable. "Good."

Harriet let them in. There had been the windfall of an unscheduled babysitter, and they had snatched at the opportunity. They would have a quick drink, and then leave Jane and Harriet in peace, go on to supper somewhere . . .

"No you won't," Jane said firmly. "You'll stay here and eat with Harriet and me. Won't they, Harriet?"

It was like one of the old evenings and unlike the careful dinner that Harriet had given in the Hampstead flat. Imogen was put to bed in her cot upstairs, and Jane made omelets and salad while Charlie opened bottles of wine and poured liberal drinks. Harriet could see that he was pleased, and that he was keeping whatever it was that he was pleased about to himself until the right moment. She entered the game, and asked no questions about his discoveries.

They ate at the kitchen table, looking out at the little square of garden and the patches of gardens and lighted windows belonging to the backs of the houses opposite. Harriet felt a rekindling affection for London, reassuring her that she was not running away to Birdwood. She was going out to Birdwood because there was something to do there, she was convinced of it.

She stopped thinking about it then. She ate, and talked, and laughed as they had done a long time ago.

At last, Jane made coffee and put the pot in the middle of the table. Charlie filled up the glasses with a theatrical flourish like a preface to his big speech, so that Jenny laughed at him. Her latest pregnancy was visible under her loose shirt, but she looked much better than she had done at Harriet's dinner.

"Past the worse," she had explained. Now she said, "Charlie's just like Harry with a secret. He can't wait to tell it. Go on, Charlie."

Charlie raised his eyebrows and looked at each of them in turn.

"Go on, Charlie," Harriet echoed. Her attention was refocused, pin-sharp.

Charlie said, "I talked to someone who has a good friend inside the Castoria Development Company."

The light from the lamp hanging low over Jane's kitchen table drew them into a circle, like a cabal. Harriet felt a draft of excitement, potent as a drug, and knew what she had suffered from its withdrawal.

"Who revealed some interesting details, after a certain amount of persuasion." Harriet knew that it was not her place to inquire too closely into what the methods of persuasion had been. She should take the information and use it, as the dues that Charlie owed her.

Charlie told them that Keith Bottrill had been in pursuit of the Birdwood site for almost five years. He had been slowly and painstakingly signing up a jigsaw puzzle of option agreements, fitting his potential acquisitions together, across what was most probably a forty-acre site. Charlie had not been able to discover from his informant exactly how much of the ground he had already placed under option, or even the exact dimensions of the site itself.

"But I do know that he must be close to whatever he needs. He's putting his plans forward to the country planning committee at their meeting in five weeks' time. Once he has even outline planning permission, he's more or less home and dry."

Harriet nodded slowly. Five weeks was hardly long enough for her to set about acquiring her own options or even buying outright whatever land she might be able to discover. There was hardly time for her to appoint a team of architects, let alone to produce rival plans of her own.

Her only chance was to oppose the Castoria scheme at the planning committee stage, using whatever grounds she could come up with, and to lobby support for her own tenuous proposal.

She thought of Everden, and the Wheatsheaf, the village shop, and decaying Birdwood house in its deceptive seclusion.

I can do that, she thought. *I can do at least that much.*

"Two more things," Charlie said. He was trying to sound casual, but Harriet knew that he would have kept the good news until last.

"There's one parcel he does want and can't get. Two acres straddling the natural lie of the main access road."

"They belong to a Miss Bowlly," Harriet told him. "I've met her, and I liked her."

Charlie suppressed his flicker of admiration. "That won't

matter much, in the end. He can put his road somewhere else, at a price, and make your Miss Bowlly's life as uncomfortable as he's no doubt already threatened."

"What's the second thing?"

"He doesn't own the old house either, or the garden, which is another couple of acres more centrally placed in relation to the site as a whole."

Patiently Harriet asked, "So who does own it?"

Charlie looked at each of them again. And then he announced, with the air of a conjurer brandishing the rabbit, "Everden parish council."

Harriet stared at him for an instant, and then she started to laugh. "I should have gone to see the vicar, like they told me in the Wheatsheaf. I should have asked the right questions, and I could have found that out for myself in five minutes. But do you know what? It's the best piece of news I've had for months."

She pushed her chair back and went around the table to Charlie. She put her arms around his shoulders and kissed the top of his head.

"Charlie, thank you. Listen, drink a toast with me, Jane, Jenny. To the Birdwood Project."

They lifted their glasses, looking at each other with resignation, and repeated, "The Birdwood Project!"

Harriet was already reckoning. If Bottrill had not been able to acquire the house and grounds from the parish council, then some or all of the councillors must oppose his plans. And if there was opposition to one scheme then, through the forces of reaction, she might be able to muster support for another. If it was the right scheme, the village's own. If she could make hers theirs.

"Don't you want to hear how the parish council comes to own two acres of prime development land and a Victorian mansion?"

"Tell me."

Harriet could have worked it out for herself. The last owner, an old lady of eccentric habits had sold off the parkland belonging to the estate in small slices to various buyers over a number of years. They were the same buyers, or their heirs, on whom Keith Bottrill was assiduously working in the process of his site assembly. The house and its diminished garden had remained in her possession and then, on her death, had been willed to "The village of Everden, for the use of the community in perpetuity, under the care and administration of the members of the Parish Council."

"It's probably an embarrassment," Charlie said cheerfully. "Falling into decay, and so not much mentioned by anyone. Bottrill must be waiting for embarrassment to reach the point of overcoming apathy, so the vicar and the rest of them are driven to selling out to him. They'll have no hope of doing anything useful with it for the benefit of the village, because there won't be any money."

"There is money," Harriet said.

The small silence that acknowledged the mysterious power of her wealth followed the words. "I thought you wanted to live in the house," Jane said at length. "You invited me and Imogen to share it with you."

"I wish you would. You said you wanted to make your own plans. I do want to restore it, it's a beautiful house."

"And what about the village?"

"What are the alternatives? To have someone restore it to live in is better than standing back and seeing it knocked flat for development, isn't it? If I buy the house from Everden, in return the village will get a development on its doorstep that caters to local needs. Including a hall, or council chambers or a Scout hut, whatever it is they happen to need. To benefit Everden *in perpetuity*."

Jane was laughing. "Will there be a crèche and a pensioners' drop-in center? It sounds clever on your part, and at the same time much more my sort of thing than yours. I don't believe it will work, but I can't disapprove of the plan on paper, can I?"

"Don't disapprove of it. It's a fair scheme; it offers something for everyone."

"Including the entrepreneur, of course."

"Of course," Harriet said.

Charlie reached out for the bottle. "Shall we finish this?" he asked mildly.

They sat up late, the four of them. And then, after Charlie and Jenny had gone, hospitable Jane was pleased by Harriet's agreeing to stay the night in the spare bedroom she had occupied before, and Harriet was happy to be there instead of feeling the necessity to go back to her pale, silent flat. She went to bed more ready to wake up again than she had been for weeks.

It was the beginning of May.

Harriet parked her car in the shelter of a tall wooden hoarding and picked her way through the site entrance. A fork-lift truck passed in front of her loaded with yellow-gray London stock bricks, old bricks that were already faded and weathered. At the far end of the row of emergent terraced houses the roof joists were still exposed, but nearer to Harriet there were sash windows already in place and carpenters were working inside the raw brick rooms. There was a buzz of machinery underscored by the rhythmic churning of concrete mixers.

Ahead of Harriet the ground was a yellowish quagmire bridged by planks. Harriet glanced down at her leather pumps. A boy came toward her pushing a barrow, the wheel centered on the plank pathway. In the first sun of the summer he was already stripped to the waist. He stopped wheeling and whistling for long enough to give Harriet a thorough stare.

"I'm looking for David Howkins."

The boy pointed toward a trailer at the opposite end of the site and trundled his barrow onward. Harriet set off along the planks, past the carpenters and the concrete mixers. A chorus of whistles pursued her. At Winwood they hadn't whistled, she remembered, but then at Winwood she had been the boss. She thought of Winwood inconsequentially now, without the twitch of a severed limb.

When she looked up she saw David, walking in the mud in reinforced boots. His pugilist's face seemed less surprising in this setting.

"Didn't you know that building sites are dirty places?"

"The first on-site lesson," Harriet answered composedly. "I'll wear overalls next time." They shook hands. They had spoken on the telephone to arrange this meeting, but it was the first time they had met since Jane's Christmas party.

"Come into the office."

The little cabin was stuffy after the sunshine outside. It was furnished with metal desks covered with site plans and architectural drawings, typists' chairs and builders' merchant calendars. It took Harriet back to the days of grim bargaining with Mr. Jepson in his cubbyhole at Midland Plastics. Only she hoped that she wasn't going to have to bargain with David Howkins.

At the thought Harriet was overcome by a sense of overpowering urgency. There was far too little time, and everything that needed to be accomplished must still be done slowly, and tactfully. She perched on the corner of one of the metal desks, ready to jump up again. A girl clicking at an electric typewriter stopped work and looked at her.

"Would you like tea, or coffee, Harriet?" David asked.

I want to get down to business, she might have answered. But she said economically, "Coffee, please, milk but no sugar."

David dispatched the typist to make it.

"I was sorry to read about Peacocks," he told her. Harriet was aware that he was looking closely at her. It made her want to shift her position on the corner of the desk, but she held herself still.

"It's given me the opportunity to develop other ideas." She did move then, to reach down for her briefcase that stood at her feet.

"And what happened to your face?"

Harriet put her hand up to her jaw. She had forgotten about it. "It was just an accident."

She was reflecting that her relationship with David Howkins had moved in the opposite direction from the norm. He had begun by trying to kiss her and she had resisted a strong urge to follow him home, to wherever that was. They had progressed to conversation tinged with abrasiveness at a Christmas party, and now they were formally and politely embarked on a business meeting at his site office. The corners of Harriet's mouth lifted involuntarily. David went on looking at her.

The coffee came, still revolving in the mugs. Brown eyes of powder circled like planets. Harriet drew a mouthful before snapping open her briefcase.

"Tell me what your plan is," David said, settling in his chair to listen.

Harriet described Birdwood, drawing the expanse of it in the stuffy air and cupping her hands for the hollow that held the house. She had had more time since she had sketched the first ideas for Jane, and she had done her research. She brought out prospectuses of other new-village schemes, plans, photographs, newspaper articles. She described the starter houses for local couples, the houses for rent and the sheltered community with covered walkways and communal center, the bigger homes for families and the landscaping that would set the whole development in place without blighting the surrounding countryside.

David cut her short. "Yes," he said. "It's familiar territory."

"There could be some workshops, too. Providing employment for local people . . ."

"Craftsmen making hand-carved rocking horses and glass terrariums?"

"Why not?" Harriet answered.

"Nothing too dirty or industrial, then."

"That would be inappropriate in a village setting, wouldn't it?"

"If you say so. I only hope you can find enough young

couples looking for affordable houses in a village Utopia who are
also able to carve a decent rocking horse or cut a clever terrarium."

Through the window that looked out over the building site
Harriet had been watching a bricklayer working on a garden
boundary wall. He moved rhythmically, larding each brick with
mortar and then laying it on the course beneath, setting it with a
sharp tap of his trowel and slicing away the surplus with a
flourish. He came to the end of the new course now, and stood
back to examine what he had done.

To do what she was trying to do, Harriet reflected, was
equivalent to seizing bricks and mortar out of the air and compressing them with one movement into a solid brick wall. She
turned away from the window.

"Does that mean you're not interested in the scheme?"

David smiled. "Not at all. You've described a good-natured
entrepreneurial vision, to touch the heart of any planning committee. The reality may turn out to be different. Property development isn't the sweetest-smelling business."

"I know that," Harriet said.

After a moment David answered, "I'm sure you do. Where's
the money coming from?"

"From me, to begin with. For outline plans, initial acquisition of land, lobbying and the rest. After that, from investors. I
can raise it."

"Yes. And with the site assembly, how far have you got?"

Outside, the bricklayer laid the first brick of another course.

"Nowhere," Harriet said.

"So what do you want with a building contractor?"

"Not *a* contractor. You. And your partners." David had
explained to Harriet that he worked only in conjunction with a
group of architects who designed as he wanted to build. But at
Jane's suggestion, Harriet had already visited some of their suc-
cesses. She had been impressed by what she saw.

David was waiting. Harriet made a wide gesture in the air,
the nearest she could come to drawing down the bricks and
mortar in their concrete form.

"It's all a balancing act, or a juggling feat. It's making everything look right and sound good just for long enough, long
enough to block the competition and win out ourselves. I can do
one vital thing, but I need you for the rest. I want you and your
partners to come and look at the site, do some drawings, perhaps make some models. I want you to come with me to the
parish council meetings. I want you to be on the platform with
me at Everden village hall when I describe our scheme. We'll get

the support of the village, and with local opinion behind us we can go to the planning stage. With local opposition properly directed we can overturn Bottrill's proposals, and if I can secure the piece of land I want I can use it as a lever against him.

"If we can blow a bright enough bubble in a short enough time, we'll attract all the attention and the applause. Reaction against Bottrill will be action for us."

"You're talking like a propaganda poster."

Harriet's eyes were brilliant and her face was warm. "It doesn't matter. It doesn't matter if our bubble doesn't last once we've seen Bottrill off. You'll have time after that to work on the plans properly, even if you don't believe in my Utopia."

David was going to interrupt her, but she held up her hand to stop him. "It's a marketing exercise, don't you see? I can market the Birdwood Project. I can market a new village to an existing village. I can market myself, and I can market you."

"A bubble," David repeated.

After a moment he stood up and went to the window, to look at the work going on outside. "Come and have a look at the job," he said, after a moment.

Harriet contained her impatience. "I'd like that," she told him.

He took a pair of Wellington boots from behind his desk, and gave them to her. Harriet put them on and waded after him into the sunshine.

Two new, short terraces of little houses were emerging within a pattern of similar streets. Weathered old bricks were being used for the frontages, so the unfinished houses seemed already to belong to their Victorian setting. Each house had a small garden front and back, more private than those of an ordinary terrace because the line of houses was stepped. Harriet saw that although the scale was small, the architect's achievement had been to create a sense of intimacy rather than any impression of overcrowding.

"The density is fourteen per acre," David remarked. "Quite high, even by urban standards." As he spoke, something in his expression told Harriet that he found it incongruous, and amusing, to be walking across the site talking to her about housing density. She dismissed her own urge to say something irrelevant in response.

"We're working in association with a community Housing Trust," he went on smoothly. "We have a certain amount of leeway in what we can do, but there are corresponding restrictions."

"It all looks very attractive," Harriet said, in her most busi-nesslike voice.

They had turned in at an open doorway. The door-frame was in position, but there was no front door as yet. The staircase, in pale new wood littered with the flat coils of woodshavings, led upward directly in front of them. David motioned to his right and they stepped into the living room. The walls were freshly plastered, and sash windows were ready for the glazier. Harriet had caught a glimpse of him working in the house next door. She breathed in the smells of raw plaster, sawdust and putty and brickdust. It was satisfying to have a sense of the solid little houses rising out of the loaded pallets and dumps of raw material.

As she turned around in the light room, putting her fingers out absently to touch the cold plasterwork, she realized that the house reminded her of Jane's. This one was separate from the other by a hundred years, but they were constructed with the same plain, unvarnished logic. And it was in Jane's living room that she had danced with David, years ago, at the beginning of "Meizu." Harriet thought of the colored balls, rolling and click-ing, and remembered what she had lost.

She had been afraid, then, of what it might mean if she let David Howkins kiss her to a background of *The Police* and teach-ers talking.

And now she was here in pursuit of different things. David was standing with his hands in the pockets of paint-encrusted jeans. It came to her that he was ridiculously attractive. She felt her face changing color, and her susceptibility made her angry.

"When will the houses be ready for occupation?"

"These first ones, in two months' time. The others in various phases thereafter."

"I'll have a quick look upstairs, shall I?" The bare boards were hollow under her feet. There were two light, square bed-rooms and a bathroom with the fittings in place, but still swathed in the manufacturer's tape. There was a litter of cardboard pack-aging in the bath. It was in Jane's bathroom, Harriet remem-bered, that she had taken refuge.

She descended the stairs once more, in full possession of herself.

"Thank you for showing me around," she said crisply.

"I'll walk you to your car. Keep the boots on, until you're out of the mud."

They crossed the site once more, past the barrows and the piles of sand and the concrete mixers, and the builders who didn't whistle at Harriet in David's hearing. She looked back across the yellowish quagmire at the skeletons of the nearest houses, and it struck her that the trailer office was a long way from the svelte premises of Landwith Associates that had once impressed her so much.

David must have been thinking in parallel, because he asked her, "How is your friend, the financier?"

"Venture capitalist. Well, as far as I know. We parted company."

"At the same time as you parted company with your company?"

"More or less."

"I'm sorry."

They had reached Harriet's car. She put her hand on the bonnet, feeling the sun-hot gloss of it. Harriet smiled suddenly, with perfect openness.

"Don't be," she said.

David took the keys of the car from her hand and unlocked the door for her. Harriet tossed her briefcase onto the passenger seat and then turned to him.

"Well?" she asked. She felt a fierce determination that he should not turn down her project.

David said, "I'll talk to Anthony about it." Anthony was his architect partner. "And we'll come down and look at your site."

"Don't talk too much or take too long. There's not much time."

"Bubbles never last long, do they?"

Harriet was already in the driver's seat. "Do you think I'm crooked? Or crazy, or both?"

"Neither. I think you're deeply impressive."

The car began to slide forward. Harriet was still wearing the Wellingtons. "Keep the boots," he called. "You'll be needing them."

"They're four sizes too big."

"Room for growth, then." He waved, and turned back to the site entrance.

Harriet whistled as she drove. She negotiated the south London traffic, and headed out toward Everden. She had told David no less than the truth, there wasn't much time, but she was convinced that somehow she could make it enough.

"Back again?" said Miss Bowlly.

"May I come in?" Harriet asked. Miss Bowlly didn't say yes or no, but the door seemed to inch wider of its own accord.

"I don't know what keeps bringing you down here," she remarked in the mounded-up nest of her kitchen. "I don't suppose it's my tea, is it?"

Harriet sipped at the brown brew in the mug rimmed with tannin scum. "I called to ask you if you'd like to come for a walk with me. It's a fine day."

"A *walk*?" Harriet might have been proposing a crime, or an act of exhibitionism. Miss Bowlly scrutinized her with distrust. The old lady's eyes were set in pouches that seemed surprisingly fleshy in comparison with the rest of her bony frame. With her gray hair sticking out in wisps around her face she looked like some small but threatening mammal.

Harriet calculated briefly, and then offered, "I thought we might go over and take a look at Birdwood House. And the grounds, too. No one will accuse us of trespassing, will they?" Miss Bowlly was calculating as well. For a moment they stood still, weighing each other up.

"I'll get my coat on," she said at length.

It was another warm, still day. Harriet had walked over from Everden in shirtsleeves, her attention fixed on the house in its hollow and the curves and undulations of the land around it. But Miss Bowlly pulled on an ancient brown tweed coat that only stopped short at her ankles, and covered her hair with a kind of fawn knitted bonnet. They made an incongruous pair as they set out on the short walk to the gates of Birdwood House. Miss Bowlly was not inclined to make conversation, Harriet discovered. Harriet was also busy with her own imaginings that each car sweeping past them might contain one of Keith Bottrill's emissaries, or even Bottrill himself, circling his target like some bird of prey. The idea of herself and Miss Bowlly slipping in through their guard, dismissible as an eccentric old lady and her daughter out for a dutiful stroll, was pleasing and also exciting. Harriet knew that the thought was also farfetched, but that was part of her pleasure in it.

The entire scheme was farfetched, and that was its strength as well as its weakness. The surprise would be greater and the impact more powerful when the time came.

Harriet was smiling. She walked briskly, and Miss Bowlly showed no difficulty in keeping up. The hedges on either side of them were heavy with the creamy froth of May blossom. They reached the end of the driveway and edged around the heavy gate without trying to push it open any farther. The shade of tall trees closed over them at once.

"I used to come up here, you know," Miss Bowlly said

abruptly. "When the house was still kept right. Christmases; and for the village festival in the summer, that was always held in the garden; cricket matches sometimes, that my father played in."

"Tell me about it," Harriet asked her.

"Oh, all a long time ago now."

It was a familiar story, Harriet thought. Before the war there had been indoor servants and gardeners, and after the war a slow decline to the point where one elderly survivor lived a confused existence in two barricaded rooms. They reached the house.

"Shame to see it like this, isn't it?" Miss Bowlly said.

They made a slow circuit. The afternoon's sunshine promised summer, but still the house seemed dark and cold in its morbid setting of overgrown shrubs. The fanciful wrought-iron work of the veranda was hanging in places in truncated ocher fragments that denied the symmetry of filigree scrolls and wreathed acanthus leaves. As they passed the wooden screens roughly nailed over the windows Harriet examined the black scribbles of graffiti once again. She was right, there was nothing sinister here. Only children, announcing their allegiances in spray paint that would probably outlast them.

There was more fine iron-work over the elaborate porch. By the height of summer, buddleia would be raising its purple spikes out of the stone on either side. Up against the heavy double doors there was a deep drift of dead leaves, cigarette packets and empty drinks cans.

Harriet wanted to stoop and clear it away, exposing the heavy stone flags beneath, making a path to the doors so that she could push them open and step inside onto the exuberant pattern of the Victorian hall tiles. Instead, the marked wood nailed where there must once have been panels of stained glass solidly confronted her.

Yet her first instinct had been right, Harriet thought. It was a magnificent house. It drew her like a magnet. She was not afraid, but galvanized.

She stood ankle-deep in the litter at the door.

"I wish we could get in," she whispered.

Miss Bowlly had sharp ears as well as eyes. "Tom Frost's got the keys," she said. "But why would he let you in? The place belongs to Everden."

"I want to buy it."

The old lady laughed. "You've got the money, have you?"

Harriet turned away from the padlocked doors. "I'm rich enough," she said.

She couldn't remember having admitted it so simply before. She was neither apologizing nor advertising, but stating the fact.

The possession of the Peacocks money had begun to have a significance unconnected with Peacocks and defeat. If it enabled her to rescue Birdwood House, then that was well and good. And with Birdwood House, enticingly linked, came the Birdwood development.

Miss Bowlly looked differently at Harriet now. Not with direct suspicion or mistrust but sidelong, speculative. They began to walk away from the house, through the rim of the shrubbery and under the big trees on the far side of it. Green bramble snares caught at their ankles and soft, rotting branches split underfoot. They came to a sagging fence of metal rails that marked the boundary of the garden. Looking behind her, Harriet saw that the house was masked by spring growth.

Miss Bowlly spread her hands on the top rail of the fence and rested one boot on the lower. The fields fanned in front of them, green alternating with ribbed brown, marked out by hedges and gates and narrow lines of trees. Once again, Harriet noted that the seclusion of Birdwood was deceptive. From here she could see the outskirts of two of the three villages in the enclosing triangle, and there was a handful of houses scattered between them. She was wondering again which acres of land belonged to which of them, and how many of the landowners had signed Keith Bottrill's enticing option agreements.

Free money now, and a percentage of the take when the property bonanza finally came. Miss Bowlly had not taken the bait, at least.

Harriet said quietly as they looked out over the saucer of land, "There will be a housing development of some sort here, you know. I think it's inevitable now. Planning permission will be granted to someone in the end, for something. Only it doesn't necessarily have to be boxes for commuters, which is what Bottrill intends."

Miss Bowlly turned her back on the view. She only said, "I'll get back home now. I can't be gadding about here all the afternoon."

They walked back again, almost in silence, as they had come.

At the cottage Miss Bowlly held open her front door, clearly expecting that Harriet had not finished what she had come to do. And Harriet, who had planned to walk straight back to Everden and let Miss Bowlly cogitate for a precious day or two, took her chance.

"I want to put a proposal to you."

She was looking around the dim kitchen at the heaped-up newspapers and the cardboard boxes overflowing with empty jars and old saucepans and pieces of ironmongery. The sense of familiarity came back to her, but she knew that Miss Bowlly was no Simon. Miss Bowlly was shrewd and suspicious, and she was well able to take care of herself.

"I guessed that," the old lady said, looking at Harriet without blinking. The resemblance to a small, unfriendly mammal grew stronger.

"I want to buy your property."

"I told you the first time. I'm not signing or agreeing or selling."

"Won't you listen to what I'm proposing, and then decide?"

"If it doesn't take all night."

And so, speaking softly and without emphasis, Harriet made the offer that she had been thinking about for days.

She would buy Miss Bowlly's cottage and two acres of garden, outright, and not under an option agreement. While she was talking she watched Miss Bowlly's face carefully, but she couldn't detect the smallest flicker of interest. So when she came to naming the price Harriet revised it upward by ten percent. It was such a large sum of money she almost regretted it as soon as she made the offer. It was beyond what was necessary, a long way beyond. Harriet stopped and waited, with the figure resounding in the air between them.

Miss Bowlly had never even blinked.

"Why so generous?" she demanded.

"There are two reasons. The first is that I need your land, to use as a wedge to drive into the Castoria holding. And I can offer to buy it outright because I have made money elsewhere, and I'm not a big-scale developer with a dozen similar deals under way. There's also the chance that, knowing you and hearing that you have decided to support my scheme rather than the rival one, other local owners and the village and the parish council might be influenced in my favor, too. I'm being generous because I need to be."

Harriet was candid, because there seemed to be no point in dissembling.

"And the other reason?"

The table they were sitting at was crowded with the empty glass jars that seemed to be Miss Bowlly's chief collecting interest. Most of them were as yet unwashed. Harriet watched a fly making progress around the rim of a jar that had once held raspberry jam. In between the jars there were boxes of cereal, and white sliced bread in cellophane wrappings. Miss Bowlly appeared to live on Weetabix and jam sandwiches.

Harriet tried to imagine what it would be like for Miss Bowlly to live in another place, in one of David's sound, modern cottages constructed on approved traditional lines, for instance, or in a sheltered unit in an old people's community with a warden who called in to see her every day, and nagged her about eating properly and attending the evening whist drives in the common room.

It was, she was aware, only partly an act of generosity on her own part to offer Miss Bowlly a chance to direct her future. The terms were more than generous, but they were based on self-interest. Harriet understood that, and she also knew that she would have to learn to live with many similar self-accusations if she was to progress beyond Miss Bowlly's garden boundary. If she was going to blow up her bubble and let it catch the wind over Birdwood.

Her presence in Miss Bowlly's kitchen was an intrusion. She remembered the steps by which she had intruded into Simon's life, both consciously and with careless ignorance, and the conclusion, in the deep cutting under the bridge.

She met Miss Bowlly's suspicious stare full on. "I took something from someone else, when I started out in business. I didn't pay him in the right currency. I don't want to do that again. I want to make sure there are no debts."

Miss Bowlly gave her laugh that sounded like an animal's yelp.

"Making atonement with me, are you?"

It was ridiculous to imagine that anything that could be done for Miss Bowlly was an atonement for Simon. Miss Bowlly would not look at her and see Kath's young face gazing back; Miss Bowlly would never wish that Harriet might have been her daughter.

Simon was dead.

In the end bulldozers would arrive at the gate outside, and whether they came on Harriet's account or via some faceless developer operating out of his distant office suite would not, finally, make very much difference.

The decision whether or not to accept Harriet's offer was Miss Bowlly's alone.

"I can't atone, in this case," Harriet said. "But you asked why I was being generous, and this is the second reason."

Miss Bowlly sniffed. One nostril collapsed and she puffed heavily out again.

"I'll have to think about it," she conceded.

Harriet knew it was as much as she would get, for the time being. "Thank you," she said warmly.

She left Miss Bowlly to do her thinking, and walked back to Everden.

When Alison returned from London for another weekend, Harriet asked her, "Do you mind my still being here?"

She had cleared the chaos of her papers off the long kitchen table and packed them neatly away in the blue bedroom, and she had made a lengthy and very accurate list of the dozens of telephone calls she had put through in Alison's absence. The cottage was tidy because Harriet had hardly moved around in it, and she had taken uncharacteristic care to make sure that there was food in the refrigerator as well as cold white wine.

"If you do, there must be some sort of pub or hotel I could stay at, or a cottage to rent somewhere."

Alison sank into a paunchy armchair and drank from the glass that Harriet put into her hand.

"I don't mind you still being here. I told you, stay as long as you like."

"It's already been long. And you didn't expect me to treat the place like an office."

"That's true. I expected you to come and have a rest. To read a novel or two and potter about in the garden and perhaps strike up an offbeat friendship with someone from the Wheatsheaf."

"I don't play darts well enough for that."

"That's also true. But what do I find? Within a couple of weeks you're in the middle of creating a property empire. You're planning to buy up half the village and build a theme park for community-conscious country folk. You intend to take on one of the major bad-boy developers and beat him at his own game." Alison closed her eyes, and then forced them open again. "It's very tiring. I'm exhausted by the spectacle of your energy and industry."

Harriet said gently, "It's all speculative. Nothing exists, yet, except a few architect's outlines, a pile of posters and some invitations to attend a meeting in the village hall."

"Which makes your energy and enthusiasm all the more awesome."

"It's what entrepreneurs run on."

"You're an entrepreneur, Harriet. You must have been born one."

"Do you mind what I'm doing?"

"As I said when we talked about it at the beginning, this is a small country, and people have to live somewhere. Why not next to the village of Everden, Kent? And if some developer is going to pocket a pile of money out of it, I'd rather it were you with your artisans' cottages than Keith Bottrill and his Kentish executive homes. Only one thing worries me."

"Which is?"

Alison looked up at her. She was thinking that for all Harriet's warmth there was an obliqueness about her when it came to analysis of her own feelings. Coupled with her formidable determination it could make her seem unapproachable. Alison chose her words with care.

"When we were here together the first weekend, you told me that you hadn't given any consideration to happiness since, you couldn't remember when. And that now you would, because you had plenty of time."

There was a silence. Involuntarily, Harriet put her hand up to her jaw. The marks left by the attack had all but disappeared, and she remembered that to touch them was to draw attention to them. She dropped her hand again and fiddled with the bottle of wine to occupy her fingers elsewhere.

"I was miserable when I had nothing to do. I felt sick, dismembered. I don't know about happiness. I don't know what else to do, if I don't do this."

Alison went on looking at her. Harriet could detect only interest in her expression, not pity or sympathy nor any trace of disapproval. It came to her that although she could not benefit from Alison's warning, she was deeply grateful to her for troubling to make it. She was aware of the value of new friendship that took her as what she had become, rather than as a reminiscence of other times. She got up now, and went across to Alison's armchair. Awkwardly, because she was not physically demonstrative, she put her arm around her and as quickly withdrew it. It was Jane who hugged and patted hair and linked hands, and when she thought of her Harriet remembered other friendships, different and possessed of their own value. The warning found a kind of mark, then.

"Thank you," Harriet smiled at her. "I'm happy, doing what I'm doing."

She reached into her pocket, and took out a pair of heavy old keys. "Look. Tom Frost has lent me the keys to Birdwood."

Harriet had been to see the chairman of the parish council, just as she had also discreetly visited the vicar and the individual members of the Everden Association, and all the other local residents who, on Alison's advice, were judged likely to be receptive to her ideas.

"I waited for you to come home, so that we could go and see it together."

Alison sighed, but she was already on her way up and out of the depths of the armchair. In the middle of May there was plenty of light until nine o'clock. There was enough time to go with Harriet to see the house of her dreams, and to be back home again before dark.

"More like a nightmare," Alison shivered, as the heavy doors creaked open. A soft tide of dead leaves and litter drifted in at their heels.

Harriet and Alison stepped into the hallway of Birdwood House. The light was dim, and Harriet switched on the big torch she had brought with her. The tiles were there, just as she had imagined them, an intricate plaid of buff and terracotta and olive-green, chestnut and startling blue, criss-crossing and receding into the depths of the house. The torch-beam moved upward. It traveled up the wide staircase, illuminating elaborately turned fat newel posts and mahogany globes furred with gray dust, and the intricate pillars and balustrading of a first-floor gallery.

Alison shivered again, more theatrically, but Harriet walked slowly forward. Through tall doorways and Gothic archways they could see dim rooms, inward-turning, blinded by the wooden screens nailed over their windows. The torchlight penetrated more deeply. There were bare floorboards marked by unvarnished rectangles that the soap manufacturer's fine Turkey carpets had once generously covered. Marble mantelpieces that had displayed wax fruit trapped under glass domes, colored glass, silver candlesticks were naked now, decently veiled by the blankets of dust. Plaster ceilings garlanded with leaves and pendulous with fruit showed the brown archipelagoes of damp stains, and in places the bare teeth of laths above where the plaster had crumbled away.

The corners of the rooms held a flotsam of screwed-up newspapers, broken chairs, and swept-up plaster. In one room a broom leaned at an angle against a wall as if the sweeper had suddenly found himself unequal to the task; in another an ancient garden rake had been similarly abandoned.

Harriet and Alison walked on, in silence, until they came to

the farthest reaches and found the stone-floored kitchens where
the big old flat butler's sinks sheltered colonies of spiders, and
blue-green crusted deposits were frozen under the copper taps.
On the farthest wall a dresser with racks and hooks for a huge
dinner service was empty except for cobwebs.

"Let's look upstairs," Harriet whispered.

They went back again and climbed the stairs to the gallery.
Alison put her fingers out automatically to the banister rail, and
then quickly withdrew them, padded with dust. The windows of
the bedrooms leading off the gallery were unscreened, and the
evening light filtering through the murky glass seemed dazzling
after the darkness below. Harriet clicked off the torch. They put
their heads back and looked up at the broken ceilings and the
cornices leprous with damp, and at the fireplace littered with
rubbish and the doors of yawning cupboards that sagged on
their hinges to reveal blistered brown interiors and shelves lined
with yellow sheets of newspaper. The walls of successive bedrooms were a gallery of wallpapers, fading roses, and birds in
leaf garlands and peeling *toile de Jouy* shepherdesses.

Another staircase, narrow and bending at an awkward angle
under the pitch of the roof, brought them to the top floor and the
maids' bedrooms. The little black grates up here were narrow,
almost slits, looking hardly big enough to burn two coals at a
time. The floors of splintering boards were puddled with ugly,
greenish patches of slimy moss, and when they looked up this
time they could see the whitish evening sky through the rotting
beams and broken slates. Birds were circling overhead, preparing
to roost in the tall trees. Harriet thought of their predecessors,
generations ago, who had given the house its name.

Finally, at the highest corner of the house, they came to the
little half-rounded room at the top of the turret.

"I wanted to come up here," Harriet murmured.

Tiny leaded windows with arched tops gave a view over a
two-hundred-degree sweep of the surrounding countryside. Harriet bent down to look through one of them, out at the houses
and prosperous farms and the twists of roads marked by the
double lines of hawthorn hedges.

The turret room had the feel of an observatory, or the look-
out point of a much older building, a fortress or a castle.

"Mr. Farrow's castle," she said aloud. Almost directly beneath her, in the middle of the wide vista, she could see Miss
Bowlly's cottage.

Alison was angry. "It's a crime," she said, "Letting it decay
like this."

"Didn't you know that the house belonged to Everden?"

"No. Not until you told me. I'm not surprised no one talks about it."

Charlie Thimbell's guess had been right, of course. Harriet had learned from her round of discreet visits that Everden was not proud of its neglect of Birdwood House. But, as the vicar had sighingly told her, it was an impossible position to find themselves in. The house had been willed to the village, in perpetuity, but there were no resources available to maintain it. No one had even hinted as much, but Harriet knew that they would let it slip until it was past saving, and then they would quietly and regretfully sell it. The demolition men with their ball and chain would move in, to make way for the new, profitable houses. Keith Bottrill was waiting.

"Can we go, now?" Alison asked. "It's extremely depressing."

"Or equally challenging," Harriet answered. "Yes, let's go home."

They descended through the house. Through the clumping of their feet on the old boards Harriet imagined that she could hear other noises: the insidious drip of water, the crack of timbers and the sudden rattle of falling plaster, the sounds of Birdwood House falling into ruins.

She thought of her money like concrete, that she could pour in to shore it up.

My castle.

Would Everden part with it, in exchange for a fitting extension to the village? Or would they prefer to see Keith Bottrill demolish it altogether? Harriet didn't believe so. Alison's dismay at what she had seen fueled her optimism. As she locked the double doors on the dust and the damp once more, she was thinking that Birdwood House would interest David Howkins.

It was a soft, gray evening and the darkness came quickly. Alison and Harriet needed the torch again as they walked back up the lane to the cottage.

When Alison pushed open her front door, they saw a brown envelope lying on the doormat just inside. Alison picked it up and peered at it. When she saw the name on the front she handed it to Harriet.

"For you."

There was a single sheet of cheap lined writing paper folded inside.

Harriet read the brief message. It was written in an old-fashioned, carefully crossed and dotted script.

Dear Miss Peacock, I do not intend to accept your proposal. Money cannot buy everything, whatever you may believe. It will not by you my house and land.
Yours, E.V. Bowlly.

And she read it again, to make sure. Without Miss Bowlly's land, Harriet knew she didn't have any ammunition at all with which to mount her attack against Keith Bottrill. All the ideas and architects' schemes and posters were hot air, if she didn't control the wedge of property that drove into the site. If she had offered Miss Bowlly *less* money, she thought. Or offered it in a different way, or handled her more subtly. Harriet could have shouted aloud in her disappointment and frustration.

Alison stared at her. "What's wrong?"

"Miss Bowlly won't sell."

Alison breathed. "Oh dear. Is that the end of it, then?"

The question answered itself within Harriet, immediately and clearly. It wasn't the end, of course. She would get what she wanted somehow, sooner or later.

"No. Certainly not. We'll have to bluff it somehow, win the village over, do it just by getting public opinion behind us." She folded Miss Bowlly's note and stuffed it into her pocket. "Alison, have you got any champagne?"

"There might be a bottle somewhere."

"Then let's open it and drink to the Birdwood Development, Phase One, and to hell with everything else."

Alison shook her head at her, but she was smiling. "All right. If you say so. Phase One, by sleight of hand."

Nineteen

EVERDEN VILLAGE HALL WAS a four-square breeze-block building
standing back from the main street, a little beyond the Wheatsheaf,
on its own fenced patch of rough grass. A notice-board beside
the gate gave details of a Summer Fayre and the cricket team's
summer fixtures, but the center of the board was occupied by a
poster, square black lettering on a not-quite-fluorescent pale green
backdrop.

The words read, ACTION FOR EVERDEN. Beneath the heading
was a date and a time, invitation to a public meeting to be held in
Everden village hall. Harriet had had her poster professionally
designed. It could not have looked more different from the Everden
Association's pale pink message that she had first seen in the
village shop, and identified with the playgroup's bring-and-buy
sale.

She did not look at the green poster as she passed it. It was
familiar, and there were copies of it at every prominent point in
and around the village. She took a short cut across the hummocks of grass, her attention fixed on the door of the hall. But
once she was inside, she did stop. She was subjecting the hall
and the arrangements that had been made to critical examination.

The hall's stacking chairs were arranged in loose semi-circles
around the platform at the opposite end. Straight lines were
formal and intimidating. She wanted the Everden residents and
ratepayers to feel that this was their meeting, not hers. She
walked a few steps forward now and rearranged the seats in the
back row, pushing them a little further apart. If only a few
people came the hall should at least look as full as possible; if
there was a crowd more chairs could be hurried in from the store
behind the stage. There were fewer chairs than the number of
people she was hoping her meeting would attract; it would look
good to have to augment the seating.

The walls displayed more of the green posters, and between
them there were big, grainy, blown-up photographs. On the
left-hand side were pictures of Bottrill developments, and on the

right pictures of some of David Howkins's completed schemes, and of the half-finished development that Harriet had visited. She was pleased by the contrast they made. Over the platform hung a big banner. She was pleased with the banner, too; it had the right homemade village celebration feel. The hand-painted words read, REACTION AGAINST BOTTRILL IS ACTION FOR EVERDEN. Harriet would not let a good slogan go to waste just because David Howkins had made mild fun of her for coining it.

Underneath the banner, sitting at a trestle table, David Howkins and Anthony Fell, the principal architect, were drinking beer out of cans and waiting for her. David's feet were propped on the table, inches away from the architects' scale model of the proposed Birdwood development. Only Harriet, David and the architects team knew just how hastily the model had been put together.

David waved his beer can at her.

"Everything to your satisfaction?"

"I'm sorry I'm late," Harriet said. She was nervous, and admitting the nervousness to herself instead of trying to suppress it, as she might once have done. She was late because she had set out once from Alison's cottage and then turned back again to change her formal suit with its wide shoulders for something softer. She looked at her watch now. The meeting was timed to start in half an hour. If she judged village curiosity rightly, the first few sightseers would begin to drift in at any minute.

"Would you like a beer?" Anthony Fell drawled.

"No thanks." Harriet ignored her sharp inclination to tell them to sit up properly and put the beer cans away. That was her own style, not theirs. She settled for making a few more adjustments to the chairs, then took her place on the platform between the two men. They waited, with the banner above their heads drifting in the draft from the open door.

What if no one comes, Harriet thought. *No one at all. What then?*

But they did come, almost as soon as the anxiety took hold of her. They filtered in slowly, in couples and trios, occupying the seats farthest from the platform first, murmuring in low voices almost as if they were in church, peering at the three of them on the platform. As soon as the first arrivals took their places Anthony and David became businesslike, sitting behind their model with its matchbox houses and tiny, fuzzy green trees, but none of the Everden people ventured up onto the platform to examine the layout. *Afterward*, Harriet resolved, she must encourage every single one of them to come and look. It didn't matter that the dimensions of the site itself were based on conjecture, that the little model cottages in their rural streets had been hastily borrowed from the models of other developments, that the whole layout represented an idea instead of miniature reality. It was the idea that Harriet wanted to sell. She wanted the people of Everden to admire her bubble. Once they admired it, she could begin work.

As the half-hour passed the murmur of conversation swelled to a loud buzz, the earlier arrivals began to wave to latecomers, chairs were rattled together, the occupants of the platform were stared at more openly. Looking calmly back at the rows of faces, while David and his partner talked in low voices beside her, Harriet saw that her audience was made up of all kinds of people. Young couples sat alongside businessmen in suits and women in earrings and old ladies with ridged white perms, waiting to hear what she had come to say.

￩ There was no real resemblance at all, but Harriet was suddenly reminded of a Peacocks shareholders' meeting. And the thought brought a bite of pure, delicious adrenaline into her blood.

Over the heads of the vicar, Tom Frost and the other parish councillors, her friends from the Wheatsheaf and more faces that she didn't recognize, Harriet saw Alison sitting at the back of the hall. It was a Wednesday evening and Harriet had not expected to see her, but she was glad that she had come. She was remembering the question that Alison had asked her, and her warning. But it came to her now that what made her happy was doing this; she was happy at this instant. She was doing what she was good at, and it was enough to make herself content with that.

Alison lifted her hand, as if she read her thoughts, and made a small, ironic salute. Miss Bowlly stumped in, alone, and sat on the far side of the hall. Her small mammal-look was particularly pronounced. Harriet gave her a welcoming smile that she hoped was untinged by either disappointment or acquisitiveness.

Harriet looked at her watch once more. At the stroke of the hour she stood up. She was nervous, but her nervousness was an ingredient of the biting high. On her feet she felt tall, and elastic, as if she could stretch to touch what had once been out of her grasp. The hum of talk diminished, falling away into silence.

Harriet said simply, "Good evening. Thank you for taking the trouble to come here tonight. I hope we won't keep you too long, but I believe that what you are going to hear is important for Everden and for the new community on the Birdwood site."

As she spoke she knew that they were all watching her face. She didn't smile or frown; the tiny muscles worked smoothly under the clear, healed skin. She thought, *They can look. There's no harm.* Some of them had come to stare at "Meizu Girl," the old tabloid name still trailed her. They were looking at a name that had been linked with Caspar Jensen's; the men in suits would know the Peacocks story, part or all of it. Harriet found that she was indifferent. If they had come to the hall because they had read about her or seen her picture in the newspapers, if they had come out of curiosity, then her name had at least achieved something. They would stay to listen, she would make them hear.

Harriet's fingers separated and spread, as if she would lift them to touch the outline of her features, but she held them still and flat on the top of the trestle table. There was a lump at the angle of her jaw, an imperfection in the knitting of the bone, but it was detectable only to her own touch. There was no swelling to see, her eyes had reappeared from the yellow cushions of flesh. The face was the old one. She had been attacked and she had recovered, that was all. She forgot, now, the associations of defeat.

It was a public face, but she could spend its currency this evening and live behind it as it suited her. If it helped to bring her Birdwood then she was grateful to it; if she was happy now it must be in the realization that this hall gave her satisfaction.

"Let me explain the idea," Harriet said to the listeners.

She began by describing the village laid out in miniature in front of her. She did lift her fingers this time, to touch the roofs of the little houses and to trace the narrow streets.

Harriet talked about Birdwood as if it already existed, making it sound as real as Everden itself, and she took her audience on a tour of it. "Here *is* the village green," she said, "and these, here, are bigger family houses, and here are starter cottages, for rent or partial purchase." She never said, *Here will be.* She described the workshops as if the knitwear designers and potters were already at work, and the community center under its steep pitched roof as if the activities program was fully under way and the toddlers of Birdwood were happily playing in the enclosed garden.

The people sitting in their loose lines gave her their full attention.

Listening to her, Alison could not help but be admiring. Harriet possessed remarkable, infectious conviction. Up until now Alison had been privately convinced that the entire Birdwood scheme was an elaborate fantasy of Harriet's. She had mistrusted the watery utopianism of it as much as the clear opportunism of the Bottrill scheme, but she had made no comment. She had assumed that the planning and the preparations provided a necessary outlet for Harriet's energies after Peacocks; she had also assumed that the plans would come to nothing. But this evening, for the first time, it occurred to her that the Birdwood development might be more than a fantasy. When she had first met Harriet, she had been struck by her single-mindedness, and her absolute determination to say what she intended and in the way she thought best. It had made her an awkward but interesting interviewee; the same determination tonight conjured Birdwood village out of the air, solid as brick and stone. It had persuaded Anthony Fell, the community architect about whom Alison had read something admiring, somewhere, to rush a model together and to come and sit on a platform in front of the curious and suspicious of Everden. It was, already, some kind of an achievement.

Alison folded her arms and tipped back an inch in her chair, waiting to see what would happen next. She remembered Harriet telling her that the same conclusions in life could be reached by going straight for them with full force, or by hoping to be swept there. The thought of Harriet being swept anywhere made her smile.

Harriet talked for another five minutes. She spoke fluently but simply as if to a single listener instead of a roomful. At the end of her guided tour she introduced Anthony and David, and made a gesture of handing the meeting over to Anthony. When she sat down there was a small silence, as of disappointment.

Alison thought, *That was extremely good.*

The meeting went on. The architect explained his theories of new, integrated communities and David spoke briefly about their previous collaborations, pointing to the big photographs on the right-hand wall.

The audience began to fidget. Chairs creaked, and there was a rustle of whispering and yawning. But when Harriet stood up again there was silence. The man in front of Alison leaned forward, to hear better.

Alison knew then, *She's got them.*

"You've listened very patiently to our proposals," Harriet said. "As I told you at the beginning, Birdwood is only an idea. It will never become any more than that without your support, your belief in it. I hope you will go home tonight and talk about it. But before you do go, you should know that there is an alternative scheme. Most of you already do know, because you will have seen the posters and listened to the local speculation. I can tell you a little more about it and the developer behind it." Harriet extended her hand to point at the photographs on the opposite wall. The big, square diamond shone in the light.

Alison turned her head with everyone else. She didn't know for sure, but she guessed that Harriet had dispatched a professional photographer, a very clever one, to capture some unusual angles of Castoria Developments. In these pictures blank walls and thin fences seemed to press together, and windows that seemed too small to admit light eyed each other at awkward angles across narrow strips of churned-up earth. One picture showed identical houses, with mean porches like coffins and slits of windows, stretching away in a jumble as far as the lens could capture. There seemed to be hardly room for two people abreast to pass between them. It was a theatrical contract with the pastoral idyll of Anthony Fell's Birdwood proposal.

Harriet looked at the photographs too.

"High-density housing for young executive families," she announced cheerfully. "The maximum number of identical or near-identical units shoehorned into the site, for quick sale, and maximum return on investment, to identical or near-identical Middle-management families, almost all of them incomers."

The photographer had been expensive, but he had done an excellent job. She had come a long way from the black and white parachute silk and the rickety polystyrene-block sunburst of her very first display at the Earl's Court Toy Fair.

"A typical Keith Bottrill development. His proposal for the Birdwood site, which goes before the planning subcommittee in a matter of days, will be substantially the same. Mr. Bottrill is a property developer, and he is interested in profit. Some of you will be familiar with his reputation. Others will not."

As Harriet talked, Alison felt the hairs rise at the nape of her neck. She looked around the hall at the rapt audience, wondering how many of the men in suits were Bottrill's spies. Harriet was probably being careful, probably none of the allegations she made were directly slanderous, almost certainly the majority of them were factually verifiable. Her journalist friend Charlie Thimbell must have helped her to dig the necessary dirt, Alison thought. But it was a startling performance. As an assessment of Bottrill's methods and achievements, it was no less than savage.

It occurred to Alison that even though she had never met Harriet's venture capitalist, she had a sudden clear idea of what he must be like. The two of them would have been formidably well-matched. It was a pity that they had not been able to run on together. Observing her now, as she commanded the hall, Alison was convinced that the antagonizing of Robin Landwith had been one of Harriet's rare mistakes. Personally, as well as professionally.

"And so I ask you," Harriet was softly concluding, "to consider whether you would let this man build his version of a village in that green and pleasant land next to Everden?" It was her only cheap theatrical flourish, and Alison recognized that it was well-judged.

There was another silence and then it was broken by a huge outburst of applause.

It was Anthony Fell who held up his hand at length. "If there are any particular questions we would be glad to answer them. Now, or individually after the meeting. And the model is here, for anyone who would like to examine it more closely."

His hand lingered, expressively, over the lanes and gardens and clumps of little, crusty artificial trees.

A man stood up. Harriet recognized Ron, one of the darts players from the Wheatsheaf. He was embarrassed to find himself on his feet in front of so many people and he spoke quickly.

"Question is, what are we supposed to do? Pictures and models and ideas are all very nice, and I don't believe there's a soul in Everden who wants that other lot to put up their expensive boxes over there, but those of us ordinary people in the village, not councillors or any of the rest of it . . ."

He had recovered himself enough to direct a sharp sideways glance across the hall, to where most of the parish council were sitting. Harriet could only half-guess at the subtle undercurrents of village politics, and hope that they would flow with her rather than against.

". . . it's not in our hands, is it? We have to take what comes, whoever wins."

Harriet smiled warmly at him. "You can help us to win. That is, if you know you would prefer *this* to *that*."

The diamond on her right hand glittered briefly again as she pointed.

"You can write to the Planning Department. Write to your M.P. Join the Everden Association. Display and distribute Action for Everden publicity material. There are a dozen things you can do, if you are willing to help us."

It was the enthusiasm and the positive warmth in Harriet's voice that affected them, Alison thought, rather than anything she said. The hall was buzzing again, a low hum of interest and determination rising from the rows of chairs. Ron sat down, looking pleased with himself. From her vantage point at the back, Alison could see the backs of nodding heads. Tomorrow the letters to the authorities would start dropping into the letterbox on the wall outside the village shop.

More questions followed, to do with increased traffic and provision of services and whether buying priority would be given to local people. David and Anthony dealt with them smoothly. There was not a very high level of interest in the specifics, Alison noticed. The meeting had grasped the outline of Harriet's scheme and had been willingly beguiled by it.

Then a woman who Alison didn't know stood up. She was wearing a navy-blue vaguely marine-looking jumper and a striped shirt with the collar turned up. Alison guessed that she was an Everden outskirter, from one of the big houses outside the village with tennis courts in the secluded gardens and the tops of new conservatories just visible from the lane. Her husband would be a City commuter.

"There is one obvious question that no one has asked." Her voice confirmed Alison's guess. Harriet faced her pleasantly.

"What account, if any, does either plan take of Birdwood House itself?"

Harriet had expected the question and she had prepared herself for it. Perhaps the woman in the striped shirt had taken walks past Birdwood House, ventured up the drive as Harriet herself had done, maybe fantasized about selling the comfortable old rectory and restoring the half-ruin to its Victorian-Gothic glory, to the envy of the neighborhood. Maybe she was a genuine conservationist, or was simply curious. Harriet swallowed. Ever since she had stepped inside the tiled hall with Alison and looked upward in the torchlight into the ornate gallery, Birdwood House had been part of her dream. She was defensive of it, although it was no more hers to defend than it was the striped-shirt woman's.

"I can't tell you what the Castoria plan is. They don't send me any free information . . ." there was a polite ripple of laughter, now ". . . and so I can only guess. But judging by their past performance, I imagine that if they were able to purchase the house and its land . . ." Harriet didn't look at the councillors. She held the questioner's eyes instead ". . . they wouldn't hesitate to demolish the building and squeeze as many new units as possible onto the site. That is only my guess, of course."

"And what about your own scheme?"

Harriet could feel a small pulse ticking at her jaw, on the

point where it had been broken. She resisted the impulse to rub it away.

"The house would be saved. It would be fully restored, with the most sensitive care."

"As a private house?"

"That was its original function. Mr. Farrow built it as a home for his family, and it has been privately occupied ever since, except for the last few years when it has been unfortunately empty."

"But the house was willed to Everden, for the use of the village, wasn't it?"

The woman's husband, sitting beside her, was a plump man with glasses. He looked up at her now. Harriet couldn't tell whether he wanted to encourage his wife or to signal her to sit down and let someone else ask the awkward questions.

"That is true. But crumbling old houses are expensive to restore and then to maintain, as I'm sure you know. The original bequest didn't provide for that. It's an awkward dilemma. I don't think I have the right to make any further comments."

Harriet did allow herself to glance sideways, now, deliberately.

The woman persisted. "Do you intend to buy Birdwood House under the umbrella of your development scheme and restore it as a private house either for your own use or for resale for profit?"

Harriet had made her offer to the parish council. It was a very generous cash offer. But when she made it she had also indicated, with the utmost delicacy and reticence, that any further progress of the Birdwood scheme was dependent on her acquisition of the freehold of the house and garden. She had left them, to consider the proposal.

And so Harriet smiled at the woman now. The smile was a masterpiece of friendly regret, Alison noted. Harriet said, "There is only one potential buyer for Birdwood House. If it is sold it will be restored with all the available loving care, and it will be occupied as it always has been, by a responsible owner. It will not be put up for sale again." The support of the meeting was still with Harriet. There were two or three low mumbles of encouragement and some impatient shifting of feet and chairs.

"I don't think I can tell you any more," Harriet said, with gentle finality.

The woman sat down, but from his place beside her her husband surged to his feet. He pushed his spectacles back up the bridge of his nose and surveyed the hall. "We've listened to the pros of one development and the cons of another," he intoned.

"My question is a very simple one. Not for the people who have given themselves the platform, but for those in the body of the hall, Everden residents and friends. Do we not live in Everden because we value its rural beauty? The Birdwood site is a beautiful piece of our countryside. Why must it be built on by anyone at all?"

There was a rumble of voices.

From across the room another man in a suit, who had listened to all the discussion with folded arms, now unfolded and shouted back, "I endorse that entirely. The village character of Everden must be preserved at all costs."

And as if some secret password had been spoken, the Everden outskirters sprinkled all through the hall suddenly revealed themselves. Voice after well-modulated voice rose to cry no to Bottrill, and no to Harriet, too.

Beside her, Harriet glimpsed Anthony Fell masking the lower half of his face with his hand and exhaling gustily behind it.

The outskirters had bought into their rural idylls, into the big houses behind the close hedges, and they had come to defend their tranquil corners against whoever might try to squeeze on with them. They had taken the measure of Harriet's proposal and now they would shoot it down.

Too confident too soon, Alison thought. In front of her a man jumped up. She saw that it was Geoff, born in the house in Everden main street that he still lived in. He roared over the raised voices, "Our village? Whose bloody village, did you say? What do you do for the village except bugger off out of it at eight o'clock in the morning and bowl back in at eight at night? You don't even buy a pound of sugar in the shop, do you? Don't talk about the precious community, mate."

There was another barrage of shouting and the long-haired girl from the Wheatsheaf yelled over it, "We want *houses*. We want houses we can afford, not houses for people like you. We want this development, and we'll get it. It's what this dump needs, a shot in the arm."

More people sprang to their feet. The village hall became a sea of angry faces and waving arms. Alison felt the swelling tide of pent-up hostility between the incomers and the natives. The mood of the meeting swung from acceptance to combative in a matter of seconds, and Alison saw at once that the anger was not only rippling between the two factions but was also directed at Harriet, David, and Anthony up on the platform. She looked to Harriet, to see what she would do.

Harriet stood up, resting the knuckles of her clenched fists on the table in front of her. For a moment she stood in silence, watching the faces and listening. The sudden eruption of buried resentment was dismaying, but something in the rawness of it caught at her. The meeting up to this moment had gone too smoothly; there had been nothing in it for anyone to remember. Now everyone present would recall this, and each one would have an opinion. Harriet knew that it rested with her to capture those opinions.

She lifted her head. "It's a good question. Why build anything at all?" Her voice was clear, and it carried. Faces turned to her, and the noise diminished.

Tell them, Harriet exhorted herself. If she had learned anything from "Meizu" and Peacocks it was to fight her corner, and to try to turn disadvantage into advantage. In her head, for a brief second, she could hear the rolling and the clicking of the colored balls. "Listen to me and I'll tell you why," Harriet shouted.

She didn't try to convince the incomers that it would be socially beneficial for Everden to gain a whole subcommunity of affordable houses in the traditional style. Instead, in the City language familiar to herself and the men in suits, she made it clear that if neither Castoria nor her own company gained the site, then another developer surely would. Birdwood had been defined, and in the end it would succumb to development.

"The question can no longer be whether to develop, but *which plan you would prefer to see.*"

There came a roar of support, but it didn't drown the voice of the opposition.

"Not so," shouted the man with glasses. "Development is not inevitable. Why don't we ask Miss Bowlly, over there? Miss Bowlly doesn't want it, does she?"

The entire meeting turned and craned forward to look at her. Miss Bowlly scowled furiously in response. But then, still scowling, she levered herself to her feet and clumped forward in her perennial Wellington boots. She didn't mount the two steps to the platform but positioned herself in front of it, a small, conical, brown figure.

Harriet stared frozenly at the back of her fawn knitted bonnet. Now it would be made public that she had failed to buy the crucial tongue of land. Now Bottrill would hear that her only ammunition was ambitious talk, and pretty plans. The pulse in her jaw seemed to beat like a sledgehammer.

Miss Bowlly jabbed her finger at the big photographs. "It might seem a one-sided show to some, looking at these things. You might think it's an unfair representation of a man's work, those of you who like to think, seeing clever photographs that bend it and shrink it like these here do."

Harriet didn't dare to look to either side, at David or Anthony, nor at the striped-shirt woman or any of the rows of faces that peered at Miss Bowlly now, not at her. She fixed her eyes on the top of Alison's head, away at the back of the hall, and waited for whatever it was that was coming.

"Well, I can tell you something for nothing. I've met some of the young men who work for *him*." The finger jabbed again at the Bottrill pictures. "I didn't like them. All nice while they wanted something, they were, and when they found out they weren't going to get it they turned nasty. They weren't afraid to threaten me, with what would happen if I didn't be good and sell them my property. Noise, and big lorries, and workmen, and then no one would want to buy my place at all."

Miss Bowlly gave her meaty chuckle. Harriet sat quite still, unable to move.

"I wouldn't sell a pound of hedge blackberries to that lot." And she stabbed her finger again at the photographs.

There was a splutter of laughter. Miss Bowlly didn't smile. She turned to indicate Harriet sitting behind her. "Then this one came. It wasn't an option she was after, wrapped up in fancy language. *She* was prepared to put her money up, no strings, no promises to buy someday if it happened to suit her. She's probably no better than the rest of them, but she made me a fair offer, and I've got a nose for these things. I'd say she's honest, since you're asking what I think."

Miss Bowlly searched for the incomer couple and fixed them with a glare of dislike. "And since you've chosen to single me and my opinions out for public discussion, I'll tell you that I've listened to what's been said tonight. I'll say *she*'s right. There'll be houses on that bit of land whether you and your posh friends like it or not."

There was a rattle of applause. Miss Bowlly marched down the hall toward the door and the clapping followed her. Harriet wanted to let her head drop forward into her hands. But her hands were trembling, and she held her head upright.

"Thank you, Miss Bowlly," she called after her.

She couldn't have orchestrated the moment any better if she had planned and rehearsed it. *I didn't deserve that*, Harriet told herself, *but I'm grateful for it*.

She thought of Simon then, in his house, and the game she had taken.

She became aware of the pressure of David Howkins's hand

on her arm. People were leaving their chairs and flooding up onto the platform. Faces loomed over the model.

"Are you all right?" David asked her.

"Yes. Yes, I'm all right. I . . . didn't expect that from Miss Bowlly."

"You have admirers in every quarter," David dryly remarked.

There were more questions to answer. Anthony's finger traced the outlines of the village again and again as the heads bent over it. Young couples came to Harriet, wanting to put their names down on the list for starter houses.

"It's too early," she told them. "There is no list. There's no site, as yet. This is only the beginning." She made her gesture of drawing the bricks and mortar out of the air, trying to hold them together. "None of this can go any further if Mr. Bottrill is given planning permission, if the county planning committee refuses to consider our rival submission."

"We'll write to them," a girl said. "We'll do everything you told us. Please, take our names anyway, won't you? There's no other way me and Keith can get a house of our own, not near here."

Harriet took their names, writing them down on a page in her notebook. She saw Alison at the back of the crowd, seeming to nod in approval.

The questions persisted for more than an hour. At last, seemingly all of a sudden, the last people filtered away and the hall was empty. Only Alison was left, sitting in the front row with her legs stuck out in front of her.

What now? Harriet was thinking. Just what has all this gained us?

Then the doors banged open once more, and Miss Bowlly reappeared like the bad fairy. With all four of them staring at her she traversed the hall again and positioned herself squarely in front of Harriet.

Harriet found her voice and the initiative. "Have you come to tell me you're ready to sell, Miss Bowlly?"

"All right," Miss Bowlly answered, gracious to the end.

It was a brief meeting and exchange of promises. When Anthony had courteously escorted the old lady back to the door, Harriet sank back into her chair in unbelieving exhaustion. It was David who slapped his hand on the trestle table and gave a crow of triumph.

"I think Miss Bowlly's just handed the deal to us," Anthony said.

Harriet sagged in her chair. She was surprised to see the

delight in the three faces. Now the performance was over the adrenaline was seeping away. Even with Miss Bowlly, did they have enough?

"Will they come around to us?" she asked. "Do you think they will?"

It was Alison who answered. "Listen. I believed in Birdwood, as if it was already there. I felt I could walk down the streets and admire all the houses, as if I could touch all the good brick walls . . ." she glanced at David, and it was a glance that Harriet even in her lowness interpreted as flirtatious, ". . . even pick the flowers in the damned gardens. Everyone else in this room believed in it, too. They imagined it and they loved it. You could have collected down-payments on a couple of streets full of houses at least, if you'd only asked for them. I'd probably have parted with real money myself, and I don't need part-ownership of a two-bedroomed cottage in the authentic Kentish vernacular style. I've got a nose for these things as good as old Miss Bowlly's. Birdwood'll make your fortune. Your second fortune, of course."

Harriet knew that she was joking, but that there was a mixture of truth in what she said.

She reminded them, "There's a long, long way to go yet." But she found that her spirits were rising once again. The euphoria was infectious. And she had Miss Bowlly. Miss Bowlly was what she needed, more than all the goodwill in Everden.

"We covered a good distance tonight," Anthony said. They all smiled, dazedly, acknowledging it.

"So let's go and have a drink on it. Come back to the cottage," Alison invited.

They took down the posters and the big photographs and the REACTION AGAINST BOTTRILL IS ACTION FOR EVERDEN banner, and stacked the chairs once more, leaving the hall all ready, just as the Committee had stipulated, for the use of the playgroup the next morning. The last job of the evening was performed by David, who extracted a set of flat-packed boards from under the stage and reerected the Wendy house.

Then they went back to Alison's cottage and drank whiskey, growing noisier and readier to laugh as the bottle emptied. Alison watched David Howkins, carefully estimating the exact degree of her attraction to him. She also saw that he only looked at Harriet. A little later she stood up and when she had turned away from the group the corners of her mouth pinched in, compressing her lips, so that she looked older and disappointed.

Then she opened a cupboard and took out a second bottle of whiskey. She poured herself another measure, and when she sat down she was laughing again.

In the time before the planning committee meeting, Linda came home from school to stay for a weekend with Harriet. To settle it, there had been elaborate four-way telephone negotiations between Harriet, Ronny Page, Clare Mellen's secretary in California, and Caspar.

"She so much wants to come," Caspar said.

Harriet listened to his resonant voice. It was unmuffled by the miles between them, but there seemed to be longer silences between their careful words than could be explained by the distance.

"I'd like to see her."

"You've a way with the kid. She listens to what you say. Always did, since that first god-awful day." Caspar laughed at the memory, without self-criticism.

Harriet wanted to cut through the whiskey bluster. She could imagine him, at the wide window with the view over Los Angeles to the Pacific, and the diamond pool glimmering outside. She knew just what level in the bottle he had reached, and she felt neither affection nor sympathy for him.

"She listens to whoever takes the trouble to talk to her. Linda will be okay. How are you, Caspar?"

"Good. I'm looking at a couple of ideas."

"I meant, about the accident."

The longer silence again, before he said easily, "That's all been handled."

Harriet could imagine the lawyers and the agents, the calls and the deals, and the ears of the right policemen and deputy prosecutors that would have been employed in the handling. The discreet money and handshakes and silence.

"That's all right, then," she said, tonelessly.

"And you, Harriet?"

Even at this distance, even knowing what she did, his warmth and charm seemed to touch her. She answered, more expansively than she had intended, "I've got a new project, too. A kind of property deal, a community development." She told him about Birdwood, and the tense wait for the news of the planning committee decision. "If Bottrill gets the outline permission, that's the end. If he's turned down, we can submit our own scheme."

Caspar said, "It always was business that turned you on, Harriet, wasn't it?"

She could have bitten back. *Not just business. You did, until I knew better.* But she did not. She let the silence speak. There was no warmth, after all.

"You and Linda enjoy yourselves, won't you?"

"I'll take good care of her. Good-bye, Caspar."

That was all.

Harriet collected Linda from the school on a Friday evening. She was to deliver her back again on Sunday afternoon, in time for tea.

"Two whole days," Linda chanted. "Two whole days' freedom. What shall we do?"

Linda was taller and thinner. The unflattering uniform dress was too short for her, and her collarbones showed at the neck of her maroon sweater. She had been wearing her hair in regulation off-the-collar bunches, but as soon as Harriet drove out of the school gates she pulled out the maroon hair-ribbons and banished them to the winds out of the car window. Harriet caught sight of them out of the corner of her eye, whipping away over the hedge.

"For God's sake, Linda. What we *will* have to do now is spend two days combing John Lewis's for exactly the right shade of ribbon to replace those you've just chucked over the hedge."

Linda laughed. "Arabella Makepeace's got about twenty yards. I'll snip a teeny bit off the end of hers and she'll never notice the difference."

"Poor Arabella Makepeace. Still the unknowing provider, is she?"

"Still the total pain in the ass."

Linda seemed older, too, with a new veneer of confidence acquired with the bewildering speed that Harriet assumed was normal at her chameleon age. It seemed much longer than the bare year since Linda had crept out of the privet hedge, defiant and miserable, to confront Robin and herself. Harriet wanted to look hard at her, studying the new angles and shadows in her face, but she kept her eyes firmly on the road.

"I haven't seen you since the day we went to Santa Monica," Linda said.

"It was a good day," Harriet agreed.

It was a measure of Linda's new maturity that she let the rest of the Los Angeles topic lie quiet between them. There would be time to come back to it, proper time, not now in the car bowling toward Hampstead against the weekend traffic.

When they came in through Harriet's gate, Linda shuffled a sideways kick at the privet and giggled. Harriet laughed, too, and put one arm around her shoulders. They went up the steps and into the flat together.

Harriet had come up from Everden only that morning, in time to stock the refrigerator and make up the spare bed. To her the rooms felt chilly and unwelcoming. But Linda looked around at the pale walls and unobjectionable pictures with an admiring sigh.

"I really love your apartment," she said.

"Do you?" Harriet was startled. In comparison with the house at Little Shelley, even this neglected place must seem homely, she thought. "I . . . went off it, for a while. I've been staying with a friend of mine, in the country. But I like it when you're here."

Harriet had planned the evening's entertainment. They were going to the cinema, and then to have a Chinese supper. Linda had said that she loved Chinese food.

They were all ready to leave when the telephone rang. It was David, needing to talk about an aspect of financing the Birdwood scheme. Harriet sat down at her desk table at once, and drew some papers toward her.

Behind her back Linda stood waiting in silence. After a moment or two she crossed to the window and stared out, resting her forehead against the glass.

The conversation lasted for about eight minutes. When it was over, Harriet cheerfully said, "Sorry about that. Shall we go now?" Then she turned to look at Linda. The scowl that met her was an exact replica of the first expression she had seen, in Annunziata Landwith's drawing room.

"What's the matter with you?"

"I thought now you didn't work for Peacocks anymore it wouldn't be business all the time. This is our weekend. I really looked forward to it."

Harriet was angry. "I didn't *work* for Peacocks. I made it. It was mine and I lost it, and that hurt me. I don't expect you to understand what happened, but you're old enough to know what loss means. Now, I'm telling you that I'm trying to set up a new business. It's work, yes, but I do what I do because I enjoy it, because everyone needs to do something, because if I don't I'm like nothing. Like an empty paper bag. Can you understand that, Linda?"

She paused, then, realizing that she was shouting, surprised by the heat of her own response. She rubbed the back of her hand against her mouth, to contain the unnecessarily harsh words.

"If you like being here, if you like me, you'd better accept that work's a part of me. There *is* no me without it. You'll be spending weekends with a paper bag."

The attempt at lightness was too late, and lame-sounding.

Linda clenched her fists. "You'll have no time for *me*."

In her fear and indignation, the words came out as a squawk. Harriet heard in them all the resentment and bitterness at her parents' neglect.

"Oh, *Linda*."

She ran to her and tried to hold her. Linda struggled away but Harriet dug her fingers into the child's hair and twisted her head so that she was forced to look at her.

"You're hurting me."

"Listen then."

Linda was crying now. Unwilling tears smeared her cheeks.

"I have got time for you. I have, I always will. But you have to have time for me, too. It has to be mutual. That's what adult relationships are."

Harriet thought, *The hypocrisy of it. As if I were an expert*. She guided Linda to a sofa and made her sit down, still within the circle of her arms.

"I promise I will always have time for you, if you have time for me. Having time for me means accepting my work, what I do, as part of me. We can't cut the nice bits out of each other and ignore the rest. If we could, I'd keep all your fun and liveliness and cut out the scowling and the ribbon-throwing. But we can't do that. I take calls, you have tantrums. Shall we agree to go on as we are?"

Linda sniffed furiously, but she accepted the handkerchief that Harriet gave her. Harriet waited, pointedly.

At last Linda mumbled, "It's our weekend. I looked forward to it."

"I looked forward to it, too. It still *is* our weekend, unless you wreck it. Come on. Crispy fried duck, remember?"

"I'm not a baby. You don't have to bribe me with things to eat." Linda lifted her head and looked Harriet straight in the eye. "Is he your latest boyfriend?"

Harriet was momentarily bewildered. "Who?"

"Him. *David*."

She had said, *Hello, David*, of course. "It was a private conversation, Linda."

"I was standing four feet away, wasn't I? You didn't ask me to leave the room, did you?"

"No, I suppose I didn't."

"*Is* he?"

It was, Harriet reflected, the exact opposite. Their relationship had continued to make reverse progress from personal to professional. It was now conducted upon an entirely bloodless business footing.

"No, he isn't. I don't have anybody, at the moment, as it happens."

"Hmm." Linda rubbed her eyes with the handkerchief and screwed her nose up into a snout before blowing it thoroughly. "That may be the problem, you know. A woman needs a man. Everyone knows that."

"Then *everyone* is adopting a very old-fashioned and inaccurate view," Harriet snapped. "I'm surprised at you, Linda, for thinking anything of the kind. Now. Are we going to the cinema, or not?"

Linda's dignity was restored. With pursed lips and skeptical expression she went to fetch her jumper. "Whatever you say, Harriet," she murmured.

Harriet hid her amusement, and her relief. They went off to the pictures arm in arm.

On Saturday they went to the market at Camden Lock that Linda loved, and came home with armfuls of T-shirts and a small pair of Doc Marten's.

"Are you *sure* people wear these?" Harriet had asked doubtfully.

"Sure I'm sure. You're brilliant, you know, Harriet. Ronny will only buy me those stupid sandals with sunburst holes in the toes. Like in some dumb school story from nineteen *fifty-*something. But you understand."

"Some things." Harriet remembered her own battles with Kath over miniskirts and Twiggy lashes. The memory made her laugh.

"Actually," Linda said seriously, "You understand about most things. I'm, you know, sorry about last night. I guess it was unreasonable of me, was it?"

"About as unreasonable as it was for me to shout back at you. So I'm sorry, as well."

Abruptly, Linda said, "Do you miss my Dad? I wish it could have worked out. You'd've been my stepmom, and I'd really have loved that."

Harriet tried for the right words. Linda was perceptive, and she didn't delude herself with unrealistic hopes. She said *would have*. "I miss him a lot. I've never known anyone like your father; I don't think there is anyone like him. I miss his voice, and the way he talks, and his energy, and his sense of humor. All kinds of different things about him. But will you understand what I'm saying if I tell you that all the things didn't add up to make a necessary whole? Not for me. Nor did I for him, you know."

"Some things about him you didn't love." Linda was resigned. Her realism touched Harriet more deeply than the tears had done. She did examine her small face now. The expression was earnest, not despondent.

"No," Harriet said gently.

Linda considered. "I understand. You know you said about not believing that a woman needs a man?"

"Yes."

"I thought about it. I think *some* women do. Like Clare; you know, as if there's no show without a man there to watch it? But you're not like that. When I think about you I don't think about you being a woman. You're just a person."

"Thank you. I accept that as a compliment," Harriet said, meaning it.

"That's okay. Shall we do the cooking, now?"

Linda had announced that she wanted to learn to cook. Harriet had protested that she was hardly the person to enlist as a teacher, but Linda was adamant. She said she loved the way the kitchen was a real part of Harriet's apartment. In the Bel Air house, she said, Mercedes didn't like her to go in the kitchen at all, and when Caspar was at Little Shelley there wasn't any chance to cook.

"He can make all kinds of food, though. He's really good at it."

"Yes, I know," Harriet said.

So they had agreed that they would have supper at home *à deux*, and Linda would prepare it under Harriet's direction. Between them they had settled on grilled lemon chicken and stuffed baked apples as a menu Harriet felt they might reasonably manage. Linda put on an apron and pushed back the sleeves of her new T-shirt. Together they laid out the ingredients. Linda put a tape in Harriet's cassette machine and hummed exuberantly.

"Watch that knife, it's sharp," Harriet warned her, as she attacked a handful of fresh herbs from the market.

"I can *handle* it," Linda answered patiently.

They worked side by side, comfortable with one another.

Harriet hoped that Linda found the same satisfaction in their collaboration as she was discovering for herself.

When the telephone rang Harriet assumed that at six o'clock on a Saturday evening it would be Jane, or Jenny, or perhaps Alison. Unthinkingly, she lifted the receiver from the wall next to the work-top in a buttery hand.

"Harriet?" a man's voice answered. "This is Martin Landwith."

It was so unexpected that Harriet could only repeat, conventionally, "Hello. How are you?"

Months had passed since she had spoken to him. Her dispatch from Peacocks had been entirely organized by Robin; Martin had written her a carefully worded letter of sympathy afterward.

"Very well, thank you. Harriet, Annunziata is with some friends of ours in Hampstead, and I'm meeting her there for dinner. It's not very far from where you are, I believe. May I drop in and see you for fifteen minutes on the way past?"

Harriet didn't think quickly enough to manufacture an excuse. She was still too startled by finding herself in conversation with him at all. She could only say, feebly, "Um, yes, I suppose so."

Martin was as smooth as the butter that Linda was busy rubbing into the chicken skin.

"About seven, then," he said. Harriet was left listening to the dial tone.

"Are you okay?" Linda asked.

Harriet sighed, foreseeing trouble. "That was Martin Landwith. Do you remember him?"

Linda gave a theatrical grimace. "Ugh. That house. All those drapes and cushions."

Harriet supposed that because Bel Air was home, Linda didn't look with the same critical eye at Clare's decor. She remembered thinking that the Bel Air mansion made Little Shelley look bleakly understated.

"Mmm."

"What did he want?"

"I don't know, exactly. He's going to pay us a little visit in an hour's time."

Linda put down her knife. Harriet watched her, side-on. She took a deep breath, raising her skinny shoulders, controlling herself by being seen to control herself.

"Is *he* staying to dinner?"

"Definitely not."

Linda picked up her knife once more, exhaling steadily.

"Good. Have I chopped enough of this stuff?"

There was no complaint this time about *our weekend*. Linda had listened to what she had been told.

"Yes, that's plenty," Harriet said. They went calmly on with their preparations.

At seven o'clock exactly Martin rang the doorbell. Harriet thought, *If he turns up on a Saturday evening, he can take us just as we are*. She showed him straight into the kitchen where Linda was perched on a stool, arranging her stuffed apples in a baking dish, surrounded by the debris of their cooking.

"You remember Linda Jensen, Martin?"

"Of course I do." Martin was about to extend an avuncular hand but then, seeing Linda's, he thought better of it. Linda favored him with a blank stare, and then turned her attention to licking the sugar and cinnamon off her fingers.

Martin accepted a glass of sherry and stood in the middle of the kitchen looking around him. For a Saturday evening in Hampstead he was dressed a shade less formally than on a weekday. The dark blazer was still magically tailored to make him seem taller and slimmer than he really was. Harriet found it almost comically incongruous to see him standing among her pots and pans. She caught herself staring at him, and turned abruptly to hustle Linda's chicken into the refrigerator.

Linda watched it disappear. "Harriet and I are having dinner," she said coldly. "I did the cooking for her."

"Jolly good. This all looks very cozy."

Harriet concealed a smile. She thought, *If you turn up more or less unannounced . . .*

Linda's chilliness was adult in its potency.

"Ah, I was hoping, Harriet, that we might have five minutes' talk?"

"Linda, would you like to go and watch some television?"

"How long for?"

"Until I have finished talking to Mr. Landwith," Harriet said severely. Linda would have to learn to gauge the dividing line between the unencouraging and the simply rude.

"I'll go in the garden."

She swung her legs off the stool and strolled out. A moment later they saw her appear in the overgrown garden. She sat down in the late sun, on a bench under a heavy swathe of roses. She settled down with her back to the kitchen window, her knees pensively drawn up to her chin.

"Not a very easy child, that one," Martin said.

"On the contrary. She's extremely bright, and excellent company." *Only not an easy child in the prize-winning, captain of cricket, father's-footsteps fashion of* your *child,* Harriet thought. *I know which I prefer.*

"Yes. Well. Harriet, you won't mind if I come straight to the point?"

"Please."

He was looking at her in the old, calculating manner. He seemed, if it was possible, younger and fitter than when she had first met him. His appraisal of her contained the same elements of shrewd business evaluation and sexual challenge. Harriet felt impatient, and at the same time alarmingly susceptible. Martin was as attractive as ever. She wondered how it would be, after all this time, if he had come to proposition her?

The truth is, she told herself, I'm a sucker for a clean limb and a chiseled profile. After all that high-minded stuff I preached to Linda, too.

She became aware that Martin's expression had changed. He was looking oddly at her. It must be because she was smiling. It was his son who had accused her, a long time ago, of too often looking as if she were enjoying some private joke.

"Go on," she encouraged him, resettling her face. Of course he hadn't come to proposition her. Not in fifteen minutes, surely?

"I heard—someone in the city told me, it doesn't matter who—that you're involved in a new venture?"

There were no secrets in business, Harriet thought.

"Not yet. It's no more than an idea."

"I heard it was more than that." Martin went to the window, as if to check that Linda was far enough out of earshot. He turned abruptly. With his back to the light his features were blotted out. He became a dark outline against the sunshine.

"I came to say, be careful."

Harriet repeated, "Careful?" She couldn't see his face, only the black shape of his head haloed with yellow light. "What do you mean?"

"Just that property and construction are dirty businesses."

"I'm not afraid of dirt."

"I don't think you understand me. If you're trying to block a deal of Keith Bottrill's you should know that his battles are not always fought on paper. His methods can be unconventional. Not personally, of course. But you could find a couple of burly individuals stepping out of the shadows one night, and suggesting that you let Mr. Bottrill pursue his legitimate interests without opposition."

In the warm light, in her own kitchen, Harriet shivered. She saw windy, empty streets and foul-smelling tunnels, and the

echoing vaults of underground car-parks. She knew how it would
be, when the two men slid out of shadows to block her path,
because it had already happened. She wrapped her arms around
herself, rubbing her chilled fingers against her bare arms.

It isn't cold, she told herself. Looking past Martin's bulk she
could see Linda, stretched out flat on the bench now, pulling at a
spray of creamy roses. But still, she glanced up at the locks and
bolts that protected the tall window overlooking the garden.
Simon had locked his doors and windows. He had pasted
newspaper over the glass. Simon. Harriet lifted her head. *Nothing will happen. It's happened already. I'm immune, now.*

"I didn't mean to frighten you," Martin said.

"I'm not frightened."

Martin walked away from the window. He crossed to the
work-top, where the scattered remnants of Linda's cooking lay,
and the sherry bottle beside them. He lifted his empty glass.
Harriet could see his face again.

"May I?"

"Please, help yourself." She picked up a cloth and began to
wipe up spilled crystals of brown sugar. Then she straightened
again, and still holding the cloth with the sugar in her cupped
hand she said, "Thank you for the warning. I'll remember what
you said."

Martin nodded. With one hand resting on her kitchen table,
the other holding his sherry glass by the stem, tilting it as if he
were going to comment on the color of the wine, Martin seemed
to be contemplating something new.

Harriet only had to wait a moment.

"Yes," he said thoughtfully. "I knew there would be no
putting you off."

"Hardly."

His dark eyes moved across her face. "I very much admire
your spirit, Harriet. And your capabilities. Tell me, are you
raising capital yet?"

Harriet almost laughed out loud. "Did I *hear* that?"

Martin made a small gesture with his manicured hand, an
urbane, smoothing-away gesture that indicated what was past
was gone, and so need not disturb them. Harriet wanted to crack
his composure. She wanted to make him hear. She shouted
at him.

"Martin, have you forgotten what Landwith's did to me?
Levered me out of Peacocks overnight, while I was on holiday,
after creeping around lying to my shareholders and my family?"

He was quite unperturbed. People must often shout at him, Harriet thought.

"Not Landwith's, specifically. Robin. As you will remember."

"It's the same damned thing."

"Not quite. Have you talked to Robin lately?"

He was impervious. Harriet's incredulity bounced off him, making no impression. She sighed, impatient rather than angry. "Of course not. Nor will I be talking to him in the future."

"Ah. Well then, you won't know that we have decided to separate the business. Probably not before time. Robin is a grown man and a shrewd brain, and it has probably been my mistake to keep him too much under my eye. He needs to spread his wings now. In the future, we shall be operating much more as separate entities."

"I see." Harriet could only guess at which transgressions of the favored son, or what breakdown of the subtle powerplay between the two of them, had led to such a severance. She could only wonder, too, if Robin had at the end refused to play with the right emphasis the role for which his father had groomed him. The thought, surprisingly, made her feel sad. She wondered what else Martin and Annunziata had to turn to for consolation.

Martin went briskly on. "If you're looking to raise capital for your development, Harriet, I hope you would come to me. I'd spread the investment, of course, we could look into that when the time came. But as a basic principle . . ."

She interrupted him, gently but with all the firmness she could command. "Martin. I wouldn't come to you for capital if you were the last person on the earth. Even if you and Robin are no longer in partnership. I couldn't, you see. But thank you for the offer, and for coming all the way here to tell me to look after myself."

Was there any dinner party in Hampstead, she wondered?

Martin set down his glass, empty once more. "No need to thank me. I like you, Harriet, you know."

He took her hand and shook it. The appraising look came, and a crooked, perceptive, likable smile with it.

"Good-bye, Martin. Would you like to say good-bye to Linda? I'll call her in."

"Don't worry." He went to the window and sketched a wave. Harriet saw him to the front door and watched him down the steps, a smallish, dandified, confident man who didn't impress her as much as he once had done.

Linda came back into the kitchen, peering warily around the door.

"Gone?"

"Yes, gone."

"Let's grill the chicken now, I'm starved." They smiled at one another.

Later, after they had eaten the meal and praised one another extravagantly for it, and after they had watched television together for an hour, they made Linda's bed up once again in the living room. Harriet wished that she had a proper spare bedroom, so that she could think of it as Linda's room when she was at school, or in Los Angeles. When Linda scrambled under the covers Harriet sat on the edge of the bed, looking at the way her fine hair fanned out on the pillow.

"I've had a lovely day," she told her.

"Me, too," Linda sighed. She put up her arms and locked them around Harriet's neck. "I love you," she said.

Harriet whispered to her, "I love you, too."

Thinking of the other times she had said the same words it came to her that it was only for Kath that they had lasted. Only now she believed that they would last for Linda, too.

Before she went to her own bed, Harriet checked the bolts on every window, and the locks and chains that secured the doors. She wasn't afraid, she had been telling the truth when she told Martin so. But she wanted to be sure, while Linda was under her roof, that her house was secure. It was as if Martin's visit had made her realize how valuable the little girl was. She was glad he had come, for that.

Two things happened, in quick succession, after Linda went back to school.

The first was that Harriet received a letter from the Clerk to Everden Parish Council, informing her that the Council, on behalf of the village of Everden, was willing to accept her offer to purchase Birdwood House and the gardens thereof.

The second, at the end of June, was the announcement that Castoria Developments' proposal for the Birdwood Estate had been turned down by the County Planning Committee.

Harriet walked briskly along Leadenhall Street toward Piers Mayhew's offices. She was early for the meeting and it was a pleasure to walk, passing women in summer dresses and bank messengers and pin-striped men who strolled, for once, instead of rushing. With the arrival of high summer and the prospect of holidays, the City seemed to have taken on a festive air. Harriet had been working hard, but she felt as full of energy as if she had just returned from a holiday. She looked up at the sky, and at the roofline of the banks and financial institutions, in a kind of salute. She was passing near Morton's, the bank where she had made a visit to the three wise monkeys in an effort to raise capital for Peacocks, and she made another acknowledgment to the black glass edifice. Today's meeting would be the opposite of what she had experienced at Morton's. She had been waiting for today for a long time.

Piers Mayhew's office suite was done up in English country house style. His English-rose receptionist came out from behind her walnut desk and showed Harriet into the sanctum. Piers jumped up and came to shake her hand. He was noticeably glinting with anticipation.

"All ready for the off?" Piers often talked in racing or sporting jargon.

"All ready," Harriet said composedly.

At eleven o'clock, Piers's secretary announced that Mr. Bottrill and Mr. Montague had arrived.

"Show them in," Piers said. He was rubbing his hands with pleasure. "Show 'em in and let's see what they're made of."

The two men were ushered into the room.

Keith Bottrill was a big man. The sleeves of his suit creased horizontally around his biceps and rose up in protest over his wide shirtcuffs. His striped tie lay like an exhausted tongue over his convex chest. His eyes, small points in a fleshy, suntanned face, went straight to Harriet. He made his solicitor, thin and dark with black-rimmed spectacles, seem by contrast as elegant as Martin Landwith.

Bottrill's hand enveloped Harriet's. She felt that he could easily grind her bones, and the thought of dark places and empty corners came back to her. She withdrew her fingers, and forced herself to look into his eyes.

"Thank you for coming to meet us today."

The man smiled, showing crowded teeth. "We've got interests in common. Important interests have we not? It's a pleasure to be here."

The four of them sat down around Piers Mayhew's conference table. Keith Bottrill leaned forward, knitting his thick fingers together. He was wearing a gold bracelet.

"The Birdwood site," Harriet said softly. "Shall we get straight down to business?"

"By all means," Keith Bottrill answered. "It's what we're all here for, isn't it?"

"I don't think it will come as a surprise to you if I tell you that I have acquired the site access, will it? And you probably also know that I am in the process of acquiring Birdwood House and the surrounding ground?"

"I did know as much. As you also know that the clowns in the planning department have turned down my first proposal." The man leaned back, crossing one tree-trunk leg over the opposite knee. Harriet was not sure whether the accompanying facial tremor was intended as a wink. She stared back at him, stone-faced, and waited.

"So we've come to make a proposal to you, Miss Peacock, in return. A commercial proposal. That's what you're intending, isn't it?"

Harriet and Piers let him talk. Montague slid a sheet of notes in front of him, and Bottrill unfolded his plan. As they had known it would be, it was a proposal for amalgamation, Harriet's interests with those of Castoria Developments. Keith Bottrill's creases softened, and his thick fingers danced and riffled through his plans and notes. His voice became almost musical as he extolled the beauty of the site, the desirability of the development, the opportunities that would thickly present themselves once the small obstacles had been cleared. It was, he told her, hardly surprising that a businesswoman of Harriet's caliber had been similarly attracted. And it was in their mutual, entirely mutual interests to present a united front now. As a team, they would be formidable.

The crowded teeth showed again.

It was just a question of agreeing the detail, the mutually acceptable terms, was it not?

Mr. Montague put his pale fingers together, indicating his alertness in working out any details to their mutual satisfaction.

When she was quite sure that Bottrill had finished his pitch, and was leaning back in pleasure awaiting her agreement, Harriet spoke. She took pleasure in letting her words fall like cold stones into the pool of oily warmth that Bottrill had spilled.

"Our interests are by no means common," she said clearly.

The temperature in the room dropped by several degrees. The solicitor let his fingers fall apart again.

"You are proposing an in-and-out development that will do nothing to enhance the existing village. I am interested in helping to create an integrated community that will bring direct benefits to local people. I have to tell you that there is no basis for an amalgamation of our interests. None whatsoever."

Angrily, the man started forward in his seat. "I don't think you appreciate quite what the financial opportunities are. Quite what the returns on this project will be. Even if, as I am willing to agree, they are divided equally between us."

Harriet said, "I do appreciate the opportunities. And I reject your version of them."

The man was not used to rejection. A dull red flush spread under his suntan. Silence turned solid in the pleasant room. Harriet held herself still in her seat, against a sudden urge to run. Beside her, reassuringly, Piers unscrewed the cap of his fountain pen.

He began, "If I might propose—"

Bottrill snarled, "Propose nothing, friend." And then he turned to Harriet. He thrust out his big hands, front and back, like a huge, meaty, aggressive child presenting them for adult inspection before eating. "Take a good look," he shouted at her. "Look at them. I've worked with my hands. I started out, shoveling rubble. I've made a living at this business. I'll go on making a bloody living out of it."

Oh yes, Harriet thought. A living, all right. Your gold bracelet and your Rolls-Royce initialed KGB, and your ranch house with the swimming pool, all made out of people's land and hopes and security. *I've got you now. I'm not afraid of you.*

She listened to him ranting. He was trying to make an honest living. He had had years of the privileged classes, Harriet and her kind, blocking his path and spouting their lily-white ideals at him, they should try to live life the hard way, live it as he had been forced to do. Then they would know what he stood for.

The coarse words crashed around the listeners' ears. Piers studied the blotter in front of him, and Mr. Montague sat with one hand shading his eyes, his body curved away from his client's bulk by the merest suggestive millimeter.

The voice went on. The man changed his tack, from self-justifying to threatening. He would buy more land and block Harriet's scheme. He would sell his interests to a third party and defeat her in that way.

Harriet lifted her head. She had heard enough. She looked full at him, as cold and reasonable as he was sweaty and incoherent. She used his name for the first time.

"Mr. Bottrill, there is only one buyer for the Birdwood land.

And that buyer is me." The pleasure of it was better than any sensation she had ever known. She sat still, and let the fire of it burn through her veins.

Keith Bottrill subsided. As if the wind was blowing out of him, he seemed to grow smaller and quieter. Harriet knew that there was nothing to fear from Bottrill, neither for herself nor Linda. There would be no men stepping out of the dark to bar her way. Another kind of silence occupied the room now. It was thoughtful, even calculating. And then Bottrill's sausage fingers made a surprisingly fine, snipping movement, as if severing an invisible thread.

"Let's cut through all the talk, shall we?"

"By all means."

"What are you offering?"

Harriet said, "You bought in the region of two thousand pounds per acre. I will give you fifteen hundred, for the portions of the site you already own. I will take over your options, and give you ten thousand pounds for the lot." She spoke colorlessly but she thought, *Count yourself lucky, too.*

The man and his solicitor murmured together. Piers stood up, as if to stretch his legs, and wandered to the window to look down into the street. Harriet waited.

"All right," Keith Bottrill said, as if he were agreeing the price of a used car.

It was the lawyers' turn, then. Piers returned to his seat, and the blood seemed to flow back into Mr. Montague's frozen limbs.

Fifteen minutes later, the meeting was over. The English rose came to the doorway, and escorted the property developer and his solicitor away.

Piers Mayhew held out his hand to Harriet. "Congratulations," he said.

Harriet took his hand. The moment of triumph was like a physical thrill.

She thought, *If only Robin were here to see me now.*

Twenty

THE WHITE VAN MARKED "Decorations for All Occasions" was still parked in front of the house and, even though the November evening was chill and murky, the double doors stood open, letting the night's dampness seep inside and bead the old tiles with tiny drops of moisture.

One of the caterers' assistants came in, two cardboard boxes filled with glasses balanced in his arms. He passed through the hall toward the kitchens at the back of the house, where food for two hundred fifty people was being assembled.

Harriet leaned on the smooth wood of the gallery rail, looking downward and letting her eyes follow at random the stars and diamonds and octagons of the tile patterns. The wind blew in a flurry of wet leaves that stuck themselves down like defects in the geometrical repeat. It didn't matter, Harriet thought idly. It suited the theme of the party. She straightened up and went slowly down the wide stairs. Her fingers ran down the mahogany banister, moving with the fat curves of it. The carving had been dusted, but not very thoroughly, and she could still feel the faint furring of the years under her fingertips. The bare boards of the stairs had been swept, but there were still fine particles of grit that made a tiny crackle under the soles of her shoes.

The evidence that the slow decay of Birdwood had been barely interrupted did not disturb her. It gave her, rather, a sensuous awareness of what was waiting to be done. She would do it; she could do it, now that the house was hers. The roof would sit taut and dry again, the wind and the rain would make no impression, and beneath the roof the proper mahogany and glass and tiles and marble would shine once more.

Mine. Harriet looked up into the dim space over her head. Three or four of the first-floor bedrooms had been hastily cleaned for this evening, and lights shone in them as if they were already lived in. *My beautiful house.* She felt a pride of possession as strong as she had once felt for Peacocks.

"Sorr-y. The boys keep leaving this door wide open."

The cheerful, hearty girl who ran the party organizers came through the hall in her white apron. She grinned at Harriet, standing at the foot of the stairs. "Gosh, you look nice."

Harriet was already dressed for the evening. She had stared at her own reflection and the unfamiliar dress of ivy-green velvet in a faded and spotted mirror in one of the bedrooms. The dress seemed to suit the house.

"Thank you. Don't worry about the door, I'll do it."

She crossed the hallway and slipped out onto the porch, pulling the big doors behind her. Through the broken ironwork she could see the sky. The moon was briefly visible behind torn clouds.

Harriet had lost her fear of the dark. She found comfort in the shelter and anonymity of it once again. She walked slowly now across the bitten grass, listening to the creaking of the huge trees that sheltered the house. The bare branches slapped and twisted in the wind.

Away from the house and the trees, at the farthest point of the patch of Birdwood ground that she now owned, Harriet saw another van parked. Torch beams streaked across the grass, turning it momentarily green. The men were setting up in readiness for the fireworks display.

Harriet kept away from the farthest-reaching arcs of light. She came to the shrubbery and stood for a moment in the shelter of the evergreens, breathing in the musty smell of recent rain. There were lights in all the downstairs windows of the house, shining out where two of David Howkins's men had torn down the black-scribbled boarding. Birdwood had come to life again.

Harriet did not know how long she stood there, looking at it. She only became aware that the damp soaked up through her shoes, and that the velvet dress did not keep out the cold. She retraced her steps, across the grass and under the broken porch. The double doors stood ajar, showing the jewel colors and the brightness inside. There was the smell of cooking, and the sound of laughter. Harriet went inside again, leaving the doors as an invitation.

She walked from room to room, looking at what had been done.

It was not the big corporate party that she had once imagined herself giving. This was a party for Everden, and the prospect of it pleased her more.

"Decorations for All Occasions" had done their job well, assisted by the builders and contract cleaners. The house was semi-derelict and unfurnished, but a theatrical scene had been set. The big, empty rooms were low-lit, and the light was enhanced by log fires burning in the open hearths and hundreds of candles set in sconces. The designers had taken sheets of white fabric, and dipped them in plaster of Paris. Then they had hung them up, to set in ripples and folds. The effect was of broken marble pillars and crumbling classical balustrades, set within the rooms to create dim alcoves and receding grottoes. The pillars were wreathed in garlands of ivy and mistletoe, and great branches of fir were draped on the marble mantelpieces and over the doors, to give off their celebratory, Christmas scent in the rooms' warmth.

In the plaster recesses there were simple benches and folding chairs; in the biggest room a dance floor had been laid and a band would play; in another round tables were covered with floor-length white cloths, ready for supper.

Harriet approved of what she saw. The fire- and candle-light cast wavering shadows of the temporary pillars on the intricate moldings of the ceilings, and shone on the glossy tendrils of ivy. The old house had been transformed for one night into a part-Gothic, part-Arcadian fantasy. Soon the people would come. If Harriet had taken Birdwood with one hand, she was trying, tonight, to give it back with the other.

The big, white invitations with the deep embossing had gone out to as many local people as she felt could squeeze into these rooms. The parish council was coming, with wives and husbands, and the Wheatsheaf regulars, and the vicar and the churchwardens and the outskirters from the big houses with the new conservatories. The local farmers and their wives were coming, and the big landowners, and the smallholders who had sold options on their parcels of land to Keith Bottrill. The Women's Institute was coming in full force, and the Young Conservatives, and the Pensioners Club, or most of it. Even Miss Bowlly was coming.

They were coming, Harriet knew, to peer into the rooms and to nudge each other and to take another look at "Meizu Girl," if they hadn't seen enough of her already. Part of her, in her pride, wanted to take their breath away with the house's splendor for the night. But another part of her, a better part, wanted them to see that Birdwood House was still here, and to convince them that it still belonged to Everden.

Harriet was wandering between the broken pillars when she heard a sound behind her. She turned, and saw Alison.

"What do you think?" She spread her arms wide. She was

proud of the renaissance, even though it would last for only one night.

Alison looked, at the ivy garlands and the blazing candles and the dark, massed weight of the fir branches. "Like I said. When you do something, you give it your full attention. No half measures. It looks—wonderful."

"I'm nervous," Harriet confessed. "Do you think they'll come? Will they enjoy themselves?"

"Will they *come*? Nothing else has been talked of in Everden for weeks. When I came through tonight, the excitement was palpable. But I can't pretend what will constitute enjoyment for the Pensioners Club. Spotting Tom Frost with the vicar's wife behind the plaster groves, perhaps?"

They laughed, but Alison was thinking that, for all her capability, there was an uncertainty in Harriet that could make her seem oddly vulnerable. It must be the combination, of fragility with her undoubted power, that made her attractive to men. Alison had seen the eyes that followed her, but she didn't suppose the admiration compensated for the thinness of Harriet's skin that aroused it. It would be easier, she thought, for an entrepreneur to have an elephant's hide.

"Come and see the rest," Harriet invited.

They toured the house, walking through the expectant rooms where waiters and waitresses were taking up their stations, and penetrating into the kitchens where a canvas encampment had been erected beyond the back doors. There seemed to be dozens of people, all working like clockwork.

To Alison, Harriet seemed lonely in the midst of it all, in all the briefly made-up crumbling splendor of her big house. They came back to the hallway and stood at the foot of the sweep of stairs. Harriet was looking out into the darkness.

"They'll be here soon," she whispered.

Suddenly she turned to Alison. She took her hand, with a slight awkwardness. "It's because of you that I'm here," she said. "Because you were generous, and invited me to stay with you when you hardly knew me. I wanted to say thank you."

Alison was touched. The impressions that had drifted around her as they toured the house swam together now, and coalesced. Harriet was powerful, and she was very rich, and very busy, and she was in need of friends. It was so obvious that Alison was irritated with herself, although she prided herself on being perceptive, for not having expressed it to herself before. She had been deceived by the facade, as others were.

"I'm glad I did," she said. "Although there's no need to

thank me for anything. I wouldn't have missed tonight for all the world." She held Harriet's hand for a moment, and then let it go.

"Look," Alison said. She pointed, out through the open doors. There were car headlights, turning in at the Birdwood gates.

Harriet put her hands to the skirt of her green velvet dress, and then stood up straight. They came, in a steady stream.

There were the pillars of Everden, the women in best dresses topped off with woolens, as if they couldn't bring themselves to believe that the derelict rooms would be warm enough, and the men in stiff suits. There were the outskirters in last-season's designer outfits and some of their husbands in dinner suits, and the farmers and their wives, and the pensioners, and the young people, who came in bigger groups exuding noisy, nervous bravado.

Harriet shook every hand, and welcomed each arrival back to Birdwood.

The people flooded into the rooms, whispering at first and peering skeptically at the theatrical decor and nudging one another, but they swept the glasses of champagne off the silver trays held out by young waiters, and the volume of talk and laughter swelled until it filled the rooms and drowned the soft music played by the band.

David came with Anthony Fell, bringing a double contingent of their staffs so that brawny, suntanned young men and black-clad design people filtered between the cardigans and outskirter taffeta. Harriet, who had worried that there would be an imbalance of elderly ladies, began to see that there was no need. Anthony Fell bore down on Miss Bowlly, and pressed another glass of champagne into her hand.

A hand touched Harriet's shoulder, and she turned to see David beside her.

"It looks spectacular. Just what they need to convince them that anything can be done, with a will."

She turned her face up to his. David didn't remove his hand. "Will it be a success?"

"It is a success."

Harriet looked away from him, abruptly, at the throng around them. "Mingle, mingle," she begged him.

"I know what do to," David said. He half-smiled at her, and went away into the crowd. Harriet found that her eyes followed him. She allowed herself to take a glass of champagne from a passing tray.

A small nucleus of Harriet's own friends came, Jenny and

Charlie and Jane and Karen among them. Jane stood in the big room, framed by ivied pillars. Candlelight shone through her faintly frizzed hair, making a nimbus around her head, as she surveyed all the people and the waiters and the musicians circulating under the grand plaster ceilings.

"Jesus," she breathed.

"Thank you for coming," Harriet said warmly.

"The lady of the manor commands, and we can only obey."

"Don't say it like that."

Jane turned to her. "I was only joking."

"I know, but don't."

Charlie came between them, put his arm through Harriet's. "Show me everything," he commanded. They wound away, between the knots of chattering people, and Harriet pointed eagerly past the decoration for the night and described the work that would be done, must be done, to put the house back into order.

"You really love this place, don't you?" Charlie asked.

"Yes. I never felt I had a home before. Charlie, I have to go and talk to people."

He let her go, watching her with amusement as she plunged into the task.

Harriet worked her way through the rooms, talking and laughing, shaking hands and making introductions. The separate groups began slowly to mingle and then to coalesce. The party was moving under its own momentum. Harriet drank another glass of champagne, and began to enjoy herself.

Among Harriet's own guests were Kath and Ken. Ken had gravitated naturally toward the building contingent, and Kath pecked at the edges of the Everden ladies groups, with Harriet watching her from the corner of her eye. After two drinks Kath's fair skin flushed pink and she grew animated, laughing at something Anthony Fell told her and then resting her hand confidingly on Karen's arm.

When the people began to drift into the supper room and settle themselves at the round tables, Harriet found herself sitting with Kath on a garden bench in one of the plaster grottoes.

"Are you all right, love?" Kath asked, as she almost always did.

"Yes, Mum, I'm all right."

"It's a very grand party. It's not what I was expecting, not at all."

"What were you expecting?"

When Kath laughed, in a certain half-apologetic way she

had, Harriet was reminded of the young girl she had once glimpsed behind her mother's face. She saw the girl now. Kath's fingers came up to smother her laughter. "Something more like a village fete. Iced cakes, tea urns, and wet grass. I should have known better, shouldn't I, since you had the planning of it?"

She was looking across the room, into the heart of the log fire. Her expression was a mixture of pride and awe.

"It must all be costing a fortune," she murmured.

What Harriet saw was the anxiety that habitually overlaid her mother's face.

"It's all right," she reassured her. "It's important, and the cost doesn't matter."

Kath sat up straighter, as if determined to make a confession. "I never said I was sorry. I *was* sorry, Harriet, but I did what I thought was right."

"I know you did." Harriet wasn't going to say that it was all right, offering yet another reassurance, because it was not. With Kath, she could have saved Peacocks from Robin Landwith. "I know why you did it."

Kath nodded. They saw Ken, red-faced and beaming his enjoyment, beckoning from the doorway.

"There's your Dad. He'll be famished. He wants us to go in with him to have dinner."

"You go. I'll be in when I've made sure of everyone else."

Harriet kissed her mother's cheek, and watched her walk away, taller than usual on dressed-up high heels.

Not my Dad, she thought. And she also knew that even though they didn't speak of Simon it didn't mean that he was forgotten. Harriet thought of him every day, and wished for him.

She left the shelter of the grotto, and went in search of the last of her guests who might need accompanying into dinner. Harriet was the last to go in herself, on the arm of Anthony Fell. She had grown to like him, as well as to admire what he did.

They surveyed the crowded tables. Anthony said smoothly, "This is a very nice piece of P.R. It won't do the planning application any harm."

"It's not just P.R. I wanted people to come to Birdwood, to feel that it hasn't just been taken up by some stranger. I'd like to do other things here, village things, when the house is restored. The place was willed to Everden, in the beginning."

"Very commendable," Anthony said. Harriet sensed that he was making mild fun of her, but she let it pass. She didn't know, yet, how she would establish the links without adopting the lady-of-the-manor role for herself. Jane's sharp remark had struck home. But she determined that she would do it, somehow.

Across the table Miss Bowlly was dispatching a large plate of duck with great enthusiasm. She had removed her Wellingtons and her knitted hat for the occasion, but otherwise she seemed to be dressed much as usual. She leaned forward, and winked at Harriet.

"Nice to see everyone mucking in," she remarked.

It was not quite the elegant phrase Harriet might have hoped to have applied to her elegant party, but it conveyed some of the spirit she intended. She beamed back at Miss Bowlly. "It is, isn't it? Long may it last."

There was only one short speech after the dinner. Harriet delivered it herself, standing informally at her table. She welcomed the guests to Birdwood, and thanked them for coming. She hoped there would be many more such evenings to come, celebrations for Everden and the new community together. She asked them to raise their glasses and drink a toast to that association. They drank, and there was loud applause.

"Well done," Anthony murmured in her ear when she sat down again. She didn't try to convince him that she meant what she said.

After dinner the dancing began.

With her speech over, Harriet took a third glass of champagne. She was beginning to float on a sea of well-being. When she danced with the vicar the faces around her seemed to belong to friends. She saw Kath dancing with the farmer whose land adjoined Miss Bowlly's, and Ken with Miss Bowlly herself. Anthony Fell was dancing with the striped-shirt woman from the village hall meeting, the woman herself barely recognizable in peacock-blue taffeta tiers.

The tempo of the music grew quicker. The vicar relinquished Harriet, and she found herself with one of the dinner-jacketed outskirter men. As they whirled over the floor, in and out of the pillars, in a throng of young dancers, Harriet found herself sentimentally hoping that if Caz and Fran of the spray-paint vows were not here themselves, then at least their parents were, or their older siblings. It seemed symbolically important that they should have penetrated past the unboarded windows tonight.

Harriet passed from partner to partner. The party was alive, moving without her direction. Some of the pensioner ladies were already leaving, thanking her and beaming with their own daring in having come at all; the younger contingent was settling in for a much longer night. The dancing continued, but some of the couples were separating out to sit in the plaster groves. The pairings would fuel village gossip for months.

Harriet remembered that once, at a party of Jane's, she had felt that her life was separated into two compartments, and the occupants of one compartment could not be allowed to stray into the other. But tonight she knew that all the parts of her life worth reckoning with were here, under one decaying roof, at Birdwood.

Then Harriet saw Jane herself. She watched her dancing with David Howkins. In that instant by recognizing something in the way they touched one another, with familiarity and yet a kind of constraint, or perhaps by making the kind of connection eased by champagne, Harriet knew that they had been lovers.

It was like a bright, unwelcoming light flicking on in a darkened room.

Harriet had been dancing with Charlie Thimbell but she faltered, and then stood still. She was winded by recognition of her own obtuseness, and by a shaft of jealousy.

"Are you all right?" Charlie asked her.

"Yes, I'm all right." Disconnected images began to form a picture in her mind. The jealousy startled her, but she was also shamed to know that she had been too blind and too busy to see what was happening to her friend. She understood just as plainly as the love affair had existed that it was over now. "I can be very stupid," she added, more to herself than to Charlie.

"You always seem as sharp as a razor to me," Charlie said, with the comfortable air of having forgotten everything that he did not find palatable to remember. "You seem to have everything very tidily sewn up."

"Not everything. Not quite everything."

Charlie wasn't listening. He had taken her hand to lead her out of the dance, and now he lifted each of her hands in turn and kissed them. "Listen, we've got to go. I wish we didn't, but there you are. It's a wonderful party."

They found Jenny sitting on one of the benches. Her latest baby was only a very few weeks old. She looked plumper than she had done. She lifted her head to smile at Harriet.

"I'm dragging him away again."

"And I wanted to see the fireworks." But Charlie was only pretending to be aggrieved.

"There will be plenty of other times." Harriet was thinking again of other evenings, of the small accretions of experience shared that built up into friendship. "There will. There must be."

Charlie and Jenny didn't notice her ferocity. She went with them, across the hall to the double doors, and kissed them both.

"Good night. Good night."

She let them go, to drive home to their children. Their babysitter had charge of Imogen, too, for this one night. As Harriet retraced her steps she was thinking of sleeping heads on pillows, as she had seen Linda's. A sense of the intricate responsibilities of parenthood admonished rather than attracted her. Although she had imagined that she would have children of her own someday, some unspecified day, it came to Harriet on this surprising evening that perhaps she had long ago chosen and already moved too far down a different path. She felt a lightening, as of relief. She thought of the work she had to do, of the Birdwood development and of other threads moving outward from that beginning, drawing her with them. An awareness of happiness that had nothing to do with champagne carried her in search of Jane.

She found her sitting at one of the cleared supper tables. She had been talking to one of the youngest Everden couples, but they melted away when Harriet sat down. Jane met her head-on.

"I'm sorry about the lady-of-the-manor dig. Charlie ticked me off for it."

Harriet waved her hand, taking in the dimming room all the way across to the great open hearth where the burned logs were collapsing into the hollow red heart of the fire. It was after eleven o'clock. At midnight, the fireworks display would mark the beginning of the end of the party.

"It wasn't quite unjustified, was it? I'll try not to turn into the lady. Will that do?"

Jane sat back in her chair and laughed at her. "We'll have to see."

They were both aware of the shifting sands of their friendship, and of their wish to secure it again. They sat for a few moments, facing each other across the white tablecloth with their champagne glasses between them. They talked about the party, and about the Everden stalwarts who passed by them, and the new village that Harriet hoped to see built across the fields.

"Good luck," Jane said at last, tipping her glass and emptying it.

Harriet took a breath. "You never told me about you and David Howkins."

After a glance, Jane said, "You never asked."

She couldn't gauge if it was meant as a rebuke, but Harriet accepted it meekly. "I know. I'm sorry."

"It doesn't matter. It all finished quite a long time ago."

"Were you hurt?"

There was a pause. "No," Jane lied to her. And then, with a renewal of the act of generosity that Harriet could just begin to guess at now, she offered, "It's you he's interested in. Did you know that?"

Harriet answered simply, "Yes. I think I did."

Briskly Jane gathered up her evening bag and her empty glass. "Well, then," she said, without bitterness. "I'm going to have another drink, and find somebody to dance with. A night without Imogen doesn't happen all that often. Not that I'm complaining, you understand."

She winked at Harriet, a lewd wink, and went away into the room where the dancing was still in full swing. Harriet sat on, alone at the table. The white cloth made a blank page for her thoughts.

She had made the party, it was her own creation. All these people were here, the guests and the waiters and the cooks, because she had brought them together. Their enjoyment was her achievement, and in watching the faces Harriet felt the fragile bubble of her Everden dream grow stronger. Harriet was proud of her evening, but now that it was reaching its climax the success of it did not surprise her. She knew what she could do, she expected success from herself. But it also came to her as she sat there that she should arrange her own life with the same decisiveness.

A long time ago, at the very beginning, when she had met David in Jane's kitchen full of teachers, she had believed that she had no time for the absorbing conspiracies of love. And now, as she sat painfully remembering her marriage, and Robin and Caspar, her own failures and smallness of heart as well as her partners', she was sure that she had made a true reckoning. Other things drew her, taking out her energies and allegiances. Love as a pursuit was too exacting, and the responsibilities daunted her.

Harriet felt no particular sadness. Rather a kind of elation, at a truth finally recognized and categorized. But there was, she decided, another kind of truth to be reckoned with. She could recall, from the days when she was trying to start Peacocks, how grim her denial of everything unconnected with her business had been, and how rigid her determination to succeed. She thought she must have been very unlikable, in those days. *But I did succeed*, she told herself. The severed limbs of Peacocks still hurt her, but she knew how to contain the hurt. *I'm mistress of myself. Or I should be.*

The choice of phrase made her smile, intensifying her private-joke expression as she sat with her chin in her hands.

Harriet felt suddenly happy, possessed by a happiness that managed to shake off guilt, that was nothing to do with champagne or the elation of the party. She didn't want to go in pursuit of love, as if it were some threatening Grail, as she had tried to do with poor Caspar Jensen. But that was no reason, she understood, why she should not enter into all the other human conspiracies—of sex, of friendship, or simple enjoyment, as she had discovered in one dimension with Linda. There was time. The initiative was her own, as in everything else she did. The truth was so simple, and so obvious, that it almost took her breath away.

David Howkins had offered her something long ago, and she had anxiously rejected it. She had *hidden in the bathroom*. The memory made Harriet laugh out loud. A passing couple looked curiously at her.

Tonight it had made her jealous just to see him dancing with Jane, just to think of what was plainly over.

And if you want something, Harriet told herself, *then you can go and get it.* She surveyed her room, from the ceiling moldings to the oak floorboards, acknowledging a partial truth. But she was not so elated as to allow herself total conviction.

She took a deep breath, and then went to look for David.

She found him almost at once. He was standing on the first-floor landing, leaning on the mahogany rail and looking down onto the heads in the hallway. Harriet knew that he had been waiting for her.

She gathered up the hem of her green velvet skirt and went slowly up the wide stairs to meet him. When she reached his side he moved along, making room for her. She leaned on the rail beside him, feeling the warmth in the wood where his arms had been.

They bent forward, shoulder to shoulder, watching the scene below them. There were small groups of people gathering together, talking and laughing. Coats and wraps were being brought out, and helped on. The doors stood open, and there were more people filtering out into the darkness. It was almost midnight, time for the fireworks.

Harriet said, "Perhaps I should go out with them. Give some directions." Then she turned to David. She examined his face, wondering that she had ever thought he looked like a boxer. She was microscopically conscious of the texture of his skin, the way his mouth moved. She smiled at him, a lazy smile. "Or perhaps I shouldn't."

"There's no need. It's their party." David was smiling, too.

Harriet knew that he was right. She had presented them with Birdwood for the evening, and it was theirs to enjoy. They didn't need her, and she wanted something else. She wanted it very much.

David stood upright. They faced each other, and he put one arm around her waist. Then he leaned forward and touched the tip of his tongue to her mouth. Harriet lifted her arm and curled it around his neck, drawing his face to hers. Their mouths met and opened.

Downstairs, all of Everden streamed out to watch the fireworks.

When David lifted his head again it was to demand, "Where?"

Harriet might have said, *impossible*, but this evening she would not. Instead she took David's hand, thinking quickly. In the room with the faded and spotted mirror where she had changed into her green dress there was a pile of sheets left by the decorators.

"This way."

They slipped along the gallery, hand in hand, bumping into each other and laughing like conspirators. Harriet pushed open the door. The sheets lay in a heap on the floor, but there were also coats left by the waiters, a shopping basket and a crash-helmet.

"No," Harriet said. But David gathered up the sheets and took her hand again. He led the way now, along the gallery and up the much narrower, dark and crooked stairs that took them to the servants' floor above.

The only light came filtering up from below. Harriet could hear his breathing as he pushed open the nearest door. It was almost completely dark, but Harriet knew that it was one of the maids' rooms, fitted awkwardly under the eaves, with a little slit of iron grate, seemingly hardly wide enough to burn a single coal.

She saw the faint blur of gray as he unfolded the sheets and then, looking upward as her eyes grew accustomed to the dark, she saw the different navy-blue darkness of the jagged sky through the hole in the roof.

David took hold of her, drawing her against him. Their mouths explored each other; Harriet turned her face, feeling the heat of her own skin reflected back from his. His hands went around her, smoothed over her bare back, then undid the long zip in the green velvet bodice. The dress fell away and left her shoulders bare.

David put his mouth to the exposed skin, and Harriet's head fell back. They knelt down, very slowly, facing each other on the spread sheet. The truant laughter had died, now. There was only the echo of their breathing.

They lay down, stretching along the length of each other.

From outside there came a *rip*, and a great crackle.

Looking upward, Harriet saw an instant's flicker of fire, and then a great shower of scarlet sparks falling toward the earth.

From a long way off, she heard a chorus of voices saying, "Ahhhh . . ."

David put his fingers to her mouth, to suppress the renewed laughter.

Harriet said, *"Yes."*